Little White Lies

Little White Lies

Lesley Lokko

First published in Great Britain in 2013 by Orion Books,
an imprint of The Orion Publishing Group Ltd
Orion House, 5 Upper Saint Martin's Lane
London WC2H 9EA

An Hachette UK Company

1 3 5 7 9 10 8 6 4 2

A CIP catalogue record for this book
is available from the British Library.

ISBN (Hardback) 978 1 4091 4247 8
ISBN (Trade Paperback) 978 1 4091 4248 5
ISBN (Ebook) 978 1 4091 4249 2

Typeset at The Spartan Press Ltd,
Lymington, Hants

Printed in Great Britain by
Clays Ltd, St Ives plc

The Orion Publishing Group's policy is to use papers
that are natural, renewable and recyclable products and
made from wood grown in sustainable forests. The logging
and manufacturing processes are expected to conform to
the environmental regulations of the country of origin.

www.orionbooks.co.uk

Acknowledgements

This is a novel about three families, originating in very different parts of the world, whose histories encompass some of the best- and least-known moments of the twentieth century. In the case of the Harburgs and the Betancourts, I have relied on three works in particular: Ron Chernow's excellent *The Warburgs: the Twentieth-Century Odyssey of a Remarkable Jewish Family* (Vintage: New York, 1990); *The World's Banker: the History of the House of Rothschild* (Weidenfeld & Nicholson: London, 1998) by Niall Ferguson; and an online essay, *Afro-Brazilians in Togo: the Case of the Olympio Family 1882–1945*, by Alcione M. Amos, (http://etudesafricaines.revues.org).

Although this novel concerns an entirely fictional family, the Betancourts, some of their story will be at least partially familiar to those who know the history of Togo. In order to fashion their tale, I have taken enormous liberties with historical facts and I must stress that this is, above all, a work of fiction. The chronology of events and the historical reasons for the fall of the Betancourts are not indicative of anything that happened to any one family in Togo, nor should it be read as a factual history of that beautiful country in any way. I borrowed heavily from the history of the Olympio family and anyone wishing to read more about them would do well to begin with the online article mentioned above. Sadly, much of what I know about the Olympio family comes from my beloved friend, Natasha Olympio, who died tragically in July 2011, and whom I miss every single day.

As ever, thanks go to my *über*-agent, Kate Shaw (simply the best); my lovely editor Kate Mills and the whole team at Orion; friends in London, Edinburgh, Johannesburg and Accra; and of course, my whole family, Debbie, Megan, Nick, Lois, Simon, Paul, Mae-Ling, Noe and Dad, spread as they are across the globe. I enlisted the help of several dear friends and colleagues to help with the various foreign languages. To Stephan Ata, Marilí Santos-Munné, Nenad Cvetkovic, Konstantin von Eggert, Bart Goldhoorn, Inessa Kouteinikova, Delphine de Blic, Sandra Dorville, Igor Marjanovic and Joy Terekiev, I'd like to say an *enormous* 'thank you.' I'd also like to thank two very dear, very special 'teenage-hood' friends with whom I've recently reconnected (though, thankfully, not on Facebook!) – Roy Engel and Lori Rose, who'll recognise parts of the scenery we once shared a very, *very* long time ago. I hope I've done it (and you) justice.

Contents

GODMOTHERS

'Always a godmother, never a mother. That sucks.'
Courtney Cox

Prologue
2013

Martha's Vineyard, Cape Cod, USA

She lay on the ground with her cheek pressed flat against the Persian rug, her mouth stirring sporadically, as if she were about to speak. Her hands were tightly balled fists at her sides and her breathing was laboured and shallow. Outside, amidst the muffled noise of running feet and barking dogs, a child cried out: David, perhaps, or Joshua? She couldn't tell. Whoever it was, he was hurriedly picked up and hushed. It was nearly six p.m. and the hard, high ball of fire that was the sun had started slipping towards the horizon. It was only May but already the days were long and hot. A week ago, just before her guests arrived, she'd ordered the covers off the swimming pool. Every morning, the servants unfurled the large white patio umbrellas and plumped up the blue-and-white striped cushions, making the shimmering turquoise pool the centre of the day's activities. Every day, including today. *Today*. Her skin began to crawl.

For the hundredth time, her mind skittered over the hours that had passed since that morning, trying to make sense of it all. The day had begun like every other day. She'd gone out early, just as dawn was breaking, drink in hand – orange juice, with the barest splash of vodka – just enough to get the day going. She'd dipped her feet in the heated water at the shallow end, enjoying the early-morning quiet. Toys, the debris of games begun and abandoned, lay scattered around the grey birch decking that ran all the way around the house. *Toys. Children's toys.* At the thought of the toys, her lips began to tremble all over again. She moved her head a fraction and the rich, dense colours of the carpet rose up to meet her half-closed eyes. Yellow: *pomegranate, chamomile, egg-yolk*. Red: *blood, wine, burgundy, ruby*. Black: *walnut, bark, night*. It was a beautiful carpet. Large and soft, it stretched from one end of the study to the other. Expensive, too. She'd lied to Adam about the price, of course, knocking off a few thousand dollars, though she'd no reason to – it was *her* money, after all. But Adam was so unpredictable these days, especially where money was concerned. Her stomach gave a horrible, twisting lurch. Oh, God, Adam. He would be back from New York any minute now. What would he say? He would blame her, of course. Everyone blamed her and why the hell shouldn't they? It was her fault. She was to blame, no one else.

Her mind began to wander uncontrollably again, darting back and forth over the day's events but without any sense of order. *When* did it happen? Before or after breakfast? After she'd come in from the pool? Had she *really* told Clea to take a break? 'No, no, *you* have an afternoon off, Clea. I'll look after them. Come *on*, four kids . . . it's not rocket science!' She'd grinned at her. Clea. Lovely Clea, the cousin of one of the girls who worked for the Lowensteins, her neighbours. Betty Lowenstein introduced them soon after Tash arrived; she'd hired her on the spot. She seemed so nice. And so capable. It was *she*, Tash, who wasn't capable.

You've got to get up. Her own voice. She tried to lift her head. It felt wobbly, as though it wasn't properly attached. Footsteps approached suddenly; someone was coming up the stairs. Heavy. A man's tread. It must be the inspector. No, not inspector – detective. Wasn't that what they called inspectors over here? Detectives? Officers? Sergeants? No idea. The steps slowed and he came to a stop. She could hear his breathing through the door. She held her own breath. *Please don't come in. Not yet.* A minute spooled slowly by, then another, and another. She waited. Just when she thought she might scream at him to go away, she heard him turn back. She exhaled very slowly, the breath leaving her body in short, sharp gasps. He was wary of her; she'd sensed it straight away. Something in the way he couldn't quite hold her gaze, despite the seriousness of the occasion. His eyes kept slipping away from her to the cars parked in the driveway, the enormous house, the works of art, the furniture and the Persian rugs and the servants who kept flitting in and out like lost bees. She knew exactly what he was thinking. *Rich bitch.* Rich, foreign bitch. The line dividing the residents of the luxurious holiday homes along the water's edge from the locals who lived in Edgartown was clear. *Them and us. Rich and poor. The idle and working classes.* But he knew nothing. He knew nothing about her, where she'd come from, what she'd done. He had no idea. And, idle or not, rich or not, the absolute worst had come to pass. Tragedies can happen anywhere, to anyone. She, of all people, should have known that.

4

He walked down the stairs, his heels clipping out a sharp, crisp rhythm that slowly faded to silence. Somewhere on the ground floor a door opened; there was an exchange of voices but she couldn't hear what was said. There was the short, staccato burst of a walkie-talkie or a radio. A car swept into the driveway, scattering gravel; the dogs barked wildly. More voices. The house was beginning to fill up with people. More police. She struggled upright. Her knees and hands were shaking; her mouth was bone dry. It was time to call Rebecca.

PART ONE
TEENAGERS

'Adolescence: a stage between infancy and adultery.'
Ambrose Bierce

1

1993

TATIANA BRYCE-BRUDENELL
Chelsea, London

With the sort of anxious concentration that only teenagers can muster, seventeen-year-old Tash Bryce-Brudenell carefully examined herself in the tiny bathroom mirror. Things weren't looking good. Mousy brown hair pulled back into a ponytail (a style she'd sported since the age of six); pale blue eyes (set much too far apart); short, barely there eyelashes (blonde, not brown, highlighting their absence even further). At least her skin was reasonably clear – a few spots, a few freckles – not as bad as some of the girls in her class. Not Annick, though. Or Rebecca. She sighed. What kind of malicious deity had made *her* so goddamn plain and her two best friends so goddamn pretty? She had no answer.

She soldiered grimly on, baring her teeth in an approximation of a smile. She grimaced. Her teeth were dreadful – too many, too long, too crowded, too crooked. Smile *only* when absolutely necessary. Chin? Weak, but at least it wasn't receding. She'd been lucky there. She'd never met her father but in the few photographs her mother had shown her, he had an unmistakably receding chin. She turned slowly sideways. Her nose now came into its problematic own. It was large and long with an uncomfortably high bridge that made it difficult to keep her glasses on. Another typical Bryce-Brudenell feature (or so her mother said).

'Tatiana?' Her mother's voice came barrelling through the door. '*Chto ty tam delaesh?* What you doing in there?' As ever, Lyudmila said everything twice, once in Russian and then (as if Tash didn't understand) in English.

'Nothing,' Tash yelled back unconvincingly. 'I'll be out in a second.' She hurriedly turned on the taps.

'*My budem pozdno.* We gonna be late.'

We're going *to be late*, not *we* gonna *be late*, Tash automatically

9

mouthed. Not that Lyudmila would take any notice. She'd lived in England for almost twenty years but her voice, syntax and grammar had lost none of their sensual, throaty Russianness.

'What you *doing* in there?' Lyudmila asked again, exasperated. Hers was a voice that could penetrate lead.

'I'm *coming*,' Tash hissed. She rinsed her hands and yanked open the door. 'What's the bloody rush?' Her eyes narrowed suspiciously as she surveyed her mother. Lyudmila was dressed as though ready to go out – a long, floor-sweeping fur coat that, although it had clearly seen better days, was still impressive; black high-heeled boots and a soft black beret over her blonde, waist-length hair. Almost every penny of the meagre allowance that came through every month from the Bryce-Brudenell family solicitors in Edinburgh was spent on clothes – Lyudmila's, not Tash's. Lyudmila spent *more* than enough on Tash's school fees, she lamented. Daily. 'Why you not ready, *dushen'ka?*' she asked, impatiently tugging on her gloves.

'Ready? What for?' Tash frowned. 'Are we going somewhere?'

Lyudmila rolled her eyes. '*Dushen'ka*, I *told* you. We have invite. Lady Soames invite us. You and me. We must to go *now*.'

Tash groaned. 'Oh, God, Ma, no! Not Lady Soames! Why do *I* have to come? No one'll even notice if I'm not there. Why don't you go by yourself?'

Lyudmila shook her head firmly. '*Nyet.* I promise her you coming. Hurry up. You know she doesn't like it when we is late.'

'When we *are* late,' Tash corrected her sulkily.

Lyudmila shrugged. 'Is. Are. No difference. Come. Where is coat?'

'Where I left it.' Tash sighed. She followed her mother reluctantly down the corridor. Lyudmila was up to something; she could tell by her excited, distracted air.

'*Dushen'ka*, why you always so *nezgovorchivaya?*' Lyudmila paused to view her reflection in the mirror before opening the front door. *Nezgovorchivaya.* Disagreeable. It was her favourite word, especially when it came to Tash.

'Because that's the way you made me,' Tash said, tightening her ponytail defiantly.

'Not true,' Lyudmila said calmly. 'I try everything make you nice girl.' She opened the cupboard door and pulled out Tash's coat, a sensible black woollen schoolgirl number. 'Okay, here is coat. Come. We late.' She marched ahead.

We are *late,* Tash mouthed silently, crossly. She followed her mother disconsolately out the door.

'Taxi!' Only in Lyudmila's mouth could the word come out as 'texy'. A black cab on the opposite side of the road, spotting the long blonde hair and fur coat, turned immediately and screeched to an abrupt halt.

'Where to, love?' The driver looked Lyudmila appreciatively up and down. Tash hung back instinctively.

Lyudmila grasped the door handle and climbed in. 'Christchurch Street. You know where is it?'

'Christchurch Street? What . . . the one round the corner?' The driver sounded disbelieving. Tash's face began to burn.

'Yes.'

'You'd be quicker walking, love.'

'I like drive.' Lyudmila pulled out her compact and started powdering her nose. For a second, Tash caught and held the driver's incredulous gaze. She looked away. He pulled out into the traffic without a word.

'*Dushen'ka,* be nice today, hmm?' Lyudmila turned her attention away from her own face just briefly. She reached across and tucked a stray lock of lank hair behind Tash's ear. Tash only just resisted the temptation to smack her hand away.

'Why?'

'Because,' Lyudmila answered cryptically.

Tash turned her face back to the window. Yes, her mother was definitely up to something. She caught a glimpse of her own reflection. She looked down at her hands. It wasn't easy being Lyudmila's daughter, especially not her *ugly* daughter.

'Lyudmila! How *lovely* to see you, my darling! What a surprise! Do come in! Come in. It's absolutely *perishing* outside! And here's the lovely little Tatiana. How *splendid* of you to come! You know the way – of course you do!' Lady Pamela Soames stood in the hallway, practically (and inexplicably) rubbing her hands in glee. She looked like a cross between a sumo wrestler and a poodle, Tash thought to herself uncharitably. How on earth could it be a *surprise* when she was clearly expecting them? And who in the world would ever call her 'lovely' – or, even more ludicrous, 'little'? Her height was the only thing she'd inherited from her mother. At seventeen she was nearly six feet tall. 'How *are* you, darling?' Lady Soames looked up at her indulgently.

'Who? Me?' Tash scowled down at her and was rewarded by a sharp prod from Lyudmila.

'Teenager,' Lyudmila said helplessly, making it sound like a terminal illness. 'What I can do?'

'Oh, don't I know it,' Lady Soames said conspiratorially, tucking her arm into Lyudmila's as she led them towards the conservatory. 'It's a dreadful time, absolutely dreadful. For *all* concerned.' She lowered her voice. 'Now, listen, darling. I've asked Rupert to come downstairs but he's a bit reluctant, I'm afraid. You know what they're like at his age.'

Tash stopped dead in her tracks. Rupert? Rupert was Lady Soames' eldest son. So *that* was why she'd been dragged along. Oh, Christ. Lyudmila was playing matchmaker. A wave of embarrassment washed over her. She could have *killed* her! Wasn't it enough that she had to endure the pitying glances of all Lyudmila's friends? Did she have to endure their sons' sniggers as well? She glared daggers at her mother's rapidly disappearing back. Not that Lyudmila would notice. Or care.

2

'So what's he like?' Annick was eager to hear all the details. It was half past ten and the most embarrassing day of Tash's life was finally drawing to a close. 'Is he good-looking?'

Tash snorted derisively. 'God, no! He's about half my size.' She wedged the phone between her chin and neck, attempting to talk and paint her toenails at the same time. 'And he's got ginger hair. He's repulsive, actually. Besides, I don't *want* a boyfriend, and even if I did, I'm hardly going to ask my mother for help. I'm perfectly capable of getting one on my own. *If* I wanted one. Which I *don't*.' She enunciated her words clearly, keen for Annick to get the point.

'Darling, if we wait for you to sort yourself out in that department, we'll be waiting for ever. You're so bloody picky.'

'I am not. Besides, I'd rather be picky than a slut.' She grimaced. 'Sorry. Didn't mean that.'

'Yes, you did. Anyhow, we're not talking about me. Can we get back to the subject, please?'

'There *is* no subject. He came downstairs, took one look at me and fled.'

'Oh, Tash! He did *not*! You're making it up.'

'I'm *not*. You should've seen his face. I'd just stuffed a scone in my gob and a bit of cream oozed out, so I scooped it up with my finger and licked it off in front of him. He nearly *died*. His mother looked at me as though I'd gone mad. It *was* funny, though. You should've seen Ma's face. Anyway, I'd better go. I've still got that history essay to finish. Have you done yours yet?'

'Nope.'

'Er, it's due tomorrow.'

'Yeah, I know.'

'You hassle me about boyfriends and I hassle you about homework. How does that *not* make you a slut?'

'All right, point taken.'

'I'd better get on with it, then. You'd be advised to do the same.'

'I might. I'll see how I feel.'

'Fine, you'll get an "F". See you tomorrow.'

'Mmm.' Annick sounded about as interested in her essay as Tash had been in Rupert Soames. 'Meet you outside the gates at nine.'

Tash put down the phone, lay back against the pillows and held out her hand. She looked at the tattoo nestling in the fold between her thumb and first finger. It was almost healed. A week earlier, she, Annick and Rebecca had walked past a tattoo parlour on the way home from school. Without saying a word, they'd all stopped in front of it. They looked at each other.

'Won't it hurt?'

'Oh, Rebecca.' Both Tash and Annick turned to look at her.

'Sue Parker's brother got one done the other day. She said he said it hurt like hell.'

'Yeah, but I bet his covered half of his back, or something stupid like that. We're only going to get something small.'

'Like what?'

Annick shrugged. 'How about a rose?'

Tash rolled her eyes. 'Bo-ring. Let's get something that actually means something. To all of us.'

'Like what?' Rebecca's curiosity got the better of her.

'How about something . . . something like that?' Tash pointed at something in the window.

'Which one?' Annick stepped closer to see.

'That one. The triangle. Three points – that's us, right?'

'How about a triangle set in a circle?'

'Genius. Fucking genius.' Tash grinned. 'The three of us, together, always. I love it. Here, right here where we'll always see it.' She pointed to the spot between her thumb and forefinger.

'Come on, before Rebecca chickens out,' Annick laughed.

'I won't. Does . . . does it have to be right there?' she looked at her hand. 'Can't it be somewhere more . . . well, hidden?'

'Scaredy-cat. You're afraid of what your mum's going to say. Don't worry, when your hand's closed, you'll hardly see it.'

And that was it. They exited the shop half an hour later, each looking a little paler than before, holding a little wad of cotton wool over their bleeding hands. They'd chosen the design together – a thin blue triangle, enclosed in a circle. 'Best friends for ever, huh?' The tattoo artist grinned approvingly at his handiwork.

'Yup.' They all spoke at once. The triangle had been Tash's idea, the circle enclosing it, Rebecca's. Annick concentrated only on not crying. Unbelievable how something barely the size of a ten pence piece could hurt so much, she said weakly. Lyudmila nearly fainted when she saw it, as did Aunt Mimí, Rebecca's mother. Annick's mother hadn't seen it yet and probably wouldn't notice it anyway. Her parents were barely there, and when they were, their attention was always claimed by someone else, someone more important.

Tash traced the still-puckered flesh with her fingers. She rolled over onto her stomach, burying her face in her pillow. She didn't like lying to anyone, least of all Annick. The afternoon hadn't been quite as funny or as entertaining as she'd made out. Lyudmila and Lady Soames disappeared as soon as Rupert finally came down, leaving the two teenagers locked together in a silent agony of sullen resentment. Every so often, a tinkling laugh could be heard down the corridor, making the silence between them even more uncomfortable. Rupert looked at his shoes. Tash looked down at her hands. The silver tray of scones and tea lay untouched in front of them. Tash racked her brains for something to say.

'So what's Eton like?' she asked finally.

He looked up. His expression hovered somewhere between boredom and disgust. ''S'all right,' he muttered.

Tash felt a rush of feeling at the tip of her nose; any second now it'd turn red and shiny and she'd burst into tears. She forced herself to look away. 'D'you want some tea?' she asked after a moment.

'No.' There was another monumentally awkward pause. Then he jumped to his feet as if he'd been bitten – or possibly shot. 'Look, I'd better go. I've forgotten something—'

Tash opened her mouth to say something – *anything* – then snapped it firmly shut. He ran out and suddenly the room was quiet. She looked around her slowly and poured herself a cup of tea. In a flash of inspiration, she poured a second cup and drank that as well. Then she polished off the scones. When the adults returned half an hour later, two empty cups sat side by side on the tray. Not even a dollop of cream remained.

'Did you enjoy yourselves?' Lady Soames said, beaming. 'Where's Rupert?'

'You just missed him. He'd forgotten his homework or something,' Tash said calmly. It was half true. She saw Lyudmila glance at the empty teacups with a small, self-satisfied smile. Job done. She beamed at Tash. Tash blinked slowly and looked away.

3

ANNICK BETANCOURT
Mayfair, London

Several miles and an entire world away from Tash's cramped little basement flat, in her own enormous but empty apartment overlooking Hyde Park, Annick Betancourt sat down and opened the history book she'd been half-heartedly thumbing through before the phone call. She struggled to concentrate. *How far was Henry VII's government threatened by rebellions in the years 1485 to 1509?* She stared at the question. The problem with it – as with most history questions – was that she didn't actually care. She found it hard to summon up any kind of enthusiasm for things she had absolutely no interest in . . . and therein lay the problem. Although she wasn't the *only* girl at St Benedict's Sixth Form College who wasn't academically inclined, she was certainly one of its most high-profile. In a school filled with the offspring of rock stars and royalty, Annick Betancourt was both. Her father, the handsome, charismatic Sylvan Betancourt was the president of Togo (not that anyone knew where Togo was). Her mother, the gorgeous, glamorous

Anouschka Malaquais, was a bona fide film star. Rarely a day went by in her native France without some mention of her in the press. She was perhaps lesser known in Britain for her roles than her robes, but Annick had long got used to the sight of her mother's face staring impassively back at her from the cover of *Hello!*

With two such illustrious parents it was inconceivable that their only child should turn out to be a dunce. But that was exactly what had happened. When it became known that Annick Betancourt would, in all likelihood, fail her A-levels, the school suggested (perfectly nicely) that she might perhaps be better off somewhere less, er, *stringent* in its pursuit of academic excellence. Anouschka immediately flew from Lomé to London (via Paris and the haute couture shows, of course), to protest. In person. As the excited girls whispered to each other afterwards, the headmaster was so overcome at the sight of Anouschka Malaquais-Betancourt, all high heels, flowing blonde hair and the unmistakeable whiff of power and wealth that clung to her like perfume, that he immediately capitulated. Annick stayed on.

Annick herself wasn't sure whether to be pleased or annoyed. She was relieved *not* to have to leave – that would have meant leaving Tash and Rebecca behind, in itself an unthinkable prospect. Between St Benedict's and the Hyde Park apartment, she had little else to call 'home'. Her father spent most of his time in Lomé, the Togolese capital, where she holidayed once a year – twice, if she were lucky. Her mother flitted back and forth between Lomé and Paris with the occasional stopover in London if the fashion shows were on. Annick very occasionally joined her at the beautiful Left Bank apartment in Paris for Christmas but it had been several years since she'd spent Christmas anywhere other than at Rebecca's – which was daft because Rebecca was Jewish and didn't celebrate it. Still, Aunt Mimí always put on the most fabulous lunch for the thirty-odd friends and relatives who always came to Harburg Hall on the day itself – and it sure as hell beat sitting in her own living room, alone or having Christmas dinner with the housekeeper, which was worse.

A sharp tap at the door interrupted her.

'Come in,' she muttered.

'Everything all right, Annick?' Mrs Price asked, her eyes quickly sweeping the room. Like a lighthouse, Annick thought to herself irritably.

'Everything's fine, Mrs Price,' she murmured. 'Just doing my homework.'

'I thought I heard you on the phone earlier and I know you've got a lot of homework on.'

'Yeah.' They both hesitated. Mrs Price was clearly waiting for Annick to elaborate further and Annick was determined not to. Annick always found it difficult. Although the palace in Lomé was stuffed full of servants, Mrs Price unnerved her. She didn't quite fit the category of servant, at least not in the way the servants back in Togo did, and yet she was definitely *not* a family member. Still, there were times when Annick came home from a particularly bad day at school or she'd been waiting a week for one or other of her parents to call and the only person in the world she had to talk to was Mrs Price. On days like those, instead of going straight to her room, she hung around the kitchen, watching Mrs Price expertly slice onions or roll out a sheet of pastry for a pie and for a few minutes she could pretend she was like all her other friends with a mother to talk to, a father somewhere in the house . . . people who *cared*. Not that her parents didn't care, she always reminded herself quickly. They just happened to live six thousand miles away and each had a job to do. They were busy people.

'Well, don't stay up too late, then,' Mrs Price said finally, acknowledging defeat.

'I won't.'

'Goodnight.'

'Goodnight, Mrs Price.'

The door closed behind her. Annick blew out her cheeks and began to tidy her desk. She didn't like thinking about her parents, especially not before going to bed. At night, without the distraction of traffic outside or the occasional sound of the neighbours, the flat was at its most silent. It was the silence she dreaded. When she went home in the holidays to Lomé, the house was always full of noise and laughter, people talking, arguing, debating, shouting. Life flowed around them: it was everywhere, in every visitor, every car that swept up the impressively long driveway; in the noisy, excited chatter of the many servants who lived in the quarters to the rear of the palace . . . noise, *noise* everywhere. In Lomé it was impossible to feel alone. London was the opposite. There were nights she felt as though she were the loneliest person alive.

She shut her eyes tightly, trying to picture them – Maman, Papa and her – sitting in the sunny, spacious *salon de thé* in the apartment on rue Matignon. As always, she could see herself quite clearly but whenever she tried to focus on her mother or father, the image slipped, becoming fuzzy and unclear. She could picture certain things – the colour of her mother's hair, especially after a visit to the hairdresser, or the small gold necklace with the three diamond circles that she always wore; her father's dark tweed suits, smelling faintly of cigar smoke and aftershave and the way his beard always showed up dark and bruised under his skin. But not the whole picture. Not the three of them, together, complete. That image stubbornly refused to come. She closed her eyes tightly and tried to think of something else. Anything. No point in ruining another weekend by feeling homesick. Although how could you be homesick when you didn't really have a home?

4

REBECCA HARBURG
Hampstead, London

Sitting opposite Adam Goldsmith, her second cousin on her father's side whom she'd never met, Rebecca Harburg was in an agony of embarrassment – and, face it, lust. The object of her desire sat with his legs (in ripped and faded Levis) spread insouciantly apart, a cup of tea calmly balanced on his muscular thighs, chatting easily to the elderly aunts, spinsters, mothers and three other cousins who'd come to gape at this Goldsmith from the Belgian branch of the family, a creature from another planet. Blonde, blue-eyed, athletic and well over six foot tall, Adam Goldsmith looked like no other Harburg, dead or alive. He was twenty-three years old, fluent in half a dozen languages, now a trainee banker with the family firm and had recently returned from a two-year stint in the Israeli army. This last, of course, was the icing on the cake. No Harburg had ever done anything like it. He'd *volunteered* to serve in the Israeli army? What a *mensch*! Despite those rather uncomfortably Aryan looks, no one could accuse him of not being Jewish enough. In a sea of dark-haired, dark-eyed, pale and sensitively intelligent faces, the man who looked as if he'd stepped off the catwalk was going down a storm.

Embeth Hausmann-Harburg, known to friends and family as Mimí, was sitting opposite him, her teacup and saucer balanced daintily on her knees, trying unsuccessfully to suppress a frown. The Friday afternoon gathering was at *her* house and it was *her* daughter whose mouth was hanging open. She stared at Rebecca, trying to get her attention. Pointless. Rebecca, along with everyone present – a half-deaf grandmother, three elderly great aunts, four girlish, simpering cousins and the maid – were dumbstruck. Orit, the maid she'd brought back from Tel Aviv, had almost dropped the tray when she saw him. She'd gone beetred when he opened his mouth and said, 'Shalom' and then had to leave the room, quite overcome *and* without serving anyone to boot. Silly women. Had they never seen a good-looking man before? 'Rebecca,' Mimí hissed. 'Rebecca! *Cierra la boca*! Close your mouth!'

But Rebecca was beyond hearing. She was sitting close enough to reach out and touch him. Those long, lean, finely toned thighs; the broad chest underneath the cream Fair Isle sweater that offset his tan; the bulge of his biceps; the thick, sandy blonde hair; and those tanned, rugged cheeks with a morning's worth of beard already showing through. She was rendered completely dumb. He reminded her of the marble statue of Adonis, the beautiful Greek god who stood outside the library at school. An image of the statue's limp penis suddenly slipped into her head and she choked on her scone, sending crumbs flying out of her mouth.

'What's matter with her?' Eleanor, the oldest of the great aunts, suddenly spoke up. She was hard of hearing and squinted anxiously in the direction of the noise.

'She's choking! Get her some water!' Another great aunt sprang into action.

'The girl's choking?' Aunt Eleanor fumbled for her spectacles.

'Will someone get the girl some water?' Aunt Rosa yelled. 'You want she should choke to death?'

'I'm . . . I'm fine,' Rebecca stammered, furiously wiping away her tears. The embarrassment was almost as bad as the coughing fit. 'No, really . . . I'm fine.' She waved off their concern.

'She's fine. It just went down the wrong way, that's all.' Mimí soothed her anxious relations. 'Why don't you go and wash your face?' she turned to Rebecca calmly. 'And get some fresh air,' she added firmly.

Rebecca jumped to her feet, stealing a quick glance at Adam. He was eating his scone as if nothing had happened.

'Poor thing,' she heard one of the aunts say to another as she left the room. 'Such a fright she gave me! D'you remember the Meyerson boy? The tall one? Had an allergy to nuts. Dropped dead, just like that! One minute here, the next . . . gone!'

'Oooh, don't remind me, please! *Terrible* business, terrible. It took them *years* to get over it—'

'Such things you don't get over, Miriam. Never.'

Rebecca stifled a giggle as she closed the door behind her. Every Friday, her mother served afternoon tea for a never-ending stream of aunts and great aunts, followed by the traditional Friday night *seder*. Lesser family members fought over the invitations like dogs over scraps of meat. Embeth's *seders* were beautiful occasions, more social than spiritual. An invitation to Harburg Hall on a Friday night was a sign that you'd *arrived*. There was to be a special *seder* that evening to welcome Adam to London. He was about to join the family bank, starting with a position right at the bottom. It was the way they did things at Harburg's. In three generations, no one had ever made director without having worked everywhere, 'from the mail room to the board-room,' as Lionel, Rebecca's father, liked to say. It seemed rather unlikely that Adam would be delivering mail, Rebecca thought to herself as she hurried to the bathroom. If she was lucky and found herself seated next to him at dinner, perhaps she could ask him what he would be doing? At the thought of dinner and possibly being seated next to Adam, she brightened.

She bent down and splashed cold water onto her face to cool down her still-burning cheeks. She eyed her reflection anxiously, tucking a few stray strands of hair behind her ears. Her eyes, normally a clear dark-brown colour that often verged on black, were unnaturally bright. She traced the line of her eyebrow tenderly with a finger, slicking it into shape. Her skin was pale, lightly dusted with freckles across her cheeks and the bridge of her nose. Her long, poker-straight hair fell on either side of her face from a centre parting, which she hated but everyone said suited her. She longed for Annick's wild masses of dark-brown corkscrew-tight curls that drew gasps of admiration from everyone – even total strangers – when she let them spring free. 'Why can't I have hair like yours?' she moaned to Annick, endlessly.

'Because.'

Not a lot you could say to *that*. She checked her reflection for the last time, turned off the taps and opened the door. Her heart missed a beat. Adam was there, right in front of her, crossing the hallway towards the front door.

'Hey,' he said lightly. 'I was just nipping out for a fag. Want one?'

Rebecca gaped at him. She didn't smoke. No matter. She did now. 'Yeah,' she said, as nonchalantly as she could manage. '*Love* to.' She trotted obediently after him. He held the front door open for her and they both stood in the portico, sheltering from the rain. He fished a packet of Marlboro Lights from the pocket of his jeans and handed one over. A bolt of lightning shot through her as their hands touched. A second bolt hit as he cupped her hand to help her light it. Annick and Tash smoked; she didn't. She tried desperately to recall how they did it. *Bring cigarette to mouth. Open mouth. Inhale. Slowly. Exhale. Quickly.* The fit of coughing that overtook her brought tears to her eyes.

'Easy,' Adam said, smiling down at her.

Her heart did a slow somersault. 'S . . . sorry, just . . . it's that bloody scone again.'

'Sure it is.' His voice was full of teasing laughter.

She took another, less enthusiastic draw, and cautiously looked up at him from underneath her lashes. He was just so goddamn beautiful – blue eyes, the colour of the sky on a hot summer's day; blonde hair that reminded her of sunlight; skin that glowed with rude health. 'Adam, can I ask you something?' she said suddenly, the words tumbling out of her mouth before she could stop herself.

'What?'

'Ha . . . have you ever killed anyone?'

It was the dumbest thing she'd ever said. The way he looked at her just confirmed it.

'He just *looked* at me,' she wailed half an hour later on the phone to Annick. 'I mean, what kind of an idiot asks a question like that?'

'So what did he say?' Annick asked breathlessly.

Rebecca paused to blow her nose. 'Nothing. He just looked at me. Then he stubbed out his cigarette and said, "Funny, every girl I meet asks me that." So not only am I dumb, I'm just like all the others.'

'Well, there are worse things to be,' Annick said cheerfully.

'Like *what*?'

'I . . . well, I can't think of them right now,' Annick said carefully. 'But I'm sure there are. So where is he now?'

'He's going back to Belgium for a couple of weeks. It's funny, he's completely English when he speaks to me – to us – and then he speaks to his mother in French and he sounds so different. He's just like you.'

'I'm hardly six foot three, darling, and I certainly haven't come back from some army camp.'

'You know what I mean. Sometimes when I'm with you and I hear you on the phone to your mum, or your friends from home, or whatever . . . you *look* like you, but I don't recognise your voice. It's weird. He spoke Hebrew to Orit and she nearly dropped dead.'

'He sounds lovely,' Annick said loyally. 'But he's your cousin. You can't.'

'Can't what?'

'Marry him, silly.'

'Who says I want to marry him?' Rebecca asked indignantly. 'And anyway in our family it's allowed. It's practically enforced.'

'Well, there you go. It's settled then. You'll marry the gorgeous Adam, you'll move to Israel and live on a – what d'you call it again? A kibi? You'll have fifteen kids and live happily ever after.'

'It's a *kibbutz*, you idiot, and in any case, with my luck, they'll find me some distant cousin from Poland who's thirty years older than me with no chin and no hair and I'll have to move to Lódz,' she said glumly.

'Oh, you're so melodramatic, Rebecca. You ought to move to Hollywood.'

'Maybe I will. Anyway, I didn't call just to talk about Adam. Have you made your choices yet?' Rebecca asked, reminding them both of something of far greater importance. University. Rebecca knew Annick was worried about getting in. Their exams were four months away and at the rate Annick was going, she would never get the grades she needed. She ought to at least pass French – it was her mother tongue, after all – but you still had to read the set novels and have more than a passing acquaintance with the characters. Annick just didn't seem to care. Her concern about university wasn't the university itself or the course of study she'd chosen, or even whether or not she'd find it difficult. Annick's real concern, Rebecca knew, was not to be left behind.

'No,' Annick said glumly. 'I keep putting it off. Have you?'

'History of Art.'

'You guys are so lucky,' Annick said enviously. 'At least you're good at something. I haven't got a clue what to do.'

'I thought you were going to do languages?' Rebecca asked carefully.

'Well, that's only because it'll be easy.'

'So choose something harder.'

'Me? Since when do I ever do anything hard? I just hope I get *in*, that's all. I couldn't bear it if you two got in and I didn't. Knowing me, I'm the one who's going to wind up in . . . where was it? Lobs?'

'Lódz,' Rebecca giggled. '*Now* look who's being melodramatic. Anyhow, I'd better go. I'm blessing the candles tonight and I'd better not screw *that* up. Mum'll kill me. Aunt Rosa's always complaining that they don't teach me how to do things properly. I wish you could meet Adam. Actually, no, I don't. One look at you and it'll be all over for me. He won't be able to take his eyes off you.'

'Don't be silly.'

'I'm not,' Rebecca said glumly. 'That's just it. I'm not. Tash is so fucking clever, you're beautiful . . . me, I'm just average. Tash is going to wind up some hotshot lawyer or something, you're going to marry someone rich and famous and I'll be the one who gets left behind. Just you wait and see.'

PART TWO
ESCAPE

'To slip away from pursuit or peril; avoid capture,
punishment, or any threatened evil.'
The Oxford English Dictionary

5

1935

LIONEL HARBURG
Hamburg, Germany

He turned away from the table, impatient with the talk. His uncle
Abraham, eyebrows working magnificently like two thick, hairy *Raupen*
– caterpillars – was holding court. To Uncle Abe's left sat his mother,
Sara, the matriarch of the clan. Sitting bolt upright, those dark, attentive
eyes missing nothing, she listened without speaking. His older brothers
were ranged around the table in order of age and importance: Felix,
Otto, and George. And then him, of course. At eighteen, he was the
youngest. Ordinarily he wouldn't have been here at this time. He would
have been in uniform, doing his military service, like millions of other
young Germans. But six months earlier that particular tradition had
ended abruptly. Jews were now banned from serving in the army.

A tram rumbled past; on the polished sideboard the wine glasses
rattled gently. He fished in his pocket for a cigarette, avoiding his
mother's disapproving frown. Couldn't they all see what was happening?
A month earlier, at a rally in Nuremberg, Hitler had announced a new
law *for the Protection of German Blood and German Honour*, making
marriage between Germans and Jews illegal. Barely a week later, another
one had been passed. This time it was the *Law for the Restoration of the
Professional Civil Service*. It meant Jews could no longer work in government. The picture was sharpening with each passing month. Slowly but
surely, they were being shepherded back into the very same ghettos from
which their forefathers had escaped. For the Harburgs, and families like
theirs whose very fortunes depended on trade and the freedom to move
around Europe, it was a death knell. *He* could see what was happening.
It was crystal clear. He drew angrily on his cigarette. It was absurd.
Whilst Hitler and his cronies plotted their strangulation, Uncle Abe sat
and talked and his own father locked himself up in his first-floor study

and listened to Brahms. They were slowly being strangled, 'strangled to death!' Lionel had burst out the week before. Uncle Abe laughed gently. '*Ach*, such fantasies! We're *German*,' he insisted. 'Always. First and foremost. You think they'll get rid of *us*? Rothschild? Warburg? Harburg? It's inconceivable. Inconceivable. They *need* us! This nonsense will pass, you'll see. It's not the first time, you know.'

The sound of girlish laughter from the adjoining room floated through the partially open door. His sisters – Lotte, Barbara, Rebecca and the youngest of them all, six-year-old Bettina – were playing cards. They rarely joined in these family discussions. Only his mother sat amongst the men, as she'd always done. She was more of a man than anyone he knew, he thought to himself suddenly, admiringly, watching her. For a second their eyes caught and held. She knew exactly what he was thinking.

He turned away and looked back down at the street. Snowflakes swirled in ever more intricate flurries, drifting eventually towards the ground. On the spires and steeply sloped roofs around them, huge piles of white, fluffy *Stoff* had gathered, softening the city's edges. It was December and Hamburg was in the grip of winter. He smoked quietly, his mind running ahead of itself, weighing up the options, thinking about potential destinations, contacts, people on whom he could call. They were running out of time. He'd lunched that afternoon with Uncle Sigmund and that dreadful friend of his, Chaim Weizmann. Weizmann was en route to New York, trying to persuade rich American Jews to support his vision of a Jewish state. Otto seemed charmed by him but Lionel was ambivalent. Emigrate? To where? Palestine? It meant little to him. For nearly three centuries the Harburgs had operated successfully in that lucrative, fluid area between the Jewish and Gentile worlds. They were on excellent, first-name terms with statesmen, politicians and business leaders across Europe. Of the great Jewish banking dynasties – the Rothschilds, Warburgs and Harburgs – the Harburgs were the smallest but they were by no means the weakest. Three centuries of slow but steady advancement – he saw no reason to give it up and flee halfway across the world to some barren, dusty patch of land and grow what . . . *oranges*? They were bankers, not farmers.

He ground out his cigarette and pulled out his watch chain. It was nearly eight in the evening. From his parents' elegant villa on Rothebaumchaussee it was a short walk to his own small apartment on Feldbrunnenstraße. The opulent home where he'd spent his childhood was a far cry from the cramped little apartment that was now his. Sara, though restrained enough in her outward emotions, was a woman of surprisingly rich, decorative tastes. She favoured the neo-Classical style of the German haute-bourgeoisie – dense, colourful patterns, heavy wooden panelling, ornate picture frames, potted plants, mirrors and pictures on every conceivable surface. Although he would never say it out loud, Lionel sometimes felt stifled by the surfeit of colours and patterns and textures that he'd grown up with. When his father and Uncle Abe (or the other way round, to be more precise) had made a gift of the bachelor apartment five minutes' walk from the family home, he was relieved. He was drawn to the clean lines of the Modern movement, to the spare, elegant architecture of Gropius and the young Mies van der Rohe who'd taken over the running of the Bauhaus. But the Bauhaus too had fallen foul of the new regime. Lionel had heard, amongst other, more disturbing things, that the school was to be closed down the following month. None of it augured well.

'Lionel,' Sara called out, drawing him back to the dining table. 'Uncle Abe is leaving.'

Uncle Abe levered himself up from his chair, gripping each of his nephews by the shoulder in a gesture that was meant to bolster them after a Friday-night dinner shadowed by fear.

Lionel walked over to him. 'Uncle,' he murmured, feeling the older man's heavy grip on his own shoulder.

'Chin up,' Uncle Abe said in what he thought was a reassuring voice. 'This will pass. You'll see.' Lionel was on the verge of telling him what he really thought but Sara's eyes flashed a quick warning. Uncle Abe pulled on his coat and lumbered into the drawing room where the girls sat listening to Bettina play the piano. There was an outburst of laughter and squeals as he flirted with them, cracking jokes and playing the role of favourite uncle.

'Don't,' Sara murmured in an aside to him, as Lionel's fists clenched involuntarily. 'Don't say anything, *mein Liebling*.'

'Mama, this is absurd!' Lionel hissed. 'Chin up? He's *insane!*'

'Shh. Your brothers'll hear. I'll see Uncle Abe off, and then let's you and I have a glass of port together in the study. Calm down, Lionel. It's not good for your blood pressure.'

He said nothing but watched her move regally through to the drawing room. His brothers were still arguing mildly over the merits of some play or another. He turned away in disgust. What was the phrase? *All of*

Rome is burning and the band plays on. He lit another cigarette and moved again to the window. Outside, seemingly oblivious to the impending doom, snowflakes continued to fall.

SARA HARBURG

It was nearly midnight by the time Lionel stopped talking. 'England?' Sara put up a hand to nervously touch the locket she wore around her neck. It was a small, uncharacteristic display of weakness. But in her next breath she rallied, caught hold of herself. She was aware of how much he depended on her. 'England,' she repeated slowly, but it wasn't a question this time. 'Have you spoken to Uncle Paul?'

He nodded, drawing on his cigarette, taking care not to blow the smoke anywhere near her face. 'He's confident he can get us in. But only if we leave soon. We can't wait any longer, Mama. We've got to go. *Now.*'

Sara nodded slowly. She looked at the room, at the wood-panelled walls laden with bookshelves, pictures, the plump, comfortable furniture; the beautifully aged leather chairs with the red, ruched-silk cushions she'd had specially sewn. Over in the corner, there was the standard lamp with its fringed shade and the gilt and rather gaudy Blackamoor that Uncle Paul had bought at Sotheby's and brought over to Germany as a gift . . . it was their home. *Her* home. *This* was their life. Generation after generation had worked hard, saved and sacrificed personal gain. *For those that come after*, the mantra by which every man in the Harburg family lived. That they'd come from such humble beginnings had never been forgotten, not like some she knew. You worked hard in this life to provide for those whose turn it was next. And by God, they'd worked hard. What was more, the accumulation of their wealth had nothing to do with the display of it. The Harburgs had *never* flaunted their success, never taken it for granted. That old, ancestral fear of displacement had never quite left them, though in Sara's generation the fear had been buried, sublimated under the libraries and art collections and the patronage for which she, Sara Harburg, was so renowned.

But what use was all of that now? What use was a Harburg box at the *Staatsoper* when they were banned from stepping inside? Lionel was right. Slowly but surely the Nazis were stripping them of everything that made them human, made life worth living. Scores of families they knew had left Germany, many of them to Palestine. But, just like Lionel, Sara was alarmed by the thought of leaving the world that she knew – music, good food and wine, conversation, the ballet – for an unknown culture in a corner of the world she knew little about. She had no desire to go to Palestine but she wasn't delusional, either, like Abe. If others like Max Warburg was talking openly of rescue, Lionel was right. They had to leave. And quickly. And yet . . . every one of her eight children had been born in that house. Leaving this would mean leaving some essential part of herself behind.

As if sensing her thoughts, Lionel suddenly put out a hand and touched her arm. 'It's a hard choice, Mama. God knows. But it's no choice at all. It's this . . . or nothing.'

She looked down at his hand, and then covered it with her own. She nodded slowly. 'Do what you can, Lionel. Make the preparations. Your brothers won't come, you know that?'

'I know. But *you* will. And Lotte and Bettina, of course. But Rebecca . . . I don't know about Rebecca. There's the thing with the Rosenberg boy—'

'You're a good son, Lionel,' Sara interrupted him slowly. 'A good son. Strong. I couldn't have asked for better, you know that. You've made me so proud of you. Your father—' She hesitated, and then stopped. They both knew what it was she couldn't say. She got to her feet heavily, brushing his arm aside and walked to the door. 'Do what you have to. Get us out of here. Those that will come.' She closed the door firmly behind her and made her way upstairs.

He would remain there, smoking quietly, thinking things through, she knew. The comment about his father, though she'd stopped herself just in time, would have hit the mark. Although still so young, Lionel would be the one to save them, not her husband. She'd married a weak, vain man: loving and kind, yes, but weak. It pained her to say it but it was the truth. She shook her head at how things had turned out. The daughter of a prominent Altona banker, she was seventeen when she married, not yet a woman. At first she was delighted with the charming young man, whose arrival in their solemn house brought warmth that was previously lacking. But she misunderstood the charm, believing it to be his real nature. It was not. He was weak, feeble. In another life, he might have been an academic or a poet, a man of letters and words, not actions. In another life, *she'd* have been a man. She was married before she could have any real idea of what the world might offer her. She saw at once that a dreadful mistake had been made but she was a practical girl. She produced her children, one after the other . . . ten in all. Eight of them survived.

When her fourth child and last son, Lionel, was born, she knew that she'd been saved. Of all her offspring, only he was like her. Now that he was almost a man, the ambition that she'd suppressed in herself for so long was born again. They would move to England, reinvent themselves, as they had to, and find a way to survive. It came as no surprise to her now, after nearly sixty years, that it would be her son, not her husband, who would save them – those who had the courage to follow, of course.

6

1939

FOUR YEARS LATER

LIONEL
London, England

A hush fell over the small knot of employees gathered in the banking hall. The secretaries exchanged nervous, half-excited glances. It was rare that the great business of banking ever ground to a complete halt, even rarer that the men for whom they all worked ever came down to the hall and stood with them, cigars and cigarettes in hand, just waiting. Even the telephones were silent. Everyone held their breath. There was a short burst of static, then the strong, confident voice of Chamberlain filled the hall.

'I am speaking to you from the Cabinet Room at ten Downing Street. This morning the British ambassador in Berlin handed the German government a final note stating that unless we heard from them by eleven a.m. that they were prepared at once to withdraw their troops from Poland, a state of war would exist between us. I have to tell you that no such undertaking has been received, and that consequently, this country is at war with Germany.' Lionel quickly glanced across the room to where his uncles, Siegfried

and Paul sat. Both men wore looks of impassive, impressive calm. *'Now may God bless you all,'* Chamberlain continued. *'May He defend the right. It is the evil things that we shall be fighting against – brute force, bad faith, injustice, oppression and persecution – and against them, I am certain that the right will prevail.'* There was complete silence as Chamberlain's voice faded away. It was as if the morning was holding its breath. A second passed, then another and then suddenly the air was ripped apart in a heart-stopping, heart-thumping shriek. The air-raid sirens had gone off.

In the chaotic scramble to get to the basement of the building that served as the street shelter, he found himself pressed up against a young girl, one of the many secretaries who worked on the second floor. Her pretty face was distorted by fear. He quickly looked away. There was something about seeing in the faces of others what he kept buried in himself that made him deeply uncomfortable. It stirred memories of their escape from Germany. It had taken them four days to make the crossing from Hamburg to Rotterdam and he'd been afraid every single second of the way. With his mother and two sisters beside him, he couldn't give in to the dread seeping through him whenever the train stopped or a bell sounded or he heard the voices of the guards coming down the corridor. For their sakes, if not his, he maintained an air of unflappable calm, much as his uncles were doing now. They stopped once in the middle of the night at a shunting yard somewhere in the no-man's land just before the official Dutch border. It was the absence of noise that woke him. The great creak and sway of the train that he'd grown used to, ceased suddenly. He got up carefully so as not to disturb the others. He could hear his mother's laboured breathing. The journey, which had already taken the better part of two days, had been hard on her. And it wasn't over yet. He opened the door and shut it quietly behind them. In the dark, silent corridor, he could hear nothing other than the thump of his own heart. The train gave the odd twitch and creak as it stood still, patiently yoked to the tracks like an ox. It was cold; there was an open window about halfway down the corridor. He moved towards it, his heart hammering, and carefully stuck his head outside.

The night air was sour; a yellowed smell of urine and brake fluid rose sharply from the ground. He could see lights ahead and the ominous hit-and-miss of flashlights as shadowy figures moved up the tracks towards him. Fog swirled around one of the sodium-orange floodlights. Somewhere dogs began to bark; there were shouts and he could feel reverberations of doors slamming further down the train. A few minutes passed, spooling out towards infinity. He could feel rivulets of nervous sweat prickling his underarms, his back. His hand went to the two tiny packages in his left trouser pocket. In one, a small black velvet pouch contained several beautifully cut and polished diamonds. In the other hand, a small pillbox containing three vials of cyanide. Two packages, two choices. Live or die. Hans von Rilke, a classmate and one of the few left who still took his calls, had tipped him off. 'Take diamonds,' he said guardedly. 'They might come in handy, you never know.' Diamonds were the insurance of choice. It was too risky to be caught carrying cash.

The sound of footsteps grew louder, but it was a single footfall. The door at the far end opened and someone stood in the doorway, a dim, yellowy light spilling around him. Lionel's fingertips went to the velvet pouch. The officer – there was no mistaking the measured, confident tread – walked down the corridor towards him and stopped. They were almost of equal height. There was a moment's pause as the officer looked at him, sizing Lionel up. There was no tell-tale yellow star, no 'J' pinned to his dark grey overcoat.

'*Ausweiß, bitte.*' The words were clipped, measured. What happened next depended entirely on Lionel.

He withdrew the small velvet pouch and carefully, very carefully, placed it in the officer's palm. There was no mistaking his intent. In complete silence the officer weighed it up, jiggling the little pouch, assessing its contents.

'*Gute Reise.*' He slipped it into the pocket of his uniform and turned on his heel. For the rest of his life, Lionel knew he would remember that moment as if it were yesterday.

Now, as he watched the faces of the young girls and men around him, blinking dazedly in the dim, weak underground light, the fear of that journey washed over him like a sweat. He desired only to be safe. A second later, as if in answer, the shriek of the all-clear sounded, mingling down there with the groans and cries and sighs of relief. A false alarm.

Uncle Paul's hand was on his shoulder as they all trooped noisily up the stairs. 'Narrow escape, eh?' he murmured. 'Let's hope there'll be more of those.'

Lionel nodded, not trusting himself to speak just yet.

'D'you have a moment, my boy?' Uncle Paul asked as they both reached the first-floor landing together. 'Come up to my office. There's someone I'd like you to meet.'

Lionel nodded. 'I'll just get my cigarettes,' he said, opening the door to the small office he shared with his cousin Henry, Uncle Paul's oldest son.

Uncle Paul chuckled. 'They'll be the death of you, those sticks,' he said. 'Hitler might not get you, but they will.' He continued on his way.

There were three gentlemen in Uncle Paul's office. He recognised Samuel Warburg immediately. He was chairman of S.W. Warburgs, their bigger, more established rival on Cheapside. The Warburgs had been in England for decades, although they were originally German, like most of the Jewish bankers in the City. He looked at the other two gentlemen, whom he'd never seen before. The man who sat with his back partially turned to the window was vaguely familiar – Lionel had seen his photograph somewhere – a newspaper, perhaps? He couldn't quite place him. The man standing by the window was different, in all senses of the word. Olive-skinned, with thick, jet-black hair, a proper handlebar moustache of the kind that had long ago gone out of fashion, he was dressed in a smart black suit, silk cravat and a snowy white shirt straining over an impressively domed stomach. He looked Italian, or Spanish, perhaps, certainly not English, or German.

'Ah, Lionel.' Uncle Paul looked up as he came through the door. 'Come in, my boy, come in.'

The three men turned. Samuel Warburg looked him over gravely, then turned to his Uncle Paul with an eyebrow cocked, as if to say, *So, this is whom you've been talking about?* Lionel recognised the look. *He's young. Very young.* It accompanied most introductions that came his way.

'Good afternoon, gentlemen,' Lionel said, crossing the room to shake hands before the invitation to do so had been issued. He could see the wary approval in everyone's eyes. A confident young man.

'Fred Schultz.' Uncle Paul made the introductions. 'And Georges Malouf.'

Ah, Lionel thought, recognising the name. *Frederick Schultz.* A colleague of Uncle Abe's from Hamburg – not Jewish, a Gentile. What was he doing in London? he wondered. And the other man? From the name – Georges Malouf – he presumed the man was an Arab but what was he doing in Uncle Paul's office?

'Gentlemen,' Uncle Paul began, without delay. 'Shall we get down to business?' He indicated the polished oval table with its eight chairs in

35

the centre of the room. Lionel waited until the four men were seated and then took his own opposite his uncle. Uncle Paul sat down and cleared his throat. He looked up from the dossier of documents in front of him. 'Thank you for coming, gentlemen. You all know the situation we find ourselves in. We have two options. Either we abandon the bank to the Nazis or we effect a temporary transfer of control. Samuel, I believe you're in the same boat, which is why I've asked you to be here. I do not wish for this firm, which has been my life's work, as yours has, Samuel, to be destroyed. I'm therefore proposing we take the latter route. I'm proposing we transfer control to you, Fred, until this is over.'

He looked up again. There was an expression in his face that Lionel hadn't seen before, a kind of openness . . . an appeal of some sort. Before he could ponder it further, Uncle Paul continued. 'This . . . this *madness* will end one day, gentlemen. And when it does, the whole world will have changed. I believe in being ready for those changes. *We* must be ready, which is why I've asked my dear friend Georges Malouf to be here. Gentlemen, our fortunes are inextricably linked. Germany, Britain, the United States and Palestine. I'm proposing an alliance, my dear friends, that will see us through the coming years. And I've asked Lionel, my youngest nephew, to be present because it will be *his* task, just as it has been mine for the past thirty years, to build on what we've been given.'

7

The office felt strangely emptied after they'd gone, as though the very air had been sucked out of it, replaced by a melancholy that produced in both himself and Uncle Paul a strained reluctance to speak. Neither seemed willing to break the spell. Lionel lit a cigarette and smoked quietly. Uncle Paul got up from his seat at the polished oval table and walked to his desk. He sat down heavily, removing his spectacles to pinch the skin between his eyes, a gesture that struck Lionel as ineffably sad.

'So this is it,' he said after a moment. 'Three hundred years we've been in business. I never thought *I* would be the one to make such a decision.'

Lionel's mind was moving quickly. 'It's the right thing to do,' he said carefully, stubbing out his cigarette. His uncle was seeking some other form of reassurance, separate from the hard-nosed business decision he'd just had to make. Something deeper, another form of consolation. 'And you're the only person who could have done it. Uncle Abe won't listen. He thinks Hitler will be finished within the year.' He gave into a hollow laugh. 'And as for my father . . .' He shrugged. There was no point in saying anything further.

Uncle Paul nodded absently. His mind seemed elsewhere. The minutes ticked by slowly. Lionel finished his cigarette and was just about to get up when Uncle Paul spoke suddenly. 'Listen, my boy, I want to tell you something. It's about your father. Something I think you ought to know.'

As he spoke, Lionel saw that he was retreating into another relationship with him, as if the role of banker was another, different matter. 'It's not because I want to excuse him,' Uncle Paul said, wagging his finger from side to side. 'No, not at all. I know what a disappointment he's been, not least to your mother.' He swivelled his chair around so that he was facing the impressive portrait of Samuel Harburg, the founder of the bank. He fell silent for a moment. Lionel was aware of the ornamental clock on the mantelpiece behind them, ticking away. 'There are things you need to know, to understand,' Uncle Paul continued. 'Not for his benefit, mind you, for yours. No man should have to make his way in the world thinking of his father as a failure. He may have failed certain, shall we say, *challenges*. But he's not a failure, no. Not when you understand what he came from.'

'What do you mean?'

Uncle Paul sighed. He rested his elbows on his desk, steepling his fingers together. 'I don't suppose anyone's ever told you, have they?'

'Told me what?'

'That your father's not . . . not quite who you think he is.'

Lionel stared at him. 'What are you talking about?'

'I expect you've always thought of him as simply one of us. A Harburg. Oma Rebecca's son. Well, he's not. He's a Harburg. Yes, he's Samuel's child, but not Rebecca's. No. Your grandfather had a – a *liaison*, shall we call it? – early on in his marriage and your father is the result. The woman died not long after he was born. Rebecca took the baby in immediately. Brought him up as her own. Many women wouldn't, you know, but she did. But, there was always a slight lack of *warmth*, shall we say? Your father suffered terribly. Still does, I imagine. And then there was the question of . . . well, the woman wasn't Jewish.'

Lionel stared at him. 'Are you saying my father's not Jewish?'

'Well, *technically* speaking, no. He's not. But that doesn't matter. He's a Harburg, that's all there is to it. That's all that matters.' He frowned at Lionel. 'But none of this has any bearing on *you*, my boy. You're Jewish, as Jewish as the rest of us. And you're your mother's son, make no mistake. There's almost nothing of your father in you. Well, a little around the eyes, perhaps. But you're Sara's boy. Which is why you're here. You watch; you listen; you act. Just like your mother.' He sighed. 'The most capable woman I've ever met. I must confess to . . . to a certain *admiration* for Sara, not that she'd ever accept it.' He stopped abruptly. 'I digress. Forgive me. My point is that your father's had quite a lot to deal with. His position within the family has always been difficult. There's been a lot of . . . insecurity. Yes, insecurity. He is an insecure man, Lionel, not a *failure*. It's important you understand the difference. Do you?' Uncle Paul looked up from his position at the desk. A sternness had crept into his voice that hadn't been there before, as though he'd staked out certain big, immutable facts and was now daring Lionel to make sense of them and accept them.

Lionel was silent. He thought of his father. A quiet man, with a weakness for the softer, sweeter things in life – sweets, puddings, rich tortes and sticky buns that the girls in the kitchen used to make especially for him. He was mild-mannered, not at all given to the outbursts of sentiment and fierce debate that characterised every other member of the household, the girls included. He spent most of his time in his library or, if the weather was fine, in the gardens beyond the lawn. When he was younger, Lionel sometimes wandered over to help him with whatever gardening task was at hand – pruning, planting, weeding and cutting. He spoke little, hummed a lot under his breath. That was all. Very occasionally, out of some strange, hidden provocation that none around him could see, a mood would come upon him that took him out of himself, turned him momentarily into someone else. He would shout and shake his fist at the world, some darkness having descended upon him. They heard the incomprehensible shouts and steered clear. Oddly enough, it was only their mother, Sara, who could calm him at such times. She would sit quietly with him until he had shouted himself out and the storm of whatever it was that had overtaken him had worn itself thin. When all was quiet again, he would suddenly pick up whatever task he'd been engaged in and continue, as if nothing had happened. His mother would sit there for a few minutes longer and then with a look upon her face that Lionel had never been able to fathom, she would simply get to her feet and leave.

He got to his feet slowly. He felt suddenly overwhelmed. His view of the world, which had until that point remained refreshingly simple, was becoming more complicated by the second. The family that he'd always thought of as solid and immutable was crumbling. They were scattered now: some of them stubbornly waiting it out in Germany; his mother and sisters here in London, under his care. There were uncles here and there, new business associates in America and Palestine. New opportunities were presenting themselves and with them, of course, came new risks.

It was then, in that moment, that he saw very clearly what it was his uncle was asking of him. The question wasn't whether or not he accepted Uncle Paul's version of the facts as he'd told them to him. The question was deeper, altogether more urgent. Was he ready? *That* was the question. Was he ready to be the thread that would pull and hold the fragmented pieces of his family's past together?

8

1963

TWENTY-FOUR YEARS LATER

EMBETH ELEANORA HAUSMANN
Cornell University, Ithaca, New York

'You are just so *lucky*, Em.' Betty Schroeder rolled over onto her stomach and cupped her chin in her hands, watching Embeth pack.

'Lucky? Why d'you say that?' Embeth held up a pale-blue cashmere sweater in her hands. Was it worth taking back with her to Venezuela? No, probably not.

Betty held out her pink-tipped hands in front of her, inspecting her nails. 'Well, *you* don't have to find a husband or get a job. At least not right now.' She rolled over onto her back again, sighing deeply. Unlike Embeth, whose wealthy parents had gladly footed the bill for Embeth's education, Betty was an SG, a scholarship girl. She was bright and ambitious and everything, but her scholarship hadn't *quite* covered the cost of four years at Cornell University. There was now a considerable amount of debt, which had to be paid back somehow. Betty was pretty and wholesome in the way of many girls from places like Buffalo, New York and Marshalltown, Iowa, and her mother was desperate for her to make a good match – the sooner the better, too. What was the point of such an expensive education if it didn't mean meeting a different calibre of man? A *better* calibre? Betty had no answer.

'Neither do you,' Embeth said calmly. 'The husband bit, I mean.'

Betty sat upright and smoothed down her skirt. Her dress, a stiff, layered confection of pink cotton with splashy, over-sized roses and a nipped-in, belted waist, was creased. 'You try telling my mom that,' she said wryly. 'Oh, Em, I wish I was going with you!'

Embeth shook her head. 'No you don't. Believe me, you don't.'

'I do, really I do. It all sounds so . . . so glamorous. Your life *is* glamorous, Em. All those parties, the beach, the hot nights . . . it sounds divine, it really does,' she said passionately, earnestly.

Embeth smiled, a wave of affection for her best friend washing over her. Betty really was the most earnest person she'd ever met. They'd been friends since their freshman year. It was almost impossible to believe it was all over. 'Well, what things *sound* like and what they're *really* like aren't always the same,' she said firmly, closing her trunk. She heaved it off the bed and onto the floor. In the corner of the room, three further trunks stood, bursting at the seams. Four years' worth of clothing that she would probably never wear again and books she would never touch again had been stuffed into those trunks, soon to be dispatched to Caracas. Every fall, for the past four years, she and her mother had spent a wholly enjoyable week in New York, shopping for the upcoming winter. They'd bought the soft wool and luxurious cashmere outfits that her mother remembered from her own childhood in Switzerland. But there was no need for cashmere in Caracas. 'And anyhow, I'll be under just as much pressure as you, just you wait and see,' Embeth added.

'No you won't. I've met your parents, don't you remember? Your mom is just the most glamorous person I've ever seen. I wish she were *my* mother.'

'Don't say that,' Embeth said quickly. 'Don't ever say that.'

'Why not? It's true. And as for your father . . . oh, *my*! He's just so . . . so suave! So sophisticated!' She rolled over yet again, kicking her legs up into the air. 'They're both just so goddamn *fabulous*! Everything about your life is fabulous, Embeth, *everything*!'

Embeth shook her head, smiling. She knew better than to argue with Betty. If it suited Betty to think Embeth was jetting back to South America to a life of cocktail parties and hot, steamy, tropical nights, well, so be it. *She* knew the reality was very different. Of course she'd have her fair share of parties to attend, and there'd be soirees and trips to the opera and the ballet and so on, but underneath it all, she'd be under just as much pressure to marry as Betty – more, if anything. The pool of eligible young Jewish men in Caracas was tiny. She already knew most of them and the thought of marrying any one of the weak-chinned Ababarnel, Guzmán, Braunstein or Kaufmann sons was enough to make her weep. After all, she'd been the one to beg her parents to do things differently. She'd wanted them to send her to America. She wanted a college degree. To her surprise, they'd readily agreed. Her mother in particular had been supportive of her only daughter's wishes. 'If Mimí wants to study, she should. I see absolutely no reason *not* to send her.' She ought to have spotted the difference. Finding no reason *not* to send her wasn't quite the same thing as wanting to send her. But she was sent abroad to one of the best schools, no expense spared, just as she wanted. In her four years at Cornell, her parents made sure she lacked for nothing.

Now, on her return, she would be expected to make good on their investment. It wasn't about the money. The Hausmanns 'had more money than God', as she'd once overheard someone say. It was about something more elusive, less graspable. They wanted her to make a good *match*, the right sort of man from the right sort of family. Betty had *no* idea just how claustrophobic it could be. Venezuela had been good to those Jews who'd come in the 1920s and 30s as professionals. These immigrants were not *shtetl* Jews, fleeing pogroms and living timid lives in their new, adopted homes. No, the Jewish immigrants who arrived in Caracas were prosperous, influential people. They settled into palatial homes in Altamira and the like, and the Hausmanns were no exception. Within a generation, the Hausmanns produced two Nobel prize-winning scientists, scores of doctors, two judges, a novelist and three government ministers, including her uncle, Jorge Hausmann, *el ministro*. The Minister. Everyone knew Jorge Hausmann. One summer when Embeth was in high school, there'd been talk of a match between Embeth and Julio, Uncle Jorge's middle son. Fortunately, her mother had seen the look of horror on Embeth's face when the subject was first broached and she swiftly put an end to the hopeful speculations.

At the thought of her mother, Embeth's stomach gave a little lurch. Hard as it was to imagine, in just under a week's time she'd be back there in Caracas, back amongst her family, sitting under the soft, warm glow of the chandelier that hung above the dining table. The maids, Sophia and Mercedes, who'd been with the family as long as Embeth could remember, would bring in the many dishes. Her mother, Miriám, would serve herself first, then indicate Embeth's turn, watching her carefully to make sure she didn't overeat. Miriám needn't worry. The puppy fat Embeth had had at thirteen had long since been shed. Now, at twenty-two, she was every bit as slender as Miriám. She would never say it out loud, least of all to Betty, but when she'd first met Betty's mother at the end of their freshman year, she'd offered up a silent prayer of thanks. She couldn't *imagine* having a mother like Betty's. Enormous, with triple chins that quivered every time she spoke, a cigarette hanging permanently from fleshy, over-ripe lips and those *feet* . . . like pink sausages stuffed into scuffed, pointed shoes. She'd stared at her, unable to recognise in her the fresh-faced Betty she'd come to know and love. There was almost nothing of Betty in Sally, or vice-versa. How could that be? Miriám was everything Embeth wanted to be. And more. What, she wondered to herself, must it be like to have a mother like *that*?

She hauled the last suitcase onto the bed. One more to go. What would her mother be doing right now? It was almost five o'clock in the afternoon in New York, four p.m. in Caracas. It was a Tuesday. She would just be returning from tennis. Her mother's life was a never-ending stream of social engagements, charity functions and exercise. She played tennis, rode horses and practised daily the tortuous calisthenics that kept her slender and firmly toned. But mostly she did nothing. Embeth had never seen her mother read anything other than a magazine or a novel. Very occasionally, she picked up a newspaper, which she generally put aside with an expression of dismay. She'd never worked in her life. Work was for men, or for women of a much lower class. And work was certainly not for her daughter, Embeth. In fact, the whole conversation about sending her to America had been couched in terms of *improving her chances*, but not of the professional kind.

'Here . . . what d'you think?' Betty said suddenly, jumping to her feet and interrupting Embeth's rather dismal train of thought. Embeth looked up from the suitcase. Betty was standing in front of the mirror, admiring herself. She'd pinned her hair up with one hand. 'Too Grace Kelly?'

'A little,' Embeth agreed, smiling. 'But that's not such a bad thing.'

'Reckon I could get me a prince too?'

'Well, *you'd* probably stand a better chance than me,' Embeth giggled. She quickly hopped over the bed and came to stand behind her. For a moment the mirror held the two of them: Betty, cool, serene-looking and blonde and Embeth, dark and fiery. With raven-black hair, almond-shaped eyes, high cheekbones, she was darker than either of her brothers. *Un toque de alquitrán. A touch of the tar brush, a shadow behind the ears.* There were many sayings in Spanish to explain why some within a family might have a duskier complexion than others. Miriám paled when she heard them and forbade Embeth from going in the sun. By the time Embeth was in her teens, she couldn't recall the last time she'd had a tan. Now, in her early twenties, her skin was pale and soft with only the faintest hint of colour rising in her cheeks when she was embarrassed or upset. 'Why don't you wear it loose?' she suggested, looking at Betty. 'It suits you best.'

'Yeah, maybe you're right. D'you think I gained weight?'

Embeth rolled her eyes. '*Betty!* I don't believe you. Here we are, a week after graduation, and all you can talk about is hair and weight? Come on, there are so many other things worth talking about.'

'Yeah? Like what?'

'Well,' Embeth said, considering, 'like . . . like the war, for one thing. Did you hear about Medger Evers?'

'Who?' Betty yawned at her in the mirror.

'Medger Evers, the civil rights activist. He was murdered yesterday.'

'Oh, *him*.' Betty inspected her nails. 'The problem with you, Embeth,' she drawled lazily, 'is that you think too much. There are so many other things to focus on.'

'Like what?'

'Like what are you wearing tonight?'

'Oh, *Betty*.' Embeth shook her head. But perhaps Betty was right, in her own, rather myopic way. What was the point of getting all steamed up about a war that was being fought ten thousand miles away? She picked up another cashmere jumper. It was pale pink, a Betty sort of colour. 'Here . . . I'm never going to wear these again. Would you like them?' She pointed to the growing pile of pastel-coloured sweaters and cardigans.

'Are you *kidding*? Ohmigod! *Thank* you, honey!' Betty squealed, pouncing on the pile. 'You're an *angel*! These'll look *so* good with those new pedal pushers I just bought – you know, the black ones? They're *so* fashionable right now! Jackie Kennedy had on a pair the other day, did you notice?'

'I was too busy focusing on what her husband was saying,' Embeth said drily.

It was Betty's turn to roll her eyes affectionately. 'Like I said, you *think* too much, Em. Oh, I can't *wait* to try these on.' She clutched the sweaters to her chest, pressing her cheek into the luxuriously soft wool. She gave a deep sigh of heartfelt contentment. 'You're so *lucky*, Embeth.'

And this time Embeth had no idea what to say.

9

SIX MONTHS LATER

EMBETH
Avenida San Carlos, Caracas, Venezuela

The conversation at the dinner table was conducted, as ever, in Spanish, English and German, and occasionally all three at once. The discussions ranged far and wide – the war in Vietnam; Hurricane Flora, which was threatening Cuba; the Profumo Affair rumbling on in England; Martin Luther King's Washington speech; the local presidential elections. The Hausmanns had a particular interest in the latter. The incumbent president was at the end of his term and there'd been talk of Uncle Jorge assuming leadership of the party. As always, opinions were sharply divided.

As the tenor of the talk around her rose and fell, Embeth laid her knife and fork to one side to indicate she'd finished, leaving half of her food untouched. Her mother glanced over approvingly. A lady *never* finished what was on her plate. She leaned back in her chair, only just managing to stifle a yawn. It wasn't that she was bored – on the contrary. She found the men's talk fascinating, but joining in was out of the question. Like the other women present, her job was decorative. She was wearing white, a splendid contrast to Miriám's burgundy silk.

44

Earlier that evening, just before descending the staircase to join the others, Miriám had threaded a beautiful ivory silk rose through her dark hair. 'There, that's better.' She surveyed her daughter critically. 'I *still* don't understand why you cut it,' she murmured, smoothing her own luxuriously long tresses in an unconscious gesture of protection.

Embeth sighed. It was a conversation they'd had practically every single day since her return. 'I like it short,' she said, careful not to let the irritation she felt slip through.

'So unbecoming,' Miriám murmured. 'Anyhow, it'll grow back. You look beautiful, my darling. Are you ready?'

'About as ready as I'm ever likely to be.'

'Oh, for goodness' sake, Embeth! A little graciousness wouldn't go amiss.' Miriám didn't wait for a reply but swept out of the room, her silk evening dress fanning out splendidly and fluidly behind her. Embeth had no option but to follow. Mother and daughter descended the staircase to the slow, appreciative applause of the men gathered below.

'Mercedes!' Miriám hissed at the now-elderly maid. Miriám couldn't bear seeing half-empty plates strewn across the snowy white table. 'Mercedes,' Miriám whispered again, louder this time. She signalled urgently but discreetly across the table. *Fill up the empty wine glasses! Clear away those plates!* The penny dropped. Mercedes nodded and hurried out. Within seconds, the offending plates were gone and empty glasses were topped up. No one except Embeth noticed a thing. That was the way her mother ran the household, Embeth thought to herself, watching her, smooth, silent performance. Even the candles in the chandelier above the table lasted the exact length of the meal, no more.

She looked down the length of the table to the living room beyond, and beyond that, framed by the gently billowing white muslin curtains, to the veranda where they sometimes held cocktail parties overlooking the emerald pool. The night air was quiet and still. After the wintry silence of upstate New York, the soft buzz of the tropics, a mixture of warm, humid air and the barely audible hum of insects, was a welcome return. She could see their reflections in the huge gilt mirror at one end of the dining room. Maria-Luísa Gomez de Santander, the wife of the finance minister, was on her left, murmuring something inconsequential to her mother. Her perfume was thick and heavy, clinging to her skin like fog. She'd detected the faintest wrinkle in her mother's nose as she was ushered into the hallway. Miriám disliked excesses of any kind.

Embeth stifled another yawn. She'd been back for almost six months and in that time, had done little else than attend dinner parties, the ballet, and opera . . . just as Betty had predicted. There was little else to do. The highlight of every dinner party held at home was gossiping afterwards in the kitchens with Sophia and Mercedes.

'Did you *see* that one?' An hour later, the men safely in the study with cigars and brandy and the women on the patio with coffee, Mercedes' eyes widened in disbelief. 'Like a turkey! She could hardly get her bosom into her dress! Any tighter and she'd pass out.'

Embeth and Sophia giggled together conspiratorially. Sophia and Mercedes took a lively interest in the comings and goings of the household. They knew more than their employers did about what really went on. Both had been with the Hausmanns for ever. Mercedes was a couple of years younger than Miriám . . . Embeth couldn't exactly remember the intricate route of relationships by which she'd come to them – her mother had worked in service for Miriám's mother, or some such – but she genuinely was one of the family. Sophia had been there almost as long – thirty years at least.

'*Ay Dios*,' Sophia murmured quietly, putting away the remains of a beautifully pink poached salmon. 'And as for Señora Cabral . . . well, I wouldn't like to guess where Señor Cabral was this evening.'

'I *know*. D'you notice how they never go out together?'

'*I* heard he's got another little apartment in town—'

'No, don't tell us. You heard it from that little *puta* who works at the Madrigál place?'

'How do you know?'

'You're not the only one with spies, you know—'

Embeth was comfortable in the way of a child, sitting at the table with her arms folded across each other, resting her cheek in the crook of one elbow. The gossip ebbed and flowed. The two women bustled good-naturedly around her, stopping occasionally to exclaim or protest or giggle. Miriám came in and frowned when she saw Embeth slouched over the kitchen table, but said nothing, just raised an eyebrow in that way of hers that said more than words ever could. Sophia hurried after her with the silver tray of coffee pots and exquisite porcelain side plates of *petits fours* that always accompanied the after-dinner coffees on the terrace.

'So, I saw Señor Hahn here yesterday,' Mercedes said as soon as they'd gone out, casting a sly, sideways glance at Embeth as she carried a stack of plates to the sink where the girl who did the washing up was waiting.

Embeth inspected her nails. 'So?'

'Don't gimme that look,' Mercedes grinned. 'What did he want?'

'Nothing,' Embeth said lightly. She sighed deeply. Why couldn't anyone find anything to talk to her about other than potential suitors? 'He just came to say hello.'

'*Claro que sí* and Prince Charming just stopped by to see *me*. Come on, spill the beans, girl!'

'There *are* none,' Embeth insisted. She slid off the seat. 'Besides, he's barely out of high school.'

'*No exageres!* He's older than you!'

'Doesn't look it. Anyhow, what's the rush? I've only just got back.'

'You gonna be an old maid if you don't watch out,' Sophia giggled, coming back into the kitchen. 'Like me and Mercedes.'

'You speak for yourself,' Mercedes piped up. 'I ain't gonna be here for ever, you wait and see.'

Sophia cackled heartily. Both women were in their fifties. Their chances of finding husbands were long gone, though neither seemed to display any resentment. They'd both given their lives to the care and running of the Hausmann household. What, Embeth wondered suddenly, was their reward? She looked at them as though seeing them for the first time. Mercedes was almost completely grey haired; her once thick, black hair, springy at the roots (yes, definitely 'tar' in the family in *her* case), was pulled back into a rather severe bun at the nape of her neck. Her body that had once been slender and slight had thickened; she looked every inch the plump, well-fed matriarch, except she was no matriarch. No family to speak of other than the Hausmanns, no children, no husband. What would happen to her when she was no longer able to work? What would happen to them both?

She brought the subject up the following morning as she sat watching her mother get dressed. 'What on earth do you mean?' Her mother turned from her mirror to look at Embeth. 'What do you mean, what will happen to her?'

'When she's too old to work, I mean.'

'Gracious, Embeth, what a thing to worry about! She'll be pensioned off. She'll return to her family, of course.'

'But she's lived here all her life. We *are* her family.'

47

'Embeth, that's just the way it is. What on earth has brought all this on?'

'Nothing,' Embeth mumbled, picking at a loose thread in her skirt. 'Nothing.'

She looked beyond the dressing table where her mother sat to the hills that were just visible through the half-open shutters. It had rained the night before, one of those sudden tropical downpours that come seemingly out of nowhere, shake the very foundations of the buildings with tremendous thunderclaps and flashes of steely white lightning, and then disappear, rolling over the hills to the south of the city and the vast *interiór* of the country beyond.

She let her mind roam free, as if the glimpse of green in the distance had sparked a restless, unspoken desire to break out of the confines of the house on a Saturday morning with its familiar rituals – a long, leisurely bath, followed by a breakfast of fruits and coffee on the terrace with the pool shimmering just out of sight; wandering into her mother's room, watching her get dressed; then the drawn-out preparations for lunch. There would be guests, of course, and Mercedes and Sophia would be in charge of making sure the junior staff swept and polished every surface until it gleamed. Her eyes shifted unconsciously between two dimensions – the one, far off in the distance, a line of hills marking the limits beyond which she couldn't see, and the other, the intimate, claustrophobic world of the house. Her skin tingled in rejection of it all.

'Mama,' she began again, more hesitantly this time.

'*Sí, mi amor.*' Her mother was dreamily distracted.

'Why do I have to get married? Couldn't I . . . couldn't I get a job, or something? If it's about money, I—'

'Embeth, will you *stop*? What is the matter with you? Of course it's not about money! What a thought! Don't you want to have a beautiful home, children, a good husband . . . a good life?'

'But why . . . why can't I have those things *without* a husband? Why do I have to get married? And in any case, what's the rush?' Embeth looked at her mother and then wished immediately she hadn't started the conversation in the first place. Her mother's look was one of sheer incomprehension.

'Oh, don't be so *silly*! How can you have a child without a husband? No, don't answer that. I don't even want to *hear* it.' Miriám turned back to her image. 'Now go and find Mercedes for me. Tell her to bring me some salts. You've given me a headache and it's not even noon.'

Embeth got up hastily from the bed and left the room. She'd been back for six months and there were days when it felt as though the centre had somehow fallen out of her world. Nothing made sense anymore, least of all her own thoughts. It was as if a veil that had previously obscured her vision of the world had suddenly been lifted. It was strange and bewildering. In her four years in Ithaca, safely away from her family and their silent but powerful demands, it had never occurred to her to rebel, to break free. She'd done what was asked of her. She attended her classes, attained and maintained her grades, the model student in more ways than one. But now that she was home again, a strange, unspecified longing had broken out in her, which she only now realised had been dormant all along. The pulls and ties that she'd subconsciously resisted now began to reassert themselves – a suitor, an engagement, a marriage . . . a family and a household of her own to run. She shrank instinctively from the gifts that were being offered but found that she had no substitute to take their place.

She pushed open her bedroom door and quickly closed it, leaning against it as if for support. Up there on the third floor, overlooking the gardens and the shimmering pool, the silence was of a different order. She looked over at the large double bed with its pretty counterpane and matching pillows, the thin, delicate mosquito net that hung draped above the bed and which Sophia untangled every night before she went to sleep. *This* was her life. *This* was what she'd been brought up to believe in, to cherish, and to want. So why didn't she want it?

10

SIX MONTHS LATER

LIONEL
London, England/Caracas, Venezuela

He went through the formalities with a weary acceptance that surprised even him. He'd lost count of the number of flights he'd taken between London and New York in the past year alone. He was a veteran, now. How quickly we become accustomed to the unaccustomed, he thought to himself wryly as he followed the now stooped figure of Uncle Paul through the various checkpoints before they reached the lounge where businessmen like themselves met before a flight was called. Tickets, passports, boarding cards . . . he produced them mechanically, one after the other until they were finally on board.

Dirk Schofeld, their business associate from Holland, was uneasy. It was his first flight. 'I'm a virgin, would you believe it?' he'd quipped nervously, much to Lionel's amusement. It was obvious. Once inside the lounge, he quickly downed one brandy after another. Uncle Paul looked on in faint but marked disapproval. He was not a drinker. Neither was Lionel, to be honest. His mother (*Baruch HaShem, may she rest in peace*) had developed an appreciation for brandy that had lasted right up until her death and Lionel still missed those evenings by the fire when he would come home, hang up his coat and hat and find her in the study, reading, a glass of brandy waiting for him, and a plate of those small English digestive biscuits that she so liked. He felt the habitual pull of sadness. Yes, it was two years since her death but there were days he felt the loss as though it were yesterday.

'Perhaps *now* you'll marry,' Uncle Paul had said to him, a few months after the elaborate funeral to which every single bank employee had been invited. He'd always maintained it was Sara that had kept him from the *chuppah*. Lionel shook his head. No, nothing like that. He'd just never met a woman he wanted to marry. At forty-seven he was a confirmed bachelor. He lived in the same, very comfortable set of apartments in St James's Park that he and Sara (*Baruch HaShem*) had shared for over twenty years. Her bedroom was exactly as she'd left it. In the living room was his vast collection of books, their beloved artworks that had been retrieved from the Altona house in Hamburg after the war, and three dogs.

His sister Lotte had married shortly after their arrival in England and now lived with her husband and two children in the countryside, a few miles from Cheltenham. She rarely came up to London and when she did, she was full of complaint. Bettina – fiery, hot-headed Bettina – had run off with a group of young, idealistic Zionists at the unbelievably tender age of seventeen to join a *kibbutz*. He'd come home one day to find her gone; it was a new world – there was nothing he could do. She refused all offers of financial help; she was a *kibbutznik*, not an heiress. He and Sara, once they'd got over the shock of it, shared many an evening alternately wringing their hands and laughing in admiring disbelief. It was in her blood; the girl couldn't help it.

Of the remaining siblings in Germany, three had eventually found their way to the United States and Barbara was safely in Australia. Otto was dead. He, along with other lesser members of the family who'd stubbornly refused to leave, was caught trying to make for the Dutch border in 1942, a year too late. He died at Auschwitz, together with his wife and two small daughters, the only members of the Hamburg Harburgs to have met such a fate. In some ways thankfully, his father had died of a heart attack shortly after Lionel took his mother and sisters to England – at least Hitler hadn't got him. All in all, Lionel reflected in those sombre moments when he allowed himself to think on it, they'd been fortunate. But it didn't ease the pain of Otto's death. His own brother: gassed, dumped, disposed of, like an animal led to slaughter. He had never been able to visit Auschwitz and he never would. Never.

He shook his head quickly to clear it and tried to concentrate on the business ahead. For the second time in his career, he sensed great changes in the air. *He* could see, even if Uncle Paul couldn't, that the era of the gentleman banker was almost gone. Clients no longer shook hands on a deal, expecting the handshake to hold firm against competition, dips in the market, losses and risks and circumstances beyond one's control. Now clients and bankers spoke to one another through their lawyers. But the changes didn't stop there. Between bankers themselves, the old rule about not treading on each other's toes or poaching clients by offering better deals elsewhere, was dying. Advertising and marketing, those anathemic 'professions' that seemed to him to be a mixture of everything he despised – flattery and pseudo-psychology – had crept into the industry with disastrous results. Suddenly everything was up for grabs, including loyalty. Their competitors were now stealing accounts that had been in the firm for decades. Colleagues appeared to have no qualms about stabbing each other in the back, all in the name of increased profits. Yet Uncle Paul wouldn't countenance the thought of striking back. He was proudly adamant. The Harburgs did *not* do business that way. They would not lower themselves by joining in the frenzy. *Their* clients would never leave them. Relationships at Harburg's were for life.

He was wrong, as it turned out. He was now an elderly man, almost bent double with curvature of the spine but he was stubborn. His wife had passed away almost five years earlier. With no children or grandchildren to occupy him, Uncle Paul lived for the bank. He came in every morning by chauffeur as he had done for over half a century and clung to his seat on the board.

But Lionel was a very different type of banker. He was a twenty-first-century man. He'd been born at the *fin-de-siècle*, at a moment when the old order of things was being swept aside. His decision to flee Germany and what he saw as his failure to save other members of the family from Hitler had made him wary, both of the past and of the future. He kept a wary eye on both but trusted in neither. He'd come to the painful conclusion that the only place that mattered was the here and now. He was a man of action, not words. In an unconscious rejection of his own father, perhaps, he stuck to his belief that what mattered most was the *ability to act*.

The trip to Venezuela was one such act. It was time for the bank to move away from the European upper-middle classes who had been their traditional clients and find other avenues for business. If they didn't, he told Uncle Paul flatly, there would be no banking legacy to pass on. It was a touchy subject. P. N. Harburg & Son, the London branch of the family business, was Uncle Paul's baby, the replacement for the children he'd never had. With Lionel's unexpected arrival in London, the delighted Uncle Paul had added the '& Son' to the bank's name. It mattered little that Lionel was not his son. He was a nephew but more of a son than anyone could ever have guessed. Now, in the twilight of his life, it pained him dearly that there might be nothing left of the bank worth handing down. It didn't make for the most cheering conversation between them.

Lionel drained the last of his champagne and fiddled with the radio headset, turning the dials until he found a station playing the sort of classical music he favoured. The strands of Mahler drifted over him and he felt immediately calmer. Venezuela was a young country, rich in raw materials and with a newly elected president who seemed pro-market, pro-reform and, crucially, pro-European. It also had a sizeable and affluent Jewish community. Oddly enough, it was Dirk Schofeld who'd made the first approach. He had associates in the Dutch Antilles and through them he'd managed to secure an invitation to dine with the influential Hausmann family at their Altamira home. Lionel was no fool. The first round of introductions was certainly important but after that it was anyone's guess which way the wind would blow. The name Harburg was still a force to be reckoned with – but so too were Rothschild and Warburg and Lehman and Loeb and there were no longer any guarantees that any one of them wouldn't be on the lookout for the same business opportunities as the Harburgs. Indeed, times had changed.

He lifted the window cover and looked out. The ground lay under a thin blanket of fog. Caracas would be sweltering, so they'd been told. The tropics. He'd never been to the tropics, he thought to himself as he felt the engines revving up below them. His trips abroad had always been across the Atlantic, to New York and Washington, or to Europe, and to Israel, of course, with Sara (*Baruch HaShem*) and to visit Bettina. He'd found it mostly hot and baffling.

There was a loud 'ping' above his head. They were ready for take-off. He felt the familiar rumbling shudder that was both sound and feeling that seemed to go on for ever. They taxied slowly out to the runway; there was a few minutes' wait whilst Dirk drained the last of his bottle of wine, pausing to mop his sweating face. There was a pause as they lined up down the long length of the runway, then a tremendous burst of energy as the plane began to race towards the horizon. He felt his whole body being pressed backwards into the seat as though some giant hand had come down on him, then the breaking free, the moment of flight, a bumpy, upward thrust as the plane lifted itself into the air. He remained with his face pressed against the window – no matter he'd seen it all countless times before. A few bumps and dips then the aircraft steadied itself and ploughed on blindly through the fog. It was a miracle, a modern miracle.

The fog thinned and lifted, wispy clouds zooming in and out of focus until suddenly they were properly free, sailing onwards into the vast, iridescent blue. A tremendous feeling of wholeness came over him, a renewed sense of his own power and energy and strength. The faint anxiety – not yet sadness, not quite depression – that had been with him all week lifted and he felt himself freed of his own dark moods. As they soared above the clouds he felt as though he could reach out and touch them, just as he might reach out and touch the future he couldn't yet see. *London–New York–Miami–Caracas*. The journey before him was all the proof he needed. The flight from Germany, their twenty-odd years in England, the horror of the death camps and the loss of so many members of their extended family . . . the immense pain of it all was suddenly lifted from his shoulders. He felt alive again, thrillingly alive.

11

EMBETH

At dinner that evening, sitting opposite him and in front of her mother's disapproving glare, she found herself unable to drag her eyes away. He had an energy that burned so that she felt the heat of it, even yards away. It burned through his shirt, spilled out into his eyes and was there in the quick, restless way his hands moved as he talked. He was full of plans. Ideas. Opportunities. Her father was similarly captivated. She wondered how old he was. Forty? Fifty? It was hard to tell. She didn't think he was married. He wore no ring and spoke of no wife or children back in London. Unlike so many of the men who dined *chez* Hausmann, he actually addressed the odd question to *her*.

'Did you enjoy America?' he asked her after the first introductions had been made and they found themselves next to one another as they strolled into the dining room.

'Er, yes . . . yes, I did.' Embeth suddenly found her voice. 'Ithaca was . . . is beautiful.'

'I've never been. I hear it's magnificent in winter.' *Vinter*. His voice was deep, with a rich layering of many accents. He was German, so she'd been told, although he'd lived in London for long enough to be considered British. 'And do you ski?'

'Er, yes . . . yes, I do, actually.'

'Here in Caracas?'

'Oh, no, no, we—' She looked up at him uncertainly. He was smiling. Teasing her. She blushed. 'No, of course not. In Europe. We go to Switzerland most years.'

'Ah.'

And then her mother placed her hand on his arm, deftly steering him away.

'He's not *that* old,' Mercedes said firmly, dipping the giant battered prawns into a large copper pot of boiling oil. There was a satisfying hiss as they hit the oil, puffing up immediately. She deftly ladled them out a few seconds later, hot and glistening, onto a paper plate. 'Here, try one.'

Embeth picked it up gingerly with her fingertips and bit into one end.

A hot fragrant rush of coriander, chilli and lime flooded her mouth. It was delicious. She devoured it in seconds. '*Está bien,*' she said, nodding in approval. 'So . . . you don't think he's too old?' She returned to the all-important topic at hand. It was two days since the dinner party and she'd woken that morning to the news that Lionel Harburg was coming back. To dinner. Alone, without his elderly uncle and that dreadful Dutchman whom they'd all disliked.

'For what?' Mercedes looked at her slyly. 'For you?'

Embeth blushed and looked away. 'No, not for me,' she mumbled. 'I was just wondering, that's all.'

'Hmph.' Mercedes wasn't fooled. 'S'better like that,' she said knowingly. 'S'better when the man is older.'

'So how old *do* you think he is?' Embeth asked, ignoring her somewhat suspect advice. How would Mercedes know what was better? As far as Embeth knew, the closest she'd ever been to a man was her father.

'Forty-seven,' Mercedes said, not without a hint of triumph. '*And* he's not married.'

Embeth's eyebrows went up. 'How d'you know all that?'

The corners of Mercedes' mouth went up, almost mockingly. 'What? You think I don't know things?'

Embeth suppressed her own smile. She was right. There was little Mercedes and Sophia *didn't* know or see. Forty-seven. It seemed veritably ancient, though Lionel Harburg certainly didn't *look* ancient. 'How d'you know he's not married?' she asked after a decent enough pause.

Mercedes shook her head. 'His collars. They're not pressed properly. No wife lets her husband out of the house like that. No, there's no wife. You want another one, *chica*?' she indicated the battered prawns.

Embeth shook her head and slid off the stool. She was already thinking ahead to what she might wear for dinner that evening. 'No, I'm not hungry,' she said dreamily.

'Black,' Mercedes said firmly.

Embeth looked at her blankly. 'Black?'

'Wear your black evening gown. You know, the one with the sleeves like this,' she crossed her hands across her chest in imitation of the Halston pleated silk gown that was sheathed in tissue and plastic in her wardrobe upstairs. 'And put your hair up. It'll make you look *más sophisticada*. Not so young.'

Embeth blinked slowly. Truly, there wasn't a thing the woman missed. 'Okay,' she said meekly.

He was *very* quick, not just in the way he talked, but in the way he listened. He caught every glance, every shift in mood at the table without ever seeming to look. She liked that. There was a knowing subtlety about him that contrasted sharply with the flamboyance of her own family, whose voices seemed permanently raised. She liked the way he listened, quietly, with the finger of one hand pressed into his cheek. There was always a small smile at the corner of his mouth, which he tried hard to conceal, as though he were permanently amused by something no one else could hear or see. A rather unsettling combination of lightness and intensity came off him, like a faint buzz. She heard it and was drawn to it, and to him. She'd done as Mercedes suggested and pinned her hair up, catching it with a red silk rose just above her left ear. The Halston gown offset the faint tan she'd acquired (without her mother catching her) since she'd been back. She saw from the way his eyes kept coming back to her that he was aware of her in a different way from the others around the table. He was a difficult man to gauge but the feeling that he approved of her made it possible for her to talk to him lightly, almost teasingly.

Her mother saw it, too. After dinner the men retired to her father's study for port and cigars. Miriám waited for her as the women left the table. 'He's nice, no?' she said quietly, tucking her arm into Embeth's. 'Very proper, although I don't find him so English, I must say.'

'Well, he's German, isn't he? I mean, from before?'

'Yes, of course, I keep forgetting. Well, what do you think?'

Embeth blushed again. She kept her face slightly averted. 'He's . . . he's nice,' she said lamely. Nice seemed such a weak word to describe someone so powerful.

'Nice?' Is that all?'

'I don't really know him,' Embeth said weakly.

'Then *get* to know him,' Miriám snapped suddenly, disengaging her arm from Embeth's. She strode ahead, leaving Embeth staring after her in stunned disbelief.

He stood with his back towards her, just inside the pool of light cast by the dining room chandelier. She was in the doorway, hidden from him by the curtain that rose and fell in the breeze like a veil. They were so close she could have reached out her hand and touched him, had she dared. He was smoking, quietly, with slow, unhurried precision. He shifted slightly, but still did not see her. He ground out his cigarette with his heel and stood for a moment, looking at the ground. His expression was different from the one she'd seen at table – less guarded, more open as if he was too deep inside his own thoughts to be aware of what he might have to hide. As she watched him silently, she felt her stomach tense, but the little frisson of fear she'd experienced as soon as she saw him there was gone. She was calm, content to continue looking at him in absolute, perfect silence.

'Who's there?' he asked suddenly, but his voice was low, as though he half-expected the answer. She must have made some sort of sound, a drawing in of breath, perhaps.

'It's me,' she whispered.

'Embeth?' He put out his hands and it had become a kind of game now. His fingertips brushed her arm through the curtain and he stepped towards her. He was so tall. She had to tilt her head quite far backwards to see him. The light was fully upon him but she was drawn not to the outline of his body or the gradual coming into focus of his face, but to his eyes, to the look she'd seen earlier, a kind of nakedness that she'd never seen in a man. But strong, not weak; there was no vulnerability in it. Just an openness that was utterly disarming. It seemed as though he was letting her see straight through him, right to the centre of who he really was, not who he showed himself to be to others. They stood very still for a moment or two, not touching, with the curtain rising and falling all around them with the breeze. Behind her she could hear Mercedes and Sophia clearing the table and behind them, further still, the muted sounds of conversation coming from the living room. Soon her mother would come looking for her, she knew, when a decent enough interval had passed. She had again the strong sensation of being part of some well-worked-out game in which she, despite its importance to the course of her own life, was only a minor player. Her parents, the dinner invitations, the enigmatic older man from overseas . . . there was a pattern and a strategy at play but what astonished her now was her willingness to join in. After so many years of growing rebellion, she was falling in with a suggestion that hadn't even yet been made.

He took her wrist very gently, tightening his grip. 'Don't,' he said, so softly that at first she wasn't sure he'd spoken. 'Don't be afraid.'

She looked up at him. They were suddenly in an intimacy that was so strong they both had to pull back from it. 'I'm not,' she said slowly, wonderingly. 'No, I'm not afraid.'

12
1965

SYLVAN
Paris, France

There was a telephone in the other room, shrieking its head off, like his grandmother used to when she felt those around her had ceased listening. His head was buried somewhere in a tangle of sheets, ladies underwear, and in his mouth, the fragrance of a woman's skin mingled with the rather unpleasant taste of stale cigarettes. Not just *any* woman's skin, he reminded himself as he blearily roused himself and forced himself upright. Anouschka Malaquais. It was *her* perfume, *her* sweat, *her* sweet secret fluids that were still on him. Anouschka Malaquais herself lay snoring lightly beside him.

He staggered out of bed, his penis bobbing stupidly, proudly before him as he strode to the adjoining study. He picked up the phone. '*Allo?*' His voice was that particular gruff mixture of drink and cigarette smoke and the bleary torpor of one who hasn't yet properly slept. There was the faint *bleep* of the international call and he felt, just for a moment, the fleeting tremor of disquiet that accompanied every overseas call. A short burst of static, like gunfire, then the high-pitched whine that said the caller had hung up. He stared at it for a second, and then shook his head. He turned, running an appreciative hand over the hard plane of his stomach. He could hear Anouschka Malaquais (he found it hard to think of her simply as 'Anouschka') stirring next door. The sun had come out and threw long, luminous streaks across the carpeted floor. He was almost at the door when it started up again. He walked back and picked up the receiver. '*Allo?*'

'Sylvan?' It was his stepmother. She was gasping for air. He felt the hackles of fear across the back of his neck. 'Sylvan? *C'est toi*, Sylvan?'

'Yes, yes, it's me,' he said impatiently. 'What's the matter?'

'*C'est ton père.* Sylvan—' The line crackled and fizzed alarmingly. '*Que Dieu le protège . . . il est mort.*' He gripped the phone. His stepmother had been his enemy in that far-off place called childhood. His own mother had died when he was too young to really remember her, but now that he no longer lived at home, or even in the same country,

58

the ages-old enmity between them had lessened slightly. She was a religious woman with a worldview that had clashed with his own. It was not surprising, really. Drink, drugs, women. Everything he did, she abhorred.

He gripped the phone again. He'd broken out into a cooling sweat. It wasn't the time to think about that. 'Dead? What d'you mean? He wasn't ill.'

'No, not ill. There was an attack,' her voice dropped several octaves. 'Last night. *Il a été assassiné.*' She began to cry, a fearful sobbing noise that sent a shiver down his spine. The throb of dread rose up, up in his throat.

'Assassinated?' he repeated slowly. He could hear Anouschka Malaquais yawning next door. He shook his head, trying to clear it. 'How? When?'

'Don't come home. Not now. Stay where you are. For now.'

'But . . . I don't have . . . I don't have any money,' he heard himself say. *That* was the real and immediate fear. He'd overspent last night at the casino. Wildly. His monthly allowance was gone before the month was even a quarter way through. It had been on his mind when he went to bed the night before. He'd gone to sleep with Anouschka Malaquais's mouth on his cock and his head full of the ways he might ask for more.

There was a long, horrid silence. He thought she might have hung up. She did, but not before the word exploded out of her mouth like a gunshot. '*Cochon.*' Pig. And that was it. The line went dead.

13

ANOUSCHKA MALAQUAIS
Paris, France

'Cut!' The director yelled out the command. There were audible sighs of relief from the crew who'd been struggling to please him for over an hour, not least from Anouschka. She'd stumbled on set that morning after barely getting an hour's sleep. Sylvan had been woken up by a telephone call just before dawn and had rushed from the hotel room without saying a word. She'd phoned François to send a driver to pick her up. She yawned as discreetly as she could. The rhythm of a day on set with Patrice de Santis was always the same: sixty, seventy, sometimes even *ninety* minutes of intense concentration, then an hour or more of waiting around, then another burst of frenetic activity, hair and make-up people fussing, teasing, powdering, soothing, smoothing . . . and then another period of waiting about . . . and then back on set for it all to begin again. Film sets had their own rhythms that seemed to have nothing to do with the outside world. Perhaps, Anouschka thought to herself in a momentary flash of insight as yet another junior stylist approached with eyeliner and a powder brush, that was the whole point? That it *wasn't* like real life?

But it was certainly her life now. Ever since that fateful Friday afternoon when she'd been spotted coming out of her school gates with a group of friends and a photographer had spotted her, aiming his camera at her like a gun. She'd stuck out her tongue and he'd snapped away, one frame after another, and then he'd come over to talk to her. His name was François Languet. *Her* name back then was Anne-Marie. Anne-Marie Malaquais. She was sixteen. He was much older, charming and camp as hell. She knew immediately she was safe with him. He said she was prettier than Bardot. That he would make her a star. That together they'd become rich and famous. She didn't know why but she trusted him, right from the start. It took him six months but then he sold the photograph to *Time* magazine. Paris in Spring. *Paris au printemps*. François and *that* photograph set her on the course that changed her life. Anne-Marie Malaquais became, quite simply, Anouschka. She started modelling, skipping classes at school without saying a word to her parents or her friends. She slipped her mother the extra money, claiming she'd been working part-time in a bar. Within a year, just as he'd said, François moved her on and up in the world. After her first catwalk appearance, her first proper pay cheque arrived – more than her father earned in a year. The game, so to speak, was up. She left school without a single qualification – who needed one? In one year she'd earned more than her father had his whole life. He was a factory worker. She was on her way to becoming *une vedette*. A star. How was he supposed to argue with *that*?

But it wasn't all smooth sailing. Having made her a model, François wasn't content to stop there. He wanted her to work on television, in commercials, in films. It took nearly ten years but he got her there in the end. Now, at twenty-nine, she was a bona fide movie star, one of the most photographed women in France. The fact that it had been two years since her last movie made no difference. She'd finally crossed the magical line from 'actress' to 'star' and was as famous for her outfits and lovers as for any roles she might have played. Her latest conquest, Sylvan Betancourt, was the icing on the cake. François was beside himself. They made such a striking couple: Sylvan with his dark, mocha-coloured skin and political pedigree, and she, blonde and honeyed, a French Grace Kelly. 'Good move,' François said approvingly when the very first picture was taken of them coming out of a hotel together. '*Very* good move.'

She yawned again and got up from the chair. She was listless and needed a cigarette. Out of the corner of her eye she could see Patrice eyeing her nervously. He needn't have worried. Unlike *some* stars she could name (but wouldn't, of course), Anouschka Malaquais was a consummate professional. She showed up on time, learned her lines, didn't throw tantrums or make outrageous demands. She got along with cast and crew alike, was unfailingly polite and displayed the sort of good-humoured willingness to pitch in at all times, in all weathers and at all hours that had gone a long (*very* long) way to making her the darling of all who met her and several million more who hadn't. A quick drag would perk her up – that was all. Christ, if Patrice or any of the other directors knew how long and hard she'd worked to get where she was, they'd *know* she wasn't about to throw it all away by behaving badly.

'*Chérie*,' she murmured to one of the many assistants running haphazardly around the set. 'You couldn't find me a cigarette, could you, *ma p'tite*? I'm *dying* for one!'

'But of *course*, Miss Malaquais! Just one second!' And the girl rushed off to do exactly as she was bid.

She was sitting on one of the plastic chairs outside on the terrace, finishing her cigarette when she became aware of the static buzz of a radio presenter's voice, coming from the street below. A word caught her ear. *Betancourt*. She stubbed out her cigarette and leaned over the balcony. There were two workmen in white overalls painting the wrought-iron balustrades outside the hotel where the film was being shot. A tiny portable transistor stood on the ground between them. Neither saw her; they were both engrossed in their work. She strained to hear. *At 11.27 last night, the president of the tiny West African country of Togo was assassinated in what appeared to be a military coup d'état. The president, Cristiano Betancourt, was pronounced dead at 5.18 this morning.*

His only son, Sylvan Olympio Betancourt, is currently residing in Paris but it is believed he will be recalled . . . Anouschka almost toppled over the railings.

'François! François!' she ran back into the room where they were filming, ignoring the looks of surprise. François was in the editing suite with Patrice. She burst through the door. 'François! Quick! Get me a car!'

'What's going on?' François looked up in alarm. 'What's the matter?'

'It's Sylvan! His father . . . it's his father. His father's been *assassinated*!' She put a hand to her throat. 'Last night. Get me a car, *please!*'

14

'Phosphate?' Sylvan looked uncertainly at the man who had just spoken.

'Phosphate,' the man repeated firmly. 'The largest deposits in Africa. Who knows . . . perhaps even the world?'

'Er, I see.'

'With all due respect, Mr Betancourt, I'm not sure that you do.'

'It's like this, Sylvan.' Dominique de Valois, whom Sylvan remembered from his teenage years, turned to him. He'd been deputy foreign minister under Pleven and was now minister of finance and economic affairs. Sylvan remembered him primarily for his cigars (Cuban) and his sense of humour (dry). There'd been many a night he'd stayed up listening to his father and de Valois talking and laughing in the Paris apartment whilst he pretended to do his homework next door. But de Valois wasn't laughing now. 'We sent out a team of French engineers in May to take a preliminary look at the Hahatoe site. Their initial reports were encouraging, but it was the chief engineer's report last month that we believe set the whole thing in motion.'

'Wh . . . what do you mean?' Sylvan's mouth was dry.

'You guys are sitting on potentially the largest lime phosphate deposits on the continent. As Antoine said, perhaps the world. There's *no way in hell* the timing of this *coup d'état isn't* connected to the report. D'you know how much all of this is worth?'

Sylvan shook his head. He'd never even heard of lime phosphate until that afternoon. 'How much?'

'Enough. It's used in fertilisers and there aren't many places on earth where it's found in such concentrated quantities. Moscow's got its eye on Hahatoe. And I'll wager that the thugs who killed your father on Monday were armed by the Soviets. This isn't a game, Sylvan. Moscow's been looking for ways to get into Francophone West Africa for decades. This is as close as they've ever come and if you think, *for one second*, that de Gaulle is going to sit back and allow *that* to happen, think again. You're on a flight first thing tomorrow morning. Pack your bags. You're going home.'

'Phosphate?' It was Anouschka's turn to look blank.

'Phosphate.' Now he was the one to sound firm. He paused in the task of flinging more clothes into a suitcase. 'Lime phosphate. It's used in making fertilisers.'

'But what does that have to do with . . . with *this*?' Anouschka all but wailed, pointing at the wreckage of the hotel room. Three suitcases lay open-jawed on the enormous bed, partially filled with his clothes. 'Why are you leaving *now*? I thought it was dangerous?'

'It is.'

'But I . . . I don't understand what the rush is all about. When are you coming back?'

Sylvan turned to her. He felt the presence of history like someone standing behind him. He had never, in all his thirty-four years, felt anything like it. He was *needed*. For years he'd resigned himself to feeling (and behaving) like a louche playboy, a handsome no-hoper on whom no one could depend. He was his father's only remaining son but could never shake off the feeling that he'd been – and always would be – a disappointment. His older brother, Epiphanio, had died in a car accident when Sylvan was fifteen and it seemed as though the Betan-courts would never get over the loss. Epiphanio, or Épi, as he'd been known, was everything Sylvan wasn't. Clever, conscientious, disciplined. All the traits one would expect in an heir and leader, except handsome, unfortunately. *That* was Sylvan's domain. With Épi's death came an-other realisation: not only was his beloved brother gone, so too was the shield that had protected him from everyone else's expectations, allowing him to do what he did best – nothing. Suddenly *he* was in the spotlight. He'd spent the next fifteen years apologising inwardly and outwardly for letting them down. Now his chance had come to turn it all around.

But there was also another, less noble reason for his enthusiasm:

money. If he'd understood things correctly (and he was fairly certain he had), there was lots of it to be made, especially if *he* took control. He had the backing of the French and the Americans, and, as politically inexperienced as he was, if there was one thing on which he was absolutely clear it was this: neither the French nor the Americans would give a fig for who got their grubby little hands on Togo's phosphate deposits if there wasn't money at stake. He'd never quite recovered from the humiliation of his stepmother's last words. *Cochon*. Pig. For not having enough money. It would never happen again.

'I don't know,' he said slowly. 'I'm supposed to take over.'

'Take over what?' Anouschka's cornflower-blue eyes were on him. He felt the familiar stirrings of an erection.

'The government. I'm to take my father's place.'

15

Hahatoe, Tsamé, Sevagan, Lomé. Anouschka sat with François, pronouncing the musical names with some difficulty. Her fingers danced over the map. The solitaire diamond on her left hand sparkled fabulously. She lifted it every now and again to admire it. 'Beautiful, no?' she turned to François, holding it out for his approval.

François said nothing. He was sulking. His meal ticket – the girl he'd staked his career on, his closest friend and confidante, the better part of *him* – was going. Leaving him.

'But I'm going to be *La Première Dame*,' Anouschka said, genuinely astonished at the depths of his despair. 'How can you possibly ask me *not* to do this?'

'I'll *miss* you!' François wailed.

'Well, I'll miss you too, *chéri*, but it's not as though I'm going to the moon, come on! It's half a day's flight! You can come and visit. Visit me in the palace . . . just think of that! You and me, François, in the palace!' Anouschka jumped up and grabbed his arm, attempting to drag him into a waltz.

He shook her hand off angrily. 'It's not a palace, you idiot! It's a dump! It's the *Tiers-Monde*, not the Champs Elysées!'

Anouschka stopped. 'Don't be so childish,' she snapped. 'Yes, I *know* it's the Third World. I'm not stupid, you know. I *love* him. Why can't you just accept that?'

'Because *I* love you,' François muttered.

'You're gay,' she said drily. 'It doesn't count.'

He flung her a murderous look and got up from the sofa. 'I'm going home,' he announced huffily, picking up his scarf.

'Fine.'

'Fine.' He stomped off, slamming the door behind him. Anouschka sighed and collapsed back into the sofa. He would come round soon enough. After all, she still had another week to go. A week spent shopping – she hugged one of the silk cushions to her chest in glee. *La Première Dame*. It had such a *ring* to it, so much more interesting than plain old 'wife', or 'mother'. She'd been surprised, even shocked, at her own unhappiness in those first few weeks after Sylvan left. She, who was so used to seeing herself on television, had been astonished to see *him*. For a good fortnight, as the French army fought alongside the Togolese to install the assassinated president's son in Lomé's *Palais National*, the previously unheard-of West African country had been on everyone's lips – *and* on the nightly television news. The fact that the president-in-waiting was good-looking, with oodles of charisma *and* had been seen stepping out with France's best-known and loved actress only added to the drama. Suddenly there was another reason to add Anouschka Malaquais to the evening news list. Oh, it was all too delightful for words. Now, when he appeared on the news, she could practically *smell* the aura of power and authority. Overnight Sylvan had become a contender. The spoilt, fun-loving playboy was gone. The image staring back at her was that of a *man*. A powerful man. There was nothing sexier *on this earth*, she declared passionately to François. Nothing at all.

A month later, when the last remaining junior army officers who'd instigated the coup had been rounded up and 'dealt with', as he put it, and the thirty-four-year-old son of the assassinated leader was finally inaugurated, a man approached Anouschka with an airline ticket. *Air Afrique*. Paris-Dakar-Lomé. First class. She almost snatched it from his fingers. She couldn't wait to go.

16

She stepped awkwardly out of the car that had been sent to the airport to fetch her and looked around. Once, as a very young child, she'd been struck by the sight of a field of sunflowers, heads dropping towards the ground as if the stalks could no longer hold their weight. She'd asked her mother why the flowers looked so sad. 'Sad?' 'Yes, like they're crying.' 'Oh, it's the heat, silly. It's too hot for them. They'll perk up as soon as the sun's gone in.' Today she felt – and looked – just like those wilting sunflowers. The *heat*. She'd never in her life experienced anything like it. From the moment the aircraft doors opened and she was faced with the blast of hot air – reminiscent of a hairdryer – she could feel herself begin to droop. 'Where's Sylvan?' she asked the silent, stern-faced man who collected her bags. 'Didn't he come?'

'*Monsieur le Président* is busy.' He looked her up and down insolently. His look said what his mouth wouldn't. *Too busy to come for his wife.* She recognised the sentiment as if he'd spoken it out loud. 'Please to follow me.'

The palace certainly *looked* like a palace. Neo-classical, with a long, double row of peeling white pillars and a driveway of raked gravel, leading to a long sweep of identical barred windows, three storeys high . . . Like a palace and an army barrack at once, she noticed with a small chill. Where the hell was Sylvan? *Monsieur le Président* indeed! The car braked noisily to a halt and the door was flung open, allowing the air-conditioned cool to escape and the fierce, hot breath of the outside to rush in. A hand reached in – a large, pink-palmed black hand with a signet ring squeezed tightly into the flesh. She stared at it for a second, and then gingerly stretched out her own.

She was helped down from the car and brought abruptly face-to-face with a long line of unfamiliar faces. Servants were lined up; she recognised the uniforms from photographs Sylvan had once shown her (white drill, khaki shorts, red cummerbunds and, incongruously, white gloves); they wore the same disinterested, impassive faces of servants the world over – blank, almost haughty in their indifference. A man in a navy-and-white striped suit with a white carnation pinned to his lapel moved swiftly forwards.

'*Madame! Bienvenue!*' His outstretched hand and proprietary air marked him out as someone of importance, if only in his own estimation. She shrank from him instinctively. 'Welcome to Lomé. Please, come this way. This way, *madame*, this way.' He ushered her deftly past the line of blank faces and up the front steps. It was marginally cooler inside the portico. She lifted the heavy curtain of her hair away from her neck, wishing she'd had the foresight to pin it up instead of leaving it flowing down her back. It was Sylvan's fault, she thought to herself crossly. He liked her hair loose and flowing. Oh, where the hell was he?

'*Chérie*.' His voice suddenly broke through the din surrounding her arrival. She looked up. Sylvan was standing at the top of the stairs, looking down at her with an amused, playful smile on his face. She opened her mouth in surprise. It had been just over a month since she'd last seen him.

'Sylvan?'

'*Chérie*.' He descended slowly, grandly. His stomach, once flat and solid, was now bloated. He'd broadened in almost every direction. Anouschka's eyes widened.

'Sylvan? What . . . what the *hell* have you been *eating*?'

She saw by the quick, severe frown that appeared between his brows that she'd angered him before she'd properly opened her mouth. With a quick, peremptorily dismissive wave, he shooed the small crowd who'd clustered around her away. 'Go on, get lost. I'll call you when I need you. Yes, you too, Atekpé. *Even* you.'

'But, *M'sieur le Prési*—'

'Buzz off! Now!' Sylvan cut him off. He stood on the second or third step, staring imperiously down at them as they backed out, one by one. Anouschka's mouth was still hanging open as the door at the bottom of the stairs closed and they were finally alone.

'Don't ever do that,' Sylvan said, waiting for her to mount the last few steps to join him. 'Don't criticise me in front of them. In front of *any*one, for that matter.'

'But I—'

'Don't.' His voice was cold. Then he relented. His face – broader now than it had been a month ago – broke into a smile. 'You look beautiful, *chérie*. Come.' He held out a hand. 'Come and see your new home.'

It was a role to be played that was no different from the roles she'd played on screen before. *La Première Dame*. Within a week of her arrival into a world that was as unfamiliar to her as if she'd landed on the moon, she realised she had to find a way to make sense of it or she'd simply sink. Aside from the heat – which seemed to her to be a living, breathing human being, another *presence* in her life – there were dozens of other things to consider. Protocol, for one. Africans, she decided, were big on protocol. Who went through a doorway first, who was the first to speak, who spoke to whom and in what tone . . . it was exhausting. Then there were the functions – dinners, lunches, state openings, state addresses, television and radio appearances, openings of schools, new offices, churches, churches, *churches* . . . she hadn't been in a church since she was sixteen, she protested to Sylvan after their fourth visit in as many days.

'Well, you're making up for lost time,' he chuckled, adjusting his tie. He turned to face her. 'This one or that?'

'The blue one. But you're not even religious!' she protested, selecting a pair of pearl earrings.

'I am now.'

And that was that. A role, no more, no less. She would have to quickly inhabit it as though her life depended on it – which, in a way, it did. They were surrounded by people who made the beaming, professional ploy of making Sylvan's interests their own. They were not to be trusted. She could see, even if he chose not to, the ravenous, wolfish aspect behind their smiles. Sylvan's father had been disposed of – *pouf!* – in spite of their pledges of allegiance and undying loyalty. She knew instinctively they wouldn't hesitate to do it again. In the scramble for power and resources which followed Sylvan's ascent to power, there were promises made which had to be kept. She came upon the conversations when she wasn't supposed to. So much to this one, so much to that. Sylvan seemed to revel in it all. 'It's a game, *chérie*, that's all. Just a game.'

A few weeks later, at a dinner one night, Anouschka listened to Maurice Couvé de Murville, the French foreign minister, give both the happy couple and the country's newly restored commitment to democracy his blessing. She stole a surreptitious glance around her. All down the length of the elegant table with the heavily starched cream napkins and the gleaming plates that she'd personally polished all afternoon were Sylvan's government ministers, French mining bosses, West African oligarchs from the neighbouring states and the usual clutch of sycophants and professional hangers-on. Sylvan sat at the head, accepting the congratulations and praises being heaped down upon him with a smile as long and wide as the table at which they all sat. A man in his element. Almost overnight, it seemed, he'd developed a way of speaking – long, flowery sentences, then a pause, allowing space and time for his audience to murmur appreciatively to one another, then to him, their voices growing louder, stronger, his own swelling and echoing in response – that made her feel quite faint. A chill stole over her. It was horrible; it was as if they drew something out of him, some essential, secret life force . . . like flies feeding on a corpse. Sylvan thrived on it. Later, in the car on the way back to the palace, he abruptly ordered the driver to pull over and asked him to step away from the car for a few minutes. He fucked her hurriedly but with great passion on the back seat. He adjusted his clothing, straightened his tie and called the driver back. He, unlike her, was in his element. *La Première Dame*. Yes, it had a certain ring to it. And it was now her life.

17

1975

TEN YEARS LATER

ANOUSCHKA MALAQUAIS-BETANCOURT
Palais National, Lomé, Togo

She was obliged to feel her way in the darkness down the path towards the pool. Nothing moved, not even the leaves on the palm trees to her left and right. No moon, no light, nothing other than the thick, soft night above her and no one to witness her going. She'd fallen asleep earlier in the evening whilst waiting for Sylvan to return from some meeting or other and woken up drenched in sweat. The electricity had gone off and the air-conditioners had stopped. Nothing other than a swim would cool her down. She was out the door before she could change her mind.

She stumbled, brushing her calf against one of the wiry bushes and drawing blood with a sharp sting. She didn't stop to look. She reached the tiled edge of the pool, shrugged her dress over her head and kicked off her flip-flops impatiently. She walked to the edge, sat down, and then slowly slid in. The pool drank her in: feet, ankles, thighs . . . she sank gratefully into its cool, wet mouth with a relief that brought tears to her eyes. She submerged herself again and again, feeling the rush of water around her ears as it swallowed her up. The night air, which had been so hot and oppressive up there in the bedroom, was now cool against her burning cheeks.

Half an hour later, her midnight swim was over. She hauled herself out of the water, droplets falling like diamonds all around her. She was stark naked. It was nearly ten years since she'd come to Lomé and she *still* hadn't got used to the heat. She never would. The heat. The heat. An oppressive, never-ending refrain. It was the first thing she thought about in the morning when she opened her eyes and it was invariably the last thing she thought about at night, lying in that enormous circular bed of theirs, praying the electricity would last through the night. Heat and electricity. Electricity and heat. In her entire life she never thought she would think of either, let alone in the same breath. And yet, here she was, First Lady of Togo, wife of the *Président de la République*, dreaming of the cold, of autumn and winter and of France, her breath scrolling before her like a signature on frosty December mornings. Some mornings she woke up parched, her skin stuck to the drenched bed sheets, and she could have wept for the realisation that she *wasn't* at home, in Paris, somewhere where the lights always worked and the air wasn't as thick and hot as soup. Here in Africa, the heat stuck to everything; it turned her make-up to sludge, her hair into a damp, frizzy cloud and although there were noisy air-conditioners installed in practically every room, a constant supply of electricity was required for the damned things to work. Another of life's essential commodities she was learning to live without – electricity. It was enough to make you weep, she thought to herself bitterly – and she frequently did.

She bent down to pick up her dress. A sudden rustle in the bushes made her pause. '*Est-ce-qu'il y a quelqu'un?*' she called out, her voice strong and clear in the night air. There was no answer. It didn't occur to her to be afraid. She slipped the dress over her head, fastening it and felt her way into her flip-flops. '*Est-ce-qu'il y a quelqu'un?*' she called again. There was still no answer. Probably one of the guinea fowl that wandered in and out of the gardens all day long, she thought to herself as she made her way back up the garden path. Every now and then she would hear a loud squawking as one or other of the guards managed to catch one; she didn't like to think how they were killed. Women at the roadside grilled them over open charcoal fires with a spicy pepper sauce that made the eyes water. Sylvan claimed it cooled you down. She wasn't so sure. Whatever the case, she drew the line at eating *there*, by the side of the road. Dirty, she said, wrinkling her nose. And common. Not for him. He said it was good for the local people to see him eating just like them.

'You mean, not like some bourgeois Frenchman?'

'Exactly.'

'But you *are* a bourgeois Frenchman,' she said innocently.

He glowered. '*Je suis Togolais,*' he said, displeasure showing around his mouth.

She knew better than to argue. After nearly a decade she'd come to understand, better perhaps than he did, that the line separating him from his fellow countrymen wasn't quite as invisible as he made it out to be. She'd come to his country ignorant not only of where it was in the world but even more ignorant of its history. The Betancourts belonged to a tiny minority, a privileged elite, descendants of freed Brazilian slaves who'd returned to Africa in the late 1800s. These Afro-Brazilians, as they were known, banded together, worshipped together, did business with one another, married each other's offspring and generally considered themselves a cut above the local population. Anouschka had never met people like them before. They fawned over *her*, of course, praising Sylvan for his 'good taste' and 'excellent choice', euphemisms, she eventually realised, for her blonde good looks, fair skin and blue eyes. They were mostly insufferable gossips with nothing to say. The world Sylvan had brought her to was smaller and more claustrophobic than anything she could ever have imagined.

She walked unsteadily in the dark back towards the terrace, heat licking her face like a furred tongue. A mosquito sang insistently somewhere near her left ear. She swatted it impatiently. Another twig snapped; something rustled in the blackness behind her. She turned and waited. The clouds parted suddenly to reveal a sheeny, luminous moon that threw an eerie light across the ground. The rains were due shortly. The air was pregnant with sweat. Every glass she took from the refrigerator would bead almost immediately with condensation. At the same hour every afternoon, a sudden gust of cool-smelling wind would blow across the lawn, followed by bursts of air that flattened pieces of paper against the fences, sending up little scurries of dust into nowhere. Ten or fifteen minutes later, a low drumming would begin, turning to a deafening roar within seconds. It rained so hard and noisily you could barely hear your own thoughts. An hour, occasionally more . . . then it ceased as quickly as it had started. She'd never known rain like it.

She sighed as she continued up the steps to the front door. So many things to get used to. Would she ever get the measure of the damned place? Probably not.

One of the armed security guards was suddenly come upon in the dark. He sprang guiltily to his feet. *'Vous désirez, madame . . . ?'* He'd been napping on one of the plastic chairs on the veranda.

She waved him away with a hand. *'Non, merci,'* she said and walked slowly up the stairs. It was nearly one o'clock in the morning. Sylvan still wasn't home.

18

A week later, she was on her way back from the *grand marché* in the centre of town, delicately picking her way through the piled-up garbage, accidentally caught up in the crowd, when she heard a noise behind her, a long rolling sound, like thunder. She stopped. The silent bodyguard who accompanied her everywhere and whose name she didn't even know almost bumped into her. 'What's that noise?' she asked, tilting her head to the air, like a dog sniffing the approach of strangers.

'Nothing,' the bodyguard shrugged dismissively. 'Just the market women. They make too much noise.'

'No . . . there's shouting. Listen.' The sound grew louder, a drumming from somewhere behind Rue Tokmaké. 'What's happening?' The sound was growing louder, a rhythmic, swaying chanting of some kind.

He shrugged again. He was carrying her bags, pushing people rudely out of the way as they tried to make for the car. In one, she'd packed a few precious slabs of cheese that she'd bought herself from the Lebanese trader on rue du Grand. It was pointless sending the maids to buy cheese. The poor women couldn't tell if something had gone off. In the other, there were several bolts of the beautiful local fabrics she liked to turn into those striking dresses she wore on state occasions. There were few white women who could carry off the elaborate headdresses and the strikingly bold patterns and colours, but she could. She had three seamstresses – Nadine, Isabella and Marie-Antoinette – on permanent duty. Together they pored excitedly over the magazines she brought back from Paris, turning out ever more intricate and cleverly fashioned *haute couture à l'africaine*. 'It's nothing,' he repeated. 'Let's go.'

Suddenly the air was ripped apart by gunfire. She turned and saw a crowd of men running towards them, hands linked, some of them carrying crude banners that she couldn't make out. Everything around them had come to a complete stop. Suddenly the market women who normally sat cooking and gossiping comfortably got to their feet, shouting and screaming. There was another burst of gunfire and the crowd began to dissolve as people broke into a run. A few stray dogs and chickens, picking up on the sudden burst of fear, began to bark and squawk, adding to the confusion. She saw the first line of soldiers advancing down the road, guns trained on the crowd, who by now were running in every direction around them.

'*Madame . . . go!* Get inside the car!' she heard the bodyguard yell above the noise of gunfire as people began to push and shove. A woman balancing a wide pannier of bread on her head broke into a run, sending the loaves flying. '*Madame!*' The bodyguard was shoving his way through the women crowding round to get to her. She caught a glimpse of her pink basket spiralling upwards, cheeses wrapped in greaseproof paper flying through the air. Someone grabbed her arm. She gasped and struggled to break free but it was her bodyguard. He'd abandoned her purchases and was shoving her roughly in the direction of the car. 'Get in, *madame*! Get *in*!' He pushed her forwards until they reached it. He yanked open the door and shoved her in the back. There was no time to argue. The driver already had the engine running. More gunshots rang out, pinging crazily against the parked cars around them. The driver turned round, shot them a terrified glance and responded automatically to the bodyguard's scream, '*Go!*' The car lurched forwards, narrowly missing a woman whose mouth opened as if in slow motion but no sound came through the thick bulletproof glass. Anouschka covered her head with her hands, too terrified to scream.

They zigzagged their way in fits and starts down the road that was now thronging with running men and women until they reached *Avenue de la Présidence*. It was almost empty. The driver put his foot down and they went sailing across the intersection with *Avenue de Gaulle* and straight up the boulevard that led to the palace. The car screeched to a halt in front of the main entrance and the bodyguard leapt out. He was in a state of high excitement. He opened the door for her and then ran towards the rear of the palace, his firm, high buttocks pumping furiously as he went.

'*Madame?*' Ophélia, the cook and housekeeper, was standing in the hallway, surprised to see her back so soon. '*Est-ce-que ça va, Madame? Tout va bien?*'

'Yes, yes,' Anouschka said breathlessly, aware that her hair was dishevelled and her face bright red and sweaty. 'There was some trouble . . . in town.'

'Trouble, *madame?*'

Anouschka nodded. 'Yes, I'm not sure what was going on . . . there was a crowd . . . and some gunshots. I don't know what—' She stopped herself just in time. How many times had Sylvan warned her against saying too much in front of the servants? 'I'm going upstairs,' she concluded.

Ophélia looked at her but said nothing. As Anouschka turned to go, she saw someone standing in the doorway to the kitchens, just to the left of the stairway. She saw Ophélia make a quick, concealed gesture with her hand but the gesture was so swift and so fleeting it was hard to tell what it was. A dismissal? Warning? She didn't know. She suddenly felt rather overwhelmed. Where was Sylvan? It was nearly eleven o'clock on a Tuesday morning. He was normally downstairs in his study with half a dozen ministers and officials. The driveway was usually full of the dark green Peugeot 504 cars that every government official seemed to use. Today it was empty.

She climbed the stairs wearily to their room and closed the door. She switched on the rattling air-conditioner and kicked off her shoes. She sat down on the edge of the bed and looked at her hands. They were shaking. She saw very clearly again the faces of people in the crowd. A young man who turned his head to see where the shouts were coming from and whose face almost collided with her own. The details flashed before her eyes. Yellowish-brown skin, pocked by tiny raised pimples and straggling whorls of tight black hair. Near the mouth there was a tiny puckered strip of light pink, a scar, perhaps. She wasn't aware of even seeing it at the time. The pregnant woman whom the driver had nearly knocked down in his haste to get away. The pinkish wet inside of her mouth as it opened on a scream, row upon row of beautifully even teeth. A hand flattened against the window as the car tried to move through the crowd. The pale imprint of the palm, lines etched clearly in darker brown and, turning slightly as the hand moved away, the clear line where the velvety blackness of the outer hand met the salmon pink of the palm. A watch; a frayed cuff-sleeve; the flash of earrings and someone's headdress, which had slipped. Everything, every little detail, came flooding back. She let herself slide off the bed until she was sitting on the ground. Her head felt heavy and her heart was thumping fast. Nothing had actually happened. They'd got away, driven home. But something might happen, no? If not now, then one day. Soon.

19

SYLVAN

Like many things he read about himself, it wasn't quite true. He had not been his father's favourite son. There were even some who whispered he wasn't his father's son at all, not that he paid them any attention. He folded the newspaper carefully and put it aside. In all likelihood, it was his stepmother who had started the damned rumours in any case. Even now, so many years later, she could not accept that a young French actress, *une femme blanche*, had supplanted her in her people's affections. The woman who was now – and who had been for the past nine years – *La Première Dame*.

Across the room, staring at herself in closed, dreamy self-absorption, *la Première Dame* herself sat, mid-point in her preparations for a state dinner. A visiting delegation from his 'old friends', the French. That was the line the journalist had used. *Ses anciens amis*, the statement somehow managing to be both benign and sinister in the same breath. He looked down at his bare feet after their hour-long pedicure. It was in Paris that he'd acquired the taste for such small luxuries. Pedicures, massages, bespoke tailoring. Nothing in the world like the attention money could buy. Nowadays his suits and shirts came directly from Dege & Skinner in London and a local girl came in once a week to attend to his hands and feet.

His mind drifted back to the article. In spite of himself he was impressed. It was cleverly done, subversive rather than inflammatory, written in the flowery, somewhat overwrought language that the journalist, Kweku Ameyaw, liked to use. He knew Ameyaw. They'd actually been students together in Paris at the same time, though their social circles had never really overlapped. An intense man, given to protests and demonstrations and Trotskyite sentiment. Sylvan remembered him well. He'd returned to Lomé long before Sylvan. He sighed. It was high time someone paid Ameyaw a visit. He pulled the soft flesh of his lower lip into his mouth, biting gently. Whom should he send? Attipoe? Gbédéma? He scratched his elbow. Of the two, Gbédéma was certainly the more brutal. Still, brutality had its uses, he mused. There were some, including his so-called friends, the French, who thought he was too soft. Too friendly. That his marriage, and the trappings of luxury it had provided him with, had weakened him. It seemed not everyone was as thrilled with his movie-star wife as the Togolese public.

He let go of his lip with a soft 'phut' and sighed deeply again. Yes, he would send Gbédéma to pick Kweku Ameyaw up. Rough him up and scare him a little. Not enough to make him leave – no, that would be counter-productive. He didn't want the subversive little shit writing about him from the safety of Barbès. He wanted him close, nearby, here where he could keep an eye – and a thumb, if necessary – on him. Make him toe the line. The last thing he wanted was to give free rein to every journalist with a typewriter and access to liberal French editors with axes to grind. It was ironic. Those very editors with whom he and Anouschka had once danced and dined were now only too ready to give voice to those weaselly little agitators like Ameyaw. He found it almost laughable. The editor of *Le Figaro* – Didier Cohn – he *knew* him. Hadn't they spent many a winter evening in the same Pigalle bars, drinking from the same bottle, even slept with the same girls? For him to turn around and print the kind of mealy-mouthed rubbish about 'press freedoms' and 'unpopular economic reforms', not to mention all that nonsense about the glass factory at Agouenyive that had provoked the bloody demonstration in the first place . . . unforgivable. A betrayal, really.

He yawned, his attention distracted by Anouschka, who had risen from her *toilette*. She was wearing a loose silk robe and a pair of high heels. She put one high-heeled sandal down carefully in front of the other as she crossed the room, like she used to in the old days when he'd sat in the front row of those warehouses and hotel lobbies and train stations that they'd converted into catwalks or whatever they called them, packed with beautiful women and their gay, flamboyant male counterparts. He'd sat amongst them drinking the free champagne, making small talk, watching with the rest of them as those absurdly slender, elongated creatures from another world strutted up and down, stopping in front of him, hands balanced jauntily on that piece of bone that could hardly be called a hip before turning and swaying, swaying as they sauntered back and forth. He felt the strong stirring of desire within him, deep inside his belly. He looked down at himself, watching with detached fascination as his penis thickened, tenting his shorts. His suit lay draped over the chair by the window. He glanced at his watch. It was nearly eight o'clock. The dinner was due to begin in half an hour. Anouschka took for ever to get ready. If he approached her now they would surely be late. She would be hot and sweaty and her hair would require 'fixing'. The thought did nothing to dampen his sudden ardour. He got up purposefully, his cock now fully erect and throbbing dully. They would be late. So what? The French would wait. They would all wait. Wasn't he *le* fucking *Président*? He laughed suddenly, delightedly, at his own wit.

20

SIX MONTHS LATER

ANOUSCHKA

The sour, metallic taste in her mouth was a dead giveaway. That and her swollen breasts. She put her hands on her abdomen and drew a deep, shaky breath. It had been six weeks since the night Sylvan had practically forced himself on her just before the all-important dinner with the French ministers and members of his cabinet. Yes, that was the night she'd conceived. It had to be. She'd been so angry with him that she hadn't allowed him near her since. She'd had to take a hasty shower, re-dry her hair and then the bloody electricity went out and it took them half an hour to find the damn garden boy with the key for the generator . . . all in all, by the time she'd managed to make herself presentable again, she was over an hour late. She was furious. The dinner had gone badly. Everyone except Sylvan, of course, was in a foul mood. He left shortly afterwards on one of those interminable, pointless multi-country trips around the region. Niger and Chad. Did she want to accompany him? *Hell*, no. She felt her stomach turn again. Well, if she really *was* pregnant and she managed to hold on to the baby, it would

77

mean leaving Lomé for the next few months. She hadn't been back to France since Christmas and she was desperate to go.

She leaned her forehead against the marginally cooler surface of the mirror and took a few deep, shuddering breaths. Four pregnancies in ten years, all of them over before they'd properly begun. Sylvan didn't know; no one knew. Did she actually *want* a child? Aside from the obvious danger a baby would pose to her figure, the prospect was daunting. Feeding, washing, cleaning, spending hours with it dangling a set of plastic baubles above a cot, all that ridiculous-sounding baby-talk that she heard others make – could she, Anouschka Malaquais-Betancourt, actually *do* that? She'd never been the maternal type. If the truth were told, the miscarriages she'd suffered had actually been a relief. And yet . . . there were worse places to have a child than Lomé, she mused, flushing the toilet on the thin trail of vomit that was surely the evidence of a pregnancy. There were servants galore. Housekeepers, cooks, nannies, drivers, gardeners, an endless supply of other children. Anyone and everyone to make the day-to-day running of the household and the bringing up of a child as trouble-free as possible.

Except, of course, it was anything *but* trouble-free. Supervising the damn staff was a full-time job, nowhere more so than Lomé. She thought of the two young girls whose job it was to keep their Parisian apartment clean and tidy and nearly wept. Here she had to remind everyone not once, not twice, but *every single day*. Clean this, wipe that, dust here, sweep there. One of the girls, that sullen girl whose name she could never remember, just looked at her with the cow-faced, mutinous expression that was impossible to read . . . and then continued to do what she'd always done – almost nothing – despite her screaming instructions to the contrary. There were days when, exhausted by the effort of arguing with them, she retreated to the bedroom, switched on the air-conditioner (if the electricity was on) and lay down on the bed, stunned into sleep by defeat. In some ways, despite her position as *la Première Dame*, they had the upper hand. Who cared if the dressing table hadn't been dusted? *She* did. Who cared if there were no fresh flowers to greet guests in the huge marble lobby? *She* did. The head cook in the palace was a Moslem and therefore didn't drink. Pointless, therefore, expecting him to judge the merits of one wine over another. In the battle to apply her own exacting standards to a wayward, reluctant household, she'd lost. Sylvan didn't understand her despair. He didn't want to be bothered with tales of how no one listened to her, how difficult it was, how sulky and uncooperative the staff were. *Just get it done*. He had a whole country to run. She'd been given a house. Surely she could manage *that*?

Seen from that perspective, then, a child might be both blessing and curse. It would get her out of the place for at least six months, probably more. She'd be cosseted and looked after, fussed over by her mother – well, perhaps that was stretching things a little far – but she'd see all her old friends again, and François . . . she began to brighten up. A baby would mean an excuse to stay in Paris a little longer. A chance to see her friends. A *change*. Some new outfits, a new hairstyle, new shoes, a complete makeover. She'd be back in the papers again, back in the public eye. She hurried into the bedroom and fished a notebook out of her bag. By the time she'd finished making a long list of all the things having a baby might mean, her bad mood had all but disappeared. She took a long, leisurely bath, did her hair and dressed for dinner. The foreign minister and his wife were invited; she made sure to look her best. Sylvan was delighted with her; she'd been walking around with that grumpy expression for *weeks*, he whispered, as they walked together towards the dining room. Tonight she looked beautiful, just like she used to.

Towards the end of dinner, with just the two of them left sitting at the long table, she broke the news to him. He was happy; how could he not be? Finally, the news he'd been waiting almost a decade for. Yes, of course she should go back to Paris. The sooner the better. It was all settled. No bad thing, either, he murmured as they walked upstairs together, for the child to be born in France. *One never knows*. She kept her fingers crossed as he undressed her, tenderly laying his head against her abdomen. *Finally*, after nine years . . . a child? His obvious delight delighted her. A good thing she hadn't mentioned the pregnancies that had been – and gone – before, she thought to herself as she stroked his head. Sylvan, for all his obvious strengths, was a surprisingly sentimental man.

21

1974

LYUDMILA
Krylatskoe, Moscow, USSR

Vladimir and Elsa Gordiskayo gingerly turned over the leaflet as though it might bite. *Split. The Socialist Federal Republic of Yugoslavia.* A week.

'A week, eh?' Vladimir stroked his moustache.

His fifteen-year-old daughter, Lyudmila, nodded confidently. 'A week.'

'How . . . how will you get there?' Her mother, who, as far as Lyudmila knew, had never been further east or west than Moscow (or north or south, for that matter), turned the leaflet over again, as though there might be something she'd missed the first six or seven times she'd read it.

'By train. We'll go from Moscow to Kiev, then from Kiev to Belgrade. It's easy.'

'Easy?' Elsa murmured apprehensively. 'It's so far. And your teachers will be with you the whole time?'

Lyudmila nodded again. 'The whole time,' she said emphatically. 'The whole team's going, Papa. Everyone.'

'Everyone,' her mother murmured again. She looked nervously at her husband. 'If they're *all* going,' she said slowly. 'I don't suppose there's any harm?'

'No.' Vladimir said decisively. 'No harm at all. It's an honour. She's fifteen now. Next year she'll join the Komosol . . . it'll be her last chance to prove herself.' Her father looked at her, pride shining in his eyes.

'Thank you, Papa,' Lyudmila said fervently.

'Well, if Papa says it's all right, then of course you should go. It's only for a week, though, isn't it?'

'That's right, just a week.' Lyudmila wondered how many times she'd have to reassure her mother. 'We leave on Monday and we're back the following Sunday. There'll be two games – the semi-final and the final – and that's it.'

'I think this calls for a small celebration, don't you?' Vladimir looked at his wife. 'Just a small glass. And one for Lyudmila.'

'She's only fifteen!' Elsa protested. 'I'll get her some raspberry juice.'

'Mama! It's not as if I've never had vodka before,' Lyudmila exclaimed. Her father winked at her.

'Get three glasses, woman!' he roared. Elsa hurried to the kitchen, returning with three glasses and a half-empty bottle. '*Tvoye zdorovye*' Vladimir poured a generous measure for each of them.

'*Zdorovye!*' Lyudmila tipped back the small glass and downed her vodka in a single gulp. Her mother looked nervously at her father. Nothing further was said.

The night before she left, a pale half-moon hung in the sky, sending out a thin trickle of light across the slate rooftops. She sat in the bedroom window with her legs drawn up underneath her. Her parents were in the sitting room. Theirs was a standard two-roomed apartment, like all the others around it. One room housed the dining table and four chairs and a sofa which was usually reserved for Papa when he came home from work; the other, partitioned by a screen, housed two beds – one double, for her parents; the other a single one, for her. The kitchen, little more than a narrow cupboard leading off the hallway, was where her mother spent most of her day. She baked almost incessantly – *sharlotka, syrniki, blinchiki* – whatever she could, whenever she found the ingredients. Elsa could make a cake out of thin air, she'd often heard her father say proudly. She bartered with their neighbours for extra food – without it, there were times they'd have gone hungry. Vladimir was a foreman in the steel plant that lay half a kilometre down the road; Elsa had once worked as a nursery-school teacher. Housing in the Soviet Union was free, as was Lyudmila's schooling and heating and lights, but food was sometimes scarce. Not that anyone complained – it was just the way things were.

She felt in her back pocket for the single cigarette she'd put there and drew it out carefully. She and Tatiana had pooled their pocket money for a single packet of ten *Poctobs*. Five each. They'd smoked one together after volleyball practice the other night, giggling hotly together. She passed the cigarette under her nose; the strong scent of tobacco flooded her nostrils pleasurably. She practised holding the cigarette between her index and middle finger, just the way she'd seen Sophia Loren, the most glamorous woman in the whole wide world, do. Sophia Loren. The sound of her name alone sent a shiver down Lyudmila's spine. Sophia Loren was the most beautiful, most voluptuously decadent film star the fifteen-year-old had ever clapped eyes on. The mere fact she even knew of Sophia Loren's existence was something of a miracle. In one of the inexplicable cock-ups that occur every once in a while, even in the most repressive of regimes, the Youth Workers' Club of Krylatskoe had screened *Arabesque*, a film starring Loren and Gregory Peck, which had somehow slipped past the censors. Everyone in Krylatskoe – not just the youth – had watched it every night for an entire week. When the party official responsible for community entertainment realised his mistake, he'd hurriedly pulled it, but the damage had been done. Every teenage schoolgirl at the Joseph Gymnasium in Krylatskoe dreamt of being a dark-haired, dark-eyed beauty with a heaving bosom. Lyudmila, whilst undeniably pretty, looked nothing like Sophia Loren, however. She was just over six foot tall, with long blonde hair, light, hazel-brown eyes and the sort of athletic, muscular figure that made her one of Joseph Stalin High School's star volleyball players . . . but sadly not a sexpot actress. Not that it mattered. Whatever else Lyudmila lacked, she certainly didn't lack ambition. One of these days she would find her way out of Krylatskoe, out of the depressing grey that surrounded them . . . one of these days. It was just a matter of time.

She lit her cigarette and inched her way a little further out of the window. Tomorrow morning, for the very first time in her life, she would be leaving Moscow. The Communist Youth League volleyball match in Split was hardly an invitation to the Paris *haute couture* shows but still . . . she was leaving. That was the main thing. She circled her knees with one arm, hugging herself tightly. 'It's a long way away,' she whispered to herself. 'A very long way from here.' Their little apartment was on the fourteenth floor of the eighteen-storey, horseshoe-shaped block of flats. In front of them, behind them and on either side were similar units, stretching all the way down Osenniy Bul'var. They were in 18K2. Opposite, where her best friend Tatiana lived, was 18K1. Beyond the flats were the forest and the two-lane highway, Rublevoskoe Shosshe, that led straight into Moscow. Krylatskoe was at the edge of everything, including ambition. She finished her cigarette and flicked the butt away with her fingers. She watched it fall, arching away from her then plummeting straight to the ground. In one of those rare flashes of insight that occasionally happened to her, she wondered if the falling cigarette butt were a metaphor for her own life.

22

It was the first time she'd ever seen the sea. On the second day of their week-long holiday, the Russian teenagers were bundled into a bus that took them from Zmovnica, the suburb where the matches were being held, down to the harbour. The entire bus fell silent as the enormous and elegant Diocletian Palace loomed into view, and beyond it, the shimmering, hazy, azure sea. There were gasps from the girls whilst the boys tried to look as though they'd seen it all before. Lyudmila grabbed Tatiana's arm. In her bag was a brand-new swimsuit – red, with small white dots – which her mother had carefully wrapped and left on her bed the night before she left. It was a little small – that was the problem with being so damned tall – but she knew just how good it would look. She still had her summer tan and she'd just started shaving her legs and underarm hair, which few of the girls did. She couldn't wait to sink her feet into the soft sand, pull her hair out of its ponytail and run into the cool, clear water. Dimitri Petkanchin, the star of the boys' team, would be watching her every move.

Dimitri wasn't the only one watching her that afternoon, she saw. At the water's edge, protected from the fierce midday sun by a jaunty yellow-and-white striped umbrella, was a group of middle-aged men whose eyes were firmly locked onto the red-and-white dotted swimsuit as she and Tatiana alternately swam and floated nearby. They were both good swimmers but neither had ever swum in the sea before. To Lyudmila, everything about the trip seemed like a fairy tale. Even the bleak, uniform dormitories where they were staying had an air of mystery and romance about them. She closed her eyes against the sun and let go of the breath she'd been holding, feeling it go out of her body in a slow, powerful sigh. The water was warm and clear; it held her gently, tipping her from side to side, Tatiana's dark, streaming hair just visible out of the corner of her eye.

Someone spoke suddenly. A man's voice. *'Vy Russkaya?'* Schoolboy Russian, spoken haltingly.

She opened her eyes. A middle-aged man was bobbing beside her, fleshy neck and shoulders breaking free of the blue. She nodded cautiously, looking surreptitiously around for Tatiana. She was nowhere to be seen. '*Da*,' she said after a moment. He was one of the group who'd spent the afternoon watching her.

'I'm Martin,' he said, smiling and holding up a hand to shade his eyes against the light. 'And you're Lyudmila. I overheard your friends calling you,' he said with a smile. 'D'you speak any English, by any chance? I'm afraid my Russian's atrocious.'

'Little.' Lyudmila was pleased to be able to say at least that. There'd been an English girl who'd married a Russian engineer – Lyudmila forgot how she'd wound up in Krylatskoe – living across the hallway from them for a couple of years. Whatever little Lyudmila had picked up had come from Rosie. 'Little bit.'

'Very good,' Martin grinned at her. 'I'll speak slowly then. Where did you learn it? Are you on holiday?'

She shook her head. She understood the word 'holiday'. 'No. Tournament.' She mimicked hitting a ball.

'Ah. Volleyball.'

'*Da. Voleibol.*' They smiled at each other. He had short, greying hair, plastered flat against his skull. Blue eyes, crinkled at the corners, like her father's. He looked like the kind of man who smiled a lot. 'Are you English?' she asked.

He shook his head. 'Scottish. From Dundee. You ever been to Dundee?'

They both laughed. Lyudmila shook her head. 'I've never been anywhere,' she said in Russian. 'First time leave Russia,' she added in English.

'Really? Your first trip abroad?' He sounded disbelieving.

She nodded. 'First time.'

'How old are you, Lyudmila, if you don't mind me asking.'

'Eighteen.' She dared him to challenge her. He didn't.

'Lyudmila! *Ty chto delaesh?*' It was Tatiana. She'd swum up to her, bobbing a few yards away.

Both Lyudmila and Martin turned at the sound of her voice. 'And you must be Tatiana,' Martin said, beaming.

'*Poshli, poshli,*' Tatiana said anxiously. *Let's go.* She looked nervously back at the shore where their teachers were waiting.

'We have to go,' Lyudmila said reluctantly. She submerged her face, pushing her hair away from her eyes à la Loren, just as she'd seen her do in the film. His eyes narrowed appreciatively as she came back up.

'How about a drink, girls?' he called out to them as they turned tail and headed back for the beach. 'Tonight? We're at Hotel Luxe . . . it's on the Riva, right beside the ice-cream shop.'

'Maybe,' Lyudmila shouted over her shoulder.

'Are you crazy?' Tatiana hissed as they swam towards the shore. 'He's an old man!'

'He's not *that* old. Besides, it'll be fun.'

'Fun? You really *are* crazy, Lyudmila! How're you going to get out of the dormitory, anyway?'

'We. How're *we* going to get out? You're coming with me.'

The air inside the bar was thick with smoke. Outside, amidst the bustle of waiters and conversations in foreign languages, cars drove slowly up and down the promenade; motorcycles wove in and out; all was noise and light. One eye narrowed against the bluish haze, Lyudmila looked around her in delight. She couldn't believe how easy it had been. Their teachers, already emboldened beyond belief by the freedom of being on holiday and in another country, were already in the bar at the community centre where the team were staying. They were drunk. No one had bothered to do a roll call after dinner; she and Tatiana merely slipped away from the crowd of students returning to the dormitory and made their way to the bus stop. Tatiana, the scaredy-cat, kept looking over her shoulder as if she expected to see the Red Army hot on their heels.

But look at her now. Lyudmila smiled to herself. She'd knocked back two gin and tonics in rapid succession and her hair had come out of its pony-tail . . . she looked happy. Relaxed. Sexy. They *both* looked sexy. It was obvious from the way every head in the bar turned as they walked in and no one looked happier to see them than Martin. He was sitting in the corner with the same group of friends whom she'd seen on the beach. He jumped up, almost knocking over a chair in his haste to get their attention. 'Whoo hoo . . . Lyudmila! Here . . . we're over here!'

'He sounds like a schoolboy,' Tatiana muttered under her breath.

'I told you he wasn't that old.'

'Hello, *hello* girls . . . fantastic you could make it!'

Both Tatiana and Lyudmila giggled. He was right. His Russian accent was ridiculous. In his mouth, the word 'fantastic' had come out sounding rather silly. *Eto fantastika!* Accent on the wrong syllable.

'Another one?' Martin leaned towards her now, indicating her half-empty drink.

Lyudmila shook her head. 'Not yet.' She was in no rush whatsoever. It was an evening to savour, slowly. It was hardly the first time she'd drunk alcohol but it was certainly the first time she'd done it in the company of four middle-aged men, in a bar in a foreign city, outside the USSR and she was in no hurry to see the evening end. She took another sip of her drink, letting the ice cubes swirl around in her mouth before swallowing them whole. Martin's eyes were like saucers, watching her.

An hour later, she got up from her seat. One drink had turned into two, then three, then four . . . it was time to stop. She looked across at Tatiana. Her hair had come completely free of its ponytail, falling in long, looping curls across her face. Her lipstick, too, had smeared; there were more traces of it on the face of the man sitting next to her. Lyudmila had already forgotten his name. There were three men with Martin. Businessmen. *Biznesmenov* – one of those new Russian words that had crept in via black-market American TV shows. Martin was eager enough but he seemed out of his depth. *Chelovek – glupets! Nothing so foolish as a man.* It was one of her mother's favourite sayings. If Martin thought she'd been taken in *in any way* by his tales of success then he was even more foolish than he looked. That wasn't the reason she'd agreed to meet him that night.

'Tatí.' She hissed at the now-drunk Tatiana. 'Get up. Come with me to the bathroom.'

Tatiana looked up, slightly befuddled. 'Now?'

'Now.' Lyudmila's voice brooked no argument. Martin looked up the length of her legs and his eyes immediately glazed over. 'Come on.'

'Okay, okay. I'm *coming*.' She detached herself with some difficulty from Dirk – or whatever his name was – and stumbled into the toilets after Lyudmila. 'This is so much *fun*,' she trilled happily over the partition between them. Lyudmila zipped up her skirt and flushed the toilet. She stood outside Tatiana's cubicle until she heard her do the same. Down the long mirror a couple of local girls stood looking haughtily at them. Lyudmila ignored them and calmly reapplied her lipstick. 'Don't you think so?' Tatiana asked, fluffing out her hair in the mirror.

'*Nyet*. It's boring. *They're* boring.'

'So . . . what are we doing here?' Tatiana asked, looking at her uncertainly.

'You'll see.'

*

86

She didn't even tell Tatiana what she was up to. During the day she practised her volleyball strokes alongside everyone else, or joined in the activities at the beach. On their third day, the day of the semi-final match between the Joseph Stalin Gymnasium of Krylatskoe and the Josip Broz Tito Gymnasium Split, she excelled, driven by some invisible inner force that saw her take most of the winning shots. Afterwards, accepting congratulations from her teammates and teachers, she caught Tatiana's eye. There was a new wariness in her friend that she hadn't seen before, as though Tatiana were trying to work out what it was that Lyudmila was thinking. What *was* she thinking? Sitting in the bar on the Riva with the Englishman and his friends had offered her a glimpse of a different sort of life – champagne, cigars, beautiful clothes, older, wealthy men who could buy her things . . . Split was hardly Paris or London; she wasn't stupid. Martin was no Jean-Paul Belmondo and he looked and sounded nothing like Gregory Peck. She thought about the tiny, two-roomed apartment back home in Moscow, her mother's tired and drawn face, her father's distant, preoccupied gaze; the bored, indifferent look of her teachers, the bleak greyness that stretched all around . . . she felt her very skin shrinking away from it. She wanted something different, something better. She listened to Martin's ramblings about the lucrative Eastern bloc and their taste for whisky which he, Martin Donaldson could provide, with half an ear, one eye on the clock above the door, the other on some distant point in the future when she wouldn't have to put up with the incoherent fantasies of a middle-aged sales rep.

On the fourth night, she made up her mind. It was Thursday. In another couple of days, the team would be heading home. The final match was scheduled for Saturday afternoon. There would be a party that evening for all the students and teachers who'd taken part in the tournament – the perfect moment at which to slip away. Their teachers would all be too busy with their new-found friends and the free booze that was laid on each night to pay much attention to the teenagers they'd brought along. Especially if they won the final match. She drew long and hard on her cigarette. Leaving. It was the toughest decision she'd ever had to make.

23

Afterwards, she would remember that hour as the longest of her life. She'd walked out of the hostel without saying a word to anyone, not even Tatiana. She'd taken only half her clothing, leaving a remaining jumble of jeans and T-shirts on her bed so as not to arouse suspicion. She headed for the main road leading out of Split, where she'd seen the huge lorries with their foreign licence plates heading north towards Germany and Italy. She didn't care where she ended up, so long as it was outside the Communist bloc. In her back pocket was her Russian passport and a small bundle of useless roubles – and an English ten-pound note Martin had given her. She'd wanted to hold and feel the contraband currency in her hands and he'd readily obliged. She had no idea what it was worth – a meal? A night in a hotel? Or neither. No matter. There was only one way to find out. It didn't occur to her to be afraid. With her tight, cut-off shorts and T-shirt and her long, wavy blonde hair falling over her shoulders, she knew it would only be a matter of hours, if not minutes, before she found a lorry driver willing to smuggle her across the border. She'd seen the way they all looked at her, honking their horns as she and Tatiana strolled towards the bus stop. She had Martin's name and address; as soon as she was safely in England she'd call him. He'd promised her all sorts of things – little did he know just how soon he'd be called upon to make good. Fifteen minutes after leaving the hostel she clambered into the cabin of a truck heading for the West. Giuseppe Zanotti was a middle-aged, balding, paunchy father-of-six who was on his way back home. His headlights picked out the statuesque blonde in her tight shorts standing just off to one side of a traffic light and he almost lost control of his vehicle. He was on his way back to Trieste with a truck full of *slivovitz*, the local plum brandy that his countrymen loved, which he'd exchanged for the usual consignment of Western goods that the Yugoslavs couldn't get enough of – perfumes, jeans, imported cigarettes – whatever the businessmen who employed him thought would sell. He didn't care what was in the truck. For the past ten years he'd been driving the thousand-odd kilometres down the coastal road from his home city towards the pretty Yugoslav towns of Brgat and Dubrovnik. It was a pleasant journey. He knew the towns and villages along the route off by heart – Rijeka, Crikvenica, Senj, then further down, Zadar, Sibenik,

Split. But the evening he stopped to pick up a young Russian teenager on the run from a father who beat her every chance he could was the first time he'd ever knowingly broken the law. She was so sweet and pretty, dammit . . . he clenched his fists when he thought of what she'd been through. She was tough, though. Seventeen years old and making a new life for herself. You had to admire her. His own daughter, Giuliana, was eighteen and bright enough but she had none of the Russian teenager's gutsy determination. She chatted to him in her husky, broken English – she didn't know a word of Italian and he knew no Russian – but between them, on the twelve-hour-long ride through the night, they somehow managed to fathom each other out.

He stopped the truck just outside the border crossing as they'd planned and she got out of the cabin. He made a space for her in the rear, amidst the crates of *slivovitz* and the boxes of soft, furry peaches that he'd picked up for a quarter of the price in Hvar. His wife and two eldest daughters would do the canning – they'd sell the jars in the months coming up to Christmas to supplement his salary. It was an arrangement that had been in place for years and one of its unforeseen advantages was that he knew most of the border guards who manned the checkpoint between Plavje and Trieste proper.

'*Dobra vecer!*' he called out cheerily as he approached the checkpoint. '*Kako je stari?*'

'Ah . . . Giuseppe. *Come va?*' Zoltan, a middle-aged guard with a handlebar moustache whom he'd known for the past few years, grinned up at him. 'What you taking back tonight?'

'Oh, the usual. *Slivovitz*, peaches . . . couple of boxes of pears.' He reached down and pulled up a plastic bag from the floor beside him. 'And these, of course.' He handed the bag down to Zoltan.

'Ah. *Grazie*, my friend, *grazie*.' Zoltan peered inside at the box of cigars and two bottles of perfume for his wife and daughter. He slapped the side of the truck. '*Sve najbolje moi prijatelju. Dobra vecer.*'

'*Arrivederci*,' Giuseppe called, starting up the engine. He gave the Yugoslav a half salute as he was waved through the barriers. He drove carefully onto the freeway that led to the city of Trieste and then put his foot down, putting as much distance between himself and the border post as quickly as possible. He drove directly into the centre of the city – deserted, now that it was nearly midnight – and pulled into the fore-court of a small petrol station. He killed the engine and ran around to the back of the truck.

'You okay?' he called out anxiously as he opened the rear doors. '*Tutto bene?*'

Lyudmila's blonde head appeared above a stack of boxes. She grinned at him. '*Da*. Is good.' She stood up, her head nearly touching the roof, and clambered unsteadily towards him. He gave her a hand and she jumped easily downwards. She was at least a couple of heads taller than him and he could only look up at her helplessly.

'Where you go now?' he asked finally.

She looked across the deserted forecourt. She shrugged. 'I find hotel. No problem.'

He hesitated, then reached into his pocket. He pulled out a thick wad of lire. 'Here,' he said, peeling off several thousand. 'Take. No good have no money. Take,' he urged her. 'Take.'

She looked down at him and at the notes in his hand, an unreadable expression in her young face. 'Thank you,' she said softly, stuffing the notes into the back pocket of her shorts. He scratched his head. Aside from the small bag that couldn't have held much more than a tooth-brush and a spare T-shirt, she had nothing. How would she manage? She seemed to understand his unspoken question. 'Thank you,' she said again, flicking her thick blonde hair over her shoulder. 'I go.'

'Where? Where you go?'

She shrugged and smiled. Her limited English didn't allow her to say much. 'Is okay.' She turned and began walking towards the main road. It was his last glimpse of her. Those remarkable long, tanned legs, the frayed denim shorts and the thick curtain of heavy blonde hair . . . she was quickly swallowed up by the night.

24

A YEAR LATER

She ran her finger down the long length of the sideboard, checking it for dust. In half an hour's time, her employer would do exactly the same. And if there were a speck to be found, Lady Bryce-Brudenell would find it. Lyudmila inspected her finger anxiously. It was clean, not even the faintest smidgen of dust. She nodded to herself. If there was one thing the teenager from Krylatskoe knew how to do, it was *clean*. Elsa had taught her well. She pulled a quick, disappointed face. She was a cleaner. It wasn't exactly what she'd imagined when she stepped off the train that had carried her from the continent to London's Victoria station but . . . shit happens. Things don't always pan out the way you expect. Working for Lady Bryce-Brudenell, however fussy she was, beat working in (respectively) the seedy Blue Spot Café on Great Peter Street, behind the bar at the Lamb and Flag just off Piccadilly, handing out leaflets outside King's Cross station and, very briefly, collecting ten pence each from unsuspecting sunbathers who'd dared sit down on one of the wooden deck chairs in Hyde Park. At least here, in the family's large, somewhat gloomy flat in Chelsea that they occupied during the week, she had her own room with plenty of hot water and thick, fluffy towels, the likes of which she'd never seen. Her room was at the top of the third flight of stairs with its own en suite bathroom and (tiny) kitchenette. Lady Bryce-Brudenell had opened the door to it saying, 'It's a bit on the small side, but I think you'll find it cosy enough.' She'd had to look up 'cosy' in the dictionary (*uyutnyi*) but the comment still made her smile. A bit on the *small* side? Clearly Janet Bryce-Brudenell had never been to Krylatskoe.

She plumped up the cushions on the two sofas, straightened the thick, oriental rug and quickly wiped the coffee table. She made sure all the magazines were neatly stacked away and that the flowers in the vases were still fresh. One last tweak of the heavy damask curtains and the living room was done. She still had the dining room and the hallway to do before her employer came home but it was only halfway through the morning. Lady Bryce-Brudenell wouldn't be back from her twice-weekly bridge session until at least noon. Plenty of time.

She wandered into the kitchen and pushed open the back door. It was damp outside, the sort of cold, grey English weather that reminded her of home. She shut the door behind her and lit a cigarette. The smoke curled and burned its way pleasurably down into her lungs. A red-breasted robin fluttered into view, landing delicately on the dewy grass, beak dipping and darting before fixing her, an unfamiliar presence, with a careful, beady eye. They remained there together for a few moments, she finishing her cigarette with languid, unhurried grace, the bird pecking around for a worm or some morsel that wasn't a cigarette butt but something useful, perhaps even edible. From behind the closed door she could hear the tinny, persistent shrill of the transistor radio. Dionne Warwick's voice swelled mournfully. *I'll never fall in love again.* She inhaled deeply, drawing the smoke down into her lungs. She preferred the chirpier, more upbeat sound of bands like the Beatles and the Jackson Five. *It's Been a Hard Day's Night* and *ABC* and *I Want You Back*. That sort of stuff. She didn't care for these lonely-hearts ballads. They put her in a bad mood.

A sudden noise made her jump. It was the front door, opening and closing. She quickly dropped her cigarette and ground it underfoot. She opened the kitchen door and slipped back inside. She could hear footsteps coming down the corridor. Suddenly a man's frame appeared in the doorway. It was Sir Peregrine Bryce-Brudenell, Lady Bryce-Brudenell's husband and a rare sighting in London. He spent most of the time on their family estate somewhere in Scotland. Lyudmila stared at him. She'd only met him a couple of times in the three months she'd worked for them. He was a tall, heavy man in his late fifties, a good fifteen years older than his wife, with a large, high forehead and a receding chin that lent a somewhat melancholic edge to his otherwise frosty manner. The telephone was ringing in the background; he held out a cellophane-wrapped bunch of flowers and there was a moment of embarrassed awkwardness between them.

'I'll just—'

'Should I—?'

They both spoke at once. She hesitated. The phone continued to ring, shrilly.

'I'll get that,' he said finally. 'Here. Unwrap these and put them in a vase. It's Janet's birthday. Lady Bryce-Brudenell,' he added, as though she might not know her employer's first name.

'Yes, yes, of course.' She hastily took the bunch from him. Red, velvety and barely unfurled roses, their heads pressed against the cellophane like faces against glass. He disappeared back down the corridor. She ripped the flowers free of their squeaky transparency and quickly buried her nose in the deep, earthy perfume.

His disembodied voice floated down the corridor. 'Yes, I just got in. No, not yet. Oh, around eight, I should think.' She fished out one of the heavy glass vases from beneath the kitchen sink and filled it with water.

She was just arranging the last of the stems when he came in again. 'Ah, that's lovely, thank you.' He looked closely at her, taking her in. They stood together again in a lightly held embarrassment for a few seconds, servant and master of the house, neither quite sure, it seemed, of what to say. Then he cleared his throat, the sound breaking the silence. He turned and left the kitchen. His tread died slowly away down the long corridor like an echoing sigh.

25

The room was shrouded in darkness. 'Wake him at five with a cup of tea,' Lady Bryce-Brudenell had instructed her as she was leaving the flat. 'He'll sleep past dinner if he's not careful.' She tiptoed in, the tray carefully balanced in her left hand as she moved past him so as not to disturb him before she'd laid it down. The air was heavy and dark; the scent of pipe smoke and books mingled together. She kept her eye on him as she laid the tray down on the table beside the heavy black leather Chesterfield on which he slept.

'What time is it?' He was already awake.

She stopped, like a child in a game of statues. 'Five o'clock. Nearly.'

'Bring it here.'

She hesitated. There was a ringing sensation in her ears, as though she'd submerged herself under water. She looked closely at him; in the dim half-light that came in from the barely opened door, his face was a concentration of expression, not a set of individual features. 'Wh . . . would you like milk?' she stammered.

He shook his head. His hand reached out, as if for the toggle on the lamp beside the sofa, but went instead to his head. 'I've a terrible headache,' he said, levering himself upright. 'Terrible.'

'Oh.' She didn't know what to say. Her own hand hovered over the tray. 'Milk?' she asked again.

He shook his head. 'No. No milk.'

She hesitated again. 'Lemon?' Their sharp scent hung in the air.

'No. No lemon.'

There was another awkward pause. 'Shall I . . . do you need something? For your headache, I mean,' she asked.

His hand went to his temple. 'Right here,' he said, tapping it forcefully. 'I don't know when I've had such a headache.' He seemed to be waiting for something from her. The flat was completely empty. Lady Bryce-Brudenell was at a dinner; the children were still at school. The silence was almost palpable. A shape moved; it was his arm. He reached out and took hold of her arm. 'Here,' he repeated, pressing her hand towards his forehead. 'Right there.' His skin was damp, almost leathery. She swallowed. Darkness, fear and confusion were running together in her mind as one – what did he want? Outside against the darkened windowpane, a light, furry snow was falling.

His fingers moved from her own, beginning a trail down her forearm that was a caress. They were close: he, half-sitting, half-lying on the Chesterfield, she bent awkwardly over him, still frozen with nervousness and indecision. Part of her wanted to jerk her hand away but there was a part of her that recognised there was more to be gained from the situation if she only allowed it to develop. 'Sit,' he said, releasing her hand and patting the space beside him. She sat down gingerly. The leather squeaked and protested slightly under her weight. He got up and went to lock the door. The room was still dark; if there was to be a protest from her, now was the time to make it.

She did not.

26

FOUR MONTHS LATER

'You can get dressed now,' the nurse said to her briskly, pulling back the curtains. 'The doctor'll be in to see you in a minute.'

Lyudmila sat up, hurriedly pulling the sheet awkwardly over her legs. 'Is . . . is result?' she asked.

'Yes, yes. The results are in.'

'What is result?'

'The doctor will discuss that with you.' The nurse's lips were drawn together in a thin line.

Suka. Bitch. Lyudmila looked away from her and down at her stomach. She knew what the results would be. She didn't need a doctor to tell her *that* – but she had to be sure. She'd waited as long as she could but time was fast running out. It was getting harder by the day to hide the growing bump underneath her jumper. Only the other day she'd caught Lady Bryce-Brudenell looking at her closely as she'd straightened up from cleaning the oven. 'Are you all right, Lyudmila?' she asked, her tone oddly brittle.

'Fine,' she'd replied hastily, hoping her cheeks wouldn't betray her. 'Just a little . . . tired.' It was true. She *was* tired, and dizzy.

'You look . . . you've put on a bit of weight, eh?'

'*Da*. Good food. Good English food.' She'd tried to make a weak joke of it.

Lady Bryce-Brudenell had stared at her for a second, and then nodded. 'Yes. I dare say.'

The door opened suddenly and the doctor appeared in the doorway holding a clipboard in his hand. The stern-faced nurse threw her a final disapproving look and left the room.

'Well, Miss Gordiskaya,' he pronounced her name smoothly. 'As I'm sure you already know, yes, you're pregnant.'

Lyudmila ran a tongue around her lips. 'How much?'

The doctor looked confused. 'How much what?'

'How much pregnant?'

'Oh, I see. Between twelve and thirteen weeks, I'd say. I take it you're not—?' he left the question delicately unsaid. His demeanour indicated there might be other options than the one he'd left out.

'No. No married.' Lyudmila wasn't one for delicacies. 'But is okay. I will have baby.' She looked him straight in the eye. 'I am not first, you know.'

'Er, no. I don't suppose you are.' The doctor was the one to drop his eyes.

'I see.' The voice on the other end of the telephone might have been discussing the weather, or a sudden drop in share prices, or a friend's performance on the green. Anything, in fact, other than the real reason she'd called.

'So what do you want?' His voice was clipped.

Lyudmila's hand gripped the receiver tightly. 'Money,' she said slowly. 'Money for baby.'

There was a moment's hesitation. 'Fine. But just for the child. Not for you.'

'Okay.' She let out a breath. *Chelovek – kuznets svoego schastya. You make the bed you lie in.* She could almost hear her mother's voice. Well, she'd certainly *made* the bed – countless times. And yes, it was now hers to lie in. Hers and her baby's. He would have no part in it. He'd made that perfectly clear. 'Okay,' she said again, slowly. 'Money for baby. Is okay.'

'The solicitors will contact you.' And that was it. The line went dead. She put the receiver down and sat there for a few minutes, her hand slowly going round in circles over her swollen belly.

PART THREE
BEGINNINGS

'The beginning is the most important part of the work.'
Plato

27

1997

TASH
Cavezzana, Italy

Somewhere up there in the corner of the vast panorama that was the sky, a ghostly moon hung, pale and translucent, waiting impatiently for evening and the inevitable dying of the light. It was June and the late-afternoon sun had retained its lush fullness of warmth without tipping over into humid slackness. Down there in the valley away from the house, Tash stood ankle-deep in the cool river, poking around her bare feet with a stick. There were probably fish darting about in the shallows, and worms and algae and all sorts of other creatures she couldn't name but for once she didn't care. She was enveloped in a shimmering shawl of green, the branches of the trees around her all dipping towards the stream. The wind moved gently, stirring the leaves. Up there on the terrace, out of sight but not out of sound, were the various members of the Harburg family, who came to the beautiful old mill house in Cavezzana every summer.

It wasn't the first time she'd been invited – every year Rebecca begged her to come – but it was the first time she'd actually been able to come. Somehow, from some source Tash didn't care to know about, Lyudmila had produced the necessary wad of cash that made the trip not only possible, but also enjoyable. She and Tash had spent an unusual and unusually exciting few days shopping for new clothes and shoes – the sort of stuff Lyudmila somehow always managed to buy for herself but never for Tash. They'd gone to Selfridges on a Thursday morning and had coffee and a croissant in the cafe on the ground floor before going up the escalators to the warehouse of clothing that was the women's department, where Lyudmila was evidently known, if not exactly appreciated. She was clearly the sort of customer who demanded lots of attention but spent very little. There was a hint of a sneer in the eyes of the various snobbish sales assistants whom she summoned every other minute, but Tash didn't care. That morning she discovered that whilst she didn't have the kind of face that would launch a new outfit never mind a thousand ships, she did have the rangy, loose-limbed body that was suddenly in vogue. 'You're practically as tall as Stella,' one of the girls cooed, standing behind Tash in the mirror. Tash resisted the temptation to smirk.

'How much is jeans?' Lyudmila snapped. She wasn't used to her daughter receiving more attention than her.

'Expensive, I'm afraid.'

'Ma,' Tash hissed, squinting at the sales tag. 'You can't possibly spend that sort of money on *jeans*.'

'Is okay. Is investment. Maybe you gonna find *khoroshego mal'chika*?' Lyudmila lapsed into Russian. Tash rolled her eyes. A nice boy? Fat chance, even if she *were* looking.

'Ma,' she began, but Lyudmila had already turned back to the snooty sales assistant.

'I take one pair white, one pair blue. And shoes.'

Half an hour later, mother and daughter stepped through the revolving door with more bright yellow bags than Tash had ever seen in one go and flagged down a cab.

Sitting beside Lyudmila on the way back to their tiny flat, Tash experienced a desperate, almost crippling surge of envy. She longed to be rich. *Properly* rich. Like Rebecca and Annick. Although her school fees at St Benedict's had been paid for by the Bryce-Brudenell family, it had long been understood that once Tash had finished her A-levels that would be the end of it. There would be no further remittances from the Mortimer & McKenzie offices on George Street, Edinburgh, whose cheque sailed through the post box on the first of every month and had done since she was born. Whatever 'arrangement' Lyudmila had come to with the father of her as-yet-unborn child, eighteen years of support was as far as it would go. University was out of the question. Lyudmila, whose own schooling had ended abruptly after a high-school volleyball tournament, couldn't see the point. She was desperate for Tash to put her expensive education to good and proper use and *go out and get a job*. But she hadn't reckoned on Tash's stubborn ambition. Rebecca and Annick were going to university – why shouldn't she?

After a long, argument-filled summer, Tash finally got her way. She continued to live at home and took the bus every morning to the LSE. Lyudmila thought she was crazy. What the hell was she going to do with a BA (Hons) in economics? The best way to study economics, Lyudmila declared irritably, was to go to work. Tash thought otherwise. She got a grant easily enough – Lyudmila's official earnings amounted to almost nothing – and she knew she'd have to find a job whilst she studied, but she wasn't afraid of having to work hard – she'd done that most of her life. The important thing was not to be left behind. Annick had chosen law and Rebecca art history, and despite their obvious advantages, Tash had always managed to keep up her end of things – that wasn't about to change now. In September, along with the others, she duly began her degree course, full of trepidation but determined to do her best.

Now, three long, hard years later, wearing the short white denim skirt they'd bought that day at Selfridges, she looked down at her bare feet in the water and knew she'd made the right decision.

From the terrace beyond the trees came a sudden burst of laughter. The guests were sitting under a bowery of young, translucent vines at the cloth-covered table now heavy under the weight of dishes. In addition to the three girls, there was Rebecca's mother and two aunts, three cousins of similar age, an uncle, and a great-uncle who'd come over from Israel, hard of hearing, but who sat amongst them with a beatific, contented smile. The mill house was at the end of a narrow, winding road that led from the town of Pontremoli up into the hills and then plunged down again into a steep, wooded valley. Sitting in the back seat of the car that had come to Genoa to pick the three girls up, Tash thought she'd never seen anything quite so beautiful as the Tuscan countryside in early summer. Rebecca's father had bought the place several years before, another holiday home in addition to their place in the South of France, their Hampstead home, the flat in Blooms-bury where Rebecca had spent her university years and their Tel Aviv home . . . the Harburgs' wealth was almost inconceivable. When they rounded the last bend and drove over a narrow, rickety bridge suspended over a rocky gorge, she had to bite down on her tongue to stop herself from squealing out loud. The mill house spread itself over three levels, all the way down to the azure pool at the rear of the buildings, away from any prying eyes. As far as the eye could see were steep wooded hills with their small patches of clearing; tall, narrow, red-roofed houses clustered together under a thick canopy of vine leaves and grey-green olive trees, small vegetable plots appearing like a neat chequerboard of colour in an otherwise lush, green landscape. The sky was a deep, clear blue, misted over here and there by faint wisps of cloud. Tash got out of the car and stood in the driveway, her nostrils prickling pleasurably with the scent of unfamiliar flowers, gazing out on a day without landmarks other than the anticipation of an afternoon at the pool.

'Come on, dozy,' Rebecca giggled at her, leading the way. 'I'll show you to your rooms.'

'But . . . what about our bags?' Tash roused herself to ask.

'Oh, don't worry . . . Stefano'll bring them up. He knows where everyone is.'

Tash glanced at Stefano, who was already busy directing two other young lads with the mountain of luggage that had come with the various guests who'd just arrived. He was a pleasant-looking man in his late twenties, she guessed, with limited English but a ready smile. He'd already noticed Annick in that way that all men noticed Annick – staring at her for a fraction longer than necessary, eyes locked on her when speaking to others . . . Annick had that effect on everyone, not just men. She'd been an outrageously pretty teenager; now, at twenty-one, she'd grown into the promise of her mother's beauty, coupled with her father's dark colouring. Masses of light brown, tightly curled hair, hazel-green eyes, clear coffee-toned skin *without a single blemish*, a figure to die for . . . life, Tash reflected to herself as she followed Rebecca under the stone archway and into the main house, was generally unfair.

She gave the water another vigorous poke. It was their fourth day of a fortnight's stay – ten days to go until they returned to London. Someone had asked her the night before, 'And what do you plan to do with yourself when you get back?' She'd been unable to answer. A degree in economics seemed about as useful to someone in her circumstances as a degree in geography. Useless, in other words. 'Get a job' seemed to be the correct – and only – answer, but even then . . . what sort of job?

And that, mused Tash, flinging the stick onto the opposite bank, was the difference between her and her two best friends. Wealth was nothing other than freedom: freedom to choose, freedom to think, freedom to do whatever the hell you liked. Well, there were no such freedoms for her. She had to find a job, and quickly, too. Lyudmila had been dropping hints like boulders – it was time for her to either move out or start contributing in a more meaningful way to the family economy. She'd been indulged for long enough.

'Tash? Tash?' Someone was calling her. It was Annick. She could see her curly head bobbing above the geraniums that lined the terrace edge. 'Where are you? It's lunchtime.'

'Coming,' Tash yelled, pulling her feet out of the water with a 'plop'. She scrambled onto the bank and picked up her plimsolls. She walked back up the short track to the house, the voices from the terrace becoming stronger and louder as she went.

As usual, a vigorous discussion was underway. The Harburgs loved to argue. No meal was complete without raised voices, flashes of wit and laughter, complaints from those members who were either hard of hearing or who knew too little to join in. In contrast, mealtimes with Lyudmila, when they occurred, were usually silent affairs, Lyudmila's full concentration spent on making sure she didn't overeat. Tash usually had her nose in a book – when they did speak, it was usually only to ask for something. Pass me the butter. Where's the salt? Here, it was different.

—What time did he say they'd be open? I was there yesterday – no one, not a soul! Eleven o'clock in the morning. No wonder you can't get anything done in this country. *One of the aunts pulling a face.*

—Oh, don't be ridiculous, Embeth. It's never going to happen. Never.

—Don't listen to him. That's what they said in '39, remember? Why, I still recall . . .

—Who's asking you? *The scraping of a chair as someone moved back from the table.*

—Don't start all that again.

'Oh, there you are! Rebecca, look who's here. It's Tash. Such a lovely name, don't you think? Come, my dear . . . sit. Sit next to me. That's it. Now, what can I offer you?'

Great plates of food were carefully passed down the length of the table. Enormous platters of salad, green leaves so light and delicate they appeared almost translucent; purple-red radishes, split open to reveal their creamy, frilled flesh; long languid tongues of grilled sweet peppers, their flesh glistening with oil like sweat. A local woman from one of the neighbouring farms supervised a clutch of young girls bringing food from the kitchen to the table and back again. Down below by the swimming pool, thousands of wasps clustered around the rock-hewn steps, seeking some relief from the heat in the spray that bounced off the boulders. The younger children – Deborah, Rosalie, Gabrielle – rushed back and forth in bare feet, squealing as they narrowly escaped being stung.

Tash helped herself to a simple but delicious dish of tagliatelle, seasoned with olive oil, torn basil leaves and small, bittersweet anchovies, topped with flaked almonds. 'It's a speciality of the district,' Rebecca's mother explained, making sure everyone had enough food and wine before settling herself at the head of the table. 'Luisa makes it at least two or three times every summer. Do you like it? *Te gusta?*'

Tash nodded, swallowing quickly. She marvelled at the way Embeth moved graciously from guest to guest, always making sure everyone was comfortable and provided for, without ever making it seem like a chore. She dutifully divided her attention between her guests but seemed to reserve a special welcome for Tash. There was something in her frank gaze that implied a special awareness. Embeth had only once met Lyudmila, at a school play, some years earlier – an unhappy event that Tash had tried to ban from her memory – but she could see now that Embeth remembered it only too well. She took extra special care to make sure Tash felt at home and Tash was grateful. 'It's delicious,' she mumbled, hoping none of the sauce had escaped her mouth.

'Some more wine? We've got a Sancerre that's particularly good,' Embeth motioned to Rebecca to pass the bottle. 'Or there's a Pouilly-Fumé somewhere . . . where's the Chamoux?' she called down the table. 'Have we finished it already?'

'Luisa!' someone shouted. '*Può portare un'altra bottiglia, per favore.*'

'*Va bene,*' came back the answering shout. Seconds later, one of the girls came running out with another ice-cold bottle. Glasses were quickly topped up, toasts made and the conversations resumed.

Tash finished off her pasta and took another sip of her wine. She leaned back in her seat, aware of the conversations and activities that were taking place around the table, but she also felt oddly separate from them, as if viewing them from afar. Rebecca and Annick were engaged in an earnest discussion with one of the aunts; there was an argument further down about whether or not some cousin or other was going to show up; the old, hard-of-hearing uncle was dozing quietly at the other end. It was a family gathering of the sort she'd never before encountered. She felt a sudden unexpected clawing at her heart and to her horror, felt her eyes growing wide with tears. She blinked quickly, but not before Embeth had caught her eye.

'Are you all right, my dear?' Embeth laid a hand on Tash's forearm.

Tash nodded, unable to speak. She got up, avoiding everyone's concerned glances and practically ran from the table. Her rubber-soled plimsolls made the searing squeak of fingers dragged across a blackboard. Her chest was rising and falling in an effort to control the tears.

She pushed open the door to the pretty, low-ceilinged bedroom that had been hers for the past four days, closed it firmly behind her and lay down on the bed. She thought of Lyudmila at home in the small flat, carefully cutting out coupons from the free magazines that floated through their letterbox every day. In the large wooden wardrobe that blocked the door to the living room were her clothes, her 'investments', as she called them. Lyudmila would sooner go hungry than pass up on a new pair of shoes (in the sales, of course), and she frequently did. For years Tash had wondered at her mother's priorities – hair, clothes and make-up before everything else, including Tash – all in the vain hope of catching a man who might, just *might*, provide some of the same comforts. She loved her mother – of course she did – but that afternoon, sitting amongst those rich women of an entirely different order, she'd experienced an ache of sympathy for Lyudmila that was mixed with shame. Lyudmila longed for the kind of lifestyle that Embeth Harburg had, but she had none of the skills or tools at her disposal that would have secured it. Rebecca's father had yet to make his appearance; he was in Israel, overseeing one or other of the vast projects that bore the family name, but Tash knew instinctively that he too would be a man of an entirely different disposition from the men whom Lyudmila so desperately entertained.

She rolled over onto her side, hugging the lavender-scented pillow to her chest. Something was being told to her. Part of it had to do with wealth, and the getting and display of it – and her mother's failure to either grab hold of it or keep it, but there was another side to it that she hadn't quite grasped. She would never be like Lyudmila – she had neither the looks nor the temperament – but she had none of the advantages that Rebecca did. She didn't envy Annick either. In many ways, Annick was just as lonely as Tash, perhaps even lonelier. Although her parents were both undeniably rich and glamorous, they were absent. Tash knew all about absence. She'd never met her father and as far as she could work out, Lyudmila had barely known him either, yet his shadow was upon them both. When she was younger, in an attempt to make the situation seem more acceptable, perhaps, Lyudmila would sometimes evoke his presence in a way that Tash hungered for but was never convinced by. Little things, little off-hand, tossed-aside comments – 'your father likes milk in his tea', or 'he doesn't like marmalade'. Trivial details that, spoken in the present tense, made it seem as though his absence was only temporary. Tash understood her mother was pretending – for one thing, the details never changed or deepened. What Lyudmila knew of Tash's father was the sort of thing an *au pair* or a cleaning girl might know; how he took his tea, what sort of scones he liked, whether or not his socks were to be ironed. She sensed it was for her sake, and it hurt her to think her mother thought it necessary.

And then, of course, the day arrived when she stopped believing the myth and the whole absurd circus came to an end. She decided to seek him out. It had actually been Rebecca's idea. 'Why don't you just go and see him?' she'd asked one Friday afternoon as the three of them trooped home from school.

'Where? I don't even know where he lives.'

'Thought you said he was Scottish?'

'No, that's just where the money comes from. He's got solicitors in Edinburgh.'

'Well, why don't you start there?' Annick's eyes lit up. She loved happy endings. 'Just go up to Edinburgh and tell them you won't go away until you've seen him . . . or they tell you where he is.'

'How? I haven't got any money. How'm I going to get to Edinburgh? And what would I tell my mum?'

'We'll give you the money, silly. And tell your mum you're staying with me,' Rebecca scoffed at her excuse.

'Why don't we all go?' Annick broke in excitedly.

Tash shook her head. 'No, I'd rather go alone.' She turned to them hesitantly. 'Are you sure? I'll pay you back—'

'Don't be daft. Come on, let's go to the cashpoint. How much d'you need?'

'I've no idea. How much is a train ticket to Edinburgh?'

Three hours later, she was on her way. She took the sleeper train from King's Cross with nothing in her schoolbag other than a three-pack of underwear purchased at Marks & Spencer and a ham sandwich that Rebecca had pressed into her hands just before the train pulled out.

She got out at Waverley Station at seven a.m. the following morning, having slept almost all the way – a combination of nerves and fear. It was cold. It was autumn in London but early winter up north and she pulled her school blazer tightly around her as she made her way up the steps towards Princes Street. She had only the foggiest idea of where she was going. She knew the law offices of Mortimer & McKenzie were at 114 George Street, Edinburgh . . . but where was George Street?

Ten minutes later, she was standing outside a dark blue painted door with a large brass ring and a small brass plate announcing the presence on the second floor of Mortimer & McKenzie, Solicitors-at-law. It was just past seven thirty and George Street was still practically empty. Well, at least now she knew where it was, she reasoned, looking up and down the wide, handsome street for a cafe. There was one at the end, just before the square . . . she could see people hurrying in and out with Styrofoam cups. Her stomach rumbled angrily; she'd had nothing to eat since the rather soggy ham sandwich almost twelve hours earlier.

'Mornin', darlin', what can we get ye?' A plump, cheerful-looking woman turned as Tash approached. 'Brrr,' she mimed a shiver. 'Nippy out there, isn't it? You warm enough wi' only that on?'

Whoever it was who'd claimed Scots weren't friendly clearly hadn't been to Edinburgh. She nodded quickly. 'Yes, I'm quite warm, thank you. Could I have a coffee, please?'

'From down south, are ye?'

Tash nodded again. 'I've just arrived. I've come to visit my father.' The words slipped out.

'Oh? Lives up here, does he?' the woman asked as she began the complicated-looking process of making a coffee.

'Yes. He lives just up the road,' Tash said confidently.

'On George Street?'

Tash nodded firmly. 'At 114 George Street.'

The woman paused and looked more closely at her. 'Didnae think there was anyone left actually living on George Street,' she said after a moment. 'They're all offices now. Oh, well . . . he must be very wealthy, your father, then.'

'Er, yes. Yes, he is. How . . . how much is that?'

'That'll be a pound, love.' She made a great pretence of holding up Tash's English fiver. 'Ooh, d'you think I ought to take it?' she turned to her colleague. Everyone laughed. Tash took her coffee, mumbled her thanks and fled. *My father lives just up the road.* She had no idea why she'd said it – it had just popped out. She hurried along George Street. At the opposite end was another small garden, now filling up with office and shop workers beginning their day. She took a seat on a bench at the far end and slowly sipped her coffee, waiting for Mortimer & McKenzie's offices to open.

The receptionist looked her up and down slowly, her eyes resting on Tash's regulation school shoes. 'D'you have an appointment?' she asked finally.

Tash shook her head. 'No, I . . . I just . . . I was just passing by,' she stammered. Now that she was here, in the dark, gloomy oak-panelled reception room, the bravado and confidence that had brought her from King's Cross to Waverley overnight was quickly seeping away. 'I just thought . . .' Her voice trailed off.

'I'll have to see. Mr McKenzie's awfully busy at the moment. Take a seat, Miss Bryce-Brudenell.'

She disappeared through the connecting door to the office behind her. Tash looked around her. The room was quiet. Outside, the sounds of George Street coming to morning life filtered up from the ground. A clock in the far corner of the room slowly counted out the minutes. She was bursting for the loo. She looked around; the toilet was probably in the hallway. She hesitated for a second or two. There was no sound from the adjoining office. She jumped up, unable to hold it in any longer. Leaving her satchel on the chair, she quickly nipped out of the door. She was right; the second door on the left was indeed a toilet. She locked the door behind her and sat down, relieved.

It took her a second or two to understand the conversation going on in the room behind her was actually about *her*.

'But I can't just send her away.' It was the frosty receptionist.

A man's voice. Deep, with the barest hint of a Scots accent. 'Which one is it? The Lithuanian?'

'No, well . . . I don't know. Tash, she said. I suppose she *could* be Lithuanian . . . Natasha?'

'Oh for Christ's sake. Well, you'll just have to deal with her. His instructions have always been the same. No contact. School fees until they're eighteen, no more.'

'She's come all the way up from London . . .'

'Silly girl. What on earth did she expect? To find him here?'

Tash didn't wait to hear another word. She stood up, forgetting in her haste to flush the toilet or wash her hands. She opened the door and ran down the stairs. It was only when she was out on the street, her whole body burning with embarrassment and shame, that she realised she'd left her satchel behind. No matter. She'd stuffed her train ticket and a crumpled ten-pound note in her blazer pocket. Mortimer & McKenzie could keep her schoolbooks, her house keys and the cellophane-wrapped M&S knickers. She ran all the way back to Waverley Station, ignoring the curious glances of passers-by. She was in luck; there was a train leaving in twenty minutes. She bought herself a can of Coke and a baguette and boarded, her lips drawn into a tight, angry line.

*

A tap at the door brought her abruptly back to the present. She sat up, rapidly scrubbing at her cheeks. 'Come in,' she called out, hoping her voice was steady. It couldn't be Rebecca or Annick – they would simply come barging in.

It was Embeth. She was carrying a small tray on which two tiny espresso cups were balanced, together with a plate of pale, crisp almond *biscotti*. 'I thought you might like some coffee,' Embeth said with a smile. 'Luisa made a batch of these this morning – the smell woke me up. Too delicious for words.'

Tash struggled upright. One plimsoll was still on; there was a dusty streak on the pristine white counterpane. She hastily brushed at it with her hand, embarrassed. 'Sorry,' she muttered, kicking it off and drawing her legs up underneath her.

'Oh, don't worry about that . . . it'll go in the wash tomorrow. Now, how d'you take your coffee?' She perched elegantly on the side of the bed and passed over one of the small porcelain cups. 'Milk?'

To Tash's horror, for the second time that day her eyes filled with tears. She shook her head, praying they wouldn't overspill and slide down her already-damp cheeks. 'No, no milk,' she said shakily.

Embeth said nothing for a moment. A light breeze came in through the window, stirring the sheer muslin curtain so that it billowed into the room, then was sucked back out again, a mouth opening and closing with the wind. Against the perfectly still blue Tuscan sky, a line of dark cypresses stood as though they were painted. They could hear the faint shouts of the younger children in the pool and the silvery tinkle of splashing water. 'Is it your first time to Italy?' Embeth asked gently and they both understood a different sort of question was being asked.

Tash nodded slowly. 'It's my first time . . . well, anywhere,' she said. 'My . . . we don't really . . .' She stopped, embarrassed, and picked at the counterpane instead.

Embeth smiled. 'You don't have to explain,' she said gently. 'Not everyone's as fortunate as we are. You work hard, Tash, and that's the main thing. Not whether you go on expensive holidays.'

Tash looked up at her uncertainly. It wasn't the sort of conversation she usually had with anyone, least of all a friend's mother. There was a deep and kind expression in Embeth's eyes that suddenly left her feeling out of her depth. She wasn't used to tenderness; it was a breath of something she'd somehow missed. 'It's just my mum and me,' she said slowly, looking up nervously to see if Embeth understood what she herself was unsure she was trying to say.

'And your father?'

She hesitated before answering. 'I've never met him. He . . . he has another family.'

'Ah,' Embeth nodded sympathetically. 'It happens. It's hard, especially for the children. But it doesn't alter the fact that you've done well, Tash. From what Rebecca tells me, you've achieved a great deal.'

Tash looked down at the bedspread. She knew Lyudmila was grudgingly proud of her, despite her inability to show or say it, but hearing the words from someone else was almost too much to bear. 'Th . . . thanks,' she stammered, cursing the awkwardness that had crept over her.

'Have another one,' Embeth smiled, proffering the *biscotti*. 'No one makes them like Luisa. Now, I'd better see about dinner. Mr Harburg's arriving tonight and I'd better make sure there's no *pancetta* in any of the recipes. Luisa seems unable to cook without it.' She gave a low, warm chuckle, dispelling any awkwardness between them. The bed springs creaked gently as she got up; when she closed the door behind her, a faint trail of her perfume followed her, like a delicately scented cloud. Tash remained where she was, her whole being suddenly lightened.

28

REBECCA

The Courtauld Institute, London

'Just stop here, Garrigan, please,' Rebecca said, nervously clutching her bag. 'Here's fine.'

'Are you sure, Miss Rebecca?' Garrigan, her father's elderly chauffeur, turned his head to look at her. 'We're still a couple of streets away. Why don't you let me drop you at the front entrance?'

'Oh, no, this is fine, honestly.' Rebecca's hand was already on the door handle. 'This is perfect.'

'But what about your bags?'

'I'll manage them,' Rebecca said and hurriedly got out of the car. There was no way she was going to make the mistake of arriving for the first day of her course in a chauffeur-driven Rolls-Royce. She'd made *that* mistake in her first year at the Slade and she would never do it again. She'd driven up Oxford Street to Goldsmid House in the Bentley and run into three new fellow students coming out the front door. *Poor little rich girl.* The charge had stuck. This time it would be different. This time, she'd arrive on foot, like everyone else.

She hauled her bags out of the boot before Garrigan could even get out of the car and breezily waved him on his way. She watched the Rolls glide out into the traffic and gave a sigh of relief. A few minutes later, she looked up at the entrance to the Courtauld and, had her hands been free, she'd have hugged herself in delight. A one-year, postgraduate degree in Art and Renaissance Society – she could hardly wait for the course to begin. Her parents were planning to bequeath a number of their artworks to the Tel Aviv Museum of Modern Art and her choice of study suddenly seemed absolutely fortuitous.

She grabbed her bags and stepped under the archway. She had to register with the departmental secretary, find the study that had been allocated to her and find a locker. She looked down at her outfit. A tweed, dark-brown A-line skirt, tan knee-high leather boots, a cream sweater and a faded denim jacket. Tash had chosen it. For someone who had such disdain for fashion, Rebecca often thought, Tash had an uncannily good eye. She could size up a situation, fling open your wardrobe doors and put together a 'look' in less time than it took Rebecca to wriggle out of her jeans. She drew in a deep breath, hoisted her leather satchel onto one shoulder and followed the signs to the Registry.

29

ANNICK
College of Law, Store Street, London

Sitting in the second-to-last row, trying very hard to look as though she belonged there (or at least not as though she so patently *didn't*), Annick struggled to follow the lecturer. Equity and trusts. Tort. Contractual law. She felt like burying her head in her hands and howling. It was hopeless. Sooner or later they'd find out that she wasn't supposed to be there. The phone call that her father had had to make to the dean in order to get her onto the course would be exposed as a complete and utter waste of time. The president's daughter was too stupid to have been allowed *in the door*, never mind enrol on the bloody course. She'd *never* be able to keep up. Her mind drifted back to that fateful conversation she'd had with her parents at the beginning of the summer. If it hadn't been for that odious little creep Traoré, the foreign minister from Burkina Faso, the conversation might not have taken place at all. He'd turned to her in that idiotic, *faux*-chummy way her father's friends and associates had, pretending to take an avuncular interest in her, yet staring openly at her breasts. 'So, *mademoiselle*,' he'd chuckled, his eyes slipping from her face. 'You've finished your studies, eh?'

'Yes, sir.'

'And what did you study, if you don't mind me asking? Ha, ha.'

She didn't understand what was so funny but she answered demurely, 'French, sir.'

'*French?*'

'Well, French and Modern European Languages. It's . . . it's a joint honours degree.' It wasn't worth telling him that she hadn't quite made the honours grade.

'*Qu'est-ce-que c'est que ça?*' He turned to her father for clarification.

Sylvan waved a spoon. 'Some nonsense they study over there at the undergraduate level. She's going to do law.'

'Ah. Law.' Traoré nodded knowingly. 'You're going to become a . . . how do they call it in England? A barrister? *C'est bien ça, non?*'

'No, I'm actually going to be a solicitor,' Annick hastened to correct him. There was no way in hell she'd ever survive a pupillage to become a barrister.

'A solicitor? No, surely not? If I understand the English system correctly, it's not quite as, shall we say, prestigious, *non?*' Traoré was keen to show off his understanding of the finer points of English law.

'Oh, no, no, it's practically the same thing—'

'Don't be ridiculous.' Her father looked up from his plate. 'You're going to be a barrister, not a solicitor.'

Annick's heart sank. She looked quickly at her mother, who quickly looked away. 'Er, well, the thing is, I've had a think about it . . . I spoke to the tutors at the Law College and they all agreed—'

'A solicitor?' Her father spat the word out again like a piece of gristle. 'No. No. No daughter of mine is going to become a second-class lawyer.'

'But it's not like that, Papa,' Annick began, feeling the hot blood rush into her cheeks. 'Not any more. It's not like—'

'Silence. You are going to become a barrister.'

She should have recognised the threatening finality in his tone. She didn't. She began to try and explain again but was stopped by his fist banging down on the table like a thunder crack. Even the servants jumped. There was a moment's startled pause, then one of them rushed forward to try and mop up the wine that had accidentally spilled from Anouschka's glass.

'*Chérie*,' Anouschka murmured, trying to divert his attention before his temper got the better of him. 'Shall we switch to the Bordeaux?'

Annick watched her father draw in a deep breath. Despite his anger, she felt almost elated. The attention he'd shown her that evening was more than he'd shown all year. Her own breath was shallow and tense as she waited for the explosion. But it didn't come. Nothing further was said. Her mother got up from the table and the sight of her taut bottom in skin-tight white jeans and the thick curtain of wavy blonde hair that fell down her back distracted both men. When they turned their attention back to the table – and to talk of a different kind – Annick and her career choices were forgotten.

So, now here she was, in the second-to-last row, fingers tightening nervously around her pen, surrounded by students who were more eager, more qualified, more intelligent and certainly more motivated than she was. Criminal law. Land law. Public law. Not only were her eyes glazing over, her brain had suddenly stopped working. The lecturer droned on. 'You'll need an analytical, enquiring mind and the ability to draw out key issues from a mass of information. You'll need clear verbal, listening and written communication skills to gather information and pass it on, articulately, to others.' *An analytical, enquiring mind?* She had nothing of the sort. *The aptitude to solve problems in a practical way that helps your client?* Nothing could be further from the truth. She had no practical skills whatsoever. She couldn't even change a light bulb and it wasn't for the reasons Tash once claimed: it wasn't because she'd grown up with an army of servants who catered to her every whim. It was because she couldn't be bothered. Annick's world was neatly divided into two categories: things that were of interest to her and things that weren't, and unfortunately the latter seemed to outweigh the former. She'd once assumed the whole point of university was to somehow redress that balance, to make the world more interesting and students more curious. It hadn't quite worked in her case. It was her own fault, really. She'd gone for the easy option at university. French. She *ought* to have done well. French was her mother tongue, after all. Only studying it wasn't quite as easy as speaking it, as she soon found out. Study required learning, and learning took effort.

'Confidence is key.' The lecturer's voice suddenly interrupted her musings. 'To be a good barrister, you need to have the ability to build relationships with a wide range of people.' Annick brightened visibly. Well, that was *one* thing she was good at. People. Talking to them, putting them at ease, finding things out. Nothing made her happier than a good conversation and she didn't mind with whom. At home in Lomé her mother was always chastising her for chatting to the servants when she ought to be studying.

'D'you have another pen, by any chance?' The young man to her left suddenly leaned over and whispered in her ear. 'Mine's run out, worse luck.' He held up a leaking ballpoint pen.

'Oh, yeah. Sure.' Annick pulled her bag up to her knees. She had a handful of pens somewhere in the bottom. 'Here. No, keep it. I've got a couple.'

'Thanks.' He smiled at her gratefully, holding her gaze for just a second longer than was necessary. She blushed and then saw the lecturer look directly at her. It was a look she recognised only too well. *Pretty. Silly. Fluffy.* She sighed. She ought to be used to it by now. It was a look that had followed her most of her life. The lecturer was still looking at her. She saw two girls in the row in front slowly turn their heads. *Flirting already?* One of them, a studious-looking redhead with over-sized black spectacles smirked knowingly at her companion. They bent their heads together, laughing at her, of course. Annick felt the familiar flush of anger travel up her face. It wasn't her fault that men seemed unable to pass her by without a second or a third glance. She had nothing to do with it. Her looks were *a fact*. She was tired of having to be extra nice to other girls so that they wouldn't hate her. She was tired of fighting off men, even those old enough to be her grandfather and tired of everyone's mistrust. She wasn't a classic beauty, like her mother, she was a *sexy* beauty, which was far worse. Her beauty was of the cheaper, more inconsequential kind and it meant that Annick neither enjoyed it nor learned how to use it properly. She made a sudden grimace.

'What's the matter?' The young man who'd asked for a spare pen sensed an opening. He put his face very close to hers. *Too* close. Annick stood up suddenly. She grabbed her bag and her coat and quickly left the lecture hall. She'd had enough. Of everything.

30

TASH
Lady Davenport Public Relations, Flood Street, London

'We always answer the phone on the third ring. Lady Davenport doesn't like it to be picked up any sooner.'

'Why's that?'

The giggling blonde named Priscilla, who was showing Tash around, paused. Her slender shoulders went up and down . . . once, twice, three times. 'No idea, actually,' she said at last, as though the question had surprised her. 'I never asked her.' She gave a small, incredulous laugh. 'D'you know, I've never even thought about it. Have you?' she asked her twin, who was sitting at her own desk, rifling through a magazine. The girl looked up, stared at them blankly and then slowly shook her head. 'I *must* ask her,' Priscilla said breezily. 'Now, coffee's in there. Lady Davenport takes hers black. She doesn't take milk in her coffee.'

'Presumably what "black" means,' Tash murmured. She regretted her tone as soon as the words were out. It was only her first day. She oughtn't to frighten everyone off just yet.

Priscilla looked at her uncertainly for a moment, and then the penny dropped. (Slowly, so fucking slowly, Tash swore later to Rebecca and Annick, she could practically *see* it falling.) 'Oh, right. Yes, I see what you mean.' Priscilla gave her irritating tinkling little laugh. 'Gosh, I'm not being very bright today, am I?'

It was on the tip of Tash's sharp tongue to say she couldn't quite imagine her being bright on *any* day, but she managed to rein herself in. *Be nice.* Those were Rebecca's strict instructions. *Be nice, Tash. And if you can't be nice, just be quiet.* 'Sorry,' she muttered.

Priscilla affected not to hear, opening the door to a second office.

'Oh, hu-*llo*!' Two further identical blondes were sitting behind a long glass table. 'I'm just showing the new girl round; hope I'm not disturbing?' Neither girl said anything. 'So,' she went on gamely, 'that's Tiggy and that's Tilly.' She pointed at each girl carefully in turn – useful, since Tash couldn't possibly have told the difference. So far at LDPR, everyone she'd met was tall, leggy and blonde. Where on earth did *she* fit into the picture? 'And this is Tash,' Priscilla said finally, beaming at Tash. She's new,' she added unnecessarily. Tiggy and Tilly stared at her blankly.

'So,' Tash said briskly. 'That's us. The, er, team, as it were.'

'Yes, that's us,' Priscilla said brightly, sensing an exit. 'I'll just show you where the photocopier lives and the coffee machine . . . and that'll pretty much be it, I shouldn't wonder. There's not actually *that* much to do around here, you know.'

'You don't say,' Tash muttered under her breath, following her through the doorway. The offices of LDPR occupied the top floor of a small mews house on Flood Street, just round the corner from the cinema. The rooms were tiny, the central heating seemed to be perman- ently on, making it even stuffier than it ought to be, *but* it was off the King's Road, (which, as everyone except Tash seemed to know), was absolutely de rigueur for PR agencies. Lady Davenport was a thrice- divorced woman in her early fifties, with the sort of blonde beehive hairdo that Tash thought had gone down with the Titanic. She'd been (variously) an interior decorator, an art-gallery owner, a jewellery-shop owner and now she owned a PR agency. To Tash's irritation, it was actually Lyudmila who'd found her the job. There weren't *that* many career openings for a girl of *extremely* modest means with a bachelor's degree in economics and Lyudmila would sooner have cut off her right hand than fork out the money for a masters (which seemed to be what was required for a career in economics). Tash sat at home for a month, growing increasingly despondent until Lyudmila dragged her out one night to Lady Soames's on the pretext of 'introducing' her to Lady Davenport. 'What for?' Tash asked bitterly. 'Don't tell me they're looking for maids?'

But Lady Davenport wasn't looking for a maid. An assistant, she explained to an eager Lyudmila and silent, sulking Tash. Over dinner, Lyudmila sang Tash's praises whilst Tash fingered her tattoo resentfully, trying to look as though she wasn't there.

*

No one was more surprised than Tash, therefore, when Lady Davenport rang a few evenings later, asking for Tash. She appeared to be offering her a job. 'Salary's not up to much,' she said cheerfully, 'but you'll get *loads* of experience. When can you start?'

'Start what?'

'Start work, of course.'

'You want *me* to work for *you*?' Tash almost dropped the phone. Lyudmila, realising what was going on, leapt up and practically wrenched it out of her hands. By the end of the three-minute conversation, it had all been decided. Tash would start work. On Monday morning.

And now, here she was, sitting at an empty desk in a stuffy little office somewhere in the bowels of Chelsea, wondering where it had all gone wrong. *This* wasn't what she'd imagined her future would be.

The front door suddenly burst open and Lady Davenport swept into the room trailing perfume, two wicker baskets, a handful of fabric samples and a scatter of Post-it notes, which she promptly dropped onto Priscilla's desk. She turned to Tash. 'Tatiana! How *lovely* to see you! All settled in, are we? Has Priscilla shown you the ropes? *Dear, dear* Priscilla. D'you know, I don't know what I'd do without her.' She smiled beatifically at Priscilla, who immediately blushed scarlet and affected not to notice.

'Now, listen up, gels. We've got a new client. Hurrah! A rugby player's been caught with an under-age schoolgirl and just before the World Cup, too – can you *imagine*? His agent's in a complete spin. Oh, those *boys*. Too dreadful for words, don't you agree, gels?'

'Dreadful,' they murmured dutifully.

Lady Davenport turned to Tash. 'Would you be a darling and get me a coffee, Tash? Quick as you can, there's a good girl. I'm absolutely *parched*.'

Tash's eyes widened. Coffee? She was here to make Lady Davenport *coffee*? She glanced at Priscilla. There was a tiny, self-satisfied smile playing around the corner of her lips. Now it was Tash's turn to feel the penny drop. Not only was she the new girl, she was the gofer, the coffee maker *and* the errand-runner. With Tash's arrival, Priscilla had moved one tiny notch up the ladder.

A familiar feeling of dread slowly rose in her. In the two months that had passed since they'd all left university, the line that separated her from her two best friends had gradually solidified. The truth of it was simple; neither Rebecca nor Annick actually *had* to work. Annick had been pushed into studying law, not because she had any great desire to be a lawyer. She didn't. Tash knew better than anyone else that the only reason Annick was enrolled at Store Street Law College was because of her father's vanity. He liked the idea of having a beautiful, clever lawyer daughter. What Annick herself wanted was of no consequence. Sadly, Annick had never been able to stand up to either of her parents. What they wanted, they got. And she had no alternative plan for her own future, in any case. She could go on living in the Hyde Park apartment for the rest of her life. At some point, she'd once told a shocked Tash, they'd find a suitable husband for her . . . and that would be it. It had been on the tip of Tash's tongue to yell out, 'Oh, for God's sake! Don't be so bloody feeble! Tell them what you *do* want to do! Jesus, we're not living in the Middle Ages!' But she couldn't and shouldn't. Annick was bright; she just didn't *think* she was. Tash had never herself been in a position *not* to have to worry about how the rent would be paid or how she'd live. Perhaps if she had, she'd understand it. And Rebecca? Rebecca would never have to work, *ever*. She'd enrolled at the Courtauld mostly because she rather liked the idea of swanning around in a dark grey polo-neck and knee-length boots, a stack of art history books under one arm, rushing from one obscure lecture on Byzantine art to another. 'Look,' she explained to Tash airily one morning over coffee, 'not *everything* you do has to make sense. In terms of the future, I mean. Sometimes . . . well, sometimes you just have to do what pleases you.' Tash didn't know quite what to say to that. Rebecca and Annick had the luxury of money; she didn't. It was as simple as that. The gulf between them had begun to yawn.

There was another thing too that troubled her. She understood now that if *she* was able to see them with new eyes, then the distance must work both ways. They too would be able to look at her across the barriers of wealth and privilege and see *her*, and she dreaded being the object of their pity. Tash Bryce-Brudenell, for all her brains and ambition, was now an office junior. Yes, the gulf between them was beginning to widen; one day it might be too wide to cross. She swallowed down hard on that little knot of fear.

31

REBECCA

'Ancient Greek and Roman art is embedded in the culture of recent centuries and it often appears all too familiar to us. But how did it come into existence to begin with? Who made it? And why did they make it?' Dr Jeremy Garrick paused dramatically. Around the seminar table, sixteen pens hovered nervously. Was it a genuine or rhetorical question? Was he asking *them*? Rebecca risked a cautious sideways glance to her left. Sitting next to her was Hugh Fraser, frightfully clever and (luckily) already something of a friend; to his left were the three frighteningly confident and snobbish girls she had dubbed the Cruellas – the improbably named trio, Luella, Bella and Ella.

'Is that a question?' One of the Cruellas spoke up, her horsey voice full of confident flirtation.

'No.' Dr Garrick barely looked up from his notes. 'Over the next couple of months,' he continued, as if the student in question had never spoken, 'we'll be examining some of art's functions, forms and meanings within ancient society.'

Rebecca looked back down at her own notes, relieved she hadn't had the confidence (blind or plain stupid) to raise her own voice. For the next half hour she concentrated on taking down as many of his pearls of wisdom as she could.

An hour later, the seminar finally over, she was crossing the beautiful courtyard of Somerset House when she heard footsteps behind her. It was Hugh. He caught up with her, taking care not to spill his Styrofoam cup of (terrible) canteen coffee.

'God, I nearly bust a gut when he snubbed Luella.' He took a sip of coffee and pulled a face. 'Christ, this is shit. Almost as awful as she is. Mind you, Garrick's almost as bad. He's such a pompous ass.'

'Oh, I don't know,' Rebecca said dreamily. 'I think he's rather good-looking.'

'Good-looking?' Hugh nearly spat out his coffee. 'He's *fat*! *And* he's old!'

'Not *that* old. And he's just *big*, not fat.'

'You need spectacles, darling. He's *fat*.'

'*I* think he's rather sexy, if you really want to know.'

'You're clearly blind,' Hugh said sniffily. At that precise moment, a gust of wind blew across the courtyard, taking Rebecca's scarf with it. She snatched at the air, whirled around and found herself practically pressing against the imposing mound of Dr Jeremy Garrick's belly. She let out an audible gasp.

'Your scarf.' Dr Garrick's voice was as dry and disinterested as it had been when snubbing Luella Maxwell. He held out the offending article of clothing as though holding a snake.

Rebecca took it from him in silence. Her whole body was stained with a blush that travelled from the crown of her head to her toes. She crumpled the scarf in one hand, too embarrassed to speak. They watched him stride off, his coat flapping imperiously behind him.

'Oops.' Hugh was fond of stating the obvious.

'How much d'you think he heard?' Rebecca asked anxiously.

'I've no idea. But at least *you* were complimentary.'

'He might *not* have heard me,' Rebecca said hopefully.

'Yeah. Deaf as well as fat and old.'

'Shit.' It was Rebecca's turn to state the obvious. There wasn't much else she could say.

32

Almost a week later, she was standing in a small knot of people in front of a painting by Modigliani at the National Portrait Gallery on yet another wet Saturday morning in mid-October. She was a month into her course, and was loving it. She had her sketchbook in hand and her headphones on, oblivious to the people around her. Slowly the knot of people around her thinned and drifted off. She turned to go and almost bumped into the person standing next to her. It was Dr Garrick. Again. He inclined his head gravely as their eyes met.

'Morning.'

'G-good morning,' she stammered, uncomfortably aware of the blush spreading up through her neck and chest.

His eyes flickered over her face for the briefest of seconds, then he turned back to the painting. 'Exactly the sort of thing one should see on a wet Saturday morning. A timely reminder of the finer points of life.'

'Er, yes. It's . . . it's beautiful.'

'No, not "beautiful". Striking, yes. Complex. Profound. But not "beautiful". Never that. Beautiful is too simple for Modigliani. His work's hard to place and that's what makes him so special.' He paused. She gazed up at him, too impressed to speak. 'He's the bridge, the link between two worlds,' he went on. 'Influenced by the Cubists, but not part of their movement. Still, the antecedents of Art Deco are already there in the work. One of those in-between artists without whom we wouldn't understand what went on before or what followed.'

She swallowed nervously. What on earth was she supposed to say in response to *that*? 'I . . . I love the portrait of the Lipchitz couple,' she said hesitantly. 'I used to sneak downstairs to stare at them when I was a child. It's funny. I thought I *knew* them. I thought they were relatives or something. I used to run my fingers over the canvas. If my father ever knew, he'd probably kill me.'

He turned to look down at her and frowned. 'Downstairs? Down-stairs where?'

She blushed. 'Um, at home.'

'You have a Modigliani at home? An *original* Modigliani?'

She blushed even more violently. She hadn't meant to show off. 'Um, yes,' she mumbled. 'My father . . . he sort of collects . . . different artists.'

'And what does your father do?'

'He's . . . um, he's a banker.'

'What's your name again?'

'Rebecca Harburg.'

'Ah.' He pulled a face. 'Well, Miss Rebecca Harburg, enjoy the *Red Nude*,' he said gravely. He inclined his head, taking his leave. 'And the rest of your weekend.'

'Er, thank you, sir,' she stammered, wishing she didn't sound quite so breathless and . . . and *stupid*. She waited until she heard his footsteps die away and then she turned. He was standing in the doorway. Their eyes caught and held again, and she felt her whole body slowly start to dissolve.

She ran into him a fortnight later on the stairs in the entrance hall.

'Miss Rebecca Harburg.' He inclined his head. There was that same narrowing of the eye, as if trying to decode something about her. She found it deeply flattering. Dr Jeremy Garrick, trying to work something out about *her*.

'Oh. Oh, good morning, sir,' she squeaked.

He gave a slight smile. 'We're all on first-name terms round here. You ought to know that by now. It's Jeremy.'

'Oh.' She turned brick red. 'Right. Of course, Jeremy.' Saying it out loud sounded almost sacrilegious.

'So, where are you off to?'

'A . . . a lecture. It's "Art in Venice". Dr Crawford. I mean, James.'

He grimaced. 'Dear God, he's not still teaching that, is he?' he asked with another faint smile. She looked up into his light blue eyes, watching with fascination the network of laughter lines that radiated from their edges, hinting at a side of him that was lighter than that which his students were allowed to see. A delicious prickling of pleasure broke out across her skin. Something of it must have communicated itself to him. 'I've got an idea,' he said suddenly.

'An idea?' she repeated and the thought of it made her knees tremble.

'Mmm. Fancy a stroll?'

'Right now?'

'Yeah. I'm going to show you something that'll put James's *Art in Venice* in its proper perspective.'

She swallowed. 'Um, yes. Yes, I . . . I'd love to.'

'Good. I'll meet you on the corner by the bridge.'

She turned and watched him walk off. He was a strange contradiction: the large, solid man who looked as though he'd be more comfortable on a rugby field than in a lecture hall, combined with the curious, sensitive face of the intellectual. She was absolutely transfixed.

He took her to a small antiquarian bookstore, just off Charing Cross Road. There was a bell above the door that jangled as they entered. Like Alice tumbling after the White Rabbit, she followed him in. It was dark and fusty inside. The owner clearly knew Jeremy, greeting him like an old friend and waving them through. 'You know your way around here,' he chortled. 'Shout if you need any help.'

Jeremy led her through a series of corridors until they were in the very back of the shop, in a tiny room that housed not much more than three old wooden chests. He slid open the top drawer of the chest closest to the window, and beckoned to her to come closer. She could hardly breathe. Inside, separated by layers of fine, crinkled tissue paper that let off a scent of mothy, yeasty decay, were a series of original sketches.

'Recognise these?' Jeremy asked, his voice breaking the reverential silence that the tiny room seemed to demand.

Rebecca looked closely at the pencil and ink drawings nestled in the sleeves of tissue before her. They were studies – quick, sharp flicks of the wrist and hand, frozen moments of time and place in the construction of a painting that was yet to emerge. They were of a couple locked in a close embrace. As he gently peeled the layers of drawings, one from the other, the sensation was of watching something in motion, of a series of moving parts. She stared at the sketches. She'd never seen anything quite so expressive. On each, she could almost feel where the artist's soft lead had bitten into the creamy surface, the paper resisting at first, then giving way to the dent, then the mark, and then all the marks combining to provide an opening into the soul. 'No,' she whispered, because it somehow seemed appropriate to whisper. 'Who's the artist.'

'Francesco Hayez. Eighteenth-century Venice. These are the study drawings to his most famous work, *Il Baci*. The Kiss.' He looked down at her, his expression unreadable. 'It's the most passionate representation of a kiss in the history of Western art.' He turned and opened another drawer. He pulled a drawing out, placing it on top of the chest. 'Look how he's holding her. See? She's leaning backwards, away from him. We can't see their faces. For the first time in Western art, it's not important *who* they are, but what they're *doing*, what the embrace represents. It's the *kiss* that's the centre of the painting, the expression of *feelings*, rather than rational thought. But look at it a bit more closely.' He bent forward slightly. Rebecca followed suit. Her heart was racing. 'Look at his clothing. He's wearing red, white and green. Those were the colours of the *Risorgimento*, the Italian patriots fighting for independence from the Austro-Hungarian Empire. She's wearing pale blue, the colours of France. In the same year as he painted this, France made an alliance with the Kingdom of Piedmont and Sardinia, which allowed the states of the Italian peninsula to unify under the Italian flag. It's a kiss, yes, but it's also the birth of Italy. And in these sketches,' he turned back again to the first drawer, 'you get a glimpse into the layers that constructed it, that whole vision of independence . . . the beginning of a new identity. That's *art*, Rebecca Harburg. Here, in this bookstore, in these drawers, between the tissue paper and the reproductions and what we know of the period. *This* is where it lives. Not in some lecture hall.'

She was moved beyond words. He made no gesture towards her but just stood there next to her, lifting the sheets with a gentle, careful hand, letting them fall, touching, stroking, lightly caressing them . . . and all the while it was her skin he was touching. That much was thrillingly, shockingly clear.

33

THREE MONTHS LATER

TASH/ANNICK

'What're you drinking?' Tash shouted above the racket, trying to catch the barman's eye.

'Glass of white!' Annick yelled back. 'But something decent. *Not* Blue Nun.'

'Give me a break!' Tash rolled her eyes. She finally caught the bartender's attention and fixed him immediately with a beady glare. 'Glass of white, please. And a double whisky. On the rocks.' She slapped her debit card crisply on the counter. No point in ordering for Rebecca. She was late. She collected their drinks and turned back to Annick. She rolled her eyes again – in the time it had taken Tash to turn round and order drinks, two men had sidled up to Annick.

'Here you go,' she said, quickly elbowing them both out of the way. 'A glass of the Rising Sun's finest.' The men took one look at Tash, opened their mouths to protest and then quickly changed their minds and sloped off. She was six foot tall with an expression neither wished to question.

Annick picked up her glass. 'Is it safe to drink?'

'Don't be such a snob,' Tash said, taking a sip of her own drink. After a couple of shots, she mused, she felt ready to take on anything, including the embarrassment of standing next to Annick whilst half the men in the room drew near, ignoring her. Not that anyone would guess – she'd long since perfected the mask of bored insouciance that protected her from most of life's indignities. 'Where the hell *is* Rebecca? And why's she always late these days? She never used to be.'

Annick shrugged. 'Dunno. I was supposed to meet her on Saturday on Oxford Street and she never showed up. Said she forgot.'

'What were you doing on Oxford Street?' Tash felt a sudden pang. She hadn't been invited.

'Shopping. Well, *she* wanted to go shopping. She's got some dinner party or the other coming up. She's acting very weird these days.'

'Why don't you ever ask *me* to come shopping with you?' she asked, already cross with herself for sounding plaintive.

Annick looked at her in surprise. 'You *hate* shopping!'

'That's not true. I just hate crowds.'

'That's why we didn't ask you, silly. Oxford Street on a Saturday afternoon? You?'

'Yeah, okay.' Tash was partly mollified. She looked at her watch. 'So what d'you want to do? I don't much fancy sitting here all night watching every bloke in the room try and get off with you.'

Annick laughed. 'Don't exaggerate. Just because *one* person came up to me—'

'Two, darling. Two men came up to you as soon as my bloody back was turned. Oh, well, whatever.' It was still her favourite expression. What-*ever*. Delivered with a small shrug of the shoulders and the faintest twinge of an American accent. It suited her perfectly. What*ever*.

'There she is.' Annick pointed to Rebecca, who had just hurried in through the door. She looked flustered. Her hair was prettily dishevelled and her face was flushed. She looked as though she'd just woken up.

'What time d'you call this?' Tash said, pointing to the clock above the bar as she rushed up to them.

'Sorry, sorry . . . I . . . I got caught up.'

'In what? Bed?'

Rebecca flushed scarlet. 'No,' she mumbled, turning away and busying herself with her coat.

Tash and Annick exchanged quick, surprised glances. 'You've been in bed all afternoon. You have, haven't you?' Tash said slowly, incredulously. 'With who?'

'Shh!' Rebecca's head jerked backwards. 'Not so loud!'

'With *who*?' Tash repeated, her eyes as wide as saucers.

Rebecca's face was buried behind her hair. She began fishing around in her bag for something as a distraction. She mumbled something inaudible but didn't look up.

'Rebecca?' Annick said, more gently than Tash. 'Is something wrong?'

Rebecca shook her head furiously, still keeping it down.

Tash and Annick looked at each other again. Neither had any idea what was going on, or what to do. 'D'you want a drink?' Tash asked finally. 'Red?'

'Yes, please.' Rebecca finally looked up. Her face was still flushed but she was a little more composed. 'Sorry . . . I'm just a bit tired, that's all.'

'Tired? How can you be tired if you've been asleep all afternoon?'

'I'm just not feeling very well,' she mumbled. 'I . . . I think I might be coming down with a cold or something.'

Tash's eyes narrowed. 'What aren't you telling us, Rebecca Harburg?' she asked finally. There was an awkward silence. Annick and Tash glanced at each other. Rebecca continued to stare at her hands. Finally she lifted her head. She cleared her throat, an odd, high sound, audible even above the racket of the bar.

'He's . . . he's one of my professors.'

There was a further moment of stunned silence as Tash and Annick stared at her. Then Annick drained the rest of her wine, set her glass carefully down on the counter and picked up her coat. 'Coming?'

'Where to?' Tash asked, already grabbing her own coat.

'Follow me,' Annick said grimly. The other two had no choice but to do as they were told.

'Good evening, Miss Betancourt. Welcome to the St James's.' The doorman at the front door was quick to welcome them in. 'Will you be dining with us this evening?' he asked, relieving them of their coats.

'Yes, please, William. Is the corner table upstairs free? The one in the alcove?'

'I'll just check, miss. Won't be a moment.' He picked up the phone nestling discreetly behind the desk. Two minutes later whoever had been seated at the table by the window was gone. 'If you'll just follow me, ladies,' William said, bowing slightly.

Even Rebecca, who was no stranger to members' clubs, was impressed. 'The St James's? How'd you manage *that*?' she whispered as they walked up the stairs behind him.

Annick shrugged. 'My dad's been a member for ages,' she whispered back. 'And it's quiet. It was the only place I could think of round here with a decent enough wine list.'

'Clever girl,' Tash murmured, looking round, only just remembering to keep her mouth shut. Was there no end to the wealth surrounding these two? She'd never in her life been in a place like this.

There was a few seconds' wait as the table was expertly cleared and then the three of them were seated. 'I wanted us to be somewhere comfortable whilst we hear *this*,' Annick declared, picking up the wine list. 'Now, darlings, what're we having? Something nice and expensive, I think. It's on the house. Well, on my dad, at least.' She looked down the list. 'That one.' She pointed to a bottle of Chateau La Mission Haut-Brion. 'Nineteen eighty-five. Ought to be good.'

'*Very* good, miss.' Their waiter disappeared happily.

'So,' Tash said, taking charge as soon as their glasses were filled. 'Tell us what the hell's going on. And don't spare us the details, either. We're your *friends*, Rebecca.'

Rebecca fiddled around with the stem of her glass for what seemed like ages. 'His name's Jeremy,' she whispered finally. 'He's my seminar tutor. He's the most intelligent person I've ever met and he . . . he likes me.'

'Why's that such a surprise? When did it start and, more importantly, *how far have you gone?*'

Rebecca bit her lip. 'Quite far,' she said after a moment. The other two stared at her.

'Is he married?' Tash asked finally.

'Tash!' Annick glared at her.

'What? Most professors are,' Tash retorted. 'It's a fair question. Well, *is* he?'

'I . . . I don't know,' Rebecca said, looking at her hands.

Tash and Annick looked at each other again, both lost for words. 'What does that mean?' Annick asked at last.

'It . . . it means . . . well, I haven't actually asked him.' Rebecca's face was the colour of the wine.

'Why on earth not?'

'I . . . I don't know.' Rebecca turned her face up to look at them both. 'I . . . I guess I just don't want to know.'

There was silence for a few moments as the three of them looked at each other, then at the ground as Rebecca began helplessly to cry.

ANNICK

Almost two hours later, Annick clambered gratefully into the taxi that the doorman at the club had flagged down for her. 'Park Lane, please. Bishop's Court.' She sank back against the seat. A light drizzle had begun to fall. It was past midnight and all of London looked as if it were draining, draining slowly away. Her head was swimming, a result of the wine and the conversation. She still couldn't quite grasp it. Rebecca Harburg was sleeping with one of her professors? A *married* professor at that. She'd sat opposite her, her chin propped in her hand like a child listening to a bedtime story. It seemed so . . . so unlikely! Rebecca was such a *good* girl. The one with the inner moral compass, the one who never, *ever* went astray. She didn't even *smoke*. Rebecca was so goddamn sensible and however reluctant she might be to face the truth, sleeping with one of her married tutors was the goddamn opposite of sensible. Annick could see it already – disaster was looming.

She was just about to fish in her pocket for a cigarette when she saw the sign. NO SMOKING. She pulled a face; she was dying for one. So, Rebecca was in love, she mused, watching the traffic slip past in a watery blur. Properly, madly in love. Annick felt a surprise pang of envy, listening to her.

After the second glass of wine, she confessed to being unable to eat or sleep. Annick simply couldn't imagine it. She'd sooner have died than admit it to either Tash or Rebecca, but she couldn't actually remember the number of men she'd slept with. Not because there'd been hundreds, but because she hadn't technically been in a relationship with most of them. In her first year at university she'd woken up several times after one party or another, not really able to remember fully what had happened, or how she'd wound up at midnight in some flat in Camden or Kensington with a boy whose name she might – or might not – recall. She hadn't really thought anything of it. Most of the girls on her course did exactly the same. She rather liked the feeling of grabbing up her clothes, pulling on her coat and walking out of the door without stopping to think what *he* might think. It seemed a neat reversal of the usual order of things. Silly female histrionics over who should call whom, when, how, for how long and so on, simply bored her. One of her boyfriends had once accused her of being more like a man than most men. He was baffled when she laughed. It was a compliment! But listening to Rebecca's account of the past few months, her first reaction was one of jealousy. A man! A proper, grown-up man with a whole life outside the Student Union and Friday-night parties that were really just excuses to go out, drink as much cheap beer as possible and then tumble into a generally unwashed sack.

The cab stopped suddenly. 'This it, miss?' the driver enquired.

'Yes. Thanks.' She pulled a ten-pound note from her purse. 'Keep the change,' she said, suddenly feeling generous. She got out, ignoring his wide smile, and hurried up the steps. The whole façade was in darkness. The entrance hall and the short corridors were ghostly and empty. There were months when there was no one else in the entire building except for Annick and Mrs Price. A few years earlier, in her last year of school, there'd been a Saudi family on the floor above, who'd stayed for longer than the usual three or four months. Six or seven small children, a gaggle of Filipina maids and several indistinguishable women in floor-length burqas came in and out all day long. One day she'd accidentally come upon two of the women in the lift, *sans* burqas, and they'd struck up a conversation. Dina and Amina were cousins in their mid-twenties, and both spoke excellent English. Dina was a medical student; Amina was studying pharmacy. A rather hurried invitation followed to tea, which Annick accepted with alacrity. From that day, she went upstairs to tea at least once a week. The rules surrounding social engagements in their culture were stricter than anything Annick had ever known, but there was a warmth and intimacy about the way the women lived together that drew her in. She would knock on the door at the appointed hour, remove her shoes and follow one or other of the maids in. There would be scarves beside each chair in the unlikely event that one of the husbands, uncles or brothers walked in, and warm cries of welcome. She would sit down, cross-legged on the floor as they did, opposite the older women who spoke no English but who smiled and nodded at her as they received cups of sweet mint tea from the younger ones. The same maids would bring in trays of delicacies from Fortnum & Mason and the children would be temporarily banished.

Weekends were no longer stretches of empty time to be endured. But their respective courses ended and Dina and Amina returned home.

It had been a couple months since then and now the corridors seemed lonelier than ever. She slid her key in the lock and opened the front door. The flat was silent. Mrs Price was away, visiting her daughter. The central heating gave off its usual soft hum, the only audible sound. She stood uncertainly in the doorway for a moment. She was home. The loneliest place she'd ever been.

34

REBECCA

Seeds of doubt, once planted, will grow. *Is he married?* Rebecca climbed into bed that night with the question ringing loudly in her ears. She had no idea. He wore no ring and certainly hadn't mentioned a wife. It had been going on for almost three months and not once in all that time had he ever brought the subject up. As mad as it sounded, even to her, neither did she. They met once or twice a week at her place or in college, never at his. They'd done it once in his office with her bent backwards (most uncomfortably) over his desk, her mouth hanging open as much in surprise as anything else at the force with which he'd grabbed her in the corridor and pulled her in. He was the most interesting person she'd ever met. He was some twenty-odd years older than her, but, like an actress, was vague about his age. He could talk about anything and everything: art, history, politics, literature, philosophy, film . . . his was a mind of extraordinary depth and talent. But emotions were off-limits, especially his. Whenever she tried, however lightly, to express what she felt about him he swiftly turned away. He had a way of deflecting anything that touched upon the personal (unless it involved his own career), turning things quickly into the abstract. Abstract ideas were safe. Despite the age difference, within a fortnight she saw quite clearly that for someone who made a living out of his head, he had remarkably little understanding of what went on inside it.

She lay in bed, trying not to think. Where was Jeremy at that very moment? She didn't have his telephone number. He always rang her. She didn't even know where he lived. Somewhere near Belsize Park, he'd said once. She'd tried to ask something further, a little more detail, but he'd neatly side-stepped the question by opening a book, deftly steering the conversation elsewhere. She pulled her duvet cover up to her chin and stifled an involuntary sob. There were times when the longing just to be near him overwhelmed her. Up until that point, it seemed to her, her life had been ordered, predictable, everything planned. Now, for the first time she was confronted with something she couldn't control and certainly couldn't predict and if there was one thing she'd learned about Jeremy Garrick, it was that he was unpredictable. She never knew what to expect. She was a postgraduate student, not an undergraduate, which meant that any relationship they might have was at least permissible. But he'd made it perfectly clear that open acknowledgement of what was happening between them was not an option. It wasn't anything he'd ever said. No, that would have been to talk about 'it', about his feelings for her. It was simply clear in the way he behaved towards her in public as if he didn't know her, or if he did, only distantly, as one student amongst many. She understood that. From the outset, he set boundaries that she had no option but to keep, which she did, willingly. Until tonight, when Tash, typically, asked her the most obvious question of all, one *she* should have asked him herself in the beginning . . . but didn't.

And now she couldn't. She lay in the dark, the horrible realisation slowly breaking over her that even if he *were* married, it would make little difference to the way she felt. It was too late. He'd *got* her, right where he wanted her. At a distance.

35

TASH

'Gels, gels, *gels!*' Lady Davenport's voice rose above the cacophony in the office. '*Please!* I'm looking for something *constructive*, gels. A *constructive* suggestion, not just noise.'

'But everything's already been done before,' Tiggy wailed.

Lady Davenport only just managed to hold on to her eyeballs. 'Oh, for goodness' *sake*, Tiggy! How can you even *think* that? What on earth do I pay you for?'

Tiggy turned bright red and looked imploringly at the other two. Tash looked from one to the other. Her heart was thumping. She rarely got involved in client discussions. For three months she'd kept herself to herself, certainly making no friends but not making enemies either. She tried to stick to Rebecca's mantra: *if you can't be nice, be quiet*. Well, she was certainly quiet. She answered the phones, made coffee, did the photocopying when asked and, when there was absolutely nothing to do, flicked through the endless copies of *Hello!* magazine that the 'gels' dropped into the pile every Tuesday morning. Lady Davenport was rarely in the office and when she was, she breezed in with a distracted air and breezed out again. She did most of the actual day-to-day work of the agency. The 'gels', as she called them, aside from answering the phone, were expected every now and then to come up with new 'ideas'. Like now.

PINK, the breast cancer charity, was LDPR's biggest and most lucrative client. In fact, PINK more or less paid everyone's salaries. Tash knew because the bookkeeper that came in once a month had asked her to photocopy the accounts and she'd subsequently spent an hour in the photocopy room reading them. She'd been pleasantly surprised to see that Priscilla, Tiggy, and Tilly earned little more than she did, despite their superior airs. Now, looking at their blank, terrified faces as Lady Davenport tried to extract an original thought from each, she understood why. Her mouth opened of its own accord. 'How about doing it a bit differently,' she asked, as nonchalantly as she could.

All four heads swivelled round to look at her. 'Differently? What d'you mean?' Lady Davenport frowned.

'Well, I don't know much about it but it seems to me that all the fundraising stuff to do with cancer's terribly depressing. Worthy, but depressing. It's all about gloomy statistics and suffering and running marathons – why not do something a bit more glamorous? Get celebrities involved – everyone knows someone who's been touched by cancer, even famous people. Get someone like Elton John to host a dinner each year . . . one year it'd be fancy dress, the next a masked ball, the next a pink ball . . . that sort of thing. We could get Anouschka Malaquais to be the official "face" of the ball . . . tickets at five hundred pounds a pop . . . why not?'

Tiggy's eyes grew as wide as saucers. 'Look, thanks for the suggestion,' she began in a tone of voice that suggested anything but gratitude. 'But really, this is a bit out of your league—'

'No, no, let her finish.' Lady Davenport cut Tiggy off and turned to Tash. 'Anouschka Malaquais? Now, that's not a bad suggestion. I'm not sure I've got her number, though . . .'

Tash's heart was beating fast. 'I do.'

All four of them looked at Tash. 'You *do*?' Lady Davenport asked.

Tash nodded firmly. No point in telling them how.

Lady Davenport smiled at her. 'Why don't you and I have a little talk?' she asked, getting up from her chair and indicating her office.

'But—' Tiggy turned a desperate face towards her. 'But it's *my*—'

'Tiggs, darling, won't you bring two coffees in?'

There was a sudden shocked silence as yet another penny made its way to the floor. *Bring two coffees in?* It was a demotion. 'What a *bitch*!' she heard Tilly whisper loyally as the door closed. 'She practically *stole* your job!'

'Take no notice,' Lady Davenport said briskly, sitting down behind her desk. 'If there's one thing you'll learn in this business it's to pay attention to the things that really matter. Now, where were we? Do sit down, darling. You make me nervous standing there like that. How tall *are* you, anyway?'

Tash sat down hurriedly, wondering if the question were rhetorical. Lady Davenport pulled out a notepad from the drawer and plucked a pen from the delicate ceramic pot, which was practically the only item on her glass desk. Tash looked at it closely. It was beautiful.

'Billy Lloyd,' Lady Davenport murmured without looking up. 'I've been collecting him since I was in my twenties. Lovely use of colour, don't you think?'

'Er, yes,' Tash nodded. You had to hand it to her, she thought to herself as she waited for Lady Davenport to finish scribbling. She had an eye for detail. Although her style wasn't exactly to Tash's taste, she liked the way she put things together. The other day she'd come into the office wearing a tan trenchcoat, the sort of coat practically every man, woman and teenager in Chelsea wore; she'd tied a leopard-print scarf around her neck, but not in the usual black-and-tan colour combination – deep pinks and purples instead. Against her bright orange bob, the colours could have seemed garish but they didn't. As she waited, it occurred to Tash that she would do well to take note of the woman's style.

'So, tell me, how do you come to have Anouschka Malaquais's phone number?' Lady Davenport asked.

Tash blushed. She sensed it would be better to tell Lady Davenport the truth. At all times. 'I'm best friends with her daughter,' she said reluctantly. 'We were at school together.'

'Ah. Two things I like. Honesty and directness. Don't waste your time telling people what you *don't* want to do – like that lot out there. Forever complaining, never proposing. Tell people what you *do* want to do, as clearly and quickly as possible. And then just get on with it. A masked ball. Lovely. Let's get started.'

*

A week later, everything had changed. Tash was now sitting where Tiggy had once sat, up front, just outside Lady Davenport's office. Tiggy had been relegated to the back room alongside Priscilla and Tilly. They no longer spoke to her; just threw her bitter looks every morning as she came in, but Tash could have cared less. In under a week, she'd gone from office dogsbody to being in charge of the PINK masked ball. Now, instead of arriving in the office every morning half an hour before everyone else, she generally started her days with a quick meeting at Lady Davenport's home, a few streets away from the office.

'It's the only place I can *think*,' Lady Davenport explained, throwing open the doors to the dining room. 'I can't *hear* myself think with all that chatter going on around me in the office. The girls drive me to distraction, I promise you.' A tray of coffee and miniature croissants had silently appeared. Lady Davenport led the way to the polished mahogany dining table, yellow lined notepad in hand. 'Venue's been sorted.' she continued, clearly eager to get down to business. She swallowed a croissant whole. Tash watched, fascinated, as it disappeared down her throat. 'Lord Hetherington's lending us his pad. It's in Hampshire. Di*vine*. Everyone'll want to come now. *And* we've got a date. The sixth of May. If we're lucky, the weather'll be good. That gives us four months. Where are we with the guest list, darling?' She reached for another croissant. 'Has Anouschka Malaquais confirmed yet?'

'Yes,' Tash nodded firmly – a tad *too* firmly perhaps.

'Oh, fabulous. Well *done*, darling. Let's get cracking, shall we? Ooh, this *is* exciting!'

'What you mean?' Her mother looked at her suspiciously. 'Who? Which stars?'

'Well, people like . . . like Emma Thompson.'

'Who?'

'Emma Thompson. You know, the actress . . . she was in that film you liked so much, *Remains of the Day*. The one with Anthony Hopkins.'

'Oh. You think *she* gonna come?' Lyudmila's expression softened suddenly.

'I think so. I'm going to ask Annick's mum, too. It'll be ever so glamorous.'

'Hmm. If you say so.' As Tash passed by, she reached out and took hold of her arm, pulling her towards her.

'Is good project you have, darling,' she said, hugging Tash, much to her surprise. 'Is *very* good project. You see . . . I told you. Is all my idea.'

'What's all your idea, Ma?' Tash asked, her face pressed against Lyudmila's shoulder. She couldn't remember the last time she'd been that close to her mother.

'Work for Lady Davenport, of course. I *knew* you gonna be big success.'

Tash was too astonished to reply.

'I *think* so,' Annick said, sounding rather doubtful. 'I mean, if I tell her there'll be lots of other famous people there. So what is it? A party?'

'No, not exactly. Well, of course there'll *be* a party. We want to get people to pay for a table, but it's a masked ball,' Tash said, warming to her theme. 'The thing is, it won't be a one-off. We'll do it again next year, with a different theme, and the year after that. If you could get your mum to agree to be one of PINK's ambassadors, that'll practically guarantee the glamour bit.'

'Will it be sad?'

'No, no, that's the whole point. It's about surviving cancer, beating it. Gloria Gaynor's agreed to headline. *I Will Survive* . . . get it?'

'Of course I get it. I'm not *that* stupid.'

'It's for a really good cause. Just ask your mum, please?'

'Course I will. Can we come? Me and Rebecca?'

'Of course you're coming. There's no way I'm organising this without you two there.'

'I can't believe you thought this up on your own,' Annick said admiringly. 'It's fantastic. Okay, I'll speak to my mum tonight and let you know what she says. What're you going to wear, by the way?'

'Annick, it's four months away,' Tash laughed. 'Let's get your mum on board first. *Then* I'll start thinking about what to wear.'

'Not a moment too soon. That's what Maman always says. She plans her outfits a year in advance.'

'That's why *she's* the movie star and I'm not,' Tash said drily. 'Just make sure she comes, won't you?' She put down the phone before Annick could ask anything further.

'A *charity* ball?' Her mother made the pairing of the two words sound not only incongruous but absurd.

'No, no . . . it's a masked ball. It'll be ever so glamorous, Maman. Lots of people are coming.'

'Like who?'

'Oh, Elton John and . . . and Elizabeth Hurley. It's for a really good cause and—'

'Elton? That's odd. I saw him last week and he didn't say anything about a charity ball.'

'That's because it's still all completely under wraps,' Annick said quickly. 'Tash said they had a . . . what d'you call it? A press embargo,' she lied, hoping it would impress her mother. It did.

'Oh. A *press* embargo. Well, they must be expecting lots of important people. When did you say it was?'

'Sixth of May. It's ages away. Besides, I haven't seen you or Papa for ages.'

'Of course you have. Weren't you here at Christmas?'

'No, Maman, I wasn't.'

'Oh. Well, we'll see you soon,' Anouschka said cheerfully. 'May, you said? And Elton's definitely coming?'

'*Oui*, Maman.' There was a lump in Annick's throat. It was time to get off the phone. Anouschka positively hated what she called 'a scene'. It was Tash who'd pointed out once, long ago, that one reason they all got along so well, especially in the beginning, was because they were all only children. But for all Tash's complaints about her mother and for all Rebecca's moaning that she wasn't at the centre of her parents' lives in the way she wanted to be, at least they were *there*. Annick wasn't even on the periphery of her parents' attention, never mind its centre.

'Well, bye then, Maman,' she said finally, hoping she sounded more cheerful than she felt. 'See you in May.' She put the phone down, swallowed hard and picked up a book. She knew the drill.

36

REBECCA

She ought to have seen it coming. It happened on a Thursday afternoon, wet and windy, as it had been all week. She and Jeremy had had dinner on Friday but he'd declined her invitation to come back to her flat that night, claiming he had papers to mark. He'd jumped in a taxi as soon as dinner was over, leaving her standing on the pavement in an agony of doubt. Had she said, or done, something wrong? Was she the cause of his bad mood? She took a taxi back to her own empty flat, drank half a bottle of wine on her own and cried herself to sleep.

He wasn't at work on Monday or on Tuesday, and didn't respond to either of the two messages she left on his office answering machine. Pride kept her from making another call, but by Thursday she was desperate.

She was hurrying down the corridor, on her way to the phone box, when she saw him coming out of his office. Her heart missed a beat. There was someone with him. A young blonde girl, whom she dimly recognised, followed him out of his office. Rebecca promptly dropped her pile of books. She bent down to pick them up and the girl rushed off in the opposite direction. Jeremy stopped and looked at her for a second, then turned and walked off without saying a thing. Rebecca straightened up slowly. A cold sweat broke out across her face. Why had he ignored her? Who was the girl? And what was she doing in his office?

She shoved her books into her bag and rushed upstairs to the library. Pinned to the wall just before the librarian's desk were thumbnail portraits of all the students at the Courtauld. She scanned the rows anxiously, her heart beating fast. There she was. She peered at the picture. Lucy Creswell. She was also a postgraduate student. She felt sick. There was no way she could face her two o'clock seminar. She blinked back her tears and rushed from the building.

As soon as she got home, she yanked open the fridge door and grabbed the half-empty bottle of wine left over from the other night. She didn't even bother with a glass. She took it straight into her bedroom, sat down heavily on the edge of her bed and took a long, hard swig, trying to calm herself down. She had to talk to Jeremy. She had to find out what was going on. But how? She had absolutely no way of contacting him. Suddenly something occurred to her. He'd stopped by her flat the previous week on his way home from college. He'd been carrying a stack of letters in his hand . . . she'd poured him a glass of wine in the kitchen as he opened them and, if she remembered correctly, he'd chucked the envelopes in her bin. She'd emptied the bin at the weekend, she remembered, but with any luck they would still be there. She jumped up and galloped downstairs. She pushed open the back door and ran into the small yard at the rear of the flats. It took her a couple of minutes to find the black bin that belonged to her flat. She dragged it out, squealing aloud at the bits of potato peel and soggy banana skins that fell out as she rummaged through it. She pulled out half a dozen envelopes, still folded together, several of them stuck together with damp. Her heart hammering, she flattened them out carefully on the ground. There it was! *Dr Jeremy Garrick. Flat 1, 44 Howitt Road, London NW3*. She had his address! She raced back up the stairs, yanked her coat off the door and grabbed her purse.

She flagged down the first cab. 'Howitt Road,' she said breathlessly through the window.

'Howitt Road . . . Belsize Park? Just off Haverstock Hill?'

She nodded. 'I think so.' She yanked open the door, sweating with fear. She'd never done anything like it in her life. She had no clear idea of what she would do once she got there but, suddenly, getting there seemed the most important thing in the world. To get there.

There was no one at home. She pressed the buzzer several times but no one came to the door or the window. She'd managed to work out from the buzzers that his was the ground-floor flat but the curtains were drawn. She stood on the doorstep, wondering what to do. She shivered in her thin coat. It had stopped drizzling but the wind was cold. There was nothing for it but to wait for him to come home. It was nearly three o'clock. With any luck he'd be back within a couple of hours, or so she hoped. She looked down at her feet. She was wearing her fluffy bedroom slippers. She hadn't remembered to change into her boots! A short sob suddenly escaped her throat and her cheeks felt warm with shame. Had she gone quite mad? But she couldn't think of anything else to do and there was no way she could go back home without seeing him. He didn't come into college on Fridays and then there'd be the whole of the weekend to get through. What if – her mouth suddenly went dry at the thought – what if he never contacted her again? No, there was nothing for it but to wait for him, even if it took all night. She sat down on the low wall outside the house.

She didn't have to wait for nightfall. Just before four, when the light was only just beginning to fade, she saw a figure she recognised at the top of the road. Her heart almost stopped beating. It was Jeremy. He wasn't alone. A woman and a child walked alongside him, the young boy holding on to the woman's hand. Jeremy carried the shopping bags. She watched, open-mouthed, as they approached. They were having the sort of mild domestic argument she'd heard a thousand times before, in other circumstances, in different places.

'But Dad, you *promised*! You said I could—'

'That's enough, Steven,' the woman said, bending her head to his. 'We'll do it together after supper.'

'But *Dad* said—'

'Oh, for goodness' sake, Jeremy. Why on earth did you—'

Something must have made him turn his head as they walked up the steps to their flat. He stopped when he saw her. His eyes narrowed, as he looked at her. But this time, there was no interest; just the odd expression of something that looked like triumphant contempt. He held her gaze for a few seconds as his wife fumbled with the front door key and Rebecca was powerless to turn away. Then the moment passed, he followed his wife and child into the flat and shut the door. Rebecca sat there for a few more minutes as though her feet had taken root. Then with a stifled sob, she got up and fled.

37

There were dark shadows under her eyes and her hair was lank. She quickly washed her face, praying that the storm of weeping that had descended upon her that afternoon had left few traces. She was dreading the upcoming *seder*. Her mother, who always had a nose for whatever wasn't being said, wouldn't be easily fooled. She patted her face dry, ran a quick comb through her hair and pinched her cheeks to give them a little colour. She faced herself in the mirror and to her horror, her eyes started filling with tears again. *Stop, stop, stop.* She gave herself a shake. Deep breath in, slow breath out. She had to get a grip on herself. It was going to be a big dinner – her father would be there, for once, and various members of the extended Harburg clan. It was no time to appear dishevelled and distraught. She blew her nose again, took another deep breath and opened the door.

The house was redolent with the rich smells of cooking. The two girls who came in on Fridays to help Embeth would have been in the kitchen all day; everything made from scratch, just the way Embeth liked it. The beautiful long dining table, covered in snowy white linen and polished silverware, would be groaning under the weight of food: roast lamb, sprinkled with apricots and cinnamon; traditional gefilte fish and the braided, home-made challah; *shakshuka*, the coriander and green pepper stew that was a childhood favourite of her mother's; porcelain tureens of light, clear broth with delicate matzo balls . . . all the traditional *seder* dishes she'd grown up with.

She paused on the landing for a moment, looking down the great staircase into the hallway below. The chandelier that had hung in the same position through all the long years of childhood had recently been polished. Its cut-crystal edges threw light onto the silky warm colours and textures below – the oriental rugs, cherry- and satin-wood furniture, and the ornate gilded mirror on the opposite wall.

As she descended the staircase, she caught a glimpse of herself. She'd lost weight; her jeans were baggy and her neck and collarbones stood out above the neck of her jumper. She could feel another wave of sadness threatening to break over her but she was nearly at the foot of the stairs. Any second now one of the many doors that led off the circular hallway would open and someone would step out. She couldn't afford to start crying. Not now.

'Ah, *there* you are.' Her father came out of his study. 'When did you arrive?'

'About an hour ago, Papa.' He too had lost weight, she noticed suddenly. She looked at him closely, seeing him properly for the first time in ages. He seemed shorter, too. He was wearing an old grey cardigan that fell in folds around his shoulders. Her heart rose alarmingly in her throat. He was old.

'What's the matter, Rebecca?' He peered at her over the top of his spectacles.

She shook her head. 'N . . . nothing. Here.' She picked at an imaginary piece of fluff on his sleeve to give her hands something to do.

'What's that?'

'Just . . . just a bit of fluff. You must've picked it up somewhere.'

'*Ach, laß es doch*. I'm sure I'll just pick up another bit somewhere else. Tante Brigitte's here – have you seen her?'

She shook her head. That was another thing. He often lapsed into German these days, something he'd never have done when she was younger. When she was very young, she didn't even realise he *was* German. She remembered coming upon him once, in the very same study, speaking German to someone on the telephone. She'd listened, stunned, for a few minutes, then run to find her mother. 'Papa's talking all funny!' she'd shouted, much to everyone's amusement. The sudden memory prompted a fresh load of tears and she had to turn her head away. 'Come on, Papa . . . they'll all be waiting.'

'*Ja, ja.*' He put a hand on her arm, as if waiting for her to lead him through. But as she moved forward, he exerted a gentle pressure, making her stop. 'Rebs,' he asked enquiringly, using his childhood name for her. 'Is everything all right?'

She swallowed. The desire to lean into him in a way she hadn't done in nearly fifteen years was overwhelming. She saw him so sporadically, especially now. She rested her head for a moment on his shoulder. It wasn't the firm, solid pad of muscle and flesh she remembered from childhood but he was still her father, still the most dependable, most trustworthy man she'd ever known. 'Papa,' she began hesitantly, but stopped. What would she even *say*?

'Everything will be all right, Rebecca,' he murmured, reaching around to catch hold of her hand. 'Everything will be fine. *Ist nichts*. In a month's time you'll have forgotten all about him.' He patted her arm and then moved on, leaving her standing there, open-mouthed with surprise. How on earth could he have known? Suddenly she caught her mother's eye. Embeth was standing on the other side of the table, nodding faintly in a way that let Rebecca know *she* too understood. As she took her place amidst cries of welcome from those who knew and loved her best, she felt their obvious affection and warmth behind her like a solid presence, a reminder of who she was and why the events of that morning would pass. Just as her father said.

38

TASH

The evening was all going splendidly according to plan. She slipped away from the hordes of event managers, their assistants and assistants-to-the-assistants, bodyguards, chefs, bartenders, security chiefs and general all-round gofers whose job it was to keep everyone happy and in line. Lady Davenport was somewhere in the great entrance hall together with the host, Lord Hetherington, doing what she did best – meeting and greeting, air-kissing and cooing delightedly over the masked guests, the glamorous ball gowns, dresses, hairdos and jewellery. The rules were strict – no entry without a mask, and pinned to everyone's back was a beautiful gilt-edged card with a single word or statement that alluded to their identity. In the two-hour mingling-and-cocktails slot before dinner, guests were asked to guess who was behind the mask and, if the answer was correct, the wearer was obliged to unmask. By dinner, Tash hoped, most people would be unveiled, with a prize going to the person who'd correctly identified the highest number of masked partygoers. The atmosphere was gay and festive, exactly what she'd wanted; even the waiters had joined in the fun. Some of the clues were hilarious. Lady Davenport had enlisted the help of yet another friend who set out crosswords for the *Sunday Times* – it was all very witty and jolly.

She opened the door to one of the smaller rooms on the ground floor, closed the door firmly behind her and walked over to the window, extracting a cigarette from her handbag. She lit it with slightly shaking fingers and opened the window, carefully wiping the sill before arranging her white silk dress so that it wouldn't crush. The dress had been a gift from Lady Davenport. Lyudmila cried when she saw it. She inhaled deeply, blowing the smoke out carefully. Far below her, the gardens sloped away to the river. There were dozens of taut, cream silk tents, decorated with lilies, garlands of tiny white spray roses and giant bouquets of pale flowers whose names Tash couldn't even pronounce, let alone remember. Under each marquee there were three or four circular tables, decked out in silver, gold and white, with matching chairs and linen. Thousands of tea lights and silver-and-gold hanging chandeliers provided the rosy glow under which everyone, even the ageing celebrities would look gorgeous. It had all been organised by the event planner, the formidable Lady Caroline Ashford, another friend of Lady Davenport's whose connections stretched across six continents and most of Europe's royal houses.

She stubbed out her cigarette and closed the windows. She picked up her purse and opened the door. Rebecca and Annick were somewhere in the crowd eagerly anticipating the stars, the show . . . the whole damned event. Rebecca's parents had politely declined the invitation. The Harburgs had their own discreet brand of philanthropy in which movie stars and actors rarely featured. No matter. There were more than enough millionaires in the crowds waiting under the tents. Her heart began to beat faster. It was time to don her own mask – a gorgeous, diamanté-studded pair of green cat's eyes, complete with whiskers made out of peacock feathers and jewelled tassels. Her note read, *A Left-handed Marriage. One of Eight. A Cousin.* She couldn't remember the complicated history by which Princess Tatiana Konstantinova of Russia had seven siblings, a cousin and a morganatic marriage, but it was the name 'Tatiana' that was the link. No one present would guess it, anyhow, she thought. Annick's card was equally obscure. *Two Presidents and a Daughter*, a reference to her father and the president of Venezuela, Rómulo Betancourt. Embeth Harburg was possibly the only person who might get it – and she wasn't there, of course. Rebecca's was easier. *Captivating. Dreams of Manderley.*

She smoothed down her skirt and took a deep breath. It was time for the show to begin.

39

SYLVAN

He stood a little way behind his wife, who was resplendent in crushed dark green silk, her beautiful face hidden behind her mask as she stood chatting to people. Whose idea was it for everyone to wear those damned masks, he thought to himself irritably. Although, he mused, the black velvet behind which he hid and surveyed the crowd had its advantages. He wasn't expected to know or recognise anyone, which was something of a relief. It had been so long since he'd been involved in Anouschka's world that he was no longer up to date. He had no idea who anyone was, who'd married whom, who'd divorced whom, who was on his or her way up or down . . . and besides, they were all English. Anouschka seemed to know everyone, or at least she appeared to know everyone. It was often only when they were alone, afterwards, in the hotel room or official residence, that she confessed she didn't actually know who anyone was.

There was a woman to his left wearing what looked like a motorcycle helmet, not a mask, chatting to someone who'd taken hers off. Their voices were shrill and clear. They were talking about someone – a mutual friend, it seemed – who'd been diagnosed with cancer. All of a sudden, without warning, his mind gave a violent jerk, catapulting him backwards in time and place. He was four or five again, perhaps even six, and his mother was dying, slipping agonisingly slowly from one world to the next. She'd been doing it for more than a year and since the humidity of Lomé had proved unbearable to her, they'd all decamped to Paris, to the big, half-empty apartment on rue Louis Pasteur in Boulogne-Billancourt. It was near a tennis stadium, he remembered dimly, and there was a large park, a forest, nearby. One day, his grandfather took him to watch a match. Afterwards, they walked back along the main road, one hand held loosely in his grandfather's and an ice-cream in the other. He remembered two things – the pleasurable, almost-forgotten sensation of his smaller hand in someone else's and the melting ice-cream that trickled down his sleeve.

His mother was too sick to hold his hand anymore. She was too sick to do much other than lie in that bed in the big room on the first floor that overlooked the forest and smelled of terrible things. Her days, which in Lomé had seemed rather idle, were now given over to a strict routine: breakfast sent up to her on a tray; then the nurses trooped in, washing her in bed, arranging her pillows and her hair, doing their best to disguise the scent that he didn't know until much later was the scent of death. Then he was allowed into the room to kiss her before her mid-morning nap. Grandfather came in and sat with her until lunch, after which the nurses took over again. In the late afternoon he was brought in once more. He perched gingerly on the end of the high bed whilst her temperature was taken and various pills administered. After a few minutes murmured conversation she slipped away into sleep.

Her dying gave form to the temporary household that didn't have one. Until that point, Paris had been a place he associated with summer holidays. The rules were relaxed; there was no homework, no maids, and no school friends, just him, his mother and his grandfather, alone in a way that the families of presidents never are. It was just after the war and there was little traffic on the roads. He was at last allowed to have a bicycle and could wander off down the road to the park as he pleased. Late in the afternoon when the household was preoccupied, he would cycle off, exploring the side streets and roads that led to the Bois de Boulogne. He made friends with the women who emerged from the bushes and trees, standing on the side of the road in belted coats, in all weathers, even rain. They called him *chéri* and occasionally gave him sweets or a *sou* or two. He would cycle homewards, feet furiously pumping the pedals, his cheeks bulging with liquorice or those small butterscotch sweets – what were they called? *Berlingots*. That was it! *Berlingots*. All of a sudden, their sweet, silky taste of them was in his mouth and he gave out a stifled groan. Anouschka turned her head and frowned at him. What was wrong? He couldn't explain. He had to get away from it, and from them.

He blundered onto the terrace behind the marquees. His whole body was taken over by a kind of sadness that was a physical pain. He scrabbled in his pocket for a cigarette to move his mind off the path it had taken. He walked around the terrace to a smaller one, at the rear of the house, where he could no longer be seen.

It was dark back there on the small stone-flagged patio that looked across a fuzzy landscape of garden and trees to the long valley beyond. A rich, fruity smell of earth and the delicate scent of roses came up to him as he leaned on the balustrade, its edges worn smooth like a piece of soap. He wrenched off his mask, passed a hand over his face, closing his eyes briefly, and was horrified to find his cheeks were wet.

'You're crying.' Someone spoke to him out of the darkness behind him. He hurriedly shoved his mask back on and turned. A young woman, still wearing her own mask, was standing in the doorway leading into the house. She was very tall, dressed in a long white dress that seemed to glow in the darkness. She too was smoking; he watched the red tip of her cigarette trace out an arc in the darkness. 'You're crying,' she said again. It wasn't a question.

He nodded and swallowed with some difficulty. He was thankful he couldn't see her face, nor she his. There was a calmness about her that touched him. 'Yes,' he said after a moment. 'I heard someone say something . . . I found it moving.'

'Was it someone close to you?'

He blinked. She was young – he could tell that, but not much else. She stood in the doorway, her hand moving slowly towards her lips again as she took another drag. He saw the butt fall to the ground and felt, rather than saw, the way her leg moved as she ground it out. A long, fluid movement . . . full of grace. 'Yes. Yes, my mother. Oh, it's a long time ago now. Many, many years.'

'So it's not true, then?'

He blinked again. 'What's not true?'

'That time heals all wounds.'

He gave a small laugh. Young as she was, she had a presence. 'Well, yes and no. It's funny . . . I haven't thought about her in years. Maybe even a decade. It's the theme of the event, I guess. It makes you think.'

She nodded. There was a moment or two of easy silence between them. 'I've never known anyone who's died,' she said slowly. 'Not anyone close, at least.'

'That's your good fortune,' Sylvan said. 'That, and youth. You're young.'

'Not *that* young,' she said and there was a smile in her voice.

'Would you like another one?' He moved closer, holding out his packet.

'Thanks.' The smile was still in her voice. She bent towards him, cupping her hands around his as he lit the cigarette for her. She was very tall and quite plain – even with her mask on he could see she was no beauty. But there was something powerfully attractive about her. He caught a faint whiff of her perfume as a breeze fanned across the terrace and she moved from the doorway, brushing past him to sit on the edge of the balustrade. She raised the hem of her dress, as women do, and balanced herself carefully. They were looking at each other but their faces were concentrations of expression in the darkness rather than individual features. He put out a hand to help her up and was suddenly overcome with an awful, helpless desire of the kind he hadn't experienced since he was a youth. 'I—' He stopped. His face was inches from hers. There was a few seconds' pause then he leaned forwards slowly and with great delicacy and erotic hesitancy, kissed her, drawing her soft, willing lips into his own.

40

REBECCA

There was a burst of clapping and laughter as someone correctly identified Robbie Williams that sent the startled nighthawks circling into the night sky. Rebecca, whom no one had even spoken to, let alone unmasked, was growing impatient. She looked around for the others. As usual, Annick was in the middle of a group of young men; Tash was nowhere to be seen. She walked over, holding her own mask firmly in place.

'Have you seen Tash?' she asked, raising her voice over the noise of the crowd.

Annick shook her head. 'Haven't seen her for a bit. You know what she's like. She's probably running around making sure nothing goes wrong.'

Rebecca nodded glumly. Annick's young man was clearly keen to get back to business. She left them to it and wandered into the main hall. The staff rushed back and forth with trays of food and champagne. A woman with a headset clamped to her ear was shouting out instructions, military-style, a complete contrast to the genteel, tasteful sophistication outside. It was clearly going well. She glanced at her watch; from what she remembered of the timetable, dinner was about to be served. Where the hell was Tash?

She wandered around to the rose garden at the rear of the house. The band was playing a song she recognised. She walked up the side steps to the terrace, humming lightly to herself. She stopped suddenly. A man was standing a few feet away from her, bending over someone whose hands clawed roughly, passionately at him, pulling him into her. Her jaw dropped. It was Tash. She recognised her dress. But who the hell was the man standing over her? His dinner jacket was stretched tightly across his broad shoulders. She peered at the card on his back. *Sliver of A Country. Takeaway (US)*. Recognition crashed over her like a wave. It was Annick's father. She and Rebecca had chuckled over the card earlier. She stared at them for a second, a tidal wave of embarrassment and disgust rising up through her body. In the moonlight she caught a glimpse of Tash's face, her head moving slowly from side to side, her mouth open. She moaned softly, her voice a gentle counterpart to his ragged breathing. They were utterly absorbed in each other. She backed away silently, too shocked to breathe. She found herself flattened against the climbing roses, their small thorns pricking her through the thin fabric of her dress. Tash and Annick's *father*? She clapped a hand over her own mouth, then inched her way backwards. After what seemed like ages, she reached the grass where she could no longer be seen. She picked up her skirt and ran back towards the house. She rounded the corner and stopped abruptly. Annick was coming towards her.

'Did you find her?' Annick shouted. 'Dinner's just about to start.'

Rebecca shook her head, still too shocked to speak. Her fingers were twisting themselves nervously against her dress. 'No, I—'

'What's the matter? You look as though you've seen a ghost.' Annick drew level with her, putting an arm on hers.

'Nothing! I . . . I just . . . I'm just feeling a bit . . . hungry.'

'Well, dinner's about to start. You sure you're okay?'

'Yes! I'm fine. I'm fine,' Rebecca insisted. She couldn't bring herself to look Annick in the eye. Some awful remnant of what she'd just seen must surely be reflected in there?

'Have you seen my dad anywhere?' Annick added, looking around. 'Maman's looking for him. I think he's bored.'

Rebecca opened her mouth to speak but nothing would come out. It was her best and worst quality, her inability to lie. She could feel the hot, shameful wave of horror seep up through her neck and throat, staining her cheeks. Annick looked at her queerly.

'What on earth is the matter with you?'

'Nothing.' She turned away before Annick could question her any further and began to walk back in the direction from which she'd come. She had no clear idea where she was going, just that she wanted to get away from Annick, but just at that moment, Tash appeared from around the corner, smoothing out the crumpled skirt of her dress. Her hair was dishevelled, dragged loose from her ponytail and her mask was off.

'Oh, *there* you are!' Annick caught up with them both. 'I was wondering where the hell you'd got to.' She stopped suddenly and looked at them both. 'What on earth's the matter with you?'

Tash looked up. In that moment, her guilt couldn't have been plainer than if she'd confessed out loud. The three of them looked at each other. A few seconds passed without anyone saying anything, and then Annick's father walked round the corner. He too stopped. All four of them looked at each other. There was a large, wet stain on the front of Tash's dress; she put out a hand instinctively to cover it.

Sylvan Betancourt looked at the girl he'd just screwed on the balcony behind the house and then the penny dropped. He realised who she was. '*Merde*,' he said quietly. '*Merde.*'

Annick put up a hand to her mouth. It was a moment Rebecca knew she would never forget. 'Tash?' The sound dropped into the silence like a stone.

Rebecca watched Annick's father pass a hand over his face in an acknowledgement of shame. For a few minutes they all stood there, locked in the grip of a terrible, fearful inertia. Tash looked at the ground. Sylvan looked at his hands and Rebecca slowly backed away. Annick's ragged breathing was the only audible sound.

PART FOUR
SINK OR SWIM

*'If my critics saw me walking over the River
Thames they'd say it was because I couldn't swim.'*
Margaret Thatcher

41

2003

FIVE YEARS LATER

ANNICK
London, England

She rushed into the meeting ten minutes late, flustered, full of muttered apologies and sat down next to the client. Just before her bottom hit the seat there was the unmistakable feel of tearing fabric. Her skirt had split neatly up the seam. There was a startled, stifled giggle from Claire Hungerford, the other trainee solicitor present, and a withering, despairing look from Justin Clark, her boss. Annick went scarlet.

'Right, shall we get started?' Justin's voice made it clear he was in no mood to do dress repairs. 'Annick . . . would you mind bringing everyone up to speed on where we are?'

'Er, yes, absolutely.' She took a deep breath. She couldn't risk standing up so she remained seated. For the next half hour, she did her best to forget her ripped skirt and explain instead to the irate young man opposite her why his stepmother had managed to get her paws on his dead father's £3.5 million estate.

Forty-five minutes later, her ordeal was finally over. She waited until they'd all filed out of the meeting room before daring to stand up. She twisted round to look at the damage. Her heart sank. The skirt had split neatly up the central seam. She fell back into the chair in despair. She knew *why* it had split. It was too tight. Simple. She buried her face in her hands.

'Annick?' Justin suddenly appeared in the doorway. 'Are you all right?'

'Yes . . . yes, I'm fine,' she stammered, mortified. 'Just . . . just a little tired.'

'Tired?' He raised an eyebrow. It was eleven o'clock in the morning. 'Long night?' he asked mildly.

Annick almost laughed out loud. 'Oh, no . . . nothing like that. I've . . . it's the case. There's a lot to go through, that's all.'

'Ah. Well, gird your loins.' He put a sheaf of papers down on the table in front of her. 'Mrs Hall's just had these dropped off. I'll leave you to it,' he grinned. At the door he turned round. 'And there's a dry cleaner's on the corner,' he said, not unkindly. 'They'll be able to help you out.'

'Thanks,' she muttered, hoping that he couldn't see her face reddening. She waited until he'd gone then got up and ran for her coat.

It took the nice lady at the dry cleaner's ten minutes to fix her skirt.

'There you are, love.' She bit off a last thread and handed it over. 'I've put in a double seam. It'll last you for the rest of the day at least. You're never a size ten, though, if you don't mind me saying. Fourteen's more like it. Sixteen, even.'

Annick felt her cheeks reddening again. 'I . . . it's an old skirt,' she mumbled.

'Well, I'd buy a new one if I was you. That'll be a tenner.'

'Thanks,' Annick muttered, pulling out her wallet. Size sixteen indeed! She fished out two fives and hurried through to the back. She squeezed herself back into the skirt, let out the top three buttons and hurriedly left the shop.

She walked back down Cheapside, her cheeks still burning with a mixture of embarrassment and shame. Deep down, she knew the woman was right. In the past year alone, she'd gone up at least two dress sizes. She just couldn't stop eating. She couldn't pinpoint when it had begun. She'd always enjoyed her food, but for most of her teens and early twenties, she'd found it easy enough to pass on a second helping or a chocolate bar or two if she thought her jeans were getting a little tight. Now, however, things were different. She thought about food *constantly* – what she'd just eaten, what she was about to eat, what she was going to have for breakfast, lunch, and dinner . . . and almost every waking hour in between. She generally had breakfast alone in the kitchen before Mrs Price surfaced and was at her desk by nine, having stopped off somewhere en route to buy a croissant and a cappuccino. Another cappuccino and a biscuit or a muffin broke the morning's routine at eleven and then she spent the next couple of hours deciding what to have and where to go for lunch. And as soon as lunch was over, she began to think about dinner.

Her life had somehow narrowed itself down to two things: work and food. Aside from the odd drink with colleagues after work, most of whom she didn't really like anyway, her social life was practically non-existent. After that terrible evening when it became clear what had happened between her father and her best friend, something inside her had snapped. She just couldn't face her mother: what she'd seen that evening would be written all over her face. Her father simply pretended it hadn't happened. '*Merde*. Shit.' That was it, that was all he said. That was all he would ever say, she knew. It made it impossible for her to return to the palace in Lomé or to the apartment in Paris when he was there. Slowly, as the weeks of silence deepened into months, then a year, followed by another year, she found herself so far removed from the person she'd once been – bubbly, carefree, *slim* – that there didn't seem to be any way to bring her back. Anouschka didn't help. On the odd occasion she saw Annick, all Anouschka could talk about was how fat she'd become. She railed against what she saw as a betrayal of her own beauty. *Why must you eat so much? Why don't you exercise more? Why don't you have a boyfriend? Where are those two friends of yours . . . what're their names again? Natasha? Rebecca? Don't they say anything to you?* What could she say? The words wouldn't come. She turned her face away from her mother's accusatory glare and thought about what was for dinner instead.

It was nearly two o'clock. She bought her sandwiches and a brownie and hurried back to the office, passing the Jaeger store on the way. She glanced in the window; there was a sale on. She hesitated. She really ought to get a new skirt. She glanced at her watch. A plain black skirt would go with the jacket she was wearing, though to be honest the jacket was uncomfortably tight as well. Perhaps she ought to try a size fourteen. She walked in, hurriedly pulled a few items from the bulging racks and headed to the changing rooms.

Nothing fitted properly.

'I'm afraid fourteen's our biggest size. We don't go any bigger. Have you tried Marks & Spencer?' The sales girl spoke to her from the other side of the shut cubicle door. If they'd been standing face-to-face, Annick would have slapped her.

'Fourteen's fine,' she muttered. 'It's just a *fraction* too tight.'

'*If* you say so.'

Annick looked at herself in the long mirror. Her stomach flopped over the waistband and there were large rolls of flesh poking out of the side of her bra. There was no long mirror at home, just the small vanity mirror in the bathroom above the sink and it had been ages since she'd seen herself like this. A lone tear began its slow journey down her cheek. She brought a hand up to wipe it and caught sight of her tattoo. It took her a few moments to steady herself. It was five years since that terrible night and the end of a friendship she'd thought would last for the rest of her life. Rebecca had tried to patch things up, of course, but even she couldn't understand how it had happened. And Tash refused to talk about it. There'd been no coherent explanation, however painful, that would allow them a way back into their friendship . . . and so it ended. It had taken months for the anger inside Annick to die down and then it had been replaced by something else that was oddly familiar – a horrible, aching sense of loss. It simply slotted in neatly with all the other losses, all the other people about whom she cared deeply but who always, in the end, left her behind.

She wiped the tears hurriedly away with her sleeve. She wasn't about to let the damn salesgirl see her crying. She picked up the size-fourteen skirt and jacket and walked out with as straight a back and as neutral a face as she could muster.

'I'm afraid your card's been declined,' the snotty salesgirl said haughtily, a few minutes later.

Annick blinked in surprise. Such a thing had never happened to her. 'Declined? Why?'

'They don't tell us why. Have you got another one?' Her very tone implied Annick wouldn't.

'Yes, of course I do,' Annick snapped and pulled out her gold American Express card.

There was a few seconds' wait as the salesgirl swiped the card, then she looked up again. Now she sounded positively triumphant. 'This one's not going through either.'

There was an irritated cough from the person behind her. Annick's face began to burn. 'Um, I might have enough cash,' she said, quickly rifling through her purse. No such luck. Her purchases came to over £300. 'Could you just put those to one side for me?' she asked. 'I'll go to the cashpoint.'

'If you like. *So* sorry about the wait, madam.' The girl looked past Annick.

She ran outside and looked around for a cashpoint. There was one across the road. She ran across, fished her card out of her purse and put it in. She waited nervously for a few seconds. A message flashed up on the screen. *Please contact your bank.* She stared at it in disbelief. The card was not returned. She slid the second one in and waited. A few seconds later, the same message appeared and the machine swallowed her card. What the hell was going on? She looked at her watch. It was almost two fifteen. Guimard et Cie, her father's bank, was on the Strand, at least a ten-minute cab ride away. She was already fifteen minutes late for the office, but what else was she supposed to do? She hesitated, and then stuck her hand out. She would explain everything to Justin later. A cab swerved round and she clambered in. It had to be a mistake. Nothing like this had ever happened to her before.

The cashier glanced at her screen, then up again at Annick. She seemed oddly nervous. 'Could you just hang on for a minute?' she asked. 'I'll be right back.' She slid off her stool and disappeared. A minute ticked by, then another, then another. Annick looked nervously around her. She'd only ever been inside the bank a couple of times: once, when she first arrived in England with her mother and once with her father, waiting for him to conduct whatever business he had behind the wooden-panelled doors.

'Miss Betancourt?' She jumped and turned round. Standing next to the worried-looking cashier was a young man with a badge pinned discreetly to his lapel. *Steven Hewlett. Personal Wealth Management.* There was an odd look in his face. 'Would you mind coming with me for a moment, Mrs Betancourt?'

'Is something wrong?' Annick asked, anxiously. What the hell was going on?

'If you wouldn't mind coming with me . . . just this way, Mrs Betancourt. My office is just down here. It'll be easier to talk in private.'

She followed him, her heart starting to accelerate. 'Is something wrong?' she asked again.

He waited until she was seated opposite him. He laced his hands together and cleared his throat. 'Are you aware of any . . . of anything unusual happening in Togo?' he asked carefully.

Annick shook her head. 'No, nothing. Why?'

He hesitated. 'We've been issued with a TRO on all your accounts.'

'What's a TRO?' Annick asked, puzzled.

'It's an assets freeze. Your accounts are frozen, in other words.'

'Why?' Annick's heart was thumping.

He looked extremely uncomfortable.

'I think you'd better contact your embassy. I think that would probably be the best thing to do.'

Annick stood up. She felt dizzy. 'My embassy?'

He nodded vigorously. 'Yes, I'm awfully sorry, Miss Betancourt. It's the first time . . . I've not had to deal with a situation like this before,' he said apologetically. 'I'm sure everything'll be fine. It's probably just a temporary thing, a blip. You know, until things calm down.'

She stared at him uncomprehendingly for a second, then picked up her bag and walked out. There was a phone box on the corner, just outside the bank's main entrance. She yanked open the door, slotted in a few pounds' worth of coins and dialled her mother's private line. The phone rang, the familiar, high-pitched single ring, but there was no answer. She dialled her father's office with shaking fingers. Again the phone rang and rang but no one picked it up. She tried all the various different numbers in the palace that she knew off by heart – the chief protocol officer, the press secretary, the kitchens . . . but again, nothing. She hung up, her heart thumping. Something was seriously wrong. She stumbled dazedly out of the phone booth. And that was when she saw it. The headline, splashed across the *Evening Standard* board. *West African Leader Assassinated. Wife and aide also killed in blast.* Her knees suddenly buckled under her.

'Hey, you all right, love?' A passer-by shot out a hand. 'Woa . . . easy.' He grabbed hold of her as she stumbled, half slumping to the ground.

'No, no . . .' Annick couldn't get her words out.

'Here, you'd better sit down.' He helped her across the pavement to a bench. He was an older man, in a suit and tie. He looked concerned. 'What's the matter?' he asked in concern.

She felt as though she'd been punched in the stomach. She couldn't breathe. Everything around her had slowed down. There was a terrible, insistent blush of fear that had burst inside her, rapidly spreading up through her body, all the way through the muscles and organs and flesh and skin. She brought both hands up to her face, pressing them against her cheeks, her ears, her neck.

'Are you all right?' the man repeated. 'Is everything all right?'

She couldn't hear him. She would never understand how to tell him, how to tell anyone, how to get it all straight.

42

Mrs Price was waiting for her at the flat, her eyes reddened from weeping. It was the first time Annick had ever seen her cry. 'Oh, Annick,' she said as soon as she walked in the door. 'Oh, Annick.'

Annick opened her mouth but terror blocked her words. The dread was like a taste in her mouth, sharp and bitter. She stumbled again and Mrs Price quickly dragged out a chair, helping her into it. 'I . . . I just saw—' Annick's mouth wouldn't close properly over the words.

'I know, I know. Your aunt phoned a couple of hours ago, that's how *I* heard. I didn't have the news on this morning, like I normally do. We've been trying to reach you at the office but they didn't know where you'd gone. You're to go to her immediately.' In Mrs Price's anguish her Scottish accent suddenly became more pronounced. 'She says I'm to pack you a few things. No one knows what's going on down there.'

'How? It said . . . the newspaper said . . . both of them . . . ?' Annick looked up at her in fear.

'I know, I know. It was a grenade. Someone in the crowd. They were on a parade . . . oh, Annick. Your poor, *poor* mother. And your father. I don't know what to say, really I don't. I don't know what to think.' Mrs Price's voice cracked.

'My aunt wants me to go to Paris?' Annick tried to focus on what she'd just said. 'Which aunt?'

'Aunt Libertine. She says I've got to get you on a train immediately. She's afraid they'll come after all the properties and the money—'

'What money? My accounts have all been frozen,' Annick said dazedly.

'I don't know. She just said it's best for you not to be here. She thinks you'll be safer in Paris, that's what she said. Oh, dear . . . oh, Annick.'

Mrs Price's voice kept receding off into the distance as more and more urgent, terrible thoughts took hold. One part of Annick's brain received the information mechanically processing the words, but the other was flooded with a choking sense of terror. 'What shall I take with me?' She heard the words as if they'd been spoken by another.

'As much as you can, that's what she said. You might have to be there for a wee while,' Mrs Price said, looking around her fearfully as though expecting someone to burst through the door any second. 'I'm going down to Kent to stay with my sister until . . . until well, until things settle down. I'll help you pack. Come on, we'll do it together.'

Annick allowed herself to be taken by the arm and led her into the bedroom. She looked around her dazedly. 'What should I take?' she asked again helplessly.

'Let's start with your clothes and any personal things you might want, photos and such. We . . . we don't know when you'll be back, that's the thing.'

Annick couldn't speak. She watched as Mrs Price hauled down two of the big suitcases from on top of the wardrobe. They were covered in dust, which she hurriedly wiped off with her sleeve. It was such an unlikely gesture for someone as fastidious as Mrs Price; Annick's sense of panic deepened. She began to cry as Mrs Price flung clothes into the suitcase, pausing every now and then to hold up something, a wordless question. *This? How about this?* Clothes, photographs, books . . . all quickly disappearing as she efficiently packed up Annick's life.

At last it was done. She put an arm around the still-weeping Annick and led her back into the kitchen. 'You'd better have something to eat,' she said, opening the fridge.

'I . . . I can't,' Annick shook her head. 'I can't.' She looked round the kitchen, at the pale green walls that hadn't been painted in years; at the new white fridge that she'd bought only the other month to replace the one that had stood in its place since she'd moved in; at the worn Formica countertop and the stainless steel kettle that sat to one side. There was a vase of flowers on the windowsill – Mrs Price must have put them there. Her eyes filled with tears again. Her world was coming apart. Again.

43

TASH
London, England

Trouble was brewing. As soon as she stepped out of the lift she could sense it. The office was quiet; always a bad sign. Genevieve, the bubbly receptionist wasn't at her desk. That too was a bad sign. Genevieve was *always* at her desk. She walked into the large, open-plan office over-looking the High Street that she shared with four others and found it empty. That was the worst sign of all. An almost empty office meant one of two things: either everyone was in the bathroom, crying their eyes out, or they were upstairs in Rosie Trevelyan's office, possibly also crying. Neither scenario appealed. Rosie Trevelyan, Tash's boss, was the glamorous editor-in-chief of indeterminate age of *Style*, one of the most respected magazines in the fashion industry. They were three weeks away from signing off on the July issue. Tash had been at *Style* long enough to know that the last three weeks were always the most stressful. She was also smart enough to find as many reasons to be outside the office as possible in that time. Today she'd slipped out early to scout out a couple of locations for an upcoming shoot and had managed to turn it into an all-day event. Her colleagues, Michelle Riddle, the senior fashion editor and Holly Wilkes, the fashion features editor, could handle whatever Rosie chose to throw at them, or so she hoped. The fact that neither was in the office, however, was ominous.

She walked over to her desk, shoved a pile of papers out of the way and sat down. If the entire team was upstairs receiving a drubbing, there was little that could be gained from joining in. Better to just sit tight and get on with her own work. If Rosie felt like yelling at her too, she'd summon her soon enough.

She surveyed her desk with a mixture of dread and satisfaction. There wasn't a spare inch of its surface that wasn't covered by layouts, print-outs, photographs, torn-off newspaper and magazine articles, scraps of fabric samples and (the one thing she'd learned from working at Lady Davenport's), dozens of yellow Post-it notes covered in her trademark scrawl. *Call Testino re. Rome. Get milk. Call Mama re: doctor's appointment. Don't forget Emma's birthday Friday.* There was nothing of such importance that it couldn't wait until she got home. She quickly suppressed the urge to smile. Home. After three long, horrid years of flat sharing, she'd finally, *finally* got her own place. At thirty-seven square metres (not counting the bathroom, thank God) it was hardly big enough for a bed *and* a sofa (a sofa-bed solved that problem) but it was in Earl's Court, not too far from the flat in Kensington where she'd spent the first twenty-three years of her life with Lyudmila.

It was a funny thing, she mused to herself as she waited for her computer to boot up. For years Lyudmila had nagged her to move out and find her own place. No sooner was she gone, however, than Lyudmila began to complain she was lonely. It was true. Lyudmila had few friends and, these days at least, even fewer gentleman callers. She spent most of her days at home, watching TV, drinking cheap wine and smoking. When Tash came round, which was at least three or four times a week, she'd begun reminiscing about life in the Soviet Union. Food, clothing, holidays, life . . . everything in the Soviet Union was better. It was patently untrue. Tash wondered if it was simply old age. How old was Lyudmila? She was vague about her age . . . fifty-something, perhaps even sixty? She'd always been vague about it. Tash tried to compare her to Embeth, Rebecca's mother, but couldn't. There was a gulf between the two women that had little to do with age.

She brought up a hand to her face. It had been five years since she'd spoken to either Annick or Rebecca. The truth was, she just didn't know how to. She didn't know how to explain things to herself, let alone to them. When Sylvan Betancourt came upon her on the terrace that night, she didn't know who he was at first. It was dark, for one thing, and she'd had quite a lot to drink. She'd lost count of the number of quick slugs she'd had that evening – she knew of no quicker way to calm the thudding in her chest and her clammy palms. It was in that state of mind that he'd stumbled across her on the terrace. She'd been so surprised to see a grown man crying that it had made her forget her own nervousness. He'd offered her a cigarette and then one thing led to another and by the time she figured out who he was, well, by then, something else had taken hold of her and she couldn't have stopped herself, even if she'd wanted to. When he bent his head to kiss her, she couldn't believe *it was happening to her!* At long last! Rebecca and Annick had no idea what it was like to always be the one no one wanted, to be the girl no one ever looked at, especially when Annick was around. She brushed it off, of course, and she'd have sooner ripped out her tongue than admit it, especially to them, but it hurt. It hurt like hell. And now here was someone – a grown man, old enough to be her father if she'd ever had one – *and he wanted her*. It was both more shocking and exciting than anything she'd ever experienced. The voice in her head that shouted out, 'Stop!' was drowned out by the unexpected thrill of it all . . . and then it happened so fast that she didn't even have time to think. He *wanted* her. That was all she could think about and her body responded quicker than her mind. That was it, really. She'd followed his lead until the moment she walked round the corner and saw Rebecca and Annick . . . and that was when it really hit her. That was when she realised who he was and what she'd done. She'd crossed a line then and there was no going back.

Rebecca tried to talk to her in the days that followed. Annick couldn't, of course, and as for Sylvan . . . he promptly disappeared. But she couldn't get the words out, not even to Rebecca. What could she have said? *Deep down I wanted it.* Why? Admitting to wanting to be like Rebecca and Annick would have been to admit to something she couldn't even bring herself to think about, much less say out loud. Around them, she felt lesser, somehow, in a way that wasn't just to do with money and her perpetual lack of it. She'd grasped pretty early on in life that poverty was something to be overcome. If you worked hard enough and made sure you never let go of your ambition in the way Lyudmila had done, you could manage, perhaps even come out on top. But the other stuff – being beautiful or interesting enough to *attract* someone wasn't something you could control, at least not in the same way. Her failure in *that* department was a failure of the deepest sort precisely because she could do nothing about it. It didn't happen. Month after month, year after year, from the sidelines of the friendship, she watched Rebecca and Annick plough through suitors. Not once in all that time had they ever asked her what it felt like not to have one. Not *once*.

Her phone rang suddenly, jerking her out of her uncomfortable reverie. 'Hello?' she picked it up warily. It was Michelle.

'Upstairs,' Michelle said brusquely. 'We've got a bit of a problem with one of the layouts.'

'I'll be right there.' Tash grabbed a notepad, her heart sinking, and headed upstairs.

Walking into Rosie's office never failed to produce a sharp thrill of pleasure whatever the occasion. Rosie was sitting at the head of the oval glass table that occupied roughly a third of the room. She had the entire penthouse suite to herself; everyone else at *Style* was pushed into the three lower floors of 65 Marylebone High Street that *Style* occupied. The entire glass-walled, 200-square-metre space on the fifth floor was hers. As it should be. Just standing in the doorway, looking out over the treetops towards Regent's Park and down onto the fashionable bustle of Marylebone High Street below, was a potent reminder of the power and sheer style of London's most influential *fashionista*.

'Ah, Tash. At *last*!' Rosie barked out. In a bad mood, Rosie was the most terrifying person Tash had ever encountered. She'd never quite recovered from the experience of having an ashtray hurled at her head over some mistake or other she'd made – she still wasn't sure what. She hadn't known whether to duck or laugh. Today, Rosie was dressed in a stunning lemon-yellow silk dress that matched her auburn hair perfectly – Stella McCartney, Tash noted. A slim, snakeskin belt and matching snakeskin high-heeled court shoes – Fendi, possibly Prada – and a chunky black-glass necklace completed the outfit. But for all her rages, Rosie was not only the most stylish person Tash had ever clapped eyes on, she was also *fun*. She *played* with fashion, was endlessly inventive, curious, daring, bold . . . all the things Tash secretly longed to be, but wasn't.

'Sorry,' Tash said, slipping into the nearest vacant seat. 'I . . . I was out. Location scouting.'

'Something's not quite right with this.' Rosie paid her no heed. She pointed to a series of A3 sheets spread out across the table. She tapped one with a perfectly manicured fingernail. *Chanel. 576. Beige Pétale.* Tash made another mental note. It paid to pay attention to what Rosie was wearing. 'I've asked everyone else and sadly, no one seems to have a *clue.*'

There was complete silence around the table. Tash could see Michelle fidgeting nervously out of the corner of her eye. She scrutinised the offending image. 'It's the colours,' she said finally. 'They're too strong for the period. We either need to touch them up post-production, or re-shoot.'

Rosie looked at the layouts again. 'You might be right,' she muttered finally.

There was an audible sigh of relief around the table. A 'might' in Rosie's mouth was as good as a 'Yes, you're right.' Michelle mouthed a silent 'thank you' to Tash as they crowded round the prints again.

'Look, it's Paris in the 1920s. It's Louise Brooks and Jeanne Lanvin . . . delicate colours, simple lines, lots of draping, embroidery. But it doesn't work here. Her make-up's wrong. Reds and blacks are far too overpowering. She needs a more muted palette. It's fantastic that we're actually using Lanvin again. Ortiz's got the same eye for detail . . . look at that dress, the colour. That was Jeanne's favourite shade, the Quattro-cento blue, but we need *pale* make-up, not bold. The models look out of place – that's what's wrong. The exact historical details aren't all that important,' Tash said firmly, casting a quick glance at Rosie's impassive face, 'but I think that's what's caught your eye. Colours are wrong.'

'Right. Let's re-shoot.' Rosie straightened up, clearly buying Tash's explanation. 'See what happens when Lucy's away?' she asked no one in particular, though everyone heard the remark as though it were directed at them. Lucy Brocklebank was *Style's* art director and the one person whose job Tash absolutely coveted. Rosie *adored* Lucy, which meant that there was no chance of moving up the ladder into Lucy's spot, but she'd recently had a baby and Rosie had (exceedingly reluctantly) agreed to six weeks' maternity leave – which was why there were problems with the *Flapper Girls* shoot in the first place. Lucy would never have made the same mistake. 'Will someone *please* call the photographer and get the new prints to me by the end of this week. Right. Any other business?' There was none.

Six relieved *Style* executives beat a hasty retreat. 'Oh, Tash?' Rosie's voice rang out just before she'd reached the door. 'Just a minute.'

Tash hung back, her heart suddenly beating fast. 'Of course, Rosie.'

'MoMA's opening a new exhibition next week. *American Glamour*. I'd like you to come.'

Tash's brain refused at first to work. MoMA? Where the hell was MoMA? MoMA in New York? Rosie wanted her to go to *New York*? 'New York?' she spluttered in disbelief. 'You want *me* to go to New York?'

'Is there something wrong?' Rosie's large green eyes were on her. 'Do you have another, more pressing engagement?'

Tash shook her head vigorously. 'No, no . . . of course not.' She swallowed nervously. 'W-when is it?'

'We leave on Thursday night. Opening's on Friday. There are a couple of people I'd like you to meet. Back on Monday morning. Give Katie your passport. She'll sort out your tickets and your visa. The car'll pick you up from home.'

Tash quickly gathered her wits. 'Er, yes, thanks. Thanks, Rosie.' She backed out of the office, still dazed by the news. As she walked down the stairs to the floor below, dizzy with delight, she realised that still, even after five years, the only people in the whole world she wanted to call were Annick and Rebecca.

44

Sitting in the back of a New York yellow cab, next to Rosie who was already on her mobile, Tash did her best to remain calm. *Everything* about the journey was new and exciting – from the moment the sleek black Mercedes had pulled up outside her Earl's Court flat to the smiles of the British Airways ground staff as they ushered her and Rosie through the separate check-in for first-class passengers. She didn't dare confess to Rosie that this was only her third flight – and her first in such style. She grinned to herself at the pun and looked out of the window. It was April and although it was still cold, the sun was brilliant and high in the pristine, cloud-free blue sky. She hadn't seen a sky that colour in months. Her mouth dropped open, as the cab turned onto 5th Avenue and then onto 58th Street. The Four Seasons hotel was suddenly in front of them.

A bellhop eagerly leapt forwards as the car stopped in front of the entrance. 'Right this way, ma'am.' He ushered Rosie up the steps first, then turned his attention to Tash. 'Welcome to the Four Seasons, ma'am.'

Welcome indeed. Tash gazed up at the spectacular marble-and-gilt lobby as they ascended the steps. Rosie was on her mobile, sorting out meetings. She was immaculately dressed – a short, camel-coloured angora tunic top with wide, ruffled sleeves, straight black woollen trousers and a pair of Jimmy Choo suede ankle boots that occasionally revealed a tiny micro-strip of black fishnet stockings. A giant black Prada handbag and over-sized shades completed the outfit. She looked every inch the most powerful woman in British fashion. Behind her, in a pair of skinny jeans, a white shirt and a midnight-blue Gérard Darel leather jacket that she'd borrowed from Michelle, Tash felt like the proverbial country hick. If the bellhop, receptionist or duty manager who personally came forward to greet them (well, Rosie, at any rate) thought so too, all were far too well-mannered to show it. She was shown to her seventh-floor room with as much aplomb and deference as Rosie was to her suite on the forty-ninth.

'Cocktails are at six sharp,' Rosie said as the lift doors closed. '*Sharp.*'

Tash nodded vigorously. She'd be there an hour early. She followed the bellhop down the corridor and gasped as the he flung open the doors to her room. At nearly one hundred square metres, it was more than twice the size of her entire London flat. She only just managed to shut her mouth on a squeal as he opened the door to the bathroom. 'Th-thank you very much,' she managed to squawk as he arranged her bags neatly on the upholstered stool that (she assumed) had been custom-built for that very purpose. 'Thanks. Here. Um, that's for you.' She remembered at the last minute to produce a ten-dollar note. It was received with the utmost speed and discretion, and he withdrew from the room just as quickly and discreetly. She stood in the middle, turning round slowly, hugging herself with glee. It was all so much more glamorous and opulent than she'd dared expect.

'You?' Michelle and Holly had both squeaked when she told them the news. '*You're* going with her to New York? Why *you?*' She hadn't been able to answer them. She knew everyone at *Style* thought her a bit of an oddball and not the kind of young woman who routinely walked its corridors. Bookish and serious, with a congenital inability to flirt, that funny nose and that strange haircut . . . no, not your typical *Style* exployee. Oh, she was clever enough. There wasn't much about the history of fashion that Tash Bryce-Brudenell didn't know – but was that enough to wrangle a trip to New York? She was the most unlikely fashionista at *Style* – lanky, beanpole-thin with that dreadful haircut and those awful teeth – how come *she* got to go? Tash could read their faces as if they'd voiced their complaints out loud. Well, labels or not, Fendi or no, here she was. In New York. In a suite at the Four Seasons with a suitcase of hastily packed clothes, a camera and two pairs of new shoes. It didn't get much better than that.

The bar on the fourth floor of the hotel was everything a bar in New York should be . . . and more. Dark, supremely elegant and comfortable with an enormous, backlit bar and an impossibly good-looking barman. Tash arrived half an hour early, tightly clutching the sequinned over-sized purse that she'd pinched from one of the photo shoots she'd worked on, longing for a cigarette.

'What can I get you, ma'am?' Mr Good-Looking Barman was in front of her in a flash. He slid a leather-bound menu across the counter.

'I . . . I think I'll just have a Martini,' Tash said weakly.

'Very good, ma'am. We have several flavours to choose from . . . here, take a look.' He flicked open the menu. Tash's eyes bulged. *Abbey Cocktail. Algonquin Cocktail. Apple Cider Martini. Apple Martini. Apple Pie Martini. April Rain. Aviation Cocktail. Bamboo Cocktail. Big Breezy. Biltmore. Black and Gold. Black Martini. Blood Martini.*

She pointed to one halfway down the list. *English Rose*. 'I'll have that one,' she said decisively. She had no idea what was in it, but the name was serendipitous.

'Very good, ma'am,' he repeated, flashing those amazing teeth. 'And a little something to snack on, perhaps? We have an excellent carb-free menu.'

It was on the tip of her tongue to ask him why he thought she'd be interested in a carb-free menu but the sheer choice involved shut her up. *Traditional Shrimp Cocktail with Cream-free Horseradish Cocktail Sauce; Spicy Tuna Tartare with Daikon Sprouts; Avocado and Smoked Salmon with Capers; Jersey Heirloom Tomato Burrata with Balsamic Reduction Crème Fraîche; Tempura Shrimp with Miso-and-Pineapple Glaze.* 'Er, that.' She pointed to the *Spicy Tuna Tartare*.

'Excellent choice, ma'am.' He withdrew, still smiling. A few seconds later, her cocktail appeared in front of her.

'What's in this?' she asked, taking a cautious sip.

He rattled off the ingredients. 'Two ounces gin, one ounce dry vermouth, an ounce of apricot brandy, half an ounce of lemon juice, splash of grenadine and a maraschino cherry for garnish. Slightly sweeter than a traditional martini, but you don't look as though you need to worry about that.'

'Oh.'

Rosie suddenly appeared. 'An old-fashioned Martini, no olives,' she said briskly to the bartender. 'And no snacks,' she said severely. At that very moment, of course, Tash's *Spicy Tuna Tartare* arrived.

Tash swallowed nervously. 'I . . . uh—'

'Oh, go ahead. You obviously don't have to worry about your weight,' Rosie said, uncharacteristically gracious. 'Yet.'

'Ah, Tom's here,' she said, catching sight of an exceedingly dapper, exceedingly good-looking man who'd just walked in. Tash nearly fell off her stool. It was Tom Ford. 'And there's Charlie.' Within minutes there was a small coterie of the most powerful people in fashion surrounding them.

Tash immediately moved off to one side. She wasn't about to join in their conversations. She was content to observe them, especially Rosie. With her short, orange bob, chiselled cheekbones and impeccably porcelain skin, she was certainly elegant and attractive, but was she actually beautiful? It was hard to say. She looked a good ten years younger than she actually was – somewhere in her mid-fifties, Tash had heard – but Tash couldn't decide which was the more apt adjective –

beautiful or stylish? She sipped her drink and tried not to look as though she was listening.

'So, who're you seeing tomorrow, darling?' Tom asked Rosie playfully.

'Oh, the usual suspects,' Rosie quickly deflected the question. 'We're seeing you in London next week, aren't we? You're opening a new store. How exciting.'

If Tom recognised he was being put off, he was far too well-mannered to show it. It was all a game, Tash realised, draining her glass. The designers courted powerful editors like Rosie. With one well-placed comment, she could make or break a designer's career, but at the same time, she needed them. She needed to be seen within their inner circle, to be snapped by the paparazzi with them at bars like this one, at events like the MoMA exhibition where they were headed, and at the after-hours parties. She needed invitations to their summer homes on Capri or to go skiing with them in Gstaad. In turn, they needed *Style's* support. The first ten to twelve pages of each issue were reserved for the biggest brands – Gucci, Dior, Chanel, Vuitton, Cartier and YSL. Their adverts appeared before anyone else's. It was all an intricate game of seduction and withdrawal – you had to be available, but not *too* available – and there was no one more practised at it than Rosie Trevelyan. Watch and learn, Tash whispered to herself as they finally collected their coats and bags and headed out into the night.

A fleet of cars was parked kerbside; she instinctively waited for the last one. She saw from the way Rosie turned briefly to nod at her, that she'd done the right thing. It was odd, she mused, as the driver pulled away and they headed towards the museum. She and Rosie had barely exchanged ten words on the flight over from London. Rosie had accepted a glass of champagne, pulled on one of those funny sleeping masks and gone straight to sleep. At the bar at the Four Seasons she'd ignored Tash once the brief introductions had been made. Yet, for all that, Tash and Rosie somehow understood one another. Just as it had been with Embeth Harburg and with Lady Davenport, Tash felt. Something valuable was being offered; if she wasn't quite aware of it now, she understood intuitively, she soon would be.

45

ANNICK
Paris, France

Two days later, after a terrible train journey to Paris where she half-expected to be stopped at any second, Annick sat in the living room of the flat on rue Malville with her aunt, listening to the news broadcast in grim concentration. Neither woman spoke. Annick's knuckles were white where she gripped the armrest. Finally, after what seemed like hours, the presenter's voice died away.

Aunt Libertine sighed and got up heavily from the sofa. She shuffled into the kitchen, leaving Annick alone. It was three days since she'd arrived and they were expecting yet another guest. Every flight that landed at Charles de Gaulle from Lomé brought with it fresh people and news. The French media gave only the scantiest details. It was from the guests who arrived in the flat every hour that they began to piece together the events of that terrible day.

Claude Touré arrived a few minutes later and was able to fill them in. He'd been one of Sylvan's closest friends. It was a *coup d'état*, he told them wearily, yet another revolt by a group of junior army officers, much like the one that had restored her father to power. It had begun in the early hours of the morning. A small group had stormed the broadcasting station and the airport, seizing control from the overwhelmed guards. The element of surprise clearly worked; within an hour, all of the country's communications centres were in the young soldiers' hands. The surprise of it was that no one yet knew. The parade was due to begin at eight a.m. By seven, the streets were already lined, crowds gathering to cheer on the president and his glamorous wife. At the central *Place de l'Indépendance*, where the celebrations were due to reach their climax, the canopied dais was already erected along with rows of the ubiquitous white plastic chairs that are a staple of African ceremonial life. The entire diplomatic community had turned out for the ceremony along with military top brass, important business leaders . . . everyone who was anyone in Togolese society. But, Touré said, his voice cracking with exhaustion, the signs were already there. The mood in the country was tense. Just weeks before, there'd been a brutal crackdown of striking workers at a factory in Kpalimé, north of Lomé. Twelve were killed. By soldiers acting under direct orders from the president, it was rumoured. And then there was the case of the two journalists, one of them here in France, murdered, it was said, again on direct orders of the president. Tragic, tragic.

Annick listened to him in bewilderment. 'Wh-what journalists? Wh . . . when?' She glanced nervously at her aunt; Aunt Libertine's gaze slid away.

Touré seemed not to hear. He was lost in his own description of events. The open-top Rolls Royce bearing the president and the first lady turned slowly down Independence Avenue, moving towards the *Place*. They waved at the crowds as they did every year; Anouschka was wearing a brilliant blue headdress. He saw it move from side to side as she waved to the crowds.

'There was a helicopter; it circled above our heads, drowning everything out. We didn't know then that the rebels were controlling it. The car came up the road, very slowly – everyone was waving. Some of the women, you know, the market vendors, they were dressed in their traditional cloth with Sylvan's picture printed in the middle. It was a bit strange, seeing his face like that . . . on their stomachs, their breasts, their backsides. Someone commented – I think it was one of the European ambassadors – he was sitting behind us. I don't remember exactly what he said. There were many ambassadors – France, Germany, Spain. I don't know about the British – so maybe they were there; maybe not.

'And the crowd was very good. Every few minutes, somebody would shout, "Vive le Président!" And everybody would shout . . . you know the way our women are. They were making that sound, the one they make at funerals and weddings. It was crazy. We found out later that those in the crowd shouting "Vive le Président!" were actually the agitators. They'd been hired by the soldiers . . . the ones who were behind it. I saw the car coming towards us and the shouting and screaming got louder. There was all of a sudden a lot of gunfire and there was a brass band playing a little further up the road and the soldiers were all lined up for inspection so it was hard to tell if it was intentional, you know, part of the parade. It was a volley . . . *papapa-papa*. Back and forth. It was some sort of drill parade, that's what we thought the gunfire was, at first. But those people who were shouting, suddenly their shouts turned into screams. That's when we thought there was something strange going on.

'I saw the ambassadors, the ones who were sitting behind us – they got up, and someone shouted something . . . "watch out!" or "look!" something like that. And then I saw a soldier take aim, pointing towards the car. It was all so confusing. Some of the soldiers in the parade broke ranks and started running towards the car. One of them was shot – the colonel who was leading the band turned round and saw him and he just pulled out his pistol. Just like that. That's when the first grenade went off. It was so loud. Jesus! The whole place was heaving. And the helicopter overhead. It came very low over our heads so there was a lot of confusion. Then we heard a second grenade and the car stopped. One shot. *Bang!* I saw it with my own eyes. It hit him on the side of the head. Clean, just like that. He fell forwards, you see, towards the floor of the car, and that's when I saw that your mother was already down.'

Annick listened to Touré with the stunned detachment of someone hearing a story told of others. The tears that had flowed almost non-stop since she'd left London now refused to come. She felt numb. When he finally stopped talking, she heard someone panting, a horrible hoarse sound. After a moment, she realised it was *her*. She got up quickly, embarrassed, and went into the kitchen. She poured herself a glass of water from the tap. She drank slowly, the cool liquid filling her mouth, her throat. She was thirsty; she was alive. They were not. Now what?

'Well, you must stay here.' Aunt Libertine looked at her after Touré had gone. 'You'd better stay in Paris. They'll have taken the house in London already, the bastards. Were you, er . . . were you able to bring any money with you?'

Annick shook her head. 'No. Nothing. All the accounts have been frozen.'

'*Merde.*' Aunt Libertine's face fell. 'But you have a profession, no? You're a lawyer?'

Annick nodded. 'But I studied in England. I don't know what it will be like here. Will they accept my qualifications?' She looked anxiously at her aunt.

Aunt Libertine shrugged. '*Merde,*' she said again. She shook her head slowly, sighing heavily. She was the youngest of Crístiano Betancourt's children with his third or fourth wife – Annick couldn't remember – a half-sister to Sylvan. Annick scarcely knew her. She'd spent an Easter holiday with her once when Anouschka failed to show up and she'd visited them in London a couple of times at home. *Home*. The word seemed almost surreal. Where was home now?

'Well, you just have to try.' Aunt Libertine got up heavily from the table. 'You can stay here for a while. Until you find your feet. It's small, but . . . what can we do? You'll sleep in the bedroom down the hallway and we'll have to share the bathroom. Have you eaten?'

Annick shook her head. The thought of food was repugnant to her. 'No. I . . . I'm fine,' she stammered.

'You should eat. You're a big girl. You need to eat. There's some rice and stew in the oven.' She paused, looking down at her. 'It won't bring them back, you know. I don't mean to be harsh but it's true. It's just the way things are with the Betancourts. It's always been like this; it always will be. It's what happens, always.' She shrugged with an air of indescribable finality.

'Wh . . . what do you mean?' Annick stammered. 'Why? Why does it always happen?'

Aunt Libertine looked at her oddly. 'How else could it be?'

'I don't know what you mean,' Annick said uncertainly.

Aunt Libertine made a small sound of impatience. 'It's because of *this*,' she said, rubbing her hand along her forearm. It was a gesture Annick dimly remembered seeing other relatives make. 'Yes, it's because of this . . . our colour. And our name. Betancourt. That was your great-great grandfather's name: Epiphanio Betancourt. He came to Africa in, oh, in 1840, I think it was. After the slave revolts. That was the beginning of it. Thirty families made the crossing – the Olympios, the Baétas, the da Souzas . . . you know the names. All those families. And they married each other . . . this one with that, this one's daughter promised to that one's son, this one's nephew to that one's niece. That's the way they kept us apart.'

'Apart? Apart from what?'

Again Aunt Libertine looked surprised. 'From the Africans, of course. That's how we've kept this.' She made the same gesture yet again, rubbing her finger back and forth across the surface of her coffee-coloured skin.

'But Papa's dark. Not *black*, but he's not my colour, either.' She spoke of him in the present tense.

'It's true. Sylvan's dark.' Aunt Liberline pulled the corners of her mouth down. 'Some say that's where the trouble began.'

Annick shook her head. 'What trouble? What are you talking about?' She could feel tears starting to well up behind her eyes. 'I don't understand. What difference does it make who married whom, who's darker than whom . . . why does any of it matter?'

'Don't be so naive,' Aunt Libertine said sharply. 'It was a mistake to set ourselves so far apart. Pride, pride. A terrible thing. We all – Betancourts, Olympios, Ribeiros, all – we thought ourselves *better*. Different.' She paused. 'But your father . . . it was more complicated for Sylvan. The bloodline wasn't straight, you see. Your great-grandfather, Sylvanus, wasn't a Betancourt. He was adopted. Your great-grandmother took him in, though I'm not sure anyone spoke of adoption in those days. She couldn't keep her own children alive, that was the problem. One by one . . . they all died. And your great-grandfather desperately needed an heir. So they found this child – his mother was one of the maids in the house. He was a little lighter-skinned, you see. It wasn't clear who the father was, and the mother didn't want to say. In the end, your great-grandmother just took him in, raised him as her own. He was *your* great-grandfather, Annick, my grandfather. And then when *he* married, he didn't choose one of us, from one of the families. He took a native wife. An African woman. Dark-skinned. *That's* why Sylvan is so dark.'

'But why . . . why aren't *you* dark, like Papa?' Annick asked, struggling to keep up with the complicated, convoluted web of family alliances about which she knew next-to-nothing. Neither her father nor her mother had ever said much about the past. To be fair, she hadn't asked either. Her grandfather had been president; there was a stepmother lurking somewhere in the background whom her father disliked . . . that was all she knew.

Aunt Libertine looked away. 'These Betancourt men,' she said after a moment. 'It's hard to say who's really who. Who fathered which child? There were twenty-four of us in the end. Some dark, some light, some favoured, some not. In the end it was good for Sylvan . . . that he came out that way, that he was so dark. It made it easier . . . politically. For some of us, it was clear after independence that Togo was no place for us. We were a liability, you see. A reminder of the old colonial order. That's why some of us came here to France. But where else should we go?' she asked, a touch defiantly. 'Brazil? Portugal? We don't even speak Portuguese any more!'

'But what does any of this have to do with Papa? It's all ancient history,' Annick burst out.

'Nothing in Africa is ancient history,' Aunt Libertine said crisply.

'Nothing. And the sooner you realise that the better.' She got up heavily. 'You'll have to excuse me,' she said. 'I'm a little tired.' She pulled her cardigan around her shoulders, picked up her walking stick and slowly left the room.

Annick sat where she was, immobile, the only sound in the room her own breath, rising and falling, and outside, distantly, the sound of traffic on the street below. At some point in the afternoon she'd got up to make them a pot of tea, which they'd both left untouched. It stood now, gone cold, on the table in front of them. Her legs were stiff and her shoulders ached. She'd been hunched over, almost from the moment her aunt began talking until the last words died away.

She got up awkwardly, levering herself off the floor. She tried to picture her father, but failed. When had she last seen him? A year ago? She could recall certain things – his size, his bulk, his splendid white army uniform and the sound of his voice down the telephone line . . . but it was all fragmented; nothing was whole. Even her mother. What did she *know?* Her scent - Chanel No. 5; the flash of silky blonde hair when she'd just come out of the salon, hair that Annick had longed for all her life; blood-red toenails and the ruby-and-emerald ring that sat on the third finger of her right hand . . . details, fragments, disjointed bits but never the whole.

The urge to vomit came upon her suddenly, with no prior warning. She ran down the corridor to the bathroom, pushed open the door to the toilet and dropped to her knees. She crawled to the bowl as her stomach turned in convulsions, expelling everything that she'd been trying so desperately to swallow. Up it all came: all the pain and the terror, the awful imaginings of what the last few seconds of their lives must have been like, the anguish. She lay her head against the cold white porcelain, tears and slime and spittle streaming from her eyes, mouth and nose, unable to do anything other than gasp for breath.

46

TASH
London, UK

The fork was halfway to her mouth when she first heard the word 'Togo', followed rapidly by 'assassinated'. It clattered to the ground without her even realising she'd dropped it. She stared at the TV screen in disbelief, but the short bulletin was over. 'In other news today . . .' She remained frozen to her seat. Where . . . what . . . how? She put aside her bowl of pasta and stood up, feeling suddenly dizzy. The president of Togo and his wife . . . *assassinated*? She rushed to the hallway, yanked her handbag off one of the hooks and scrambled in her bag for her mobile. Annick. She had to call Annick. She dialled the still-familiar number with shaking fingers. It hit her then, hard. Back then, five years ago, when they'd last spoken to each other on a daily basis, there were no mobiles – or if there were, neither she nor Annick had one. But she still remembered Annick's number. With her free hand she switched channels, desperately seeking more details. The line was dead. She rang it again, her heart thudding inside her chest. There was nothing further. She put down her mobile and ran to her desk. It took her two seconds to bring up Google and type in the words 'Togo' and 'president' . . . and suddenly, there it was. *Togolese President and Wife Assassinated. BBC – 2 hours ago.* She clicked furiously, sweat breaking out all the way down her back. Her mouth opened in horror. 'No, God, no . . .' The details unfolded on the screen in front of her. *Two gunshot wounds, one to the head, the other to the chest . . . his wife, the French actress and movie star Anouschka Malaquais, died of injuries sustained as the result of a grenade thrown into the car as it passed. Two bodyguards were also killed.* She closed her eyes. Annick. She had to reach Annick. The news was already a week old . . . where the hell was Annick?

The flat was exactly as she remembered it. *Bishop's Court.* She pressed the buzzer for number sixteen and stood back, her heart thumping. The entire second floor – Annick's flat and the smaller flat that Mrs Price occupied across the corridor – was shrouded in darkness. Tash bit her lip. She pressed the buzzer again. There was no answer, just an eerie silence. She pressed it a third time. A sound close by suddenly made her jump and turn. Out of the corner of her eye, she saw a man take a step backwards, slipping back behind the building. She held her breath, waiting for him to emerge. A minute passed, then another, but he didn't reappear. It was probably nothing, she told herself sternly. Bayswater was a busy area. Even now, at eight thirty in the evening, there were people walking up and down in twos and threes . . . probably just someone who'd changed his mind. She turned and walked back towards Marble Arch. There was only one thing for it. She had to phone Rebecca.

If Rebecca was surprised to hear Tash's voice, she hid it well. There was only the slightest hesitation, the faintest intake of breath, then the warm, slightly throaty voice that Tash remembered so well came rushing down the line.

'Tash? Tash?'

'Rebs, it's me. Yes, it's me.' Tash wasn't prepared for the way her throat thickened painfully. She swallowed hard.

'Where are you?'

'I'm here . . . I'm in London, I mean. I'm standing outside Annick's place . . . have you heard?'

'Heard what?'

'The news. It's her parents . . . her father,' Tash swallowed hard again. She cleared her throat. 'He's . . . there's been a coup . . . in Togo. Her parents were killed—'

'Wh-what? What're you talking about?'

'I heard it on the news earlier this evening. It was just a two-second announcement so I Googled it . . . it happened a week ago, apparently. Some junior army officers. I rang Annick straight away but there was no answer and I don't have her mobile number so I jumped in a cab and came down to the flat—'

'I'm coming with you. I'll be right there—'

'No, that's the thing . . . there's no one there. I've been standing outside the flat for the past half hour but it's completely dark.'

'Where's Mrs Price?'

'I've no idea. I don't even know if she still lives there. The phone's been cut off.'

'Oh, God . . . her mother too?' Rebs sounded even more distraught than she was. 'Why didn't I hear about it?'

'I don't know. It was only at the tail end of the news this evening. I

didn't see it in the papers, nothing. I don't even know if she was there.'
She hesitated. 'When . . . when did you last see her?'

'About . . . maybe three years ago? I tried, you know, after . . . well,
for a while afterwards but she didn't really want to meet up anymore.
What are we going to do? D'you know where she works?'

'No. I haven't seen her since that night. Jesus, Rebs . . . I . . . I don't
know what to do.'

'Where are you?'

'Marble Arch. Just outside the McDonald's.'

'Stay there. I'm coming. I'll be there in half an hour.'

47

ANNICK

She followed the flapping trouser legs of an estate agent as they climbed
up a flight of stairs. Up and up they went – third, fourth, fifth and . . .
please God, let this be the last . . . sixth flight, Annick holding onto the
bannister for support and hoping to God that her breath would return.

'It's a bit of a hike,' he said cheerfully, as they rounded the last curved
flight. 'That's why it's cheap.'

No, it's cheap because it's a dump, Annick thought as he opened the
door and the smell of stale cooking rushed out. She followed him in.
Her heart sank further. The flat was tiny. One room with a kitchen that
was little more than a counter along one end of the wall and a shower
and toilet that had somehow been squeezed into a cupboard. Everything
looked as though it had been covered in a thin layer of grime. The walls
were streaked and yellowed; the blinds were broken and the floorboards
looked half-rotten. There was an old sofa in one corner of the room that
clearly doubled as a bed and in the other, a wardrobe with a door
missing. It took all of her self-control not to burst into tears.

'So . . . what d'you think?' the agent said cheerfully.

Annick swallowed. 'It's . . . it's small.'

'Bijoux,' he supplied helpfully. 'Cheap to heat, mind you. And easy to
clean.'

It was on the tip of her tongue to say that obviously hadn't occurred to the previous tenant but she shut her mouth. She had absolutely no choice. She couldn't stay with Aunt Libertine a day longer. The previous week she'd found out her qualifications wouldn't translate after all. She would have to do a conversion course to French law which would cost a small fortune – and who did she think was going to pay for *that*, Aunt Libertine demanded accusingly. Annick had no answer. She'd walked out of the flat determined that morning to find something – anything. By the time she returned in the evening, she had a job. Aunt Libertine looked at her blankly.

'In a *hotel*? A hotel receptionist?'

Annick nodded. 'Just . . . just for now.'

'I see. *Eh bien . . .*' the rest was left unsaid.

So . . . here she was. From solicitor to hotel receptionist, from Park Lane to Portes Blanches, from daughter of *Président de la République* to penniless orphan. Overnight her life had been turned upside down. There'd been days when she didn't think she could get out of bed, never mind find a job, or a place to live. Earlier that week, standing in the Métro with the warm wind of an approaching train gusting down the track, she'd felt herself begin to slide. What if she just stepped out in front of it . . . a couple of paces, that was all it would take. She heard the hooter and the metallic scream of brakes as the train began to slow down. All around her were sounds of people going about their ordinary evening lives.

Someone jostled her suddenly, and grabbed her arm. She was pulled back just as the train flashed past. It was an older man. His eyes flickered quickly over her and then he stepped back to allow her to pass. She boarded the train with everyone else, too numb to register the fact that he'd just saved her life. She reached overhead to hold onto a strap, pressing her face tightly into the sleeve of her jacket so that no one would see her tears.

'It's two months deposit,' the estate agent said as he locked the door behind them. 'And a small fee for the security check.'

'Oh. I . . . I don't think . . . I won't be able to manage two months,' Annick said, panicking. 'I don't have enough saved up.'

'You have a job?' He was obviously accustomed to hardship amongst his clients.

She nodded. 'Yes . . . at a hotel near here. On rue Championnet.'

'*Ça va, ça va*. One month is fine.' He hesitated. 'Can I just ask you something?'

Annick swallowed. 'Er, yes . . . yes.'

'You seem like a very, well, like a very well-educated young lady. I heard you speaking English in the office earlier. Are you sure you want to live around here?'

Annick swallowed again. 'It's fine for now,' she said slowly. He had stopped one or two steps below her and was turned towards her, concern showing on his face. She looked away. She couldn't bear kindnesses, especially not from strangers.

'It's just . . . well, it can get a little rough around here, you know. Are you sure you wouldn't prefer somewhere quieter?'

Annick shook her head. 'This . . . this is fine,' she stammered. 'And my work is close by. It's only for a few months.'

'I see.' He shrugged. '*Bon*. If you're sure . . . ?'

Annick nodded. 'Yes. Yes, I am.'

They continued to the ground floor in silence.

At his office – two small, smoky little rooms next to an even smaller grocery store – he produced the paperwork for her to sign. 'Here . . . and here,' he indicated, lighting up a cigarette at the same time. 'And once more. *Voilà*. Annick Malaquais.' He peered at her signature. 'No relation, eh?' He chortled at his own joke. 'Mind you, that poor woman. Should never have got mixed up with that African, if you ask me. That's how it always ends with them. What a thing to happen.'

Annick looked away. *A thing. A thing that happened.* A thing that could have happened to anyone. Instead it had happened to her. That was all; that was the difference. It wasn't a novel or a film, or an account of someone else's life that she'd read. It was her life. It had happened to *her*.

She watched numbly as he made copies of the contract and sorted out the keys. Five minutes later it was all done. She got to her feet, clutching her keys, and stumbled outside. It was nearly three o'clock. She hadn't eaten anything since breakfast that morning. She was suddenly ravenous. There was a small bakery on the corner, just before the entrance to the Métro. She had a ten-euro note in her pocket – all that was left of the money Aunt Libertine had grudgingly given her. She hurried over.

Stepping into the warm, sweet smell of freshly baked bread and pastries was like stepping into a warm, scented bath. She stood in front of the glass counter and felt the saliva rush into her mouth. She felt dizzy with hunger. *Three pains au chocolat – no, four – a ham and cheese baguette and . . . a tarte au citron. Yes, that one.* She handed over the note and picked up the paper bag. She tried to wait until she was somewhere more private before she opened the bag but she just couldn't help herself. She tore open the bag and stuffed a *pain au chocolat*, practically whole, into her mouth. Little flakes of buttered pastry fell down her coat but she didn't care. It was still warm, the chocolate thick and melting. She'd never tasted anything quite as delicious. She tore off another piece, and another, cramming them into her mouth. She ate all four, one after the other, leaning back against the wall for support. Her coat was covered in crumbs. She brushed them off, intending to go down into the Métro and make her way back home. She would save the baguette and the *tarte au citron* to have with a cup of coffee. Aunt Libertine was out; she wouldn't be back until much later in the evening. But the lingering taste of chocolate was still in her mouth. She had four euros left; she could feel the coins in her pocket. She hesitated for a moment, then turned and walked back to the bakery.

'Two more, please.' There were two young girls behind the counter. The one who'd served her earlier looked up. There was a flash of something between them, not recognition in the conventional sense – they'd never set eyes on each other before – but some private under-standing that made Annick's cheeks burn with embarrassment. The girl watched as her colleague handed over the little paper bag and as Annick turned to go, she heard her whisper, softly but distinctly, *'la pauvre.'* Poor girl. Poor thing. She pushed open the door and hurried out, shame breaking out all over her skin like a film of sweat.

Aunt Libertine seemed only too happy to see her go. Generous now that she knew Annick was leaving, she ordered a taxi. 'You can't possibly manage,' she'd said, looking at Annick's three suitcases and two large plastic bags. 'It's fine. I'll call a taxi. No, I'll pay,' she said, looking at Annick's suddenly panicked face. 'You can pay me back later.'

Annick nodded. She didn't trust herself to speak. She dragged her suitcases down the short flight of stairs. However grubby and tiny the new place might be, it was *hers*. The trembling, shaky fear that had accompanied her every waking moment over the past couple of weeks was gone. She was no longer afraid to be alone. Yes, the apartment was dirty and it was small but she could clean it. She had a job that paid weekly. She'd been told she could have lunch and dinner at the hotel. It was Sunday – on Friday she would pick up her first wages . . . only another five days to go. She stowed her suitcases in the boot, slammed the door behind her and didn't look back.

The Hôtel du Jardin on rue Championnet wasn't the sort of hotel Annick would ever have noticed, let alone stayed in. It didn't even *look* like a hotel. Aside from the small brass plaque outside on which the Tourist Board stars had been conveniently erased, there was nothing to suggest the narrow townhouse, like all the other townhouses in the street, was anything other than a series of tiny hutch-like apartments. There was a makeshift reception desk in the foyer, and a rack of keys behind her head, but other than that, little had been done inside to turn the rundown series of twenty-four rooms into anything that resembled a hotel. Everything was covered in green – walls, floors, sofas, bedspreads, curtains. Even the bathroom suites at the end of the corridors were a particularly vile shade of avocado. It was the sort of hotel in which people either stayed for an hour or a year.

The manager, a slender, sloe-eyed young man from Guadalupe with a wide smile, rattled off the rates, rules and regulations and tips for dealing with troublesome guests. Annick listened dazedly. Three months ago she'd been in meetings dealing with inheritance tax – she felt as though she'd stepped through a doorway into some parallel, hellish universe that she didn't recognise. She tried to focus. Off-duty manager. Telephone. Police. She nodded dumbly.

'*Bon*, that's it, then. I'm off. Been here since last night. I'm bushed. Lunch is through there.' He pointed to the curtained-off doorway on the right. 'He starts at one. Cook's lousy. Algerian. Bit too much harissa for my liking, but what can you do? Dinner starts at six and the night-shift guys come in at eight. Got all that?'

Annick nodded. 'Yes, I . . . I think so.'

'Good girl. You'll get the hang of it. Any problems, give the off-duty manager a ring. Shouldn't be any, though. Most of the people who come here are regulars, if you know what I mean. Watch out for old Lajeune. Room 314. Been here for ever. He'll ask you for his key and try and squeeze your ass when you turn round.'

Annick swallowed hard again. A kind of darkness had settled over her, pressing down on her. It was as if she'd narrowed her gaze so that she saw only those things that were immediately in front of her – telephone, key rack, counter top, receipt book. When she thought about the past, it made her feel dizzy. She could no longer step back far enough from her day-to-day self to see anything clearly. Hearing about it from Aunt Libertine had only made things worse. It seemed to her now that everything – every event, every circumstance – stretched around her in a tangled maze in all directions, past and future, and that everything was connected in ways she couldn't see or understand. Listening to her aunt's explanations had made her even more fearful. Her parents' death had its roots in something that had happened two hundred years before she was born, on a continent she'd never seen, in a language and culture she didn't understand. She had no hope of ever grasping it, or what it meant – for her, for them, for anyone. The only option left to her was to cut herself off. She knew now that she wasn't like Tash or Rebecca, both of whom saw life differently, especially Tash. Tash saw life as something to be acted *upon*, not just endured. Tash was afraid of nothing. As she watched the manager pick up his coat and check his phone for messages before pushing open the door, she felt a dull blow of pain just below her ribs. She'd have given anything to hear either of their voices again.

PART FIVE

SWIMMING

*'You ain't supposed to get salmon when they're swimming
upstream to spawn. But if you're hungry, you do.'*
Loretta Lynn

48

2005

TWO YEARS LATER

REBECCA
Tel Aviv

The foyer of the Israeli Philharmonic Orchestra was crowded. Well-dressed women in furs and expensive-looking coats stood around, holding flutes of champagne, laughing loudly whilst their partners chatted to one another in low, soft murmurs glancing frequently towards the door. Now that the concert was over, their minds were elsewhere.

Rebecca came up the stairs from the toilets, surreptitiously drying her hands on her skirt and caught her mother's barely perceptive frown. It was her father's ninetieth birthday and a special performance had been put on in his honour. He sat in his wheelchair in the midst of his friends and relatives, his head held high. In spite of his gruff manner, Rebecca could see just how touched he was by the outpouring of love and good wishes from everyone around him, not just those closest to him. The trip had been an emotional one; though few would ever say so out loud, there was a general feeling amongst those present that it might well be his last. He had outlived two of his sisters and all his brothers – it was time to pass the baton of philanthropic and social work to the younger generation of Harburgs, to Rebecca, his only child.

She glanced quickly at her mother. Now in her sixties, Embeth was still a powerfully beautiful woman who drew people towards her the way she'd done all her life. It wasn't often that Rebecca speculated or even thought about the nature of her parents' marriage but tonight, looking at them together, her mother now towering over her father in her elegant heels, she experienced a sudden rush of feeling that brought a thin film of tears to her eyes. Despite their differences in age and culture, they were absolutely devoted to one another. When she was younger, she was ashamed to admit she'd been irritated by Embeth –

187

what, exactly, did she *do* all day? Especially when set against her father's world, Embeth's life seemed inconsequential. Lionel had always been powered by an energy that constituted its own force-field, finding its proper outlet in his business dealings and travel. But perhaps she'd been mistaken? Without her mother, she was beginning to understand, her father would simply never have managed the burdens – emotional, financial, familial – that had been placed upon him. She was the anchor to which he attached himself, and in doing so, she gave him rein to roam free.

Was that what it would be like for her? Rebecca wondered. Perhaps *that* was what was missing? Marriage, motherhood . . . the sense of being central to someone? The vague dissatisfaction that had followed her ever since she'd left the Courtauld had intensified. It was as though she was waiting for something – a sign, a suggestion – that would release her into the future, pushing her out of herself and into a new kind of life. She'd done what everyone expected – she'd gone to university, done reasonably well – she'd followed her mother into the philanthropic causes the family supported, throwing herself into the things with gusto. But something was lacking. She could feel it.

Picking up the threads of her friendship with Tash only served to intensify her vague dissatisfaction. When they met nowadays, as pleasurable as it was, she came away each time feeling more and more restless. Tash seemed so *purposeful*, so ambitious. She worked longer and harder than anyone Rebecca knew, but she thrived on it. She seemed to love the buzz and frenzy of the fashion world; being at Rosie Trevelyan's beck and call, never knowing where she'd be sent or what she'd be asked to do. She loved the unpredictability of her life and she didn't give a shit what anyone else thought. Rebecca longed to be as tough – but she wasn't. Tash answered to no one. Lyudmila aside, she could come and go as she pleased. Rebecca's life was completely different. There was a whole generation of extended Harburg relations and foundations to answer to – she couldn't just hop off to New York on a whim, even if she'd wanted to – which she didn't. But what *did* she want? She fingered her champagne glass disconsolately. The answer, as always, escaped her.

'You look rather glum.' Someone interrupted her. She looked up. A man stood in front of her, tall, silver-haired, wearing a light grey suit with a rather beautiful pale yellow tie. His face was deeply lined but tanned and his eyes were the most astonishing shade of blue. Did she know him? 'No, you don't,' he smiled, reading her mind. 'But I know who *you* are. You're Lionel's daughter,' he offered with a slow smile. 'I'm

Julian. Julian Lovell. Another of the relatives you've probably never heard of.'

Rebecca laughed. A baritone, English-sounding voice. 'No, I'm sorry, I haven't,' she confessed.

'That's what comes of being the favoured family,' he said, smiling again. 'Everyone knows *you*. The reverse doesn't hold true.'

She blushed. 'It's my father,' she said, shrugging. '*I* haven't done anything worth mentioning.'

'Not what I've heard. You're an artist, aren't you?'

'Oh, no, no. I *studied* art, that's all. Art history.'

'Ah. My mother must've got it wrong. Funny that. She's the walking encyclopaedia on all matters Harburg.'

Rebecca laughed again. 'You make us sound a lot more interesting than we really are.'

He shook his head. 'Well, the Harburgs are *not* like any other family; that's the whole point. Can I get you another?' He pointed to her empty champagne glass.

Rebecca looked over his shoulder at her parents. The concert had ended almost an hour ago and she knew how tired her father would be. She looked back up at Julian. He was a good deal older than her, she thought to herself – late forties, perhaps even older? Very handsome in a rugged, outdoorsy kind of way, at sharp odds with the elegance of his suit and tie. 'Let me just see what my parents are up to. Not that I normally have to check with them,' she added quickly, embarrassed.

'Go ahead. I'll be here.' That slow, wry smile again. She hurried away before she made a fool of herself.

Her mother looked up as she approached.

'Did you enjoy the concert, darling?' she asked, smiling. 'I saw you chatting to lots of people. Isn't that Julian Lovell?'

'You know him?' Rebecca was surprised.

'Of course. He's just taken over the Paris branch. He's very nice.' There was something in the way she said it that made Rebecca look sharply at her.

'How old is he?' she asked bluntly.

'Oh, not *that* old. Forty, perhaps,' Embeth said vaguely, looking off into the distance.

'Mama. Come on.'

'Well, maybe a *little* older than forty.'

'Fifty, you mean.'

'Perhaps. But he's very nice.'

'How do you know him? How come you've never mentioned him before?'

'Darling, we know so many people.' Embeth sounded genuinely surprised. 'Actually, I'd forgotten all about the Lovells. Anyhow, you're keeping him waiting. Are you going for a drink somewhere?'

'Well, I was just checking . . . is Dad ready to go home?'

'Yes, but don't let that stop you. You go on and have fun. I'm sure Julian will make sure you get home safely. And we can always send the driver for you.'

'Mama,' Rebecca whispered sternly. 'He just asked if I wanted another champagne. We're not going anywhere.'

'Well, suggest it, for goodness' sake! It's the twenty-first century, Rebecca, not the nineteenth. Show a bit of initiative!' And with that, Embeth turned back to the group, leaving Rebecca with her mouth hanging half-open.

'So . . . another champagne? Or how about a spot of dinner?' Julian robbed her of the initiative she'd been busy trying to muster.

'Er, sure. Dinner, I mean. I haven't eaten since . . . well, since lunchtime.'

'Then let's go to dinner. I'll drop you home afterwards, don't worry. And I know where the house is. I don't think there's a person left standing in Israel who doesn't,' he added with a dry laugh. 'Didn't the architects win an award for it?'

'They did,' Rebecca nodded. 'But I find it a bit frightening, I have to confess. Not the sort of place you'd want to leave your washing out or your dirty dishes in the sink.'

'Presumably why your dear mother has an army of staff. Shall we?' He held open the door for her as she buttoned up her jacket and they stepped out into the cold night-time air.

'I think this is the first time I've been here in winter,' Rebecca said, pulling a scarf from her handbag. 'It's freezing.'

'Oh, this is actually quite mild. Up north is where it gets really cold. Jerusalem, too. It snows occasionally.'

'Do you live here?' Rebecca asked curiously.

'Some of the time. I spent most of my teens here . . . worked on a kibbutz, picked oranges, watermelons, that sort of thing.'

'I can't quite see you picking oranges,' she said with a laugh.

'Oh, you'd be surprised. Here we are.' He disarmed the car, a sleek, glossy-looking affair that smelled of fresh leather and the faint lemony scent of men's cologne. He held open the door for her. Rebecca slid in, unaccustomed to such good manners.

'So,' he said, getting in on the other side. 'Where to?'

Rebecca leaned back into the soft leather seats. 'You choose,' she murmured, rather surprised by her own boldness. 'You seem quite good at it.'

'I am, aren't I?'

She smiled but didn't answer and turned to look out of the window at the city as he turned onto Ibn Gabirol, heading towards the centre. It really was a beautiful city, she thought to herself as the tall, elegant hotels that fringed the seafront flashed past, one after the other. Perhaps she ought to stay on a while? After all, it wasn't as though she had anything urgent to return to. She smiled to herself. She couldn't wait to tell Tash.

49

TASH
London

One last set of proofs to oversee and then she was done. Tash picked up the magnifying monocle and peered closely at the image in front of her. It was Gisèle, the Brazilian model-of-the-moment, all long golden limbs, flowing honey-coloured hair and that incredible face. The photo, shot by Steven Meisel, was stunning. Gisèle was stunning. The *location* – in front of a sun-drenched pool in Palm Springs – was stunning. It was all stunning. It was the cover photo for *Style*'s January issue and it would hit exactly the right note of sunny happiness that dreary, weary January sales shoppers would respond to. The only problem – and it was a big one – was that she'd just heard Anna Wintour was using Gisèle for *Vogue*'s January issue. Unthinkable for two rival magazines to feature the same girl, shot by the same photographer – even if the locations were different. *Vogue* had gone to Capri; *Style* to Palm Springs. It made no difference. *Style* would be accused of copying *Vogue* and Rosie would throw a fit. Playing second fiddle to *Vogue* was *not* where she wanted *Style* to be.

Tash had two options. One would be to let the *Style* cover stand as was and claim she hadn't heard about *Vogue*'s plans. Rosie would throw her fit – and probably a crystal ashtray as well – and then threaten to sack Tash, a fairly routine occurrence. The other, involving a bit more work, was to run upstairs *now*, tell Rosie (and duck) and then be expected to come up with an alternative in twenty-four hours flat.

She pondered her options. Her eye fell upon the postcard that was pinned to the wall, just behind her computer. It had been there for ages. It was from Annick, sent long ago, on one of the long summer holidays she used to spend in Togo when they were at school. She'd found it in a box of old letters that had been lying at the back of her wardrobe for years. Looking at it produced the same old mixture of dread and longing that thinking about Rebecca and Annick always did. It was of the Gate of No Return, a monument to the slave trade in the town of Ouidah, in neighbouring Benin, not far from Lomé. She remembered receiving it, tracing the unfamiliar stamps with her finger, wondering what it must be like to be thousands of miles away from the familiar atmosphere of school.

She reached for the postcard, peeling it away carefully from the wall. She turned it over. Annick's handwriting: *On an absolutely <u>interminable</u> state visit with Papa to Benin. Got dragged to see the Porte du Non Retour this morning. Awfully hot and dusty, but still quite sad. Maman complains all day long – you know what she's like! Can't wait for school to start! Miss you lots, A.*

She stared at the image. Two silhouetted wrought-iron figures on either side of the painted stone arch. Wasn't Ouidah the site from which hundreds of thousands of African slaves had departed for Brazil? She frowned and picked up the image of Gisèle again. Gisèle was Brazilian. She had no idea where Gisèle's ancestors came from – somewhere in Germany by the look of her – but the link between her native country and the rugged, vibrant coast of West Africa might be worth thinking about. She switched on her computer. She needed to get a closer look.

An hour later she had the beginnings of a layout sketched out. She'd printed off half a dozen pictures of cheeky-faced, grinning children, lush, tropical landscapes and those stark, sombre monuments and slave castles that dotted the West African coast. She'd even thought of a title: *Going Back to Her Roots*. Her mind was whirring. They'd cancel Gisèle on the cover but they'd do a fabulous, six-page pullout spread with her inside the magazine instead. Rosie prided herself on being more creative and daring than anyone else in the business and it would be so much more than just an ordinary shoot. They'd get someone to write something about the location, the slave trade, the links with Brazil, Gisèle's ancestry. Tash's pencil flew across her notepad. A short story or two, perhaps by a well-known African or Brazilian writer, maybe showcase some local Brazilian design talent alongside the Dolce & Gabbana and Prada outfits she was already picturing. She almost bit the end off her pencil she was so excited.

Rosie looked as though she'd eaten something disagreeable. Across the table, Michelle and Andrea were silent. Tash frowned. What on earth was wrong? How could they *not* like it? It was a *brilliant* idea. 'Is there something wrong?' she asked finally. Michelle and Andrea exchanged nervous glances.

'Tash, this is a *fashion* magazine,' Rosie said finally. 'A *fashion* magazine. We're in the business of selling clothes, perfumes, lifestyle . . . *comprende?* We're not the *Economist* or *Newsweek*. If your aim is to win the Pulitzer Prize, you might want to re-think where you are. All very *interesting*,' she waved a languid hand in the general direction of the layout, 'and fascinating *if* I wanted to know something about the trans-Atlantic slave trade,' she paused dramatically, 'but I *don't*. I want to read about fashion, Tash. Not history.'

'But—'

Rosie held up an imperious hand. 'Enough.' She looked at the enormous black Breitling she wore on her left wrist. 'It's one thirty. We've got until five to come up with an alternative cover. Find me an alternative or find yourself a new job.' With that, she picked up her coat and bag and walked out of the room.

'Hul*lo*,' the woman behind the glossy white Corian counter looked up as Tash walked in. 'Haven't seen you in a while. Everything all right?'

Tash gave her a wan smile and shrugged. 'Oh, you know how it is,' she said with an exaggerated sigh.

The woman shook her head. 'No, actually, I don't. I don't understand how *you* stand it, to be honest. You're absolutely wasted there, Miss Bryce-Brudenell, absolutely wasted. Now, have you seen these?' She pointed to a rack of clothes hanging to one side, still in their stiff plastic covers. 'Diane von Furstenberg. Wrap-dresses. Di*vine*. No one else has 'em yet. I ordered them when I was in New York last month – they've just arrived.'

Tash's mood suddenly lifted. The woman she was speaking to was Edith Berman, a small, rather severe-looking woman in her late fifties who looked more like the headmistress of one of those impeccably mannered girls' schools somewhere in the New Forest than the owner of Eden's, a small boutique just off the Marylebone High Street. Just as Edith couldn't understand Tash's career choice, there was much about Edith that Tash didn't quite get. Formidably intelligent with a line in conversation that went from particle physics to the joys of organic silver, dressed mostly in Jil Sander with the most astonishing collection of jewellery Tash had ever seen, and grandmother to two adorable young boys, she'd run Eden's with her late husband since the early seventies. There was no one quite like her. Despite Eden's formidable success, they'd never opened another store; there was only one Eden's, and it had always been in the same location on Moxon Street. She had very little time for the fashion 'rat pack', as she called them – the editors, stylists and their (thousands of) assistants who dictated what was 'in' and what wasn't. Edith wasn't interested in trends. She shopped with two things in mind: quality and originality and the women who came into Eden's once, came back again. Again and again and again.

'They're lovely,' Tash said, picking up one of the dresses and peering at the print through the plastic.

'Take it out. Feel it. It's silk. Silk jersey. Lovely against one's skin.'

Tash smiled to herself. Edith sometimes spoke like royalty. *One's skin.* Only Edith could say something like that. She carefully unsheathed the dress and held it against her, turning to look at herself in the mirror. A typically striking, stylish DvF print – large white tropical flowers against a mustard background. It was stunning, though not on her. 'Lovely,' she agreed. 'She's got such an eye.'

'*I've* got such an eye, you mean,' Edith smiled. 'Though I do miss Seth. Now *there* was a man with an eye for colour – unbelievable what he'd find.'

'Did you always work together?' Tash asked curiously.

Edith nodded. 'Right from the start. We opened up in 1972, can you believe it? Over thirty years we ran the shop together. Thirty-two years. Married for forty.'

Tash didn't know what to say. She realised she knew very little about Edith's private life. 'Where's that from?' she asked, pointing to the exquisite cuff bracelet that Edith was wearing.

'This? Oh, she's one of my favourites. Kimberly McDonald. I just love the way she mixes things up. That's agate and gold, and those are geodes,' she said, pointing to the blue, purple and amber-hued stones, cut flat and polished to a high sheen. 'Lovely, isn't it?'

'Where's she based?'

'South Carolina, of all places.'

'How d'you ever find all these interesting designers?' Tash asked.

Edith gave a small laugh. 'Internet. Simple. It was Seth's idea, really. He used to spend hours looking at sites, tracking down young designers. They're all online these days.'

Tash nodded absently. She used the internet mostly for research – layouts, places, photographers and the like. The idea of Seth Berman, who must have been in his, sitting in their little office at the back of the shop, browsing, tickled her. 'But isn't it a nuisance?'

'What d'you mean?'

'Well, if you see something in—'

'Edith? Oh, thank *God* you're here!' A woman's voice cut her short. 'It's a complete disaster!'

'Excuse me a moment,' Edith said to Tash. 'Let me just see to this. Clare's a very dear customer.'

'Of course. I'll just browse; don't mind me. I won't be buying anything,' Tash said with a grin. She moved off, leaving Edith to sort out whatever disaster was looming.

'It's just so *frustrating*,' the woman named Clare wailed. She was holding out a dark grape dress that Tash recognised as Michael Kors. 'I *love* it but the colours are all wrong. I want the orange one. I saw it in Milan last week and I should've bought it there are then. I told Declan but he thought the green suited me better. It doesn't. It's a *disaster*.'

'Well, we can place an order for the orange one. I know just the one you mean – it's actually burnt amber, not orange – but you're right, it'll go so much better with your colouring. What on earth was Declan thinking?' Edith said with a placatory smile.

'Yes, but can you get it here by Saturday?'

'Clare, it's Thursday today,' Edith reminded her gently.

'I know, but it's Nadine's fortieth on Saturday night – you know, Nadine Hernandez – Pépé's wife? Well, his *third* wife, at any rate. Anyhow, it's her fortieth on Saturday and we're going to Fulton's and I so *desperately* wanted to wear it.' Clare looked almost suicidal, Tash noticed, sneaking a quick look over her shoulder. Edith was doing her best to placate the woman, pulling out one alternative after another. But there was no placating a woman who'd set her heart on a particular outfit for a particular event. 'It's *got* to be Michael Kors, Edith, it's just got to be. He's perfect for that sort of occasion. Oh, God . . . what'm I going to do?' she wailed. Clare Whatever-Her-Name-Was was clearly not just a valued customer, she was savvy too. She was absolutely right. The dress, a simple belted crepe-wool dress with small cap sleeves, fell to just below the knee. With the right belt and shoes – and Tash could already see in her mind's eye the dark brown lizard-skin Pierre Hardy shoes she'd spotted in the window as soon as she walked in, and the brown-and-cream Miu-Miu lizard-skin bag – the outfit would be stunning, yet understated. Perfect for a third wife's fortieth birthday dinner at Fulton's.

'Tash?' Edith called out as she pulled yet another outfit off the rack. 'I'll be with you in a second.'

But Tash was already halfway out the door. Something had just occurred to her.

50

REBECCA
Tel Aviv

Julian Lovell. She still wasn't quite sure how to think of him. It had been just over a fortnight since she'd first met him. She had no idea what he expected from her. If he *was* courting her, he was doing it with infinite patience. He hadn't so much as kissed her, other than the perfunctory touch on either cheek when he picked her up or dropped her off, and yet he'd come round practically every day. She'd never experienced anything quite like it. All her previous boyfriends seemed to view getting to know her as a by-product of the relationship, certainly not its main point. But Julian wanted to *know* her. He wanted her opinion of things. What did she think of Tel Aviv? Jerusalem? Was she enjoying herself? What sort of music did she like? Did she like the taste of this or that? And wine? There was a warmth to him that she'd rarely encountered in anyone, least of all a man, yet he confused her at times. For all his generosity and openness, she saw that there was also part of him that was shut off to her. In spite of his gentle, insistent questioning of her, he somehow managed to say very little about his own past. He'd never been married; that much she knew. Once, over dinner and a glass of wine too many, he mentioned a woman's name, Ruth, but then stopped, as if he'd already said too much. She'd looked at his face uncertainly, unsure whether to ask anything further, but it was already closed. And then, as usual, he'd neatly turned the conversation round to her.

The land stretched before them, an endless, gently undulating line of trees with feathery, silver tops that thinned out where the hills began. 'Where are we?' she asked as he swung the big car carefully off the road. It was a late Saturday afternoon; there was almost no traffic about. The car rode gently down a soft sandy track towards a line of trees whose branches met overhead, throwing down a shadowy, dappled light.

'Near Hadera. I thought I'd show you where I worked when I first came here.'

'The *kibbutz*?'

He nodded. 'Ein Shemer. It's about half a mile down that track.' He pointed ahead of them, and then opened his door before coming round to open hers. He helped her out. It was colder here than in the city and she pulled her coat tightly around her. The sky was clear, a lovely, watery blue-turning-to-pink colour, as dusk began to fall. She stood close to him, aware of his presence next to her as she surveyed the landscape. 'They grow everything here,' he murmured, pointing to the fields that lay just within sight. 'Apples, oranges, watermelons . . . you name it. Avocados, tomatoes . . . I don't think there's anything they haven't tried – and succeeded too. It's one of the richest *kibbutzim* in the country.'

'You know so much about this place,' Rebecca murmured, impressed. 'I feel like such an ignoramus around you sometimes.'

'*You*? An ignoramus?' He laughed.

'It's true,' Rebecca said earnestly. 'I hardly know it, or anything about it. I suppose I just never thought it had anything to do with *me*, you know?'

'Of course it does. You're Jewish.'

'No, it's not *that*. It's just that it always seemed so . . . I don't know . . . so far away, somehow. And always full of problems.'

There was a very faint muscle that moved in the side of his jaw, she'd noticed, when he was animated. It moved now, as though he were clenching his teeth. Some deeper emotion came from him, bouncing off the surface of his skin so that she felt it skim lightly across her own, like a faint, tingling shiver. She waited for him to say something more but he was quiet. Had she offended him? He inspired a strange mixture of longing and trepidation in her. His approval of her, when it came, contained such warmth and interest that she felt herself basking in it, like sunlight. His smiles were slow and not easily won, so when he did smile at her, turning his face to look at her properly, fully, she could feel her heart and stomach turning over, as if she'd been given something both precious and rare. She shivered suddenly.

'Cold?' he murmured.

She shook her head. It was exactly the same tone of voice her father used, a mixture of solicitous kindness and tolerant amusement. To her alarm, she suddenly felt a prick of tears behind her eyes. Her father was old and there were moments when the strains of running the family empire showed clearly upon his lined face. They would have liked more children, a son especially. Her mother never spoke about it but from some forgotten source, Rebecca knew there'd been many attempts, many miscarriages, before she finally came along. And after her, there would be no more. She'd overheard them once, years ago, arguing in a way they seldom did, in her father's book-lined study downstairs. 'Leave them to Rebecca? What for?' she'd heard her father ask angrily. 'She'll never read them.'

'You never know,' her mother replied soothingly. 'One day, perhaps? And even if she doesn't, perhaps . . . perhaps her husband will?'

She'd paused on the stairwell, a ripple of fear running lightly up her spine. Her husband? She didn't even have a boyfriend! She'd wanted to linger but one or other of the maids in the house came clattering through into the hallway and the quiet spell was broken.

She shook her head. 'No, not cold. Just . . .' She stopped suddenly, unsure how to continue or put into words what she was feeling.

'Just . . . ?'

'Nothing, really. I was just thinking . . . how nice it's been. Hanging out with you,' she added quickly. 'Going to different places. You've been really kind.'

'Is that why you think I'm doing this?' Julian asked quietly. 'To be kind?'

Rebecca hesitated. There was a tone in his voice she hadn't heard before. 'I . . . well, I just assumed . . . I mean, I don't know, you've been really, well, kind. Yes, kind.' She didn't know how else to put it. What was he asking? She stole a quick sideways look at him. He was concentrating on the landscape but the faint movement at his jawline indicated he was thinking of something else.

'What do you think of me?'

'You?' She was taken aback. 'What d'you mean?'

'What I said. What do you think of me?'

'I . . . I think you're . . . well, you're . . . you've been great. To me, I mean. I really enjoy—' She stopped, blushing furiously. What the hell was he asking?

'Go on,' he said gently.

She shook her head. 'I . . . I don't know what you mean.'

'Come on, Rebecca. It's not bloody rocket science. What do you think of me?'

Rebecca couldn't help herself. She giggled. Julian didn't seem the type to swear. 'Sorry . . . I didn't mean to laugh. It's not that . . . it's just you. Swearing. It doesn't seem like you, somehow.'

'Too old?'

She shook her head. 'No, it's not that. It's just . . . you're much too dignified. I've never heard my father swear, ever. Not even in German.'

'Is that how you think of me?'

The question caught her off-guard. 'H . . . how d'you mean?'

'Like your father?'

'God, no! I just meant . . . oh, you know what I meant.'

He was looking at her intently, as though waiting for something further. A strand of her hair blew across her face. With a steady hand, he reached out and tucked it carefully behind her ear. It was the first time he'd touched her, properly, and it burned right through her skin. Her face felt as though it were on fire. She put up a hand to her cheek but before she reached it, he'd caught hold of it. They stood there, at the side of the road, the cold evening air blowing around them, not speaking. A lone car drove past; she listened to the hollow roar of its tyres on the tarmac dying away. His thumb moved across her hand in a gentle rhythmic movement that somehow managed to be both soothing and erotic at the same time.

'Rebecca,' he murmured quietly, pulling her towards him. She pressed her face against his shirt, her hands reaching around his back underneath the warmth of his jacket. She breathed in deeply, taking the scent of him down into her lungs. Again he brought her father to mind – his beautifully laundered shirts, jackets brushed at the shoulders, crisply starched trousers, cigars and after-dinner drinks, the unmistakable scent of polished leather, the scent of her father's study . . . all those things that she associated with maleness, with class and good taste, wealth . . . Julian had it, in spades. 'Rebecca,' he murmured again against her hair. 'I know this may seem a little . . . well, *sudden*, but—'

'Sudden?' Rebecca couldn't help herself. 'You call this *sudden*? You haven't even kissed me yet!'

He laughed. She could feel the reverberations against her cheek. 'Okay, perhaps "sudden" isn't quite the right word. But, the thing is . . .' He stopped again.

Rebecca pulled back just a fraction to look up at him. His expression was one she'd never seen before. He was frowning intently but his face was at once remote and mysterious, out of her reach. She felt a tremendous surge of feeling somewhere inside her that was both connected to him – and to that grave, childishly serious expression – but also to the day itself. It was all jumbled up inside her, mixed up with her longing to be part of her own family's history and yet somehow set herself apart from them. She saw very clearly, and not for the first time since she'd arrived in Israel, just how adrift she was, going along with whatever was put in front of her. Julian seemed to be offering her something and although she had no clear idea of what it was – yet – it would be a *serious* offer, not something frivolous or light. He was a serious man. Whatever came next, whatever he was about to say, she knew her life was about to change. 'What?' she whispered, pushing her face back into his warm, solid chest.

'I . . . I don't know any other way to say this. I'm . . . I'm in love. Yes, I'm in love with you. I haven't felt this way about anyone since . . . well, in a long time. A *very* long time.' He seemed to be struggling with the words. His grip on her tightened momentarily. 'Ever since . . . since it happened . . . I didn't think I'd ever be able to—' He stopped. 'Look, this isn't the right place to talk. Not here, not by the side of the road. Can we go somewhere?'

Rebecca nodded. Her whole body felt as though it were on fire. A hundred and one questions were tumbling around in her brain but there was some part of her that just didn't want to let go. She'd never felt as safe with anyone in her life. 'Wherever you want,' she whispered.

'Come on. You've never been to my place. There's something I want to show you.' He held her by the upper arms and pushed her slowly away from him, his eyes never leaving her face. Then he bent his head and kissed her, gently, but with great passion. She felt her world turn upside down, and then right itself slowly. She would have followed him anywhere.

His apartment was on a beautiful tree-lined street just off Sheinkin Street, in the centre of the city. It was dark by the time he pulled over and switched off the engine. 'I'm up there,' he said, pointing up through the silhouetted trees to a white, balconied building. 'Fifth floor. It's a Bauhaus building. One of the first.'

'*Ha-ir haLevana,*' Rebecca smiled. 'The White City.'

He looked at her, impressed. 'I keep forgetting,' he smiled. 'You're the clever Harburg.'

She laughed. 'Hardly. Everyone knows *that* about Tel Aviv. It's got the biggest collection of Bauhaus buildings in the world.'

'Not everyone. Come on, I'll show you around. It's small, I warn you.'

'You must think I'm incredibly spoilt. You should've seen the flat I lived in at university.'

'No, I don't think you're spoilt at all,' Julian said, shaking his head. 'Just that you're probably used to grander things.'

'Well, that's where you're wrong. We aren't grand at all. My father still re-uses jam jars.'

'That's the war for you. They haven't forgotten,' Julian said, leading the way up the path. 'My mother's the same.'

There it was again, Rebecca thought to herself as they walked into the lobby. That strange familiarity. To be with Julian was to be with someone who was at once familiar and strange. She was irresistibly drawn to the combination.

He opened the front door and stood aside to let her pass. The lobby was cool and dark. There were ceramic pots of dark-green plants in the corners and large, abstract oil paintings on the walls. It was quiet inside. They entered the lift, not touching, but she was acutely aware of his scent and of his presence beside her.

'Here we are. Home sweet home. At least when I'm here.' He opened the door onto a large hallway flanked by double glass doors. He switched on the light. Rebecca looked around in pleasure. The flat was very much like Julian himself; elegant and refined. They walked into the compact living room. The walls were a deep, dark green and bare except for a large, striking oil painting above the fireplace of a grey-haired man standing with his hands shoved in his pockets, looking down at the ground. Julian followed her gaze. 'Stephen Conroy. It's a self-portrait. I loved it the minute I saw it.'

Rebecca nodded slowly. There was something both arresting and poignant about the image; although his face was largely obscured, the intensity of his gaze towards the unseen ground hinted at the same private struggle within himself that she'd glimpsed in Julian. 'It's beautiful,' she said simply. 'I like your flat. It's . . . well, it's just like *you*.'

He seemed unsure how to respond. He looked at her for a second, then turned away, busying himself by opening the drinks cabinet. 'What can I get you? A glass of red?'

Rebecca nodded gratefully. The easy, light-hearted aura that had enveloped them all afternoon had disappeared suddenly and in its place was a rising, slightly uneasy tension that was rapidly turning her stomach upside down. She sank down into the sofa. Julian left the room. She could hear him opening cupboards in the adjacent kitchen, the clink of wine glasses and the soft, welcome sound of a cork being eased gently out of a bottle.

'Domaîne du Castel,' he said, coming back into the room. 'From the Judean Hills, not far from where we were today. When in Rome and all that.' He put the tray down in front of them, smiling slightly. 'Cheers. God, I'm suddenly nervous.'

It was on the tip of Rebecca's tongue to say something arch, but there was a gravity in Julian's voice that prevented it. Instead she said simply, 'Me, too,' and the trite phrase was enough to relax them both. He took her hand and brought it to his lips. She wasn't familiar with the old-fashioned gesture and she turned her body towards him, laying its caress along his side. His hand lifted the heavy thickness of her hair, touching her neck gently in a way that sent a shiver straight through her. For a long time he stroked her hair whilst she waited for the next move, and he waited to speak.

'Rebecca.'

'What?' she whispered, still waiting for the next, well-known moves. He suddenly seemed very far away from her, disappearing into a memory to which she wasn't privy, or shouldn't be. She put up a hand to touch him, feeling the wonderful shock of a burning warmth of flesh that wasn't her own. She pushed her face into the hot sweet darkness of the space between his chin and shoulder. A night of her own inside that scented corner. She sank pleasurably into him, feeling his arm tighten around her. For the second time that day, his lips found hers. His free hand slipped into the opening made by her jacket, finding the thin silk of her blouse and, beneath it, the lace of her bra. His touch was both electric and soothing at the same time. She pushed herself against him, unable to believe that she'd roused such passion in him, in anyone. He kissed her again and again, murmuring her name beneath his breath. He opened his eyes dazedly, narrowing them as he searched her face, then moved his body so that she was lying underneath him, pinned against the starched linen of the cushions, her arms encircling him as though she would never let go. She was shocked at the ferocity of her own longing, and the shock was physical. She'd never been the one to take the initiative – now she pulled at his jacket and shirt like someone possessed. She was prepared for the strong, sure side of him that had been all she'd seen of him until now; what caught her off-guard was the tender, soft part of him that he kept tightly under wraps. There was a scar that ran from his navel to just before the groin, which she felt with her fingers. 'What's that?' she whispered lightly, her breath warm and fuzzy against his ear.

'Appendix,' he murmured, taking hold of her fingers and pressing them gently against it. 'When I was eighteen. Just before the army.'

Again his words sent an afterglow of delight rippling through her. There was the same blast of tender wonderment that she'd felt with Jeremy Garrick but, unlike Jeremy, Julian's hurt presented itself to her as something to be healed, not held against her. Time slowed to almost a standstill as he pulled away the last scraps of her clothing, tugging at her stockings the way a man does, impatiently, almost irritably. At last she was completely naked underneath him and there was no shame, no embarrassment, no awkwardness – it was as if everything that had happened between them in the past few weeks had simply been the prelude to this moment, the moment of entry.

Agonisingly slowly, deliciously, he pushed his way into her, eyes wide open and fixed on hers throughout. She was the one to close hers, as if the sight of his face, screwed up in a concentration that was so unlike his habitual, calm expression, was something she couldn't possibly bear. He was a skilful, thoughtful lover, better than anyone she'd known. He took his time, patiently waiting for her own sweet surge of release to coincide with his. He kissed her slowly. 'Marry me,' he whispered against her mouth in the last few seconds of conscious, rational thought. She thought for a moment she'd misheard him. 'Marry me,' he whispered again, just before the familiar tender explosion overtook them both. 'Marry me.'

51

TASH
London, UK

The screen flickered dully as Tash scrolled up and down, stopping every once in a while to check a figure more closely or read through a paragraph with greater attention. She looked up at the clock – it was nearly two in the morning. She'd been working for almost eight hours straight. She'd arrived home at five, made herself a cup of tea and immediately sat down at her desk. She had a meeting at eight the following morning, not that she cared. She couldn't have stopped herself if she'd tried. Her brain was on fire. Ever since her encounter with Edith's client, Clare, an idea had slowly been forming in her mind, taking shape, solidifying, gaining definition. She clicked onto another link and the text immediately scrolled up.

> *Online shopping is the relatively new process whereby consumers directly buy goods or services from a seller in real-time, without an intermediary service, over the internet. It is a form of electronic commerce. An online shop, e-shop, e-store, internet shop, web-shop, webstore, online store, or virtual store evokes the physical analogy of buying products or services at a bricks-and-mortar retailer or in a shopping centre. The process is called Business-to-Consumer (B2C) online shopping. When a business buys from another business it is called Business-to-Business (B2B) online shopping. In order to shop online, one must be able to have access to a computer as well as a credit card or debit card.*

She flicked through the rest of the article until she found the magic word. *Amazon.* She opened the link and began reading. Half an hour later, she pushed back her chair from her desk, lifted her arms above her head and stretched. Her heart was beating fast. She thought back to the conversation between Clare and Edith earlier that day. What Clare wanted, in essence, was a fashionista's equivalent of Amazon.

She got up and walked across the living room to the window, grabbing a pack of cigarettes en route. She pushed open the window, perched herself rather awkwardly on the ledge and lit up. The sounds of the street below drifted up to meet her. It was nearly three in the morning but Marchmont Street never slept, least of all now. From across the way came the stuttering stop-and-start of a lorry, off-loading deliveries to the dozens of small grocery shops that ran up and down the street. A street sweeper droned by, its bristles whooshing along the pavement as it swept debris up into its soft, hairy mouth. She let herself drift with the cigarette smoke for a moment, watching it curl, thick and white, around her fingers. She smoked quietly, her mind running ahead of her. An online shop selling the latest, up-to-the-minute trends in clothes, shoes, accessories. A place where women could browse at their leisure, from their desks at work, in the study, at the kitchen table. All you'd need was a computer and an internet connection. An online version of Eden's, but much bigger, better, edgier. Luxury fashion delivered straight to your door. She could almost picture the boxes – black-and-white striped boxes with different coloured ribbons – pink for lingerie, red for haute couture, green for daywear, white for formal. What would she call it? There was only one choice – www.F@shion.com.

She stubbed out her cigarette and hurriedly closed the window. She only had a few hours left before she had to get up for work again and there was still so much to be done.

52

A MONTH LATER

'So what's your question?' James stirred his coffee and looked at her with a puzzled frown on his face.

'D'you think it will work?' Tash bit her lip nervously. James McBride was an old friend from university days who now practically ran the IT department at UCL single-handedly. Tash hadn't kept in touch with many people from her days at LSE but James, oddly and fortunately enough, she still saw.

'Work? Technically, you mean? Of course it'll work. That's the easy bit,' James scoffed.

'You're sure?'

'Tash, it's not rocket science. There are literally thousands of online shops already.'

'But . . . ?'

He took a sip of his cappuccino, leaving a faint frothy moustache above his upper lip, and shook his head. 'I just don't think anyone's going to buy luxury items online, that's all. Especially not clothes. I don't know much about women's fashion, granted, but I can't imagine anyone wanting to buy Yves Saint Laurent and doing it online. Women like that go to Paris, Tash, not to their laptops.'

'I'm not sure,' Tash said slowly, stirring her own coffee. She looked at her watch. 'Anyhow, that's really all I wanted to know for now. *If* it'll work.'

'Yeah, the technical bit's the easy part. Whose idea is this, anyway?'

Tash shrugged. 'Oh, just something I was thinking about. Research . . . for my boss. Anyhow, thanks for the chat, James. If I need any more advice, can I ring you?'

'Sure. Any time.'

Tash slipped off her stool. She pulled a fiver from her purse and laid it on the table. 'I've got to run,' she said, picking up her bag. 'Thanks again. It's on her,' she added. 'My boss.'

'Oh, in that case . . . I'll have a croissant as well,' James grinned at her.

'Don't push it. See you,' Tash wriggled her fingers at him and disappeared through the doors.

'Are you *quite* with us, Tash?' Rosie's voice was laced with frost. Tash looked up. Six pairs of impatient-looking eyes were aimed straight at her. She'd been elsewhere, of course.

'S-sorry,' she stammered, feeling as though she were back in school again. 'I . . . I was just thinking.'

'Clearly, but not about *this*.' Rosie stabbed the layout in front of her. 'This has to be signed off today. *Today*,' she hissed. 'Not tomorrow, or next week, or, at the rate you lot are going, next *month*. I'm sick and—' she stopped suddenly. 'Where the hell d'you think *you*'re going, Tash? I haven't finished—'

'*I* have.' Tash ignored the six pairs of eyes that swivelled round to her, wide as proverbial saucers. No one – *no one* – ever interrupted Rosie mid-sentence. Something inside her head just snapped. Tash picked up her handbag and notepad. Her hands were shaking but she hoped no one would notice.

'What the—?'

'Tash,' Michelle hissed urgently. 'Sit down.'

'Sorry, chaps.' She took one last look at her five colleagues, grown women all, reduced to schoolgirls in Rosie's presence and, as calmly as she could, walked out the door.

'You did *what*?' Lyudmila looked at her as though she'd just grown two heads. Or lost her mind. 'You quit job? They fire you?'

'No, Ma,' Tash sighed. 'She didn't *fire* me. I told you, I quit.'

Lyudmila's mouth hung open. 'Why?' she said finally. 'How you can quit job?'

'Easy. I walked out.' She knew exactly what Lyudmila was thinking. It had been over ten years since the last cheque from Mortimer & McKenzie's and probably five since the last of her regular gentleman callers had called on anything other than a sporadic basis. Although she'd clung onto her figure and looks as though her life depended on it (which, Tash thought to herself rather bitterly, it did), the sad truth was that the men who'd thought nothing of casually dropping a couple of hundred pounds into her lap whenever she asked for it, no longer did. It was Tash who paid the rent, bought food, made sure that her council tax and her TV licence were up to date. Lyudmila still somehow managed to squeeze something out of the few men who still dropped in on her to buy the odd pair of shoes but it had been a long time since she'd visited the shops along Brompton Road that had once been her regular haunts. Fortunately, she'd been in the basement flat for so long she was now regarded as a sitting tenant, otherwise Tash would never have managed to look after them both on her ridiculously small salary. And that, she thought to herself bitterly, was yet another reason to quit. Rosie seemed to think working at *Style* was quite enough remuneration on its own, thank you very much. 'Thousands would kill for this job,' was a constant refrain. Yes, there was the bonus of free clothes every once in a while and a trip to Paris or Milan, but the clothes looked ridiculous on Tash anyway and how many Fendi handbags could a girl reasonably have? You couldn't *eat* a handbag, though Lyudmila often looked as though she'd tried.

'What you gonna do?' Lyudmila got up from her chair and walked to the sideboard. She quickly mixed herself up a stiff gin and tonic.

'I . . . I've got an idea,' Tash said hesitantly.

Lyudmila spun around. 'Idea? *Idea?* What idea?'

'I don't want to talk about it yet,' Tash said firmly. 'Not until I've thought it through.'

'And what we gonna eat while you *think it through*?' Lyudmila's tone was derisive. She took a long, deep slug of her drink.

Tash sighed. 'Ma, it's my life, okay? I couldn't take it anymore, that's all. She was driving me crazy.'

'Yes, is your life,' Lyudmila muttered dourly. She took another slug and turned to Tash. There was real fear in her eyes. 'You better get new job,' Lyudmila said calmly but her hands betrayed her. They were shaking as she gripped her glass. 'You better find job today.'

Tash turned away. The bravado that had swept over her that morning had completely drained away. Something flowed over her now – a memory so faint and fleeting she had difficulty grabbing hold of it. She'd been walking with her mother somewhere . . . somewhere in the well-heeled streets around them, holding onto Lyudmila's hand, looking up and straight into those elegant, first-floor living rooms whose windows were always wide open, inviting glances and sometimes frank, open stares. There was one – on Onslow Gardens, not far from them – she remembered it still. A white stuccoed and porticoed house. The wooden shutters were peeled back and a woman stood in the window, framed by an enormous glass bowl of lilies on one side and a plant of some description on the other. She'd watched Lyudmila and Tash walk slowly past, Tash turning her head as she went by, looking longingly past the woman to the richly decorated room beyond. Lyudmila had stopped to light a cigarette or something; Tash stood patiently beside her, her hand tucked into the crook of Lyudmila's elbow. She smiled at the woman in the window. There was something so warm and friendly and inviting about her, though she couldn't have said what. How old was she? Five? Six? Suddenly the woman's hand went up in a wave. She leant down quickly and drew up the window. She was wearing a pale pink cardigan and Tash remembered it slipped off her bare, tanned shoulders. 'Wait,' the woman called out to them. 'Wait a moment.'

Lyudmila's hand, on its way to her mouth with her lit cigarette, paused. She looked down at Tash in surprise. '*Vy znaete, etu zhenshchinu*? Do you know that woman?'

'*Nyet*,' Tash whispered. Something was going to happen; she could feel her skin begin to prickle uncomfortably.

The woman came running down the short flight of steps. She was holding something in her hand. A plate. A plate of scones, or biscuits. What happened next was still confusing, even after all those years. There was an exchange of words, a shout, and then Lyudmila's hand flew up. The scones flew into the air, tumbling and breaking apart as they hit the ground. There was a lot of shouting, mostly by Lyud-mila . . . Tash looked at the ground. Lyudmila grabbed her by the arm, so hard that it hurt, and, hurling abuse at the woman in Russian, dragged her away. At the last minute, Tash turned her head to look back. The woman was kneeling on the ground, picking up the pieces of the broken plate. She got up stiffly and the last thing Tash saw was her elegant heels, scuffling quickly from side to side, pushing the small, fluffy pieces of scone that had fallen, to one side, under the hedge, out of sight.

Charity. That was the last time she'd seen fear on Lyudmila's face. She saw it now. She picked up her bag and quickly left the flat.

53

ANNICK
Paris

'*Bonsoir.*' She looked up from her book. A man was standing in front of her, wearing a suit, unusual in the hotel's run-of-the-mill clientele.

'*Bonsoir,*' she said dully. 'Rates are on the board behind me.'

There was some sort of commotion in the far corner of the lobby where there was a bench and a small coffee table, though neither was ever used. She glanced past him to a couple seated on the bench, so close the girl was practically in the man's lap. A big man, with a broad, fleshy chest and a dark, shiny face. The girl had on a red wig and a skirt so short it barely covered her backside. 'What's your best room?' asked the suited man in front of her. Annick dragged her eyes back to him.

'The best?' It wasn't a question she was often asked. 'Well, the rooms on the third floor all have en suite bathrooms. I could give you one of those. They're a bit more expensive, though.'

He glanced at the board behind her head and peeled off a large wad of notes. 'Three . . . four . . . five. There. That should cover it.' She looked past him again. The big man was angled away from her; she could only see the back of his head and the broad expanse of his shoulders, tightly encased in a dark blue blazer. Fascinatedly, she watched as the girl lazily tickled the rolls of fat around his neck with long, pink-painted finger-nails.

'Cover it?' she repeated, confused. He'd put down five hundred euros in neat, clean notes on the countertop in front of her.

'Yes. We'll take all four rooms on the third floor. Please don't allow anyone up. Not whilst he's there.' He jerked his head backwards, indicating the man and his painted, child-like companion. 'I'm assuming there's no one there just now?' He looked past her to the rows of keys.

She nodded, and then shook her head. She was confused. His French was flawless, his manner impeccably polite – he definitely wasn't the sort of customer she met on a daily basis. 'No, yes . . . no, I mean. There's no one there.' She quickly reached behind her and pulled off all four sets of keys, laying them out in front of her.

'We'll take this one.' He picked up the key to Room 313 and turned. 'Sir,' he called out. 'It's ready.' The girl turned her head slowly, flickered a lizard-like glance over him, and then turned it back slowly. Annick watched, fascinated, as she licked the big man's tiny ear, whispering something to him, and threw her head back, laughing, laughing. The sound of laughter was incongruous in the darkened lobby.

'I'm busy, can't you see?' the big man laughed, a deep, sonorous rumbling that fought its way out of his stomach. Finally he lumbered to his feet, pulling the girl along with him. The girl carefully put her high-heeled feet down, one in front of the other. The man followed her, his eyes glued to her small, high backside, gazing blankly in the way men looked at women they'd paid for, no thought at all in their faces other than the thought of what lay ahead. The lift doors closed and suddenly, abruptly, there was silence in the lobby.

'I'll just take a seat over there.' The suited man pulled a book out of his jacket pocket and walked to the bench his boss had just evacuated.

Annick nodded but didn't say anything. After working at the front desk for so long, nothing shocked her anymore; she'd seen it all. Although, she thought to herself quickly as the man sat down and flipped open his book, she'd never seen a bodyguard who read Jean Genet. *Journal du Voleur.* Her eyes widened. She'd read it once, a long time ago. She looked down at her own book. It was a cheap American thriller of the sort she'd never even glanced at until she started working at the hotel. Those books passed the night like no other – page after page, murder after murder, clue after clue . . . all the way to the happy-ever-after. It was a lie, of course. There was no happy-ever-after. Only in cheap American thrillers.

'It's good?'

His voice startled her. She hadn't even heard him get up. She made a quick gesture with her hand as though to hide it from him. 'Er, yes. No, not really. It . . . it passes the time.'

He looked at her curiously for a moment but before she could say anything, his mobile rang. He turned away momentarily. There was a hurried conversation in a language she couldn't quite catch, then he shoved it back in his pocket. He turned back to her, gesturing towards the lift. 'Does it work?' He seemed in a hurry. She looked up. It was stuck on the fourth floor, a common occurrence.

'It's stuck,' she said, lifting her shoulders. 'It happens every night.'

He looked at it; then, with a sound that she hadn't heard in a long time, he sucked his teeth together, a sound of impatience, irritation . . . a sound only Africans or West Indians make. Her father used to make that very same sound, she thought to herself in surprise. She looked up but he'd already pushed open the fire-escape door. He disappeared; she could hear him running up the stairs. She stared at the empty, swinging door. Unexpected tears prickled behind her eyes. Who was he? It made no difference. It was unlikely she'd ever see him again.

But she did. '*Bonsoir.*' She looked up. A red, watery light from the neon sign opposite lit the interior of the lobby.

'Oh, it's you.' She felt her face grow warm. Other than the few people she worked with, she rarely spoke to anyone.

He smiled, his white, even teeth startling in the dark, smooth face. '*Oh, it's you,*' he mimicked, but teasingly, not unkindly. 'It's Yves, actually. What's your name?'

She was so taken aback she had no idea what to say. 'I . . . my name? An . . . Annick,' she stammered.

'Nice to meet you, Annick,' he said, still smiling. He held out a hand. There was a moment's awkward confusion, then she took it. His grip was warm and firm. 'How long have you been working here, Annick?' he asked pleasantly.

The question threw her. They'd barely spoken three words to each other but it was already more than she could handle. 'I . . . we . . . we're not really supposed to talk to guests,' she said finally. She didn't know how else to end the conversation. She just wasn't used to making conversation with anyone, let alone a handsome stranger. And he *was* handsome, she'd noticed.

'I'm hardly a guest. But it's fine.' He held up his hands in mock defeat. 'If you'd rather I left you alone . . . ?'

'I . . . it's not that. It's just . . . where's your boss?' she asked, unable to think of anything else to say.

'He stopped off en route,' he smiled. 'He'll be here soon enough.'

'Who is he?'

He looked away. 'Just a businessman. No one you'd know.'

'Are you his bodyguard?'

He smiled. 'Sometimes. Most of the time I'm a student.'

'A student?' She couldn't keep the surprise from her voice. He looked too old to be a student.

'A late bloomer,' he grinned, reading her mind. 'No, actually, I'm doing my doctorate. It's just taken longer than I thought.'

'Oh. What are you studying?'

He grinned at her as if to say, *But I thought you weren't encouraged to talk to guests?* 'Engineering.'

'An engineer who reads Genet?' She couldn't help herself.

'Engineers read all sorts of things,' he said mildly. 'Even American thrillers.'

She blushed and looked down at her hands. She who had once been the class flirt couldn't handle a simple conversation. 'Well, I'd . . . I'd better get back to work,' she said eventually.

He raised an eyebrow but said nothing. He put down the money – in cash again – and picked up the keys to Room 313. He gave her a quick two-fingers-pressed-against-his-temple salute and walked back to his bench. A second later, his mobile rang. His boss was clearly on his way. A few minutes later, a second bodyguard pushed open the door and shadowed him in. As ever, he was accompanied by a young, heavily made-up girl whose arms were entwined around his thick fleshy neck as he lumbered into the lift. Annick watched the doors close slowly behind them. The girl was busy pressing herself against his bulk; he paid no more attention to her than he would a buzzing fly.

Less than an hour later, they were gone.

The rest of the night passed without incident. Customers straggled in and out: men in cheap, badly fitting suits, girls – young, old, haggard, innocent-looking – trotting obediently after them. She'd seen it all before. Occasionally, one of the people who more or less lived in the hotel permanently came in, smiled at her briefly and disappeared. Why would anyone choose to live here? she often thought to herself. There was one elderly woman who'd been at the hotel for almost a year, with whom Annick felt a strange, secret affinity. She'd given her name as Madame C. D. de Férrier-Messrine, and although it was true there was something faintly aristocratic about her bearing and her speech, it was clear that she'd fallen on hard times. Annick knew from the gossip she overheard when the cleaners exchanged shifts that the woman practised a frugality that would have made the social services cry 'famine!'. She ate nothing but boiled rice. The chambermaids brought back the empty packets without a word. She was very thin, always dressed in black with one ornate piece of jewellery, a gold bracelet that hung off her bird-like arm, coins and medallions clanking every time she moved. She always said a polite, gravelly 'good morning' to Annick when she came upon her early in the morning. Where did she go, Annick wondered, at seven a.m? Once or twice she'd caught Annick coming out of the bakery opposite, her arms full of crusty batons of freshly baked bread and sometimes a bag of croissants, still oozing butter through their paper skin. They'd flashed each other a quick, guilty look of complicity but nothing was ever said. They both harboured secrets; that was enough.

At seven on the dot, she picked up her book, bag and coat and got ready to leave. Wasis, a sour-looking, taciturn man from Chad or Mali or Burkina Faso, depending on who was asking, took over. '*Tout va bien?*' he asked in his gruff, staccato French.

She shook her head. 'No, no problems.'

'*D'accord. Bonne journée.*'

'*Toi aussi,*' Annick replied automatically and pushed open the door. It was cold outside; a nippy, chilly wind blew around her ears and ankles, the only parts of her that were exposed. She pulled her scarf up more firmly, settling her neck into her collar and shoving her hands in her pockets. She had no gloves; maybe next month. Her salary covered the absolute basics – rent, bills, food – and precious little else. She walked to and from work every day to save on transport and once a month she took the train to visit her aunt. That was it. She'd never had the dubious advantage of knowing how to live on very little. Most of her life had been spent cossetted in the kind of luxury that seemed unending. Not once had she even had to worry or even enquire about the price of food, the cost of transport, or the tariffs on gas. She'd never owed anyone money, or asked for an advance against earnings to come. In Paris, she'd learned quickly. She had to. After those first few months, she wised up. She took her weekly pay, deducted her rent and bills and put the remainder in one of the kitchen drawers. Everything came out of that drawer – food, the odd bus ticket, the odd book, a scarf, and even, once, a lipstick . . . not that she had any use for it. She'd seen the shade in the window of one of the small pharmacies that lined her route to work. *Rouge Allure. Impertinente. Chanel.* She stopped and put a hand to her mouth. Her mother had worn the very same shade. Annick lost count of the number of sleek, shiny black tubes she'd pilfered from the bathrooms in the Paris apartment, or the enormous, marble-floored bathroom at the palace in Lomé. Where were all those tubes now? She pushed open the door, hearing the familiar, two-tone chime coming at her as if from a great, great distance and handed over the last few euros in her purse.

For a week she ate nothing but *ficelles* and drank water from the tap but it was worth it. The tube sat unopened, month after month, the only item of luxury in the tiny flat six floors above a butcher's and a baker's, between them home to at least a dozen rats. She knew – at night she could hear them scrabbling around in the rafters.

She walked up Boulevard Barbès and, at Marcadet-Poissoniers, crossed the busy intersection into Boulevard Ornano. The rows of small shops sold everything from fake hair and the sorts of vegetables one would more readily expect to see on the streets of Algiers and Tunis and Lomé and Dakar than Paris, to cartons of dinner plates at knock-down prices. There were always sales on in La Goutte d'Or, the neighbourhood she now called home. It was another Paris. Dim, dank stairwells that opened out onto the view of the white onion-domes of Sacré-Cœur, tiny, bent balconies over which housewives hung brilliantly coloured rugs out to air; people swirled in and out of shops displaying rows of bright, sticky-sweet pastries with signs scrawled in flowery, Arabic script. She walked past the bakery where she often stopped, past the Métro stop at Simplon, down rue Neuve de la Chardonnière . . . *Le Bar Yemen. Coiffeurs Hommes. Bar Taba.* She walked on, blindly.

At the bottom of the road, just before rue de Roi d'Algers, she stopped suddenly. There was a hairdresser on the corner, next door to La Semeuse, a restaurant and bar that appeared to be housed in some-one's sitting room. She peered through the light-blue curtains. Inside were half a dozen women, sitting in mismatched chairs, reading magazines, laughing and talking – there was even one smoking a cigarette. She hadn't been to a hairdresser for three years; it too seemed to belong to another life. But there was a fifty-euro note tucked into the lining of her purse – an unexpected gift from Aunt Libertine the last time she'd visited. She caught sight of herself, a large, bulky object, muffled up against the cold with no discernible sign of anything remotely feminine, or, God forbid, attractive. Her hair, which had once been her pride and glory, was perpetually scraped back into an untidy bun. She'd been trimming the ends herself ever since she'd arrived in Paris and she couldn't remember the last time she'd worn it loose outside of the anonymity of her own bed.

She pushed open the door without thinking. The chemical garden-sweetness of the salon hit her like a slap. Several of the women looked up but there was only warmth in their faces. '*Salut chérie, besoin d'aide?* The woman who was standing in the corner, smoking and supervising, looked up with a smile.

'I . . . I was just wondering . . . I wanted to . . . how much is a cut and wash?'

'For you, *ma belle, c'est pas cher*. Come in, come in.' She beckoned to Annick to come forward. 'Have a seat, *ma belle. Tu veux boire quelque chose? Un café?*'

Annick's eyes prickled. 'Yes,' she nodded quickly. '*Un café.*'

'*Ouh la la . . . regarde ça!*' The woman expertly unpinned Annick's bun and her hair tumbled over her shoulders. The other women looked over enviously. All were paying for their hair to be straightened, teased, primped and tamed – Annick's thick, curly locks were the envy of all. 'You are a *métisse, non?*' The woman asked her, but again there wasn't a shred of hostility in her voice. 'Lucky you. She got the good hair, *non?*' she asked the others and there was a general, laughing murmur of assent. 'So, *ma biche*, where are you from? *Tes parents, je veux dire. Des Antilles?*'

Annick shook her head. She hesitated. 'My father is – was – Togolese. My mother was French.'

'Was? *Ils sont mort?*' the woman asked, parting the thick brown curls and inspecting the ends. 'When did you last cut your hair, *ma belle?*' she went on, without waiting for an answer.

The two questions carried the same weight. 'A long time ago. My hair? I . . . I can't remember . . . two, three years ago, maybe?'

'Three years?' The woman gave a mock scream. 'No wonder you walked in here today. *D'accord*. Sophie . . . take the *jeune mademoiselle* to the sink by the window, yes, that one . . . give her scalp a good massage. *Three years . . . mon Dieu.* So you're an orphan, like Arlène here.

Dommage, non? Bon, Sophie is going to wash your hair and then I'm going to cut it myself, *personellement*. Three years?' She turned away, shaking her head in disbelief.

'*Togolaise?*' One of the women, whose head was buried under the second, steel crania of the dryer, craned her neck to take a look at Annick. 'You're very *clair*,' she said, noting Annick's pale skin colour. '*Très clair*. Whereabouts in Togo are you from?'

'I . . . I've never been to Togo,' Annick said quickly. 'I was brought up here.'

'Ah.' She seemed satisfied by the response.

'Just as well,' someone else piped up. 'Terrible what's happening there. Ter-rible.'

The women began to talk amongst themselves again as Annick was led to the basin by the window. She listened, fascinated. They were from all over the African diaspora – Sénégal, Congo, Rwanda . . . Martinique, Guadaloupe, Toronto. There were a dozen women in Céleste's living room, which, as Annick had correctly surmised, doubled as her salon. They were all friends, or customers who'd been coming to her for so long they'd become friends. It was light-years away from the salon on the King's Road that she'd gone to ever since her mother had taken her there at the age of eight, but there was a familiarity in the togetherness of the women – of all ages, all complexions – that soothed her instantly. They reminded her of her grandmother's house in Lomé where the women of the Betancourt family met at family occasions – the births, deaths and funerals that were their rites of passage, a kind of female freemasonry that, even though she was too young to take part in it, she'd been given to understand would one day be hers, too.

She closed her eyes as the girl's fingers deftly massaged her scalp. It was practically the first time someone had touched her in months, perhaps even years. In the warm, chemical fuzz of the dryers and steamers around the living room, she was suddenly eight or nine years old again. Her mother sat in the salon with her fingernails steeping in oil, her hair hidden under a rubber cap with holes in it, the hairdresser pulling through strands with a crochet hook to tint it. She'd be given money – a few pence, if they were in London, a franc or two if in Paris – to go out and buy sweets for herself. 'Not too many, *chérie*,' Anouschka would call out anxiously. 'Just one or two.' She would trip back happily, a lollipop or some such in her hand, whispering to herself with the curled contentment of a kitten.

'*Viens*.' The girl squeezed the last drops of water out of her hair and beckoned to Annick. She got up with some difficulty – the chairs were small and narrow – and shuffled with the towel draped across her shoulders to the mirror where Celeste was waiting, smiling beatifically.

'Just a little trim, *non*? With curls like yours, it'd be a crime to cut them off. Just enough for it to grow again, *c'est tout*.'

Annick closed her eyes. She didn't want to see the image of herself staring back at her, her once-beautiful face now fat, swollen out of all recognition. What was it that had sparked the desire to get her hair cut? She shifted uncomfortably in her seat. She didn't like to admit it, but the conversation with Yves, brief as it was, had catapulted her back in time to her old self, to the Annick who deflected men's attention the way some people swatted flies. She wasn't that person any longer but the longing for her remained.

54

REBECCA
London

For once, the weather had decided to cooperate. It was a beautiful early summer's day – fresh and crisp, a cloudless, blue sky with no threat of rain. At Harburg Hall, everything was in full swing. A marquee had been set up on the lawn behind the house. White, with stiff, peaked folds, its edges had been artfully scalloped with enormous bunches of white and pink roses; there were garlands of pink gerberas and rosy carnations, palm fronds and in the centre of the garden, the *chuppah*, the traditional Jewish canopy where the rabbi would bless the union. From her bedroom window overlooking the gardens, Rebecca watched the teams of waiters streaming back and forth, carrying glasses, champagne crates, wine bottles, more flowers . . . she could see her mother calling out to one of the wedding organisers, a formidably efficient woman called Ruth. The two women huddled together, consulting a list in Embeth's hands . . . probably working out some last-minute relative who'd ignored their repeated RSVPs and who'd just now phoned from Heathrow, demanding to know why a car hadn't been laid on.

She turned away from the window and walked over to her dressing table. For the first time in weeks, she was completely alone. She savoured the silence. She sat down, taking care not to crease her dress. It was a pale ecru silk dress, very simple, gathered in tightly at the waist and falling in stiff, billowing folds to the floor. Her mother had chosen it – a modern version, she said, of her own wedding dress. She looked at herself in the mirror. She put out a hand to touch her image dreamily. It was her wedding day. The day of her marriage. When she'd told her mother of Julian's proposal, Embeth's eyes had immediately welled up. She'd put out a hand and covered Rebecca's in a gesture that was both blessing and relief. Julian was hardly part of the inner circle of Harburgs but there was the sense that Rebecca was being passed from one pair of safe hands to another. She'd never thought of her own family as a tribe; now she saw that they were, and that for all their warmth and openness, they guarded themselves against outsiders through the very same codes and values with which they welcomed others in. *A safe pair of hands*. She felt the presence of her family behind her, a solid, breathing, living presence. She caught sight of her face. She'd been frowning, her forehead marked by a single, deep crease, as though she were struggling to grab hold of something. 'It's your wedding day,' she whispered to her own image. 'Your *wedding* day.'

She stood up, flattening the folds of her dress with the palms of her hands. Her dark hair was swept up off her face in a loose chignon, with a few curly tendrils escaping to frame and soften the look. Her mother had given her the most exquisite headband of tiny silk roses to wear. She picked it up just as the door opened and her cousin Rachel walked in, followed closely by Tash. They both stopped; Tash gave out one of her customary low wolf-whistles. 'Don't make me cry, please,' Rebecca begged, half-laughing, half-crying. 'I've just had my make-up done.'

'I've been crying all bloody morning,' Tash announced, throwing herself on the sofa beside the window. 'Let someone else take over. I don't *care* if you're the bride.'

'Don't, it's bad luck,' Cousin Rachel said primly. She sat down on the edge of the bed, carefully arranging her skirt around her. 'To cry on your wedding day,' she added, in case they'd missed the point.

'Fuck it. It's *your* party,' Tash grinned.

'And you shouldn't swear, either.'

'All the time, you mean? Or just on one's wedding day?'

Rebecca threw Tash a pleading glance. *Not today, darling.* 'Are all the guests here?' she asked quickly.

Rachel nodded. 'There's one more carload from the airport – Uncle

Morris, I think, and Aunt Ellie. Oh, and Adam's just arrived. He brought his fiancée. Have you seen her?'

Rebecca shook her head, aware that a faint blush had crept into her cheeks. Adam. Her teenage crush. It all seemed so long ago. 'Ready?' she asked lightly, turning for one last look at herself.

'Uh, give us a moment, Rachel,' Tash asked. 'Alone.'

'Why?'

'We won't be a minute,' Rebecca jumped in quickly. 'Be a darling and just let Mama know I'll be down in two ticks.'

'Okay. But only a minute,' Rachel said reluctantly. 'Everyone's waiting.'

'Jesus, she gets on my nerves,' Tash said, loudly enough for Rachel to hear as the door closed slowly behind her.

'Shh, I know, I know . . . but she's my *cousin.*'

'And I'm your best friend.'

'I . . . I wish . . . well, you know what I wish,' Rebecca said, bringing up a hand to her eyes again. 'I wish Annick could be here. Oh, shit, I promised I wouldn't cry.'

'And you're not going to.' Tash put her arms round her. 'It's your wedding day, Rebecca. I can't *believe* you're fucking getting married.'

'Don't swear,' Rebecca said shakily.

'I know. It's not nice.'

'Is your mum here?'

Tash nodded, pulling a face. 'Unfortunately. Had to persuade her *not* to wear white. You know what's she like . . . she'd have upstaged everyone. Right, are you ready?'

Rebecca took a deep breath. 'Yes. Yes, I suppose I am.'

'Come on, then. It's time to get you married.'

She circled Julian carefully for the seventh and last time. Out of the corner of her eye, she could see her mother dabbing at her eyes and her father's broad smile. The rabbi carefully laid the cloth-covered glasses on the ground and Julian raised his right foot. There was a moment's hush, everyone held their breath, then he stamped, breaking them loudly, and the garden behind them erupted in cheers. Embeth was crying openly now; even her father was fumbling for a handkerchief. She felt Julian's arm on her waist and turned her face up towards his. His eyes were the deepest shade of blue she'd ever seen. She felt his lips against hers and the pressure of his hand at her back.

'*Mazel tov!*' someone shouted behind them. There were answering cheers; people clapped. Blushing and smiling, Rebecca was turned around to face the crowd. The waiters in their smart black and white jackets were standing by, trays of champagne in hand, canapés ready . . . the celebrations were about to begin. There would be speeches and a few tears, lots of laughter and smiles and congratulations all round. Some of Julian's colleagues had come over from Paris and they stood around in small groups. One or two of them had come with their wives or partners. These women, in their late thirties and early forties and contemporaries of Julian's, regarded her warily, their expressions revealing what their words couldn't. *So young. And a Harburg, too.* The Lovells were hardly third-rate relations, but there was no denying Julian had made himself a good match – a *very* good match. Julian was a safe choice for a young girl like her. Lovely man. A safe pair of hands. Rebecca could read their faces as if they'd spoken aloud.

55

TASH

It was hard not to be jealous and she hated herself for it. Rebecca deserved every ounce of her happiness. And she *was* happy. You only had to look at her to see it. She was glowing with the sort of happiness that gave rise to pop songs and Hallmark cards. Tash tried to imagine what it must be like to have someone interested enough in you to want to spend the next few weeks together, never mind the rest of your life. She couldn't. The memory of the one and only time she'd ever felt the force of someone else's passion – Sylvan Betancourt, Annick's father's – was mingled with such shame and guilt and try as she might, every time she thought about a man kissing her, wanting to be near, his body anywhere close to hers, her whole body burned with embarrassment. No one had ever looked at her the way Julian gazed at Rebecca. Once, a while back, one of the sub-editors at *Style* had rather clumsily asked her out. Tim. Tim Collier. Nice enough, in a harmless, unthreatening sort of way. They'd worked together for a few weeks on some inane article about Britain's most eligible bachelors. One night, a couple of days before deadline, they'd wound up in the office together until almost midnight, checking photo permissions. They got along fine; he was witty and droll and laughed when she said something funny . . . a friend, nothing more.

'So, who'd you pick, if you had to,' he asked, straightening up in his chair.

'Pick? What d'you mean?' She hadn't understood him at first.

'Of the bachelors.' He indicated the dummy sheet in front of them.

'Oh, I don't know . . . they all look the same to me,' she quipped.

'No, really. Which one's most like your boyfriend?'

'*My* boyfriend? Which boyfriend?' Tash was almost too surprised to speak. 'I haven't *got* a boyfriend.'

'No? How come?'

She stared at him. Was he blind? 'I . . . I haven't got the time,' she said brusquely. 'Too busy.'

'Too busy to enjoy yourself?' It was his turn to sound incredulous.

'Yes,' she snapped. 'Now, where are we with these? How many more to go?' She turned the conversation briskly back to work.

He looked at her queerly for a moment, then acquiesced. 'Couple more,' he said, bending his head back down to the photographs. 'Here . . . take a look at this. She's just out of focus . . . d'you think we'll need to clear it with her publicist?' He handed her a photograph. As she took it, their fingers touched for a second, his lingering a fraction longer than necessary. Tash jerked her hand away as though she'd been burned and got up quickly from her desk. She hurried to the bathroom and opened the window. Tim's comments and that odd little moment had set off an alarm in her that she couldn't quite control. She lit a cigarette and leaned out of the window, smoking furiously until her heartbeat had returned to normal. She was being ridiculous, she knew, but his unexpected interest had set off all sorts of alarm bells ringing deep inside her, and she had absolutely no idea why. Better to steer clear of him. He was nice enough, but clearly bonkers. Why would anyone be interested in *her*?

The next evening, as she was getting ready to leave the office, she found herself walking towards the lift with him.

'Doing anything special tonight?' he asked cheerfully as they fell in step.

Tash looked at him warily. Was he making fun of her now that he knew she didn't have a boyfriend? 'No,' she said quickly. 'Nothing special.'

'How about a drink, then?'

She opened her mouth in surprise. Now he really *was* making fun of her. The panic rose before she could suppress it. 'What? With *you*? No thanks,' she said swiftly. A terrible, painful confusion broke all over her like a sweat. She pushed the emergency exit door and let it slam behind her. She'd been rude, she knew, and cruel. She'd seen the look in his face as she'd said it but she just couldn't help herself. Better to knock him down than run the risk of humiliation. With *you*? She'd hurt him, she knew she had. *Jesus Christ*, she muttered furiously to herself as she clattered down the stairs. *What's wrong with you? He was only asking you for a drink!* She shoved down hard on the metal bar and pushed open the door, bursting out onto the street, embarrassed beyond belief.

'Don't you *dare* talk to me like that!' A woman's voice interrupted her thoughts. She turned, catching sight of a tall, leggy blonde, her beautiful face distorted with anger. She brushed past Tash and disappeared into the toilet, slamming the door behind her. Seconds later, the front door opened again and a man strode into the hallway. It was Adam, Rebecca's gorgeous cousin. He stopped and ran a hand through his hair, clearly annoyed. Then he caught sight of Tash and grinned. 'It's Tash, isn't it?'

'Yes, yes it is.' She was surprised he even knew who she was.

'You haven't got a light, by any chance, have you?' he asked, pulling a packet of Woodbines from his jacket pocket.

She nodded. 'Yeah. But I'm not sure we can smoke in here,' she said hesitantly.

'You're absolutely right. Join me outside?'

She was too surprised to do anything other than nod and follow him through the doors. 'Er, what about your girlfriend?' she asked, casting a backwards glance towards the toilet.

He shrugged. 'She'll calm down eventually. She always does.' He offered her a cigarette.

'What did you do, if you don't mind me asking?'

'More a case of what I *didn't* do. You know how it is. Didn't say she looked nice often enough. Didn't introduce her quickly enough. Didn't introduce her properly. Didn't, didn't, didn't . . . relationships are just one long string of "didn't"s, don't you find?'

'Wouldn't know,' Tash said cheerfully. She inhaled deeply. 'Never had one.' She blew the smoke carefully out of the corner of her mouth.

Adam looked down at her. There weren't many men who could look down at Tash. 'You're joking, aren't you?'

Tash shook her head. 'Nope.'

'How come?'

Tash shrugged. 'No reason in particular. Just never met anyone I—'

The door behind them opened suddenly. It was Adam's girlfriend. Her face was a mask of sulky beauty. 'I'm going home,' she said sulkily.

Adam swore softly under his breath, then glanced at Tash as if to say, *See what I mean?* 'You can't go home now,' he said patiently, as if explaining something to a child. 'There's dinner first, then the speeches.'

'I'm going home,' she repeated, though her voice wasn't quite as strident as it had been. She was weakening.

Tash dropped her cigarette, stubbing it out with her toe. It was clearly a ritual they'd been through many times before. She gave Adam a quick grin, and left them to it. He was right. A relationship? Who'd want one? Not her. *Liar*, a little voice inside her spoke up suddenly. *Liar.* She suppressed it and hurried over to find someone to talk to. The last thing she wanted was to be alone with *those* sorts of thoughts.

A few hours later, when the dancing inside the house was in full swing, she wandered outside for a quick cigarette and found herself in the company of a group of men, including Julian, Rebecca's new husband. She was suddenly shy; he smiled at her rather gravely. 'You're Tash, aren't you?' he asked curiously, breaking away from the group.

She nodded. 'Yes.' It was the second time someone had asked her that question.

'Well,' he looked down at his own wedding suit. 'You know who *I* am,' he said, and laughed.

She laughed with him. She felt curiously tongue-tied in his presence. 'Congratulations,' she said, not knowing what else to say.

He looked at her keenly. 'Thank you.' There was a slightly awkward pause. She was one of Rebecca's best friends and yet their wedding day was their first real encounter – there was an awkwardness there that neither could fully admit to. 'You're the entrepreneur,' he said, and again, it was more of a statement than a question. 'Rebecca's always talking about you. She's been telling me a little bit about your business idea.'

Tash blushed immediately. 'Oh . . . well, we've still got a long way to go,' she said quickly, wondering how much Rebecca had actually told him.

'Not much,' he said, reading her mind. 'But I'm intrigued. I'm an investor. I look for good ideas to invest in and this sounds interesting.

You should come and see me. In the office, I mean. Here . . . let me give you a card.' He slid a hand inside his jacket. 'Just give my secretary a call. We're in France next week but we're back at the weekend.'

Tash nodded. 'Th . . . thanks,' she said uncertainly. She liked the way he said it. *We're in France next week.* 'I'll give you a ring when you're back.' She saw Rebecca out of the corner of her eye, coming towards them. She was tipsy, Tash saw. The rosy colour was up in her cheeks and her eyes shone with warmth, in spite of the cold.

'So . . . you've met,' she laughed, slipping an arm around them both. 'Finally. It feels a bit strange, doesn't it?'

'Why's that, darling?' Julian looked at her indulgently.

'Here I am, getting married. No, I *am* married,' she corrected herself, giggling. 'And yet you've never met.'

'Well, we have now. And I've asked Tash to come and see me when we get back.' Julian put his arm round his wife.

'Oh?'

'Mmm. We've got business to talk about.' He winked at Tash and they turned to greet someone else.

The party sounds around her rose and fell, shattering lightly against the clear night sky. Tash turned, walked back towards the house. She pushed open the front door. There were a few people standing around in the vestibule; they looked up as she came through the door but she didn't stop to say hello. She wanted to be alone somewhere.

There was a small living room just off Rebecca's father's study. She tried the handle; the door swung open silently and she slipped in, shutting it quietly behind her. There was an open fire in the grate, sending out glowing streams of warm, coppery light. The door to the study was partly ajar but it was quiet inside the small living room. She looked around her. She'd always liked this room. Its dark wood-panelled walls held thousands of books, just like her father's private rooms up at Portmore. She stood in the doorway for a second, breathing deeply. There was an old, smoothly worn Chesterfield in front of the fire. She walked over to it, sinking gratefully into its soft, comfortable leather. She, Rebecca and Annick had spent many a night curled up on it when they were younger, playing cards, gossiping, escaping from the rest of the world, especially their respective families. There was a cosy warmth to the room, in spite of its sombre air. There was history here, and continuity, and the sense that one's own dramas, however threatening, couldn't possibly overturn the larger order of things to which the house and its wealth and history belonged.

She closed her eyes, breathing in deeply. As happy as she was for Rebecca, she'd found the day oddly overwhelming. Seeing Rebecca surrounded by literally dozens of close family members brought a keen sense of her own loneliness into sharp relief. If Tash were ever to get married – and the thought of it seemed about as remote a possibility as dying, or flying to the moon – who would come? Her mother, Rebecca, a handful of colleagues from work . . . that would be it. For all Rebecca's complaints about not doing anything with her life, she was *loved* and cherished in a way Tash would never be. She pressed the palms of her hands against her eyes. It wasn't a day to cry. Suddenly, she became aware of a low murmur coming from behind the half-closed door. She struggled upright. She wasn't alone.

'She'll find someone, don't worry.' It was Rebecca's mother, Embeth. 'It just takes time.'

'No. You don't know her.' Tash drew in a sharp breath. It was her mother's voice. Sulky, irritated. 'Tash very difficult. Not like *your* daughter.'

'Tash is a lovely girl,' Embeth said loyally. 'She's so *bright.*'

'What is point of brains?' Lyudmila said sulkily. 'Better she should be beautiful.' She sighed heavily. 'Is curse, you know. Having ugly daughter.'

'Tash isn't *ugly*, Lyudmila,' Embeth said gently. 'She's a lovely girl. She'll find someone, just be patient. Wait and see.'

'I wait how many years now? She never has boyfriend. Never.'

Tash was aware she was holding her breath. She exhaled slowly and stood up. Her whole body was flushed with anger – how *dare* her mother discuss her with Embeth Harburg? She crept across the carpet, shaking with rage. *Is curse having ugly daughter.* The words were like a slap in the face. Of course she knew her looks were a disappointment, and probably not just to her mother. She knew her colleagues at work sniggered behind her back about her hair and her teeth and the fact that she never, ever wore make-up. She was used to it. But hearing it stated so baldly and with such despair . . . she swallowed hard. She picked up her coat and bag and walked towards the main road. Let Lyudmila find her own fucking way home. She'd seen and heard enough.

56

EMBETH

She watched her own Bentley bearing Tash's mother pull slowly out of the driveway and breathed a sigh of relief. What an unbelievably disagreeable woman, she thought to herself, shutting the front door firmly behind her. Lyudmila had been one of the last guests to leave. It was well after midnight and she was exhausted. Rebecca and Julian had departed for the hotel where they were staying before going on to a fortnight's holiday at a beautiful villa at Le Dramont, near St Raphaël, her and Lionel's gift to the honeymooning couple.

Now, with the house slowly returning to itself after the excitement of the day, the staff still busy clearing the grounds and making sure their various guests were all comfortably accommodated, Embeth allowed herself the luxury of drawing breath. The entire day had gone off without a hitch. She switched off the lights in the study; Lionel had long since retired to the suite of rooms on the first floor. At ninety one, amazingly, he still had the curiosity and zest for life that had so attracted her all those years ago, but not the stamina to match. It was to be expected, of course. She'd never met anyone with as much energy. At an age where her own father had slowed to a near-halt, not moving from their Altamira home in Caracas, Lionel still went to the bank every day, still oversaw all the deals that the younger generation made . . . he could no more have stopped working than he'd have stopped breathing and there were times when Embeth feared that that was exactly how it would end – suddenly, in the middle of a telephone call or whilst chastising an employee. She was forever telling him to slow down, take things easy, think about retirement. *Retirement?* He'd looked at her as though she were mad. 'We're Jews, Embeth,' he said incredulously. 'What d'you expect me to do? Take up golf?'

She shook her head as she slowly made her way upstairs. Dear Lionel. It was sometimes hard to believe they'd been married for over forty years. She remembered their own wedding as though it had been yesterday. She, like Rebecca, a young bride marrying a man more than twenty years her senior. Had she done the right thing in marrying her off so soon, she wondered, thinking of the strange, unsettling conversation she'd had with Tash's mother, Lyudmila, concerned only with her daughter's looks – or lack thereof. She couldn't *imagine* talking about Rebecca in that way to anyone, let alone her best friend's mother. Neither could she understand Lyudmila's despair. Granted, Tash was no beauty queen but she was a bright, articulate and – from what Rebecca had told her – extremely ambitious young woman. Who cared whether or not she'd taken after her mother in the looks department. It had been on the tip of Embeth's tongue to say she hoped she'd inherited better manners than her mother but she'd stopped herself just in time.

She'd never cared for Lyudmila, to be honest. On the few occasions she'd met her over the years she'd found her uncouth and over-bearing . . . and with that dreadful accent that made it almost im-possible to understand what she was saying. She brandished her 'Russian-ness', if that were the right word, like a weapon – but why? She had no idea who or what the woman had done before her arrival in England – Rebecca had said something once about Tash's mother being a model – but in truth, Embeth had never taken much interest in her and had assumed the feeling was mutual. Whenever she'd bumped into Lyudmila at school or at some function when they'd been unable to avoid each other, they'd air-kissed briefly, chatted about their respective daughters for three or four minutes – not longer – and gone their separate ways. It was a shock to find the woman in Lionel's private living room earlier that evening, a glass of champagne in one hand and a snail's trail of tears rolling down her cheeks. What was she crying about? The fact that *her* daughter was unmarried and, according to her distraught mother at least, destined for ever to stay that way. Embeth hadn't known quite what to say. She'd offered the usual platitudes – *of course she will; don't worry; she's lovely* – but, in truth, she had absolutely no clue about the state of Tash's love life. From what Rebecca told her, Tash had set her sights firmly on other things – her own business, her own career, making her own way in the world . . . and what was so wrong with that? *She'd* never had to work; neither would Rebecca, unless she wanted to. Julian was certainly well off, and besides, Rebecca had her own trust fund, just as Embeth had had hers. Despite it being a different time, especially for young women, it was so important for Rebecca to enter into her marriage already independent.

She opened the door to their rooms quietly. Lionel would doubtless already be asleep. For nearly a decade now, they'd slept in separate but adjoining rooms, each with its own dressing room and en suite bath-room, connected by the large, comfortable sitting room where they often sat together in the evenings, watching a film or reading quietly together. It had been a successful marriage, though not without its ups and downs, like any marriage, she supposed. She sat down on the edge of her bed and eased off her shoes, sighing in relief. She'd worn a dark-grey silk dress with the same lace detail at the neckline as Rebecca's wedding dress and a pair of ridiculously high grey suede court shoes – Tash's choice. She'd looked at them dubiously when Tash brought them over. Jimmy Choos? At my age? But Tash was adamant. 'They're *divine*, Mrs Harburg. You'll get used to the height.' Embeth smiled tolerantly and slipped them on.

Earlier in the day when they were all getting ready, she'd slipped into Rebecca's room and they'd stood together for a second, looking at their reflection in the mirror. Mother and daughter. It was a little uncanny, seeing herself not only as she was now, a woman in her mid-sixties, but also seeing herself as she'd been once, a bride, just as Rebecca now was. The resemblance was strong, though Rebecca had always taken after her father, not Embeth; but they were both tall and slim, with glossy, dark-brown hair and the same wide, easy smile. 'You look beautiful,' Embeth was moved to say, kissing Rebecca's forehead lightly. 'Just beautiful.'

When they both walked out of the house into the garden later that afternoon, Embeth had accepted the compliments from all their guests, knowing all the while that there was something else being said beneath the admiring glances and the hugs. She'd done a good job. She'd been a good wife and a good mother. Who could ask for more?

She stood up, reached around rather awkwardly and unzipped her dress, stepping out of it carefully. She folded it and placed it in the pile marked 'dry cleaning'. She took off her undergarments and peeled off her stockings. She opened the huge wardrobe doors and stood for a second, looking at herself in a way she rarely did anymore. She lifted one arm, watching her skin stretch and fall away. Where had the time gone? When did her body begin to register the passing years? She put up a hand to her neck; just like her mother's had been, the skin beneath her chin was fine and papery. She turned again so that she faced herself. An attractive woman, but no longer beautiful. The squared jaw and high cheekbones that had held a hint of tomboyish beauty in her twenties had given way to slightly drooping jowls, a certain heaviness around the chin. She wondered if Rebecca would inherit the same.

In the adjoining room, she heard Lionel stir, mumbling something in his sleep. She closed the wardrobe doors quietly and picked up her dressing gown from behind the door. She tiptoed through to his room. He had his back to her and was snoring gently. All was well. She left the door slightly open and pulled back her own sheets. She slid in, feeling the cool crisp cotton sheets against her skin. In the nearly forty years she'd lived in England, she'd never quite managed to shake off the tropical habit of sleeping naked. It was hard to remember that in the beginning of their marriage, it had been the source of so much private eroticism. Now, Lionel told her frankly, she'd catch her death of cold. She smiled to herself. She remembered something her mother had said to her, on her wedding night. 'It's fashionable nowadays to wish your children's lives turn out better than your own.' She'd paused. 'But even if your marriage is only half as good as mine has been, I'll die happy.' She'd never had the final reckoning with her mother; she'd passed away shortly thereafter. But she remembered the sentiment now, as she lay waiting for sleep to claim her. She wished the same for Rebecca. Hers had been an exceptional marriage; there was no way of telling if Rebecca would be as lucky. Julian was a kind and decent man but was he another Lionel? She closed her eyes. It was a blessing, she thought to herself drowsily, as she settled herself further down in the cool sheets. Yes, a blessing. Three generations of women, wishing only that their daughters' marriages would be as successful and happy as theirs. Poor Tash. It seemed as though there would be no such wish for her.

57

TASH

She turned the card over in her hand. *Julian Lovell. Private Equity & Venture Capital Management.* Two phone numbers, both mobiles – one, a UK number and the other she didn't recognise. An email address. Nothing more. She took another gulp of coffee. Her hand hovered over the phone. It was three weeks since the wedding, three weeks in which she'd sat at home all day and practically all night, working on the proposal she now held in front of her. *F@shion.com. An online shop-a-zine.* It wasn't the snappiest byline she'd ever seen, but it was the best she could do. Besides, she knew already Julian would much rather study content than the cover page. And she'd certainly done her homework in that regard. Sixteen pages of history, analysis, market projections, market share, competition . . . it was nerve-wracking. It was the first time she'd ever done anything without the protective umbrella of a magazine or an organisation over her head. F@shion.com was *hers*.

She snapped the report shut, took a deep breath and picked up the phone. There was the soft, familiar two-tone ring, then Julian's deep, beautifully modulated voice. 'Hello?'

'Oh. Hi, Julian . . . it's, er, Tash. Tash Bryce-Brudenell. Rebecca's friend. I . . . I don't know if you remember—'

'Tash.' He cut short her babbling. 'How are you?'

'Great. Fine. Um . . . I . . . I hope I'm not disturbing you or anything but—'

'Not at all, but I've a feeling you're about to tell me something of great importance. Why don't we meet for lunch?'

'Lunch?' Tash's voice went up an octave. She cleared her throat. 'Lunch would be lovely.'

'Great. How about my club? The Lansdowne – d'you know it?'

'No. Yes. Yes, of course.' Tash had no idea where it was but she'd find out.

He chuckled. 'Fitzmaurice Place, near Berkeley Square.'

'Yes, I . . . I've heard of it,' Tash mumbled, embarrassed.

'How about one o'clock on Friday? That way we can have a glass of wine. I knock off at lunchtime on Fridays. Seems a more civilised way to enter the weekend.'

'That . . . that sounds perfect,' Tash said faintly. Her palms were sweating. Friday was three days away. She'd been out of work for almost a month and her savings were almost at zero. She was aware of Lyudmila's frantic, anguished look every time she walked in. '*Vy nashli uzhe rabotu?* Have you found a job yet? *I don't need a job, Ma*, she longed to say. *I'm starting my own company. I'm going to be my own boss.* But she couldn't. Not yet.

She put down the phone. Her hands were shaking. She ought to ring Rebecca and tell her she was about to meet Julian to ask for his advice – and possibly help – in setting up a company, but something made her hold back. This was *business*. Her meeting with Julian should have nothing to do with their friendship. She had to make a distinction between the two relationships and stick to it. If there was one thing she'd learned from working with Rosie Trevelyan it was not to mix business and pleasure, not that she could even imagine Rosie enjoying anything that wasn't in some way business-related. Rosie was *all* business and nothing but. She chewed the end of her pencil. It wasn't that she wanted to hide anything from Rebecca – on the contrary. She was eager to show Rebecca that even without the obvious advantages of money and security, she'd thought up something all on her own that might – just *might* – bring her into the orbit of the things that Rebecca enjoyed but had never had to provide for herself. But she wasn't yet ready, she realised.

She pushed her chair away from her desk and the phone and lit a cigarette. The report lay, cover up, in front of her. Copies of magazines were strewn all around, lying open-jawed at the fashion pages. Yellow stickies, notes and reminders to herself; a couple of sketches, print-outs . . . all this was in front of her. There was so much life and energy in the way it all looked. She drew on her cigarette and felt a deep, satisfying surge of excitement. This was the beginning of it. Her life was beginning to take shape. A different life.

58

The morning of her meeting with Julian started well. She woke up with a bolt of energy that saw her in and out of the shower in five minutes flat. She chose her outfit with greater care than usual. There was nothing to be done about her face or hair but she knew instinctively that Julian would notice what she was wearing and that he'd be looking for signs that she knew something about fashion. She picked out a dark-blue pair of Armani jeans, a crisp white blouse with a midnight-blue blazer from Zara and a chunky silver bracelet that a grateful stylist had once tossed her way. Nothing expensive – on her salary *haute couture* was out of the question – but it did show she knew how to put a look together.

Unfortunately for her, it was the wrong 'look'. At 12.55 on the dot, the two doormen at the Lansdowne looked her up and down and shook their heads in unison.

'Sorry, ma'am. No jeans.' One of them, perhaps sensing a scene, sloped off. The other folded his arms across his chest as if he were about to physically bar the way.

Tash looked at him, her eyes widening in panic. She'd already wasted ten minutes walking up Berkeley Square in the wrong direction. She clutched her report in one hand and her bag in the other. 'But they're *designer* jeans!'

'Sorry, ma'am. Those are the rules.' The doorman wasn't giving an inch.

'Look, I'm meeting someone . . . he's already in there . . . I've got a meeting at one. It's *really* important.'

'Sorry.' By now he'd dropped the "ma'am" and was beginning to sound imperious. 'Those are the rules. *I* don't make 'em,' he added sniffily.

Tash took a deep breath. 'Fine,' she said, pulling a pen and her Filofax out of her bag. She scribbled a quick note. 'Would you mind passing this along to Mr Lovell? I assume you know who he is,' she said, equally sniffy.

'Mr Lovell?' The doorman hesitated. 'Oh. Right. Er, if you wouldn't mind just waiting here for a moment,' he said, his tone suddenly changing. He disappeared up the imposing steps. She waited. Seconds later, she heard Julian's voice coming down the stairs.

'*So* sorry about all this,' he said easily, shrugging his way into his jacket. 'Antiquated rules, if you ask me.' He glanced at Tash. 'Nice jeans, too. Come on, there's a perfectly nice bistro around the corner. Better coffee too,' he added with a chuckle. He beat the doorman to the front door and held it open for her. He was so suave that any embarrassment she might have felt over her inappropriate attire simply melted away. 'It's just down here, on the left.'

A waiter leapt to attention as soon as he saw Julian. 'Good afternoon, Mr Lovell. Nice to see you, nice to see you. Usual table? Very good.' He ushered them to a window table. 'Everything to your satisfaction, Mr Lovell?'

'Absolutely, Cedric. Food first, then let's talk business and then wine . . . what do you say?' he asked Tash.

Tash nodded quickly. 'Er, yes . . . that sounds great.'

'I'll have the salmon, Cedric. And a large bottle of sparkling water for the table. And keep a bottle of the Pouilly-Fuissé in the fridge, won't you? The Guffens-Heynen, if you've got it. Had it last week,' he leaned towards Tash confidentially. 'Superb.'

'Steak for me,' she said firmly. Now was not the time to be coy. Other women might choose a salad; not her.

'Very good, ma'am. And how would you like your steak done?'

'Medium rare.'

Julian raised an appraising eyebrow. 'Right, let's see what you've got.'

Tash pulled a copy of her report out of her bag and laid it on the table. 'It's only the first draft. I've covered most of what I think are the basics but I've probably left out a fair bit. There's a summary right at the end.'

Julian fished his reading glasses out of his breast pocket. He read quickly, a frown of concentration on his face as his eyes slid from top to bottom. He said nothing, just occasionally reached for his glass of water and drank.

This is my best friend's husband, Tash thought to herself, watching him. He was terribly good-looking, his age only adding to his charm. His face was tanned and deeply lined, with spidery laughter lines that radiated from the corners of those extraordinarily cobalt eyes, made even more striking by his olive-toned complexion. *This is Rebecca's husband*, she thought to herself again. She tried to imagine him and Rebecca together – she'd heard some of the details of how they'd met, but, she wondered, what were they *really* like together? What did they talk about? Her mind skittered on dangerously. What was he like when he was—?

'It's pretty comprehensive.' Julian's voice brought her abruptly back to her senses. 'I'm impressed. One question. Times are tough, as you know. The dotcom bubble's already burst and investors are wary. Something's in the air, though we're not quite sure what. D'you think there's enough room in the pocket, so to speak, for luxury goods?'

Tash sat up very straight. Whatever else, it was clear that Julian was taking her proposal seriously. She felt a rush of excitement. '*I* think so,' she said eagerly. 'One of the people I've been talking to for the past couple of months is Edith Berman. You probably wouldn't know her – she owns Eden, the boutique. It's small but she's pretty influential in the fashion world. It's just off Marylebone High Street. We've looked at sales over the past eighteen months and there's a clear rise, month on consecutive month. It was actually in her shop that the idea came to me.' She quickly outlined the conversation she'd overheard. 'The real issue, insofar as *I* can see it, anyhow, isn't whether women have enough disposable income to *afford* the clothes. Women will *always* spend money on clothes, almost irrespective of the general economy, especially these sorts of clothes and this type of women. No, the bigger question is whether they'll go online to do it. Online shopping's always been associated with bargain shopping – *that's* the problem and the real challenge. How do I take it up a level? How do I make *our* online experience genuinely rewarding?'

Julian leaned back in his chair. He brought his hands together in a stiff, peaked 'V'. 'Well, how *do* you?'

'It's all in the packaging,' she said, leaning forward. 'If you turn to page thirteen . . . there, that's it. Beautiful packaging, not just of the goods themselves, but the whole thing. Website, boxes, customer service, speed of delivery . . . everything. Ideally, it shouldn't take more than forty-eight hours between clicking on a dress online and having it delivered to your door. *And* in a beautiful box. It's got to be luxurious or it won't work.'

Julian looked intently at the page she'd pointed out. 'Nice,' he said finally. He looked up. '*Very* nice. So . . . what are you looking at? How much?'

'A million. Ideally a million and a half.' Tash didn't even blink.

'And how much have you got?'

'Three hundred thousand. Edith Berman's my only investor. So far. But I've got a lot of in-kind help, especially around the website . . . there's a guy I used to know at college—'

'Couple of tips,' Julian interrupted her, but gracefully, not rudely. 'In-kind help's all very well and good, particularly when you're starting out, but I think you're onto something here, Tash. Let me have a think about this before you go too much further cap-in-hand. Who else have you approached? Have you asked Rebecca?'

Tash shook her head. 'No. I . . . I don't want to. I wasn't sure about approaching *you*, to be honest . . . but when you mentioned it at the wedding . . . I thought, well . . . why not? You're an investor . . . you probably have people pitching ideas to you every day. I just thought it would be good to hear what you think. And I don't want you to think you *have* to be supportive just because of my friendship with Rebecca.'

'I appreciate your reservations, but don't think for a second that I'd compromise an investment just because you happen to know my wife,' Julian chuckled. 'Okay. Leave it with me. Where are we today? Wednesday? I'll get back to you early next week.'

Tash suppressed an enormous, heartfelt sigh of relief. She was sweating. 'Thanks,' she said, hoping her voice wasn't shaky. 'Really.'

'Nothing to thank. The idea's the easy bit. You'll see.'

59

ANNICK
Paris

Annick looked up at Yves as if he'd spoken Greek. Either that or she'd totally misheard him.

'Eh?'

'Dinner. Would you like to have dinner with me?'

'Dinner?'

'Yes. You're not married or anything, are you?' he asked, glancing quickly at her hand.

'Er, no.'

'Well then?'

'Well, what?'

'Well, would you like to have dinner with me?' he repeated patiently.

'Wh-when?'

'Whenever. When do you have a free night?'

'Well, I . . . I guess . . . I guess you could . . . we could . . . um, maybe on Saturday? I'm not working on Saturday.' Annick said finally. *Dinner?* What on earth would she wear?

'Saturday it is. Where would you like to go?'

'Go?'

'Yes, where would you like to eat? What sort of food do you like?'

Annick blinked slowly, the heat rising up through her face like a blast. 'Um, anything,' she mumbled after a few agonising seconds.

'Anything? So, you're handing me the responsibility of choosing not only the restaurant, but presumably the wine, the food, the decor. Will you at least take charge of the conversation?'

She looked up at him in alarm, wondering if she'd offended him. But no, he was smiling. Her head was swimming. Wine. Food. Conversation. She felt the sudden onset of tears. She blinked furiously. 'I . . . yes, I'll do my best,' she said, struggling to smile.

If he noticed there was anything amiss, he chose not to show it. Instead he tapped lightly on the counter-top as though to indicate a deal had been struck. 'So . . . look forward to Saturday. I'll pick you up . . . where do you live, by the way?'

'Oh. Why . . . why don't we just meet here?' Annick said hastily, a fresh wave of panic sweeping over her. There was no way she could allow him to see where she lived. 'I'll be working during the day, anyway. It'll just be easier to meet here.'

Again his expression was kind. '*Bon*. Well, see you on Saturday, then.' He gave her a mock salute and sauntered out the door. She watched him go, struck dumb. A complete stranger had asked her out on a date. Well, that wasn't strictly true, she thought to herself dazedly. She knew Yves just about as well as she knew anyone else. Which was to say she didn't know anyone. At least not well enough to even contemplate sitting opposite them at a table, a glass of wine in hand . . . she got up suddenly. Thinking about the upcoming evening was more than she could handle. She ran into the toilet before one or other of the chambermaids came upon her crying into her palms.

The rest of the week passed in a blur of anxious anticipation. She'd stupidly left the choice of restaurant to him, which meant she didn't have a clue where he was taking her, what sort of restaurant it would be, what sort of outfit would be suitable . . . not that it would have made the slightest bit of difference. She had nothing to wear anyway. Her wardrobe consisted of two pairs of black trousers, two long black skirts, one of which had been darned so many times it was a miracle there was any fabric left; two white shirts, a long grey cardigan and (an absolutely ridiculous purchase) a frilled summer smock with spaghetti straps which she wore under the cardigan, making her look at least six months pregnant. She'd worn it only once. How was she supposed to fashion something to wear on a date out of *that*?

As Wednesday merged into Thursday, and then Friday, her anxiety grew. By Friday evening, she was in a fury of resentment.

'What's your problem?' Claudette, one of the chambermaids, stopped by the front desk.

Annick opened her mouth to say her usual 'nothing', but instead burst into tears. She couldn't help it. She'd been in such a state all day that the question caught her off-guard. Out it all came. Yves. The date. Her wardrobe (or lack thereof). Claudette leaned her ample hip on the wall, cupped her chin in her hand and simply listened.

When she judged Annick had quite finished, Claudette looked at her calmly. 'So . . . you need something to wear. Why didn't you just ask?'

'Ask who?' Annick looked at her uncertainly.

'Me, you idiot.'

'But—'

'But nothing. Come on, I'll wait for you. Wasis'll be here soon and then we can go.'

'But I haven't got any money,' Annick began in alarm. 'I can't afford to go shopping and certainly not just for one date. I mean, he'll probably never ask me out again and—'

'Who's talking about going shopping? I've got a whole wardrobe full of clothes I never wear,' Claudette laughed. 'You're a bit bigger than me, okay, but we'll find something. And some make-up, too. You've got such a pretty face, I never understand why you don't make more of it . . . what's the matter? *Oh, non* . . . don't start crying again, *ma petite*. We'll find you something, don't you worry. That nice young man won't recognise you tomorrow night, I promise. I'd better finish up the bathrooms. I'll come and get you when I'm done. I only live up the hill – it's not far . . . just below the Basilica. Here, dry your face before Wasis sees you. He's such a nosy little bugger, isn't he?'

Annick took the weakly perfumed handkerchief Claudette proffered and dabbed at her eyes. Her week was rapidly turning into the most surreal one she'd spent in the last few years. A date, the promise of a new outfit, an invitation to someone's house . . . she choked back a sob. Yeah, he is,' she agreed. She wiped her eyes and handed it back. 'Th . . . thanks,' she said, at once shy and embarrassed.

'Nothing to thank. See you later,' Claudette said briskly. She picked up her bucket and mop and moved off, leaving Annick staring dazedly at her retreating back.

60

'Come in, come in . . . have a seat, Annick. Here, move . . . *move*, I said!' A pimply, sullen-faced youth of about eighteen was lounging on a sofa whose shape had long ago taken on the imprint of various backsides the way a pair of favourite trousers holds an oft-ironed crease. He got up reluctantly. 'This one's my sister's first-born, Raoul. Say hello, Raoul. This is my friend, Annick.'

'*Bonsoir.*' The teenager's gaze slid past her to the television show he'd been watching.

Annick sat down gingerly. Claudette disappeared into the bedroom. She looked around. The flat was small but absolutely packed with furniture, goods, decorations, knick-knacks, rugs, photographs . . . family life. There was the smell of fried onions and something else – cardamom, cloves? – that wafted through from the tiny kitchen where two girls were cooking. Claudette re-emerged through one of those beaded curtains that clung to her face and hair like a veil, suddenly freed of the uniform by which Annick had known her for the past year and metamorphosed into someone else. Hard as it was to fathom, it was the first time in three years that she'd been inside another's home, aside from Aunt Libertine's, of course. She was carrying a baby on her hip. 'And this is my youngest,' she said, smiling. 'Araminta.' Too young to say anything, the baby clung adoringly to her, a tiny, delicately etched hand gripping her mother's as she surveyed Annick's unfamiliar face and shape.

'How many children do you have?' Annick asked, wondering how many people lived in the flat.

'Four, would you believe it? Mariam's the eldest – she's at her dad's tonight. Then there's Fatima and Rawia . . . they're in the kitchen. And then this one. She came along late,' she laughed, chucking Araminta under her fat little chin. 'We weren't expecting her at all.'

They were clearly not all from the same father, Annick saw. She'd never given Claudette much thought beyond being the friendliest of the three chambermaids who cleaned the hotel. Her world had narrowed to its barest essentials – work, food, sleep – and not always in that order. It left little time or energy for thinking about anything else. 'She's beautiful,' she felt moved to say.

'Ridiculous at my age,' Claudette said happily. 'Just ridiculous.'

Annick wondered how old Claudette was. As with so many dark-skinned women, she could have been anything from thirty to fifty. 'She's beautiful,' she repeated, meaning it. The two teenage girls who'd been cooking came through; shy introductions were made. The table was laid in a matter of minutes. Raoul, their cousin, did not budge from his position on the sofa and the girls waved away Annick's offer of help with a giggle. 'No, no . . . it's fine,' Fatima said, laughing. 'We do this every night.'

'Come, Annick. You'll sit here,' Claudette pointed to the head of the table. 'Girls . . . bring a bottle . . . yes, a bottle of red. You drink, don't you?' Claudette asked Annick, suddenly anxious. 'We're not very ob-servant, I'm afraid. The girls' father is, but not me. Life's too hard,' she grinned, holding up the bottle. She turned to everyone. '*À table*,' and everyone immediately complied, even Raoul.

The warmth that sitting at the table with Claudette and her family produced stayed with her all evening. It was overwhelming to sit at a table without being made to feel that she somehow had to earn the right to be there. Raoul, once he'd dragged his eyes away from the television screen and had had a glass of wine, turned out to be more interesting than she thought and her two daughters were a delight.

The girls all crowded into Claudette's room after the meal was over, helping their mother bring out a selection of dresses – no, too fussy; tops – too colourful; and scarves – yes, okay, a *possibility* – for her to look at. They arranged the clothes on the bed, arguing over which might suit her best.

'Look, Maman. Annick's got a *tattoo!*' Fatima and Rawia pounced upon her hand as though they might eat it. 'A tattoo!' Fatima breathed reverentially.

'*We* want to get one but Maman said she'd kill us,' Rawia giggled, looking triumphantly at her mother.

'*Qu'est-ce-que c'est que ça?*' Claudette peered at Annick's hand. 'I've always wondered what it was. You don't seem like the type of girl . . . well, it seems a bit strange, that's all. What is it?'

Annick fingered it self-consciously. 'It's just . . . it's just something I did . . . a long time ago. There were three of us . . . my best friends . . . just something silly we all did.'

'Did it hurt?' Rawia gazed at her.

Annick shook her head. 'No. Well, a little bit. Anyhow, it was all a long time ago.' She turned her head and concentrated on the shirts spread out in front of them. Getting the actual tattoo wasn't what hurt . . . losing Rebecca and Tash had been infinitely more painful. It still was. 'What about this one?' she asked, pointing to a pale-blue blouse, determined to change the topic.

'*Non, celui-là*,' Fatima shook her head firmly, pointing to an orange, green and cream flowered blouse. 'It'll go great with your hair.'

Annick looked at it doubtfully. 'Isn't it a bit loud?'

Claudette chuckled. 'Louder the better,' she declared. 'I don't know why you always wear black. So depressing. You should wear colour, *chérie*, lots of it!'

Annick was silent. There was a time she'd have agreed with Claudette, but not now. She eyed the shirt nervously. Aside from the usual anxiety over whether or not it would fit, now a whole host of new anxieties were beginning to surface. How should she do her hair? And what would they talk about? And should she offer to pay?

Claudette and her girls listened to her with looks of incredulity. Her teenage daughters appeared to be more clued up than Annick was about how to behave on a first date. 'Just be yourself,' Claudette advised finally. 'Just be yourself.'

Annick looked at her blankly. She'd forgotten how.

61

TASH
London

Tash put down the phone and stared at her hands. They were trembling. Her heart was pounding. She ought to lie down. For a bit. Just to let it all sink in. She got up and walked over to her sofa. She sat down. Her hands were still shaking. She locked her fingers together and shoved them between her knees. Two million pounds. Two *million* pounds! That was how much Julian and his colleagues were willing to invest. 'We've looked at it from a number of angles,' he said. 'Charles thinks you're mad. It's only been a few years since the bubble burst on the dotcoms and online businesses haven't picked up as quickly as everyone hoped. If you'd come to me five years ago I could've raised triple that . . . but, still, two million's a start.'

A *start*? It was almost twice as much as she'd dared hope. She stared at the phone. Whom should she call first? Rebecca, of course. She pressed her fingers together even more tightly. Her mother. What would she tell Lyudmila? *How* would she tell her? *I've just been given two million pounds.* Well, it wasn't quite true. She'd been given two million pounds of someone *else's* money in the hope that she would make it back. And more, of course. She unlaced her fingers and ran a hand through her hair, pulling it back ever more tightly. She rubbed her eyes. Then she got up, walked to the refrigerator and quickly poured herself a glass of cold white wine. She looked around uncertainly. 'Well,' she said out loud after a moment. 'Here's to you, Tash Bryce-Brudenell.'

She raised her glass to herself. 'Here's to your *idea.*' She laughed self-consciously and brought the glass to her lips. She'd just been given two million pounds. She raised the glass again and polished it off. She looked at her watch. It was nearly four o'clock. It was time to get down to business. Her own.

There were four of them around the beautifully laid table at the Orrery. Herself, Edith, James and Colin, one of James's closest friends from university and an authority on all things internet. All three were staring at Tash.

'Just like that?' James's eyes widened to the point of bursting. 'He gave you two million quid . . . *just like that?*'

'Why not?' Edith asked mildly. She was nearly sixty; she'd been in the business long enough to have seen investments of this scale, including her own. 'It's a good idea. A bloody good idea.'

Tash smiled. It wasn't like Edith to swear. She raised her glass. 'Well, it wasn't quite "just like that", but yes, we've got two million quid of other people's money to play with, starting now. So, here's to F@shion.-com. We've got four months to get it up and running.'

'You say "we",' James said cautiously. 'What exactly d'you have in mind? Where do we come in?'

Tash nodded slowly. 'Okay. So here it is. Here's what I'm thinking.'

It took her thirty minutes to outline her vision for the new company. Fifteen positions, ranging from admin to sales, fifteen people working out of her tiny Bloomsbury flat and four directorships, offered to each person at the table. Of the four, only Edith had anything other than ambition and passion to contribute – she'd offered three hundred thousand pounds of her own money to get F@shion.com off the ground.

'I know you'll never leave Eden,' Tash said, looking directly at her when she'd finished. 'But if you'd consider coming on board not just as an investor, but as a director, I'd . . . well, I'd sleep easier at night,' Tash said, laughing nervously. 'I'll be completely honest. I need your fashion savvy, not just your contacts list. You know better than almost anyone what sells, what's hot, what's not. I *could* do it without you; I'd just rather not have to.'

It took Edith a few minutes to answer. There was a faint but discernible tremor of emotion in her voice as she spoke. 'I'm sixty-one years old,' she said, looking around the table at the three young people sitting there. 'I've been in the fashion business for nearly forty years and I've enjoyed every moment. But it hasn't been the same since Seth died. Oh, the shop's still going . . . we've got such a loyal group of customers. But it's not the same. I don't have the appetite for it anymore. Our two sons aren't interested . . . it was never their thing. If we'd had a daughter, maybe . . . who knows?' She stopped and took a small sip of her wine and looked directly at Tash. 'I'm in. Properly in, I mean. You need an editor-in-chief, it seems to me. And you need somewhere a little bit nicer to work. Working in your flat's all very well if you're trying to save money, which we should do, no question. But there's a perfectly good shop on Moxon Street going . . . why don't we work from there?'

Tash's mouth dropped open. Aside from the stunning news that Edith had fully bought into the new venture, what was she saying? That she was about to close Eden's down? 'But . . . you can't,' she spluttered eventually. 'You can't close Eden's.'

'Says who?' There was a sparkle in Edith's eye that was entirely infectious. Everyone around the table was smiling, even the rather reserved Colin. 'It's my shop. I can do what I like.'

'I think it's a bloody marvellous idea,' James said slowly. 'I've always rather liked that end of town.'

'Good sandwich shops.'

'Lots of boutiques.'

'Easy to find.'

'Good address.'

'Close to the tube.'

'Lots of taxis.'

'Okay, okay . . . I get the point,' Tash said, laughing. 'Edith . . . are you sure?'

'Absolutely.'

By the end of the meal, it was all decided. Tash would be CEO of F@shion.com. Edith was editor-in-chief. James would be the director of e-commerce and IT and Colin would be operations director. In addition to their small salaries, each would receive a fifteen per cent share. Julian had recommended a lawyer; the next job would be to draw up the formal legal documents that bound them to their vision and to one another. The premises had been found; fifteen positions had been created . . . they had four months to pull it off.

She had four months to pull it off, Tash thought to herself as she waited for the bill to arrive. It felt good – no, it felt marvellous – to have such a talented, passionate team behind her. She trusted Edith and James implicitly and Colin, despite the fact that she hardly knew him, seemed the perfect antidote to the flamboyance and gregariousness of the other three. But in the end, it was down to her. She would be the one to hold it all together; it was her baby. Hers. She signed the credit-card slip with a flourish, savouring the rush of pride that swept over her as the waiter deferentially handed her card back. At just under three hundred pounds, it was more than she gave Lyudmila in a month. If she played her cards right and worked all the hours God sent, she would, one day, be able to give her mother far more than three hundred pounds a month. She wanted to be able to give Lyudmila everything she'd ever wanted and so spectacularly failed to earn for herself.

62

REBECCA

At about the same time that Tash was walking back to Marchmont Street along the now-deserted streets of Soho, Rebecca was lying next to Julian listening to how he'd given her best friend two million pounds. Rebecca was shocked. Not by the amount but by the fact that neither Julian nor Tash had said anything to her about it.

'When did she come to you?' she asked for the umpteenth time.

'I told you, darling. About a month ago.'

'And you didn't say a word to me?'

'It's business. That's the way it's done. It would've been premature to talk about it until I'd put the whole deal together.'

'But she's my best friend! I can't believe the two of you didn't talk to *me* about it!'

'Why should we?' Julian sounded genuinely baffled by Rebecca's anger. 'It's business, Rebecca, that's all. It's not like I was seeing her for any other reason. God, no,' he gave a short laugh.

'Why d'you say it like that?' Rebecca pounced on him.

'Like what?'

'The way you said it just now. "*God*, no." As if the very idea—'

'Rebecca, you're being unreasonable. It was a business deal; that's all there is to it. And yes, the very idea of there being anything more is absolutely ridiculous. Aside from the way she *looks*, she's your best friend, as you keep pointing out.'

'What's wrong with her looks?'

Julian sat up. It was dark; Rebecca couldn't see his expression properly, which was probably just as well. His voice, when it came out of the darkness, wasn't a voice she'd heard him use before. 'I've had enough. Deal with whatever ridiculous insecurities you have, Rebecca. I'm sleeping next door. I've got a six a.m. flight. I can't be bothered with this.' And with that, he slid out of bed, picked up his dressing gown from the back of the door and banged it shut behind him.

Rebecca lay where she was, too shocked to move. What had she done wrong? She'd only been asking a question! She could hear him pulling out the sofa bed in the study. Should she go after him and apologise? He'd got it all wrong. She hadn't meant to insinuate that there was anything between him and Tash that wasn't strictly business – it was just that she felt left out of the loop. A very important loop, too. Suddenly she heard his voice; he was on the phone. She struggled upright. It was just after midnight. A cold, unreasonable wave of fear swept over her. Who was he talking to at this time? She strained to hear – was he talking to Tash? No, don't be silly, she admonished herself severely. Why would he be talking to Tash at midnight? It was probably just another business call – Julian seemed to do most of his business with people on the other side of the world – Shanghai, Bangkok, Tokyo. His phone was always at his side, always going off at odd hours. It was only natural that he'd be talking to someone at midnight. It was in the middle of the working day in Tokyo.

She lay back, her heart beating faster than usual. She felt suddenly exposed and vulnerable. She was envious, she realised with a growing sense of shame. Jealous, even. She was jealous of the way Julian talked about Tash. What was the expression he'd used? "She's got balls, your friend. Cool as a cucumber. She'll make it, mark my words." Who would ever say that about *her*?

She slid out of bed and almost ran to the study. Julian had just hung up the phone. He looked up at her, puzzled.

'I'm sorry,' she blurted out before he could speak. 'I didn't mean to upset you.' She found, to her amazement, that her cheeks were wet. 'I d-don't know what came over me,' she stammered.

'Hey . . . it's nothing,' Julian got up and came towards her. 'It's nothing. Not worth crying over, at any rate. Rebecca . . . it's nothing.'

She was crying openly now, unable to stop herself. What was the fear that had broken out all over her like a light sweat? That Julian would find her disagreeable? She turned her face into his chest, felt his arms tighten across her back. She breathed in deeply, desperately seeking some reassurance in his broad, still oddly unfamiliar body that she hadn't 'blown' it — a phrase and sentiment from her schoolgirl days. 'Julian?' she whispered. 'Are you angry with me?'

He shook his head vigorously. His chest heaved, as though he were laughing. 'Angry? Whatever for?'

'Because of just now . . . what I said. About Tash and the deal and everything,' she hiccuped, like a child.

'Oh, for goodness' sake, Rebecca. I was irritated, that's all. Come here,' his fingers went under her chin, drawing her face firmly up to meet his. 'What's wrong with you? It's just a little disagreement, that's all. It happens.' He kissed her, slowly, deeply, his tongue thick and urgent and forgiving.

Her relief was so great it was almost orgasmic. She felt herself opening up, quite literally, all through her body. His hands were in her hair, pulling her even closer to him. There was a sudden urgency in him that she hadn't felt before, a need that he'd never shown her. His next moves happened so fast she didn't have time to think. One minute her head was in his hands, the next he'd pushed it down to his waist. It was so out of character — in all the time they'd been together he'd never once indicated that he'd even so much as heard of oral sex, never mind expect her to perform it. But he was certainly expecting it now. He thrust himself into her mouth impatiently, his hands still gripping her hair. His mood reminded her of Jeremy Garrick and his odd, frequently unpleasant sexual demands. What surprised her was her willingness to perform. At some obscure, deeply subconscious level, she was desperately trying to atone for something she wasn't even sure she'd done.

Her face in the mirror. There was a faint bruise already beginning to show up underneath her skin. Her mouth was swollen and her lips felt numb. Nothing had been said. When she'd finished and brought her face back up to his, he'd pushed her away from him suddenly. 'Julian?' she'd whispered. 'Julian?' But he seemed very far off from her. He'd belted his dressing gown and walked into the bathroom, then beckoned her back to bed. She'd followed obediently, leaving the un-slept-in sofa bed in the study for the maid to clear away the following morning.

She brought her fingers up to her lips again. There was nothing wrong. She looked down at her wristwatch, a beautiful *Ballon Bleu de Cartier*. He'd given it to her just after their wedding. Its cold, steel-silver face glinted in the semi-darkness. It was almost four o'clock. She'd lain awake for hours after he'd fallen asleep, unable to sleep herself. She cast her mind back again over the events of the evening. Dinner, a good bottle of wine, the conversation about Tash and the small argument that followed . . . so far so good. She had a handle on that. But the way he'd left the room had left her in a state of panic so great she'd almost been unable to breathe. And then the sex . . . it was strange, urgent, and horribly crude. So out of character. But her willingness to *perform*, to do whatever he wanted, shocked her even more. In that instant where he'd grabbed her hair and she'd felt herself melting into submission, she was ashamed to admit that it excited her. She wanted more. *That* was it, she realised suddenly, a flush that was both shameful and exciting rising up through her belly and breasts. She'd wanted his roughness. Julian was quick to pick up on it. When he'd held her face in both hands, pushing her away from him, she'd seen from his eyes that he'd caught her moment of weakness. It was *that* she was afraid of, she realised slowly. She'd allowed him a glimpse into herself and into something she wasn't yet sure of. She let her fingers fall. Some fearful aspect of herself was out there, between them, waiting to be filled.

63

ANNICK
Paris

'Try this.' Yves reached across the table and motioned to her to open her mouth. Annick glanced quickly to her left and right – what if someone was watching? – closed her eyes and did as he asked. Her mouth was flooded with the taste and scent of something that was simultaneously delicious and strange at the same time. She chewed slowly . . . what was it? Duck? Chicken? Fish? 'How's that?' he grinned at her, waiting for her reaction.

'Um . . . it's . . . it's lovely,' she said, swallowing quickly. 'What is it?'

'Quail. With caviar. Good, eh?'

She nodded. 'Good' was an understatement. She took another quick look around her. Chez Vong was the sort of small, known-to-a-few-important-people restaurant that her father had loved. It was in the Les Halles district of the city, close to the river. She hadn't been down here in years, she thought to herself, half-guiltily. She'd often strolled with Anouschka down the rue Saint-Honoré or the rue du Pont Neuf, stopping off at the shops and boutiques, sometimes even stopping off for *un café* and *petits-fours* before Anouschka had to return home for a fitting or a visitor, frequently both. A memory of sitting in the Café du Pont Neuf with her mother suddenly came back to her. It was spring, but still cold, and they'd stopped to have a coffee. Anouschka was wearing a beautiful black leather coat with a fox-fur collar. Her blonde hair was tucked under her dark grey trilby, a few strands floating prettily around her face. She fished in her handbag – a lovely, slouchy cream-coloured bag from Dior. She pulled out her cigarettes, tapped one out of the box, and looked around for the obligatory waiter to spring in front of her with a lighter.

'Can I have one?' Annick piped up suddenly.

Anouschka's eyes widened. 'You're only fourteen,' she protested.

'*Fifteen*,' Annick corrected her. 'And I've been smoking for ages. Everyone smokes at school. It's no big deal.'

For a second they stared at each other, Annick wondering if she'd gone a step too far. She was on the verge of blurting out something ridiculous like 'only joking!' or some such feeble retraction when she saw Anouschka smile suddenly. 'Fifteen,' she murmured, tapping out a second stick. '*Déjà?*'

Annick nodded, taking the cigarette she'd been offered. 'But I don't smoke every day,' she added. For a few minutes they smoked in silence together, a smile still playing around the corners of Anouschka's lips.

'Better not tell Papa, eh?' she said finally, conspiratorially. It was a rare moment: mother and daughter, enjoying a moment together that neither would share with Sylvan.

'What's wrong?' Yves's voice suddenly brought her back to the present. She blinked slowly, focusing her attention on him. 'You look like you've seen a ghost.'

She gave a small, wan smile, forcing herself to concentrate. 'Oh, it's nothing . . . I just . . . I was just thinking about something . . .'

'Something sad?'

She hesitated. They were only halfway through their meal. So far, it had been the most enjoyable evening she'd spent in the past three years. He'd met her outside the hotel, as they'd arranged. There was a car waiting; not the fancy BMW or Mercedes in which he waited whilst his boss finished up whatever 'business' he had in the hotel, but a small, clearly second-hand hatchback. He'd apologised for the papers on the back seat – not that she'd have noticed or cared. He complimented her on her blouse and if he'd noticed that she was wearing the same long black skirt that she usually wore at work, he'd said nothing. He drove to Les Halles; they parked close to the restaurant and walked up the street together, not touching or anything, but in the manner of two people clearly getting to know one another. Annick felt as though she were wading through fog. At one level, the game was so familiar to her . . . the shy sideways glances, the awareness of another's presence, the faint but pleasurable scent of male aftershave every time he turned towards her . . . she wanted nothing more than to close her eyes and wallow in it. But at another level, it was as unfamiliar to her as her life now was – alien, unnatural and unreal. She'd lost count of the number of times she'd caught sight of herself in a shop window or in a mirror in one of the wardrobes at the hotel and stopped – was that really *her*? She who used to spend hours examining herself from all angles – back, front, sideways – how long had it been since she'd seen herself in anything other than a passing glance? The strangest thing was, Yves didn't seem to notice her size. Or if he did, it didn't seem to bother him. Was it possible that he just didn't care? The temptation to talk came over her like the urge to laugh or cry. It was so strong she had to clamp down on her lips to stop them opening of their own accord, forming words, sentences, paragraphs, her whole life history spilling out before she had the chance to think.

'I . . . I was just . . . it's my . . . it's a bit complicated,' she stammered, embarrassment seeping up through her pores like sweat. 'My . . . my life, I mean.'

'How d'you mean?' Yves' eyes, darkly brilliant, watched her intently.

She looked down at her hands. If she did open up to him, he would immediately withdraw. Who would want to take on the burden of a girl whose parents had been murdered, whose life had been turned upside down, whose future was so murky and undetermined that it wasn't possible to see a month ahead, let alone six. Who would want that? 'I . . . you don't know much about me, do you?' she said at last.

'I know enough,' he said carefully. She looked up. His expression was hard to read.

His answer caught her off-guard. 'It's just . . . I'm probably not who you think I am,' she said slowly. She picked up her chopsticks and began to fiddle with them. 'I'm . . . well, the thing is . . .' She stopped again, unsure of how to go on.

He made a sudden, oddly familiar movement with his hand – a gentle flick of the wrist, fingers splayed outwards, as though chasing something off. It was a gesture she'd seen her father make, many times before. 'What does it matter?' he said slowly. 'You're a bit of an enigma, Annick, but I like that. You're interesting, you're kind. You have a good heart. Those are the things that count. That's all I need to know.'

Interesting, kind, good-hearted . . . they weren't the sort of compliments she was used to hearing, but then again it had been so long since she'd actually received a compliment, who was she to argue? She bent her head back down to her food, hoping the blush staining her cheeks didn't show.

64

REBECCA
London

'But you can't *not* have a launch,' Rebecca said, quickly scanning the menu. 'I'll have the Caesar salad,' she said to the hovering waiter. 'And a sparkling water.'

'Same here, but I'll have glass of the Sauvignon Blanc,' Tash said, folding her menu with a snap. She turned back to Rebecca. 'We'll be going live at midnight the night before. I don't think we need a launch.'

'It's not about what you need, darling,' Rebecca said mildly. She waited until their drinks had been carefully put down and the waiter had disappeared. She looked at Tash closely. There were dark circles under her eyes and her hair, whilst never exactly glossy or full, was lank. She watched her pick up the glass of wine and down it in one gulp. 'Tash,' Rebecca murmured. 'Go easy.'

'What?'

'The wine, darling. You're meant to *sip* it, not swill it.'

Tash rolled her eyes and signalled to the waiter. 'I'll sip the second one,' she grinned.

Rebecca bit her lip. It was the third time in as many weeks that she'd had dinner with Tash and she'd been shocked by Tash's ability to knock back one glass of wine after another. The last time they'd eaten together, Tash had barely touched her food. She'd always been slim; now she was positively scrawny. 'Is everything okay?' she asked hesitantly.

Tash paused, the glass already on its way to her lips. 'Yes, of course. Why d'you ask?'

'No particular reason. You just look . . . well, a bit tired.'

'Of course I'm tired. I've hardly slept all week. Fuck, I've hardly slept since March. But we're close . . . we're nearly there.'

'Don't you think you ought to . . . I don't know . . . get some rest?'

'I'll rest when we're ready to go,' Tash said firmly. The waiter interrupted them again. Their salads had arrived.

Rebecca watched Tash chase a piece of limp lettuce leaf halfway round her plate before putting it reluctantly in her mouth. 'So . . . what else needs to be done?' she asked hesitantly.

Tash looked up and grinned. 'Everything. God, it just never seems to end.' She rattled off a list of things that left Rebecca reeling. IT, finance, merchandising, packaging, logistics – words that Rebecca had barely heard of, let alone imagined that her best friend had a handle on. Despite her appearance, Tash was formidable when she was in full flow. 'Packaging's one of our biggest costs right now and Julian thinks I'm going overboard, but I think it's crucial. Every box has to seem like a gift, d'you know what I mean?'

Rebecca nodded hurriedly. 'Yes, yes, of course.'

'And then there's the bloody designers. They're a complete pain in the arse. Edith's great – she does most of the pitching – my contacts are mostly editorial, you know, not the designers, but still . . . this one wants to know who's signed up before she makes a decision, that one doesn't want this one on board . . . Christ, they're worse than schoolchildren. They just can't seem to get it through their heads that the more they sign up for it, the more we all win.'

Rebecca nodded again, this time uncertainly. The truth was, she couldn't imagine shopping for *anything* online, much less designer clothes. She'd bought the occasional book from Amazon but that was about it. Embeth was more of an internet user than she was, much to Embeth's amusement. She thought Tash's idea was absolutely genius, as did Julian, though he had reservations of a different kind. He thought that Tash herself was a terrible advert for an online fashion business. 'She's got to do something about those damned teeth,' he'd said to her on more than one occasion. 'And that awful hair. Why can't she just go to a hairdresser like everyone else?'

'That's just Tash,' Rebecca said, sighing. 'She's not interested in herself.'

'She ought to be. She's selling beauty and glamour and sex . . . and she's the bloody polar opposite of it all. No wonder she doesn't have a boyfriend.'

'Julian!' Rebecca said, shocked at his vehemence. 'Tash is lovely, you've said so yourself.'

'Lovely person, yes, but hardly lovely to look at. Come on, admit it. Not everyone's as beautiful as you, darling, but she really ought to make more of an effort.'

She looked at her friend now, trying to see her as Julian – or another man – might. She was in the middle of recounting how she'd walked into some showroom on New Bond Street – with an appointment! – and hadn't managed to get past the receptionist. Perhaps Julian did have a point? Not about not being able to find a boyfriend, but about her stubborn refusal to do anything about her teeth, hair, face, skin. She had bags of style but seemed totally unwilling to change anything about herself. What was it? She had an almost pathological fear of appearing feminine in any way – perhaps it was because of Lyudmila? Despite the fact she'd known Tash for almost half her life, Rebecca barely knew Lyudmila. She found her accent almost impenetrable, but it wasn't just that. She found Lyudmila childish – sulky and petulant in a way that Tash had never been allowed to be. At times, when they were teenagers, she'd found it hard to believe that Lyudmila was actually the mother. 'Tash,' she said hesitantly, wondering whether it was a good idea to go down this particular road.

'Mmm?' Tash looked up when nothing more seemed to be forthcoming.

'Have . . . have you thought about maybe seeing a . . . a dentist? You know, about your teeth? My dentist is brilliant . . . you know where I go, don't you? Dr Haslam, on Great Titchfield Street. I could make an appointment for you and—'

'You're beginning to sound like my mother,' Tash interrupted her. 'I've got a gazillion things to do that are far more important than my damned teeth,' she said impatiently. 'Here I am, trying to get this enterprise off the ground, working day and night, taking on all this debt and all you lot care about is whether or not my teeth are straight and my hair's been cut. I can't believe you sometimes.'

'But, Tash—'

'But nothing! You've got no idea what it's like, Rebecca. You've always had Mummy and Daddy behind you, supporting you all the way, making sure everything's perfect and just the way their little girl likes it. You've never had to work for anything. It's all there. Well, *I* haven't. There's no one behind me. No one. So excuse *me* if I'm not bothered about fixing my teeth or getting a boob job or whatever the fuck it is you think I need. I've got other things to worry about.'

'I never said anything about a boob job,' Rebecca protested, dismay rising in her like a tide. 'That's not what I meant!'

'Oh, no? You mean Julian didn't mention that I could do with a little sprucing up? Let me see . . . how would he put it? Lovely girl, Tash, but Christ, she could do with a makeover—'

'Leave Julian out of this,' Rebecca said hotly. 'He would *never* say anything like that.'

'Come off it. I *know* you, Rebecca. I know when you're lying and you're lying now. Why don't you just admit it? And what did you say in my defence, eh?'

'You're being horribly unfair.'

'Am I? Really, Rebecca? Come on, you don't have to pretend.'

'I'm not pretending!'

'Then why even bring it up?'

'I just—' Rebecca stopped, floundering. Her cheeks were warm and, to her horror, she realised they were wet. She was crying. She drew in a deep breath, trying to calm herself down. Tash had it all wrong, as usual. She wanted to help her, for God's sake. 'I'm on your side, Tash,' she said shakily, wiping away her tears. 'Why d'you always have to be so damned prickly about everything? I'm only trying to help.'

'Then leave my looks out of it,' Tash hissed angrily. 'We can't all be as perfect as you, Rebecca. Some of us have to *work* at it. At everything. So do me a favour and shut the fuck up about dentists and doctors and hairdressers. If you really want to help me, do something practical.'

'Like what?' Rebecca asked helplessly.

'I don't know. Figure it out.' Tash stood up suddenly. She grabbed her bag, yanked it open and pulled out her wallet. 'Here, I'll get this. I've lost my appetite.'

Rebecca looked up at her, shocked by the anger and frustration etched on Tash's face. 'No, no . . . don't be silly, Tash. I'll get this. Don't waste your money—'

'This isn't about the *money*, you idiot!' Tash flung two twenty-pound notes onto the starched white tablecloth. She picked up her jacket. By now everyone in the restaurant, including the two waiters, was staring. 'Don't you understand *anything?*'

'I—' Rebecca started to protest her innocence but it was too late. Tash grabbed her coat from the back of her chair and was gone.

'No, no . . . I'm fine. I'll just . . . can I just have the bill, please?' Rebecca brushed aside the waiter's concern. 'No, I'm fine.' She dabbed at her eyes with her napkin and fumbled in her bag for her purse. She picked up the money Tash had flung at her and folded it away. She handed over her credit card, studiously ignoring the curious glances of the other diners and, at last, was able to get up and walk out with as much dignity as she could muster. She hurried down the stairs, her heart thumping. She hurried out into the street, holding her handbag above her head against the drizzle and flagged down a cab. 'Flask Walk. Just off Hampstead High Street.'

'Right you are.' The cab swung around and sped off towards the Euston Road. She leaned back against the seat and rubbed her temples. She had a splitting headache. It was just after nine. Julian was in Paris – she wanted to talk to someone about what had just happened, but whom? Outside of Julian, Tash and her immediate family, she had few really close friends. She closed her eyes, squeezing them shut against the headlights coming towards them. It was raining; the light droplets fell against the cab windows in spittle streaks, the tyres making a dull splashing sound as they headed towards Hampstead. It was a Wednesday night and there was little traffic about. Half an hour after she'd climbed in, she was at home. She fished out a twenty-pound note and told the driver to keep the change. She climbed the steps to the pale-blue door that was theirs, slid the key into the lock and shut it firmly behind her.

The smell of the flat that was already specially and uniquely theirs, washed over her. A combination of the candles that she bought every other week from The White Company, the scent of whatever the house-keeper had been cooking that day and her own perfume. She inhaled deeply. As soon as she and Julian were married, Martha, Embeth's housekeeper of thirty-odd years, had insisted on sending over one of the young women who worked at Harburg Hall. Liz was a pleasant, exceedingly capable woman, just a little older than Rebecca, who came in three times a week. Rebecca's protests that she didn't *need* a housekeeper had fallen on deaf ears. Embeth was gently insistent. Embeth won. But it was worth it, Rebecca had to admit to herself. The house, a tall, three-storey Georgian property on the north side of the street, set back from the main road by a narrow strip of grass and the most magnificent cherry tree in their small front garden, would have been impossible for her to keep sparkling clean, polished and dusted in the manner that Julian liked. Liz didn't just cook and clean – she transformed the house into the sort of gloriously pristine environment that soothed you just to look at it.

She looked down the hallway to the kitchen and dining room beyond. The walls were painted a light, muted grey – Julian's choice – which complemented his artwork beautifully. There was another Stephen Conroy hanging above the mantelpiece in the living room, and several striking photographs by Gursky, including his famous *Shanghai* in stunning yellows and golds that he'd hung behind the olive linen sofa in the living room. She'd always thought of herself as having good taste but Julian's taste was bolder. It worked well.

She walked into the living room, kicking off her shoes and letting her coat fall to the ground in a way she wouldn't have dared do had Julian been home. The whole house was quiet, thrumming to the hidden, silent beat of refrigerators, freezers, immersion heaters, radiators, the paraphernalia of the modern home that renders everything inside it comfortable. She wriggled her bare toes in the luxuriously soft pelt of the sheepskin rug that lay before the fire and sank down into the warm embrace of the sofa. Her hair was damp; she could feel the moisture at the nape of her neck where her coat had failed to stop the rain. A round glass bowl of deep purple and pink peonies – another of Liz's gifts; she knew exactly what sort of flowers Rebecca liked and where to get them – sat fat and snug on the antique coffee table. She stared at the petals as if seeing them for the first time. There was a beautiful gold and agate necklace lying across the coffee table; she smiled, remembering that she'd left it there that morning as she was getting dressed. She picked it up, letting the delicate gold chain run through her fingers. Her tattoo jumped out at her from the creamy fold of skin between her thumb and forefinger. She touched it lightly and closed her eyes. She could remember the day they'd got them – all three of them, as if it were yesterday.

*

254

They all stop. The sign above the door reads Delaney's Tattoo Parlour. 122
King's Road, Chelsea. It's Annick who voices what they're all thinking. 'Shall
we? Shall we all get one?'

'The same one?' That's Tash. 'All of us?'

'Won't it hurt?'

'Oh, Rebecca.' Both Tash and Annick turn to look at her.

'Sue Parker's brother got one done the other day. She said he said it hurt
like hell.'

'Yeah, but I bet his covered half of his back, or something stupid like that.
We're only going to get something small.'

'Like what?'

Annick shrugs. 'How about a rose?'

Tash rolls her eyes. 'Bo-ring. Let's get something that actually means
something. To all of us.'

'Like what?' Rebecca's curiosity gets the better of her.

'How about something . . . something like that?' Tash points to the
window, which is covered in stickers and posters and drawings of all the
things that, for a modest fee, can be yours, anywhere you want on your own
body.

'Which one?' Annick steps closer to see.

'That one. The triangle. Three points – that's us.'

'How about a triangle set in a circle?' Annick's idea.

'Genius. Fucking genius.' Tash grins. 'The three of us, together, always. I
love it. Here, right here where we'll always see it.' She points to that tender
spot between thumb and forefinger, that little fold of skin which, when the
hand is spread, opens out.

'Come on, before Rebecca chickens out,' Annick laughs.

'I won't.' Rebecca suppresses the small tremor of fear and apprehension in
her stomach. A tattoo. What on earth would her mother say? 'Does . . . does it
have to be right there?' she looks at her hand. 'Can't it be somewhere
more . . . well, hidden?'

'Scaredy-cat. You're afraid of what your mum's going to say. Don't worry,
when your hand's closed, you hardly see it.'

It was the 'scaredy-cat' that did it. That and the fact that Tash was
right; when her hand was closed, it was barely visible. A thin blue line
on either side of the fold. When Julian first saw it, he'd hooted with
delight. 'You, with a tattoo? I can't think of anything more unlikely.
Sexy.'

She opened up her hand, flexing it awkwardly. They were only two points on the triangle now. Herself and Tash. And if tonight's conversation were anything to go by, she'd soon be left with one.

She put her elbows on her knees and cupped her chin in her hands. She looked at the books laid carefully on the mahogany coffee table – books on African art, tribal pattern-making, modern architecture in Brazil, glossy books on photography and Oriental rugs . . . the usual display of educated tastefulness, wide-ranging and erudite in the way she'd been brought up to be. Her mother's interior designers had worked on the house and seemed to have instinctively understood the need to modernise Embeth's tastes, but not so much that the younger version broke off all connection with the past. Where the Old Masters hung in Harburg Hall, younger, more contemporary works were displayed here, supplemented by Julian's tastes, which ran somewhere in between. Sitting there like that, her feet splayed on either side of her knees, a strange mood of childish resentment began to steal over her. She was completely alone. Julian wouldn't be back until the following day. Somewhere in the kitchen a chime sounded. Ten o'clock. She had absolutely no one to talk to and nothing to do. She ought to pick up the phone and ring Tash, find out if she was all right. She hesitated. Knowing Tash she'd refuse to pick up and then Rebecca would spend the rest of the evening in a frenzy of worry.

Her mobile buzzed suddenly. She fished it out of her pocket. She bit her lip. It was Julian. The silly, high-pitched ring tone droned on and on. She *ought* to answer it. Her fingers hovered. Then it stopped abruptly. *Missed Call. Julian (mob. Fr)*. She stared at the screen for a few minutes, then she got up slowly, slipped the phone back into her pocket and walked out of the living room.

She pushed open their bedroom door. The long, mauve silk curtains at the far end shrouded the room in a dusky, rosy light. The light grey carpet was soft underfoot. Humming a little to herself, she walked across the room, pulling off her clothes as she went. She dropped her silk blouse into the laundry basket and slowly unbuckled her jeans. She slipped off her bra and underwear and walked naked into the bathroom. She switched on the lights and stood for a moment in the doorway, looking around her. Despite her vast array of cosmetics, perfumes, creams and potions, it was a resolutely masculine space. The floor and walls were of grey-and-white marble, including the two side-by-side washbasins which sat proud of a thick, marble slab. At one end was the shower, a vast, black-tiled room of its own with two impressive showerheads and a complicated nozzle-and-showerhead affair that

Rebecca seldom used. A clawed cast-iron bath stood in the middle, which, again, she seldom stepped into. One wall was entirely mirrored; she looked at her naked profile as she began to pin her hair up in preparation for a shower. She still carried the faint tan lines she'd acquired on holiday with her family in the South of France. She'd worn the same bikini every day, worried about a criss-cross of mis-matched lines on her skin that, despite its creamy whiteness, turned olive at the merest touch of the sun. That was Embeth.

She turned the shower on and stepped back, waiting for it to warm up. Within seconds, small clouds of steam were puffing towards the ceiling. She stepped under it, gasping as the hot water cascaded over her. She turned her face carefully towards the jets, keeping her hair averted. Her hand went out blindly, automatically, towards the bottle of Chanel No. 19 shower gel that sat on the ledge. Its rich, sweet perfume mingled with the steam as she began soaping herself, long firm strokes from her clavicles, across her breasts and down the flat plane of her stomach to her thighs. She closed her eyes against the spray at the same moment her hands went over her breasts again. Her nipples hardened and she was aware of a faint, tingling heaviness in her abdomen; the beginnings of desire. How long had it been since that strange night with Julian? A week? She let her hand slide slowly down her stomach, now covered in sweetly-scented foam and then stop, hovering above the cleft between her legs. She could feel the corners of her mouth tug upwards as she parted her legs enough to allow the hot water to run between them, flowing over her clitoris and engorging it further. She turned and put a hand up against the wall, supporting herself with one as she pleasured herself slowly with the other. She was thinking about Julian as she stroked herself, but she was also aware of another hunger building inside her for something else . . . not Julian, not anyone she knew or recog-nised . . . someone else. Someone unknown. A vague face materialised in front of her, in her mind's eye – a hand, a thigh, a glimpse of unfamiliar skin, a stranger's touch. She turned her mouth towards her arm, biting her own skin, hard, almost drawing blood. She was Rebecca, Julian's wife, and yet she was not. She bit herself again and heard her own groan as if it had come from someone else. Someone else. She both longed for it and longed to *be* it – someone else. She felt herself go weak at the knees and had to grab hold of the chrome pole of the showerhead to stop herself from falling.

65

YVES

The big fat man with the broad shoulders of someone accustomed to stopping others stood at the stove, shaking the curling rinds of bacon in a large frying pan. He paused to wipe his forehead. 'Idiot,' he snarled. 'Fucking idiot.' The two men standing by the window, casting a glance out every now and then to the ground floor, said nothing. He repeated the word to himself, lifting the pan off the flame and giving it a good shake. 'You sure it's her?'

One of the men nodded. 'Yeah. We checked.'

The fat man moved the hissing pan from the gas hob and carried it over to the table. 'How many?' he asked.

'Just us, boss.'

'So where is he now?' With a practised gesture he tilted the pan and the curled rinds, still sizzling, slid off and onto the waiting plate.

The man by the window shrugged. 'No idea. Haven't seen him since yesterday.'

There was a sudden rat-a-tat-tat at the door. All three froze. 'Who is it?' the fat man called out.

'It's me. Yves.'

The three men looked at each other. The fat one made a silencing gesture. 'Not a *word*,' he hissed, before ambling over to the door and flinging it open. 'Where's the boss? Weren't you supposed to be with him tonight?'

Yves shook his head. 'Na. He's with someone. A new girl.'

One of the men by the window gave a mirthless laugh. 'Man, you ever known anyone to get as much pussy as Chief? Every night it's a different one. Good-looking ones too, eh? D'you see that one the other night, at the club? The *métisse*, what the hell was her name?'

'Who cares?' The fat man staggered back to the kitchen. He wiped his greasy hands down the front of his trousers.

'I'm just saying—' the man's tone was aggrieved.

'Well, don't. Ain't none of your business. Now, who wants fried and who wants scrambled?'

'Fried.'

'Yeah, fried's good. Whatever's going, Guido, man.' The second of the two, having been reprimanded once, was eager to show the accommodating side of his nature.

'You, Yves? What you want?'

'Oh, nothing, Guido. I'm fine. I just ate.'

'Yeah. And we all know who you ate with, too.'

'Jesus,' the fat man glared at him. 'What did I just tell you?'

Yves felt a slight prickling at the nape of his neck. He looked at the three men, two of whom regarded him with grins that appeared almost insolent. Guido was back in the tiny kitchen, made even tinier by his bulk, which took up most of it. He looked over at the small dining table. The bacon was pooling in its own fat on the flowered plastic plate and next to it, there was a glass bowl of what looked like fried liver and onions. He felt suddenly nauseous, though the sinking sensation in the pit of his stomach had little to do with the food.

66

TASH

Now. Today. Today's the day. At midnight tonight. The words drummed through her like blood in her veins. *Now. Tonight. Today.* She lay in bed, the duvet pulled up halfway over her head as though she were hiding, not just from the world beyond her front door, but from herself. Outside, beyond the lightly curtained window, dawn was just breaking. Her breath rose and fell, stirring a feather that had somehow poked through her pillow case and lay trembling on the pale-blue bedspread. The early-morning sounds of the street below floated up: deliveries to the Sainsbury's across the road, the stop/start, stop/start of the various vans that came to unload their wares. A street sweeper moved past slowly, steel brushes moving methodically across the uneven pavement; the sound of glass being hauled out of the recycling bins . . . all the dawn sounds that had become as familiar to her as her own breath over the past few months as she lay awake each morning in that semi-pleasurable, semi-fearful state of half-wakefulness. It was the time of day she liked best, that hour or so before the rest of the working world rose up. Sometimes she moved from dream to waking in a heartbeat, her mind already full of whatever problem she'd been trying to solve the night before. At other times, she floated slowly into consciousness, drifting along as her mind slowly emptied itself of a dream, recognisable only by its surreal quality.

She pushed away the duvet cover impatiently and swung her legs out of bed. She reached across and switched on the bedside light. At once the room was flooded and outside receded into darkness. She looked down at her legs in her flowered cotton shorts. They were pale and thin – paler and thinner than they'd been in months. She couldn't remember the last time she'd been in the sun. She couldn't remember the last time she'd been anywhere other than behind her desk, on the phone or in bed, asleep, or trying to sleep.

Today. Now. Tonight. She yawned and stood up, stretching her equally pale and thin arms above her head. She headed to the bathroom. It wasn't yet six a.m. but there was still so much to be done. She had a meeting at nine thirty a.m. with Susie Morgan at her Bond Street store – a last-minute, desperate pitch to get her to sign up. If it failed, she'd still managed to reach the target figure of ten. Ten well-established, cutting-edge designers who'd agreed to show their ranges via her website. It had taken her and Edith nearly four months to reach that number and they'd all agreed they wouldn't go 'live' with less. She would spend most of the day in the office with the boys, crunching numbers, making sure there were no glitches on the site and that everything was ready by midnight. She was glad now that she'd stuck to her guns. With everything that still needed to be done, there was no way she'd have had the energy, let alone the attention span, to organise a launch. They would be up until well past midnight tonight – and probably every other night that week – checking, making sure, double- and triple-checking everything to make sure that their first customers had as smooth and pleasurable an experience as was possible. She felt an unfamiliar flutter in her stomach. It was excitement. The past few months had been run on adrenalin, fear and nerves. Now, with everything in place, it was time to get excited again.

She turned on the shower, pulled her T-shirt over her head and wriggled out of her shorts. The hot water hit her like a slap, blasting her properly awake. *Now. Today. Tonight.* She closed her eyes, savouring the peculiar combination of pleasure and fear. There would never be another day like this one, she thought to herself as she turned the taps off and pulled a towel off the rack. No matter what happened, whether they succeeded or failed, nothing would ever match it. She'd borrowed just over two million pounds of other people's money and staked it and everything she had on an idea she'd had one afternoon in the middle of someone else's shop. If she stopped to think about it – which she tried very hard not to – the thought of it was overwhelming. What if she were wrong? What if everyone else was right? She could see the doubt in their eyes. Luxury fashion? Online? Online shopping was for bargain hunters, not for the rich and famous, and certainly not for clothes. *She* knew they were wrong and she'd managed to persuade a few others to follow her in her vision of a brave, new, online world. But the doubts were still there. No matter how hard Rebecca tried to hide it, especially after their horrible argument, Tash knew that deep down she was worried on Tash's behalf. It wasn't just that she'd borrowed the money from Julian. In fact, that was the least of it; Tash knew the money wasn't the issue. Julian was an investor who specialised in risk. If he didn't think they had an outside chance of succeeding, he'd never have lent her the money. But that wasn't the same as a guarantee that they'd succeed. Win some, lose some – that seemed to be the mantra he lived by, and whilst it was clear he hoped they'd be part of the former, it was also a given that they might not. Rebecca's nervousness about her new venture was of an altogether different order but Tash couldn't quite work out what, or why. All she knew was that it made her nervous too. After the row, Rebecca had done her utmost to be supportive, and encouraging, and Tash loved her for it, but there were moments when she caught Rebecca looking at her quizzically, as if trying to work something out. But what? She sighed. She had to stop thinking about it – there were other, far more pressing things to worry about today.

She towelled her hair dry, yanked her dressing gown off the back of the door and opened her wardrobe. It had been raining all week and although today it looked as though there'd be a break in the thick blanket of cloud that had swaddled the capital for what seemed like for ever, there was no guarantee that the sun would actually shine through. She took out a thin, woollen, black polo-neck sweater and a long midnight-blue pleated skirt. She held them up in front of the mirror – too sombre? She pulled a quick face. It was a sombre day. She would liven it up with a bold piece of jewellery. She turned away from the mirror, her mind already impatiently racing twenty paces ahead. Ten minutes later, her hair still damp and curling around her ears, she picked up her giant handbag, stuffed the last of the papers she'd been working on into it and closed her front door firmly behind her. Her mobile was already ringing by the time she reached the bus stop. Doubts or no, the day had finally arrived. *Cometh the hour.* She smiled to herself and was so wrapped up in her own thoughts she failed to notice the return smile the bus driver gave her.

Surprisingly, she wasn't the first to arrive at the office. Both James and Colin were already at their desks, their faces lit up by the bluish-green glow of their screens. The three young interns they'd brought with them – Justin, Jake and Freddie – were busy behind their own screens. All five looked as though they'd been there all night.

'Hi,' she said, shrugging off her coat and bringing up a stool to perch beside James. A thrill of excitement ran through her. The logo – *her* logo – flashed across the screen, followed by the opening shots of the four fashion shows – London, Paris, Milan and New York. They'd tracked down the photographer, a young German, whose fresh portraits of the frenzied, behind-the-scenes creativity of the shows were exactly what Tash was looking for – beautifully composed without ever appearing contrived. Just like us, she mused.

'Looks good, doesn't it?' James murmured, scrolling briskly across the pages. 'Izzy's working on putting the last few touches to everything. We'll test everything in about half an hour.'

'Fantastic,' Tash murmured. 'Yup, it's all coming together.'

'What d'you want to do about these?' James pointed to a list of links on the right-hand side of the screen. 'We still don't have copy for them.'

'Give me ten minutes.' Tash hopped off the stool. 'I'm on it.'

'Good girl.' James went back to his own job. *Fourteen hours, thirteen minutes, twenty-two seconds and counting.* The countdown to midnight was projected against the rear wall. Tash looked up and down the long desk to her right and left. Everyone was busy – she ran down the list of names; aside from herself, Colin, James and Edith, they now employed Justin, Jake, Freddie, Günther, Izzy, Delores, Tabitha, Caleb, Ashley, Anna B and Ana V – 'B' for Bridgeman, 'V' for Vasconcelos. Fifteen people. If things went well, Julian told her, in six months' time she'd double that and by the end of the year, she'd have quadrupled her staff. *If* things went well.

She turned back to the task in hand and switched on her own screen. *Trends. As seen on. Occasion.* She paused for a second, then her fingers hit the keyboard and she furiously began to type. It took her ten minutes to complete the first draft and by the time she'd finished, her fingers were shaking. The moment she'd been waiting for all her life had finally arrived. All she could think about was how badly she needed a drink.

PART SIX

ARRIVING

'Arriving at one goal is the starting point to another.'
John Dewey

67

A YEAR-AND-A-HALF LATER

TASH
London

Music was blaring from the giant speakers placed at the entrance to the former church. A row of bouncers who wouldn't have looked out of place at an East End nightclub were holding back the crowd of exceedingly well-dressed and exceedingly desperate-looking women trying to get in. Standing a little way behind them, her fur collar turned up as far as it could go, Tash took a last drag on her cigarette and ground it out underfoot. She shoved her hands in her pockets and moved forwards, trying to avoid catching anyone's eye, especially the bald-headed bouncer who was busy sorting out the wheat from the chaff, or whatever the expression was. 'You, yeah, you . . . in the pink coat. Yeah, come on in.' He lifted up the cordon and the girl in the pink coat skipped gleefully through. 'And you, love, yeah . . . that's right. I remember you.' Another anointed young woman was beckoned in. 'No, not you. By invitation only. Yeah, well, she showed me her invitation earlier. Hey, I said *no*!' He stretched out a hand to catch someone who was trying to slip in unnoticed. Nothing got past him.

Tash's heart was beating fast as she inched her way forward. It was the third night of the hottest show in town, the St Martin's end-of-year student show. Cody Sabin's eclectic, electric prints were the talk of the style crowd everywhere and she was one of the young designers showing that night. Tash *had* to talk to Cody face-to-face. Although they'd yet to turn a profit, the signs were encouraging. The website had grown from thirty pages to fifty, there was a monthly online magazine, an editor's letter, editor's picks, clips from the shows, three girl-about-town columns and a blog . . . it was all happening so fast. Every day there were at least a handful of sales that *hadn't* come from friends and family: word-of-mouth, Edith's connections, her own contacts, the wives and girlfriends of Julian's clients . . . all of it had had a knock-on effect that was only just beginning to be seen and Tash was anxious to capitalise on it. She wasn't big or important enough to warrant her own seat at any of the shows – that would come later, she kept telling herself – but one of the things she did do well was spot what might be coming long before it actually arrived. The fashion pack were already onto Cody, Tash *had* to strike a deal to make sure her clothes were available online before they were available anywhere else. Only the other day Julian had asked her what she thought they did better than anyone else. She didn't even have to think. 'We edit.'

'What d'you mean?' He looked at her curiously.

She shrugged. 'Exactly that. We edit what's out there so that our customers don't have to. Look, you've said it yourself. There's so much *stuff* out there nowadays, most women simply don't have the time to wade through all the collections, walk endlessly up and down the high street, especially not the women who shop with us. They're business-women, working women. They're busy. Time is what they lack and that's where we come in. We do the legwork for them *and* we present them with a vision of what they already want before they know it themselves.'

Julian smiled: that quiet, confident smile of his that she'd come to trust. 'Ah, Tash. That's what I like about you.'

'What?'

'You cut to the quick. You get to the point. No bullshit and you've always got your eye on the ball.'

She flashed her invite at the bouncer and was grudgingly let through. Inside, it was pandemonium. Models, dressed in knickers and precious little else, rushed around endlessly, followed by harried-looking stylists and hairdressers, brandishing their tools. The music was deafening. Through the double doors that led to the main hall Tash could see the front-row A-listers sitting waiting impatiently for another show to begin, one skinny leg crossed over the other.

'Ms Bryce-Brudenell?' Someone interrupted her. She whirled round. It was Cody Sabin.

'Cody! Hi . . . hello,' Tash stammered, momentarily caught unawares. She hadn't expected to see her backstage. She hurriedly stuck out a hand. 'Call me Tash, please. Look, is there somewhere we could talk for a few minutes?'

'Sure,' Cody said, jerking her head over her shoulder. 'There's an office back there. Used to be the vestry, or so someone said.' She smiled at Tash. She was American, from one of those small towns in the Midwest that every so often produced a genuine genius oddball. 'Mind your head,' she yelled over the noise as they made their way through the crowds towards the rear of the church. 'It's kinda mad,' she grinned, opening the door and standing back to let Tash pass through. 'Insane, actually.'

'You've taken London by storm,' Tash said as the door shut behind them. 'Congratulations.'

'Thanks . . . yeah, it's been crazy. I never thought it would happen . . . and so fast.'

'That's the best way,' Tash said, smiling at her. 'Unexpected.'

'Yeah,' Cody nodded. 'So, what did you want to see me about? I got your messages.'

'It's pretty simple, really,' Tash said, opening her bag. She pulled out her laptop. 'I don't know if you've heard of us, F@shion.com. We're a new internet-based shopping experience.'

'F@shion.com? Yeah, a couple of the make-up artists were talking about you backstage,' Cody interrupted, peering at the screen. 'They seem to think you're pretty cool.'

'Thanks. We like to think so too. Look, here's what we do.' She pushed the laptop over to Cody. 'We're a cross between a magazine and an online store. We provide fashion content, all the latest brands, the latest looks, accessories, shoes, bags, you name it. We've been up and running for almost a year now, and we've got an amazing customer database. Look, I won't beat about the bush. I want to sign you to a F@shion.com exclusive. I want to offer *your* collection to our clients *before* it hits the stores. I want to give them not just a sneak preview, but also the opportunity to place orders before anyone else. I want our clients to be wearing one of your dresses before the average shopper sees it on the high street.'

Cody nodded, still peering at the screen. 'You want to be ahead of the pack, huh?'

'Exactly. It's all about timing. Timing and exclusivity.'

'Who else have you signed?' Cody was quicker off the mark than Tash had anticipated.

'Jessica Harding,' Tash said quickly, scrolling down the screen. 'She was the first to sign up and we're in the process of building pages for Gudrun, and for Hermann and Hesse. That's the whole point of this section. Hot new designers before anyone else has had a chance to snap them up. There's no point in offering Michael Kors or Ralph Lauren –

everyone stocks them anyway. But someone like you . . . this is about building your profile too, and boosting sales. Like I said, we've got an excellent customer database. We ship to nearly five thousand women across the UK already and we're looking to go global. The US, the Middle East, Australia, New Zealand . . . wherever there's an internet connection and an airstrip. That's the beauty of the internet. So long as FedEx can deliver, they'll buy. One click, that's it.'

Cody nodded again. She quickly scrolled down the pages. 'How long?'

'A month. You give us access to your stocks for thirty days before anyone else; we make sure your clothes are featured on the home page. There'll be an editorial section on you to start with, then hopefully we'll get some cool shots of women actually wearing your clothes in the streets, at a restaurant, a gallery . . . whatever. We aim to build a 'look' around a celebrity or a model and then we invite customers to buy into it. It's simple. And it's effective.'

'Cool. I like it. Thirty days, eh?'

'Thirty days.' Tash's palms were sweating. Cody Sabin didn't know it, nor did she need to, but this was the first time they'd ever tried anything like it. The pages she'd shown her weren't actually live – she had James to thank for that – and she'd yet to have the same conversation with Jessica Harding, Gudrun *or* Hermann and Hesse. She held her breath. Cody nodded slowly.

'Okay, I like it. Let's do it.'

Tash let out her breath. She smiled widely. She'd won her round. One down, four to go . . . look, it was a start.

68

ANNICK
Paris

The English newspaper was lying face down on the counter when she arrived that morning at work. She recognised the typeface immediately. It was the *Guardian*. She hadn't seen a copy in months. She picked it up, wondering who'd left it there, turning the pages over almost reverentially. Few guests at the Hôtel du Jardin read a newspaper, much less the *Guardian*. It was the Saturday edition, too, nice and thick. She gathered the loose pages together, smiling to herself, putting it back into some sort of order. She would read it slowly over the course of the morning. The weekend supplement fell out and she stooped to pick it up. It took her a few moments to realise who the person on the cover was. She stared at it. *One Click Wonder – The Rise and Rise of F@shion.com*. Her mouth fell open. Tash?

'Mademoiselle?' A voice interrupted her. She put up a hand dismissively. There was a client waiting to check out. He could wait. Her eyes flew across the page.

A few years ago, women only bought clothes they had seen, touched or tried on. Now, a new business venture seems set to change all that. *www.F@shion.com.* is the brainchild of young entrepreneur Tash Bryce-Brudenell. In an exclusive interview with the *Guardian*'s fashion editor, Eve Kindall, Ms Bryce-Brudenell reveals where the idea came from, and what she's done to make online shopping a destination not just for bargain-hunters, but for women looking for luxury fashion.

'Mademoiselle?' The man, sounding more impatient now, rapped on the counter with his pen. She put down the paper, stunned. She sorted out his bill automatically, her mind racing. The client, still harrumphing, walked out, leaving Annick alone with the newspaper clutched to her chest.

Tash? A successful entrepreneur? The longing to hear her voice again washed over her, leaving her weak. She stared at the cover again. Tash, just as she remembered her. The stylist had obviously gone to some trouble to make her look as attractive and stylish as possible – her hair was carefully pulled back off her face and she wore more make-up than Annick ever remembered – but there was no mistaking the stern, rather haughty stare, the way she looked out at the camera with her arms folded defiantly across her chest.

She sat down and devoured the article hungrily. If the journalist was to be believed, Tash was on her way to making her first million. She read it through a second and third time, looking for the tiny details that would give her a few more clues into Tash's life but there were few. A guarded reference to an absent father, the fact that she'd been brought up by her Russian single mother, schooled at St Benedict's and the LSE. Finally, after reading it a fourth time, she folded the paper carefully and

271

laid it on the desk, next to the phone. She glanced at it. One call – that was all it would take. But what would she say? It had been more than five years since she'd seen or heard from either of them. Her hand hovered over the phone. So much had happened. Her fingers itched. She could almost hear their voices – Tash's, full of surprise. 'Annick? Is that *you*?' And Rebecca, calm and measured, as always. 'Annick? Where the *hell* have you been?'

The phone rang suddenly, jerking her out of her reverie. She stared at it for a couple of seconds then picked it up cautiously, half-expecting to hear Tash or Rebecca on the other end. It was neither. Just someone enquiring about rates. She gave out the information mechanically, her mind elsewhere. One call. That was all. Just one call.

'So why don't you ring them?' Yves was frowning as he listened to her. 'What's the problem?'

Annick shrugged. She pushed her food around on her plate. It had been a mistake to broach the subject. It was one thing to tell him the reasons why their friendship had fallen apart but that would only mean telling him why she'd left London so abruptly, and then *that* would mean telling him who she was. She bit her lip. There was so much they still didn't know about one another. Yves rarely spoke about his own background. He'd told her he was a student and she knew he looked after the politician whose name she'd didn't even know, but apart from that, she knew nothing. He'd told her he was adopted and that he'd grown up somewhere south of Paris but he said very little about his family and she, sensitive in a way he couldn't have guessed at, didn't pry. He was a curious combination of openness and secrecy, much like her, so they each trod carefully in the present, an unspoken, mutual agreement that suited them both. But tonight she'd crossed a line. She'd opened a door to her own past that would require more information than she was prepared to give.

She hurriedly swallowed a mouthful. 'I . . . it's been ages,' she said lamely.

'All the more reason to phone.'

'I don't know what I'd say . . . after all this time,' she said doubtfully. 'I mean, I haven't spoken to either of them since I left England.'

'Like I said, all the more reason to call. What did you say she'd done again?'

'She started this online fashion business. It's doing pretty well, I hear.'

'How do you know her?'

Annick hesitated. 'We . . . we were at school together. When we were younger.' She looked down at her hands.

'That's what that is, isn't it?' He followed her glance. 'The tattoo. I often wondered.'

'Oh, *that*,' she said, colouring. 'Yeah. We did it together. Silly, really.'

'Well, if you were such close friends then, you can be friends now, no matter what's happened. Phone them.'

Annick was silent, fingering her tattoo. It wasn't just that she had no idea what to say, she was also embarrassed. The roles had been neatly reversed. There was Tash, with all the disadvantages she'd had to endure – no father, no money, an overbearing semi-alcoholic mother who relied on her for practically everything, and despite it all, she'd not only managed to keep up, she'd surpassed them all. She had no idea what Rebecca was up to but whatever it was, it certainly wouldn't be working as a receptionist in a seedy Parisian hotel. Aunt Libertine was wrong. The past was the past. It wouldn't do to go digging around in it, not now. 'Maybe,' she said finally. 'Maybe I will.'

'Here . . . try some of this.' Yves changed the subject. He held out a forkful of food. 'Go on, it's delicious.'

She blushed and opened her mouth. She chewed the piece of chicken he'd given her slowly, wondering how on earth to bring the subject up and, if she did, how to close it again without giving away too much.

69

YVES

Annick was no fool. He'd known that about her from the moment he first set eyes on her, even though she'd been unaware of his gaze. In fact, that was one of the first things he'd noticed about her. She didn't have the same self-conscious awareness that most girls did, especially when looked at by a man. She read, her arms folded about her chest or stomach as though she were holding something in as well as at bay. He must have been in three or four times before he spoke to her and she became aware of his presence. He was intrigued by her – so well spoken, such poise. The funny thing was, he didn't recognise her, at least not at first. She'd put on some weight, he realised. It suited her, though, he thought to himself when he realised who she was. Annick. Of course. Annick Betancourt. He was shocked to see her in that grubby little hotel, of all places, and even more surprised to see that she actually *worked* there. And then of course, Guido saw her. He recognised her straight off. 'You know who that is? That's Betancourt's daughter! It's her! I swear to God! Fuck, just wait 'til Big Jacques hears *this*!' And that was when it all began to get complicated.

He looked at her now, her pretty face lit up by candlelight and the flush that wine always brought to her cheeks and was again overcome by a wave of emotion – not just pity, but something deeper. He was fond of her. He felt again the sharp, almost painful tug of divided loyalties that had characterised almost every encounter with her. The instructions from Big Jacques had been very clear. Get to know her, get her to trust you, share stuff with you . . . and then get her to lead you to the money. He shook his head slowly. If he didn't realise it then, he knew it now. There *was* no money. Whatever Sylvan Betancourt had stolen from the state, he certainly hadn't passed it on to his daughter. Christ, just look at her! Working as a receptionist in the sort of hotel she probably hadn't known existed before the coup d'état . . . no, Big Jacques and the others had it all wrong. If there *had* been money at some point, it was hidden away in one of those Swiss bank accounts whose numbers went to the grave with the holder. Or else some other family member had already got their hands on it. He doubted it. As far as he knew, there was only that aunt in the suburbs who didn't appear to have a dime. There was no one on the mother's side who'd have access to state funds, either. If there *was* any money, it was stored in a vault beneath the streets of Zurich. Before they'd started sleeping together, he'd asked Big Jacques what the point was. All he'd said in response was 'Keep at her. We'll let you know.' That was a year and a half ago and in that time, he'd grown fonder of Annick than he cared to admit.

It nagged at him like a toothache. What now? The purpose – to find the millions that Betancourt had supposedly squirrelled away – that had dominated his life for the past five years was suddenly in doubt, and not just because he believed it to be a dead end. Something else had happened. A slow and growing awareness of his own inadequacy had crept up on him. Part of it had to do with Annick, of course, but part of it too was to do with his own intensifying sense of uselessness. If he were to fail in the one task that had defined him for so long, well . . . what then? What next? It wasn't something he dared admit to anyone, least of all Big Jacques, Gladwell or Guido, or any of the others, but it was slowly beginning to dawn on him that his life lacked direction. He who had had such purpose and clarity for so long. It was enough to make anyone laugh.

'What's the matter?' Annick's gentle, enquiring voice brought him up against his own thoughts.

'Nothing,' he mumbled, spooning rice quickly into his mouth. He shook his head and smiled at her, trying to reassure her. She was uncertain, he saw. Some memory of what his father had been like – all mercurial, flickering moods – flitted across his memory. From the little he knew of her life with Betancourt, he imagined it was pretty much the same. That was another odd thing: for all their differences and the fact that they'd grown up on opposing sides of the political track, they were oddly alike. Both only children born to powerful, overbearing men and beautiful, flighty women who'd disappeared suddenly, leaving little but shadows that still haunted those left behind. It was another reminder of the unintended consequences of a shared time and place. 'Nothing,' he said more forcefully. 'I just think you should phone them, that's all. Doesn't matter what happened or whose fault it was. They're your friends, Annick. You tell me you don't have a family. So your friends are all you've got.'

70

ANNICK

Early, early in the morning, when the mechanical cleaning beasts were making their way down the boulevards and side streets, their dull whirring as familiar to her now as the sound of the pigeons on their way to and from Hyde Park had once been, she woke. From her mattress on the floor, she watched the pearly pink light come up over the city. The faint chink of breaking glass drifted up to her, dustbin men tossing the bagged bottle banks carelessly into the gaping jaws of their trucks, stopping to call out to each other in the mixture of Wolof, pidgin French and Arabic that was their particular argot. A finger of cold air came in from the broken window pane above the bed and curled around her ears. She'd complained to the landlord for months but, as usual, nothing had been done.

The faint call of a nearby muezzin drifted through: time for early-morning prayers in La Goutte d'Or. She burrowed a hand through the covers and looked at her watch. It was just after six a.m. The night before, after taking her to dinner, Yves had mumbled something about having to study that evening and he'd dropped her off outside the entrance to the block just before midnight. She'd waited shyly for some suggestion from him to come to his flat – by unspoken agreement, they never spent the night together at hers – but none came. He'd kissed her on both cheeks as he sometimes did when he was distracted. His mobile phone had rung two or three times whilst they were in the restaurant and when he dropped her off, he seemed impatient to move on. At dinner the night before, it was clear that something was troubling him. She'd asked him once or twice if there was something wrong but he'd brushed off her concern.

'Aren't you going to answer that?' she'd asked when his mobile buzzed dully inside his shirt pocket for the third time.

'No.' He didn't look at her.

'Why not? It might be someone important. Your mother, maybe?'

A look flickered across his face momentarily before he quickly snuffed it out. It took her a while to understand that it was the same look her own face carried at times. He'd told her his adopted parents lived in Clermont-Ferrand, a few hundred kilometres away. He seldom seemed to visit and said almost nothing about them. When she first met him, it suited her. The less he spoke about his family, the less impetus there was for her to speak about hers. She'd told him a partial truth; both her parents were dead. A car accident, she said warily. 'When I was a teenager.' He knew there was an aunt somewhere in the suburbs but that was about it. He appeared to have no siblings. There was at least that in common – but, equally, curiously, aside from the phalange of body-guards with whom he worked, he appeared to have few friends. None, in fact. He never made reference to his studies, or what he did during the days and nights he wasn't guarding *le patron* and wasn't with her. They didn't sleep together very often and when they did, it was always followed by a strange withdrawal on his part, as though he had to put some distance between them that making love had somehow crossed.

She turned her head. Her mobile phone – a cheap, Chinese copy – lay on the pillow beside her. It was Yves who'd insisted she get one. '*I'll* get you one,' he'd said in exasperation. 'It's absurd that you don't have one.'

'You don't need to *buy* me a phone,' she'd retorted sharply. 'I'll get one myself.' A touch of the old Annick resurfaced.

'Fine. But *get* it. I don't like not being able to reach you.' It was that last comment that did it. Someone cared enough about her to be worried when she couldn't be reached.

She'd held it tightly in her hand the night before, daring herself to make the call. She didn't. She fell asleep instead. She reached for it now. There were so few numbers stored in its small memory – *Yves, Aunt Libertine, Hotel du Jardin, Claudette, Wasis* – numbers that she actually dialled from time to time. Then there were four others that she'd entered but never rung. *Tash. Rebecca. Home (London). Home (Lomé).* She scrolled down to Tash and Rebecca. But what would she say? They'd have heard about the coup d'état, of course. It had been in the papers for weeks. But she'd left everything that might have identified her behind – the flat, her possessions, her phone. There'd have been no way for them to contact her. Neither knew where she worked, not that it would have helped. She'd never seen or spoken to any of her colleagues since. It was *she* who ought to have made the first move. She fingered the buttons nervously. What to say? She stared at the screen until her eyes hurt. *Tash. Rebecca.* Then she put it slowly away from her and rolled over onto her side. She shut her eyes tightly but the psychedelic image stubbornly refused to fade.

71

TASH
Paris

Afterwards, when the buzz and the noise and the fuss had died down, there were only a few of them left in the bar. Tash, Rosie Trevelyan from *Style*, a couple of other journalists whom she recognised but chose to ignore and a restless, hyped-up photographer from *Vogue* whose name she couldn't recall but who kept looking around as if expecting one of the models to walk in and sit next to him, presumably. She sat awkwardly perched on the stool, one hand curled around her glass of amber-coloured whisky, the other lightly touching her Blackberry, nestled in her pocket. Rosie, most unusually, was drunk. It was the closing night of Paris Fashion Week and, to Tash's great surprise, F@shion.com had won one of the industry's highest awards, the Fashion Forward Award, given to the year's most innovative retailer.

'Bloody well done, Tash,' she drawled. 'Bloody well done.'

'Er, thanks.'

'Knew you had it in you, though. Right from the start. I always said it to the others,' she waved a red-tipped finger in the direction of some nameless, faceless 'other'. 'I always knew you'd go far. You had a—'

'Rosie, no offence, but I think I'm going to turn in,' Tash interrupted her quickly. She stood up, knocked back the rest of her whisky and hurriedly left the bar. The memory of their last meeting when she'd walked out on Rosie still rankled. Especially now, as the older woman tried to make out she'd spotted Tash Bryce-Brudenell's 'potential' all those years ago. Success, she mused as she made her way upstairs, was an odd thing, a very odd thing.

The lift doors opened on her suite. She stood for a moment in the doorway, taking it all in – the acres of pale carpeting, thick velvet curtains, sleek, gleaming furniture and the enormous bed that had been carefully turned down, requisite chocolate on the pillow and a flower beside the lamp. She shook her head with a sense of disbelief. How had *she* got here? She walked over to the bed and sat down heavily. She kicked off her shoes, rolled over onto her side and opened the minibar. She needed a drink. She poured out a generous measure of whisky into one of the heavy crystal glasses, slipped in two lumps of ice and a splash of soda. Taking a sip, she set the glass carefully down and picked up the phone. It was nearly midnight in Paris, eleven in London. It was late but she was the boss and there was something she had to do.

James answered on the second ring. From the background noise, she could tell he was out. 'Tash? What's up?' He was charmingly affable. Thank God.

'James . . . sorry to call so late. I need you to do me a favour.'

'Sure, of course. What d'you need?'

'I need to find someone. I don't have much to go on, I'm afraid, but it might just be enough. Her name's Libertine Betancourt. She lives in Paris, or at least she used to. Somewhere near the Bois de Boulogne, if I remember rightly. Find me an address or, better still, a telephone number if you can. I need it by tomorrow.'

'I'm on it. I'll call you back first thing.'

'Thanks, James. I owe you one.'

'Are you *kidding*?' Still chuckling, he put down the phone.

She lay back against the pillows, her heart thudding. Why hadn't she thought of contacting Aunt Libertine before? You could find anyone if you tried hard enough. She closed her eyes. The truth was, she *hadn't* tried. Until tonight. She didn't know why the idea to find Aunt Libertine had come to her now, after all these years . . . it had something to do with sitting in the bar downstairs after the awards ceremony with only Rosie and the half-smashed photographer for company. It was one of the most important nights of her life to date and she had no one to share it with. No one who mattered. Rebecca was in Israel with Julian and the family; Edith was at home in London with her grandchildren; James was out with his girlfriend. Lyudmila, in all likelihood, was asleep, a half-finished glass of brandy or port still clutched in her hand. Everyone had *some*one. Everyone except her. She took another sip. The whisky helped her think more clearly. She knew what she had to do. James was only the first step, but at least she'd taken it. It was time to make amends.

72

She got out of the train at Boulogne-Billancourt and looked around. It wasn't quite what she'd been expecting. Pretty, but ordinary. Not the sort of place she'd imagined Aunt Libertine would live. She shouldered her bag and walked to the taxi rank. 'Rue de Verdun,' she instructed him as she got in.

'*Très bien.*' He pulled away from the kerb. '*Ce n'est pas loin.*'

Five minutes later he pulled up outside a small, neat little house with a slate mansard roof and ornate wrought-iron balconies. Number fourteen. It was slightly smaller and shabbier than its neighbours, with a white wooden gate. She checked the address James had given her. Yes, this was it. She paid the cabbie and got out, listening as the sound of his tyres on the cobbled street faded away. There was no latch on the gate; it swung open easily. There was a small buzzer to one side of the peeling front door. She pressed it cautiously. She waited for a few moments, then pressed it again. There was still no answer from within. She stepped back and looked up at the windows. It was five o'clock on a

Saturday afternoon – a good time, she'd thought to herself, to catch someone at home. A sudden movement behind the curtains of the window directly above her caught her eye. She squinted. Someone was peering down at her. She hesitated, and then lifted a hand in a half-wave. She'd met Aunt Libertine once, many years back. From the little she remembered of her, she was a frosty, very formal woman who smiled little or not at all. The curtain twitched shut immediately. She bit her lip and was just about to turn away when she heard a door close somewhere inside the house, followed by the tread of feet on the stairs. Someone was coming downstairs.

Her heart began to thump inside her chest. The door creaked open; she stepped back abruptly. It had been years since she'd seen her but Aunt Libertine's face was unmistakable. The same strange, deeply hooded eyes as her brother's; the same olive skin as Annick's, the high forehead and curved, patrician nose. She was looking into a triptych. Sylvan, Annick, Libertine. The urge to cry came upon her crudely.

'*Oui?*' Aunt Libertine opened the door a little further. '*Qui cherchez-vous?*'

'Madame Betancourt? It's me, Tash,' she began in her halting, schoolgirl French. 'Tatiana. Annick's friend, from school in London. We met once, when you came to London. You took us to tea at the Ritz.'

There was silence as Aunt Libertine looked closely at her. Tash feared she'd shut the door in her face. A minute passed, then another. Finally the door opened fully and Aunt Libertine stood aside for Tash to enter. 'Upstairs,' she said, pointing to the staircase. 'The first door.' She said nothing further as they climbed the stairs together.

She opened the door. Tash's first impression was of a room floating in sparkling sunlight until she realised it was dust. There was a sofa at one end, its cushions flattened and an assortment of blankets lay on the floor. A large television dominated the window. With her paraphernalia of books and magazines and cups and glasses strewn all around her, it was clear that Aunt Libertine was not a woman who entertained much, or even at all.

'Have a seat. There, by the window.' Her English was perfect. Just like Annick's.

Tash sat down gingerly on a low chair, trying not to sneeze. There was a sweetish smell in the air that reminded her of something, though she couldn't quite place it until she saw the half-empty glass of sherry on the side-table, next to Aunt Libertine's permanent seat. Light bounced off the glass. She was instantly catapulted back into the warm fug of home. It was the same smell she associated with Lyudmila's bedroom.

'So, you're here looking for Annick?' Aunt Libertine wasted no time. She fished around somewhere in the depths of the cushions surrounding her and retrieved a pair of spectacles on a brightly coloured string. 'Ah, that's better. Yes, I remember you. The plain one. Still plain, I see.'

'Yes, well, we're not all as pretty as Annick,' Tash retorted, a little more sharply than she intended.

Aunt Libertine's eyebrows went up. 'You clearly haven't seen her lately. *Pouf!* She's an elephant. No, she's lost a *little* weight, it's true, but when I think of what she *used* to be like . . . Tragic. If her mother could see her . . .' She stopped abruptly and reached for her glass. 'Would you like a drink?'

Tash nodded. Getting an address for Annick out of Aunt Libertine might take a little more time and skill than she'd imagined. Despite her air of tetchy independence, underneath it all, she suspected, Aunt Libertine was starved of company. If she had to sit here for an hour or two with her, drinking cheap sherry in order to get what she'd come for, so be it. She accepted a none-too-clean glass of something pale and brown and brought it gingerly to her lips. Dry cheap sherry. Ugh. Still, who cared? She was here for something else.

73

At quarter past five that evening, just as the sun was beginning to sink over the trees, she was back in her compartment on the train, heading back towards the city. Held tightly in her left hand was a scrap of paper with an address. Hôtel du Jardin, rue Championnet, somewhere in the eighteenth, a district of the city that Aunt Libertine clearly despised. 'La Goutte d'Or,' she'd said, her mouth curling derisively downwards. 'Sylvan would be turning over in his grave if he knew,' she said piously.

Tash had no idea where it was but she couldn't have cared less. She had an address. She also had the beginning of a blinding headache, brought on by the disgusting sherry, but her heart felt lighter than it had in years. The only question was why it had taken her so long. She looked out at the city now slowly coming into view. *La Défense, La Grande*

Arche, the starkly elegant form of the Eiffel Tower . . . the train began to slow down as it approached Jean Jaurès Métro Station. She would jump in a taxi from there and show the driver the address. She'd no desire to begin learning the city's geography via its underground.

'Rue Championnet?' The driver looked at her a little incredulously. 'You're sure?'

'Of course I'm sure,' Tash snapped, her patience already worn thin. He was the third driver to question her – only difference was, he hadn't immediately driven off. 'It's a hotel.'

'Well, there are hotels and there are *hotels* . . .' he began, a touch pompously. His English was good.

'Look. I'll pay you double if you can get me there in under an hour. Triple if you take me there without saying another fucking word.'

He scowled up at her through the half-open window. 'Okay, okay. It's your money. *Allez.*'

She climbed into the back seat, sighing with relief. At last. He pulled out and into the traffic heading north without another word. They crossed the river, dancing their way around the complicated traffic flow around L'Opéra until they were on the Boulevard Rochechouart, heading north. *Marcadet-Poissoniers, Barbès, Rue des Portes Blanches* . . . she read the signs as they drove. The Paris into which they were headed was a million miles away from the Paris of Fashion Week and the chic hotels of the Marais where she was staying, and from Aunt Libertine's genteel suburb. Where the hell had Annick ended up? As the traffic thickened and slowed, turning first down one narrow street then another, it was as if she'd parted the veil on another life, one that lived in the shadows. Here there were no street-side cafes where handsome waiters danced between tables, carafes of wine held jauntily aloft, no kissing couples and mothers running after children, balanced precariously on pencil-sharp heels. Instead there were shops whose signs were written in another, flowing script, windows full of bright, sticky sweets; women walked along covered from head to toe, only the opening around their eyes providing any kind of glimpse into the face beneath; men in long, flowing white robes, men blacker than any she'd ever seen in shiny suits and the pointed shoes of medieval court jesters. Her eyes widened. It wasn't possible. She would never find Annick *here*?

'That's it,' the driver spoke suddenly. 'Hôtel du Jardin. Just there, across the road. See?'

Tash craned her neck. The red neon letters flashed out a rhythm. 'I guess that must be it,' she said softly.

The driver pulled up outside the hotel. 'Triple, you said? I didn't say a word.'

'Yeah, all right.' She fished out a hundred-euro note. 'Keep the change.' She got out and slammed the door shut behind her. Her heart was thumping.

'*Merci*,' the driver shouted cheerfully as he pulled back into the traffic. '*Bonne chance!*'

Bonne chance indeed. She looked up and down the brightly lit boulevard. All around her people were streaming back and forth, all lit by the same melon-green night. The hotel's sign flickered dully. She gripped her handbag, pushed through the small knot of people on the pavement and pushed open the door.

74

REBECCA
Tel Aviv

It was a few blocks away from the beach on the top floor of a four-storey building with a broad, wide roof terrace. In front of her, the sea dazzled in a long, wide expanse of rippling blue. She put up a hand to shield her eyes.

'Beautiful, no?' The woman spoke English with a jaunty mid-Atlantic twang. 'Imagine yourself out here in the summer. You could put up a . . . how d'you call it? An umbrella? A shade?'

'An awning,' Rebecca murmured. She turned to look at the view in the opposite direction. Trees, apartment blocks, more trees, more apartment blocks – the city stretched, white and sprawling, almost to the horizon. To her left the bay curved out towards Jaffa and to her right, the impenetrable barrage of sea-front high-rise blocks gazed blankly out over the glassy Mediterranean. 'I like it,' she said firmly, looking round her again. 'I'm not sure I can be bothered with seeing any more. I'll take it.'

The woman looked up, a little surprised. 'You're sure? Your husband said I should make sure you saw—'

'I'm perfectly capable of making my own mind up,' Rebecca said tartly. 'I know my husband knows the city better than I do, but *I'm* the one who'll be living here. At least some of the time. Julian's hardly ever home.' She stopped herself just in time. The woman, sensing something else was being said, looked down at her notes. Rebecca sighed. She had to watch her tongue. In London no one seemed to care that she was Lionel Harburg's daughter, but in Israel, the Harburgs were practically royalty. 'We'll take this one,' she said firmly, more calmly.

'You're sure?'

'Quite sure.' She turned away from the shimmering blue sea and opened the door leading downstairs. 'Quite sure,' she repeated, though possibly more for her benefit than the estate agent's.

She repeated the same words several times that night on the phone. First was her mother.

'You're sure?' Embeth asked, sounding a little surprised. 'It's a nice enough street but it's hardly Herzliya, darling.'

'I know. But I don't want to live in Herzliya. It's a lovely flat. Besides, we're not going to be living there full time.'

'But it is big enough?'

'For the two of us? It's huge, Mama.'

'Well, there won't always be just the two of you, you know.'

'Why? Who else is going to live with us? I hate the idea of a live-in maid, you know that—'

'I didn't mean a *maid*, darling. I meant . . . well, you'll be wanting to start a family soon, won't you?'

'Oh. That. Look, there's plenty of time, Mama—'

'You're thirty, Rebecca,' Embeth interrupted her. 'You shouldn't leave it too late.'

Rebecca had to hold the phone away from her ear, looking at it in disbelief. What the hell had got into her mother? She was thirty, not forty. Plenty of time. 'When are you coming over?' she asked, quickly changing the subject.

'Next week. You'll still be there, won't you?' Embeth sounded uncharacteristically anxious.

'Yes, Mama. I'll still be here. You can come and look at the flat with me. Give me a few decorating tips,' Rebecca said placatingly.

'That'll be lovely, *mi amor*,' Embeth purred, momentarily distracted.

'We can go shopping together and go for lunch. There's a lovely new restaurant near Dizengoff Square that everyone's talking about.'

Rebecca breathed a small sigh of relief. Shopping. Decorating. Lunching. It was what their kind did.

Her conversation with Julian was quicker, more to-the-point. 'If *you* like it, buy it, darling,' he said, his disembodied voice sounding more distant than usual. She struggled to remember where he was. Paris? Frankfurt? 'I won't be able to see it for another couple of weeks. I'm in Brussels tomorrow night, then it's Singapore on Saturday. You'll manage on your own, won't you?'

'Yes, of course. I'll . . . I'll stay out here for a bit. Mama will be here. She'll take me to meet her architects and we can decide if anything needs doing.'

'Good girl. I'd better go . . . I'll call you tomorrow from the airport.' He hung up before anything further could be said. It wasn't Julian's style to end conversations with an 'I love you,' or an 'I miss you.'

She put the phone down slowly and got up from the sofa. She walked over to the antique cupboard, which housed the stereo. She opened the doors and the warm, rich smell of polished wood floated out. She bent down and switched it on. There was a tidy stack of CDs to one side, mostly of classical music and bands whose names she didn't know. She pushed her finger along the hard plastic length of the stack until she saw one she recognised. She giggled. The *Best of Wham!* Next to Rachmaninov. It seemed such an unlikely choice for Julian. She slid it out and in the same instant, a flash of lightning lit up the room. A winter storm was on its way. The lightning flickered again and, moments later, she both heard and felt the dull rumble of thunder somewhere out there over the sea. A tree was sweeping against one of the bedroom windows; somewhere outside a shutter rattled and banged. She slipped the CD into the deck. *Wake me up before you go-go.* The upbeat melody filled the room. *Wake me up before you go-go, 'cos I'm not planning on going solo.* She began to hum along to the tune. Her feet began to tap out the rhythm on the parquet flooring. She looked around her; she was quite alone. She lifted her hands up in the air and began to sway, slowly at first, then quicker, with growing urgency, until she was dancing wildly, uninhibitedly, alone in the strange semi-darkness brought about by the storm.

75

ANNICK
Paris

She came out of the bathroom, drying her hands on her skirt (safer than any towel hanging there), and caught sight of the figure standing by the window. Her heart skipped a beat. A tall, rake-thin woman in a trenchcoat with a scarf tied casually around her neck stood with her back towards her. She turned slowly as Annick came to an abrupt halt. For a moment, the two women stared at each other. Annick's first instinct was to run – but where to? Tash was standing between her and the front door.

'Annick.' It was spoken softly. No histrionics, then. Annick felt a wave of gratitude surge powerfully upwards through her chest.

'Tash.' Annick's throat constricted painfully. An almost unbearable ache of sadness came over her. Ten years. The woman standing in front of her was dressed expensively – pale-green trenchcoat with a dark-tan leather trim; a grey-and-white hound's-tooth-patterned scarf knotted around her neck; high-heeled black shoes with a shine on them like a mirror . . . even her bag, a pale-yellow leather affair with tassels, looked as though it cost the earth. It probably did. She was acutely aware of her own plain black skirt, scuffed shoes and frayed-at-the-collar, second-hand blue jumper. Her hands went self-consciously to its hem, tugging it down. She swallowed, casting about desperately for something to say. 'I . . . I like your bag,' she said finally, idiotically.

Tash looked at it as though seeing it for the first time. 'Prada,' she said with faint smile. 'We get given a lot of stuff.' There was another awkward silence. Annick looked beyond Tash to the street beyond. She was lost for words. Then, in a gesture of almost unbearable tenderness, Tash lifted her head, loosening her scarf. Her long pale neck was suddenly exposed, giving away to anyone who cared to see it so much of her own vulnerability that all the embarrassment and the faint flickering of resentment that Annick felt at having been caught out, vanished. Everything went right out of her and she had to put out a hand, grabbing onto the reception counter.

In an instant, Tash was beside her. 'Easy, Annick,' she said gently. 'Here, sit down. I'm a *complete* idiot. I should've rung first, I'm sorry.'

286

'No, no, of course not. It's . . . I'm fine. It's just . . . it's just such a surprise, that's all—'

'A surprise?' Tash helped her to her seat behind the counter. 'I'll bloody say! Here . . . let me get you something. Glass of water?'

Annick shook her head. She could hear Claudette clattering down the stairs with her mops and brooms and that unruly snake of a vacuum cleaner. 'I'm f-fine,' she stammered. 'Just need to catch my breath. H-how did you find me?'

'Aunt Libertine. I spent the afternoon with her. She almost poisoned me with her sherry, mind, but . . . well, here you are. Here *I* am. I . . . I don't know what to say, Annie. I don't know why it took me so long . . . well, I *do* know, but that's no fucking excuse. I—'

Suddenly the side door behind them swung open and Claudette clattered into the lobby with all her cleaning paraphernalia. She looked from Annick to Tash and back again, raising an eyebrow. A woman with a Prada bag was a rare sighting in the lobby of the Hôtel du Jardin. The three women looked at each other.

'Er, Claudette, this . . . this is a friend of mine,' Annick stammered. 'From London.'

'Nice to meet you, Claudette,' Tash said sincerely, holding out a hand. 'I'm Tash.'

Claudette, unaccustomed to such open warmth, especially in one so well-dressed, held back shyly. Annick's eyes widened. It was the first time Annick had ever seen Claudette appear shy. She shook hands, stole a sideways glance at Annick and then beat a hasty retreat.

'She seems nice,' Tash said mildly as the door closed behind her. She turned to Annick. 'What time d'you finish here?' she asked as if it was the most natural question in the world.

'Eight. Tomorrow morning. I . . . I'm doing night shifts.'

'Isn't there anyone who could cover for you?'

'Cover for me?'

'Yeah. I think we could both do with a drink. I know *I* could.'

Annick bit her lip. 'Well, there's Wasis . . . he's the other receptionist. I . . . I could ask him but—'

'Ask him,' Tash said firmly. 'And tell him we'll make it worth his while. *I'll* make it worth his while. Now I *really* need a drink,' Tash laughed shakily. 'Come on. Let's get out of here.'

Annick swallowed. She picked up the phone. That was Tash. Ever so bossy. Still.

*

An hour later, having bribed a sulky Wasis with a fifty-euro note which subsequently brightened him up no end, Annick and Tash were seated opposite one another in a small cafe just off the main boulevard. It was nearly nine p.m. and rain had begun to fall lightly again. In contrast to the lightness Tash had shown earlier, in the hotel, now, sitting across the table from her, both girls were nervous. The tiny restaurant was in some kind of uproar behind them; a large party of fifteen, twenty people were seated at the long table near the window. Every so often came the loud disorder of chairs being scraped back and forth and outbursts of laughter that shattered the delicate silence that had fallen between them. Tash traced the outline of flowers on the plastic tablecloth with a forefinger, not speaking. The silence deepened.

'What happened, Annick? *How* did it happen? Can . . . can you talk about it?'

Annick looked down at her own hands, folded carefully in her lap. 'I still don't know all the details,' she said simply. 'I was at work – I think it was a Monday morning . . . nothing out of the ordinary. I went out to get a sandwich and then I went to the bank and all my accounts had been frozen. I . . . I walked down the Strand. I didn't really know what to do. I called home but the lines were down. And then I saw one of those *Evening Standard* billboards, you know, the ones on the side of the road. And I saw the headline. That's how I knew.'

'Jesus Christ. How . . . that must have been *awful*.'

Annick nodded. 'Yeah, and then I went back to the flat and Mrs Price just kept saying that I'd better go to Paris. Aunt Libertine was afraid they'd come after the property, but I don't know why. I don't even know if they did.'

'We went there . . . me and Rebecca. It must have been a couple of days afterwards. I saw it on the news and I rang Rebecca straight away. Funny, it was the first time we'd spoken since . . . well, since the party. But the whole place was in complete darkness. We must've gone back, oh, I don't know . . . four, five times after that . . . but it was always the same. The last time we passed, it was boarded up.'

Annick swallowed. Boarded up. Her home. She blew out her cheeks. 'Well, maybe it was all for nothing? Who knows.'

'So what did you do?'

'I came here,' Annick shrugged. 'I stayed with Aunt Libertine for a while. Well, you know what she's like . . . I couldn't bear the thought of having to live off her charity. So . . . I found a job.'

'Doing *this*?'

'Well, what else was I supposed to do? My qualifications wouldn't transfer over . . . I had absolutely no money, Tash. Nothing. I think I left with fifty quid on me. How long d'you think that lasts?'

Tash bowed her head. 'Weren't you frightened?' she asked after a moment.

Annick shrugged. 'Yes, of course. Not like Aunt Libertine, though. She seemed to think they'd be after her and me. I don't remember being afraid of *that*. All I could think about . . . all I *ever* think about is that I'll never see them again.' She blinked rapidly. 'That's the bit I still can't accept. So I don't think about it. I don't think about anything. I get up, I go to work . . . that's it.'

Tash put out a hand, covering hers. 'I didn't know what to do. I kept calling you and there was no answer and your work just said you'd left suddenly. No one knew where you'd gone. We shouldn't have given up so easily. I . . . I just—' She looked away, a hot flush coming up into her face. 'Well, you know why I gave up. I was . . . I was ashamed. Of what . . . happened.'

Annick shook her head. 'It wasn't *your* fault. If anyone was to blame about *that* . . . well, it was him. He shouldn't . . . he should never have—'

'I didn't know it was him at first.' The words suddenly spilled out of Tash's mouth. 'And by the time I realised . . . it was too late. I . . . I didn't know how to stop.'

Annick shook her head. 'I . . . I know. It's hard for me to talk about him like that, especially now, but I don't blame you. Not anymore. My mother told me—'

'She didn't know, did she?' Tash's hand flew up to her mouth.

'No, no . . . I don't think so. At least *I* never said anything. But she told me other stuff about him. Stuff with the servants . . . you know.' Annick fell uncomfortably silent. She looked away. Tash's eyes were bright with tears. 'It doesn't matter anymore,' she said slowly. 'You're here. I'm just sorry you found me like this.' She looked around her.

'Why didn't you come to *us*? We'd have done anything to help you, you know that.'

Annick shook her head. 'How could I? I was too embarrassed. I just couldn't bear the thought of anyone seeing me that way. I just couldn't bear the thought of anyone's pity.' She too looked away. 'I know it's hard to explain—'

Tash shook her head. 'No, it's not. I know exactly what you mean.

That's how it's always been for me. You and Rebecca . . . you lived on an entirely different planet.' Tash's voice caught suddenly. She reached up and fiercely wiped her cheeks with the sleeve of her expensive-looking shirt. Annick's eyes widened in disbelief. She couldn't remember *ever* seeing Tash cry.

'Can I get you ladies anything to eat?' Their waiter interrupted them as he topped up their glasses.

Both shook their heads. 'No, thanks,' Tash said shakily. 'But can you get us something a *bit* more drinkable than this?'

'But of course, madam,' the waiter withdrew immediately. A few minutes later he was back, bearing a bottle before him with considerable pride. Glad of the diversion, Tash made a great show of tasting it and nodding her approval.

'I saw you in a magazine,' Annick began tentatively when he'd finally left them alone. 'Not that long ago. Someone left a newspaper at the hotel. It was the *Guardian*, I think.'

'Oh, *that*.' Tash smiled faintly. 'Doing interviews is my least favourite bit about all this. Everyone's always wondering how someone as ugly as me gets to run a fashion business.'

'Don't say that,' Annick said quickly.

'Why not? It's true.' Tash grinned. She shrugged. 'Anyway, we're not here to talk about *me*, darling. We're here to sort out what you're going to do.'

'What d'you mean?' Annick's heart gave a lurch.

'You don't think I'm going back without you, do you?'

'What d'you mean?' Annick asked again, her heart beginning to accelerate.

'You're coming back with me.'

'I . . . I can't,' Annick said, panicking.

'Of course you can.'

'But what about my job?'

'Your *job*? You're a solicitor, Annick, not a hotel receptionist. Why on earth would you even care about that job? I mean it. I'm not leaving without you. If it means waiting in Paris for a couple of days whilst you sort things out, I will. You're coming home.'

'Tash, I c-can't.'

'Why? Is there something else? You're not *married* or anything, are you?' Tash asked in alarm.

Annick began to cry again. 'N-no, of course not. It's just . . . it's all so s-sudden,' she said, furiously wiping away her own tears. 'I . . . I just d-don't know what to say.'

'Don't say anything.' Tash suddenly laid her hand on the table, palm down. She spread her fingers so that the little tattoo was clearly visible. 'Where's your hand?' she asked.

Annick lay her own next to hers. The two identical tattoos stared back up at them. Neither said anything for a moment. Tash reached over and lightly traced the outline, touching each of the three points of the triangle in turn. Annick closed her eyes. She was wrong. The circle wasn't broken after all.

76

The Hôtel Gabriel seemed to belong to another city, another planet . . . another way of life. From the moment the taxi pulled up outside the four-storey building in the Marais and a bellhop jumped forward to help them out, Annick felt as though she'd stumbled into someone else's dream.

'*Bonsoir, mesdames, bonsoir.*' The receptionists couldn't have been more delighted to see them if they'd tried. Gleaming teeth, glossy hair, smiles as wide as the Seine.

Tash remained coolly unmoved. 'My friend will be staying with me in the suite. Please take her bags right up. We'll have a drink in the bar first.'

'Very good, Mademoiselle Bryce-Brudenell.' And that was that. Annick's two bags that she'd hastily packed whilst Tash waited down-stairs were whisked out of sight. It was nearly midnight but the bar, just off to one side of the lobby, was still full. Tash ignored the one or two people who looked up as they entered and walked straight to a table by the window. Annick followed, too stunned to speak. She watched as Tash ordered a bottle of champagne, wishing the ground would open up and swallow her whole. She'd never felt so out of place in her life. The glamour and opulence around her made her feel almost nauseous.

'Cheers,' Tash said, raising her champagne flute as soon as the waiter had withdrawn.

Annick's head was swimming. The two glasses she'd had earlier on in the cafe had gone straight to her head. She wasn't used to drinking alcohol on a daily, or even weekly basis. She looked around her nervously. A few years ago the roles would have been reversed. Now it was Tash who looked supremely at home in the elegant surroundings. It was Annick who was the imposter. And why on earth hadn't she said anything about Yves yet?

'Cheers,' she whispered, as though the very sound of her voice might alert someone to the fact that she wasn't supposed to be there.

'We'll call Rebecca first thing tomorrow morning. I didn't even tell her I was going to look for you, just in case . . . well, just in case I didn't find you. She'll be over the moon.'

Annick shook her head. 'I can't believe she's married,' she said slowly, playing with the stem of her champagne flute. 'It seems so . . . well, so grown up, somehow,' she laughed shakily.

'We *are* all grown up, darling,' Tash smiled. 'Comes quicker than you think, maybe, but we are. And you? I know I asked you this before but I can't believe there isn't *some*one.'

Annick hesitated for the merest fraction of a second. 'No,' she said, shaking her head slowly from side to side. 'No, there's no one.' She looked back down at her hands, aware of Tash's thoughtful gaze. She didn't dare lift her eyes. If she'd been unable to hide anything from Tash back then, she had the distinctly uneasy feeling she'd be doubly unable to do so now.

77

REBECCA
London

She galloped upstairs to take the call, leaving Annick sitting alone in the beautiful front room with a tray of untouched tea and biscuits in front of her. They'd been talking non-stop since breakfast and she was irritated by the interruption. It was Julian.

'I don't understand it. Why didn't you just call?'

'I was going to but when I phoned the airline to change my ticket, everything got so rushed. The only flight I could get was late yesterday afternoon and I didn't want to disturb you in the middle of your meetings. And then when I got here, Tash and Annick were waiting for me . . . I just forgot, Julian. I'm sorry.'

'Forgot?'

'Well, I didn't *forget* . . . I just thought I'd do it later. You're making such a fuss about it. We were up all night and—'

'Rebecca, you're my *wife*. I've got a right to make a fuss if I don't know where you are. Last thing I knew, you were in Tel Aviv. I've been phoning the flat all bloody night!'

'I know, I'm sorry. I just didn't think you'd be worried.'

'Of course I'm bloody worried!'

Rebecca bit her lip. 'I'm sorry.' She didn't know what else to say. After all, there were times when he was away on business and she didn't hear from him for a couple of days . . . it never crossed *her* mind to be worried. 'Look, I haven't seen Annick in ten bloody years . . . well, you know what happened. I was just so excited to see her again. It . . . it won't happen again, I promise.'

It seemed to be the right thing to say. 'All right. I'd better go. I'll be back on Sunday.'

'Let's go out to dinner when you get back; I'll book somewhere nice and surprise you,' she said placatingly. She couldn't wait to get back downstairs again.

'All right,' he said again, sounding somewhat mollified. He hung up before she could say any more. She heaved a sigh of relief and was just about to go back downstairs when the phone rang again.

'*Amor?*' It was her mother. 'Where have you been?'

'Mama, can I call you back? Annick's downstairs and—'

'Darling, you can't just disappear like that without telling Julian.'

'Oh, for goodness' sake! It's fine. I just spoke to him. I don't see what all the drama is about. He's often gone for days at a time. I've no idea where he is half the time, but *I* don't worry.'

'That's different. He's your husband. He's got a right to know where you are.'

Rebecca almost dropped the phone. She was almost too surprised to speak. 'What are you talking about?'

'Men are different, *mi amor*. The sooner you get *that* through your head, the happier your marriage will be. I've been married to your father for nearly fifty years. D'you think I don't know what I'm talking about?'

'I don't understand—'

'That's the problem with you young girls. You don't try to understand. Don't do it again. Now, give Annick a hug from me. Tell her I'm looking forward to seeing her soon.' She hung up. For the second time in less than five minutes, Rebecca was left holding a hollow-sounding phone.

78

YVES
Paris

She was gone. Gone without a word, without a trace. He looked at Wasis in disbelief. 'Gone? Gone where?'

He shrugged. 'Dunno. She asked me to cover for her a couple of nights ago. Last I saw of her.'

'Was . . . was there someone with her?' He struggled to get the words out.

'Not another man, if that's what you mean. No, there was some woman with her. Tall, skinny woman. Ugly as hell.' He shrugged again. 'Didn't even say goodbye. I heard she rang Christophe on Saturday morning.'

He stumbled out of the hotel, unable to think straight. Gone. Just like that.

That was a week ago. Now he stood with the three other bodyguards, waiting for *le patron* and avoiding their eyes. They all knew. It had to be that friend she was always talking about. The one who'd started some online business or other. He wished he'd paid more attention to the damned story. He couldn't even remember the girl's name. Sally? Susan? How the hell was he going to go about finding her? He knew where the aunt lived but he couldn't risk going to see her. Would she recognise him? It was unlikely but . . . you never knew. It had been more than thirty years since she'd seen him. He'd waited in the back of the car whilst his father went up to interview her. He was gone for hours, he remembered. Finally, just when he thought his bladder would burst, she'd come out the front door to see his father off. She'd seen him sitting there, his face pressed up against the window in distress. She'd taken him upstairs to the toilet and when he came down again, she reached in the pocket of her slacks for a sweet, which she gave to him. A *berlingot*. He'd sucked on the soft boiled sweet happily, entranced by the woman his father swore was more dangerous than her brother. He'd never seen anyone as glamorous before. She had long, dark brown hair, held in place by a patterned scarf and it cascaded down her back as she turned. She smelled wonderful too; he remembered that much. The hair and the perfume and the soft, chewy sweet in his mouth. That was what he knew of Libertine Betancourt.

'What's the matter with you tonight?' Gladwell sidled up to him. Yves resisted the temptation to punch him.

'Nothing.'

'You seem a bit distracted.'

'Fuck you.' Yves moved away. He was in no mood to talk to Gladwell or anyone else.

Gladwell gripped him by the upper arm. 'Take it easy, man,' he hissed through clenched teeth. 'Boss wants to talk to you.'

'Get *off* me!' Yves tried to shake his arm free but Gladwell held fast.

'They think some money's come in. That's why she's gone. It makes sense. Five years, let things lie, nice and quiet and then, when no one's expecting it . . . *pouf*. Open up the accounts. Like water running out of a tap. Find her and we'll find the money.'

It took all of Yves' self-control not to punch the man in the face. He shook off his hand angrily and headed for the windows at one end of the room. He ignored Big Jacques' concerned frown and stepped outside onto the small balcony. The night air was cool and clean, a welcome relief from the smoky, overheated interior with its tired but lethal pool of businessmen and politicians circling each other like sharks. He drew in great mouthfuls of the night air. Though he hated to admit it, he was confused. For a moment, his hand went to his pocket, looking for the cigarettes he no longer smoked. He stood there for a moment, gazing out over the city. They were on the fifth floor of a nondescript inter-national hotel somewhere near the Louvre, a bland corporate backdrop that provided equally bland food and drink and the appropriate level of inoffensive decor. The occasion was a Franco-Togolese business summit, or so the delegates proudly announced. The real purpose of the gathering, Yves knew, as with all other gatherings of its kind, was for the French to work out who was who in the new political order. After five turbulent years, France was getting tired of dealing with the unruly rabble of junior officers who'd overthrown Betancourt. Just as Chirac had once remarked of *him*, '*ça suffit*,' now he repeated it of the rebels. *It's enough.* Five years of endless internal squabbles over power, corporate mismanagement on a scale that few could imagine and almost total fiscal impunity – *ça suffit*. In that fragile period of deal-making and shifting alliances before the storm, the players – local and international – were lining up to take their shots. *Le patron*, it was rumoured, was about to see his patience with the French rewarded.

God, he wanted a cigarette. He took off his glasses, pinching the flesh between his eyes. When Big Jacques had approached him a couple of years earlier, it all seemed so clear. He was struggling. His mother's health, never good at the best of times, was ailing. He'd been enrolled at ENSTA for the second year running to take up his half-completed thesis and he'd run out of funds. He was in his mid-thirties, no wife or girlfriend, the son of a murdered and discredited journalist with no real plan. His mother too had no plan. A pretty, high-spirited but insubstantial woman, she'd all but disintegrated after her husband's death. From one man to the next, one flat to the next, one part of Paris to the next. He loved his mother desperately but he also despised her. The combination made him uneasy and, not surprisingly, turned him from the outgoing, easy young man he'd once been into the loner he'd since become.

So when Big Jacques came looking for a part-time bodyguard for the man they hoped would replace Betancourt, it appeared as though the offer had come from God. Yves couldn't have cared less about the man's politics. No one seemed to understand. For him, Africa was finished. The dream of a return died with his father's murder. France was his future now. The job seemed easy enough. Three or four nights a week and every other weekend. Enough money to ease the job of looking after his mother and allow him to complete his studies. It was a no-brainer. As soon as he was introduced, he realised he didn't care for the fat, boorish *patron* but, then again, he wasn't paid to care. His job was to look after his safety. Nothing more, at least not back then. But if there was one thing he'd learned since then, it was not to be fooled by appearances. The man was fat, yes, and boorish too. But beneath the blubber and the sly, lazy eyes was a cunning political intelligence that took Yves' breath away. Looking after him was the easy part. His habits were dull and predictable – drink, prostitutes and watching the occasional game of football. His instinct for survival was anything but. He could – and would – break bread with anyone whom he thought might further his cause.

He was halfway through his second year on the job when Big Jacques approached him with another request. Not Gladwell or Guido – the other two, who might have been more suitable for the task. But no. They wanted him, Yves. 'On account of . . . well, we thought it would interest you more.' No one would get hurt, he was promised. All they wanted was a little information. It was to do with the girl at the hotel, the receptionist. They'd seen him chatting to her but it was Guido who'd alerted them. She was a Betancourt. The traitor's only legitimate child. Yves' job was simple. Befriend her. Get to know her.

'Fuck her if you have to, we're not fussy,' Big Jacques cleaned his teeth with a toothpick as he talked. Yves tried not to look.

'Why? What's *she* done?'

'Nothing. Nothing yet. But the bastard left money. Lots of it. Switzerland, we're told. We need to find that money, my man. The country needs it. We'll leave it to the politicians to figure out what to do with it but our job is to find out where it is. She'll be able to tell you.'

'How? She hasn't got a dime! Look at her.'

Big Jacques shook his head fondly at him. 'Naive, man. That's the trouble with guys like you. No, she'll know where the money is, trust me. But first you've got to make her trust *you*.'

He wasn't naive and he certainly wasn't stupid. They didn't have a hope in hell of getting their hands on the money – *if* there was any to be had, which he doubted. But what did he care? What they'd all failed to notice was that he had no ambition to return to Togo whatsoever. He wanted no part of the struggle going on six thousand miles south of Paris and he certainly had no intention of taking up his dead father's cause. He had his doctorate to finish. If taking Annick Betancourt out every once in a while was what was required, well, no problem. But then he got to know her. And then things began to get more complicated. And now she was gone. He took off his glasses, pinching the flesh between his eyes again. He was tired and angry and he needed time to think.

'What the fuck's the matter with you?' Someone spoke out of the shadows behind him. He turned round. It was Big Jacques himself, an irritated tone in his voice. 'You're paid to watch *le patron*, not the fucking view.'

He nodded. 'Yeah, sorry. Just grabbing some air.'

'Well, don't. Keep your eye on the ball, sonny boy. Eye on the ball. Remember that.'

Yves nodded curtly and moved indoors. Dammit, the man could see *through* you. All the way through.

79

ANNICK
London

Coach. Rykiel. Céline. Joseph. Missoni. Armani. McCartney. Chloé. Annick gazed dazedly at the selection of clothes strewn across the bed – *her* bed – in utter bewilderment. These belonged to *her*? She picked up the Chloé pink mohair cardigan, fingering it fearfully. There was a card lying on top of one of the many boxes. She opened it with shaking hands. *Darling, try everything on and I mean everything. I'll stop by later on and we can discuss what works. Couple more boxes to come. All my love, T.* She turned it over. A simple, pale-grey card, embossed with Tash's logo. www.F@shion.com. She took in a deep breath and stood up. For a moment the room lurched in tears then she steadied herself. The bedroom – *her* bedroom – was knee deep in boxes. She still couldn't get over it. Forty-eight hours after arriving on the Eurostar, Tash had handed her the keys to a flat. Her own flat. A small, beautiful two-bedroom flat on the second floor of an elegant period property on Queen Anne Street, just around the corner from Tash's own flat, and her offices. Annick's protests had simply been met by a withering look. 'You need somewhere to live, darling. End of story. We can sort out the details later.' She meant it. There was to be no discussion until Annick had a) a new wardrobe, b) had spent a day in the spa and c) found a job . . . and not as a hotel receptionist, either. The flat was fully and beautifully furnished. For the first couple of hours Annick simply wandered through the rooms, too dazed to speak.

She looked around her now. There were more clothes lying around the room, on the back of the dressing table chair, on the bed, on the ottoman at the foot of the bed, in half-opened boxes and in their plastic sheaths on the floor than she'd seen since she last opened her mother's wardrobe. What was she to do with them all? Try them *all* on? And *shoes*! Jimmy Choo. Michael Kors. Valentino. Zanotti. Names she'd forgotten, brands she didn't even know. She bent down and picked up a pair of dark orange suede platform peep toes. Rochas. Who the hell was Rochas?

She hesitated, and then slipped them on. She rose a couple of inches in height − and several feet in confidence. Jesus, Tash was right. There was nothing like a pair of high-heeled, beautifully made shoes to make the world seem, well, brighter, as though the sun had suddenly come out. She walked across the parquet floor. The heels clacked satisfyingly against the wood. She reached the opposite wall and turned round. More assertive this time. She squared her chin, looked straight ahead and walked in a steady straight line, her head held higher than it had been in years. Once, twice, three times, up and down the length of the bedroom. Then she sat down on the bed and eased them off. What were Tash's instructions? *Try* everything *on*. She ran a tongue around her lips; they felt dry, probably with excitement. It was hard to grasp that so much had happened in a week. She looked around her again at the debris of Tash's generosity. She didn't deserve it; she just didn't deserve it. Not after the way she'd treated Yves. She'd packed her bags and left the city without saying a word, not even goodbye. She'd *meant* to . . . she *wanted* to . . . but the thought of explaining everything had simply overwhelmed her. How would she explain? It would have meant telling him everything. Worst of all, she'd have had to explain why, in all the time they'd been together she'd never once told him who she really was. That was the problem with silences. What started out as the simple avoidance of truth became, in the end, worse than a lie.

The door opened suddenly. It was Tash.

'You're still in your dressing gown! I told you to try everything on!'

'I . . . I was going to,' Annick stammered, half guiltily. 'I just didn't know where to start!' She looked at the clock on the mantelpiece. 'It's only three. How come you're back so early?'

Tash grinned at her. 'That's the *only* perk of being your own boss, you know,' she said happily, shrugging off her coat. She picked up the pink cardigan Annick had discarded. 'Isn't this just *divine*? Feel that . . . soft as a blooming baby's bottom. Not that I'd know what *that* feels like,' she added, chuckling to herself. 'Nice, but a bit too girly, don't you think? You need something more assertive.'

'Why? What for?'

'For your interviews, of course.'

'Interviews?' Annick asked, bewildered. Everything was happening so fast.

'Job interviews, darling. We'll have you back at the bar within a fortnight, you'll see.'

'I . . . I was never *at* the bar, Tash,' Annick said nervously. 'I was a solicitor, not a barrister.'

'Bar, courtroom . . . wherever. We've got to get you back in the saddle, Annie. Trust me. When everything else is falling around your ears, work's the only thing you can trust. The *only* thing.'

'But where would I start?'

'At the Law Society, of course,' Tash said, looking up, an expression of astonishment on her face. 'Annick, I *know* it's been hard, darling, but you've got to get out there. You've got to put a fucking huge smile on your face, put your best foot forward and start climbing your way back up. *That's* the way you'll make things happen. You've got to get back on top, Annie. You can *do* it. I know you can.'

Annick swallowed. Deep down, she knew Tash was right. She'd been knocked off course and she'd fallen further than she'd ever imagined possible. But she couldn't keep on falling. She had to stop. She had to get up, just as Tash said. She looked around at the flat, the piles of clothes and the shoes, still in their boxes, the big, fat leather handbags and all the jewellery that Tash had gone out of her way to choose for her. A ripple of admiration tinged with fear ran through her. She'd always been in awe of Tash. She'd been the poorer of the three of them, unable to afford the things that she and Rebecca took for granted – holidays, a nice home, parents you didn't have to worry about – and yet she'd have sooner died than have anyone feel sorry for her. Jesus, if Tash could forge her own way in the world with all the disadvantages she'd had, why the hell couldn't *she*?

'Pass me that one,' she said firmly, pointing to a navy, knee-length dress with gently billowing sleeves.

'Roland Mouret,' Tash said, a satisfied smile creeping up on her face. 'Isn't he just the *best*? Makes a girl look like a star, even if she doesn't feel like one.'

'And you don't think I look too fat?' Annick said anxiously, tugging down the hem of the skirt.

Tash shook her head. 'Voluptuous, dearest, not fat. Though you have put on a pound or two,' she added, cocking her head to one side. 'Suits you, though. And there's not many girls I'd say *that* to, I can tell you.'

Annick turned to look at herself in the mirror. She was unrecognisable, even to herself. The dowdy, overweight receptionist who'd manned the desk at Hôtel du Jardin for the past five years was gone. 'Tash, I haven't seen this many clothes in five years,' she murmured, looking past Tash to where mountains of clothes still lay scattered on the counterpane.

'Many more to come, darling, many more. This is what I do, remember?'

Annick nodded slowly. She wasn't *quite* who she had been. She'd lost the sultry indolence of her teenage years and there was a new hardness and wariness in her eyes that had never been there before. But the haunted, beaten look that she'd grown accustomed to seeing every time she looked in the mirror was gone.

'Put these on,' Tash commanded, handing her a pair of black patent Jimmy Choos. 'See? See what those do to your legs?'

Annick nodded. 'How much are they?' she whispered fearfully.

'Enough to put the spring back into your step and that's enough for me,' Tash grinned. 'Look,' she continued, suddenly serious, seeing the look of panic on Annick's face. 'Don't worry about what all this cost. I haven't got anyone to spend my money on. What's the point of making it all if there's no one to spend it on?'

'What about your mum?'

Tash shrugged impatiently. 'Oh, she's getting plenty of it, don't worry. Besides, she spends most of it on booze. And, speaking of which,' she reached into her giant soft leather bag and pulled out a bottle. 'Be a darling and get us two glasses, won't you?'

'Where from?'

Tash rolled her eyes. 'The kitchen, idiot. Where else?'

'Oh.' It was her second day in the flat and she'd yet to do more than go to the loo. 'Right. Back in a sec.'

'Let's polish this off and then I'd better get back to work.' She prised the cork off the already-opened bottle of champagne. 'Right . . . let's get started. I want to see what you're going to wear on that all-important first interview. Sounds good, doesn't it? The *All*-Important First Interview. I'd better make a note of that before I forget. It'd make a good feature.' She pulled a notebook from her bag. 'Okay, knock yourself out, darling.' She settled herself more comfortably on the bed, poured herself another glass and grinned at Annick. 'Get on with it, love. I haven't got all day.'

*

It took them less than two hours to sort out a week's worth of interview outfits. Tash was ruthless. Sipping her glass of champagne, she barked out her orders. *Here, try this. No, take that off. Shoes are good, awful belt. Skirt should be longer. Different colour. You need earrings with that. No, not those ones. Try these. Yeah, that's better. You look like a hooker in those.* She walked round Annick as though she were a model waiting nervously backstage before going out on the catwalk. By five, when the last drop of champagne had been drunk and the light outside was fading, she pronounced herself satisfied.

'If you're not hired as soon as you walk through the door I'll eat my hat. No, yours. Hmm. I rather like that hat . . . who's it by?' She left in a hail of kisses and promises to call before midnight and disappeared in a black cab. She had a meeting at the other end of Oxford Street and she'd be damned if she was 'going to shove and push my way through all those fucking tourists. Bye bye, darling. Let's have a drink later on.'

Annick watched her clamber into the cab, then she turned around and walked slowly back up the thickly carpeted stairs to her flat. She closed the door, leaning against it for support, breathing deeply. She walked into the bedroom and slid back the wardrobe door. She reached for the first item on the rack. It was a sand-coloured wool-crêpe blazer with matching, wide-legged trousers. She rubbed the luxuriously soft fabric between her fingers. Tash had picked out two silk shirts – one in cream, the other in a soft baby-blue. With a pair of high-heeled dark-brown snakeskin pumps and a brown handbag, she looked every inch the stylish solicitor Tash seemed to think she was – or ought to be. She walked across the room, entranced by her own image in the mirror. Was that really *her*?

The phone rang suddenly, shattering the silence. She stared at it for a moment, then, her heart beating fast, she picked it up. For a brief, mad second, she thought it might be Yves.

'Annie? It's me.'

It was Rebecca. She felt a quick thrill of relief, followed immediately by a stab of guilt. 'Oh. I wasn't sure . . . I didn't know who it would be.'

'Well, who else would it be?' Rebecca chuckled. 'Unless there's someone in Paris you're not telling us about?'

'No, no . . . of course not.'

'What're you doing? Right now, I mean?'

'Me? Nothing. Tash just left. She brought all this stuff . . . all these brand-new outfits, shoes, bags . . . you should see my wardrobe. I've never seen so many clothes in my life.'

'Are you hungry? Shall we go out to dinner, just you and me? I phoned Tash and she's tied up in a dinner meeting and Julian's out of town. I'll come over and get you. We can go somewhere near you, if you like?'

'Um. The thing is, Rebecca . . . I'd love to, but . . .' She stopped, embarrassed.

'What?'

'I . . . I haven't any money, Rebecca. I . . . everything happened so fast and—'

'Annick, if I hear you mention the word "money" again, I swear I'm going to hit you. Just get dressed. I'll be there in half an hour.'

'I . . .' But it was too late. Rebecca had already put the phone down. Annick stood where she was, blinking back yet another round of tears.

80

JULIAN
Zurich

He pushed back the heavy sliding door, belted the thick dressing gown around his waist tightly and stepped out into the pearly morning light. The air was cold and sharp. It struck his face, burning slightly in his nostrils as he breathed in. It was the end of November, late autumn back home in London, but winter already in the middle of the continent. Below him lay the city, all dark spires, streets stitched together with Christmas lights. He could just make out the dark red tiles of the Rathaus, a couple of blocks away. Beyond the jagged line of buildings was the river. He felt light-footed and his head was clear – surprising, given that he'd hardly slept. He walked over to the edge of the balcony and placed his hands carefully on the freezing wrought iron, rocking gently back and forward, flexing his muscles, stepping into the beauty of the city as it rose from its wintery night-time slumber. The ground rumbled faintly underneath his feet; a tram slowly swam into view. A flock of birds took off suddenly from one of the buildings opposite – a dark, ragged triangle in flight across the sky.

His mind drifted from the scene in front of him to the dinner the night before. He'd taken the group to one of his favourite restaurants, the Alden Gourmet, on Splügenstrasse, a five-minute walk from the bank where they'd held their meetings. They were a tight team. There was Barry from New York; Jeff from London, Frédéric de Chambord from Lichtenstein, the South African Luc Breil and then the two men from Dubai – Mohammed Al-Rasool and Saleh Mansour. And last, but by no means least, there was Miranda. Ah, Miranda.

He allowed himself the smallest of smiles as he stood there contemplating the city at dawn. He'd known Miranda Grayling for almost twenty years and never once, in all that time, had he ever dreamed he'd be relying on her to help him pave his way through a deal, least of all a deal of this magnitude. Miranda Grayling – or Miranda Smith, as she was known back then – was Doug Grayling's PA. Grayling, a transplanted American, had started out at Merrill Lynch, then moved to Bank of America's London branch, then spent a couple of years at Goldman's before being hired at Harburg's, against old Lionel's wishes. You couldn't trust a man who'd jumped ship so many times, Lionel was often heard to grumble. But Harburg's was interested in America, also against Lionel's instincts, and Doug Grayling had apparently persuaded the board that he was just the man for the job. He moved across in a blaze of self-publicity that set the old man's teeth on edge but the younger board members were keen. There were some who complained that Lionel was losing it, even back then, but not Julian. Lionel's body was failing him but his mind was still razor-sharp. He'd seen the greed in Grayling long before everyone else did. Julian, like everyone else, now only saw Lionel intermittently at Harburg Hall. In a wheelchair now, of course, and almost completely deaf. But his eyes missed nothing. Very little escaped the old man's attention. Julian swallowed uncomfortably at the thought.

A sudden shaft of sunlight pierced through the thick, woolly clouds and for a moment, hit the golden spires of the Rathaus, a brilliant golden arrow. He brought up his hand to shield his eyes from the glare, then it slid off and the city was cloaked again in milky greyness. He let out the breath he'd been holding, slowly, and turned. He'd forgotten to close the thick, velvet curtains when he came in last night. They were still bunched to one side and the sheer muslin panel that lay between the velvet and the glass sliding door was billowing outwards, like a sail. He looked beyond the glass to the rumpled surface of the bed. Dented pillows, bunched-up sheets, a pair of men's trousers and the flung-aside arm of his shirt . . . and the firm, toned and pale leg of his night-time companion. Miranda Grayling, née Smith. She'd kept Grayling after the divorce. Sounded better, she claimed.

Her tousled blonde hair made a splendid contrast with the dark-blue silk sheets. Now, as then, she slept naked, the only difference being that the flesh he'd held, touched and tasted pretty much all through the night was firmer now, expensively anointed and pale as mother-of-pearl. Back then when she'd been one of the many pretty young secretaries who flitted in and out of the various offices at Harburg's, she'd been ever so slightly chubby, slightly less blonde than she was now and a whole lot poorer. Grayling had given her a taste for the finer things in life. In the event, her divorce settlement had given her capital. Of all the things that could be said about Miranda, 'stupid' wasn't one of them. 'Greedy', 'scheming', 'ambitious', even 'ruthless', yes, but not 'stupid'. She'd parlayed her experience of being a banker's wife into an impressive portfolio that included property, smart investments and, most interesting of all, a little black notebook (metaphorically speaking, of course . . . it was rumoured she took her laptop to bed) with more names and phone numbers than anyone else in town.

Julian silently slid back the door, closing it firmly behind him. He drew the curtains, throwing the room back into shrouded darkness. Miranda slept like a man, her head flung backwards, arms outspread. She snored steadily, lightly. He remembered that about her too. He dropped his dressing gown, looked down at his penis and was gratified to see it thickening already. He walked around to her side of the bed, drew back the covers and looked down at her. He was instantly hard.

'Jesus Christ,' Miranda mumbled, opening a bleary eye as he pushed his way aggressively beside her. 'What have we here? I thought I'd have worn you out, old man like you?'

'Be quiet, Miranda. That's the *only* annoying thing about you.'

'What is?' she murmured sleepily.

'You don't know when to shut up.'

'Tetchy, are we?' She turned herself so that he lay with his cock pressed up against the small of her back. 'Wonder what your wife says about early-morning bad humour.'

'There you go again.' He shoved a knee in between her still-warm thighs, forcing her legs apart. 'Leave my wife out of this.'

'Pity. I was rather looking forward to having something over you,' she grinned into the pillow.

'Miranda, the only thing I want of yours over me are your nether regions. Now, are you going to help me in, or do I have to force my way?'

'Nether regions!' Miranda giggled, shifting herself so that he slid into her almost immediately with practised ease.

He didn't reply. That was another thing about Miranda. Ever fucking ready. He grinned as he began to move himself back and forth. Ever fucking ready. No pun intended either.

'I don't understand.' Barry looked at the departing backs of the two men from Dubai. 'I thought we were ready to sign?' An hour and a half later, all traces of the night they'd spent together erased completely and utterly, they were sitting with Jeff and Barry at breakfast. Julian viciously speared the last grilled mushroom on his plate and chewed slowly, methodically, whilst Miranda smoothly answered Barry's panicked questions.

'Al-Rasool and Mansour are good guys,' Miranda said, cutting her sliced melon into ever-finer slices. 'Don't underestimate them. But they're not the money men.'

'So who's controlling the purse strings?'

'The Al-Soueifs,' she said simply. 'Look, they're the ruling family. QCI own sixty-five per cent, but make no mistake. Unless the sheikh's signature is on the deal, nothing happens.'

'So how do we *get* his signature on it?' Frédéric asked, puzzled.

Miranda smiled and looked up at them all. 'Simple. I'll ask him. Nicely.'

Julian looked up in alarm. A sudden, disturbing image had flitted across his brow. 'How?' he barked suddenly.

'What d'you mean, "how"?'

Julian cleared his throat, aware Jeff was looking at him closely. 'I just meant it's hellishly difficult to get access to them.'

'Not for me. Soon as I get back tonight, I'll ring him. He'll take my call, don't you worry about that.'

'You're amazing,' Frédéric said, clearly impressed. 'I'd heard you were good.'

'The best,' Miranda said calmly, with no trace of irony either. She took another sip of her black coffee and dabbed her lips delicately with her napkin. 'Give me two days. I'll get back to you with the outline proposal – and my fee, of course – and we can take it from there. Now, if you'll excuse me, gentlemen, I'm meeting that group of men waiting by the door. I'm back in Dubai tonight, so I'm afraid I've rather packed you in.' She got up, smoothed down the skirt of her dark-grey suit and held out a hand. The men scrambled to their feet. 'Have a good morning,' she said briskly, picking up her large, mannish-looking but exquisitely detailed handbag. The laptop was nestled securely inside it, Julian noticed. She turned to go.

At the far corner of the room, four Arab men waited patiently for her, their long white billowing robes a perfect contrast to the sombre granite and black interior of the hotel lobby. 'She's something else,' Jeff murmured as all four men watched her cross the room.

'You've known her quite a while, haven't you?' Barry asked Julian curiously.

'A while,' Julian admitted cautiously. The breakfast meeting had turned his earlier calm into something approaching near despondency. He shook his head faintly. He was acutely aware of Miranda's reputation. It was the reason he'd brought her into the deal in the first place. He'd seen her in action before. She was good at the game. She ought to be. Doug – poor old, broke Doug – had been a master broker and she'd clearly learned much from him. Still, there was no reason for him to worry. He was every inch as good a dealmaker as Miranda. He watched her discreetly pull on a silk headscarf before greeting her next clients warmly. She clearly knew a thing or two about doing business with Arabs, he noticed. She shook hands with each, inclining her head respectfully but seating herself gracefully before they did. Every inch a woman, yet in no way deferential.

He shook his head again. As urbane and polished as he was, doing business with the patriarchs from Abu Dhabi, Dubai, Qatar and Jordan was difficult for him, a Jew. It was Lionel who'd first taught him to 'put all of that aside', as he called it. Lionel would do business with anyone, so long as they adhered to the gentlemanly rules of the game. He had little time for politics. 'Ach, underneath it all we're all the same,' he always said. But Julian found it hard. If anything, he found the younger generation more difficult. There was something in the older men that he found he could more easily identify with. For all the ways in which they were different, they were also curiously alike. Polite, inscrutable, patient, cautious . . . much like him, in fact. The old ways appealed to him. The younger men, like Al-Rasool and Mansour, he found almost impossible to read. These were men who'd been to Harvard and Cambridge; they wore designer suits and expensive sunglasses and their mobiles seemed permanently clamped to their ears. Their casual, easy familiarity with Julian's world only showed up his ineptness in theirs and it made him uneasy. Miranda seemed to have no such insecurities. Despite the fact that she was a woman – and a Western woman at that – she appeared to float easily between *all* their worlds. He'd even overheard her speaking Arabic at breakfast – somewhat accented, of course, but Arabic nonetheless. It was enough to put him off his omelette.

The whole trip had left him out of sorts, he realised, as he made his way upstairs to pack. He didn't like the way Miranda had subtly taken charge of things, or the way she'd left his business associates speechless with admiration. And what of last night? They'd left the restaurant, leaving Jeff and Barry and the two Arabs to make their own way back to their rooms. He thought it had been his idea to have a nightcap on the rooftop bar, but perhaps it had been hers? He wasn't sure if it was he who'd made the first move. Yes, they'd wound up in his room but perhaps that was what she'd wanted all along? Dammit. He'd woken up feeling so confident and strong, as though life couldn't possibly get any better. He'd been absolutely sure they'd sign the deal over breakfast and he could go back to London, confident that there'd be another few million coming into the company coffers before long. And now? Now he was questioning everything. Miranda had them all eating out of her hand. It wasn't quite what he'd had in mind.

81

TASH
London

Lyudmila was fast asleep by the time Tash let herself in, just after ten. She opened the front door cautiously, acutely aware she was several hours late. It was the third time in as many weeks that she'd left the office after nine thirty, too late to have dinner with Lyudmila, who ate around seven, if she ate at all.

She closed the front door and tiptoed into the flat. There was another scent overlaid on top of the usual smell of home, a faint sourness that made her wrinkle her nose. In the living room, the TV was on but soundlessly. Lyudmila lay sprawled out on the sofa, the remote still in her outstretched arm. She hung up her coat behind the door and looked around. The flat was a mess. There were dirty plates on the coffee table, the usual assortment of empty bottles and glasses left lying around, a new fur coat thrown carelessly over the back of the sofa. She sighed. She'd begged her mother to let Yvette, the woman who cleaned twice a week for her, come in and do the same. 'At least once a week, Ma,' she'd said only the other night. 'Just to help with the dishes and things.'

'What dishes? I live alone!'

'I know you live alone, Ma. But everyone needs a cleaner. Even you.'

'You saying I'm dirty? House not clean enough for you, now you rich girl?'

'No, Ma, I'm not saying that. I'm just saying—'

'*Nyet*. I don't need cleaner. Here, *you* clean.' She picked up a dishcloth and thrust it at Tash.

'Ma—'

'Always you *nezgovorchivaya*. Always.' Tash held her tongue.

Now, surveying the aftermath of Lyudmila's day, in all likelihood spent in front of the TV, she blew out her cheeks in frustration. How long had the plates on the coffee table been lying there? But to begin clearing the place up would mean waking Lyudmila and there was no telling what sort of mood she'd be in. She tiptoed out, eased off her own boots and walked into the tiny kitchen. Things weren't much better in there. There were piles of plates in the sink, three or four empty wine bottles on the counter and countless saucers thick with cigarette butts. She sighed. Short of bringing Yvette in by force, there was nothing she could do. She opened the fridge, pulled out a half-full bottle of Chenin Blanc and picked a glass from the cupboard. She switched her phone to silent and walked back into the living room. She carefully pushed aside a few magazines and weeks-old newspapers from the chair opposite her snoring mother and sat down, leaning back against the cushions. She took a sip of wine. Considering it wasn't a bottle she'd bought, it wasn't bad. Across from her, Lyudmila made a funny kind of half-groan, half-sob, turning herself uncomfortably on the sofa, her face now thrust into the cushions. She groaned again, then sank back into sleep.

Tash closed her eyes. It had been a long day, not helped by her decision to break it off halfway through and spend most of the afternoon looking through Annick's new wardrobe. She'd rushed from Annick's new flat to Selfridges for her meeting with Henrietta Wheeldon, the hot new designer who'd agreed to a F@shion.com exclusive, arriving twenty minutes late. Fortunately for her, Henrietta was also running late; by the time the two women met, it wasn't clear who was waiting for whom.

From there, she'd jumped in another cab to Bailey's for a quick drinks meeting with the head of women's fashion, the utterly charming Sally MacKenzie, who not only had a cold bottle of Dom Pérignon but some chocolate biscuits as well. She had two. Two bottles of champers and two chocolate biscuits – the sum total of her daily intake. No wonder she still looked like a rake, she thought to herself wryly as she closed her eyes and took another sip of her wine. Yes, it had been a long day, but worth it. For the first time since they'd started, designers were ringing *her* up, courting her instead of the other way round. She'd turned down three well-known fashion houses in the past week, much to Edith's amusement.

She poured herself another glass. 'Cheers,' she whispered, raising it to herself. What an odd scene, she thought to herself. There she was, at the age of thirty-two, well on her way to making her first million, sitting alone in a darkened, dirty basement flat in Kensington drinking cheap white wine whilst her mother lay sleeping on the sofa opposite. She'd just installed her best friend in a beautiful little flat close to hers, the sort of flat her mother ought to be in if only she could get her to agree to the move. Just what *was* it that made her so damned stubborn?

She felt a painfully familiar ache, deep in her chest, as she looked at Lyudmila. She was the most maddeningly difficult woman on the damned planet. She'd do anything for her and Lyudmila knew it. She was happy to accept the generous monthly stipend that Tash discreetly arranged for her, but aside from shoes and clothes and her weekly trips to the salon on Beauchamp Place where she had her hair and nails done, she didn't want much else. She refused outright to move. 'Is my *home*,' she said stubbornly. 'No move.' In desperation, Tash had once offered to move her into her flat. She'd looked at Tash as though she were crazy. 'No move,' she repeated firmly. 'I *like* my home.'

Lyudmila's relationship with money was impossible to fathom, Tash realised finally. It had something to do with her upbringing, of course, which Tash knew very little about. She was also exceedingly proud. It was an odd, uncomfortable equation, lots of pride, no money. Not that having money necessarily entitled one to be proud, Tash thought to herself in one of those sudden flashes of insight that always seemed to accompany a bottle of wine. But it certainly helped. What was the *point* of Lyudmila's stupid insistence that the house didn't need cleaning, or that the TV could do with being replaced? Lyudmila seemed to view *herself* – her own face, body, clothes – as the only thing worth trusting and therefore investing in. In that department, sadly, her own daughter had spectacularly let her down. It was as though she'd been slapped in the face twice. Once, by life – *zhizniu*, in Russian, which loosely translated to 'fate' – and then by Tash, who refused to honour the things that Lyudmila held sacred: her looks. Tash had always been determined to make it using a different set of criteria – her brains. Not that she had much choice, she thought to herself wryly, polishing off the last of the wine. If she'd done as Lyudmila wanted and tried to trade on her looks, she'd be homeless by now. She put the empty glass down on the floor and stood up. She'd never quite managed to balance tipsy insight with maudlin, hard-hitting truths. The last thing she felt like doing was sitting up until midnight, waiting for Lyudmila to wake up, going over things she'd rather not think about. She walked over to the sofa and laid an arm on Lyudmila's.

'Ma,' she whispered, bending down close. 'Wake up.' She wrinkled her nose again. The smell she'd first noticed when she walked in was stronger now. She looked down the length of her mother's slumbering form. Her legs were covered with a thin blanket that she must have yanked off her bed. She peeled it back slowly and then stood up, a hand going automatically to her mouth. Her mother had wet herself. The sour smell was urine. She swallowed. The dark stains appeared all down her cream woollen trousers.

A wave of profound, primitive despair flowed over Tash before she could stop it. She stared at her mother. All her life there'd been things she felt but couldn't name, fears she couldn't utter. Not having a father was one of them. Yes, she always trotted out the cheerful, well-worn phrase, 'oh, you can't miss what you never had' and she repeated it so often it was almost true. Almost. Then there were the other fears. Worrying that she'd never blossom, the way Rebecca and Annick had. That she'd never be even remotely attractive. That she'd always be mouthy and smart but never, ever desirable. That she'd be successful but unloved, or that she'd always be alone. Looking down at her mother, it was the last fear that sent a tremor of despair running through her. Something was happening to Lyudmila – was she sick? No, that wasn't it, unless it was some hidden, secret illness no one, not even Lyudmila – could see. It was more a letting go . . . it came to her now, that, in spite of Lyudmila's inherent selfishness, especially when it came to choosing between a luxury for herself or something for Tash, her mother had always been *there*. She'd more than made up for the absence of a father. She was always there when Tash returned home, always there at night when she went to bed. She never once spent the night away from home, not even back then when she'd had every opportunity. No, her gentlemen friends always came to the house, never the other way round. The sudden, painful realisation opened out onto a deeper one. What would become of her when Lyudmila was gone?

Lyudmila's eyes opened suddenly. She struggled to focus. 'Oh. *Dushen'ka* . . . w-what time is it?'

Tash, for the first time in years, laid a hand on her mother's hair. It felt soft to the touch. 'Ma, it's late. You've had a small . . . accident. You must've spilled something on your trousers. Come on, let's get you into bed.'

Lyudmila looked down at herself, frowning. 'Wh . . . what? Oh, oh, *nyet.*' She struggled upright, brushing Tash's hand aside. '*Nyet* . . . it must've—'

'Must've been the tea,' Tash interrupted briskly. 'Come on, get up.' She helped Lyudmila stand. Together, they made their way rather shakily to Lyudmila's bedroom.

'*Ya sama!* I manage,' Lyudmila said impatiently as Tash tried to help her unbutton her shirt.

'Fine. D'you want some water?'

'*Nyet. Da.* Yes, bring me water.' Lyudmila peeled her shirt off and unbuckled her trousers. There was a second's hesitation as they looked at each other, mother and daughter, neither wishing to admit to what clearly couldn't be said.

Then Tash turned and went into the kitchen. She filled a glass from the tap and took it back in. Lyudmila was already in bed. She took the glass over, setting it carefully down on the bedside table. She looked at her mother. Lyudmila's eyes were closed. She stood there for a second, and then bent down to pick up her discarded clothes. '*Dushen'ka,*' Lyudmila murmured suddenly.

'What?'

Lyudmila's hand went out, catching hold of Tash's. She held it for a second, and then brought it gently towards her own head. Tash held her breath for a second, fighting down the ache in her chest. Then she began gently stroking her mother's hair.

82

ANNICK
London

'Someone from the IT department'll be up shortly. He'll sort you out with email access and all that. Oh, and he'll programme your ID card so that you can get into the canteen and the library. I think that's everything. I'm only down the hallway so shout if you've got any questions. Shall I take you to your office?'

'Yes, please. Th-thanks,' Annick stammered. Her hands went automatically to her sides, as though she were trying to smooth her hips away. The black skirt with its kick-flare hem at her knees felt uncomfortably wrong. Clinton Crabbe might be one of the biggest and most prestigious law firms in London but her Burberry suit felt all wrong. Too stylish. So far, she'd met approximately ten of her new colleagues, ten men and women in almost identical grey and black suits without even so much as a hint of colour between them. She'd worn the beige Chloé suit to her interview with the baby-blue shirt, of course and had been told kindly, but firmly, that 'We generally stick to black at Clinton Crabbe. Sometimes grey. Maybe navy-blue.' She'd immediately relayed the intelligence to Tash. 'Bo-*ring*.' Tash was unrepentant. 'Get the job first, though. They can't sack you for wearing nice clothes.'

On her first day she'd carefully chosen the only black suit in her wardrobe. At home, in front of the mirror, it seemed conservative enough but now, catching sight of herself in one of the mirrors as she followed her new colleague down the corridor, it struck her as a little too . . . well, *feminine*. There was nothing feminine about any of the other female solicitors she'd encountered thus far.

'Ms Karol should be here soon. She comes in from Brussels on Mondays.'

'Brussels?'

'Yeah. Her husband lives there. He works for the European Commission. She flies over every other weekend. Right, well, if there's nothing else?' He seemed in a hurry to disappear.

'No, no . . . that's great. Thanks,' Annick hastily assured him. She couldn't remember his name. Neil? Nigel?

'Good luck.' He lowered his voice. 'She can be a bit fierce sometimes, but don't let that put you off. She's brilliant.'

'Oh. Th-thanks.' The door closed behind him and she was alone. She looked around the office. It was a decent-sized room with two desks and a small adjoining room off to one side where the two secretaries sat. Neither was at her desk; one had gone out to fetch coffee and the other was busy photocopying files. Whilst the secretaries – whose names she'd also already forgotten – were technically hers as well, it was clear Frances Karol's wishes would always come first. She was the most senior woman in Clinton Crabbe and Annick ought to consider herself lucky to be working with her. So everyone said.

A shadow fell across the carpet suddenly. She looked up. A young woman was standing in the doorway holding a large silver flask. 'Oh, hello. You must be the new solicitor. I'm Louise. Ms Karol's assistant.'

'Hi. I'm Annick.'

'Um, we don't call the solicitors by their first names. Not in this department, anyway.'

'Oh.'

'So, you'll be Miss Betancourt to us. That's myself and Katie.'

'Oh.' Annick didn't know what else to say. She was saved any further embarrassment by the sound of footsteps approaching the door.

'Good morning, Ms Karol,' Louise practically dropped into a curtsy.

'Morning, Louise. Ah, you must be Annick Betancourt.'

Annick nodded. Frances Karol was a tall, flame-haired woman in her mid-forties, dressed in a grey pin-stripe trouser suit with a black silk shirt and a severe, no-nonsense look on her face. 'Y-yes,' she stammered. 'Good morning. I . . . Neil showed me—'

'Coffee? How d'you take it?'

'For me? Oh, er, milk and sugar.'

'Sugar?' Frances raised an eyebrow. 'Coffee for Miss Betancourt, Louise. This side of Christmas, if you can manage it. Now, I assume someone's shown you the peripheral stuff?'

'Peripheral stuff?'

'Toilets, canteen, that sort of thing?'

'Oh, er, yes.'

'Good. Then we can get started on the important stuff. Pull up a chair and grab a notebook. I've a list of things I'd like you to take care of. It's going to be a tough week, I'm afraid. We've got several big cases coming up and I'll be alongside the barristers in court for most of it. I'm told you've a fair bit of experience in wills and probate?'

Annick swallowed nervously. It had been over five years since she'd even looked at a legal document, let alone a will, but something told her it wasn't the time to admit to it. 'Um, yes,' she mumbled. 'That's mostly what I worked on at . . . when I last worked here.'

'Good. Not a million miles away from what I do. Patience is key. Hard work, attention to detail and patience. Let's hope you've got at least one out of the three.'

Annick had no idea what to say. She struggled to keep up with the list of things Frances was rattling off. She'd only just managed to get over the shock of watching Tash at work. The brusque, no-nonsense manner that had characterised her personality for as long as Annick had known her had been transformed into a brisk professionalism that left Annick speechless. And now here was Frances Karol, several years older and several degrees frostier. The women Annick had either known or worked with before were of a much milder, more feminine disposition.

'Annick?' Frances' voice interrupted her musings.

She looked up nervously. 'Yes?'

'You've stopped writing. Unless you've got total recall, which I very much doubt, you're going to miss something. I'm going to go back a point or two and I'd advise you to do the same. It's all in the detail, Annick. But you should know that.'

Annick bent her head back to her notebook. Her cheeks were already reddening. Could she keep up?

The brain, Annick soon discovered, was like any other muscle. *Was* it a muscle? No matter. Whatever it was – muscle, organ, *thing* – it needed exercise, fresh air, and exertion. In other words, it needed to be *used*. Her brain, unused to doing anything more taxing than working out room rates or adding up the night's takings, refused at first to step up to the plate. Her first few days at Clinton Crabbe passed in a haze of panic. She felt as though she was sleepwalking and with each passing hour, the feeling intensified. She couldn't manage the simplest of tasks, like remembering where her office was. Fourth floor, exit lift, turn left (not right), second corridor on the left, fifth office down. She whispered the directions to herself like a mantra and *still* managed to take the wrong corridor, wrong turn, wrong office. She'd lost count of the times someone on the fourth floor had seen her coming, rolled his eyes and pointed her back in the direction from which she'd come. Of the six pairs of shoes Tash had thrust upon her, none had anything less than a four-inch heel *and* they clacked. Click-clack, click-clack, click-clack. Frances wore low-heeled sensible black court shoes, not stilettoes, and she approached in silence. Annick came down the corridors sounding like the Charge of the Light Brigade.

Every morning, a pile of legal briefs would appear on her desk threatening to topple over. Her job was to go through them with a magnifying glass, checking facts, figures, dates, conflicting accounts . . . making sure, in other words, that whatever landed on Frances' desk was watertight and in perfect order. 'If you can survive six months with her, you can survive anyone,' someone helpfully told her as they both stood waiting for their coffees one morning. Annick nodded uncertainly. At this rate, she thought to herself, she wasn't sure she'd survive another six days. She went to bed after midnight every night, woke up at five, usually in a cold sweat worrying if she'd forgotten something or misspelt something or omitted something, and was at her desk by seven thirty each morning, long before Louise and Katie. There was so much to learn. 'Experience is everything,' Frances tossed out over her shoulder one afternoon. 'A tax lawyer who doesn't know her taxation is useless, so you've got to be committed to acquiring that knowledge.' Annick could only nod. Her first few months were crucial, she knew. She had to establish herself not only as credible in Frances' eyes, but as a team player, someone who could roll up her (Chloé) sleeves and get down to business alongside everyone else. She felt as though she'd suddenly been thrown a lifeline and she was determined not to let it slip.

Compared to what she'd been earning in Paris, her new salary was an absolute fortune. Tash wouldn't hear of her contributing to her rent or her clothing. 'Pay me back later, darling. When you're properly on your feet.' And that was the end of that conversation.

Six months, Annick vowed to herself. In six months' time, she'd move out of the lovely little flat on Queen Anne Street and into something that, as a junior solicitor, she could properly afford. In the meantime, there were so many other things to worry about. At the end of her first week she walked into Lewin's, the shirt-makers on the corner, and bought three plain white shirts. One more raised eyebrow from Ms Karol and she'd *die*.

83

REBECCA
London

It was their third argument in as many weeks, and, as usual, it was conducted over the phone. Where was Julian? Vancouver. No, Toronto. Ottawa? She struggled to remember.

'I don't understand,' Julian said tetchily. 'It's all organised. What's the problem?'

'But you said you'd be in Israel next week. And I . . . I made *arrangements*.'

'What sort of *arrangements*? Cancel them.'

'I . . . I can't. It was just going to be the three of us. It'll be the first time we're—'

'Rebecca.' Julian's voice was dangerously quiet. She could feel a storm coming on. 'You need to make up your mind here.'

'What d'you mean?'

'You're married to *me*, Rebecca, not those damned girlfriends of yours. Now, I've got two clients coming over with me, and Jeff and Miranda, of course. I've already spoken to your mother. We're going down to Brockhurst. She'll have the place ready for us; the servants will organise lunch and dinner. Jeff and I will take the clients out for a round of golf on the Saturday morning and I'm sure you can find something to do with Miranda and—'

Rebecca slammed down the phone. Her hands were shaking. She'd been so looking forward to spending the bank holiday weekend in Cavezzana with Tash and Annick. It was to be a surprise for Annick's birthday. They'd planned to show up at Annick's flat early on the Saturday morning with presents. Embeth's driver would wait for them downstairs. They wouldn't tell Annick where they were going until they'd reached Heathrow. First-class tickets, a driver waiting for them in Genoa, the drive down to Cavezzana . . . it had all been organised, right down to the last detail. And now Julian had gone and ruined everything . . . and the worst thing was, he wasn't even apologetic! He seemed to regard it as his *right*! And her mother seemed to be in on it, too. She'd known for *weeks* what she and Tash had planned . . . how dare she just give into Julian's demands without saying a word?

The phone rang again. She ignored it. She got up off the bed and walked into her cavernous walk-in closet. She yanked a denim jacket off the rails and shrugged it on. Flicking her hair back into a ponytail, she slipped on a pair of sandals and picked up her handbag. She glanced at herself in the hallway mirror – no make-up, an angry set to her lips and a frown that seemed etched between her brows . . . but for once, she didn't care. She had to get out of the house.

The bar at the Stag and Hound was packed. It had been years since she'd been in here, she thought to herself as she pushed her way forward, trying to catch the eye of one of the bartenders. The three of them had often sneaked in as teenagers when they were staying at Harburg Hall. Like all the pubs in the vicinity, it had gone decidedly upmarket. The walls were painted a lovely, deep raspberry and the wooden floors had been stripped back and varnished to a deep, golden sheen. The clientele had changed too. It was louder and a lot more dressed up than she remembered. Rock music blared from the ceiling in the bar and in the dining area, just behind the bar, huge, sparkling chandeliers cast a soft, pretty glow over the diners.

She spotted a stool right at the end, next to the serving hatch and quickly pushed her way over. She slid gratefully onto it, and pulled her slouchy handbag onto her lap, like a pet. She squinted at the bottles behind the bar – what did she feel like?

'What can I get you?' A good-looking young bartender was suddenly in front of her. 'Glass of white?'

'Er, yes. That'll do.'

He put the glass down in front of her with a small flourish. 'Let me see . . . I've got a lovely Felton Road Chardonnay. From New Zealand. You look like the sort of woman who'd go for that.'

Rebecca smiled, her first smile of the evening. 'And what sort of woman would that be?' she asked. He was clearly flirting with her.

'Someone with a bit of sophistication, I'd say. No, make that a *lot* of sophistication.'

Rebecca had to laugh. She gestured down at herself. 'In jeans?'

'Ah, it's the bag that's the giveaway. Looks expensive. Might not be. It's hard to tell these days. But it looks it.'

Rebecca smiled. 'It was a present,' she said quickly.

'From?'

She looked up. 'My husband.'

'Lucky man.'

'Why not "lucky me"?'

'Anyone can buy a bag,' he said easily. 'You, on the other hand? Like I said, lucky man.'

'Christian! Are you going to stand there all night chatting up poor defenceless customers?' A harried-looking man brushed past, carrying a tray of steaming glasses. 'There's a couple down the other end . . . they've been waiting for ages.'

'Sorry, boss.' Christian grinned at Rebecca. 'What's your name, by the way?'

'Sally.' The lie popped out before she could think.

'Funny. You don't look like a Sally. Well, see you later, Sally-or-not.' He winked at her and was gone. She stared after him. It had been so long since she'd had the occasion to flirt she'd almost forgotten how. And what on earth had made her lie about her name? She picked up the very large glass of white wine he'd set in front of her and took a gulp. He was right. It *was* delicious.

'Good, isn't it?' She looked up in surprise. He was back.

She nodded. 'Very.'

'What did I tell you? No rush – plenty more where that came from.' And he was gone again, whistling some damn tune, obviously mighty pleased with himself. Rebecca sat up a little straighter in her chair. She wished she'd taken time to put on some make-up.

'Your name's not Sally, is it?' He turned towards her, groping for the bedside light. She put out a hand to stop him. She liked the fact that she couldn't see him properly.

'No.'

'So what is it, then?'

'Does it matter?'

He paused. She could feel his chest expand as he slowly exhaled. 'It'd be nice,' he said after a moment.

Rebecca shook her head and reached for her handbag, which was lying on the floor beside the bed. *His* bed. An untidily made bed in a shared house somewhere in Camden. She almost giggled out loud. Christian was twenty-three. A student. Anthropology. From Dorset. Those were the facts. Oh, and that she'd gone home with him after the pub closed. She fished around for her cigarettes. The room was illuminated briefly as the match flared. 'Want one?'

He nodded. They lay back against the pillows, smoking together. 'So what's your story?' he asked her, rolling over to face her.

'Haven't got one.'

'Course you have. Dunno how old you are. Not much older than me, I don't think. You're married and your husband's clearly not around. You come into the pub for a drink, wind up having most of the bottle and then you come home with me. I'd say there's a story in there, wouldn't you?'

'Christian, can we just leave it at this?' Rebecca asked, smiling at him to take the sting out of her words. He seemed nice. 'You're very sweet . . . I had a good time tonight. But I . . . look, it's complicated.'

He was quiet for a bit, concentrating on finishing his cigarette. He stubbed it out and turned to her again. His hand went round her shoulders, burrowing underneath her hair, pulling her back towards him. His brow was creased but he didn't seem angry. They lay facing each other, touching lightly as he stroked the hair away from her face. 'Fine,' he said quietly. 'If that's the way you want it.' His other hand moved slowly down the length of her naked body, teasing her as he went. He slid a finger between her hot, damp thighs, gently stroking her back to excitement.

'Harder.' Again, the words slipped out before she could think.

'Like this?'

'No, harder. Harder than that. You can hurt me, if you like.'

His finger stopped its rhythmic stroking. 'Hurt you?' He sounded genuinely surprised.

She nodded. 'Hurt me. Please.'

She turned slowly in front of the mirror. It was nearly five a.m., although it was still pitch black outside. She'd walked from Christian's flat on Castlehaven Road all the way up Haverstock Hill to the top, before winding her way through the backstreets until she reached home. It had taken her nearly an hour but she needed the fresh air. Several lone taxis had spotted her, slowing down as they passed her, but she'd made no move to hail one down. She needed the time to think.

Now, safely back at home, she took off all her clothes and stood naked in front of the long mirror in the bathroom. She examined herself carefully from all sides. She bruised easily; already she could see faint marks beginning to show up underneath her alabaster skin. There, on her upper arm, where he'd gripped her and on the inside of both thighs. She touched the marks lightly, as though testing a piece of fruit for ripeness, wincing in pain. Why had she asked him to hit her? She had absolutely no answer save one: she'd enjoyed it. Every single minute.

The couple of hours she'd spent in Christian's bed had been the most exciting of her life. She was free to do what she liked, how she liked. He had no idea who she was and never would. She was free. Absolutely, utterly free.

She turned on the shower and stepped in. She angled her face gratefully up to the powerful water jets, enjoying the sensation of being lightly hit and pummelled for the second time that night.

84

TASH

There was something odd about Rebecca that wasn't just to do with her distracted air and the way she kept fiddling with her hair. Tash frowned, trying to put her finger on it. 'Have you been on holiday or something?' she asked her suddenly. 'You're tanned.' The three of them were having dinner at Carluccio's, on Westbourne Grove. Tash had just come out of a meeting around the corner and had somehow managed to persuade the other two to join her close by.

'Oh. Yeah, I did a couple of tanning sessions. At the salon,' she added, seeing both Tash's and Annick's puzzled faces. 'I just couldn't bear being so bloody pasty-faced any longer.'

'Pasty-faced? You're always pasty-faced,' Tash couldn't help herself. 'Well, pale, I mean.'

Rebecca shrugged. 'I just got tired of it.'

'Is everything okay?' Tash asked, frowning again. Rebecca really did seem out of sorts.

She nodded impatiently. 'Yeah, yeah . . . everything's fine.'

'How's Julian?' Annick ventured. 'I can't believe I haven't met him yet. I've been back a couple of months, you know. It's gone by so quickly.'

'He's away. Again,' Rebecca said tightly. There was an awkward silence.

'It suits you, though,' Annick said timidly. 'The tan.'

'Thanks.'

Tash shrugged and reached for the wine bottle. Fine. If Rebecca wanted to pretend that everything was okay, who was she to argue? 'Where is he, anyway?' she asked, somewhat changing the subject.

Rebecca shrugged. 'New York. Brussels. Tokyo . . . I lose track.'

'So, what's the plan for my birthday?' Annick asked brightly.

Rebecca turned a stricken-looking face to both of them. 'I won't be able to make it,' she said, biting her lip. 'I'm really sorry.'

Tash's mouth dropped open. 'What're you talking about? We've been planning it for ages,' she said, astonished.

'It's Julian's fault. He's organised a weekend down at my parents' place in Hampshire. We leave on Friday, back on the Tuesday morning.'

'You're kidding!' Tash burst out. 'We had *plans*, Rebecca!'

'I know, I *know*,' Rebecca sounded close to tears. 'I *told* him. But he's bringing some clients down. He's got these two guys coming with him and they want to spend a weekend in the English countryside. He rang my mum the other day and they organised it between them. The driver's taking us down. *And* he's bringing that awful woman, Miranda whatever-her-name-is. You know, the one who's always in the news. *I've* got to entertain her whilst they tee off. It's so fucking unfair.'

Tash's mouth dropped open. It was so unlike Rebecca to swear. 'Why can't he just go down on his own?' Tash asked angrily. 'Doesn't sound as though he needs *you* there?'

Rebecca looked even more guilty and miserable. 'I . . . I can't. I can't *not* go. I'm his wife, Tash.'

'And you're our best friend.' Tash glared at her.

Annick looked from one to the other anxiously. 'It's not such a big deal,' she said quickly. 'It's fine. We'll think of something, won't we, Tash?'

'But it was all *planned*,' Tash began angrily, irritation written all over her face.

'I know, but we'll think of something else.'

'Since when did you become such an arbitrator?' Tash snapped.

'Don't take it out on *her*,' Rebecca snapped back. 'It's not Annick's fault. It's mine, I told you. And I've said I'm sorry. I'll make it up to you, Annie, I promise.'

'It's not your fault,' Annick protested.

The three of them glared at each other. Then, to everyone's relief, Tash began to laugh.

'Okay, okay . . . . we'll think of something, Annie, just you and me. It's fine, Rebecca. You trot off and play the good wife. Me and Annick'll get up to no good without you.'

For a second, Rebecca looked as though she might burst into tears but she didn't. 'You've got no idea what it's like,' she muttered after a moment, pouring herself another glass.

'You're right, I don't.' She looked at Rebecca sharply. Two tears suddenly rolled off her chin and landed on her plate. 'Rebecca?' she asked in surprise. 'Look, it's not *that* serious,' she said, trying to lighten her tone. 'It's fine. We'll do something else. Maybe we can get together the weekend after next. How about that?'

Rebecca nodded, but seemed unable to speak.

Annick's eyes were like round, panicked saucers. 'Don't,' she said, putting a hand on Rebecca's arm. 'Don't cry, Rebecca. It's fine, honestly.'

'It's n-not that,' Rebecca stammered, wiping her cheeks furiously. 'It's n-not ab-about your birthday.'

'What's the matter, then?' Tash asked, hoping her voice was gentle.

Rebecca shook her head furiously. 'N-nothing. I'm . . . I'm just a bit tired, that's all.'

Tash frowned. It was on the tip of her tongue to ask her what on earth could possibly have tired her out, but she held back. Rebecca didn't work. She didn't have to get up every morning like Tash and Annick. She lived in a beautiful flat that was entirely paid for; there were two cars in the garage – not that she ever went anywhere – and all bills went straight to her father's accountant. Tash doubted Rebecca even knew what her trust fund paid for. There were umpteen holiday homes to choose from and her most strenuous task of late had been the purchase of their home in Tel Aviv. Her mother had organised the interior designers and, by the sound of it, had bought most of the furniture. Every once in a while Rebecca went to an art gallery, the theatre or a social function in aid of one charity or another that her family supported, but that seemed to be about the extent of her commitments. She did yoga twice a week, went intermittently to the gym and was at the salon rather more often than her long, dark-brown hair actually warranted . . . but that was Rebecca. It had always been thus; the beauty of the Harburgs' wealth was that it would *always* be thus.

'Let's get the bill,' Annick suggested. 'And before anyone says a word, this one's on me. No, I absolutely insist. It's my turn and if you don't let me, I'll start crying too.'

Watching her proudly pull out her wallet, Tash felt a second wave of remorse wash over her. Annick too had changed, almost beyond recognition. Gone was the confident, almost arrogant beauty who'd been an object of envy most of her life. The woman she'd encountered in Paris bore almost no resemblance to her. In Paris, she'd found a nervous, subdued Annick who looked over her shoulder every other minute, as though fearful of what she might find there. The past month had changed that; she no longer looked so haunted and some of that old magical sparkle was back. But there was a new depth to her that surprised Tash. Of the three, Annick had always been the flighty one. Shallow. She'd said it herself so often that she believed it. It was no longer true. It was Rebecca who now appeared insubstantial and paper-thin, not Annick. And what of her, she mused, draining the last of her wine. How did she appear to the two people who knew her best? She had an uncomfortable feeling she'd rather not know.

85

REBECCA

The countryside was shrouded in thick, dense mist that parted like a heavy curtain as they approached. The large car ate up the miles as they turned down one country road after another, often coming upon a clump of trees or a low, moss-covered stone wall seconds before they were swallowed up again. Rebecca sat in the back seat, directly behind Julian and pretended to be asleep. Out of the corner of her eye she could see Miranda Grayling's shapely knees peeking out from the hem of her exquisitely tailored skirt. Rebecca knew it was exquisitely tailored because Miranda had told her so. 'Yves Saint Laurent,' she said, noticing Rebecca's gaze. She even did a little twirl. '*Exquisite* tailoring, don't you find?' Rebecca was so taken aback she could think of nothing to say. She'd looked down at her own outfit – skinny jeans, a pair of Todd's slip-ons and a black leather jacket – and felt childish and under-dressed. She'd mumbled something indistinct and turned away. Now, sitting next to the *exquisitely* tailored Miranda, listening with half an ear to the conversation between the three of them – Miranda, Jeff Morgenstein and Julian – she wished desperately she were elsewhere. More precisely, with Tash and Annick. It was going to be a long, boring weekend.

'Look, it's just common sense,' Miranda was saying earnestly. 'In

324

difficult times, people always go to prime and London's always going to be regarded as a safe investment. Look at Land Securities last month. Someone made an awful lot of money structuring *that* deal, I can tell you.'

'Who did the legals?'

'Macfarlane's. I had dinner last week with Phil Macfarlane and the Russians. I probably shouldn't be telling you this but—'

'Oh, go on. You're amongst friends. For now, at least. Wait until the Arabs get wind of the deal. We'll not be quite as friendly then, you know, darling.' There was a burst of half-stifled laughter from the car's other occupants. Like teenagers, Rebecca thought to herself angrily. How on earth was she going to get through an entire weekend with them? They talked business, business, business . . . nothing else.

'Is she asleep?' Julian turned his attention away from the road for a second.

'Went out like a light,' Miranda said smugly. 'Soon as the engine started. I used to do that as a child, you know.' Rebecca shut her eyes even more tightly. Bitch!

'She's worn out, poor thing,' Julian murmured.

'Poor thing,' Miranda echoed, though she sounded anything but sympathetic. 'Did you hear back from the Russians, by the way?' she went on, making it clear she wasn't the slightest bit interested in hearing about poor Rebecca.

'Yes, we've got a meeting set up in a couple of weeks' time. They want to meet in Geneva. Everyone okay with that?' Julian's tone returned to the serious business of making money.

'Fine by me,' Morgenstein grunted his assent. 'Damn, it's beautiful down here. You married well, my boy,' he murmured. There was an answering chuckle from both Julian and Miranda. Rebecca's jaw tightened.

A couple of hours later, she stood at the window of the Great Room looking out over the deer park. Four long, elegant windows, each framing a different view. It had been years since she'd been to Brockhurst. She remembered the first time she'd come here as a child. She'd looked out over the misty gardens and slowly understood that it was actually one stretch of land out there, and that it belonged to them – everything, the trees, the cropped, neat lawns, the wild grasses beyond, the deer who looked up occasionally and, when the gamekeeper approached, kicked up their heels gaily, their soft, pale rumps dancing from side to side, racing off into the distance. It was all theirs; her father owned the gardens down below and the fields she could see in the near distance and the one further off and the one after that, too, all the way to the powdery blue haze of the hills on the horizon, beyond which was the sea. It seemed to stretch to infinity.

The interior of Brockhurst too was unusual, an unbalanced mixture of the heavy, ornate decor that her grandmother, Sara, whom Rebecca had never met, favoured, and Embeth's lighter, more contemporary touches. It seemed odd that Embeth too had never met Sara. By the time Lionel travelled to Venezuela, Sara was already gone, yet her presence was still very much there in the St James's apartment that Lionel occasionally used and here, in Brockhurst. The shelves of the library and the hallway groaned under the weight of her books. In the early sixties, when the German government finally returned the house in Altona to the family, together with all its furniture and the precious artworks, Lionel gave in to Embeth's request. She didn't want her mother-in-law's possessions in Harburg Hall where she'd see them on a daily basis. She asked Lionel to send them to Brockhurst, as far away from London as possible. The books were yellow now, hidden under dust covers for most of the year.

She turned from the window suddenly feeling restless. It was time to get ready for dinner. A beautiful papaya-hued silk dress by Alberta Ferretti lay on her bed, something Tash had picked out for her, of course. With its long, flattering dropped waist, it was a modern take on the twenties flapper dress. It suited her and she needed the boost. All afternoon she'd felt like the proverbial third spoke (or wheel?) in the conversations between Julian, Jeff, Miranda and their guests. At one point, she'd wandered into the kitchen, bored stiff from listening to a conversation she neither understood nor felt confident enough to take part in. There was a man sitting down beside the Aga, chatting to Mrs Griffiths, the housekeeper. It was the bodyguard. One of the Arab financiers had brought him along. He jumped to his feet as soon as she entered.

'Oh, God, sit down, do. It's not 1914,' she smiled. She turned to Mrs Griffiths. 'Haven't seen you in *ages*, Mrs Griffiths. How are you?'

'Very well, thank you, Miss Harburg. Or should I say, "Mrs Lovell"? Congratulations.'

'Thanks. I'm still getting used to it. I'm keeping my name, though. It'd feel strange to change it.' She glanced at the bodyguard, who was sitting with a teacup balanced awkwardly on his thighs. He *looked* like a bodyguard, she thought to herself with a quickening of interest. Tall, broad, a solid wall of chest and shoulders, an impassive, expressionless face. Where was he from? she wondered idly. 'You're with Mr Al-Amar, aren't you?'

'Yes, ma'am.'

'Have you been with him long?'

'Yes, ma'am.'

'Rebecca? Where the hell are you?' It was Julian. Whatever conversation she'd hoped to have with the handsome bodyguard was abruptly cut short.

'Coming,' she called out reluctantly. 'Well, I'll . . . I'll leave you to it,' she said to Mrs Griffiths, who was busy rolling out pastry. She pushed herself off the counter and smoothed down her skirt. She turned to go, but not before she'd caught the quick, unspoken flash of interest in the bodyguard's eyes. She walked to the door, conscious of his dark eyes on her.

The conversation at the dinner table rose and fell around her in waves, washing over her in a sea of dull, bored incomprehension. Although it was in English, it might as well have been in Arabic for all she understood of it. Bonds, mortgages, rates, values, taxes, derivatives, markets . . . their voices droned on and on. She looked around her at their guests. They were a rather unlikely mix. Julian was at the head of the table, grey-haired, formal, a little stiff in his manner, holding forth. Next to him was that awful man from New York whose eyes oscillated between cleavages – hers and Miranda's. Both were on prominent display. She'd be damned if she was going to let Miranda's voluptuous chest outdo hers. Miranda was sitting opposite Julian; every so often, Rebecca saw his eyes wander in her direction. She was obviously enjoying it. She wore the smug, self-satisfied smile of a cat that had got its prey. What the hell did she have to look so satisfied about? Rebecca thought to herself crossly. Whatever it was, she'd managed to grab and hold the attention of every single man present, even the Arabs. Rebecca sat to Julian's left, saying little and feeling almost invisible. She stifled a yawn. No one would notice if she disappeared for half an hour, would they? She looked around her. They were all still busy talking, talking, talking.

She put her napkin carefully to one side and stood up. No one even looked up. She walked quickly from the room.

*

'Oh!' Rebecca put a hand up to her throat. 'You scared me! I didn't think anyone was in here.' *Liar*, she thought to herself.

'I'm sorry, ma'am. I was told to wait in here.' The bodyguard, who'd been sitting by the fire, immediately got to his feet.

'No, no, it's fine. I . . . I just wanted a moment alone, that's all. It's hard work, all this . . . this *talking*,' she giggled, waving her wine glass in front of her face. They were in the study on the ground floor, a few doors down from the formal dining room where she'd left the others talking business. She walked over to the window, one arm folded across her stomach, the other holding her half-empty glass. The silk of her dress fanned out in luxurious waves behind her. She could hear the material sliding softly over her bare skin, as he could. She could tell by the way he held himself – stiffly, to attention – that she was having the desired effect. *What the hell are you doing?* a tiny voice inside her head piped up. She turned, hiding her face behind her glass. 'Drink?' she asked nonchalantly, bending forward ever so slightly. The dress was cut to a deep V. From where he sat awkwardly on the sofa, she'd given him quite an eyeful.

'Er, no, ma'am. I . . . I don't drink.'

'On the job or in general?'

He seemed even more uncomfortable. 'I . . . it's against our religion.'

So he *was* an Arab. 'Where are you from?' she asked curiously.

'Tunis.' He seemed about to say something further, then changed his mind. He glanced at her cleavage, then looked away, clearly embarrassed. Emboldened, Rebecca moved away from the window and sat down on the leather Chesterfield opposite him. She lifted a leg slowly and crossed it over her knee, smoothing down the cascading silk of her dress and tossing her thick mane of hair over her shoulder. *You're such a slut*. She suppressed a smile at the sound of her own inner voice.

'What's your name?' she asked conversationally, taking a sip of her wine. 'And call me Rebecca. No one ever calls me "ma'am". Makes me feel *old*.'

There was an awkward pause as they both looked at each other. He frowned. 'What're you playing at?' he asked quietly.

Rebecca blinked. All of a sudden he sounded distinctly English. 'I . . . I don't know what you mean,' she stammered, confused. Her heart began to beat faster. Suddenly what had started out as one of her little games didn't seem quite so much fun anymore.

'I think you know exactly what I mean.' He got to his feet and looked down at her for a moment. 'You lot are all the same,' he said slowly, shaking his head.

Rebecca's mouth opened in surprise. 'You seem awfully sure of yourself,' she said, her voice hardening.

His eyes didn't leave her face. 'No more so than you.' Some new, hostile understanding had sprung up between them.

Rebecca's pulse began to race. This wasn't quite what she'd planned. 'Look, I just thought—'

'I know what you thought, Mrs Lovell. Like I said, you're not the first bored housewife to try it on.' He laughed but there was no humour in his voice. He straightened his jacket, then turned and walked out, leaving a shaking Rebecca behind. She put her empty wine glass on the carpet and leaned forwards, burying her face in her hands. What was she *thinking? Slut.* Her irritating inner voice piped up again. *Stupid, silly slut.*

86

YVES
London

He walked up Marylebone High Street, stopping every once in a while to look up at the shop fronts, checking off the numbers, one by one. New Cavendish Street, Weymouth Street, Paddington Street – his mouth moved awkwardly over the unfamiliar syllables. There. There it was. On the corner of Devonshire Street. Number sixty-one. He crossed the road, narrowly avoiding a cyclist, and stopped in front of the dark-green door. There was a brass plaque to the right; he consulted the names. Yes, halfway down, in plain, no-frills script, was the business he was looking for. www.F@shion.com. On the first floor. He put out a gloved finger and pressed the bell.

'F@shion.com.' A brisk, very English-sounding voice.

'Er, good morning. I'm . . . I'm looking for Miss Bryce-Brudenell.'

'Is she expecting you?'

'Er, no. Not exactly. I'm . . . well, I'm a friend of a friend of hers. I'm trying to find someone. I'm in London for a few days and I hoped . . . well, I just hoped I might be able to catch her.'

'Um, why don't you come up? You can speak to her PA.' The buzzer sounded loudly, unlocking the door. He stepped inside. The foyer was tiny, with barely enough room for a potted plant and a radiator. The lift doors were directly in front of him. First floor. He pressed the button and the doors slid open soundlessly onto a large, all-white space with a gleaming white reception counter. Behind it sat a young woman, also dressed in white. Behind *her*, in yellow neon, the words www.F@shion.com flickered on and off. Yves swallowed nervously. He wasn't used to such places. He approached cautiously.

'Hi. I rang from downstairs.'

The receptionist looked him up and down. 'You're the one looking for Miss Bryce-Brudenell, is that right?'

He nodded. 'I should've rung first, I know. She doesn't actually know me, that's the thing. I'm a good friend of a friend of hers, Annick Betancourt.'

'Oh, right. Um . . . hang on just a moment.' She got up and walked round the desk. 'I'll just be a sec.' She skipped across the white-tiled floor and disappeared into an adjacent office. Two minutes later, she was back. The phone had started to ring again. 'Just have a seat,' she instructed breathlessly, rushing to answer it. 'Miss Bryce-Brudenell will be out in a minute. Yes, over there. I'll get you some coffee.' She picked up the phone. 'Fashion dot *com*,' she sang into the mouthpiece. 'Good morning!'

TASH

Tash picked up the scrap of paper the receptionist had slid in front of her. She looked at the name again, frowning. *Yves Pasqual*. A good friend of Annick's? She'd never heard Annick mention him. She wondered who he was. She ought to ring Annick and check, shouldn't she? She hesitated for a moment, then her curiosity got the better of her. She got up, pulled her ponytail tight and opened her door. Annabel, her PA, was busy on the phone. 'I'll be back in a moment,' she murmured and walked out.

He was standing by the window, looking down onto Marylebone High Street. He turned as she approached. Her eyes widened. He was tall and lean, a little darker-skinned than Annick, with short, tightly

330

curled black hair and a neat goatee. He was wearing a dark tweed jacket, a round-necked jumper and jeans. He looked serious. She held out a hand. 'Hi. I'm Tash. You're a friend of Annick's?'

His handshake was firm. 'Yes. Look, I'm sorry I didn't contact you beforehand. I just happened to be in London and . . . well, I thought I'd try and find her. Is there . . . is there somewhere we could talk for a moment? Do you have time?'

His English was excellent, if accented. He seemed nervous. Tash warmed to him immediately. 'Of course. Let's grab a coffee. There's a cafe just across the road. Gemma, will you hold my calls? Tell Annabel I'll be back in half an hour.' She turned to Yves. 'So, have you come from far?' Was he a friend from Togo or Paris, she wondered?

'Paris,' he said, standing back to let her enter the lift first. Good manners, she noticed. And good shoes. It was cold and damp outside. She wrapped her arms around her, refusing his offer of his coat. 'Come on, it's not far.'

'Hi, Tash.' One of the waitresses recognised her immediately. 'Usual?'

'What's your usual?' Yves asked, scanning the menu.

'Filter coffee, dash of hot milk, no sugar.'

'Sounds good. I'll have the same,' Yves smiled. 'I can't get used to these London coffee shops. Americano, flat white, cappuccino, macchiato. Crazy.'

'So, who exactly are you?' Tash asked as the coffees were brought to the small table. 'I'm afraid Annick's never mentioned you.'

An involuntary expression of hurt flitted across his face, which he quickly suppressed. He shrugged. 'We were close,' he said after a moment. 'We met at the hotel where she worked. I heard that's where you found her.'

'How did you hear that?'

'From one of the guys who worked there. He still talks about the fifty euros you gave him.' He smiled. 'It took me a while to track you down. There was a newspaper article she showed me once. I'm afraid I wasn't really listening at the time. I had to go back through every single copy for the last six months until I found it.' He stopped, stirring his coffee slowly with his spoon. 'I know it's a lot to ask, especially considering who she is and with everything that's happened to her family, but do you know where she is? Will you give me her number?'

Tash hesitated. 'She's a solicitor – did you know that?'

Yves nodded. 'Yes, I know. I know more about her than she thinks,' he said after a moment. He looked Tash straight in the eye. 'And I suppose you're wondering why she hasn't mentioned me.'

Tash shook her head. She smiled. 'I've known Annick a long time, remember?' she said gently. 'There's lots of stuff she doesn't talk about.'

'So will you tell me where she is?'

She looked at him. He had a certain quality about him that she liked. He was careful, but not cagey. She liked his directness and his frank way of speaking, but recognised too that there was a vulnerability behind it all, as though he knew he could also be hurt. She turned to look out of the window. Annick hadn't said anything about a man in Paris and she must have had a reason. But there was something about Yves, some instinct that told her he was someone to be trusted, not pushed away.

'All right,' she said finally. 'I'll tell her you're here. Will you wait here for her?' He nodded. She turned her head to look out of the window. Yves followed her gaze. Across the road, a woman struggled with a child in a pram and two teenagers passed by, giggling hotly between them. They both turned back to look at each other at the same moment. She found she was smiling. 'I hope I'll see you again?'

He scribbled his number on a piece of paper and gave it to her. 'So do I. She ought to know my number,' he said. 'But just in case.' He signalled to the waitress. 'I'll get these,' he said, pointing to the coffees. 'And thank you.'

'Nothing to thank. Not yet, at any rate,' Tash said lightly. 'I'd better run. I hope she calls.'

'Me too.'

So, Annick had been hiding something after all, Tash thought to herself as she hurried across the road. She was impressed. Yves had impressed her. As she walked through to her office, a deeper, darker emotion pushed its way through the thin crust of her admiration. Envy. She sat down behind her desk and propped her chin in her hands. She ought to be happy for Annick. Someone cared enough about her to plough through six months' worth of newspapers just to find her! She tried to imagine what it would be like to be on the receiving end of that kind of attention. She couldn't. The truth was that for all her achievements and her burning, driving ambition, there was no one with whom she could share any of it, even if she wanted to. She stared at the phone on her desk, biting back the sudden horrid urge to cry.

87

ANNICK
London

'Oh, Miss Betancourt,' Katie looked up as Annick staggered past, carrying a stack of papers that threatened to topple her over. 'Your friend rang again. She says it's really urgent. Did you get the other messages?'

'Yes, I did, thanks. I was just about to ring her,' Annick said breathlessly. She set the pile down on her desk with a thud, moments before it all collapsed. 'God, there's a lot to go through.'

Katie nodded sympathetically. 'And Ms Karol also rang. She's on her way back now.'

Annick grimaced and glanced at the clock. It was almost five and she'd yet to go through the huge stack of notes Frances had left out for her that morning. She was drowning in paperwork. Her earlier experience had in no way prepared her for the demands of corporate law. There seemed to be no personalities involved, which was what had made wills and probate at least marginally interesting. Corporate law seemed to be made up entirely of faceless corporations either seeking damages or seeking to avoid them. It was the most impersonal, unemotional and – dare she say it? – boring area to work in but she had no choice. She didn't dare think about how much money she now owed Tash, and it wasn't just about the money, either. She'd been given a second chance, a lifeline back to her old self – she'd be absolutely mad to reject it.

Katie picked up her coat and scarf and switched off her computer. There were many differences between them, Annick thought to herself as she watched her, but none quite so stark as their respective end-of-day routines. Katie and Louise clocked off at five on the dot, unless they were specifically asked to stay. They were at their desks by nine and not a moment sooner. She, on the other hand, rarely got home before seven. Eight or even half past was the norm.

She picked up her phone and quickly dialled Tash's mobile. Her own mobile was tucked away in her bag. Mobiles were banned at Clifton Crabbe. 'Tash? It's me.'

'I know it's you,' Tash said drily. 'It says so on my screen. *Annick. Office.*'

'I'd better be quick. Frances is on her way back. What's the matter?'

'Why should anything be the matter?' Tash asked mildly. 'No, nothing's wrong, per se. But I had a visitor today.'

'Who?'

'A friend of yours. A bloke.'

A cold hand of fear crept up her back. 'A bloke?'

'Yeah. A friend. I think you know who I mean.'

There was a short, painful silence. 'Looking for me?'

'Yup. He came over from Paris.'

'Paris?' Annick almost dropped the phone. 'Yves?'

'Why didn't you mention him?'

Annick opened her mouth but no words came out. She gripped the phone. The shame and embarrassment she'd spent the past three months suppressing came rushing up through her body like a tidal wave. 'I . . . wh-where . . . where is he?' she croaked.

'He's in Black's. You know, the cafe across the road from my office. He's been waiting there since three o'clock. I rang you at least half a dozen times. He left a number—'

'I know his number,' Annick broke in, her breath coming in short, panicked bursts. 'Wh-why did he come to *you*?'

'Well, how else was he supposed to find you? He tracked me down through that interview in the *Guardian*. Pretty intrepid, if you ask me. Annick, you've *got* to go and see him. How can you not?'

'I . . . I . . . just didn't—'

'Look, whatever it was you *didn't* do, forget about that now. He's here. He's come all this way. Go and meet him.' And before Annick could offer any more excuses, she rang off. Annick was left staring at the phone.

'Everything all right, Annick?' Frances bustled into their offices carrying yet more folders. 'Did you get through the DTI files?'

Annick looked up, startled. 'No, n-not quite. I'm still going through them. I'll . . . I'll have the summary on your desk first thing in the morning.'

'The morning? What's wrong with tonight?'

'I . . . I've got a meeting,' Annick stammered. 'At six. But I'll come back straight after.'

Frances raised an eyebrow. 'Tonight?' she murmured. 'Well, so long as it's all done by morning,' she said, picking up the phone. 'I'm meeting the minister at eleven and I'll need a *complete* summary by then.' Her emphasis on the word 'complete' was deliberate. The first time she'd done a summary for Ms Karol, a few days after her arrival, she'd in-advertently missed out an entire file.

'Y-yes, Frances.' Annick picked up her coat. Her heart was hammering so loudly inside her chest it was a wonder Frances couldn't hear it. 'I'll . . . I'll be right back.'

'First thing in the morning,' Frances said smoothly. 'Or else.'

He was sitting in Tash's favourite seat by the window. She saw him even before the taxi had come to a halt. He was bent over his plate, reading something at the same time, his head bowed and his shoulders curved. She was overcome with remorse. How could she have disappeared like that, without leaving a word, without saying goodbye? She thrust a ten-pound note at the driver and jumped out almost before the taxi had come to a complete halt. She pushed open the door to the cafe and wound her way across the crowded room to where he sat.

'Yves?'

He lifted his head. There was a pause, and then he stood up. 'Annick.'

She felt her knees begin to wobble. Deep breaths snagged on a sob. She could feel the tears rushing down her face and neck. He saw it too and put out a hand to steady her. 'Y-Yves. I'm s-sorry. I'm s-sorry,' she sobbed, oblivious to the people at the table next to him who looked from one to the other in a mixture of curiosity and alarm. 'I'm s-so sorry,' she whispered again and again. She held onto the back of the chair.

'Annick.' In a second he was beside her. She breathed in the oh-so-familiar scent of him and it made it even worse. 'Let's get out of here,' he murmured against her hair. She nodded, unable to let go of the chair. 'Come on. Let's go.'

'Wh-what ab-about your n-newspaper?'

He didn't answer. He steered her gently but firmly towards the door instead. 'I've finished with it. Come on.'

'M-my flat's ju-just around the corner,' she blubbered.

'Then let's go there.' He stopped to tuck her scarf firmly around her neck. 'That's better. It's cold outside.'

'H-how long have you been waiting for me?' she asked, unable to stop crying.

He looked at her for a moment without saying anything. Then he shook his head and gave one of his wry little smiles. His fingers gripped her arm through her coat sleeve. It took him a moment to answer. 'All my life.'

*

335

They didn't even make it to the bedroom. Annick had just managed to close the front door behind her when he took hold of her arm again and drew her towards him. She pushed her face into the warm, familiar solidity of his chest, breathing deeply, taking the scent of him down into her lungs. She brought both hands up and began to unbutton his shirt. She felt his skin shudder under her fingertips. She went over him, every inch, every dip and swell, sliding across the tight, short hair on his chest, around his taut, trembling sides to the smooth dip of his back. She turned her face up towards his but kept her eyes tightly shut, allowing her fingers to do the seeing for her. Across his cheek, then down to the corner of his lips, across the lower one, resting for a moment in the hollow below, then over the prickly skin of his chin, down the smooth, powerful neck, feeling his Adam's apple swell and contract under her touch. Like a creature feeling its way across a surface in the dark.

'What are you doing?' he whispered against her hair.

She shook her head, her fingers busy nibbling at the buckle of his belt, as if he might find some answer there. She pushed his trousers down past his thighs, feeling them fall to the floor with a soft thud, his wallet or his phone buried somewhere in the pockets. His head tilted forward and found the softness of her neck. They began to tease each other in a way she'd never dared to do before. He made short work of her jacket, blouse, bra, skirt . . . within seconds, they were both naked, oblivious to the fact that the bedroom was behind them, the door still firmly shut. It had begun to rain outside, drops beating firmly against the window-panes, marking out a different kind of rhythm to the frantic, rising tempo of need between them.

Whispered confessions. Buried history. Admissions. Hurts. Old stories, new truths. Suddenly, bed seemed the appropriate place to say every-thing. Even the silences between them had the tense, quivering quality of speech. She lay beside him, her body turned inwards towards his, his hands loosely cupping her buttocks. She couldn't stop talking, now.

'I didn't know how to explain,' she whispered. 'It just seemed too much, somehow. Too much for anyone to have to deal with.'

'That's for me to decide, Annick. Not you.'

'I . . . I *wanted* to explain. So many times, but I never found the right moment. I didn't know how to even begin.'

'Begin at the beginning; isn't that what they always say?'

'But I don't know where the beginning is. When I first came to Paris, after it happened, my aunt told me a bit. About my father, and my grandfather. Where they'd come from, when they came over from Brazil, the war . . . all that stuff.' She turned her face into the warmth of his neck. She could feel his pulse beating against her lips. 'I didn't know about *them*, though. No one ever told me.'

'Didn't you ask, though? Didn't you ever wonder why you were different? Even your name's not really Togolese.'

She shrugged. 'No. I . . . I just didn't. Lots of people don't know much about where they're from.' She felt him stiffen slightly. 'Do you?' Yves was silent. His hand continued its slow, gentle caress but something had changed. She was aware of his attention in a different way. She tried to shift her body round so that she could look at him but the cover that lay between them shrouded his face. 'Yves?' she asked uncertainly. 'What's the matter? Did I say something wrong?'

He shook his head slowly. 'No, it's nothing.'

'So why won't you answer?' She propped herself up on one elbow to look at him.

His eyes didn't quite meet her gaze. 'It's complicated,' he said finally.

'But I've told you everything about *me*.' She took a deep breath. Something wasn't right. He was still touching her in that easy, proprietorial way that she'd only just realised she'd missed but behind the lazy caress she had the impression of a mind furiously at work.

'I don't know who my biological parents were.' His hand had stopped moving. His whole body was tense with the effort of holding something in. 'I don't even know where they were from. There's nothing to tell because I don't *know* anything.'

A wave of tenderness and remorse flowed over her. She moved closer to him, putting her arms around him, comforting him in the only way she knew how. 'I'm sorry, I didn't mean to pry.' She kissed his neck, the soft, vulnerable hollow at the base of his throat that sometimes tasted salty to her. 'That's the weird thing, you know.'

'What is?'

'You think you're protecting people by not saying anything, by keeping it locked up inside you.' She hesitated, unsure of her words.

'But?' She felt his attention on her now, like breath.

'But the thing is, in the end, you wind up just pushing everyone away. Because you *can't* keep it in, that's the whole point. It eats at you, right here,' she placed a hand on his stomach. 'That's why I used to . . . to eat so much.' She stumbled over the words. 'I was always hungry, always. I used to wake up in the middle of the night and my stomach would be so empty it hurt. I didn't realise then that it wasn't hunger at all.'

'What was it?'

She swallowed. She could feel the salt of her own tears in her mouth. She pressed her hand into the hardness of his abdomen, so different from the softness of hers. 'It was trying to keep everything in. It was eating *me*, just as I was eating *it*.'

He began to comfort her, desire standing in for sympathy. She had never been made love to with such intensity before. He thrust into her again and again, his body pushing and struggling against her the way she'd once seen a bird die wildly, its wings flapping frantically against a net she couldn't see. When at last it was over and he'd found his own passionate release, he lay against her as though he were dead, the only sign of life the warm wetness she felt at her neck as he dazedly drew breath.

'Shit!' She suddenly sat bolt upright, clutching the sheet comically to her chest.

'What is it?' he asked drowsily.

'What time is it?'

He lifted a hand to his face. 'Ten past eleven.'

'Oh, *God!*' She scrambled out of bed.

'Where the hell are you going?'

'To work!' She ran into the bathroom, grabbing at her discarded clothes as she went. Her heart was thumping, the blood pumping through her veins with fright. *How* could she have forgotten?

YVES

'Fool,' he thought to himself, sinking back into the pillows as the front door slammed shut behind her. 'Fool.' With every passing month, he was sinking deeper and deeper into a quagmire. Quitting Paris would involve so much more than a simple change of address. He had no idea what Big Jacques or any of the others would do but he certainly didn't want to risk finding out. They were obsessed with finding Betancourt's stash. He wasn't about to tell any of them he'd decided to run off with his daughter. God knows what they'd think then – that he'd run off with the money himself? He shook his head. But he couldn't stay. Not now.

In all the time they'd been together, he'd only once spoken of her to someone else: Martin Duris, his closest – and only – friend. They'd met at university and whilst Martin was now a lecturer, married with two kids and content in a way Yves could never imagine himself to be, they'd somehow stayed in touch. When the urge to speak to someone frankly had finally overcome him, he'd rung Martin and suggested they meet for a drink. It was the only time he'd ever confided in anyone else.

'I wondered where you'd been hiding.' Martin took a sip of his beer as Yves's voice trailed off. 'A woman, eh? Never known you to be confused about a woman.'

Yves smiled faintly. 'She's different.'

'How?'

'I . . . I'm not sure how to explain it,' he began hesitantly.

'Try.'

He was quiet for a moment. 'D'you remember your mother spraying perfume in the air then walking through it?'

Martin looked puzzled. 'I . . . I guess so. Yes, yes, she did.'

'Well, she's like that.'

'Like perfume?' Martin looked even more puzzled.

Yves nodded. 'Yeah. Just like perfume. She's still on your skin even when she's gone. That's what she's like.'

Martin took another gulp of beer. 'Better go after her then.'

So he did. And now here he was. He'd been honest with Martin and dishonest with Annick and halfway honest with himself. He no longer knew which was which. A mess. It was all one big, complicated mess.

ANNICK

It took eleven minutes to get from Marylebone High Street to Holborn. She galloped into the building, still tying up her hair as she went. She flashed her card at the security guard, who barely blinked. He was clearly quite used to the late-night comings and goings of Clinton Crabbe staff.

She punched the lift button impatiently, smoothed back the last few strands of her hair and tried to steady her breathing. All the lights were on; the building looked curiously the same as it did in daylight working hours. At the far end of the corridor, she could see the cleaners through the smoked glass, methodically lifting waste paper baskets, and the sound of the industrial hoovers echoing eerily down the hall.

She hurried down the corridor to her office and pushed open the door. Frances was sitting at her desk in pretty much the same position she'd been when Annick left. She looked up as Annick walked in. It was quarter to midnight. For a second the two women looked at each other without saying anything. Annick's heart was in her mouth.

'Good evening, I take it?' Frances said quietly, her eyes returning to her computer screen.

Annick's face was on fire as she slipped into her own chair. 'Um, yes, thanks,' she mumbled, switching on her screen. She pulled the first folder off the stack and opened it. There was silence for a few minutes.

'Well done for coming back,' Frances said. She lifted her eyes briefly. 'Do me a favour, though,' she murmured.

Annick's hand stopped halfway through turning over the page. 'Wh-what?'

'Just don't marry him.'

88

ANNICK
London

There was a hushed silence in the Yellow Room at the Old Marylebone Town Hall. Annick swallowed nervously. Her throat was completely parched. Yves was still holding onto her hand. She looked down at her third finger. The solitary diamond sparked brilliant flashes of rainbow-coloured light.

The registrar looked at them both, smiling widely. He cleared his throat. 'And now,' he intoned solemnly, 'I pronounce you man and wife.'

'Amen,' Annick said fervently and then clapped a hand to her mouth. The word had slipped out incongruously before she could stop it. Everyone laughed. There was a stifled sob from the front row of chairs. It was Rebecca, of course – so heavily pregnant they weren't sure she'd actually make it to the registry. Julian stood next to her, beaming as much with anticipation of the imminent birth as the ceremony in front of him. On the other side, Tash stood clutching a bottle of champagne, smiling dazedly, her face partly obscured by a large, rather wonderful hat. Martin, Yves' best man, was standing next to her, and, surprising Annick at the very last minute by demanding an invitation, there was Frances, Annick's boss, resplendent in grey Armani.

'Amen,' Yves whispered at her side. 'Once a Catholic, always.' He squeezed her hand and then bent his head to kiss her. It was done. They were now husband and wife.

Everyone suddenly surged forwards, shaking Yves by the hand, hugging Annick. Rebecca's stomach got in the way of everything. She half-sobbed and laughed her way through her congratulations. Annick presented her cheek this way and that; even the registrar was kissed and hugged. They were discreetly but firmly shepherded out of the small room with its daffodil-coloured walls and cream-and-mahogany chairs. Another wedding party was waiting. Annick caught sight of the bride as they passed – yards and yards of white lace and tulle, complete with a tiara and a veil. Her own dress, a simple shift of ivory satin, couldn't have been more different.

'Vera Wang,' Tash had said firmly as soon as Annick broke the news. 'I'm not letting you go down the aisle in anything else.'

'There won't *be* an aisle,' Annick pointed out. 'We're doing it at the town hall.'

'Even more reason to wear Wang. Trust me. You'll wear the dress again and again.'

Annick laughed. 'I'm only planning on getting married once,' she giggled.

'You never know,' Tash said darkly. 'Trust me.'

'I do,' Annick said simply, spreading her hands. 'I'll wear whatever you tell me.'

'Good girl.'

'Smile, for God's sake! It's your wedding day,' Tash hissed in her ear as they clattered down the steps and emerged, blinking, into the light and noise of the Marylebone Road. There was a photographer waiting, shouting instructions. 'This way, please, all together now . . . yes, you, too, darling. Great, that's absolutely fantastic. Fan-*tas*-tic!' One of Tash's many assistants was standing at the bottom of the steps with a gigantic bouquet of white roses. A restaurant had been booked; there were cars waiting to whisk them off . . . Tash, as usual, had left nothing out. Annick climbed into the front car with Yves, holding tightly onto his hand.

'We'll meet you at the restaurant,' Tash shouted through the open window. 'The driver knows where it is. They're expecting us. Here, have a glass before we get there,' she laughed, thrusting the bottle she'd been carrying through the window. 'And darling, *smile!* At least for the photographer's sake!'

'She's quite something,' Yves murmured against her ear as the driver pulled smoothly out into the traffic. 'She thinks of everything.'

'Yep, that's Tash for you,' Annick said, leaning into him. She smoothed the pale silk of her skirt. 'She's even got a change of clothes waiting for me at the restaurant.' She gave an exaggerated sigh. 'I keep thinking I'm going to wake up and this'll all be gone, that I'll have dreamt it all.'

Yves looked at her. 'Sometimes, *chérie*,' he said, sliding an arm round her shoulders, 'you say the strangest things.'

'But it's *true*,' Annick protested, smiling. 'None of this seems real. Even *you* don't seem quite real sometimes.'

'Don't say that. Don't ever say that.' There was a sudden catch in his voice.

She turned to look at him in surprise. He wasn't the type to openly show what he felt but earlier that afternoon, just after they'd finished signing the registry, she'd excused herself and gone to the bathroom, alone. She sat down in the cubicle, aware of a great pressure building up in her chest and she'd cried a little, relieving herself of some of the unspoken sadness mixed in with the high emotion of the day. She'd waited a few moments until the storm passed, then came out, still dabbing her eyes and composing herself. Tash and Martin had been dragged off somewhere to sign something as witnesses. Yves was waiting for her by the window, looking down over the street. The sheer curtain rose and fell in front of him like a veil in the breeze; he hadn't seen her yet. She hesitated. There was something in his stance that made her stop. She looked past the face she knew so well to a face she'd never seen on him before, the face of man so deep in himself he was no longer aware of what he might have to conceal. She backed away very quietly, not wishing to be seen. That same expression, she realised now, was on his face again.

She said nothing but held onto his hand tightly. Weddings, like births and funerals, she thought to herself, were family occasions. Just as the absence of her own family produced an ache below her ribs, the same must have been true for him, she realised. They were alone in the world but they had each other. It was more than she'd dared hope for and a poignant reminder of just how far she'd come.

PART SEVEN
DROWNING

'Being an old maid is like death by drowning,
a really delightful sensation after you cease to struggle.'
Edna Ferber

89

TASH
London

She picked up the colour wheel that Niall, the interior designer, had left out for her and quickly flicked through it. *Jasmine White. White Chiffon. Lemon White. Frosted Dawn. Timeless. Handkerchief White.* She paused and frowned. *Handkerchief* white? Was that before or after someone had blown their nose? She wrinkled her own nose and put the wheel back down. Her office was the last to be decided upon and under normal circumstances the thought of it alone was enough to make her smile. Not tonight. It was seven thirty in the evening on the last Friday in June. The weather was lovely: blue skies all afternoon, not a cloud in sight. In half an hour's time, she'd go downstairs with Edith, Colin and James – her most senior staff – and they'd repair to the Orrery for the very last time. F@shion.com was moving. After five years, they were moving from their rather cramped premises off Marylebone High Street to a brand-new enormous warehouse of an office in Regent's Quarter, a new district sandwiched between York Way and the Euston Road. She'd had her doubts when the estate agents first took her there but as soon as the architects Julian had recommended had taken over, she began to see it the way they did – as the most exciting thing to happen in King's Cross in decades.

Six months after signing the lease, they were almost ready to move in. Tash went to sleep dreaming about their new premises and woke up every morning with paint samples, fabric swatches and layouts uppermost in her mind. She loved every single aspect of the whole process, from sitting with the architects and planners, working out who sat where, who saw whom, who had what views, right down to the choice of mugs in the staff canteen. F@shion.com now had a staff of nearly a hundred people. There were days when Tash sat alone in her office, her head in her hands, stunned by the enormity – and profitability – of it all.

She'd always known she would make it. She just hadn't reckoned on making it this *big*. Or so fast. Turnover for 2009 was close to ten million pounds; in 2010, it jumped to twenty-six million and by although it was only June they'd already hit the forty million mark. They'd just celebrated their 250,000th order and all the indications were that they'd hit half a million before the year was out. Good news all round. Usually, reports like the ones that landed on her desk every day were enough to put a spring in her step and a smile on her face. But not tonight.

She pushed back her chair and stood up. She walked to the window and stood there, looking down at the street. Dozens of the well-dressed, well-heeled women who clicked onto www.F@shion.com every day walked up and down, pausing at Agnès B, Fenn Wright Mason or any of the dozen or so boutiques on either side of the road, occasionally popping in but rarely emerging with more than a bag or two. Tash knew why. It all went back to what she'd said to Julian a few years earlier, when they'd first started out. F@shion.com did the editing for them, stopping short of telling them what to buy, what to wear. They made beautiful, seductive, gorgeous suggestions and then let their customers' fingers do the rest. Their online magazine, *Runway*, was just as important as the collections they had to offer. Every week, she met with her creative team – Carla, Harriet, Di, Venetia and Stephen, the sole man – to go through the upcoming issue. It was here that the real genius behind F@shion.com came into play. Each week, twenty pages of the hottest looks, the sharpest suits, sexiest shoes and most on-trend accessories were put together in a format that took the best of advertising, lifestyle, celebrity culture and fashion and mixed it up, presenting their customers with page after page of the most divine images. The discreet, candy-coloured pop-up buttons that said, simply, *GET THE LOOK* were sprinkled liberally around the page. It was a simple message and it worked. Women couldn't resist the combination of stunning clothes, stunning models and celebrities and those buttons. They clicked and bought and clicked and bought. They excitedly told their friends and colleagues, who promptly did the same. A day later, their packages arrived. Candy-coloured boxes, embossed with the words www.F@shion.com, wrapped in ribbons – pink for lingerie, yellow for summer outfits, mink for winter and red for shoes – arrived on their desks to squeals and sighs of delight.

'It's better than sex,' the CEO of a multinational declared one week in *Grazia* magazine. She was more than happy to be featured on the front page of *Runway* the following week. That gave Tash yet another idea.

True to Life. An ad campaign that featured real-life women with real-life careers, making online purchases in between making phone calls, chairing meetings, dropping children off at the school gates and running into their Pilates classes. The week *True to Life* debuted, sales jumped fifty-six per cent. It was all good, and it was all go. Most of the time. But tonight was different.

It was Annick's phone call that had set her off. She'd been on the verge of packing up for the day when the phone rang.

'Tash? It's me.' It was Annick. She sounded slightly out of breath. 'Are you busy?'

'Me? *Never.* What's up?'

'Well, I hate to do this over the phone but I'm too excited to wait. I've no idea when we'll see you next.'

Tash's heart missed a beat. She knew what was coming. 'What is it?'

'I'm pregnant.'

'Oh.' Tash swallowed. She closed her eyes briefly, then rallied herself. 'Oh, Annick. That's . . . that's wonderful.'

'Did you guess? Are you pleased?'

'Of course I'm pleased! And no, I didn't guess. I'd no idea what you were going to say. Is Yves pleased?'

'We're both over the moon. We've been trying for ages and—'

'You never said you were trying,' Tash interrupted her, surprised.

Annick gave a short laugh. 'It's not the sort of thing you want everyone to know. When it didn't happen straight away . . . well, you know me, I started to worry. I thought there might be something wrong with me. Anyhow, it's happened! *Finally.* We're pregnant!'

'How . . . how far are you?' Tash asked, struggling to remember how to phrase it. And why was it that women always said "we"? Annick was pregnant, not Yves!

'Two months. That's the other thing. Yves doesn't want me to tell anyone until next month – he says it's bad luck but I couldn't wait. And there's something I wanted to ask you, too.' She hesitated.

'What?'

'Will you be the godmother?'

'Oh, Annick, no! I'm *already* godmother to Rebecca's two.' She grimaced. 'That came out wrong. I didn't mean it like that. I'm sorry. I just meant . . . well, I'm probably the worst godmother in the world, you know that. I'll forget birthdays and anniversaries and exams and—'

'Tash, stop it. You're an *amazing* godmother. You *never* forget birthdays; what are you talking about? You threw that incredible party for the twins last year – have you forgotten?'

'Annabel organised it, not me,' she protested. 'I'd never have managed it on my own.'

'Rubbish. Anyhow, we're not taking "no" for an answer. You're going to be godmother whether you like it or not. How could you even *think* of saying "no"?'

Tash pulled a quick, culpable face. 'I know. Stupid and selfish of me. No, I'm thrilled you've asked me.'

'Really? Are you sure?'

'Of course I'm sure,' Tash said firmly. 'And can I ask – boy or girl? Or is it too early to tell? I never know with these things.'

'Too early to tell,' Annick confirmed. 'And I'm not even sure I want to know, to tell you the truth. I just hope it's healthy.'

'Of course it'll be healthy. Why shouldn't it be?'

'Well, you can never tell. Anything could happen.'

'Oh, Annick. That's what doctors are for. Put that thought right out of your head. Now, the really important question is, when are we going to celebrate?'

'Soon. Soon as Yves gets back.'

'Where's he gone again?'

'Singapore. He's back on Saturday so we'll organise something. No alcohol for me, though.'

'You're French,' Tash protested, laughing. 'French women don't give up a damn thing, or so I've heard. Come on, where's your Gallic spirit?'

'You're mad,' Annick laughed. 'Look, I'd better go. I've still got to work out how to tell Frances. *She'll* go mad. She told me not to get married in the first place.'

'She'll get over it,' Tash said drily. 'D'you know how many of *my* staff are on maternity leave? Eleven. Ridiculous.'

'It's what we do,' Annick said primly. 'Anyhow, I'll call you on Saturday. Don't work too hard.'

'Do I ever?' She replaced the receiver slowly. Godmother. Again. *It's what we do.* No, it wasn't. It was what some women did. Some women had husbands, boyfriends, lovers, children. Tash didn't. She'd had sex twice in her life – once, at university, with someone whose face she couldn't even recall and the second time with the father of her best friend, who was long dead. She cupped her chin in her hand. When she met other working women, she sometimes felt like a creature from another planet. Everyone she knew was either married with kids, or

348

divorced with kids, or in what was cheerfully described as a 'stable' relationship, though most of the relationships around her seemed anything but. Yves and Annick seemed to be an exception, though on the odd occasion the five of them went out together, Yves' attention seemed to be claimed elsewhere. She liked him. He was thoughtful and seemed to dote on Annick, which, in anyone's book, made him the perfect man, but she couldn't help but feel there was either something more there or something missing.

And Julian? She smiled ruefully to herself. She had to be careful where Julian was concerned. He was her business associate, not just the husband of her best friend. He'd made rather a lot of money out of F@shion.com and his business advice was always spot on. Well, *almost* always. She thought back to the conversation they'd had a few days earlier. They'd just begun discussing a fresh injection of capital into the business. Tash, for once, was reluctant. They were growing a little too fast for her comfort, though Julian put her nervousness down to her desire to micro-manage.

'You can't oversee everything, Tash,' he'd said to her over a working lunch.

'I have to. The minute I take my eye off the ball, sales drop. Look what happened last week.'

'It was a bad week. There's lots happening out there. Nothing to do with you being at your desk or not,' Julian said mildly. He speared a tomato. 'Look, just meet with them. You don't have to agree to anything. I'll set it up.'

'Who's "them" again?'

'Sheikh Nasim Al-Soueif. He's one of the Abu Dhabi princes, one of the more powerful ones. The money's in the Gulf, Tash. The Arabs have lots of it, they're confident and they're willing to invest. Everyone else is nervous. I don't want to be a scaremonger here but we're heading towards something we can't quite predict.'

'But we're doing fine,' Tash protested. 'We're up, week on week, month on month.'

'Absolutely. And that's why it's important you keep going, build on what you've got. You've got to show *you* believe in your own product, even if everyone around you is nervous. *If you can keep your head . . .* you know the old poem.'

'*When all about you are losing theirs,*' Tash murmured. She looked at him across the bottle of wine that stood between them. It was almost empty. She signalled to the waiter for another one.

'No, not for me,' Julian quickly covered his own glass. 'I've got another meeting right after this.'

'So? So've I,' Tash grinned. 'All right, fine. Let's meet with them and talk through what they're prepared to offer. No more. I'm not making a decision on this yet. We've got the move coming up, I've got some new ideas I want to run by the team. It's still early days, Julian.'

'All the more reason to have a substantial float behind you. I'll set the meeting up.'

'Will you excuse me a moment?' Tash asked, getting up. 'I'll just pop to the ladies'. Pour me a glass when that waiter gets here, will you?'

Julian nodded, already reaching for his phone.

Alone in the toilet, Tash locked the cubicle door firmly behind her and hurriedly unzipped her bag. She reached in for the little silver hip flask and pulled it out. She unscrewed the cap, lifted the bottle to her lips and took a long, satisfying gulp. Vodka. *Stolichnaya Elit*. She wiped her lips, waited for the burning sensation in her throat and stomach to pass and leaned her head back against the wall. Within seconds, she felt better. She wiped her lips again, the slightly oily, liquorice-like taste lingering in her mouth for a few pleasurable moments. God, it was good. She pushed herself upright, smoothed down her Joseph trousers and retied the silk pussy bow at her throat. She opened the door – no one about – washed her hands and slipped out.

Julian was on the phone as she came up behind him. 'All right, darling, you win. I'll see you tonight. It'll be late, though, probably around ten.' He hung up abruptly as she walked round to her seat. There was a glass of white wine waiting beside her empty plate. She eyed it appreciatively. After the heat of the vodka she'd just had, a cold glass of wine would go down very nicely indeed.

'You sure you won't have any?' she asked.

He shook his head. 'No, I'd better run. It's all settled. We can either fly out to Dubai – have you ever been? – or we can meet them some-where. Here, Paris, Zurich, wherever you like.'

'I've never been out to Dubai. Well, why don't we go there? It'd make a change.'

'Great. I'll get Jackie to set up some dates. I'll get this,' he said, signalling to the waiter and pulling out his wallet at the same time. 'You don't mind if I leave you alone?'

'No, go ahead; I'm used to it,' she grinned. 'I'll just finish this glass. How's darling Rebecca?'

Julian shrugged. 'Haven't heard from her yet. I'm assuming they arrived safely.'

'Oh. I thought . . . ?' She stopped suddenly. 'Has she gone some-where?'

It was Julian's turn to look surprised. 'Didn't she tell you? They left last night. They're in Israel for a fortnight. Embeth wanted to see them.'

'Oh. No, she didn't mention it.' She pulled a face. 'Mind you, I haven't spoken to her in over a week. I suppose she's got her hands full at the moment.'

'Mmm. Right, I'm off. Jackie'll be in touch in the next couple of days. The sooner we get things moving, the better.'

'What's the rush?' Tash asked mildly, picking up her glass. Julian didn't answer. He gave her a quick farewell kiss on either cheek and hurried off, threading his way nimbly through the restaurant. Several heads turned as he passed. He was a good-looking man, Tash thought to herself. Whom had he been talking to? If it wasn't Rebecca, whom was he going to see at ten that night? More to the point – whom else did he call 'darling'?

She turned from the window and picked up her bag. She switched off the lights and had her hand on the doorknob when the phone rang yet again. She sighed. Should she answer it? She walked back to her desk. It was her mother. She picked up the phone.

'*Otchego ty mne nikogda ne zvonish?*' Lyudmila pounced on her as soon as she'd said hello.

'Ma, I *do* call you. Every day.'

'Not true. Always I call you. *Dushen'ka*, I want ask you something.'

'What?'

'Let's go Moscow, you and me. I want show you grandparents.'

Tash almost dropped the phone. Lyudmila scarcely mentioned them. 'Eh?'

'Why not? You big success now. And,' Lyudmila added slyly, 'maybe you gonna open Russia branch? Maybe I can help you do that?'

Tash held the receiver away from her in disbelief for an instant. And then she began to laugh.

90

REBECCA
Tel Aviv

She shut the door to the nursery quietly and tiptoed backwards, praying the boys wouldn't wake up. Her mother's driver was waiting for her downstairs.

'Are they asleep?' The au pair stood in the doorway.

Rebecca nodded. 'Yes, they've both dropped off. I'll be back around eleven. If there's anything, just call.' She smiled her thanks and hurried out the door. Lingering would only tempt fate. She took one last look at her reflection before the lift doors closed. Her hair was coming loose. She tucked a few stray tendrils that had escaped and fished in her bag for some lipstick. It was the second anniversary of her father's death. The Israel Philharmonic was putting on a concert in his honour. Julian should have come, she thought to herself distractedly as she climbed into the waiting Mercedes. He'd begged off . . . some deal or other that he was pushing through.

The big car pulled out into the traffic. She wrapped her coat around her, watching the city flash past in a blur of coloured lights. It was her biggest regret. Lionel hadn't lived to see the twins. He'd died before they were born. He'd never got to hold them, talk to them, play with them. Towards the end he was crippled with arthritis and practically deaf. Only the eyes remained. Those large, expressive eyes that had seen so much, with their magnificent, impossibly dark brows. She felt the lump in her throat thicken. She blinked rapidly. The last thing she wanted to do was turn up at his memorial concert with reddened eyes and a handkerchief clasped to her breast. She thought of the twins. She thought of their two blond heads, Joshua's marginally darker than his brother's, and her heart lifted immediately. Both had come out favouring Julian, the fair, blond side of the family. Speaking of blonds, she suddenly thought to herself, where on earth was cousin Adam? The last she'd seen or heard of him had been at her wedding, some five years earlier. He'd arrived with yet another miniature blonde in a miniskirt and left without her, or so she remembered hearing.

'Here we are, Miss Harburg. Shall I drop you at the front?' She jumped. She'd forgotten all about the driver. For some she would for ever be 'Miss Harburg', never 'Mrs Lovell'.

'Yes, that's fine.' He pulled the car to a smooth halt right outside the entrance. She got out, pulling her coat even more tightly around her. It was freezing. 'Thanks.' She nodded at the doorman and hurried into the warm foyer. She looked around, spotting her mother almost immediately. Embeth was already surrounded by friends and family. She'd cut her long, thick hair shortly after Lionel's death. Now she wore it very short, expertly layered and a lovely, silvery-grey colour. It suited her. She was still slim, with the same olive-toned skin and handsome features, every inch the elegant, gracious widow of one of Israel's favourite sons. Lionel was buried in the prestigious Mount Herzl cemetery, just west of Jerusalem. His headstone was only a few rows away from Golda Meir's. Rebecca had to smile when Embeth told her. Golda Meir was the only woman after his mother, his wife and Margaret Thatcher whom Lionel considered more than his equal. It would have pleased him no end.

'Ma,' Rebecca came up to Embeth, kissing her on both cheeks. 'Sorry I'm late. I kept the driver waiting.'

'Rebecca! Look, it's Rebecca!' Half a dozen people immediately clustered round. 'We haven't seen you in ages! Where've you been hiding? And where's that lovely husband of yours?' Rebecca squared her shoulders and began the slow dance of meeting and greeting people, half of whom she either didn't know or didn't recognise.

The gong sounded once, twice, ushering people into the auditorium. Murmuring excitedly, casting their eyes around to take stock of who'd been invited and who shunned, the guests began to file in. The last time she'd been here, it was Lionel's ninetieth birthday and it was where she'd met Julian for the first time. Now Lionel was gone and she and Julian were married with two children. Annick was back in their lives. Tash had become a multi-millionaire. Everything had changed.

And yet nothing had. The faint whiff of unhappiness that came upon her from time to time descended upon her as they took their seats. She stole a quick glance around her. The women on either side of her were practically identical. Slim and beautiful, tanned or not tanned, stylishly dressed, immaculately made up, knees and ankles crossed elegantly, hands placed patiently in their laps. She was at home amongst them; her life was no different. Au pairs were on hand to take care of their children. Housekeepers ran their various homes; money was never spoken of. The woman to her right whose name she'd already forgotten, if indeed she knew it at all, chattered away happily. Rebecca listened with half an ear.

Their host appeared on stage and there was a sudden burst of enthusiastic applause. She spoke eloquently in English, praising 'the late and dearly missed Lionel Harburg for his gifts, his insights, his commitment and passion to the qualities of leadership, innovation, creativity'. Rebecca listened distractedly, as if they spoke of someone she didn't know. The sense of alienation that had crept up on her deepened slowly, intensifying as the orchestra struck its first notes, swelling alongside the music, rousing the blood to a heavy drum-roll in her veins. She shifted uncomfortably in her seat. She was sweating. She put up a hand to push back the damp tendrils of hair that clung to her forehead and neck.

'Are you all right?' Embeth whispered, looking sideways at her in concern.

She swallowed. 'I'm a bit hot,' she whispered back. 'I feel a bit faint, actually.'

'D'you want to go outside?' Embeth asked, laying a hand on her arm. '*Mi amor*, you're *boiling*. Do you have a fever?'

Rebecca shook her head. People behind them were beginning to tut in disapproval. 'I'll . . . I'll just pop out for a minute. I won't be long.'

She got up quickly, excusing herself as she squeezed past those same elegant knees and legs. She hurried up the aisle and burst through the double doors into the lobby, fanning herself furiously with the programme. The bar staff were busy putting the finishing touches to the refreshments. A long table, covered in snowy white linen and piled with plates and wine glasses, stood at one end of the foyer. There were white spray roses everywhere and enormous bouquets of pink-and-white lilies, Lionel's favourites. A photograph of Lionel and Embeth had been placed on the wall opposite. Rebecca glanced at it, then looked away. The strange, heavy mood that had crept up on her needed no fuelling. She ignored the waiters' curious glances and headed for the main doors. They slid soundlessly apart at her approach.

The cold night air revived her instantly. She drew in a deep breath, thankful to be outside. She reached into her handbag for the packet of cigarettes she kept hidden away in the side pocket. She'd given up as soon as she found out she was pregnant but occasionally, like now, she found herself longing for one. She walked across the forecourt to one of the sculptural stone benches tucked away to one side and sat down, already feeling better. She lit up, waving the smoke away from her face, and leaned back against the smooth, cool stone. Across the lawn, behind the tall, wavering palm trees, Tel Aviv's night traffic streamed past. It had been months, perhaps even years, since she'd been somewhere alone like this, nothing and no one around her, except the sound of traffic and the wind ruffling the tops of the trees. She felt a slow tug, as though she were being dragged backwards to another time and place . . . before Julian and the children. She resisted for a moment – how could she possibly think of life before Joshua and David? – and then she surrendered herself to it, selfishly, almost voluptuously.

Her mind drifted back to her student days, to standing in front of Mortimer's painting of Harold Pinter at the National Portrait Gallery, listening to the lecturer describe the finer points of . . . she stopped suddenly. Jeremy Garrick. She hadn't thought about him in years. She felt the heat of embarrassment creep up through her face and cheeks. That look of triumphant disdain he'd thrown her as he opened the front door for his wife and child . . . she put up a hand to her burning cheek. She wondered where he was now. With some other, confused, doe-eyed student, *sans doute*. She finished her cigarette and stood up, irritated by the direction her thoughts had taken. That was the trouble with thoughts. The mind could wander off anywhere, without control or caution. She tossed away the butt and walked back towards the concert.

There was a man standing with his back to her just in front of the auditorium doors, rocking lightly on his heels, as though waiting for something. She came up beside him and put out a hand to open the door.

'It locks, unfortunately. Automatically, from the inside.'

'Oh.'

'To prevent people interrupting the performance,' he added. 'People like us.' He looked down at her with a faint, rueful smile.

Rebecca looked up at him. 'So what shall we do?' she asked.

'Well, we can wait until someone else comes out, or go in during the intermission.' He had the air of someone patiently explaining something to a child.

Rebecca looked at him more closely, frowning. He looked vaguely familiar. He sounded American but looked Mediterranean. He was deeply tanned, with smooth, olive-toned skin, hazel-green eyes behind black, rectangular glasses. His lips were full and his thick, curly dark-brown hair was swept back off his face. She struggled to place him. Had they met? Then at last, recognition dawned. 'You work with Barenboim.

You're the Palestinian.' She clapped a hand to her mouth. 'I'm sorry, that came out wrong. I've forgotten your name, I'm afraid.'

'Tariq. Tariq Malouf.'

'You're a musician, aren't you?'

He nodded. 'A conductor, at any rate.'

'Why do I get the feeling you know me?' Rebecca said, feeling suddenly and inexplicably shy.

'Because I do.'

She opened her mouth to respond but just at that moment, the auditorium door opened suddenly and someone walked out. He pulled a face, as if to say, 'Shall we?' and held the door open for her, waiting for her to pass through. She blushed and slipped in underneath his arm. He walked off to his own seat and she hurried back to hers.

'Feeling better?' her mother murmured. 'You were gone for quite a long time.'

'The door was locked. From the inside,' she whispered back. She put up a hand to touch her cheek. It was still hot. Tariq Malouf. How did he know her?

91

'The Maloufs? Surely you must remember them?' Eighty-four-year-old Aunt Bettina, the last of Lionel's surviving siblings, peered at her through her gilt pince-nez spectacles. 'One of the oldest and most respected families in Jerusalem, my dear. You and Tariq were *such* good friends.'

'An *Arab* family?'

'But of course. They've been mayors and muftis of this city since the Ottomans, you know. Old Faisal was on the *Waqf*. Tariq's great uncle. A terribly cultured man, *terribly* cultured. Very good-looking, too. Met him several times with Lionel.'

'What's the *waqf*?' Rebecca pronounced it with difficulty.

Aunt Bettina lowered her pince-nez and glared at her niece. 'The *Waqf*. The Islamic Council. They've managed the buildings around the Al-Aqsa Mosque for centuries. I thought you'd been to university, my girl.'

'They didn't teach us anything about that,' Rebecca muttered.

'Well, Tariq runs the AAC now. It took them nearly fifty years, mind you, but they managed to get back the old house in Talbiya. That's where it sits.'

'Where what sits?'

'The AAC, of course.'

'What's the AAC?'

Aunt Bettina lifted her spectacles once more. 'Rebecca Harburg. I do *not* believe I'm talking to one of Lionel's offspring! The Arab Affairs Committee! Your father was one of its patrons. How can you pretend to be so ignorant?'

'I'm not pretending,' Rebecca protested, frowning. 'He never talked about any of it.' Her head was spinning. In the past forty-eight hours, another side of Lionel had been opened up. She had no idea how to even think about it. Her father . . . a patron of Arab affairs? 'Where's Tal-what-d'you-call-it?'

'Talbiya. Oh, the name's changed. It's Komemiyut now. Such a beautiful neighbourhood. I still remember the first time we went there—'

'We?'

'Lionel and I. And Georges, of course. Dear, dear Georges.'

Rebecca struggled to keep up. Aunt Bettina's conversations could go anywhere, she'd noticed, a by-product of her advancing years. She jumped from topic to topic, wholly lucid, but often with enormous gaps in between and the assumption that Rebecca could simply keep up. 'Who's George?'

'Georges Haddad. He was a friend of your Great Uncle Paul as well as Lionel's. You won't remember him, I shouldn't think. He was already ninety when you were born. They lived long, those Harburg boys. Like me,' Aunt Bettina gave one of her great, whooping cackles, followed by a coughing fit.

Rebecca struggled to place it all. 'You said I knew Tariq?'

Aunt Bettina nodded. 'Yes, yes. You used to play with him and his sister, Maryam. The three of you were very close, practically inseparable. It was dreadful when she died, just dreadful.' Aunt Bettina's voice grew soft and her hands began working against each other in distress.

Rebecca's eyes grew wide. Why didn't she remember any of it? 'Wh-what happened to her?'

'Leukaemia. Poor little thing, she was so sickly, so sickly. Lionel took her to New York, of course, but there was nothing they could do. She was buried here, right here in Jerusalem, in the garden at Talbiya. That's why Tariq fought so hard to get the house back.'

'Why don't I remember any of this?' Rebecca asked, suddenly feeling her throat tighten.

Aunt Bettina shrugged. 'You were so little. And when Maryam died . . . well, well, who knows what goes on inside the heads of children? *I* certainly don't,' she sniffed. She stubbed out her cigarette and picked up the little silver bell to summon the woman who looked after her. A distracted frown suddenly appeared between her brows. Her face changed, becoming vague. 'Where . . . where . . . ?' Her hands moved about, as though she were trying to find something.

'What is it, Aunt Bettina? What are you looking for?' Rebecca asked her gently.

'The photographs. My album. It was just here. I was looking at it before you came. Where did I put it? Nadine?' She called for the middle-aged woman who'd been her companion for almost a decade.

'What's the matter, *Safta*?' Nadine bustled into the room. 'What've you lost this time?'

'The photo album. The one I wanted to show her, remember? We had it out this morning. We were looking at it together, but I've gone and lost it.' In her face there was a barely suppressed kind of anxiety that Rebecca understood had little to do with the missing photo album. It was to do with the recollection of a past that was fast slipping away from her. She felt her heart contract sympathetically. She knew just how she felt. Aunt Bettina had just opened a door onto a past she knew nothing about yet had clearly participated in. The yearning to know more was overwhelming.

'Here it is. We put it away together, *Safta*, don't you remember?' Nadine bent down and pulled open one of the drawers of the elegant mahogany console that stood to one side of her aunt's chair. *Safta* meant 'grandmother' in Hebrew, Rebecca knew. It was a touching mark of respect for someone who'd never even been a mother. 'Here you are. Look. It's not lost.'

Aunt Bettina's face settled happily again. She took the album from Nadine with trembling hands. 'Here you are, my lovely. Have a look through it. I'm going for my afternoon rest. Will you be here when I wake up?'

Rebecca shook her head. 'I don't think so, Aunt Bettina. Mama's coming with the twins . . . they'll be here any minute now. Are you sure you won't wait to see them?'

Aunt Bettina waved a languid hand as Nadine helped her from her chair. 'No, no, my dear. They'll only wear me out. Put the album back in the drawer, there's a dear. Don't want it to get lost.' She turned, holding onto Nadine with one hand and her silver-tipped cane with the other, a bent but elegant figure in her long, cream silk dress, low-heeled patent court shoes and, as ever, the triple string of pearls around her neck that she'd worn for as long as Rebecca could remember. She watched the pair make their way slowly out of the room, then she opened the album on her lap.

The first few pages, separated by delicate, wafer-thin crinkled paper, were unremarkable; the yellowed, sepia-tinged photographs with their clipped white corners were replicas of hundreds of photographs that lay in drawers in the library at home. She turned the pages slowly. Lionel as a young man, muscular, finely turned legs in shorts, a woollen jumper and a scarf at his neck; Lionel in a suit, surrounded by other similarly dressed men – her uncles, she supposed. There were others she didn't recognise but whose demeanour and clothing were of that age and time. There was a particularly fetching photograph of Embeth, shyly looking up at the camera from beneath the brim of a hat. She smiled to herself. There were photos of her as a baby, then as a little girl. She peered at them curiously. There were a few of her and cousin Adam, Rebecca looking determinedly at the camera, not smiling, not frowning. She recognised the face as the one she wore even now. She lifted the page, still smiling to herself and then she stopped, frowning. There it was, just as Aunt Bettina had said. A photograph of four children: herself, aged two or three at the most, a girl of perhaps four, then Adam, his arm round the shoulders of a younger boy with the beautiful, solemn face of the man she'd spoken to the night before. Right in front of her, looking at her from a distance of nearly forty years, was the face of Tariq Malouf.

92

TASH
Moscow

Tash stepped out of the cab and looked around her with a sinking heart. Behind her, Lyudmila was arguing with the taxi driver. Tash's head hurt. Her eyes hurt. Her tongue hurt. It had been so long since she'd spoken Russian on an ongoing, continuous basis, that in the forty-eight hours they'd been in Russia, the muscles in her tongue and throat had started to ache. For the past hour or so, she'd fallen almost completely silent. Lyudmila, on the other hand, hadn't stopped talking since they left London, two days earlier. Her happiness knew no bounds. It all started at Terminal Five. One of the ground staff recognised Tash as she and Lyudmila checked in for their flight to Sheremetyevo – first class, of course – and it had taken all of Lyudmila's self-control not to swoon with delight.

'Imagine! She know you . . . imagine that, *Dushen'ka*! We famous!'

We *are* famous, Tash corrected her silently, out of old habit. 'So what're *you* famous for?' she asked Lyudmila mildly.

'Me?' Lyudmila's blue eyes grew wide. 'I your mother. Is stupid question.'

Tash declined to answer. She turned away, hiding her smile. If the truth were told, she loved every minute of it herself. Not the being recognised bit – she couldn't have cared less about *that*. But she hugely enjoyed seeing Lyudmila clearly relishing every precious moment – from the chauffeur-driven BMW that picked her up to the specially reserved check-in counters for first-class passengers at Terminal Five, to the champagne-and-canapés and all the inflight magazines, free wash-bags and anything else that the BA staff could do to make their journey more pleasant, more comfortable, more relaxing. Lyudmila's eyes practically misted over when the flight attendant brought her that morning's copy of *Pravda*. '*Spasibo*,' she murmured calmly, looking for all the world as if flying first class to Moscow were an everyday occurrence.

'You're welcome,' the attendant smiled prettily at her. 'Anything else I can get you, Mrs Bryce-Brudenell?' It was only one of a handful of times that Lyudmila had been called 'Mrs Bryce-Brudenell' and it was enough to make her glow with radioactive warmth. Tash bit the inside of her lip to stop herself grinning.

But she wasn't grinning now. She turned to look up at the block of flats Lyudmila was pointing to, squinting against the fierce, hot sun – no one had told her Moscow would be *boiling* in July – and hoped the dismay she felt didn't show on her face. She'd never met her grandparents – on either side – and the thought of spending a week with two elderly strangers in a flat that looked like something out of Blade Runner (in a bad, run-down sort of way) was daunting, to say the least. At least their first two nights in Moscow had been spent in considerable style: a suite at the Ritz-Carlton, overlooking the Kremlin and right next to Red Square. Lyudmila had been unable to sleep, of course, and together they'd emptied the contents of the minibar – hence her splitting headache and hangover.

'That one,' Lyudmila pointed upwards. '*Da*, that one.'

Which one? They all looked the damned same. 'How can you tell, Ma?'

Lyudmila shrugged. 'Never forget.'

There wasn't a whole lot you could say to that. If she'd grown up in a tower block like this one, she thought to herself grimly, she'd never forget it either. She watched her mother reluctantly peel off a pile of roubles to give to the scowling taxi driver. It was impossible for Lyudmila *not* to argue over price – it was in her blood, just as it was in Tash's, though in her case, Tash preferred to think of it as business acumen rather than a tendency to haggle. 'Ready?' she asked her.

'*Da*.' Lyudmila belted the Dior dress Tash had bought her especially for the trip and pulled her Gucci sunglasses back down over her eyes. The gift wasn't *quite* as altruistic as it sounded, she'd confided to Annick the night before they left. 'It's either that or some ghastly pink meringue. Trust me, I'm not about to show up in front of grandparents I've never seen with Ma in frilly pink; I'll tell you that for free.'

'Are you nervous?' was Annick's only – and strange – comment.

'Nervous? Why on earth would I be nervous?'

'Well, they're your grandparents. They're flesh and blood.'

'So?'

'So *I'd* be nervous.'

For once a ready quip failed to come to mind. 'Well, *I'm* not,' was just about all she could manage. The truth was, of course, that she *was* nervous. There'd never been anyone except her and Lyudmila. The whole concept of 'family' was a shaky one to her. She'd often wondered why Lyudmila had gone to the trouble of naming her 'Bryce-Brudenell' and not 'Gordiskaya'. After all, it didn't make sense to carry the name of a man who'd never seen her and clearly didn't want to. Lyudmila was at first curiously vague on the subject. 'Why not?' she asked. 'Is good name.'

'But he doesn't care about me. Does he even know I exist?' She was thirteen at the time, a year or two before she'd made that fateful trip to Edinburgh, which Lyudmila still didn't know about. Tash would never tell her, either.

'Of course he knows. Why you think he give money?'

'Not enough, clearly,' Tash grumbled.

Lyudmila rounded on her. She held Tash by the shoulders, probably the last time she'd been able to, and forced her to look at her.

'Listen to me, you, *neblagodarnaya*. Is better you have his name. Gordiskaya name is curse here. You want everyone think you some poor Russian girl with no money, no education, no brain? No! Better you have his name. You can be nice English girl; no one knows anything. Is all I ask from him. Give you little money, give you name. Now stop ask me questions about him, okay?'

Tash was too surprised to do anything other than nod.

And of course, Lyudmila was right. Bryce-Brudenell *had* proved to be an advantage. A double-barrelled name, an alumnus of St Benedict's *and* a million-pound business under her belt? No one would ever accuse *her* of being a mail-order bride.

She looked up at the building Lyudmila had pointed out. In a few moments, she was about to meet the owners of the disembodied voices she'd occasionally heard down the telephone line when she could be persuaded to speak to them. When she was very young and Lyudmila had managed to place a call through the international operator to the Soviet Union, she'd have to be dragged to the phone. She hated the tears and the cries of '*vnuchka, vnuchka!*', 'granddaughter, granddaughter!' and Lyudmila's tears and dark moods that lasted for days afterwards. Later, the calls were made the other way round. There'd be a hesitant request for something – money, clothing, medicines – and then Lyudmila's sulks, as she'd have to economise in order to send whatever it was they'd asked for. But somewhere in the past couple of years, things had changed. Now, Tash knew, Lyudmila often sent them whatever money Tash had just given her. It was one way for Lyudmila to show

how proud she was – and of course, Lyudmila just loved to show off. Standing on the pavement next to them were four gigantic suitcases stuffed with clothes, gifts, food, jewellery, medicines, electrical goods. Everything Lyudmila could think of. She'd only recently learned how to shop online and could barely tear herself away from the laptop Tash had bought her. It sat on the table beside her bed, night after night, its little white apple glowing in the dark in the same way the television screen across the room flickered silently all night. In the days before their departure for Moscow, she could hardly contain her excitement. 'Look, *dushen'ka* . . . is cute, no? For Mama.' Tash would squint at the screen and nod.

'But why don't you get her something from us?' she asked once. 'Something that'll last. I'm not sure about those jumpers, you know.'

Lyudmila scowled at her. 'You crazy? Look. Shirt for four pounds. Nothing in *your* shop for four pounds.'

Tash sighed. There was little point explaining to Lyudmila that a) F@shion.com wasn't a shop and b) a jumper for four pounds would fall apart after the first wash. She bit her tongue.

And now here they were, on a Krylatskoe sidewalk in the middle of an absolutely baking July morning with four of the biggest Samsonite suitcases that Selfridges stocked, overflowing with jumpers for a tenner.

It took a good half an hour for the fuss generated by their visit to die down. As soon as one set of neighbours departed, the women in tears of joy, the men scratching their heads in baffled pride, a fresh group rolled in.

Tash sat in the middle, at once the centre of attention and yet peripheral to the celebrations. Lyudmila, resplendent in Dior, her freshly coloured blonde hair cascading down her leather-clad back, beautiful just-manicured red nails clutching her third glass of vodka, reigned supreme. It was a performance worthy of an Oscar, three Golden Globes, a Grammy or an Emmy and a handful of whatever else might be going. Tears, laughter, screams, songs, more tears, more songs, the works. Everyone in Krylatskoe who knew her (or who'd once said 'hello' to her nearly forty years ago) showed up to pay homage, sneak a kiss or even just a peek. She was in her element. Tash, whom everyone gazed at the way they might have gazed at a giraffe, sat calmly in the middle of it all, sipping her own vodka (her fourth), bemused and amused by the fuss, secretly praying their attention wouldn't turn to her. Her grandfather, Vladimir, almost totally deaf, sat in the corner of the room by the window, his face opening and closing in confusion and sporadic recollection. Alzheimer's, Lyudmila whispered. Elsa, her grandmother, shouted out to him at intervals when it became clear he'd lost the plot, 'That's Tash, our granddaughter. Míla's child. You remember Míla?'

He looked from Elsa to Tash. 'Who is that?' he asked, pointing at Lyudmila. Elsa began to explain but he dismissed her, and with a look of crafty collusion, leaned towards Tash. 'Who is she? What's she doing here?'

Elsa bustled over, adjusting the blankets over his knees, fussing with his cardigan. 'It's Míla, Vladimir. Míla. And that's her daughter. Your granddaughter, *glupets.*' *Silly man.* It was said affectionately.

The old man must have recognised something in her tone for he smiled, a wide, toothless grin. His hand went up to his mouth and he pressed it, saying angrily to his wife, 'Why haven't I got my teeth in? Where are my teeth?'

Elsa sighed. 'Your gums were sore this morning, Vladimir, don't you remember? No, wait . . . I'll go and get them. But I want to put some of that gel on first . . . no? All right, I'm coming, I'm coming.' Her grandmother got up heavily and went to fetch his false teeth. He grabbed them from her and then concentrated carefully on the plates, deciding which was which. He inserted them slowly, his mouth masticating as though chewing on some long-forgotten piece of food. Finally it was done. His voice, when it came, was different; higher-pitched and more controlled. It seemed to Tash to be the voice of a puppet, speaking in a language and at a pitch no one fully understood. No one paid him much attention anyhow; their squeals and exclamations of delight were directed at the three open suitcases on the crowded sitting-room floor. Like a demented creature in a cartoon strip, Lyudmila dived in, pulling out gifts, one after the other. Friends and neighbours stood around, arms folded across their chests as though holding in their hearts and comments, watching enviously as Elsa disappeared under the mountain of clothing, shoes, perfumes and toiletries, the likes of which she'd clearly never seen before and certainly never in such industrial quantities.

Tash got up from her seat in the middle of the room and walked to the window. She looked down at the playground, six storeys below. The ten-storey apartments stretched on for a kilometre or more, indistinguishable from each other. It was hard to think of Lyudmila growing up here, one blonde schoolgirl amongst so many others, but in some ways, it made many of her idiosyncrasies – so utterly inexplicable

364

to an English teenager – understandable, in an odd way. One of the neighbours had let it drop that the apartments in Krylatskoe were still heated for free, thank God. No wonder Lyudmila always left the lights on or the heating turned up. Someone else commented on the government's plans to start charging for prescriptions. Again, little wonder Lyudmila was a hypochondriac. She was used to free medical treatment, free dental treatment, free heating and light. The Soviet Union wasn't quite the bleak wasteland of underachievement, shortages and ruin she'd made it out to be. Tash saw now that for all their material deprivation, there was a closeness and warmth that existed between these people who'd lived cheek-by-jowl through some of the biggest upheavals of the twenty-first century. They'd emerged from it all with their humour and generosity intact, their humanity untouched and unharmed. She swallowed hard. It was light years away from London and the life she knew to be hers.

As if on cue, her grandmother got up, not without difficulty – she was a large woman, almost as tall as Tash – and lumbered over towards her, holding out a light-blue shirt. '*Davai, malysh, pomerei etu.*' Come on, little one, try this one on. Tash hurriedly wiped her cheeks. She looked at the shirt her grandmother was holding out and only just managed to hold onto her eyeballs. Topmark. Oh, *God.* Could there be anything worse?

Hours later, Tash lay on the sitting-room sofa, tossing and turning in an attempt to fold her six-foot frame comfortably into a space that was considerably less. Quite why they had to spend their nights as well as their days in Krylatskoe was a mystery. It was an hour's cab ride back to the splendour of the Ritz-Carlton and besides, people here went to sleep early, like chickens. She'd looked dubiously at the bath – a narrow, cold-looking affair with rusting taps – and thought longingly of the enormous wet room at the suite they'd just vacated. The entire flat would fit into the bathroom with bags of room to spare all round. She sighed and shifted uncomfortably, changing position for the umpteenth time. It was no bloody use.

She got up quietly. Her bladder was full, the effect of far too much vodka and truly dreadful red wine. She tiptoed out into the corridor, heading for the toilet. The front door was ajar, she noticed as she went past. She stopped to close it and then heard two people talking outside. She peered through the crack. It was her mother and that friend of hers, Tatiana, after whom Tash was supposedly named. They were standing in the outside corridor, smoking. Blue cigarette smoke curled and rose lazily towards the overhead light.

'It's a pity,' she heard Tatiana say. Her foot, encased in its high-heeled sandal, was just visible out of the corner of Tash's eye. 'A real pity. When I think of how beautiful *you* were, you know? You still are, Míla. Still beautiful.'

'Oh, no, not anymore. I *used* to be beautiful, Tatia. Not anymore. It's all finished now.'

'No, I'm telling you. Compared to us?' She gave a harsh, hoarse laugh. 'You've kept your figure, no wrinkles. You're still a very attractive woman, Míla. Lucky you. But it's a pity about Tatiana. She's done well for herself, yes, but she's not beautiful. Not like you.'

Tash felt a cool flush of embarrassment ripple lightly up her spine. Her shoulders hunched.

'No, she's not beautiful,' Lyudmila sighed. She paused for a moment, presumably drawing on her cigarette. 'And no boyfriend, can you believe it? Never. I used to think . . . well, I don't need to spell it out. But you know what? It doesn't matter. She's *rich*.'

Tash didn't wait to hear the rest. Hot with embarrassment and shame, she tiptoed down the corridor to the bathroom. *No boyfriend. Never.* What did it matter how much money she had? In Lyudmila's eyes – in *everyone's* eyes – she was an object of pity, someone to cluck sympathetically over, not someone to admire.

93

REBECCA
Jerusalem

Immense washes of summer light spilled over the hills, bathing the city in a dusty luminosity, like the great, slow blinking of an eye. First this building, then that one – the red glare struck the sandy Jerusalem stone, turning the entire city blush-pink as the sun began to sink. Rebecca read the Hebrew and Arabic street names with difficulty as she negotiated her way slowly up Chopin Street and then turned left as the map directed. She turned into Pinsker Street. Just before the park at the end of the road, she saw the small brown sign. The *Arabic Affairs Council*. She pulled up opposite and cut the engine. A giant swathe of bougain-villea shaded the entrance to the house. In the dying light, the flowers looked as though they were on fire. She locked the car and hurried across. The wrought-iron gate creaked in protest as she pushed it open and stepped inside. A narrow flagstone path led from the gate towards the house, curving gracefully away from the road before opening out onto a dramatic view of terraced, manicured lawns sloping away down the hillside. The terraces were bordered by lush, semi-tropical plants and flowerbeds, bursting with blossoms of all shapes and colours. The effect was startling. She felt like Alice, stepping through the looking glass. A sprinkler on the second or third terrace twisted wildly, its soft 'phut-phut' tapping a rhythm to her steps as she walked along seeking the entrance. At last she found it, partially hidden from view by terracotta pots of olive trees and a climbing trellis of pale pink roses. She stopped, nervously twisting her hair into a ponytail, and smoothed down her skirt. She raised a hand and knocked lightly on the front door.

Someone answered, in Arabic, then in Hebrew. She pushed open the door cautiously. A young woman in a headscarf and veil came out of one of the rooms, a pile of files in her arms. 'Can I help you?' she asked, again in Arabic first, then in Hebrew.

'I . . . I'm sorry,' Rebecca said apologetically. 'English?'

'Can I help you?'

'I . . . I was just wondering . . . I'm looking for Tariq. Tariq Malouf?'

The girl looked at her, her expression difficult to read. Then she beckoned to Rebecca. 'Come.'

She followed her into the office. Tariq was sitting at a desk by the window. He looked up as they entered. For a second she and Tariq looked at one other in mutual incomprehension.

'I . . . I . . . was just passing,' Rebecca stammered, unable to take her eyes off Tariq's face. 'And I saw the sign outside. I thought I'd just drop in and . . . and say hello. After the other night, at the concert, I mean.' She stopped, aware she was babbling.

The girl looked uncertainly at Tariq. He shook his head, murmuring something to her in Arabic. She withdrew, quietly closing the door behind her.

'Won't you sit down?' Tariq suddenly got to his feet. He pulled a chair out for her, placing it opposite him.

'Th-thanks,' Rebecca stammered, grateful for the chance to sit down. Her legs were feeling distinctly wobbly.

'So,' he said, walking back to his own chair. 'To what do I owe this unexpected pleasure?'

'I was just passing by,' Rebecca began again, flustered. 'I was in the city for the afternoon. I . . . I went to see my aunt the other day, Aunt Bettina . . .' Her voice trailed off. She was painfully aware of the hot blush spreading up her neck and face.

He leaned back in his chair, his fingers peaked in front of his face, his expression carefully neutral. An awkward silence followed. Rebecca looked at her own hands: ridiculous – they were trembling. 'How *is* your aunt?' he asked after a moment.

She lifted her eyes to meet his. What colour were his eyes? Hazel, brown, green? She couldn't tell, not from that distance. 'She's . . . fine.' There was another awkward pause. 'I wish I'd spent more time with her when . . . when I was younger,' she added lamely.

'It's a common wish.' He looked at her closely, as if trying to figure something out, but gave little away. The faintly amused air he'd carried the other night was gone; in its place was a grave solemnity that made her regret her silly decision to get in the car and drive to Jerusalem. What had she come here for? She could feel her blush deepening.

She swallowed nervously. 'Look, I didn't mean to disturb you,' she said quickly, wondering whether she ought to get up now and save herself any further embarrassment or try and talk her way out of what was rapidly turning into her most humiliating half hour since Dr Jeremy Garrick. At the thought of Garrick, she almost choked. 'Aunt Bettina said we used to . . . to play together, when we were kids. It's strange, I don't remember any of it, so I thought . . . well, I just thought I'd stop by and ask you, you know, if—'

'You were very young,' he interrupted her gently. He seemed to be weighing her up, deciding which way, in his mind, she might fall. Good or bad, friend or foe, desirable or not. A childish urge to please came over her. She suddenly wished she were better looking, more beautiful.

'I saw a picture,' she said hesitantly. 'In one of her albums. It was of the four of us. My cousin Adam, you, your sister and me. Adam had his arm round you.' She looked at him. He was listening to her with polite attention. 'Aunt Bettina told me about Maryam, your sister . . . I wish . . . I wish I could remember her.'

He took a deep breath suddenly, pulling his lower lip into his mouth, the soft, full lip disappearing underneath the row of white, even teeth. She watched as he brought up a hand to his face, fingers stroking the dark stubble beneath the skin. It was almost dark in his office. Dusk had come upon them suddenly, the light withdrawing so slowly that neither had noticed. He reached out to switch on a small desk lamp; greenish light suddenly flooded the room. Then, without any transition from the formality with which he'd received her, he placed a hand on her forearm. She stared at it for a second, her heartbeat accelerating. 'Will you come and see me?' he asked, his eyes locked on hers. 'Tomorrow evening. I'll be in Tel Aviv.'

'Yes,' she said simply. His grip on her forearm tightened. And so, right there in his office, sitting across from each other in the rather formal manner of two people who might have come together for an official meeting, there was suddenly between them the unexpected covenant of desire.

94

He came into the bar at the appointed hour. She watched him come down the steps, duck under the doorway and look quickly around. She'd been there for all of twenty minutes, a half-finished glass of wine in front of her, an unlit cigarette in the clean ashtray at her elbow. She had to have something to do with her hands. Her freshly washed hair curled loosely about her face. Jeans, high-heeled black boots, a midnight-blue silk shirt open to the third button, showing a sliver of her silver chains between her breasts – she was indistinguishable from the well-dressed, elegant men and women who were sitting at the long marble bar. The restaurant was his choice. Hamra, on Ha'Yarkon Street. He'd written down the address for her in his office.

'You're here.' He was beside her, looking down at her as he unwound his scarf.

She nodded, her heart in her mouth. 'I left the kids with Julian,' she murmured, then stopped, kicking herself. Why on earth had she mentioned her husband and children in the first breath?

'What're you drinking?' He ignored her obvious discomfort and slid onto the stool next to her. He was dressed casually: a navy jacket, light-blue shirt, jeans . . . she didn't dare look any further or closer.

'I'm not sure,' she confessed. 'I just needed . . . something.'

'Well, I'll share the "something" with you. May I?' She nodded vigorously. He lifted the glass to those full, red lips. 'Not bad.' He signalled to the waiter. 'Another one,' he said, in perfect, fluent Hebrew. She watched him, transfixed.

'I read you'd studied at Julliard,' she began hesitantly.

He nodded. 'Studied there, taught there for a while.'

'Where do you live now?'

He shrugged. 'Like you, some months here, some months there. You go where the work takes you.'

'Not like me, then,' she gave a rueful smile.

'Perhaps not.' He lifted his glass. 'And you? How long are *you* here for?'

It was her turn to shrug. 'Another week, perhaps. My husband . . . well, *he* follows the work. I just follow him.' It was difficult *not* to mention Julian. She glanced at him, then at his hands. Was he married?

He noticed her surreptitious glance. He answered her unspoken question. 'Yes. She lives in Connecticut. Two kids. All-American. Anything else you want to know?'

She drew in her breath sharply. 'Wh-what are we doing here?' she asked, hoping her voice was steady.

He turned on his stool so that they were facing one another. His knee bumped hers. He put out a hand, the same hand that had clasped her forearm the night before, and lightly drew a line down the middle of her thigh, all the way down to her knee. She felt her thighs begin to shake uncontrollably. 'I don't know,' he said slowly. He shook his head. 'When you came into the office yesterday, I wasn't expecting you. It threw me, to be honest. I guess I always knew I'd run into you again someday. I know you don't remember any of it. You were so young and when Maryam died . . . well, I guess you blocked it all out. But our histories are so intertwined. As soon as I saw you, I knew.'

'Knew wh-what?'

'That something was going to happen. Between us.'

She swallowed. 'I'm married,' she said hesitantly.

'So'm I.'

'So what is this? An affair?'

He made the same gesture of dismissal he'd made to his assistant the night before. An almost silent 'tut', the faint shake of the head, neither a 'yes' nor a 'no', a gesture from a language and culture she didn't know and couldn't place. She hardly knew him. He was a compelling mixture of something powerfully familiar and yet equally powerfully strange. He had within him the same quality that fascinated her about both Tash and Annick. One minute they were the friends she'd known all her life, as powerfully familiar to her as family. The next, speaking French or Russian, they stepped out of themselves and out of her reach. When they were all much younger, she'd bitterly resented their ability to slip like chameleons into a place she couldn't follow. Now, sitting opposite Tariq, that same irrational fear resurfaced. She had to stop herself from reaching out to grab hold of him.

'Does it matter?' he asked slowly. 'Does it matter what we call it?'

She looked at him closely, her eyes searching his face for some sign that this was all a huge joke, that he wasn't taking it as seriously as she was. There was none. He lifted his hand from her thigh and swallowed the last of his wine.

'Come,' he said, sliding off the stool. He picked up his jacket, fished in his pocket for his wallet and peeled off a note, sliding it across the bar. 'Let's go.'

She slid off her own stool with legs that trembled at every step. She walked out after him into the summer night air, every nerve in her body attuned to the figure of the man in front of her.

She raised herself carefully on one elbow to look at him as he slept, gazing at his profile as though to commit every line to a memory that couldn't be erased. Seen sideways, the red, rosy scroll of his lips parted fractionally as he drew breath, in and out. She studied the hollow of his cheek beneath the bridge of his long, delicately etched nose, noticing the dark shadow of a beard already pushing through the smooth skin of the shelf of his jaw. He was the most deeply sensual man she had ever seen.

He stirred, turning towards her and opening one eye. The dark, black lashes swept back and forth as he focused on her. At this range, his eyes were green, flecked with gold. Lion's eyes. She caught her breath and pushed her face into the heat of his neck. Ecstasy, coupled with remorse and fear – a heightened state of being like no other. Bare skin touching, sticking, she took in great mouthfuls of the warm, male-scented air, taking him deep down into her lungs, stomach, legs. Once, when she was a teenager, on holiday with her parents in Cavezzana, Adam had taken her for a ride in a convertible Alfa Romeo that he'd hired for a couple of weeks. She was fourteen, fifteen at the most. The road from Pontremoli, the nearest village, was full of twists and turns, hairpin bends and steep, narrow inclines. He drove the little sports car hard, the engine screaming in protest and in time with her own squeals of delight and fear. She lifted her arms into the air during one particularly steep drop and felt like a child on a fairground ride with the warm summer air rushing past, her cousin's tanned and capable arm beside her, her stomach still hanging somewhere up there at the start of the drop. It was the headiest combination of sexual tension and excitement and sheer, unadulterated fear. She felt it now, her tongue darting out between parched lips to touch and taste the saltiness at his neck, nibble at his earlobe, her hands already busy down below, stroking, teasing. In the wide, double bed of the apartment he'd brought her to, not far from the bar on Ha'Yarkon Street, they made love for the third time that night, fiercely, passionately, in almost total silence, achingly aware of the solemnity of the moment. Why was this different from all the others? *It will not last. It cannot possibly last.*

95

ANNICK
London

Pregnancy didn't blunt her. On the contrary, moving about the flat and her office with the unsteady gait of a sailor, she was fired up with an energy that catapulted her straight out of sleep each morning into wakefulness. She raced from home to work, work to home, alternately alarming and amusing Yves, who feared for the child growing inside her. 'Slow down,' he begged her. 'It's not a race.' He was away a lot during the first few months. He'd found a job as an engineering consultant that seemed to take him everywhere – Singapore, Kuala Lumpur, Johannesburg and Lagos. There didn't seem to be a far-flung capital that he hadn't visited. She had grown used to his many absences and in the beginning, at least, it suited her. She could 'get on with things,' she told him earnestly. 'After the baby's born, it'll be different.' Frances, openly devastated by the news of her marriage, followed by the announcement of an impending maternity leave, seemed determined to squeeze a year's worth of work into whatever time Annick had left.

'Hmm. Pregnant. I knew it. Well, I knew someone who worked right up until her due date,' she muttered as soon as Annick announced the news. 'She went straight from here to the delivery room. Didn't slow her down in the *slightest*.'

Annick held her tongue. She had no intention of working until her due date but the burst of energy that the first few months brought her spilled over naturally into her work. With Yves away so much, it was easy enough to work long days and evenings, unencumbered by a dinner waiting to be cooked or company waiting to be kept. After three years at Clifton Crabbe, she'd made a name for herself as a conscientious, meticulous solicitor who left no stone unturned, no date unchecked and no fact un-referenced. And cross-referenced again. She and Frances made an exceptionally good team. Frances was the public front, the solicitor on whom all the clerks and barristers depended to pull in the really big cases. She loved the high-profile hustle, the posturing, the after-work drinks and the socialising. Behind the scenes, paddling furiously, was her team of hard-working, methodical and meticulous solicitors who did the bulk of the legwork, none quite so methodical and meticulous as Annick Pasqual. Against her advice, Annick had changed her name as soon as she legally could.

'But *why*?' Frances would no sooner have changed her own name than grown a beard.

Annick shrugged. It was hard to explain how thoroughly she wanted to be rid of the past. 'I like Pasqual better. It's less of a mouthful.'

'Only if you're thick,' Frances snorted. 'Betancourt's got a certain ring to it. It's classy. Foreign.'

'Not where I'm from.'

'Which is?'

'Doesn't matter. I've changed it.'

Frances narrowed her eyes but said no more. Annick's name was duly recorded and changed. Annick.Pasqual@cliftoncrabbe.com. Easy as that.

Seven weeks to go. She lumbered heavily up the road towards home, the flat she and Yves had just bought opposite Morley College, just south of the river. It wasn't the sort of neighbourhood either Tash or Rebecca would have chosen, but it was what she and Yves could afford. Yves was absolutely firm on the topic. It was fine for Tash or Rebecca to have lent Annick a helping hand when she needed it, but she was his wife now, and no such hands were needed. He'd finally found a suitable position with a small engineering consultancy with projects in places with unpronounceable names, like Kyrgyzstan and Baluchistan. Places where they spoke money, English and French – in that order. Annick joked with him sometimes that the job was just a front and that he was secretly off to see a mistress or someone else when he said he was going to work. But she saw after a while that there was a sensitivity there that meant he didn't like it. Perhaps he was embarrassed that she earned more than he did? She stopped. After all, he'd been the one to give up his entire life to be with her.

'It's still a period property,' Annick pointed out when she took Tash to see it.

'Yeah. Just. Clearly the fag end,' Tash sniffed. 'And what the hell's *that* next door?'

'It's . . . it's a council estate.'

'I don't mean *that*. I practically grew up on a council estate. No, what's that yellow stuff on the façade?'

'I'm not sure,' Annick confessed, looking dubiously at it. 'Scaffolding?'

'Are you absolutely, positively, *completely* sure you won't just take a teeny, weeny little loan from me? You could get something . . . well, *nice*. Something a bit closer.'

'This *is* close. To my work, at any rate.'

'Yes, but you're south of the river, darling. I wouldn't mind if you were somewhere like . . . like, well, even *Camden*, or something—'

Annick burst out laughing. 'Listen to you! When did you become such a snob?' She chuckled. 'No, this is perfect. It's what we can afford and . . . it's *ours*. Mine and Yves' . . . and the baby's, of course. Look, we'll probably move when we have another one. Maybe somewhere with a garden.'

'Another one? You haven't even pushed this one out yet,' Tash said in alarm.

Annick smiled. 'Don't worry, I won't ask you to be godmother twice,' she said drily.

'That's not what I meant,' Tash said quickly, looking guilty. 'I just meant . . . oh, never mind. Well, if you're one hundred per cent sure . . . ?'

'We are.'

And so they were. The ground floor, one-*and-a-half* bedroom flat (Yves argued that the tiny box room off the hallway could hardly be considered a bedroom) was perfect for their needs.

She pushed open the front door and dropped her shopping on the floor with relief. The hallway was painted a pretty, dusky-pink colour, a nice contrast to the black-and-white floor tiles. At one end of the corridor, looking out over the garden belonging to the flat below, was the kitchen. On either side were the combined living and dining room and the two bedrooms. The master (and only, Yves reminded her) bedroom also looked out over the garden. She'd recently upholstered the box window so she could sit there with the baby. On a sunny day she could open the sash windows and look out over the garden.

There was a small pile of letters lying on the floor; she bent down, not without difficulty, and retrieved them. She picked up the bag again and took everything down the corridor to the kitchen. Baked beans, cannelloni beans, chickpeas, lentils . . . she put away the tins tidily in the cupboard. Skimmed milk and yogurt in the fridge, fruit in the large wooden bowl on the dining-room table. The baby kicked and turned; she put a hand on her stomach, humming to herself. She boiled the kettle, made herself a cup of tea and took it through to the living room, settling herself on the sofa. She picked up the remote. It was nearly eight. She ought to make herself something to eat – a salad, perhaps, or a piece of grilled fish – but first the news. At the thought of dinner, the baby kicked again. She smiled to herself. Greedy little thing.

It was only as she was tidying away the last of the dishes an hour later that she remembered the letters. She'd stuck them next to the toaster. Yves hadn't yet rung; he was in New York and they were at least six or seven hours behind. She made a mental note *not* to switch her phone onto silent as she usually did before bed, and picked up the letters on her way out. She flicked through them idly: two bills, a neighbourhood flyer, a wrongly addressed envelope and one addressed to a *M. Yves Guillaume Ameyaw*. She looked at it and frowned. She turned it over. A plain white window envelope, computer-generated typeface, no indication as to whom it was from. She stared at it. Yves' middle name was indeed Guillaume so it was unlikely it was wrongly addressed, but where had she heard the name 'Ameyaw' before? It was a Togolese name. She looked down at the envelope again. It was clearly an official letter of some sort. The postmark was Parisian. She hesitated, and then slid her fingernail underneath the flap. It opened up easily. She scanned it quickly, her heart suddenly accelerating. It was from the *Maître des Requêtes* at the *Conseil d'État*. It referred to a request made in July 2010 to formally register a change of name from *Yves Guillaume Kofi Ameyaw* to *Yves Guillaume Pasqual* on grounds of national security. *Nous avons le regret de vous infomer que malgré notre attention sincère aux récents événements survenus dans votre pays, la République du Togo, nous ne pouvons porter assistance à un citoyen français qui aurait renouncé a sa nationalitié antérieurement.* 'The minister regretted to inform M. Yves Ameyaw that, whilst he was sympathetic to recent events in the Republic of Togo, no credible case could be made in the case of a French citizen who had voluntarily renounced his former citizenship.' She put it down carefully. It took her a few minutes to compose herself. Swallowing hard, she left the other letters on the sideboard and carried it through to the bedroom.

She sat down heavily, her breath coming in short spurts. Yves *Ameyaw.* She'd heard the name 'Ameyaw' before, she was sure of it. She stared at it for a few seconds and then the penny dropped. Not *Kofi* Ameyaw, *Kweku* Ameyaw. The journalist. She dimly remembered hearing something about a journalist being brutally murdered in Lomé, years back. *Kweku Ameyaw.* Her head began to swim. She put her hands on her shaking thighs. It took her a second to realise that the wetness slowly spreading itself around her was coming from her. She looked down and the fear turned to horror. Her trousers were wet. She was bleeding. She flung out a hand, searching frantically for the phone. Suddenly there was a wrenching upheaval inside her as the baby convulsed and turned. She grabbed at the phone, her hands flailing wildly. She punched in Tash's number but her fingers were shaking so much she couldn't hit the buttons properly. She tried again and again, fear rising in her throat like vomit. When, after what seemed like hours, she finally heard Tash's voice, she tried to speak but the terror in her had blocked her throat. The floor at her feet was slick with blood. She looked down at it and the sound that came out of her mouth seemed to come from someone else. *Blood.* It was her last conscious thought.

96

TASH

She ran out of the house, screaming into her mobile, and almost straight into the path of an oncoming taxi. His light was on and she wrenched open the door before he'd come to a complete stop.

'Woa . . . steady on there, miss!' he turned to roar at her.

'Drive! St Thomas's! Accident and emergency . . . DRIVE!' She held the phone aside for a split second as she flung the words at him. She slammed the door behind her and spoke into the mouthpiece again. 'Is she there yet? Who's got her? Is she . . . is she breathing? Just make sure . . . who's the doctor? *Where* is he?'

Another call was coming in. *Yves Pasqual.* She cut the nurse off. 'Yves? Yves? Where are you? You got my message? No, she's still in the ambulance; they're nearly there . . . I don't know, Yves, I don't *know*. No, of course I will. I'll be there in ten minutes. DRIVE!' She screamed at the cabbie. 'Ten minutes, Yves, I promise. I'll phone you as soon as I see her.' She switched back to the A & E. 'Hello? Are you still there? Are you still there? What's your name? Mary? Mary, please, *please* just make sure the doctors are on hand as soon as she comes in, make sure they're waiting. I'll be there in five minutes . . . yes, I'm her sister. Please, Mary . . . *please.*'

The driver made it in just less than eight minutes. Tash flung a handful of notes at him and jumped out. She almost broke her ankle but she could have cared less. Her heart was in her mouth as she ran down the short slope towards the A & E doors. She burst through, startling the people sitting in the waiting area, and ran straight to the admissions desk. 'Annick Betancourt?' she almost screamed. 'No, Annick Pasqual. Pregnant woman, came in by ambulance a few minutes ago. Does anyone know where she is? Where *the fuck is she*?'

'Miss, calm down, please! Calm down!' The duty nurse jumped to her feet. 'Please!'

'Are you Mary?'

'No, that's Mary over there. No, miss, you're not allowed—'

Tash didn't hear her. She couldn't hear a thing. The blood was thundering in her ears as she ran over to where a nurse stood, talking to a young man whose arm was in a sling. 'Mary?'

The woman turned round. 'Yes, I'm Mary.'

Tash's hand went out before she could stop herself. She grabbed Mary by the forearm. 'I'm Tash, Annick Pasqual's sister. We spoke on the phone a few minutes ago.'

'Oh, yes. She's in theatre . . . they took her in straight away. Just a minute, sir,' she said to the patient standing goggle-eyed beside her. She took Tash aside. 'She lost a lot of blood but the surgeons are doing everything they can,' she murmured, her voice low.

'Surgeons?' For a second, Tash thought she might actually be sick. Her phone had started ringing again.

'Yes . . . because of the baby. *Please* don't get yourself all worked up. We won't know anything until she goes into Recovery.'

'Is . . . is she going to be . . . all right?' Tash could hardly get the words out.

The nurse looked at her out of the depths of experience. 'We won't know for a while yet,' she said gently. 'They're doing all they can. Is there someone with you?'

Tash shook her head numbly. Inside her handbag, her phone was vibrating dully. 'Her husband's in . . . in the States. That's probably him.' She pointed to her bag.

'Get yourself a cup of tea,' Mary said firmly. 'Lots of sugar. There's a canteen in the basement. And then call him. I'll come and find you as soon as she's out of theatre.'

Tash couldn't speak. She watched Mary turn back to her patient. As kind as she was, Annick was simply another casualty in a night filled with them. She needed something far stronger than tea. She looked around for the toilets. Luckily there was something in her handbag. Her phone vibrated again and again. She hurried to the ladies', locked herself in the stall and unscrewed the cap. She downed the contents of the hip flask in a single gulp. The whisky burned all the way down; she belched softly and put up a hand to wipe her lips. She drew in two or three deep breaths and then fished out her mobile. First things first.

97

ANNICK

Tubes connected her arm to various machines thrumming with life. A series of differently pitched beeps marked out the different rhythms of her body. Heart, lungs, pulse, temperature. She tried to twist her neck to see properly, but couldn't. Another, faster heartbeat, a greenish light pulsating on and off, on and off. Shadows tiptoed around her. Someone took her hand. A flashlight showed itself through half-closed lids.

'Is she asleep?' A voice broke through the curtain of silence.

'No, it's the fever. She's got a high fever. We're trying to bring it down. Speak to her . . . sometimes it helps.'

'Annie? It's me, darling, it's Tash. Can you hear me?' A pause. Then Tash's panicked voice. 'Why can't she hear me?'

'She can. Go on, talk to her. She's been drifting in and out all morning.'

Morning? Annick struggled to make sense of what was being said. She opened her eyelids, squinting in pain as light flooded in.

'Her eyes . . . they opened! Just now!'

'I told you. Don't mind me, I'm just preparing her medication.'

'Annie?'

'Ba-bab-baby?' Annick struggled to get the word out. 'Ba-baby?'

'Shh, darling . . . it's fine. The baby's fine . . . he's in intensive care, seven weeks early . . . oh, Annie.' Tash was crying. 'You're going to be fine, I promise. Isn't she?' she beseeched the nurse who was busy preparing an injection.

'Let's hope so,' the nurse was cheerful. 'Here we go, Annick,' she said, lifting Annick's arm. She felt the soft pinprick of a needle sliding in. Through her half-closed eyelids she could see Tash burying her face in her hands. She couldn't remember the last time she'd seen Tash cry. It hurt. Everything hurt.

'Where . . . is . . . where's Yves?'

'He'll be here this afternoon, darling. His plane gets in at one and he'll come straight over. He hasn't slept a wink, Annie . . . you gave us all such a fright. No, don't try and talk. Just rest. The baby's fine. You should see him . . . he's tiny, so fucking tiny. Sorry, darling, I shouldn't swear, I'm just—'

'She's going. Don't worry, it's just the Pethidine. It'll knock her out for a bit. There she goes . . .'

She heard nothing further. Her last fleeting thought was that it was a boy.

TASH

Watching someone slide into oblivion was possibly the second-scariest thing she'd ever experienced, Tash thought to herself as she watched Annick sink. The first had to be the phone call. It had taken her a good few minutes to work out that it was Annick and that she was in trouble. What happened next was a blur, even now. She dimly recalled punching in '999' and screaming for an ambulance. They'd asked her for the address and her mind had gone completely blank. 'It's . . . it's next to the college. Next to a block of flats with yellow scaffolding. It's . . . Jesus Christ, I can't remember the address! It's in Lambeth! Morley College, *fuck*, I can't remember the road. '

'Morley College . . . Lambeth, you say? That'd be King Edward Road,' the operator said, his voice miraculously calm.

Tash could have wept with relief. 'Number eight, that's it. Number eight. Get an ambulance there quick! She's pregnant. Oh, I don't know . . . eight months? I don't know what happened . . . she's bleeding . . . she just called . . .' The words tumbled out of her mouth incoherently. The operator kept her on the line, talking her calmly through it all. She could have kissed him.

Now, watching Annick sleep, the panic that had propelled her off the sofa, thrust her feet into her boots and picked up her handbag rose in her again. She felt nauseous. She hadn't slept all night; it was now nearly eleven. In a couple of hours, Yves would be there. She'd rung Rebecca a dozen times but there was no answer. She'd left messages on her mobile and on the landline but nothing yet. She was exhausted. No, *more* than exhausted. She couldn't even think straight. Annick had very nearly lost the baby and no one seemed able to tell her why.

'Miss?' A nurse had come into the room.

Tash looked up. 'Sorry, I must've just dozed off,' she mumbled.

'No, it's fine. There's just something . . . the duty nurse forgot last night. She held out a crumpled piece of paper in her hand. 'Your sister insisted we give this to you. She was ever so agitated.'

Tash reached out for it. It was a letter, bloodied and crumpled as though someone had scrunched it up many times over. 'Thanks,' she said, puzzled.

'Sorry about that. The rest of her belongings are in there,' the nurse said, pointing to the locker in the corner of the room. 'But she kept insisting we give that straight to you. Well, I'd better get on. The ward sister'll be in to see her shortly.'

'Thanks,' Tash said automatically. She waited until the nurse had left the room and then smoothed the letter out. She frowned. It was in French, from the *Conseil d'État*. She struggled to understand what was written. *Nous avons le regret de vous informer que malgré notre attention sincère aux récents événements survenus dans votre pays, la République du*

Togo, nous ne pouvons porter assistance à un citoyen français qui aurait renouncé a sa nationalitié antérieurement. Who was Yves Ameyaw? Yves? She read it again but it made no sense. She folded it carefully and slipped it into her pocket. When Annick was well enough, she'd ask her. In the meantime, there was a premature baby in intensive care to worry about, as well as an unconscious mother. More than enough.

98

ANNICK

Nothing prepares you. Nothing at all. She stared at the perfectly formed but indescribably beautiful and tiny baby in the incubator and didn't know whether to laugh or cry. Yves' hand was around her waist, holding her upright as she shuffled slowly along the corridor. She held onto the contraption that held her drip with one arm whilst the other clutched his forearm as though she'd never let it go. They couldn't stop staring at him through the glass. He looked like nothing she'd ever seen before. His skin was yellow and waxy-looking and he was completely bald. His eyes were screwed up tightly against the light, tiny little hands clenching and unclenching slowly as he slept. She stared at him, two powerful surges of emotion competing with each other within her – the most indescribable love and the most terrible fear.

'He's coming along nicely,' one of the nurses said to her as she passed by. 'He's already gained a few ounces.'

A few *ounces*? Annick stared at her, then back at him. How many ounces were there in a pound? She tried to compute what it meant, but couldn't.

'What's his weight now?' Yves asked.

The nurse flipped a chart beside the incubator. 'Let's see . . . 1.45 kilograms – that's three pounds, four ounces to you and me,' she smiled at Annick.

'No, we're French,' Annick said abruptly. 'We measure in kilograms.'

'Oh. Well, he's one and a half kilos, then. The main thing is, he's gaining weight.'

'What about the other stuff . . . his lungs, his organs . . . his heart?'

The nurse looked from Annick to Yves and back again. 'It's too early to tell,' she said kindly. 'One step at a time. The doctors'll be in to see him shortly. You should get some rest. You've been through an awful lot yourself, you know.'

Annick shook her head. 'No, I want to be here. I can't . . . I can't *not* be here. When can I hold him?'

The nurse smiled gently. She'd seen it all before, and worse. 'Soon,' she said. 'The doctors will come in and see you once they've done their rounds. We'll know more then. A day at a time.'

Yves' hand tightened around her waist. 'Come on, *chérie*,' he whispered. 'Let the nurses do their work. We'll look in on him later. You need to be in bed.'

She swallowed hard but allowed herself to be led gently and slowly by the arm back to the ward. She couldn't speak. She looked at Yves, searching his face for some clue, some sign . . . but there was nothing. He looked as he'd always done. Was she going mad? Had she imagined the whole thing? No, there was the letter. She'd held it out, all bloody and crumpled. Give it to Tash, she'd screamed. The nurse took it from her, assuring her she would, that everything would be fine, that the baby would be all right, that *she* would be all right. It was the last thing she heard before she went under. *Everything's going to be fine.* She felt the slight warm pressure of Yves' lips against her forehead and she closed her eyes. She was tired, so very, very tired. Her limbs felt heavy and leaden; the lower half of her abdomen was still numb. There were moments when she wondered if she would ever feel anything again.

99

'But what is it?' Tash asked the following day, smoothing out the letter on Annick's bedspread between them. 'I get what it says but what does it *mean*?'

Annick's fingers knotted themselves together. 'I . . . I don't know,' she whispered, looking round fearfully as though she expected Yves to be hiding in the cupboard.

'Why's he trying to change his name?'

Annick shook her head again. 'I don't know. The thing is, there *is* someone called Ameyaw. He's a journalist. He . . . he wrote some pretty awful things about my father and . . . and . . .' She stopped and swallowed painfully.

'What?'

'He died. His body was found on the side of the road somewhere in Lomé. He'd been beaten to death, or something horrible like that. It was all over the papers in France. I remember asking my mother about it but she just said she had no idea who I was talking about.'

'What're you saying? That they're connected? Yves and this journalist, whatever his name is?'

Annick drew in a deep breath. 'I don't know. I'm not sure,' she said slowly. 'About Yves. I know I shouldn't even *think* it, especially as I haven't asked him outright, but . . . I just don't know *anything* anymore.'

'What are you talking about? Of course you know Yves.'

Annick shook her head. 'But that's just it. I don't know anything about him, about his past, I mean. I've never met his parents, and aside from Martin, I've never met any of his friends or his family. I don't even know where he comes from. He told me he was adopted but I just don't know. I don't know who he really is.'

'Annick, I think you might just be making more of this than you should,' Tash said gently. 'There's probably some really simple explanation. Yves is lovely – you know he is. I don't know what you're thinking but I can't see him deliberately lying to you. It's not possible. He cried when I told him what had happened to you. I heard him crying, Annie. He was *crying*.'

Annick's hands twisted around again and again. 'It's not that. I know he loves me. I do know *that*. But where I come from, Tash, nothing's what it seems. Everything's so . . . so murky. You can't trust anyone; that's what my father always told me. D'you know how many of *his* friends tried to kill him?'

Tash gave a short, disbelieving laugh. 'You're not saying Yves is trying to kill *you*?'

Annick shook her head violently. 'No, of course not. But I can't help wondering. If he really *is* Togolese and he's connected in some way to Kofi Ameyaw, why hasn't he said so? I mean, he knows who *I* am. Why hide it from me?'

Tash looked at her and bit her lip. She had no answer. Not for the first time, in all the years she'd known Annick, she felt out of her depth. Annick came from so far away. She was right. Tash knew nothing about

383

African politics. And she was right, too, to wonder why Yves hadn't told her he'd tried to change his name.

'You've got to ask him. Just ask him outright. Show him the letter and ask him. Not now, not whilst the baby's still . . . well, not whilst you're both still here. But when you get home, after all of this is behind you, just ask him. You owe him that much. And he owes you an explanation. I don't know much about relationships, so I'm probably not the right person to say this, but I do know this . . . you can't build anything on a lie. Not even a little white lie. Ask him. *Make* him tell you the truth.'

100

TWO MONTHS LATER

REBECCA
Hampshire

Half of her was present; half of her was not. She took part in the conversations where and when she could, chewed her food methodically, paid attention to the twins when they laughed or cried and admired Didier, who, at two months, had caught up to his anticipated birth weight and was said by the doctors to be doing fine. They were all gathered at Brockhurst Hall for Christmas. Everyone was there. Embeth, Julian, the twins, Tash, Lyudmila, Annick, Didier, Yves and her. And, of course, the baby growing silently inside her. No one knew, not even Julian. She was waiting for the right moment to tell him, or so she continually told herself. Finding the right moment wasn't the only reason for her reluctance. But she couldn't think about that. Tariq. She whispered his name under her breath. Tariq. *Tariq. Tariq.* A chant, the way the devout had once whispered the forbidden name of Yahweh. She smiled faintly at that; it was the sort of irreverent historical detail he would like.

'What're you smiling at?' She jumped. Tash was standing in the doorway.

'N-nothing. I was just thinking about something one of the twins said,' she said quickly. 'Where's everyone?'

Tash shrugged. 'Doing this and that. Mum's asleep, your mother's in the kitchen, supervising the staff. Julian and Yves are down at the stables with the twins . . . I think Annick's asleep as well. Poor thing, she looks absolutely worn out.' She flopped down on the sofa nearest the window, drawing her legs up. She rested her head on her knees, her arms circling her calves. 'Y'know, for a while back there, I . . . I didn't know if she'd make it,' she said slowly. 'Thank God she did. Thank God they *both* did.'

Rebecca nodded slowly. 'Funny, isn't it? Nothing turns out quite the way you think. If you'd asked me ten years ago what I thought the next ten years would bring, I'd never have guessed. You a millionaire. Annick's parents killed, Me, married with three, I mean two, kids—'

Tash snorted. 'That's so typical of you,' she chuckled. 'Three – oops, no, I mean two – kids. How can you forget how many kids you have?'

Rebecca flushed. 'I . . . I was . . . slip of the tongue, that's all.' She turned away to face the window, watching the afternoon darken with winter outside. One hand came to rest on her stomach; she touched the soft, full skin underneath her skirt. A baby. Whose?

TASH

Tash climbed the stairs to her bedroom. It was Christmas Eve and despite the fact that not everyone actually celebrated Christmas, Embeth had made an exception this year. They'd all decided it would be good for Annick and Yves to have a proper, family-filled celebration. 'We're your family now,' Embeth said firmly. 'And it'll be lovely to give you all something to remember.' It was typical Embeth, generous to a fault. She'd forgotten nothing. There was an enormous Norwegian fir tree in the hallway surrounded by beautifully wrapped presents, exquisitely decorated, of course, with all the trimmings. There were log fires in every room, polished silver menorahs in the windows. 'Well, we've got to have something Jewish,' she laughed, 'even if it's only to stop Lionel shouting at us to take it all down!' Her eyes misted over for a second, then she gathered herself. 'Anyway, it'll be fun for the children. They're too young to understand what it all means.'

She pushed open the door and stood in the doorway for a second. She was the only single person in the house that Christmas, except for Lyudmila and Embeth, of course. She tried hard not to think about it but at times like these the sense of being alone was particularly hard. It wasn't just the fact of an empty place beside her at the dinner table, or no one to cuddle up to on the sofa in front of the fire afterwards, the way couples did, it was also the very *family* nature of Christmas. Not having a partner was one thing but at thirty-five, it was slowly dawning on her that another door might be closing too. *Don't be ridiculous*, she thought to herself sternly, opening the wardrobe door. *You're thirty-five, not forty-five. Anything could happen.*

She flicked through the three or four long dresses she'd brought with her. There was an ecru pleated silk dress – flattering, but a tad dull; or the sea-green crêpe-jersey dress from Lanvin. A black silk Donna Karan number, or an Amanda Wakeley midnight-blue jersey dress with wide, bell sleeves? She held the last against her and looked in the mirror. It had to be the Wakeley. If nothing else, it made her look taller. Not that she needed any help in that department, she thought to herself wryly as she stripped off her clothes and pulled on her dressing gown. She walked into the small bathroom and turned on the light. She caught sight of her face in the mirror and stopped. She looked at herself closely. She'd grown used to her face – she no longer really saw it. But she looked at it properly now. She turned slowly sideways, just as she'd done countless times when she was a teenager. She put up a hand to touch her nose self-consciously. Could a surgeon *really* correct it? She bared her lips. And her teeth. Crooked, overlapping, less-than-white. Could a dentist change those? She knew what people thought of her, especially those who didn't know her. She was stylish enough and genuinely loved fashion. But she was rather less concerned about how it looked on her than how it looked on others, namely her customers. What if everyone was right? What if she *did* do something about her appearance, whatever that 'something' might turn out to be? Would her life change? Would it get better? And then the question she didn't dare ask, even of herself . . . would it help her find a man?

She walked back into the bedroom and picked up the copy of the magazine she'd been reading the night before. She quickly flicked through to the back pages. They were listed in alphabetical order. Cosmetic surgeons. From Harley Street to Hungary and everywhere else in between. She closed the magazine with a decisive snap.

*

The raised voices and laughter at the dinner table that evening brought an intimacy to the high-ceilinged dining room. The children were safely tucked up in bed. Embeth had dispatched not one but *three* nannies to help keep them amused and occupied. The table was magnificent. Everywhere you looked there were sprigs of freshly cut holly and ornate, intricate Christmas wreaths. Wine was slowly poured into cut-crystal decanters and glasses. Light from the twinkling, coloured decorations bounced off the chandeliers and windowpanes, merging into the rosy glow of the fire. It was the Christmas Eve dinner Tash had never had.

Embeth sat at one end of the table with her customary glass of water. In the two years since Lionel's death she hadn't touched a drop of alcohol, yet her voice rose and spiralled gaily as if the alcohol were rising in her blood, just like the others, a special kind of self-intoxication that burnished her skin like the sun. Across from her, doing her best to drink slowly, was Lyudmila. Tash could see she was rather overwhelmed by it all. She was wearing Valentino, an early Christmas present from Tash, but despite looking every inch as glamorous as Embeth, she looked nervous. The sudden change in lifestyle over the past couple of years hadn't been easy. It wasn't quite as simple as it looked to go from counting food coupons to flying first class, especially if the source of largesse was your daughter. The change had prompted a shift in the balance of power between them and there were times when Lyudmila resented it, or was made nervous by it, like now. Lyudmila had her heart set on introducing F@shion.com to Russia, but Tash didn't know how to tell her it wasn't even necessary. Bringing F@shion.com to Russia didn't require flying out to Moscow every other week, desperately trying to get into the right restaurants and making friends with every Tom, Dick and floozy who knew an oligarch. Modern Russian women were every bit as switched on and connected as their London counterparts. They were already using F@shion.com *and* shopping online in quantities that proved it. FedEx delivered almost as many parcels to Muscovites as they did to Mancunians. What was the point of doing a launch?

A maid entered and bent down to whisper something to Embeth. Her face lit up immediately. She got up from the table, excusing herself for a second, and hurried after her. A moment later, she was back. Someone was with her.

'Look who's here!' She announced his presence like a prize. 'It's Adam!'

He stood in the doorway, holding them all in his gaze. He wore a thick, dark-blue cable-knit sweater and jeans. There was grey mixed in amongst the dirty blond hair now. He was tanned and under the strong, squared-off planes of his face, a five o'clock shadow showed through. If she'd thought him good-looking before, Tash was unprepared for the beauty of the man now. Her lips parted but nothing came out. Like the others, she could only sit and gape at him.

'Hello, chaps,' he said, shoving his hands in his pockets. 'Hope I'm not disturbing? Merry Christmas!'

101

A log crackled in the grate as it slipped and shifted, a blue-tongued flame leaping out momentarily before settling once more into the glowing embers. The fire was almost out. It was nearly midnight and Tash and Adam were the only two left in the room; everyone else had gone to bed. Julian had been the last to leave. He'd taken half a bottle of brandy with him, looking rather the worse for wear. Tash had lost count of the number of glasses she'd had. It helped calm her nerves. She wasn't drunk, though. Far from it. On the contrary, she'd never felt better in her life.

'Your glass is empty.' Adam stood up and walked over to the table. He picked up a bottle. 'Château Mouton-Rothschild Pauillac 1986.' He let out a low whistle. 'D'you know how good this is?'

'Well, pour me a drop and I'll tell you,' Tash chuckled.

He walked over holding the bottle loosely by the neck. He had the sexiest swagger she'd ever seen in a man, she thought to herself. He shone on wine. His sensuality came to the surface of his skin the way a pebble, warmed in the palm of one's hand, rubbed up to a smooth, satiny shine. He carefully poured her a glass, then poured one for himself. 'Cheers,' he said, settling back into the chair opposite her. His thighs lolled arrogantly against each other. Her eyes were drawn again and again to the curve of his jeans, the sunburned flesh of his exposed forearms, to the broad expanse of chest. She'd never before been so conscious of a man or of her own shortcomings.

Earlier that evening, when they were all still at table, she'd looked at

388

Annick and Rebecca in turn, studying them the way a man might. Annick still had the exotic, sleepy sexuality that drew everyone's eyes to her. Smooth, satiny brown flesh, unblemished by a single mark or change in tone; the thick, vibrant cascade of curls, those grey-green eyes. At thirty-five she was a woman at her peak. Rebecca, too, was in full bloom. She'd put on a little weight in the past couple of months and it suited her. Her long, dark-brown hair hung around her face like a thick, richly burnished curtain. Tash had had to look away, unable to staunch the flow of envy spilling out of her. Adam was across the table, a wine glass in one hand, gesticulating as he recounted some amusing story with the other. His skin was suffused with a glow that seemed to come from within, as if he'd been caught in the middle of some splendid physical activity, arrested in full flight. She'd never seen anyone so commandingly alive.

'So, what're you up to these days?' she asked abruptly, bringing herself back to the present.

'In what sense?' His blue eyes regarded her flirtatiously.

'Whatever sense you like.'

He laughed. 'D'you know, that's what I always liked about you,' he said after a moment. 'So damned straight.'

She looked at him uncertainly. 'Me?'

He nodded. 'D'you remember . . . at Rebecca's wedding. We bumped into each other in the hall. I think you offered me one of your cigarettes—'

'No, *you* asked *me* for a light,' Tash corrected him quickly.

'See what I mean?' He grinned at her. 'Anyhow, I seem to recall asking you something about a boyfriend . . . what you'd do if your boyfriend did something or other and you just looked at me and said, "Dunno. I've never had one." I'll never forget that.'

Tash was puzzled. 'Why? What's so unusual about that?'

He smiled. 'Most women wouldn't.'

'Wouldn't what?'

'Admit to not having a boyfriend. No, let me correct that. To never having *had* a boyfriend. How old were you? Twenty-five, twenty-six?'

'Twenty-nine,' she said cheerfully.

'And what about now?'

'What *about* now?' she asked carefully.

'Have you got one now?'

She hesitated, then chuckled. 'Nope.'

'Don't tell me—'

'Don't make me spell it out,' she laughed. 'I didn't have one then and I don't have one now. Never had one.'

'Never?'

'Never, ever.'

He sat up straight in his chair. 'Are you telling me, Tash Bryce-Brudenell, that you're still . . . ?'

'A virgin?' She took another sip of wine. She shook her head. 'No, not that. Thank God.' She laughed suddenly. 'If I told you what the sum total of my experience with men has been, you'd die laughing.'

He looked at her, suddenly serious. 'I wouldn't. You *know* I wouldn't. I'm curious. Go on.'

She drew in a deep breath. And took another sip of wine. Entirely without coquetry she shrugged. 'Once, at university. I can't even remember his name, let alone his face. And once with my best friend's father. Annick, not Rebecca. No, not Lionel,' she added with a half-smile. She saw from his face that he was shocked.

There was a moment's silence. They stared at each other, neither saying anything. Then he got up from his chair and approached her. She swallowed and put down her wine glass. Did he mean for her to stand up? She looked up at him, her heart beginning its slow, painful thud. No. He bent down towards her. The firelight was blocked out as he dropped his head and kissed her delicately, but with great passion. 'D'you know how long I've wanted to do that?' he murmured against her mouth.

She shook her head, unable to speak. The great, immeasurable, unquenchable desire that had been dormant in her for what seemed like her whole life was awoken suddenly. He was holding her by the upper arms and she had the urge not just to fling her arms around his neck, drawing him closer and closer, but to gather up her whole life and expend it on him, throwing everything onto the bonfire of love, the fire that had been denied her for so long.

He led her quietly up the stairs, still holding her by the upper arm as if he didn't trust her not to bolt. She followed him with no thought in her head other than disbelief. *This isn't happening. This isn't happening to* me. *This cannot be happening to* me. As they passed the first-floor landing, he put a finger to his lips, winking at her. Like schoolchildren, stifling giggles, they tiptoed along the corridor until they reached his room. He held her fast with one hand; in the other he carried the half-empty Château Mouton. He kicked open the door, pulling her into the room after him. Her dress lay in a crumpled heap of silk on the floor before she even realised he'd undone it. No bra, just the quivering points of her breasts that pushed themselves into the warmth of his hands. He ran the scratchy palms of his hands down her trembling stomach, his fingers slipping expertly under the thin elastic of her panties, pushing them down. They were still standing. Next thing she knew, her knees had given way. She landed with a thud on something soft. He'd manoeuvred them both so that they were already at the edge of the big double bed. His knee was suddenly between hers, pushing her legs apart. She felt the rustle of something – plastic? – then gasped in pleasure. His finger, warm, thick, hard, was moving up her thigh . . . slowly, slowly . . . she felt her stomach muscles contract in tender, delicious pain . . . then he slid it inside her, in and out, in and out. She drew his lip into her mouth, biting it, hard . . . it brought an outraged growl of pleasure from him in turn. He struggled out of his jeans, pausing only to pull his sweater off in a single move. He was wearing a T-shirt beneath it; she ran her hands underneath it, up his chest, across his hard nipples and down the hard bulge of his biceps and arms. He was back inside her, not with his finger this time, but with his whole body, pushing against her with a force that seemed to come from somewhere else, from someone else. He was no longer Adam as she'd seen him that evening at dinner, blue eyes twinkling at her from across the table. He was simply a man under the astonishing onslaught of his own passionate release. She closed her eyes tightly.

When it was over, and she could no more have said how long it lasted than she could have predicted it happening at all, he lay as someone dead, lifting his arm only to draw her head down into the furnace of bedclothes, still damp with sweat. When love comes, it comes indiscriminately. Where had she read that? *Gods come not in the places prepared for them, but appearing suddenly amongst the rabble. That* was what had happened to her.

102

REBECCA

'Have you seen Tash?' Rebecca walked into the kitchen where Annick was busy preparing a bottle for Didier.

'Isn't she still asleep?'

Rebecca shook her head. 'I've been up to her room . . . she's not there. The bed's made up, too.'

Annick turned round and frowned. 'Has she gone out?'

Rebecca lifted her shoulders. 'Either that . . . or she didn't sleep in it.'

They looked at each other warily. 'You don't think—?' Annick began hesitantly.

'She *couldn't* have . . . could she?' Rebecca's voice rose in astonishment.

'Couldn't have what?' Julian walked in, belting his dressing gown. 'Who're you talking about?'

Rebecca threw Annick a cautious look. 'No one,' she said quickly.

Julian wasn't put off. He filled the kettle and plugged it in, turning round to face them, yawning. It was almost nine o'clock. 'Oh, Merry Christmas, by the way,' he said, running a hand over his stubble. 'You don't suppose someone's had the best Christmas present ever, do you?'

Rebecca felt a flush of anger slowly work its way up her neck and face. 'Don't be unkind,' she said shortly.

Julian looked bemused. 'Unkind? Who's being unkind? I just meant—'

'It's highly unlikely,' Annick interjected quickly. 'It would be so . . . so *unlike* her.'

'Unlike who? Who're you talking about?' Someone else had wandered into the kitchen. It was Yves. Like Julian, he too was in his dressing gown.

'Oh, for goodness' sake! I can't believe we're all standing here discussing Tash and her non-existent sex life!' Rebecca burst out suddenly. 'She's probably gone out for a walk, that's all.'

Julian turned back to the whistling kettle. 'Tea bags?' he enquired, looking at Rebecca.

'In the jar that says "tea bags". Up there, on the second shelf.' Seeing he wasn't about to do it, Rebecca sighed and reached for the jar herself.

She turned back to the others. 'Look, don't make a big deal of it,' she begged. 'Even if it's true . . . which I'm sure it isn't.'

'I'll take his bottle up.' Yves turned to Annick and the slightly more pressing subject of Didier's feed. 'Will you make me a coffee?'

Annick nodded. 'She's probably gone riding. She was talking about it in the car on the way down,' she said, frowning quickly at Yves. She was just about to hand it over when someone else entered the kitchen, whistling. All four turned round.

'Morning, all.' It was Adam. He was wearing a dressing gown that the girls recognised as Tash's and a pair of boxer shorts. His blonde hair was ruffled every which way and he sported an impressive stubble. Rebecca could only stare at his open chest, covered in fine, silky dark-brown hair. It slid down his flat torso in a splendid, thick line, disappearing beneath the waistband of his shorts. He was barefoot, his hands patting the pockets of the silk dressing gown for a cigarette. He stood before them, grinning. It wasn't the first cigarette of the day, she thought to herself, disbelief spreading out all over her like a stain as she watched him light up. Her impression was not of a man who'd just got up, but of one who hadn't slept at all.

'T-tea?' she asked, holding up an empty cup. She could think of nothing else to say.

TASH

She felt Adam leave the fug of warmth that was the bed they'd shared, springs creaking lightly in protest. It was morning outside. Through the thick, dark curtains a dazzling line of light peeped out. She opened her eyes and saw him stand up, naked, totally at ease. He bent down and picked something up – his boxer shorts – and stepped into them, the gesture familiar to her only from films and novels. There was a tightness in her thighs as she moved sleepily into the warm, Adam-scented hollow in the mattress he'd left behind. He looked around him for something – a towel? He turned and caught her eye. She held her breath. How would it be between them now? He winked. Relief washed over her in waves. Easy. It would be easy.

'Morning, sleepy-head,' he murmured. 'I'm going to get us some coffee. You haven't got a dressing gown handy by any chance, have you?'

Tash swallowed. Her throat was dry and completely parched. 'In . . . in my room. Next floor up. First door on the left. It's hanging behind the door.'

'Fab.' He bent down and kissed her briefly on the cheek. 'Coffee?' he murmured against her skin.

She could only nod. 'S-sure,' she whispered. 'Coffee would be good.'

'Back in a sec. Don't get dressed.' He opened the door and padded out.

She lay back against the pillows, too stunned to speak. She took in a deep breath, holding it for as long as she could, then she grabbed the sheets to her face, stuffing them into her mouth, laughing wildly, delightedly. She bit down on the fabric bunched up in her mouth, letting out the longest, hardest and most heartfelt scream she'd ever had reason to make. She kicked up her heels, like an excited child, rolling over with a suppressed squeal. She pressed her face into the pillow that smelled of him, of Adam, of the man she'd just taken so strangely and symbolically into her body.

She was still lying there, face down, mouth tasting faintly of her own salted tears, when he returned with her coffee. And did it to her all over again.

PART EIGHT

DECEIVING

'Nothing is so difficult as not *deceiving oneself.'*
Ludwig Wittgenstein

103

ANNICK
London

The right moment. *I'll wait for the right moment.* There's a time and place for someone to give account of something that doesn't fit, a loose end or a fact that sits outside all others. But the right moment never came. In the beginning, those first few terrible weeks after Didier was born, the matter of the letter seemed almost trivial in comparison. Her every waking moment was consumed with fear. Of Didier not having survived the night; of a new infection; of something else waiting in him in to be discovered by the doctors on their twice-weekly visits; of his appetite – too little, too much – everything, in other words, that marked him out as different, as vulnerable. As the months progressed and her confidence in Didi's ability to thrive began to take root, her mind returned to the letter. If Yves wasn't who he said he was, then who was he? Did it mean *everything* was a lie? Or just some parts? But which ones?

She lay in bed with the small, warm sleeping body of her child next to her on those nights when he was away, struggling to remember the little she knew. The journalist's mutilated body found on the roadside some-where, her mother's reticence when she questioned her about it, Yves' sudden arrival at the Hôtel du Jardin, their courtship, his following her to London . . . and now the letter from the *Conseil d'État*. Things tumbled round and round in her mind, facts and truths merging and breaking apart . . . was she going mad?

The only person who knew what was going on inside her was Tash. Rebecca was too preoccupied with her children and Julian and besides, she was hardly in London anymore. But Tash too was preoccupied. After the shortest courtship in history, Tash had shocked everyone by inviting them all to dinner and appearing with the biggest rock on her finger that any of them had seen. Tash Bryce-Brudenell was about to get married. The wedding was a fortnight away and it promised to be one of the biggest, splashiest and most lavish affairs in town. A bidding war broke out between the weeklies as to who would cover it – *Hello!* won. It was estimated that F@shion.com was worth close to 50 million pounds. In a deal that gave her almost unparalleled growth potential, Tash herself walked away with nearly 20 million. Personally. She now had the cash flow to expand into other markets and ensure she retained her position at the top of the pyramid. She also had the cash and time to 'fix herself up', as she put it, shocking Annick and Rebecca into stunned silence. Within a fortnight of getting together with Adam, she walked into a clinic on Harley Street for her first consultation. A month later, the first bandages came off. The effect was startling. Within six months, Tash Bryce-Brudenell looked – and felt – like a completely different person. Gone was the mousy brown ponytail. In its place, short, bleached blonde hair, feathered long and low across that prominent brow. Her nose had been entirely reshaped. Still long, but elegantly so, and delicately sculpted, it no longer pushed her glasses off her face. She kept the glasses but changed the frames. Black, striking, square. With her newly bleached hair, the contrast was stunning. And when she smiled, the transformation was complete. Courtesy of a visiting orthodontist from San Francisco, she now had a set of perfectly straight, perfectly white, perfectly aligned all-American teeth. The effect was both dramatic and surreal. For those who'd known Tash Bryce-Brudenell since for ever, the new, improved version was going to take some getting used to.

Annick in particular found it hard to believe. Tash had always been so adamantly opposed to doing *anything*. But, a fortnight after meeting Adam, she'd completely and utterly transformed herself. There was no question she didn't look stunning. She did. But it just didn't quite add up. And now, here she was, about to get married. 'I can't believe it,' Tash kept on repeating, every time she caught sight of herself or saw a photograph.

'Well, if *you* can't believe it, think about how we feel,' Rebecca had quipped once, earning herself the most spectacular black look from Tash in return. She'd shut up after that.

Annick sighed and switched on the kettle. Didier was asleep in the living room and Yves wasn't due back until the following morning. He'd been in Shanghai on business for the past few days. Did she miss him? She couldn't tell. She couldn't tell much these days. Her whole world had been turned upside down and there were mornings when it was hard to tell which way was up.

She made herself a cup of tea and took it through to the living room. She curled up on the sofa, feet tucked up underneath her, watching her son. He slept in the swing chair Rebecca had passed down from the twins, blissfully unaware of the turmoil inside his mother's head. His eyes were tightly shut. He'd inherited her light-brown curly hair but not her green eyes. His eyes were dark, inscrutable pools, much like his father's. There was an unanswered question hovering at the edge of her consciousness that surfaced again now, as she sat sipping her tea. If she *did* bring it up, what would that mean? What would happen then? If he did admit to having deceived her, could she live with that? And if she couldn't, could she bear to leave? What was it her mother had said to her once? *Don't ask, don't tell.* She could no longer remember the context or the conversation, just that it had surprised her at the time. Did her parents have secrets? Clearly they did. And the name Ameyaw was one of them. There was only one question worth asking, and answering, on the subject of secrets. Did she have the courage to unearth them?

104

REBECCA
Tel Aviv

Two thousand miles away, unbeknownst to her, Rebecca was asking herself the very same question: when is the right time? Tash's wedding was a fortnight away. A fortnight after that, she was due to give birth. The red light of dawn flooded the room. Somewhere on the street outside, a rising wail lingered, fading away, then returning again, louder each time. She opened her eyelids. Beside her, Julian stirred in his sleep. She rolled herself carefully away from him, trying to get out of bed without waking him. She carefully levered herself upright.

A month to go. If the baby came out favouring Julian, well, at least things on the home front could – and would – stay as they were. She'd continue seeing Tariq as and when she could. Nothing would change. Tariq's wife and family were in Connecticut. He would continue to commute to them just as she commuted between London and Tel Aviv. For the past few months, they'd tried to time their respective visits so that they were both away at the same time and there was some strange comfort to be had in the synchronicity of their deception. *He* told lies; *she* told lies. He was with his wife; she was with Julian. But when he was with her, for her at least, no one else existed. Not even her children. What was it about Tariq Malouf that held her so deeply, as if in the grip of a curse? She had never tried to explain it to anyone, not even to herself. It wasn't just physical, though she never tired of looking at him, gazing at his face and body as if trying to commit every single line, every plane, every curve and contour to memory. No, there was something else. Some other, deeper attraction that had to do with the way he was both bound to, and totally different from, her.

She loved the fact that they'd known each other once, too far back in the mists of childhood for her to remember – the feeling of coming 'home', as she put it to herself, to someone who knew her not just as the empty vessel that was Julian's wife and Lionel's daughter, but as some-one *else*. Someone in her own right, her own mind, in possession of her own thoughts and opinions, many of which clashed with his. For the first time in her life, he was a man who didn't see her through the veil of wealth. Tariq's interest in her as a Harburg had nothing to do with *that*. For him, the Harburg legacy was political, social, historical . . . certainly not financial. In addition to the deep, warm sensuality he coaxed from her, and not just in bed, he'd given her an insight into Lionel that not even Embeth appeared to know. To the outside world, Rebecca Harburg and Tariq Malouf came from two opposite ends of the same equation. From Tariq, she learned that it was a definition Lionel himself would have resisted – and did. The connections between the two families bound them together in a way that she'd never expected to find, let alone understand. Through him, she did. For the first time in her adult life, Rebecca felt dangerously close to complete. It was ironic, she thought to herself with a small, unhappy smile. She had to stray outside her marriage and outside the cosy circle of her family to find out who she really was.

But what if the baby came out differently? What then? Julian had never met Tariq. There was no reason to suppose anyone would suspect him, or anyone else. But *she* would know. And then what? Hard as it was to believe, she had no idea who the father might be.

She opened the bedroom door and padded carefully into the hallway. She walked slowly down the corridor to the kitchen, her hand holding her dressing gown over her enormous belly. She made herself a cup of tea, carrying it through into the living room, and sat down in front of the sliding doors to watch dawn break over the city. The prayer call had faded away. Now all she could hear was traffic.

Suddenly a blue light began to flash at her feet. She looked down at the ground. Julian's phone was lying face down; it must have fallen out of his pocket. She picked it up, idly glancing at the screen. *Miranda (mobile). Missed calls (7). Miranda (home/Dubai). Missed calls (2). You have two new voicemails. Please dial 121. Last call: Miranda (mobile).* She frowned. What the hell did Miranda want? She couldn't stand the woman. Her fingers hovered over the screen. If she opened up one of the messages, Julian would know. She hesitated for a moment, then put it back down. Hell, who was *she* to question *him*? She was carrying a child that might not be his!

She looked over at the home phone sitting on the console next to the television. There were moments when she longed to pick up the phone and tell Tash, Annick . . . *any*one. But it was no time to burden anyone, least of all Tash. With less than a fortnight to go to her wedding, hearing about someone else's marital woes was the last thing on her mind. She gave a small, rather unhappy little smile. Who'd have thought it? After all this time, Tash was finally getting married. She had it all, now − everything within her grasp. Of the three of them, she'd started out with the least, and had made the most. And it was all hers. No one else's.

'What're you doing up so early?' Julian's voice broke the silence. She jumped.

'Oh . . . nothing. I was just . . . I couldn't sleep so I made myself a cup of tea.'

'And didn't drink it,' Julian said, looking at her cup. He looked down at the blinking blue phone. 'Oh, *there* it is. I've been looking everywhere for the damned thing.' He bent down and picked it up, scrolling through the messages. His expression changed suddenly.

'Everything okay?' Rebecca looked up at him.

He nodded distractedly and hurriedly left the room. Rebecca looked down at her hands. Yes, she envied Tash, in more ways than one.

105

TASH
London

'To have and to hold, from this day forward, for better, for worse, for richer, for poorer, in sickness and in health, until death do us part.' Her voice was steady but her hands were not. Her fingers, underneath Adam's, were trembling.

'You have declared your consent before the Church. May the Lord in his goodness strengthen your consent and fill you both with his blessings. That God has joined, man must not divide. Amen.'

'Amen.' The congregation gathered in St James's Church in Holland Park murmured reverentially. There was a sudden commotion at the front. Lyudmila had fainted.

'She just keeled over!' Annick laughed, holding Didier on her hip. 'Like a light.'

'Well, she's been waiting for this day for thirty-six years,' Tash said drily. 'No bloody wonder.'

'Is she all right?'

Tash waved a hand. 'She's fine. Needed an excuse to have a drink, if you ask me.' She looked over to where Lyudmila was sitting surrounded by concerned strangers, absolutely in her element. As soon as Tash broke the news of their engagement, Lyudmila quickly reacquainted herself with the ladies-that-lunch of Tash's childhood, Ladies Soames and Davenport chief amongst them.

'Natasha, darling . . . I just knew you'd go far,' Lady Soames trilled when she stepped forward to offer her congratulations.

'It's Tatiana, actually. And how's that son of yours? Robert, was it?'

'Er, Rupert. Splendid, splendid. Yes, just splendid.'

'Any grandchildren?'

'Er, no. He's . . . well, he's . . . um, he's—'

'Queer, or so I hear.' Tash swiftly moved down the line.

'Bitch,' Adam whispered in her ear, grinning. 'You are *such* a bitch!'

'She deserves it. And so does he. Oh, you *shouldn't* have . . . why, thank you. That's so kind of you.'

And all around them, flashbulbs went off. It was quite some wedding.

'She looks ready to pop,' Miranda murmured, looking at Rebecca from behind the honey-toned safety of her champagne glass. 'Poor thing.'

'Yes, well, can we forget about Rebecca and concentrate on the matter at hand?' Julian said tetchily.

'There's nothing you can do.' Miranda's plum-coloured fingernails were wrapped around her glass. 'You'll just have to wait and see.'

'I can't just bloody "wait and see",' he snapped.

'Why not? What's the rush?'

'Miranda, for Christ's sake, there's a lot at stake here. If Tash . . . look, never mind. Just get an agreement signed, will you? I'll feel a heck of a lot happier once there's something in writing.'

'But that's not the way they work, darling. You *know* that. They'll come through, I promise. It's a minor delay. The old man probably wants to check the property out himself. I've got it all under control.'

'You said that a month ago. I don't know how long I can keep this up!' Julian stopped abruptly. He ran a hand through his hair. 'Get me something on paper,' he hissed angrily. 'Just do it!'

'Don't you snap at me,' Miranda glared at him. 'And don't you *dare* try and order me around. I'm not your wife, you know.'

'I'm hardly about to make *that* mistake,' Julian glowered at her.

Miranda smiled, that lethal smile of hers that he'd seen reserved for others, a combination of sarcasm and seduction. He'd never seen it directed at him, until now. Underneath his elegant suit, he was sweating. It had been a hellish day. In his wildest dreams he couldn't have predicted the outcome of Adam's arrival at Brockhurst Hall . . . *marriage?* He'd expected him to make a pass at her – he was Adam Goldsmith after all – but when Rebecca told him he'd proposed – on one knee too, the prick – he'd almost swallowed his fork. 'He wants to *marry* her?' he'd choked.

'What's wrong with that?' Rebecca looked at him across the breakfast table.

'N-nothing,' he said hastily, swallowing a mouthful of orange juice. 'I'm just . . . surprised, that's all.'

'I know you don't think she's much to look at,' Rebecca said crossly, 'but Tash is a fucking exceptional woman.'

He'd stared at her, for once unable to think of anything to say. For one thing, it was so unlike Rebecca to swear. He'd finished off his breakfast in silence.

That was three months ago and now here they were, watching the happy couple move regally down the line of invited guests, invited and not-quite-invited journalists and personalities from Tash's world, and the odd figure or two from Adam's. He had no idea how intertwined Tash and Adam already were or if Adam was privy to Tash's business affairs but if he were . . . he began to sweat again, profusely.

'Excuse me,' he muttered abruptly, pushing past a surprised Miranda and heading for the toilets. He *had* to calm down. Once inside, he peeled off his jacket, unbuttoned his shirt and splashed some cold water on his face. He grabbed a wad of tissue paper and quickly patted himself dry under the arms and down his chest. He caught sight of his own face in the mirror and quickly looked away.

TASH

The day passed in a blur of good wishes and high drama – the highest point of which was her mother passing out, of course – punctuated every so often by moments of serene detachment. She'd tried to keep the numbers reasonable. There were two hundred invited guests and some two hundred-odd journalists, photographers and hangers-on, most of whom were camped on the other side of the road opposite the beautiful church with its magnificent rose garden and forecourt, lenses trained on the wedding party. She still couldn't get over how much interest her nuptials had generated. Who cared? It was good for business, her partners kept telling her. 'Everyone loves a happy ending,' James said firmly. And hers was one of the happiest around, or so everyone seemed to think. Edith was somewhere in the church, beaming with as much pride as if it had been her own daughter. It was almost comical. There she was, a successful, hard-working and ambitious businesswoman and the only thing people were interested in was how much her plastic surgery had cost and whether or not she'd snagged her man before or after she'd had it done. Snagged? She'd looked at the hapless journalist who'd asked the question and only just managed to turn away before she slapped her. *Snagged?*

She looked over at where Adam was standing talking to Julian and that awful woman, Miranda Grayling. She'd insisted on an invitation and since she and Julian were partners in a whole host of other ventures, she'd found it impossible to say 'no'. Miranda stood to one side, immaculate blonde hair carefully swept up into a chignon, wearing an Issa poppy-red, silk wrap dress, a pair of strappy navy-blue suede sandals that Tash recognised immediately as Miu-Miu and a navy-and-snakeskin clutch purse. Her entire ensemble was on the third page of that week's *On Trend*, F@shion.com's weekly magazine. Tash smiled quietly to herself. She looked at Julian. Why was he behaving so oddly? He had dark patches of sweat under his arms – *most* unlike him – and the colour was up in his face. He'd been avoiding her all afternoon, she'd noticed. Rebecca too was acting strangely, though that might be to do with the fact that she was about to give birth. Possibly even here, in the church grounds.

She drained the last of her champagne, picked up another glass and a glass of sparkling water and made her way across the gravel path towards her. 'Here, darling,' she said, handing her the water. 'You look as though you could do with a glass.'

'Thanks,' Rebecca said wanly. 'I'd forgotten how miserable the last few weeks are.'

'When's the due date again?'

'First week of July. Hottest week of the year.'

'Same place?'

Rebecca nodded. 'Next to some celebrity who's too posh to push,' she said with a faint smile. 'And with paparazzi all around. Though you must be used to it,' she adding, looking across the road.

'Oh, they're not here for me,' Tash shrugged. 'They're just hoping for a glimpse of some of our customers.'

'Don't bet on it. You look lovely, by the way. I feel like an absolute whale. I can't wait for it to be over.'

'It'll be over soon,' Tash said soothingly. 'Have you decided on a name, yet?'

'Maryam,' Rebecca said softly, a smile suddenly breaking out across her face. 'Julian thinks it should be Miriam, not Maryam, but . . . I like it. It was the name of a . . . a childhood friend of mine.' She stopped abruptly, her face clouding over.

'What's wrong?'

She shook her head. 'N-nothing. I . . . I'd better go. I need the loo.'

'Over there.' Tash pointed in the direction from which she'd just come. 'You sure you're okay?'

'I'm fine. Just . . . just tired.'

'I'll tell Julian you ought to be taken home.'

'No, don't . . . I'm fine, honestly. I'll be back in a sec.' She moved away, walking slowly across the path to the toilets. Tash watched her go. There was something definitely wrong. All afternoon she'd been aware of a streak of strain in Rebecca's face, which rose to the surface whenever the chatter around her flagged, as though she'd just heard something that other people's conversations had drowned. There was a look in her eyes that she hadn't seen since . . . well, since that silly affair with her university lecturer, all those years ago. What the hell was his name? She couldn't remember.

She looked across to where Julian stood, still chatting to Adam and Miranda. He'd clearly caught sight of Rebecca moving slowly towards the church but made no move towards her. Most odd, Tash thought to herself. Just then, Adam turned his head and caught her eye. He smiled and winked at her and Tash felt the bottom drop out of her stomach. How lucky I am, she thought to herself wonderingly. How fucking lucky. Then she saw his attention wander and she followed the direction of his glance. A young woman crossed in front of the three of them – it was Suzanne Gibson, one of the assistant style directors. In a lemon-yellow, knee-length dress and glossy, ridiculously high-heeled patent pumps that showed off her tanned and toned bare legs, she looked good enough to eat. Tash glanced back at Adam. He clearly thought so too. She felt a thin needle of fear rise within her. She quickly crossed over to them, hoping that the uneasiness in the pit of her stomach wasn't written all over her face. She quickly downed the rest of her champagne and signalled to a passing waiter. Another, please.

106

JULIAN
Dubai

He stood at the bar, taking in the scene, one hand lying slackly on the cool marble surface, the other holding a sweating glass of beer. It was six o'clock and the evening was beginning to take shape. In the corner of the long, low-ceilinged room, Miranda sat with His Excellency Sheikh Mahmoud bin Talal Al-Soueif, one of the senior crown princes, and his three advisors, who accompanied him everywhere. He took a long hard swig of beer. He would move towards them in a minute. He was willing to be sociable but first he needed to steady his nerves. Fortunately, they were in an international hotel and alcohol was on hand. He took another mouthful. What happened next would depend on a number of things, not least his own ability to muster up the required charm. It all came down to the small matter of a clause, except that the clause in question was no small matter. His clients were in trouble: they needed cash and they needed it fast. The sheikhs had the cash and were willing to invest it, but on one condition. In return for the cash, the sheikh wanted the option to buy more shares, but at a fraction of their current value. If, at some point, he reasoned smoothly, Julian's clients might require more money, then he ought to be amply rewarded. Cheaper share options seemed fair enough compensation all round.

In the scheme of things, it was a small request. The sheikh was about to buy a twenty per cent stake in a bank that was valued at 4 billion pounds. It was one of the biggest deals of its kind. Julian and Miranda stood to make 50 million pounds each on the transaction, more than either had ever made in a single deal. The problem was, Julian had already spent it. Or, more accurately, *Tash* had already spent it, not that Tash knew a damn thing about it. The opportunity on which he'd staked most of Tash's spare cash had come via a tip from Miranda. A twenty per cent stake in Two Hyde Park, a new residential tower just going up on Hyde Park Corner.

'Hyde Park, darling,' Miranda had said to him over a drink at the Lanesborough one evening. 'It doesn't get better than that. This isn't just prime real estate, Jules, it's *premium*. Everyone's in on it.'

'Are you?'

'D'you think for a second I'd put you onto something I wasn't about to make money on?'

He'd thought about it for twenty-four hours, panicked when he realised he didn't have enough himself to invest and then did something he'd never done before. He put up the capital using Tash's money as collateral. It was preferable to asking Rebecca. He was amazed at how easy it was. Everyone knew he was Tash Bryce-Brudenell's go-to man, her right-hander. He knew Tash's signature almost as well as he knew his own. No one checked in any case. It was only temporary, he reasoned. He'd leverage just enough capital to stump up his share.

When the Arabs bought their stake in FIB, he'd walk away with a cool 50 million, 30 million of which would replace Tash's 'loan' to prop up his required twenty per cent share of Two Hyde Park. He'd shred paperwork as soon as it was done and no one would be any the wiser. He'd be holding onto forged papers for no more than a month, a fortnight if he were lucky.

Well, he hadn't been lucky. What was that goddamn saying? If you want to make God laugh, tell Him your plans. He hadn't, but God sure as hell was laughing now. It had been three months since the deal was first mooted – three months in which he'd scarcely been able to meet Tash's eye. It was only a matter of time before she, her accountants and lawyer and/or Adam found out. He was running out of options. FIB *had* to accept the clause the Arabs wanted. There was *no question* of the deal going south. He, Julian Lovell, had staked everything he had on it. His reputation, his cash, his future earnings . . . hell, his *life*. If Tash ever found out what he'd done, he'd be finished. If *Rebecca* ever found out . . . it didn't bear thinking about. He felt the sudden weight of Lionel's gaze. It made him feel nauseous, and old. He drained his beer, dabbed at his lips with a napkin and squared his shoulders. He moved through the now-crowded bar towards Miranda and the sheikh. It was time to turn on the charm.

Half an hour later, the four men he'd been desperately trying to woo stood up. Sheikh Al-Soueif adjusted his robes with an impatient, practised switch of his arm. His snowy-white *ghytra* was held firmly in place by a double band of thick, black rope; its long, tasselled corners fell in billowing waves over his shoulders. He wore the traditional white *thawb*, with a long overcoat of embroidered gold. He was a short man, perhaps a whole head shorter than Julian, but there was such power in his stance and his calm, slow gaze that Julian felt he should be looking up towards him, not the other way round. His nephew and the two advisors arranged themselves on either side as the party made their farewells. The nephew, a smooth-talking, smooth-faced young man of around thirty, had translated for his uncle throughout. Julian sat back, listening to the Arabic flowing over them, and was reminded yet again of how close the language was to Hebrew – despite not speaking a word of it, the rhythm and cadence was closer than he'd thought. He sneaked a quick look at Miranda; she understood more than she let on, he thought to himself. Once or twice their eyes caught and held. *Don't panic*, she seemed to be signalling. *Let me handle this*. It was hard *not* to panic. He was sweating profusely again by the time they shook hands.

The four Arabs had started walking back slowly towards the exit when the sheikh turned round suddenly. The three younger men held back respectfully.

'One last thing, Mr Lovell,' the sheikh said in perfect English. 'Just to satisfy my curiosity. Do you race?'

Julian gaped at him. Not only did the question take him by surprise – what sort of racing was the man referring to? – but he'd spoken English. Perfect English.

'Er, n-no, sir, your Highness,' Julian stammered. 'If you mean horse-racing?'

'No other kind, I'm afraid.' He looked up at Julian from under those deep, hooded eyes and then smiled. 'I thought not.' He turned to his aides and waved his hand imperiously. '*Ya'alla*.' They moved off immediately, as one.

'What the . . . ?' Julian turned to Miranda, almost speechless with surprise. 'He just spoke English!'

'Eton,' Miranda murmured. 'Then Oxford. PPE, I believe. Or PPP . . . can never remember. Or tell the difference,' she smiled. 'Drink?'

Julian nodded vigorously. 'Christ, I need one. What an afternoon.'

'Don't worry, we'll get the clause put in. It'll happen, Julian. I don't know why you're so worried. I've never seen you this tense,' she said, stroking his arm lightly. 'You need to relax, darling.'

The urge to confide in someone almost knocked him sideways but he steadied himself. Confiding in Miranda would be a mistake. No matter how chummily intimate Miranda might get, her first instinct was self-preservation. If the chips were down she'd use anything and everything to make sure she'd come out unscathed. Miranda would throw him to the dogs if she had to. 'I'm fine,' he said tersely. 'Lot going on.'

'Has Rebecca had the sprog yet?'

He winced. 'It's not a sprog, Miranda. It's a little girl.'

'You know what I mean.'

He glanced at her. In her grey business suit with the pink silk blouse and those oversized tortoiseshell glasses, she looked like the sort of sexy schoolteacher he'd have had a crush on, had there been a schoolteacher like Miranda at his all-boys' prep school. His cock began to stir. 'Join me in a drink?' he motioned towards the bar.

Miranda shook her head. 'Sorry, darling . . . I've got plans.' She gave him a coy little smile, patted him condescendingly on the bottom in much the same way he'd have patted her if he'd had half the chance, and moved off. He was left alone in the bar of the Intercontinental in Dubai, surrounded by braying, semi-drunk ex-pats. He scratched his beard. His wife had just given birth, his business partners had no idea where he was, or what he was up to, or what he'd done . . . it wasn't quite adding up. He was fifty-seven years of age and he was horribly over-extended. It wasn't where he'd planned to be. *How d'you make God laugh? Tell Him your plans.*

'Give me another,' he signalled to the bartender. 'And make it a double.'

107

TASH
London

The brochures were spread across the breakfast table, each one glossier, more beautifully photographed and styled than the next. She cleared away a space and fanned them out in front of her. She looked at the breakfast table and sighed deeply in pleasure. The saucers that were part of the beautiful porcelain set Embeth had given them for their wedding held the remnants of breakfast – a plain scone for her, jam and toast for Adam. Two months into their married life and it sometimes felt as though they'd been married for ever. Their routines were remarkably similar. They both got up around the same time, just after dawn, took it in turns to shower in the bathroom that was the size of an entire flat and met downstairs in the pretty kitchen on the ground floor, where the maid would have laid out the breakfast table before disappearing upstairs to restore order to the rooms they'd just vacated. An assortment of honeys and jams, sometimes the odd slice of ham or prosciutto that she'd chosen at the delicatessen around the corner or some cheese. A cafetière of freshly brewed coffee. They read the papers, checked emails and messages and then left the house separately, Tash in her chauffeur-driven car since they'd moved to the new King's Cross offices, Adam to the office he shared with his business partners. Even after two months it was still a little unclear to Tash what Adam actually did: 'investments', he said airily, but she still had no idea what that meant. Whatever it meant, it kept him busy. He was gone from seven thirty in the morning until six or seven at night and seemed pleased enough with the progress.

She picked up the first brochure. She looked at the image on the cover and her heartbeat immediately quickened. *Oversea: set in an unbeatable location on Lincoln's Circle, Nantucket's premiere neighbourhood, this classic waterfront home exudes early Nantucket charm, with unobstructed views of the Sound and beyond. Oversea has been an island landmark for well over a hundred years.* Eight bedrooms, three and a half bathrooms, private beach stairs, a bargain at 15 million dollars, according to the estate agents. She picked up another leaflet. *Tranquillity sets the stage for this striking new home, set on 3.6 acres in Sconset. Designed both for domestic comfort and gracious entertaining, this richly detailed property . . .* Six bedrooms, six bathrooms, black granite pool, a guesthouse . . . it looked divine. She picked up another. And another.

It took her two hours to go through all fourteen brochures and by the time she was finished, her head was spinning. She had a meeting at eleven – just under an hour to go – and all she could think about was low-ceilinged barns, wooden rafters, kitchens the size of whole houses and wild grass lawns. Nantucket Sound, Katama Bay, Menemsha Pond, Squibnocket Bight. What on earth was a 'squibnocket'?

She hummed to herself as she tidied everything away. She didn't want Adam to see what she was up to. She wanted to surprise him. She couldn't remember when the idea of a second home had come to her. Perhaps it was hearing him talk about New York? She'd suddenly had a longing to visit New York again. It had been almost ten years since her trip with Rosie. All she could remember was the sheer excitement of it all – the yellow cabs, the vertical canyons of buildings, the lights, the buzz, the atmosphere. It was true what they said – New York was less a city than a *feeling*. She suddenly wanted to feel it again and what better way than to have a place there? Not *in* the city, per se, but somewhere just outside it. Somewhere beautiful, calm, tranquil . . . a place to entertain family and friends, to invite her godchildren.

It was at this last that her pulse really began to race. She and Adam hadn't had *that* conversation. She wouldn't have even known how to bring it up. Did she actually *want* a child? She'd never taken any precautions against having one, and neither had he, but nothing had happened. She was thirty-seven: old enough to wonder, too young to panic, as Annick delicately put it. It'll happen, she assured her blithely, 'just when you least expect it.' Tash wasn't sure quite what was meant by 'when you least expect it', but she let it pass. It seemed odd to be taking advice from Annick and Rebecca when she was always the one dispensing it.

She stowed the brochures away in the dresser in the hallway and made her way upstairs. She had a photo shoot in the studio to oversee at eleven, then an afternoon meeting with her accountants. She pulled a face. Meetings with accountants she endured; a photo shoot was a much more interesting way to spend a day.

By four o'clock, she was struggling to stay awake. Cash flow; balance sheets; off-shore investments; her portfolio; tax breaks; insurance policies; over- and under-exposure . . . she had to keep nudging herself as the accountants droned on and on. Every so often her eyes fell to her BlackBerry, nestling in the palm of her hand. Across from her sat Colin, calm and capable as ever. She trusted him to grasp the finer points of whatever it was they were discussing. Did they have enough to do what she wanted? That was all she cared about. *How* they got there was Colin's business.

She looked down at the message list on her Blackberry again. There were half a dozen emails from the various estate agents she'd contacted in Cape Cod. One was marked 'highest priority'. She glanced around the table; the four men were busy discussing the finer points of balance sheets. She surreptitiously clicked on it and her heart began to race. *12 Pohoganot Road, Martha's Vineyard. This signature home is sitting high on a bluff with breathtaking water views in three directions: the Atlantic Ocean to the south, Paqua Pond to the east and Ripley Cove to the west.* It was the photograph that caught her attention, tiny as it was. It was of a grey shingle, two-storey house with whitewashed trim, three or four chimneys, a beautiful sweep of lawn and beyond, the bluest, freshest skies she'd ever seen and an ocean view to die for. She stared at it. 6,900,000 dollars. Five bedrooms, five bathrooms, a pool, tennis courts, a guest house and – best of all – a beautiful old barn on the northern slope, away from the house. She swallowed hard. She scrolled across the screen, her pulse accelerating by the second. *Hi Ms Bryce-Brudenell. Please call me as soon as you can. This property's just come on the market and we've had a lot of interest already. It's totally special, even though it needs quite a bit of work. It's a bargain at the price! Look forward to speaking. Yrs., Janine van Wolmer.*

She glanced at her watch. It was nearly five: eleven in the morning in Martha's Vineyard. She'd better get to it before anyone else did.

'Tash?' Colin's voice brought her abruptly back to the meeting at hand.

'Huh?'

'We were just wondering . . . there's a transfer amount here,' Colin pointed to some random figures on a spreadsheet. 'It's into your private account, not one of the company accounts. It seems a little odd.'

Tash had no idea what he was talking about, but all she wanted to do was look at the pictures of the house she'd just received. She'd never wanted anything so badly before. She got up from the table, clutching the phone. 'I'm sure it's fine. Must've been something for my mother. I've got to run, I'm afraid – something's come up.' She grabbed her bag and practically ran from the room. She heard Colin's calm, measured voice as she closed the door behind her.

'Well, you heard her. She often transfers large amounts to her mother. They've been thinking of setting something up in Russia, I believe. I'll get the details later.'

She galloped back down the stairs to her office, fingers already dialling Janine's number. On the third ring, it was answered. 'Is that Janine? Tash Bryce-Brudenell here. Has it gone? The house on Pohoganot Road? Is it still available?'

'Well, hi there,' Janine's friendly voice crackled down the line, shaming her. 'How *are* you?'

'Fine, fine . . . has it gone?'

'No, not yet. It's a *very* special property, Tash. May I call you Tash?'

'Yes, yes, of course. When can I see it?'

'You're in London, England, right? I just *love* London. In fact, I love England. I was there—'

'Janine, we can talk about England when I get there. Give me two days and please, *please* don't show it to anyone else. I've got a really good feeling about the property – I can't explain it. Can you do that for me? Just keep it under wraps for a couple of days. I'll be able to tell you straight away if I'm taking it.'

'Why, of course, Tash.' Janine was practically purring. Tash could hear it down the line. 'Two days, you say? Today's what, Thursday?'

'I'll be there by Saturday morning. I'll get my secretary to forward my itinerary.' She put the phone down before Janine could extract any further promises. She hugged herself tightly. It would be her secret to everyone. She'd have to make up some reason why she had to be in the

US that weekend but she knew in her heart of hearts that it would be hers. A holiday home for everyone – Adam, Rebecca, Julian, Annick, Yves, their kids, her mother . . . everyone. She could already picture it. Long summer evenings by the pool; Christmases when the beach was knee-deep in snow; autumn walks as the children grew older, kicking at red and gold leaves, mulled wine and gingerbread cookies by the many fireplaces. The barn could be converted into a studio or an office for Adam; the guest house could be Lyudmila's pied-à-terre . . . it would be open all year round to whomever wanted it. They could use it as a location, entertain clients if she felt like it when she went over for the shows. Anna Wintour had a home nearby. Hell, half of New York's fashion world summered in Martha's Vineyard. It was perfect. The perfect backdrop for all the different facets of her life. She hugged herself in giddy, half-nervous anticipation. Was this *really* her life?

108

REBECCA
Jerusalem

Under heavy, rain-sodden skies, the last of the mourners made their way across the stony path, away from the graves and the spectacular views over the Old City. To her right lay Yad Vashem, the memorial to the Holocaust that she dimly remembered visiting as a child, with her parents. Rain fell in small, sharp needles, hitting the taut fabric of her umbrella before sliding down in pearly, crystal droplets, falling towards the ground. Maryam was struggling a little; snuggled up against her mother in a red parka with a fur trim around the hood to keep her warm, she sucked her thumb, humming to herself as she often did. 'What're you singing, darling?' Rebecca would often ask her, searching those beautiful, mysterious eyes that held her own captive as she searched for what lay behind. But Maryam would only look at her, deeply, then smile and turn away.

The party who'd come to bury Bettina Harburg, the last of Lionel's sisters, had gathered in small groups at the entrance to the cemetery, huddled under umbrellas. Julian walked slowly beside her. She felt his gaze turn from the mourners to a tall figure in a dark grey overcoat who stood on the other side of the turnstile. 'Who's that?' he asked, jerking his head in the man's direction. 'Why doesn't he come inside?'

Rebecca looked across the square. Her heart missed a beat, a whole, entire beat. She thought she might drop Maryam. 'Wh-who?' she stammered, knowing full well who it was.

'Him . . . there, over there by the turnstile.'

She forced herself to look round and look away again. 'No idea,' she said quickly. She bent her head to Maryam's, praying her cheeks weren't the colour of her coat.

'He looks a bit suspicious. Is he an Arab, d'you think?'

'Oh, Julian . . . don't be silly.'

'I'm not. Hang on a moment. Here, take this.' He passed the umbrella to her and moved off, heading for a small group of men in black coats – the rabbi who'd come to officiate and a few others. She could see her mother talking to someone; another relative whom she'd never met. Her heart was thumping so hard it hurt. Maryam must have sensed it; she stirred restlessly in her arms. She didn't dare go across to where Tariq stood. She didn't even dare look at him. She stood there, cold rain dripping down the back of her own coat, unable to think straight. She knew why he was there. He wanted to see his daughter. She was nearly three months old now and he hadn't yet seen her. It was Rebecca's first trip back to Israel. She'd baulked at the idea of Tariq coming to London. The night before their departure, she'd left Maryam with the nanny and rushed out to the shops along Hampstead High Street, her mobile clutched to her ear. 'I *can't*,' she said, tears flowing down her cheeks. 'I just daren't risk it, Tariq. *Please* don't ask me. *Please*.'

'Just tell him you're going to visit a friend,' he'd exploded. 'What the hell's the matter with you, Rebecca? I haven't even seen her yet.'

'I know, I know. I'll . . . I'll try. I can't promise anything. You don't know Julian . . . I sometimes wonder if he suspects.'

'I don't give a damn about Julian. She's *my* child, Rebecca.'

'I know.' She began to cry in earnest, like a child. Her face would be all blotchy and swollen by the time she got back to the house, she knew, but she didn't care.

And now, here he was, standing on the other side of the barrier that separated them, waiting for her. She saw Julian ask something of one of the older men, who looked over at Tariq. Something was going to happen; she could feel it. She held onto Maryam tightly as Julian and

415

two others broke away from the group and moved towards the gate. Tariq stood his ground, watching them as they walked purposefully towards him. Her heart was thumping as they drew near. She was too far away to hear what was said but, from their expressions and gestures, they were less than welcoming. She stood by helplessly as one of them – not Julian, she was pathetically grateful to see – pushed a finger into Tariq's shoulder, much the way one would chastise a child. He jabbed at Tariq several times until Tariq caught hold of his finger, forcing him to stop. Behind them, two young soldiers, their guns strapped across their chests, began to move towards them, clearly wondering what was going on. Her heart in her mouth, she watched as Tariq slowly brushed his overcoat with his palm and then turned around and walked off, leaving Julian and the three or four men who'd joined him, watching after him, obviously wondering who the hell he was.

Maryam stirred again; she was getting hungry. There were tears in Rebecca's eyes, which she quickly brushed away as she hoisted Maryam onto her hip and moved towards the gate. She wanted nothing more than to run after Tariq and beg his forgiveness, not just for the silly little incident that had just happened, but for everything.

'He *was* an Arab,' Julian said angrily, coming up to them. He brushed at his own jacket as though he feared some part of Tariq, perhaps, had rubbed off onto him. 'Why they don't stop them, I'll never understand.'

Rebecca looked up at him, a sudden wave of revulsion and shame spreading through her. 'Let's go,' she said tightly, not trusting herself to say anything more. 'Maryam's hungry.'

'Don't you want to—'

'No, I don't,' she interrupted him coldly. 'I want to go home.' She didn't wait for his answer but pulled Maryam's hood more tightly around her head and marched ahead, oblivious to the stinging rain.

Pick up the phone. Please pick up. Please, please, please. The shrill, insistent single tone droned on, and on and on. There was no response, no pick up, no request to leave a message . . . nothing. It was perhaps the hundredth time she'd call him since the funeral three days earlier and still there was no response. She was back in the flat in Tel Aviv. Jerusalem was a good hour and a half away . . . how on earth would she explain it to anyone if she simply took the car and drove off?

From the kitchen she could hear the sounds of the twins being fed. Julian had gone out to dinner with a business associate and would be back any moment. Her mother had already gone home. She tapped her fingers on the sideboard, a sudden urgency blowing up inside her like one of those summer thunderstorms, bewildering in their intensity. Should she . . . ? Maryam was fast asleep. She was such a good little baby; she only cried when she was hungry and even then, softly, as though she were talking to herself, not crying. She was so unlike her brothers. They, like Julian, were full of passions. Arguments, tantrums, quicksilver changes of mood. Not Maryam. She slept and gurgled her way through the drama surrounding her without so much as a whimper. *What are you thinking?* Rebecca longed to ask her as she stared at her face, liquid black eyes opening slowly, blinking contentedly under the scrutiny, like Tariq sometimes did.

She hesitated for a second, then snatched the car keys from the dresser and thrust her feet into a pair of sandals. She stuck her head round the kitchen door. 'I'm just going out for about an hour,' she said to a surprised Dorit, who was busy spooning yogurt into Joshua's unwilling mouth.

'Mama!' David called out in a panic. He could see she was on her way out. 'Mama!'

She didn't wait to hear the rest; from bitter experience she knew it was best just to run. In ten minutes they'd have forgotten all about her. 'Just keep an eye on Maryam, will you?' she yelled, grabbing her jacket from behind the door. 'I'll be back in an hour.'

The car was parked across the road. She jumped in, dumped her handbag in the child-carrier and started the engine. Her heart was racing. Was she mad? She pulled out, narrowly avoiding a bus, and tore off jerkily down the road. It was seven in the evening and traffic was slowly thinning out. If she were lucky, she'd make it to Jerusalem in just over an hour. She followed the signs to the motorway leading out of Tel Aviv, her foot almost flat on the accelerator wherever she could. The road ventured out of the city, parting the thinning suburbs with small outcrops of service stations and strip malls. Half an hour after leaving, the road began its slow ascent into the Judean Hills. It was dark now; in passing stretches of light, she saw the outline of the hills and the twinkling lights of settlements, Jewish and Arab, on either side. The small engine screamed in protest as she climbed the hills, her heart still racing in time to the speed at which she drove. Shoresh. Abu Ghosh. Nahalat Shlomo. Ein Naquba. The patchwork of competing names. The main junction outside the city swam into view and was bypassed; she wound her way down past the Botanical Gardens, along the roads she'd come to know so well . . . Herzog, Jabotinsky, David Marcus and finally, Pinsker.

It was ten past eight by the time she pulled up outside the villa. She quickly checked her mobile; no one had rung. Whatever else might happen next, for the moment, everything at home was under control. She got out of the car, struggled into her jacket and ran across the road. The little wrought-iron gate was locked but there were two buzzers, one for the office, and the other for the house where Tariq stayed when he was in Jerusalem. She pressed the bell for the house and stood back, smoothing her hair away from her face. She waited for a few moments, her heart beginning to race even faster, and pressed the buzzer again. It hadn't even occurred to her that he might not be at home. Panic beginning to mount, she pressed it for the third time. A few seconds later, a voice suddenly crackled through the intercom. '*Aiwa?*'

She jumped. 'Is . . . Is Tariq there? *Tariq b'bayit?*' she repeated in her halting Hebrew.

A torrent of words poured forth in Arabic, which she understood even less.

'I'm sorry . . . I don't understand,' Rebecca shouted back. 'I don't speak Arabic.'

'Hello?' A second voice came on the intercom. 'Who is this?' Rebecca recognised Aysa's voice, Tariq's shy, quiet assistant.

'Oh, Aysa, thank God. It's Rebecca. Rebecca Harburg. Is . . . is Tariq there, by any chance?'

'No, sorry, he's not here.'

'Oh. Um, wh-when will he be back?' she asked, wondering what Aysa was doing in the house.

'I don't know. He's in America. He left on Sunday. I don't know when he'll be back.'

Rebecca had to hold onto the low wall for support. 'Am . . . America?' she croaked.

'Can I give him a message?'

The words were a clench of panic, deep in her belly and chest. She must have staggered and lost her balance. She found herself leaning over the low wall, with the disembodied, disconnected voice coming from the box above her head. 'Rebecca? Miss Rebecca?' Fortunately there was no camera attached. No one there to see the look of sickening defeat spreading across her face. She turned slowly and crouched down, bringing her forehead to rest against the cool Jerusalem stone. In her bag, her mobile started to ring. She fumbled for it, half of her torn by the wild, irrational hope that it might be Tariq, the other half by the fear of something happening at home. She stared at it. It was Julian. She took in a couple of deep breaths and then picked up.

'Rebecca? Where the hell are you?'

'Is something wrong? Are the kids all right?'

'Of course they're bloody all right! Where *are* you?'

'I'm . . . I'm just . . . I just popped out for a minute—'

'A minute? Dorit said you left around seven. Rebecca . . . what the hell's going on?'

'I . . .' She had no answer for him. She had no answer for herself. She listened to his voice for a few seconds more, to the rising anger in his voice, and then she slowly ended the call. She would think of something to say when she got home, not before. Not now. Now she couldn't even breathe. He was gone. She knew he would never come back.

109

NINE MONTHS LATER

ANNICK
London

After more than two years, she had a routine again. She got up early, showered and dressed in near-silence if Yves was home, sometimes humming to herself if he wasn't. Dressed for the office, her hair and make-up in place, she would walk down the corridor carrying her high-heeled shoes, swinging them by the tip of her forefinger, and peek in on Didier. If he were awake, she would put a finger to her lips and kneel down in her stockinged feet beside him, burying her head into the sleepy warmth of his neck. If he were still asleep, she'd still kneel down and gaze at him, observing every single moment of his life passing. That half hour she spent with him early in the morning before the au pair arrived and Yves woke up was precious to her. Despite the fact he couldn't yet quite speak in whole sentences, she sensed from his solemn, quiet demeanour when she entered his room and the smile on his face as he saw her, that he too understood the significance of those moments. Moments that would never come around again. At seven on the dot,

Birgitte, their Latvian au pair whose English was as excellent as her French was atrocious, arrived. In two months, she'd never once been late. Sometimes with half a piece of toast still in her mouth, Annick would run out the door, briefcase banging against her legs as she ran. Fifteen minutes later, she was hanging onto a strap on the Underground, one of thousands of other young working women, most of whom had left behind a child or two, a partner, a whole other life imperfectly balanced between the opposing demands of each.

'Morning.' Frances breezed into the office ten minutes after Annick, an almost identical briefcase swinging from her arm. 'Good weekend?'

Annick nodded, her attention already on the screen in front of her. 'You?'

'Not bad. Hubert's been posted to Nigeria.'

Annick looked up. 'Nigeria? Whatever for?'

'God knows. I've long since given up trying to figure out why the EU does what it does.'

'But . . . won't that be hard for you?'

'Me?' Frances looked genuinely puzzled.

'Going up and down to Nigeria. It's a long way.'

'Why on earth would I be going up and down?'

'Oh, I just thought . . . no, never mind.'

'Where are we on the Dowd case?' Frances' expression indicated that the personal chit-chat was at an end.

'More or less up to speed,' Annick answered, pulling a stack of files towards her.

'More or less?'

'I've just got a few more things to check,' Annick said hastily.

Frances sat down at her own desk and switched on her computer. 'Then do so,' she said, smiling very, very faintly to take the sting out of her words.

Annick bent her head and did as she was bid.

An hour or so later, when the only sound in their office was the occasional opening and closing of the adjoining door as one or other of the PAs tiptoed in and out, Annick raised her head again and asked a question that took them both by surprise.

'What would *you* do if you thought your husband was hiding something from you?'

It was hard to tell who was more flabbergasted. Frances frowned, as if

420

she hadn't heard quite right. 'Sorry?' Neither woman was given to exchanges of such a deeply personal nature.

'No, *I'm* sorry . . . it . . . it just slipped out. I'm sorry, I shouldn't have even . . . forget it.' Annick's cheeks were on fire.

Frances glanced at her quizzically for a second, then turned back to her screen. She continued typing in silence. Annick swallowed, embarrassed beyond belief. What the hell had possessed her? She tried to concentrate on her own work, praying the heat in her face and throat would dissipate. A minute passed, then another. Then Frances spoke. 'What sort of thing is he hiding?' she asked, eyes still fixed on her own screen.

The heat returned to Annick's face. 'I . . . I don't know. I found something . . . a couple of years ago. I don't know why it came to me just now . . . it's been on my mind, I guess.'

'Two years? And you've not said anything?' The look on Frances' face said it all. 'Not a *thing*?'

Annick shook her head. She picked up a pencil from the pot on her desk and began studying it, as if she'd never seen a pencil like it before. 'I kept waiting for the right moment,' she began hesitantly. 'I . . . I just never seemed to find it. It was right about the time Didier was born and it just didn't seem . . . well, fair, really.'

'Nothing fair or unfair about lies,' Frances said quietly. 'Even small ones. Why don't you tell me what's really going on?'

Annick glanced nervously at the clock.

'And don't worry about the time.'

'I don't know where to begin,' Annick said hesitantly.

'The beginning's usually a good place,' Frances said drily. She swung her chair round towards Annick's and crossed her legs. 'Go on,' she said, her voice softening a fraction. 'I'm listening. And don't worry about this going any further either.'

Annick swallowed. She drew in a deep breath, unlaced her fingers and put the pencil she'd been scrutinising down. Frances' expression was carefully neutral, as though she were prepared to hear whatever it was Annick had decided to say. As she began to speak, she could feel the weight slowly lifting from her shoulders, unburdening her, finally setting her free.

'Go away,' Frances said slowly, after Annick's voice had died. She got up suddenly, and walked to the window. She laced her hands behind her back. 'Go away, just the two of you. You need to talk, without the emotional distraction of your child. And I'm saying that for your benefit, not his. Is there someone you can leave Didier with?'

Annick chewed her lip nervously. 'I . . . I don't know. I suppose so . . . there's Tash, I suppose. She's his godmother. I wouldn't want to leave him with the au pair.'

'Then do it. And do it now. I don't know how you've managed to keep this in for two whole years. I'd have exploded after a weekend.'

Annick nodded slowly. Now that she'd finally let it out, she too had begun to wonder how she'd managed to suppress it for so long.

110

TASH
London

It was nearly eight by the time she put the phone down and her jaw actually hurt from all the laughter and the giddy, girlish excitement of the conversation. Annick was the first person – aside from Adam, of course – whom she'd told about the house.

'A *holiday* house? Where?'

'Martha's Vineyard.'

'Isn't that in—?'

'In America? Yes, it is. Cape Cod, just north of Boston. It's absolutely stunning, Annie, absolutely stunning . . . you should see it. It's got five bedrooms and there's a barn that we've almost finished converting and there's a pool and—'

'But you never said you were buying a holiday home,' Annick protested, interrupting her. 'And in America? It's an awfully long way, Tash.'

'That's the whole point,' Tash said excitedly. 'It's a home away from home. Far away. You have to get on a plane, rent a car – or I'll have someone pick you up – and then you drive off towards the sea. It's like being on another planet, and that's exactly what I wanted. It's nearly done – we've had architects and interior designers in there for almost six months – it's perfect. And next month will be just the right time. It'll be hot, but not too hot. There's the pool and there's the beach . . . everything you need. We'll all go out for ten days or a fortnight, whatever time you can get off . . . I'll make sure there's a nanny to look after the children and you and Yves can go to New York for the weekend, or Boston . . . wherever you want. Just spend some time on your own.'

'God, Tash . . . it sounds amazing,' Annick said, excitement slowly growing. 'But . . . what about Rebecca and Julian . . . and Adam?'

'We'll all go together. It'll be *fun*, darling. It'll be more fun than any of us have had in the last couple of years . . . and God knows, we've worked hard enough. I can't wait, I just can't wait. I was thinking I'd surprise you all – you know, tickets in an envelope and all that, but this is just perfect. Let's fix the dates, I'll phone Rebecca . . . we'll get it all organised – don't you worry about a thing. Just book the time off work and let's go.'

It had been a while since she'd heard Tash sound quite so excited about anything, Annick thought to herself, smiling as she hung up the phone. It was sometimes easy to forget just how hard she worked. With no children to distract her and few interests outside the business, she lived, breathed, ate and slept F@shion.com. In hindsight, it was understandable that she'd been so preoccupied over the past few months. A holiday home on Martha's Vineyard. She began to laugh. Tash Bryce-Brudenell just didn't do things by half. All or nothing. Not for her some pied-à-terre in Norfolk, like most other people. No, it had to be Martha's Vineyard.

She was still laughing ten minutes later when Yves walked in. 'What's funny?' he asked, evidently surprised to see her in such a good mood. She felt a pang of sadness.

'It's Tash. She's gone and bought a holiday home in America. She's invited all of us for a late Easter holiday. Well, early summer, really. The second week of May. She says it's the perfect time.'

'*All* of us?' He looked at her quizzically, opening the fridge and reaching for a bottle of wine.

Annick nodded. 'You, me, Rebecca, Julian, the kids. Everyone. She'll organise an au pair for the children. It's right on the beach, apparently. A *private* beach. Can you imagine it?'

Yves shook his head. 'No, I can't.' He carefully poured two glasses and slid one across the counter to her. 'When did you say?'

'Next month. The builders and interior decorators'll be finished by then, apparently. Come on, Yves. We haven't had a holiday since . . . well, in *years*. It'll be the first time with Didi. It'll be wonderful, I know it will. You know what Tash is like. She'll have spared no expense. Let's do it.'

Yves said nothing for a moment. 'A holiday,' he said finally. 'All of us.'

'Tash said we could slip off somewhere on our own,' Annick said hesitantly. 'Just the two of us. There'll be a nanny and an au pair. We could go to New York for the weekend. I've never been, you know? It'd be nice . . . just you and me.' She looked at him, suddenly shy. There'd been a time when Yves had been her only friend in the world. Frances was right – she owed it to him to hear whatever his explanation was. Her fear, both of what she might find out about Yves, and her very real fear of confronting him, had cost them both. Like so many marriages, Frances murmured, the woman begins to withdraw first and eventually, the man follows. 'Stop it now whilst you still have time,' she'd said. 'Fix things whilst you can.'

'I suppose we could,' Yves said after a moment. 'I've got that conference in Toulouse in the last week of April. I could put in for a couple weeks' leave after that.'

'Will you? Will you really?' Annick's excitement was like that of a child's. Yves laughed at her suddenly and the sound in the small kitchen was unfamiliar to them both.

'Yes, I will. Really. And you're right . . . we haven't had a family holiday. It'll do us good.'

Annick was filled with something that wasn't quite – or just – happiness. Relief flowed through her, thick and sweet. It was only now, with the possibility of things being all right again, of a return to where they'd once been, she and Yves, that the full weight of the past couple of years began to lift. She'd been unable to see or think clearly and the distortion had spread, like poison, into every aspect of their lives together. She lifted her glass to her lips and drank, the dry, cool wine flooding through her the way relief and happiness just had.

Then Yves leaned across the counter and kissed her, as if in recognition of the new and unexpected lightness that had come between them. The place where his lips had touched her cheek glowed for a long time afterwards.

News of the holiday plans came to Rebecca via Julian, before Tash or Annick had a chance to tell her themselves. He came home early, parked his car across the street as though he were just popping in for a second and came running lightly up the front steps. Rebecca wasn't expecting him. She was in the middle of preparing dinner. The housekeeper was usually the one to do the cooking but, in a moment of enthusiasm, Rebecca had given her the evening off.

It was just after six thirty when she heard the familiar sound of his car engine. She peered outside the window, watching him run up the front steps. Moments later, he burst into the kitchen.

'Did you know about this?' he asked, flinging a folded open magazine down on the counter before her.

'Know about what?' She popped a thin slice of cucumber in her mouth. 'Weren't you supposed to be eating out tonight?'

'I cancelled. Take a look.'

'What is it?' she asked, glancing briefly at the magazine that now lay open-jawed on the counter.

'Your friend has just spent 7 million dollars on a holiday home in the US. Martha's Vineyard, if you really want to know.'

'Which friend?' Rebecca frowned. She had only one friend capable of doing anything like that but surely Tash would have told her?

'Tash, who else?'

'Tash? She hasn't said a thing to me. Why would she do that?'

'She didn't even tell Adam, apparently.'

'That doesn't sound like Tash. Are you sure?'

'Course I'm bloody sure.'

'Why are you so upset about it?' Rebecca looked at him, puzzled. 'It's her money. If she wants to spend it on a house . . . well, let her.'

'What about Adam?'

'What *about* Adam? What's he got to do with it?'

'He's her husband, for crying out loud. Doesn't he get some say in it?'

'Why? It's Tash's money.'

'It's not about whose money it is, Rebecca,' Julian said, his voice suddenly quiet.

Rebecca was genuinely baffled. 'Why are you picking an argument with me? I just said—'

'I know what you just said. Doesn't matter if you're married. What *you're* saying is, what's yours is yours, what's mine is mine.'

'That's not what I said!' Rebecca put down the paring knife. She was angry now. It was typical Julian – he'd come home in a bad mood, for reasons she didn't understand, and now he was attempting to take it out on her. It wasn't fair. 'I just said—'

'Forget it. Just forget it. I've changed my mind. I *am* going out after all.' He grabbed the jacket he'd just thrown over the back of one of the chairs and left the kitchen. Rebecca stood there, her mouth hanging open in shock. What the hell had she said? In the playroom next door she could hear the twins arguing over the remote control. Maryam was being bathed upstairs. Suddenly, her eyes filled with hot, easy tears. She looked down at her hands. They were shaking. Any minute now the twins would rush in and Brigitte would bring Maryam downstairs, freshly bathed, ready to be kissed and cuddled by her brothers. She had to get a grip on herself. She felt the blood rush to her cheeks and the faint smear of shame that lurked in her always, broke through to the fore. She tried to concentrate on the task in front of her – cut, slice, arrange – but the magic of the early evening was gone and in its place was a desperate longing to make amends . . . but what for?

The study at the top of the stairs reminded her of Lionel's study at home in the house where she'd grown up. The thick, cream carpet was soft underfoot; she felt her bare toes sinking into it like sand. It was nearly ten o'clock. On the floors below, her whole family lay sleeping; only Julian still hadn't come home. She'd resisted the temptation to call him that evening. She needed time to think. The mad, impulsive thought that had come to her as soon as the front door slammed behind him required more than just the impulse; she had to think about it carefully.

She switched on the little green desk lamp and sat down. She pulled open one of the drawers and removed a file secured with a cream ribbon. She opened it and took one of the embossed sheets of paper. *Rebecca Sara Harburg*. Her name, nothing else, at the top of the page. She picked up the heavy, black Mont Blanc fountain pen she'd used all her life, quickly and expertly blotted the nib, and began to write.

It was an instruction to her accountant, the sort of old-fashioned instruction Lionel would have sent and of which he would approve.

Dear Gideon,

Kindly transfer the following sum: £25million (twenty-five million pounds sterling) from my trust account, R.S. Harburg, held at Banque Privée Edmund de Rothschild, Zurich, to my husband's personal account, held at Coutts & Co., London. If you have any queries, don't hesitate to contact me.

Thanks, as ever, yours, Rebecca.

She looked at it for a moment, then folded it neatly in three. She placed it in the envelope, sealed it, and addressed it to Gideon Levy at his offices on the Strand. It would take a week or so for the transfer to be effected but Gideon would have no queries. It was the sort of transaction he and his firm had been doing for the Harburg family for decades. In the seven years she and Julian had been married, he'd done several such transactions, though none approaching anything like 25 million pounds. But she wanted Julian to have the money. They seldom spoke about it; at the age of thirty, Rebecca had come into a 50-million-pound trust of her own. She'd given half of it to her husband, unbidden, unasked for. The rest would go into equal trusts for the children. She had more than enough. Surely he would be pleased?

111

TASH
Martha's Vineyard

She was alone in the vast, leather-upholstered back seat of the Cadillac, staring out the window as the car smoothly glided over pebbles and small potholes, neither registering so much as a bump in the armchair suspension. After a seven-hour flight from Heathrow to Boston, she ought to have been tired, particularly as the week before her departure had been filled with tension – mostly from Adam – but she wasn't. She was alert and ready, helped along no doubt by the excellent champagne on board British Airways and partially helped by the excitement of what lay ahead. Nothing and no one, not even Adam, could dampen her spirits. A fortnight's holiday in her new, outstandingly beautiful home with her two best friends, their husbands and children – her godchildren – and half a dozen helpers, nannies, au pairs, cooks and housekeepers. Everything, in other words, to ensure the holiday would be perfect, and one they would never forget. The spectacular row she and Adam had had before she left was the worst in their year-long marriage and it had brought out ugliness in them both that Tash had done her best to forget. She gave as good as he did: for the first time in her life, she'd been able to talk back, answer back, stamp her foot and throw something – an orange Le Creuset lid. Too heavy to sail far, it had fallen well short of its target, Adam's head. And when it was over, they'd stood there in the kitchen, both breathing deeply, both startled by the fury they'd unleashed in each other. They'd fought about money, of course, or rather, Tash's control over it. How could she have gone and spent 7 million dollars *without asking him?*

She looked out of the window at the clapboard houses flashing past. The chauffeur turned off the 195 Freeway and onto the Blue Star Memorial Highway, heading towards Falmouth and the ferry that would take her across. Down Sandwich Road, past the golf courses and parks with the open blue sweep of the sea on her right, down Palmer Street, Locust Street and then finally, along Woods Hole Road that led directly onto the jetty. There was a ferry waiting; she could see it from the window as they swept down the road towards the sea. She could have flown into Martha's Vineyard directly from Boston, but there was something about the slow but steady shift from the rough and ready density of the city to the calm and majesty of the wide-open sea that moved her beyond words, and she chose to drive it instead. Yes, she was rich. She could afford all this and more. But whoever said money didn't buy happiness was correct. Her determination *not* to wind up like Lyudmila had blinded her to a host of other unpalatable truths about money. Alongside the freedom it bestowed, it also brought jealousy and envy and a whole host of other unpleasant aspects that no one ever spoke about, much less admitted to.

'There she is, ma'am.' Her driver looked up and caught her eye briefly in the rear-view mirror. 'Ferry's waiting.'

'Thanks,' Tash murmured. It was Janine who'd organised the car service from Boston, in pretty much the same way she'd organised every-thing else – architects, interior designers, landscape architects, builders, plumbers . . . there was no end to her resourcefulness, or so it seemed. 'She's being *paid* to be resourceful,' Annick laughed when she told her. 'Handsomely, too, I'll bet.' Whatever the motivation, the results were impressive.

It was a windy, blustery day. The sea was a churning, frothy skin of dark blue. Little spits and licks of white foam crested every choppy wave and overhead, in a sky so blue it hurt the eyes, white cotton-puff clouds endlessly chased one another. She joined the other passengers on deck, wrapping her arms around herself in unconscious imitation of the others. It was a short, fifteen-minute journey from Falmouth to Vine-yard Haven, and from there, a short drive across the island to Pohoganot Road. Janine would meet her at the house; together they'd go over the checklist of the final alterations and renovations before her guests arrived. Her stomach gave a little lurch. In just under a week's time, everyone would be here. The bedrooms would all be ready, each a different colour and theme. Pinks, delicate shades of blue, the lightest sage, pale buttercup yellow – every room was designed with its occupant in mind. On the second floor, much as they had been at Brockhurst, were all the master bedrooms, culminating in the enormous suite at the end, overlooking the pool. A little thrill of excitement ran through her. The pool, in anthracite black tile, had been completely remodelled and re-laid. It came with its own pretty white shingle cabaña and paddling pool for the little ones and a wide-plank deck ran all the way around, providing plenty of shade and sunning areas. She thought back to the Harburgs' holiday home in Cavezzana for a second – who would've thought that she, Tash Bryce-Brudenell, would be able to offer the same hospitality, and on her own turf? She smiled to herself at the secret pleasure of it all.

112

A tweak here, a stray leaf out of place there, a gentle correction to a picture frame above a fireplace. 'I just can't *bear* it when things are out of place, can you?'

Tash followed the interior designer around like a well-trained puppy, stopping dutifully behind every vase, nodding every time the woman threw her a quick glance. She gazed around her. The dining room looked out over a vast green blanket of grass that sloped away towards the sea. Through the tall French windows, she could see the line of wavering grasses that sat atop the dunes, slowly sweeping back and forth like shy eyelashes. The sheer, palest grey curtains billowed gently in the breeze; the walls were a pale duck-egg blue, the furniture a mixture of contemporary American and European classics. Artworks had been chosen to complement the colour scheme and the mood. Everything had been thought of, right down to the size and colour of the white pebbles that covered the driveway. The house was ten, perhaps even fifteen times the size of her London flat, but both homes felt uniquely hers. Hers and Adam's, she corrected herself automatically. At the thought of Adam, her stomach gave another lurch. It was almost a full day since their argument and she hadn't heard from him since she'd slammed the front door behind her and jumped into her waiting cab. She glanced down at her BlackBerry; there were half a dozen messages and a long list of emails, but none from Adam. She slipped it back in her pocket. She wasn't about to let Adam ruin her day, especially not from thousands of miles away.

'And these? Don't you just love these?' The interior designer was busy stroking the silk backing on one of the dining-room chairs. 'Seventeenth century, Scottish. It took us an *age* to find them.'

And a small fortune, Tash thought to herself quickly. 'They're beautiful,' she murmured. 'Just beautiful.' A wave of impatience swept through her. Now that it was finally done, she wanted to be alone. She turned to Janine and the interior designer whose name she'd already forgotten. 'Look, if you don't mind,' she said briskly, 'I've had an awfully long day. It's nearly ten p.m. my time. I've got a couple of days before my guests arrive. I'm just going to settle in, get a feel for the place, that sort of thing. I'll be in touch again in the morning.'

Both Janine and the interior designer were far too accustomed to the ways of the rich and famous to make even the slightest protest. With murmurs of 'of course' and 'you must be *exhausted*', they quickly gathered their possessions, made the few last-minute adjustments to picture frames and bouquets of flowers and exited in a stream of air kisses and tyres on gravel. Her own driver, having emptied the car of her possessions, also took his leave.

For the first time in weeks – perhaps even months – she was truly alone. She stood in the doorway, looking out over the empty driveway and suddenly realised she was crying. Idiot, she chastised herself softly under her breath. You're supposed to laugh, not cry. Crack open a bottle. At the thought of champagne, she brightened. Janine would have left a bottle in the fridge. She slipped her hand in her pocket and took out her BlackBerry. More messages, of course, but none from Adam. She tightened her lips and put it away. Damn him. So bloody typical – here she was, more than three thousand miles away, standing in the doorway of their dream home and he was sulking and unreachable. The muffled roar of the sea came to her faintly, like a voice from another planet, another age. London seemed so terribly far away, and not just in the geographical sense. The gleaming water, glimpsed from over the top of the swaying grasses, was a blur of dazzling foamy surfaces. To her right, leading away from the white-pebbled driveway, was a small pathway that led directly to the beach. She roused herself. It was almost four in the afternoon; what better way to round off her first day on the island than at the water's edge, a glass of champagne in hand?

She turned and walked through the house to the vast, white-tiled kitchen with its stainless steel appliances and refrigerators the size of whole cupboards. Janine had not only provided two giant magnums of champagne – Krug, she noticed approvingly – but a small platter of olives, tiny artichoke hearts swimming in olive oil and a thick slice of crumbling Parmesan cheese. Her mouth watered suddenly; she'd eaten nothing since breakfast. She picked up the bottle by the neck, collected a flute from the cupboard above the cooker and, balancing everything rather precariously, opened the back door and followed the narrow path that led to Ripley Cove.

The protected strip of white sand that fringed the cove was the perfect place to sit in absolute silence, nothing between her and the faint, muffled roar of the sea that was held at bay by the narrow finger of land that separated the two beaches. She squatted down rather awkwardly – no one to see her – and settled herself into the sand that still held the day's warmth. She carefully put the plate of olives and cheese to one side, spreading her jacket out on the sand and kicking off her shoes. The sand was wonderfully warm and soft against her bare feet. She burrowed her toes in it, delighting in the simple, pleasurable sensation. She eased the champagne cork out of its constricting mouth and poured herself a glass, drinking greedily before the bubbles had subsided. The azure sea moved slowly, majestically, breaking in slow, drawn-out rolls against the sand, not fifty yards from where she sat. Beyond the finger-spit of sand, the tide was out, black rocks flattened and exposed by the retreating water. Behind her, providing shade and hiding the neighbouring property, was a small but thick clump of trees in the full throes of early summer. The air was quiet and still. Tash lay back against her jacket, now covered in fine blond sand. Warmth and light faintly penetrated the thin skin of her eyelids. She began to doze, lulled by the sound of the sea, the wind in the trees behind her, the snug warmth of an early summer afternoon.

When she woke and sat up to pour herself another glass, the suffused light created a distortion of distance so that the lone figure of a bird, picking its way delicately across the wet sand in front of her, seemed miles and miles off, far beyond her reach.

113

ANNICK

All the way from London, from the moment the chauffeur-driven car picked them up outside their South London flat and deposited them at the entrance to Terminal Five, to the moment they walked, dazedly, through the exit doors at Logan International Airport only to be met by another driver, in an almost identical car, Annick felt as though she were dreaming. That she'd wake up any second and find herself pressed, cheek-to-cheek, against a fellow commuter on her way into the office at 8.07 a.m. on a normal, routine Monday morning. That the sight and feel of Didier scrambling excitedly from her seat to Yves', entranced by the way the seats slid forward until they were flat and by the small television screens and the smiling ladies in smart blue uniforms who behaved as though his every wish was simply their command, wasn't real. They would be the first to arrive. Rebecca, Julian and the kids would land the following morning and the same service would be extended to them. Tash wouldn't hear of anyone paying for anything. 'Absolutely not. And that's the end of it. Not another word.' Annick and Yves smiled at each other. Whilst a first-class ticket to Boston and a ten-day holiday on Martha's Vineyard might well be within Rebecca's reach, it certainly wasn't within theirs. But Tash was adamant. 'It's my own birthday present – hell, make that Christmas-*and*-birthday present – and that's all there is to it.'

Boston, gritty and grey, slid past the tinted windows in an excited blur. Didier slept, woke up, gazed out of the window and then fell back asleep again. For the first time in a long while, Yves' hand rested slackly, warmly, against her thigh. Annick had never been to America before and was utterly absorbed by the unfolding scenery in front of them, at once familiar to her from countless televisions shows and films, and at once strange and remote. She couldn't get over the sheer size of the roads – lanes wide enough to fit three cars, not one! Yves laughed indulgently at her observations. Frances was right; within hours of leaving London behind, a new, almost forgotten warmth had re-emerged between them. The wellspring of hope that had been buried and dampened down for so long began to cautiously rise in her again.

There would be an easy explanation for it all. There had to be. Looking at him now, his gaze preoccupied by whatever lay beyond the car window, she felt a sudden surge of love, mingled with gratitude, towards Tash, Frances, Rebecca . . . everyone.

'Look!' Yves' grip on her leg tightened suddenly. 'There's the bridge.'

She followed his finger. The outline of the island swam into view, a dusky line of land that rose out of the shimmering blue. A small plane, far in the distance, rose slowly out of the greenery, dipping gently this way and that as it climbed beyond the tree line and began to head towards the puffy white cloud mass on the horizon. Behind it she could see an unbroken line of dunes, shifting sand held together by long grasses that, even from the road, brushed the horizon in long, slow caresses. A great flock of seagulls rose majestically out of the water, flying directly out of the wet light and into the sun. She gripped Yves' hand, covering it with her own.

'Have you *seen* some of these houses?' Yves pointed to the pretty New England clapboard houses that were beginning to emerge out of the trees.

Annick laughed again. 'You wait until you see Tash's place. I've only seen pictures, mind you. I can't wait. I still can't get over it, can you? I mean, all this is Tash's?'

Yves smiled and shook his head. 'I've long since stopped being surprised where you three are concerned. Nothing surprises me any-more.'

'What d'you mean?' Annick laughed in protest.

Yves shrugged. 'Nothing,' he murmured, turning to look out of the window again. 'Everything. You're hardly run-of-the-mill, Annick.'

There was a tenderness in his voice that had been absent from it for a long time, Annick realised. 'You neither,' she said quietly, hoping her voice was steady. She was filled with a sudden impatience, not just to reach Tash's magical house, but also to begin the long, painful and yet joyous process of repairing the rift that had opened up between them, years ago.

'You're here! At last!' Tash was standing in the doorway as the driver neatly brought the car to a halt a few yards from the white front door with its oversized brass knocker and giant brass numerals. 'I thought you'd never get here!' she cried, springing forward as soon as the car stopped.

Didier was out of the car first, tumbling out with all the uncoiled energy of a two-and-a-half-year-old who'd been kept cooped up for far longer than his constitution would allow. 'Didi! Careful! Don't run, *chérie* . . . walk!' The cry was lost on him as he tore past Tash and burst into the house.

'Go on,' Yves laughed, 'yes, go right inside. Don't wait to be asked.' They all laughed. He kissed Tash on both cheeks, holding her by the elbows and giving her a warm squeeze. 'What a journey . . . and what a house, Tash. It's stunning. Everything I'd imagined it to be . . . more, to be honest.'

Tash was beaming. The colour was up in her face. It still took Annick a while to get used to the new, carefully sculpted features that she only just recognised as belonging to her best friend. She smiled a lot these days. It was as if the new Tash was simply a prettier, sunnier, more winning version of the old one. She would never be the beauty Rebecca was, or have the same exotic sultriness that could still be seen in Annick's face by everyone except Annick herself, but Tash was no longer the butt of all fashion jokes. She now looked like who she was – an exceptionally successful, driven, capable woman in her late thirties who'd finally grown into her features. Or who'd *bought* herself a new set of features, others, less charitable than her friends, were wont to say. It mattered little; she now had the looks to match the kind of person she'd always been. Annick loved her unconditionally.

'You look beautiful,' she whispered in Tash's ear as they hugged. She meant it. She was dressed in the kind of androgynous white linen shift that suited her long, lean shape. With a high Mao collar, thick silver earrings and flat white Superga plimsolls, she looked every inch a Martha's Vineyard resident – tall, tanned, lithe, with minimal make-up and no fuss. Her one touch of glamour – deep red, almost black, short nails – lifted her whole appearance into the realm of the glamorous holidaymaker, welcoming friends and family to her sumptuous home. The image was a seductive one; Annick found herself being drawn warmly and voluptuously into it.

Standing just inside the doorway was a young girl who bent down to Didier's level and welcomed him very formally but with a wide grin. She was the au pair. Clea was Irish; her voice had a soft musical lilt to it that made you want to listen closely. 'Why don't you come with me, little man. I'll show you where we're all going to sleep. Upstairs, right at the top of the house with all your cousins. Let's see who gets there first.' Without so much as a backward glance, Didier went off with her, anxious to show this new friend that he wasn't about to be left behind. The three adults looked on indulgently.

'Come on,' Tash tucked an arm into Annick's, leading them both into one of what seemed to be several sitting rooms on the ground floor. The room was stunning: pale-grey walls, a highly polished wooden floor against which the light bounced and was reflected back up towards the ceiling. No expense had been spared. Tash's exquisite taste in all things was everywhere. There were plump white sofas for lounging in, beautifully upholstered chairs to admire, a fireplace in one corner, dramatic photographs on the walls and, best of all, an almost uninterrupted view of the gardens and the water beyond. Annick's mouth dropped open. On the polished mahogany coffee table were several silver trays bursting with food and drink. It was almost too much to take in. Even Yves seemed lost for words.

'When did you do all this?' he asked finally, looking around him in awe.

Tash couldn't possibly have looked happier. 'Oh, *I* didn't do it. A whole *team's* been working on this. D'you like it?' At that moment Annick wanted only to hug her. It was so typically Tash. Her pleasure lay not in the fact that the house was beautiful, but in the fact that she was sharing it with them. She was catapulted backwards in time to the moment she and her friend stood in Tash's suite at the hotel in Paris. Then, as now, her generosity had been overwhelming. She'd looked at Tash, too embarrassed to do anything other than stand by numbly, as Tash directed and organised the events that would lead her out of the desperate hole into which she'd fallen, and into a new life. It was a moment Annick would always remember. At that moment, she saw very clearly what Tash wanted from her. Not an appreciation of her achievements, or the wealth she'd managed to accumulate. Anyone could do *that*, Tash seemed to be saying. She wanted something more, some deeper understanding of what life might be all about – love, generosity, care. Tash *cared* about them, deeply, and asked almost nothing in return, just that Annick and Rebecca see it, be witness to the person she'd chosen to become. It had taken Annick a while to see it in her, and understand it, because it was strange to her. She'd always had people to care about, and who cared for her. Tash was different. She quickly turned her head. She didn't want them to see just how deeply Tash had touched her.

114

ANNICK/REBECCA/TASH

From the lofty heights of whatever arguments, fights and private irritations they'd brought with them to Martha's Vineyard, it took the three couples less than a day to climb down. Even Adam, arriving a day later than everyone else, succumbed. By Tuesday evening, six very different people had emerged, chrysalis-like, out of the tense guests who'd arrived. The children were splendidly and blissfully entertained by Clea and Adriana and spent almost every waking moment outside, either at the edge of the shimmering blue pool, or in the gardens leading to the beach. The beach itself was very firmly off-limits; after a solemn talking to by their godmother, each child understood that to venture down there where the adults sometimes went to sit and stare at the sea was a transgression worthy of an afternoon spent indoors – and none wanted that.

Rebecca and Annick were amused to see Didier bossily taking charge of the baby Maryam, possessively hugging her to him, waiting patiently beside her as she crawled, desperate to keep up. Here, in the wide openness of Tash's home, their personalities emerged stronger than before. David and Joshua quickly made friends with the neighbour's two grandchildren, Cliff and Dean, who, although a couple of years older, were quickly entranced by the four English children. From the minute they woke up until they were put to sleep after supper, they were inseparable. For Rebecca and Annick it was a return to pre-children days, to the long evenings of early summer and university days, sitting on patios and in bars with a glass of chilled white wine and the prospect of an evening spent doing nothing but talking. Within hours of their arrival, it was clear that a different sort of atmosphere had enveloped them. Under Tash's generous, benevolent gaze, they found themselves slipping under her gentle spell.

'Did you ever think this would happen?' Annick asked Tash on their third evening. The women were sitting on the veranda facing the beach, glasses of wine in hand. The men had all gone off that afternoon to play a round of golf at the course just down the road and the children were upstairs being bathed, fed, soothed to sleep. Amid roars of delight, Cliff and Dean had been asked to sleep over. Poor Betty Lowenstein had hardly seen her grandsons but she'd reluctantly agreed. From upstairs came the occasional shriek of laughter.

Tash took a sip, considered the question for a moment and then smiled. 'By "this", I take it you mean the house?'

Annick shook her head at first, then nodded. 'Well, yes, the house, of course, but all the rest. Your business, Adam . . . all of it.'

'Not exactly. I mean, I always knew I would do *some*thing – I don't mean be successful – but I knew there wasn't going to be anything to fall back on after university.'

'Not like us,' Rebecca mused. 'Well, not like *me*, at any rate.'

'Don't say that,' Tash said quickly. 'Just because you don't work doesn't mean you haven't done anything.'

Rebecca looked at her hands. It was that time of the evening when the shadows had all but disappeared but the outdoor lights weren't yet strong enough to assume the mantle of night. The low-lying clouds that had been hovering all day at the point where the horizon met the sea had all but disappeared and a hard blue sky, now slipping slowly towards night, was busy turning pink and orange at its edges. The housekeeper had thoughtfully placed a few citronella hurricane lamps on the steps just before the grass began; every now and then a whiff of lemon-scented wind touched their noses and tongues. She lit a cigarette and put her feet up on the cushion-covered ottoman. 'Yes, I suppose I *have* done something,' she said carefully, quietly.

'Of course you have,' Tash said automatically, reaching forward to top up their glasses.

Rebecca put out a hand to cover hers. 'No, not yet. I don't want to get drunk tonight. I overdid it last night. This morning was awful.'

'Come on, you're on holiday.'

'I know, I know. But honestly, the hangovers aren't worth it,' Rebecca laughed a little shakily. 'How come you never seem to have one?'

Tash grinned and lifted her full glass to her lips. 'I've clearly had more practice. Anyhow, the boys won't be back for hours. I know Adam. He'll take them to the clubhouse, they'll watch whatever boring match is on the box, have a few more brandies . . . it'll be the wee hours of the morning before they come home, I promise you.'

'We haven't had a night like this in ages,' Annick said suddenly. 'Just the three of us . . . no kids, no husbands.'

'No one to scold, no one to soothe, no arguments to settle. Bliss.' Rebecca smiled, a wistful, almost sad smile. 'Sometimes I think I've got four children instead of three.'

'What about you two?' Annick asked Tash.

'What about us?'

'Don't you want any?'

'Any what?'

'Children, you idiot. Or is that rude of me?'

Tash shook her head. 'No, course not. It . . . it just hasn't happened. I'm not sure I'm that bothered, to be honest. Besides, I've got your four. It's hard work being a godmother, you know.' She grinned at them and lifted her glass again.

Annick was about to say something but Rebecca quickly flashed her a warning glance. There was something slightly too determinedly cheerful about Tash's response. 'They adore you,' Rebecca said, meaning it. 'And not just because of this,' she added, waving a hand to bring in their surroundings. 'Though I'd have given anything to have a godmother with a house like this,' she added impishly.

'As if you don't,' Annick laughed.

'I don't!'

'You've got that amazing place in Italy, can't remember its name now. D'you remember that summer we all went out there? Just after our A-levels?'

Annick nodded. 'I thought I'd died and gone to heaven. It was so beautiful. Your mother was amazing. So welcoming.'

'Bit like me, then?' Tash grinned.

'Exactly.'

'Funny, everything seemed so simple back then, didn't it?' Rebecca was suddenly gripped with anxiety again.

'Everything *was* simple. We were . . . how old? Eighteen? Nineteen? Everything's simple at that age.'

Annick shook her head. 'No, things just seem that way from here, looking back. I'm happy just to be here, now, in this moment, y'know? No matter what's happened or what's gone on before.'

A long mass of creamy white cloud turned suddenly mauve, like a far-off landmass, hovering above the horizon. Rebecca slowly rubbed her toe along the arch of her other bare foot. 'That's the thing, isn't it? So many things have happened. You can't go back to that state of . . . of being. Not anymore.' The unrest that had been churning within her for days, weeks, months, rose to the surface. She felt as she often did early in the mornings, when she woke before she'd completely moved out of her dream world into the present one, when time had no clear dimension – have I been awake for a minute or an hour? – and when it was possible, but only just, to imagine that the one terrible thought that dominated her waking moments might belong, after all, not to the present, but to her dream. *Maryam is not my husband's child.* It seemed such a dreadful abomination of everything she, and everyone around her, held dear. *Maryam is not my husband's child.* How would she ever explain it. To anyone?

'Rebecca? Are you all right?' Tash's eyes were on her.

She nodded quickly and stood up. 'I . . . I'll be back in a moment,' she stammered. Her hair fell forwards, shrouding her face. She hurried indoors, grateful for the momentary respite it provided. A searing hot flush of emotion had erupted over her entire body – shame, mixed with the most powerful desire to see Tariq again that she'd ever felt. She had to get away from the patio with its glasses of chilled Chardonnay and trays of biscuits and cheese, none of which she could force down her throat. She had to hear his voice again, if only for a second . . . if only for the bizarre satisfaction of hearing it on his answering phone. She slipped upstairs to the bedroom she shared with her husband, shut the door behind her and leaned against it, her face damp and flushed with that terrible mixture of conflicting emotions that had become her state of mind. She eyed the phone on the bedside table. One call. One more call. To tell him where she was, where Maryam was . . . and how much she loved him still.

'D'you think she's all right?' Annick asked Tash carefully, watching as Rebecca practically ran from the patio.

Tash shrugged. 'Are any of us?' she asked after a moment.

'What's got into everyone? A few minutes ago, everything was fine,' Annick said, surprised.

Tash reached for the bottle. She was drinking rather a lot, Annick noticed. 'Life,' she said with a sigh. 'It turns out to be way more complicated than you think.'

'Is everything okay with you . . . and Adam?' Annick asked delicately.

Tash nodded. 'I suppose so. I don't know. I don't have anything to compare it to, that's the problem. What about you two? Did you ever get to the bottom of that whole mystery about his name?'

Annick felt a hot wave of embarrassment travel up through her chest and neck. She hated lying to anyone, most of all Tash. 'Yeah,' she said, as nonchalantly as she could. 'It was nothing. Just a . . . a misunderstanding.'

'I told you it was nothing to worry about,' Tash said, draining her glass. 'Silly thing. All that fuss. You're such a worrier, Annie. I'd say you've done better out of this than any of us.'

'What d'you mean?'

Tash stood up suddenly. She yawned widely, stretching her arms above her head. 'Yves is a lovely man. I can't imagine him doing anything to hurt you or Didi. Even unconsciously. I wish I could—' She stopped abruptly, her expression clouding over. 'Don't mind me,' she said quickly. 'I've had too much to drink.'

'You're drinking rather a lot,' Annick began hesitantly.

'Are you keeping tabs on me as well?' Tash asked.

'No, no . . . of course not,' Annick hastened to assure her but it was too late. Tash had already turned away. She watched her walk across the polished, gleaming expanse of floorboards, her back very straight but her balance betrayed her once or twice.

The door at the far end of the living room closed behind her and Annick was alone. Rebecca hadn't come back downstairs. Everything was quiet. She ran her hand slowly around the sharp rim of her wine glass. Was Tash right, she wondered? Was there really nothing to worry about and was it, as she'd been roused to say, all a silly misunderstanding? She stroked the glass back and forth. They were leaving for New York on Friday night – her, Yves, Julian and Rebecca. Tash had insisted. The couples ought to have at least a weekend together alone. Adam and Julian had some business to attend to in the city and she would spend the weekend with her godchildren, alone. It was the least they could do, she'd said laughingly, making it sound as though they were doing her a favour by leaving the children with her, not the other way round. Having brought them all this way out, surely their parents wouldn't begrudge her a couple of days on her own with them? And she'd have plenty of help, she pointed out. Clea, Adriana and a housekeeper at the very least. Four adults to look after four children. What could possibly go wrong?

115

ANNICK
Manhattan

The lobby of the Crosby Street Hotel in SoHo was unlike any hotel lobby she'd ever set foot in. From the giant delicate white wire sculpture of a human head standing in front of the reception desk to the recycled plastic dogs seated docilely at the foot of a grey velvet sofa with beautiful thick purple and yellow cushions that complemented the wild streaks of colour in the paintings surrounding them, this was a hotel with a difference. It was Tash, of course, who'd recommended it. Julian and Rebecca were staying further uptown, in the sort of old-world elegance that Julian favoured but *this* . . . Annick looked around her, pinching herself hard every few moments to make sure it was all true, all real and that she was experiencing it, just as her eyes seemed to be telling her.

They were shown into the bar area as their bags were taken upstairs – a riot of colourful, striped banquettes, polished silver tables and the most exquisite collection of African-inspired artworks and sculptures on the walls. Annick gasped as they walked in and clutched Yves' arm in delight. 'Oh, look!' she squealed, pointing to a large carved mask behind the bar. 'They're like the ones at home,' she said excitedly.

'Home?' He raised a quizzical eyebrow. 'We don't have one of those over the fireplace, if I remember rightly.'

She smiled. 'You know what I mean. In Togo.'

'Ah. In Togo. You've never called it "home" before,' he noted amusedly.

'Well, it is, isn't it?'

They looked at each other, faces less a collection of well-known features than a concentration of emotion that both tried to suppress. The knowledge of who they both were came up between them. She could see it in his eyes. He put out a hand; it came to rest on her forearm. She looked at it, and then back up at him, and although there was the wonderful reassurance of his sameness and familiarity, there was something profoundly different in the air between them. It was as if, in turning to look at the artwork over the bar together, a private, deeply intimate space had opened up in which whatever previously couldn't be said, now was. 'Let's go,' he said quietly, giving her arm a little shake. 'Upstairs.'

She followed him mutely, aware of the quickening of her heartbeat as the sleeping giant of desire woke in her. It had been months since she'd felt such desire. They almost ran into the elevator, ignoring the amused but tolerant glances of the hotel staff. Theirs wasn't the illicit passion of the Mr-and-Mrs-Smith variety for which the hotel was a suitably exotic and erotic backdrop. But the staff were not to know and probably couldn't have cared less. By the time the lift doors opened on the fifth floor and Yves had impatiently fumbled the key-card out of his pocket, Annick was beyond thinking – or caring – what others thought.

The room was shrouded in darkness by the time either of them was seeing again. Yves' hand lay across her stomach; every now and then, his fingers moved lightly across her skin, touching her with infinite tenderness. It had been months since they'd made love in the middle of the day like this – and years since it had taken place in a hotel. He was both rough and gentle with her, sensing the unspoken question that had been gnawing at her was about to be brought into the open, and with it, a kind of healing that they'd never dared express.

'I thought of sweet things, just now,' she whispered, her own hand going up to touch the soft tight curls that began at his forehead. 'Condensed milk. D'you remember it?'

He nodded. His eyes were still tightly closed. 'From the marketplace at Asigamé,' he murmured.

She opened her eyes. They were talking, now. 'Why didn't you tell me?' she asked, rolling over and propping herself up on one arm to look at him. 'I found the letter, you know. The one where you tried to change your name.'

He took in a deep breath. 'You once said to me, "It's complicated, my life." Well, so's mine.'

'But I told you *everything* about me.'

'I already knew. I already knew who you were before we even spoke.'

She was aware of a faint hackle of fear settling itself around the back of her neck. 'So is that why you spoke to me?'

He nodded. 'Sort of. In the beginning. The guy I worked for – Big Jacques – you remember him? He was after something . . . some information.'

'About my father?'

'About his money.' He was awake now, his whole body slipping into another kind of alertness. As if to compensate for the distance his words were about to put between them, he reached out and drew her down beside him.

'Wh-what did he do to him?' Annick whispered, her teeth already beginning to chatter. 'My father, I mean. What did he do to your father?'

There was a long, carefully held silence. Yves took a long time choosing his words. 'I think,' he said, turning round to face her, cupping her face in his hands, 'that you already know.'

116

REBECCA
Upper East Side, New York

The Hotel Plaza Athenée on East 64th Street was exactly the sort of hotel her father would have stayed at, Rebecca thought to herself as she and Julian were ushered through the revolving doors. The thought filled her inexplicably with dread. Julian didn't seem to notice. He strode on ahead; his mind already on the evening's meeting, no doubt. It was with the awful Miranda Grayling and some associates of hers that she'd dragged over from the Middle East, another round of sheikhs and princelings whose names Rebecca couldn't even pronounce, let alone remember. She wished, not for the first time, that she'd gone with Annick and Yves. In the car driving to the small airport at Martha's Vineyard, Annick pulled out her phone to show her the pictures of the little boutique hotel that Tash had recommended to Yves and she'd had to clamp down firmly on her tongue to stop herself from blurting out to Julian, 'But why aren't *we* staying there?' It wasn't the sort of place Julian liked.

This was. She looked around her in dismay. Julian was already a few paces ahead of her, arguing with the receptionist about the size of the room they'd been given. He wanted a suite, overlooking the park. 'We're completely full, sir,' the receptionist was saying. 'I'm terribly sorry. Suite 603's taken.'

'I don't care. I *always* stay in 603.'

'I'll see what I can do, sir, but I'm afraid I can't exactly throw another guest out.'

'Julian, it doesn't matter. We're only here for a couple of nights,' Rebecca whispered, coming up beside him. She hated it when he made a fuss.

'I don't care if we're only here for the afternoon. D'you know how much we're paying?'

'Oh, *Julian*.' Rebecca moved off, irritated. She stood to one side and pulled out her phone. She glanced at the screen – still nothing from Tariq. No message, no missed call . . . nothing. Nothing but silence. She swallowed, trying desperately to keep her face as neutral as she could. She'd left another miserable message on his answering service the night before, to no avail.

'Right, that's sorted them out. Come on. We've got the suite.' Julian walked briskly towards her.

Rebecca didn't bother asking how. Julian invariably got what he wanted. She picked up her bag and followed him to the lift. 'What time's dinner?' she asked as they sped upwards to the thirtieth floor.

'Seven thirty. Wear something nice, will you? Miranda's bringing the sheikh and a couple of his advisors.'

'Thrilling.' Rebecca couldn't keep the sarcasm from her voice.

'Look, I know it's hardly your idea of fun, darling, but it's important,' Julian said earnestly. 'If we pull this deal off, Tash won't be the only one with a house in the Hamptons.'

'We could buy one now, if that's what you want,' Rebecca said, surprised.

'I don't. I'm just saying.'

Rebecca shook her head at him as the lift doors opened and they followed the bellhop out. She would never understand him. Julian wanted to win, that was all. For him, the competition was the thing, the prize. Nothing to do with what he really wanted. She wondered what he *did* want, as they were ushered into the over-done, over-decorated and overly stuffy suite. She knew what she wanted . . . and it wasn't him. 'I'll . . . I'll just have a shower first,' she said, escaping into the bathroom. 'And then I'll phone the children.'

'The children'll be fine, Rebecca. Christ, Tash has got an army looking after them. Relax. Come here.' He put out a hand absently to grab hold of her. She knew exactly what he was after. She dodged it and closed the bathroom door behind her. She leaned back against it, overcome with both sadness and guilt. Back at Tash's, things were easier between them. The kids were a distraction, as were the others . . . here, in the hotel room, with just the two of them, the feeling of wanting to be anywhere else but there, with Julian, intensified. It was only a matter of time before he saw through her thin veil of polite interest and asked her outright what was wrong. She wasn't sure she'd be able to keep the truth from him, from anyone. The longing to say Tariq's name out loud was growing in her . . . soon, like a dam whose flow couldn't be controlled, it would spill out, flooding her and everything she held dear, including, and most especially, *him*.

'Will you kiss them for me?' she spoke softly into the telephone, shielding her face from Julian. 'Especially Maryam. She likes a bit of a cuddle before she goes to sleep. I know, I know—'

'Rebecca?' Julian appeared in the doorway. His voice carried with it an almost comic arch and loop of a lament. 'You're not ready yet?'

She covered the mouthpiece with her hand. 'Just give me a moment. I'm just saying "goodnight" to the kids.'

'It's seven fifteen!' Blood suffused his brow; he was fiddling with his cufflinks. 'We're meeting them in ten minutes!'

'I'll be right there,' Rebecca hissed. She turned back to Tash. 'And will you see that Josh goes to the loo before he goes to bed? He's . . . yes, I know Clea's there, but . . . oh, all right. Tell them I love them. We'll see you on Monday. Monday afternoon – around three, I think. Yes, yes . . . he's fine. We're just going down to dinner now and—'

'Rebecca! We're late!'

'I'd better go,' she whispered hastily into the phone. 'I'll phone you tomorrow, see how they're doing, and—'

'Rebecca!' It was less of a plea and more of a roar.

She hung up the phone quickly and turned to him. 'What's the panic? I'm sure bloody Miranda can entertain them for a few minutes. Isn't that her speciality? Entertainment?' She was gratified to see Julian's eyes drop, as though he couldn't quite meet her gaze. Not for the first time the thought flitted across her mind . . . what if Julian and Miranda . . . ? She turned the thought over in her mind but found she didn't even care.

Dinner was an interminable affair, made bearable only by the distraction of listening to the sheikh and his associates speak Arabic, reminding her acutely of Tariq. If either Julian or Miranda noticed her reticence, neither made any comment. Julian seemed happy enough for her to sit calmly beside him, eating and drinking automatically, smiling prettily when the odd remark or question was addressed to her, letting her eyes and attention slip when it was not. She sipped her wine, her mind elsewhere. Once Julian looked up and caught her eye; she suddenly saw herself reflected in his gaze and brought up a hand to touch her forehead self-consciously, where a lock of hair had come loose. That too only served to remind her of Tariq and she had to turn her face away once again in case anyone present were to catch her out. How much longer could it all go on?

117

TASH
Martha's Vineyard

To say that her godchildren were exhausting was both an under-statement and a lie. The truth was that, aside from the odd ruffle of hair or comment made in passing, she had little to do with them. Clea and Adriana, whose job and vocation it seemed to be, did most of what Tash would have described as the 'looking after'. There were tears as their parents departed, mostly from Maryam, who was too little to understand the nature of the temporary separation. Didi behaved as though his parents' disappearance were normal. For him, she mused, it probably was. Both Yves and Annick went to work every morning and in the evenings, they reappeared. Their departure that morning was nothing unusual. Still, Clea and Adriana knew just what to do. After the first twenty minutes of synchronised howling, during which Tash retreated to the study on the first floor with a large glass of wine, every-thing settled into a contented hum of activities, shouts, and – when their best friends Cliff and Dean finally made an appearance – delighted shrieks and gurgles of laughter.

She stood at the study window, glass in hand, looking down on the goings-on poolside below. Would the four of them grow up to be as close as she, Annick and Rebecca? What lay in store for them? And would she and Adam ever have a child to add to the pool of potential best friends? In those odd moments of pensiveness, she saw the three of them as points of a triangle, exactly like their tattoos. She touched hers absently. Annick and Rebecca had gone ahead and made connections of their own while she remained stubbornly alone. There was Adam, of course, but she was slowly being made aware that there was nothing about Adam that felt quite as solid and dependable as the line that connected her to Rebecca and Annick. There were times when Adam felt like an interloper, a latecomer, a distraction from the real business of life. She sometimes felt herself stretching away from everyone else to some distant point over an unseen horizon, alone, always alone.

She took a mouthful of wine, letting it slide to the back of her throat before swallowing. It was only eleven in the morning – too early to be having a glass of white wine – but the rest of the day stretched out before her, half-pleasurably, half-fearfully. After weeks of frantic preparation and the excitement of arrivals, the house seemed oddly empty. All her previous visits had been to a building site, not a home. Now, with everything in place, all the beautiful furniture and artworks, pieces that ought to make the place properly hers, it was time to think of it as a home. *Her* home. Hers and Adam's, she corrected herself for the umpteenth time. '*Us*, ours . . . not mine,' she whispered to herself under her breath. 'Us. *Us.*' She looked at her watch; only eleven fifteen. She would make a few phone calls, check on the office in London, call her mother . . . and then what? It had been so long since she'd found herself alone in the middle of the day with nothing particular to do. What did people do on holiday? she wondered. A walk. A walk along the beach. Perhaps with the children? She would leave Maryam with the girls and take the boys. She brightened at the thought.

Three bobbing shoulders and sunhats; that was all she could see of them as they surged ahead, eager as a pack of dogs, to be free of the constraints of playroom and pool. Something of their animal sense of the wide-open spaces of the beach came back to her like a half-forgotten, half-imagined scent. Family holidays by the seaside had never formed part of her own childhood repertoire of memories, but she must have inhaled something of Rebecca's and Annick's, like the shared cigarette smoke of their teenage years.

There were few people about on the beach, even at midday. Her heels made a soft thudding sound that reverberated through her head. There was a young man standing ankle-deep in the water, inexpertly casting a line back and forwards, a graceful, silver arc of light that hit the water emptily, again and again. The boys ran down the grassy slope of the dune onto the wet sand to talk to him; Didi, singled out by his dark skin, no doubt, was given the dubious present of a small fish. He held it out in the palm of his hand, proudly, as though he'd caught it himself. The children were remarkably easy to supervise; they moved good-naturedly as one. A couple lay prostrate, sunbathing, a few hundred yards further along the beach. As the little troop passed, the man lifted his head, shielding his eyes from the sun and Tash was aware of her gait changing, the way a woman walks when she is being watched by a man. For a single, brief moment, she saw herself as someone else might: the harried, peripherally preoccupied look of a woman out with her children. She smiled to herself as they passed. It wasn't a role she routinely imagined for herself.

Clea had packed a small basket of snacks and drinks for them, which she shouldered on one arm. When she judged it time to eat, she called to the boys and they dutifully trotted over. She squatted down in the dry, fine sand as the boys fought amiably over the cookies and treats, sucking ferociously at their cartons of juice but somehow remembering to hand back the empty packets to her for tidying away. Whatever else Rebecca complained about, her boys had impeccable manners. They looked at her impatiently; they wanted to be off again in their own world of make-believe soldiers or cowboys, or whatever else little boys dreamed of. She waved them off, content to sit for the moment in the warmth of the sand, smoking, one cautious eye on them, the other on the far-off horizon and the glittering skin of the sea.

The simple, single narrative of the beach began to occupy her. A couple of older kids, some way up the beach, were teaching a younger child how to paddle. At the same point, over and over again, the rubber canoe overturned and the story began again. The fisherman they'd seen earlier cast his line, then moved up a few yards and cast it again. The sea gave off a strange light that blunted the sun, creating a different sense of distance. The sunbathing couple could have been a couple of hundred yards away, or a mile . . . she couldn't tell. She leaned back into the scooped-out hollow of sand made by the basket and let her shoulders fall into it. The warm sand spread its heat pleasurably across her neck and shoulders. She hitched up her white sundress to mid-thigh, enjoying the unfamiliar sensation of the sun's heat on her legs. She closed her eyes, enjoying the warm moment of superb idleness. She'd brought a book with her but she was aware of the need to keep a watchful eye on the children and couldn't switch herself off long enough to read. It was strangely restful; lying in the warm sand with nothing to occupy her other than making sure the children were still in sight.

She woke with a start. The silence around her had intensified into something that was louder than sound. For a split second, she lost her sense of where she was. The distant roar of the sea hummed and shimmered all round her. The children. Where were the children? The thought clutched at her in terror. She scrambled to her feet. How long had she been asleep? She looked wildly one way and then the next . . . there was no one. She opened her mouth to shout their names but fear blocked her throat. She stumbled up the rough, tussocky incline of the dune behind her. Tiny dragonflies hovered, stopped on the air as she approached, then darted away again, blazing like matches where the sun caught their glassy wings. She stumbled forward, aware only of the blood drumming in her veins. Then she saw them – clustered around something, heads tightly bowed together – and the relief was so great she fell to her knees.

Back at the house, she found herself shrinking away from the excited chatter as the children fought with one another to show Clea and Adriana what they'd found, shout excitedly about what they'd seen. 'There was a man with a fishing rod – he gave Didi one of his fish . . . see?'

'And then we found this! Look!'

'It's *mine*, not yours, Josh!'

'But I saw it first!'

'No you didn't! You just picked it up, that's all!'

She turned away from the cacophony and yanked open the fridge door, avoiding Clea's concerned glance. She pulled out a bottle of white wine and shut the door with her knee.

'Will you have some lunch, Mrs B?' Clea asked. 'I can bring it up on a tray.'

'No, no . . . I'm fine.' She held up the bottle. 'This'll do me. I'm just going up to my room. Give me a shout if an emergency occurs.'

'Will do. All under control, Mrs B, don't you worry.'

Tash escaped before anything further could be said. The children didn't even notice her going; they were absorbed in the all-important task of determining what belonged to whom, who'd seen it first, whose turn it was to tell Clea what they'd seen. She closed the door behind her and fairly galloped up the stairs.

It hadn't gone too badly, she thought to herself as she switched on the television, poured herself a glass and lay back against the enormous white linen pillows. She'd spent four hours – four! – on the beach alone

449

with her godchildren and, aside from that one dreadful moment at the end, it had all gone off smoothly. She wasn't *quite* as bad at the whole looking-after-children thing as she'd feared.

118

TASH

She woke very early the following morning, soft, pale light filtering in through the curtains at the far end of the bedroom. Something had pulled her from sleep; she lay still for a moment, collecting her scattered, dream-like thoughts. A sound? A voice? Whatever it was, it had disappeared. There was nothing save the slow, even ticking of an unfamiliar clock on the dressing table and the even more unfamiliar sounds of birds as they swooped from the clump of trees bordering the gardens to the pool and back. The windows were open and the damp, sweet scent of flowers she didn't recognise drifted in. She yawned and stretched luxuriously; another day of holiday, her last day on her own before Rebecca and Annick came back and the house filled up once more. Adam was due back first, then Rebecca and Julian and finally, in the late afternoon, Annick and Yves. She'd gone over all the arrangements for flights and pick-ups half a dozen times with Janine, who had given over the use of her personal assistant almost entirely to Tash. No glitches, no hitches. A holiday they would never forget, remember? She grinned to herself. So far, so good. Even the little blip yesterday afternoon on the beach hadn't ruined things.

She got up, stretching her arms as far above her head as they could go. She pulled back the curtains and looked down at the trembling blue pool. A cool, early-morning breeze had sprung up, lightly stroking the surface of the water. It was too cold to swim at that hour but suddenly, the thought of a drink down there at the water's edge, before the rest of the house awoke, appealed to her. She belted her dressing gown, pulled out a pair of Birkenstocks from the vast cupboard and opened the door. The house was completely still and quiet; she ought to just peep in on the children whilst they were still asleep. She crept up the one short flight of stairs and paused, then pushed open the door as quietly as she could. The room was full of their breathing: David and Joshua slept spread-eagled in the centre of their beds; Didi was laid out straight with his toes pointing to the ceiling and the sheet tucked firmly under his chin. In a slightly smaller cot beside the window, Maryam lay on her side, one soft, lightly tanned arm dangling from the bed. The long, slow outpourings of their breath seemed to come together as one. She stood in the doorway, tracking the sound to each individual child so that she held each one in her mind's eye. Joshua muttered something in his sleep, his sleepy voice puncturing the silence, but no one stirred. She stood for a further minute or two, then turned and carefully made her way downstairs.

She walked into the kitchen and stood for a moment, eyeing the fridge. A scene suddenly flashed in front of her eyes before she could stop it – something coming up to her from the depths of her own memory. She was in the kitchen in the tiny flat in Kensington. She'd wandered in, rubbing the sleep from her eyes. She was six. Lyudmila was standing in front of the fridge in much the same way Tash now was, her hand reaching for a bottle when Tash's voice interrupted her. 'Mama?' Lyudmila spun round, almost dropping the bottle in her hand. She grabbed it by the neck. For a second, mother and daughter stared at each other. Tash could still remember the hairs standing up on the back of her neck as she surveyed the scene, realising there was something wrong with it. 'I'm thirsty,' Tash remembered saying. 'I want a drink.'

'In a minute,' Lyudmila said. *'Mama zanyat*. Mummy's busy.'

But she wasn't. She was just standing there, gripping the bottle of whatever it was, a strange look of determined anticipation on her face. It was a look Tash hadn't seen before and it was connected in some awful, terrible way to the bottle Lyudmila held tightly in her hand. Even as she was part of it, she knew there was something strange, even horrible about the picture they formed, drunk mother and six-year-old daughter, both looking for a drink but of a different kind.

The image came back to her now. She was only thankful there was no six-year-old present to see it the way she had back then. She yanked open the fridge door and grasped the first bottle that came to hand. Stolichnaya. Vodka. It would do. And a carton of orange juice. She poured herself a generous measure into a glass, splashed in enough orange juice to render its appearance harmless and unlocked the back door. Something moved somewhere behind the pool house – a shadow of something that caught her eye. She stood, frowning into the distance. A bird flew out from the darkened mass of trees but there was nothing, no sound, no movement . . . nothing. She took a sip of her drink; it was bright and deliciously sharp. She took another, waiting for the momentary warming glow as the vodka hit her empty stomach. Ahh, that was better. She looked around at the debris of yesterday's games still lying scattered around the decking: bicycles, three-wheelers, rubber toys of all shapes and sizes – she'd sent Clea into Edgartown to buy whatever she thought the children might need or like; the rest had been helpfully delivered by the very nice man from FedEx who'd been bringing parcels to the house for weeks prior to everyone's arrival.

She slipped out of her Birkenstocks and squatted down by the side of the pool, trailing her fingers to test the temperature. It was warm enough to swim after all, despite the early-morning chill. She sat down properly, letting her toes, then her feet, dangle in the water. She took another sip of her drink. Nothing like a vodka and orange juice to get the day started, she thought to herself with a smile. Suddenly a flock of birds burst out of the woods, as though they'd been startled. She looked up again with a frown. Something was out there. She stood up, dripping water onto the decking and walked towards the cabaña. Her heart was beating fast. The sun had come up properly now, and a long line of fiery light danced on the surface of the water, throwing watery shapes up against the cool white of the cabaña walls. She stood there for a moment; the only sound in her ears the steady thud of her own heart and the drumming thrum of her blood in her ears. Cicadas, crickets, the usual chorus of wooded wildlife . . . nothing out of the ordinary. No snap of twigs or the sound of human voices . . . nothing. She gave a little embarrassed laugh and drained the rest of her drink. She turned and walked quickly back into the house, arms wrapped around her although it wasn't cold. She ought to get a dog, she thought to herself, for those weeks when she might come to Martha's Vineyard alone. She brightened at the thought. Yes, one of those lovely sandy-haired, floppy-eared dogs that she could take for long walks on the beach and cuddle up to at night. She shook her head quickly. Why did she assume she'd be here on her own?

Clea was already up and about in the kitchen when she walked in. 'Morning, Mrs B,' she called out brightly, already organising the day's meals. She had the children's breakfasts all lined up – different coloured bowls, boxes of cereals, bright plastic tumblers, and cartoon-character plates. Where had all this stuff come from? Tash wondered. 'Coffee?'

'Oh, no thanks, Clea. I'm fine . . . just had some orange juice,' she stammered. Tash slipped onto one of the high bar stools to watch Clea's breakfast preparations. There was something soothing about watching her deft, neat movements. She moved briskly from fridge to counter top and back again, opening a jam jar, quickly scooping out its contents into a pretty white bowl, creamy yellow pats of butter placed just so in a glass dish, a small bowl of golden honey. In five minutes, everything was ready.

'Adriana'll get the kids up. They'll be down in a minute,' she said, looking up to see Tash watching her. 'What are your plans for the day, Mrs B?'

Tash pulled a face. 'Oh, I don't know. Got some admin to take care of. Got to make a few calls to London . . . that sort of thing.'

'It's a Sunday!' Clea laughed. 'Don't you ever take a day off?'

Tash made a surprised face. 'Sunday? So it is. The others'll be back tomorrow.'

'You work too hard, Mrs B. You ought to have a day off. Do nothing.'

'I'm not terribly good at doing nothing,' Tash smiled. She looked around the kitchen. 'But what about you? Don't you find all this a bit . . . much?'

Clea laughed. 'I've got five little brothers, Mrs B. This lot are angels compared to them. No, I'm grand. It's great having Adriana here, though. We'll have a day off in Edgartown when you're all gone. Probably spend all our wages, too,' she giggled.

'How old are you, Clea?'

'Twenty-one, Mrs B. This is my first proper job, you know.'

'You're very good at it. What d'you want to do when you go back? To Ireland, I mean?'

'Oh, I won't be going back. My cousin's in London. I'm going to stay with her for a bit . . . see what the big city has to offer.'

'Well, if you're ever in need of a job, even a part-time one, let me know,' Tash said, getting off the stool. 'And it doesn't have to be looking after children either. I haven't got any.'

'Did you not want any? If that's not too personal,' Clea asked curiously.

Tash smiled. 'No. Just never happened.' She pursed her lips with a small gesture of regret. Funny how everyone talked about it in the past tense, as though the possibility was over. 'Anyhow, I've got four god-children. That's enough to be going on with.' She stopped suddenly. 'Look, I've got an idea. Why don't you and Adriana go into Edgartown for the afternoon? *I'll* look after the kids. Go and see a film or something. You'll have a pretty full week next week . . . why not?'

Clea hesitated. 'Are you sure?'

'Course I'm sure. I'll be fine with them for a few hours. It was fun yesterday,' she added, not altogether truthfully.

'Really?' Clea looked at her dubiously.

Tash nodded firmly. 'If you get them breakfast, get them dressed and so on, I'll get the driver to run you down to town around eleven thirty. How does that sound?'

'Thanks, Mrs B . . . you're sure you won't need us? I could go on Sunday—'

'I'm sure,' Tash said firmly. 'They're my godchildren. I've got to get to know them better. You finish up here and I'll head off and have a bath. I'll get the driver to pick you up in an hour or so.'

'Well, just if you're sure?' Clea was still hesitant.

'I'm sure.'

Tash was still smiling to herself as she climbed the stairs to her room.

The outing along the beach must have accustomed the children to the absurd idea that their godmother would be looking after them for at least part of the day: no one batted an eyelid. Maryam was too young to understand, of course; she lay back in her swing chair, gurgling happily at her brothers as Clea and Adriana made their excited preparations for an afternoon off.

'Go on, enjoy yourselves,' Tash said, her fingers curled possessively around the front door as Clea and Adriana got into the waiting taxi. 'We'll all be here when you get back. We're not going anywhere. I'll just have them out by the pool for the afternoon.' She shut the door and walked quickly back to the kitchen where the children were waiting expectantly. She felt a momentary twinge of panic, then rallied herself. They were only children! She who ran a multi-million-pound business was intimidated by four children under the age of five!

'Can Cliff and Dean come?' Joshua asked as soon as they'd collected all the paraphernalia they seemed to think necessary for a quick pre-lunch paddle in the pool. Tash had never seen quite so much 'stuff'.

'Yes, of course. They're coming after lunch, darling.' Tash tried to remember what Clea had told her. Betty Lowenstein had insisted on having her grandchildren around whilst a friend from Boston paid them a visit. She hadn't seen them all week, or so their au pair had told Clea.

'Are *you* coming in?' David stood in the shallow end, waving some kind of plastic stick at her.

'Yes, yes . . . I'll . . . I'll just get my drink.' Tash bit her lip. Surely it was fine to pop indoors and make herself a drink? Maryam was nowhere near the water and Didi looked as though he'd been born a fish. Nothing would happen for the few seconds it would take her. 'Keep an eye on your sister, won't you?' she called out to David and Joshua. 'Don't let her go near the water.' Joshua, the more responsible of the two, nodded. David was busy setting up some complicated plastic toy in order either to destroy or float it and barely looked up.

She quickly went inside, made herself a large gin and tonic and hurried outside again. All was calm. The three boys were in the water. As a precaution, she called them over and, against their protests, fitted all three with plastic armbands. Now she could relax. Maryam was playing with one of those animal-shaped mobiles. At nearly a year old, she could crawl faster than most, Clea had told her, but she rarely went off on her own. She pulled a magazine out of her bag, took a large gulp and settled her sunglasses on her head. She would let them play amongst themselves for an hour or so, then Cliff and Dean would amble over, she would serve lunch . . . the boys would find their own amusement as they always did and she would take Maryam upstairs for her nap. She ran over the plan in her mind's eye; the afternoon yawned away from her in a pleasing rotation of activities. It was hot; despite it only being May, the sun was almost directly overhead. She craned her neck to see Maryam – was the sunshade on? Yes, Clea had thought of everything. There were bottles of sun lotion beside the wicker tables and she quickly got up to lather more on the boys' arms and necks, even Didi.

She lay back again, unbuttoning her own shift and letting the warm rays hit the soft bare flesh of her stomach. She finished off her drink, pulled her sunglasses down over her eyes and picked up her magazine. For the first time in a long while, she felt herself begin to relax, the tension in her neck and shoulders slowly draining away with the sound of the children's excited laughter.

She opened her eyes on an unfamiliar bird, swaying almost within reach of her hand on spindly, jet-black legs. In the pause between the pleasurable balance of sleep and the harsh light of waking, she passed a tongue over her dry, parched lips and the magazine slipped from her stomach, startling the bird, which took off in a great flapping of wings. She sat up, dazed, looking around her. For the second time in as many days it took her a second to gather her thoughts: the children. She scrambled to her feet. There was no one in the pool. 'Joshua? David?' she called out, lifting a hand to shield her eyes. There was no answer. 'Joshua?' she called again, turning round. Maryam's chair was empty. How could she have crawled out? A run of trembling went through her. She thrust her feet hurriedly into her flip-flops and ran towards the house. They must be inside. One of the boys must have taken her along.

The kitchen was empty; only the thrum and hum of the refrigerator broke the eerie silence. She felt the beginnings of a slow, terrible dread spread upwards through her belly and chest. She ran into the hallway. 'David? Didier?' Through the house, yanking the front door open, running out onto the white-pebbled driveway. Still no one. 'Josh!' The word was practically a scream. Back into the house, up the stairs, two at a time, she burst into their bedroom and still there was nothing. No sign of anyone. The beds were exactly as Clea had left them – neatly and perfectly made, as though they hadn't been slept in the night before. She stood in the doorway swaying on legs that had turned to jelly. The beach. The thought of it made her insides churn over. She ran then, banging her elbow awkwardly against the bannister, feet stumbling over one another. Outside again, feet thudding, slapping against each other, down, down the narrow path to the beach, heart racing, fear a sour, metallic taste at the back of her mouth. The beach was empty; a wave of relief flowed over her – there were no bodies washed up on the shore. She felt the beginnings of tears and a sob escaped her mouth. If they weren't at the beach, where were they? She turned in panic. Something moved just out of the corner of her eye; she whirled round and almost fell to the ground in relief. It was Cliff. He was climbing over the top of the nearest dune. 'Cliff! Cliff! Where . . . where are the others?'

He lifted his head and pointed behind him. 'They're here,' he called. 'Right behind me.'

She could have wept. She stumbled across the long grasses, clutching her shift dress to her. In her panic, she'd forgotten to do it up. 'Where did you go?' she shouted as she ran towards them. 'You know you're not supposed to go anywhere without telling me! Cliff . . . Dean . . . you should know better!' They all looked up at her as she bore down upon them with the half-fearful, half-confused look of children caught in the glare of an adult's anger. Even little Didi looked scared. She forced herself to smile. 'You gave me such a fright,' she said, slowing to a walk. 'I thought you'd got lost.'

'We were just—'

'We found—'

'Cliff, show her . . . go on, you found them'

'Where's Maryam?' Tash looked around her dazedly.

The five boys looked at her, then at each other. Joshua frowned. 'She's in her chair,' he said indignantly. 'We left her there.'

'Where?'

'Beside the pool. She was sleeping. We didn't want to wake her up.'

She stared at them, a rising fear threatening to burst out of her throat. No. She had to remain calm. For their sakes, if not hers. She swallowed. All five were looking at her expectantly. She took in a deep breath and held Cliff, the oldest, by the shoulders. 'I'm going back to the house, Cliff,' she said, in what she prayed was a calm voice. 'I want you to take the others straight back, d'you hear me? Straight back. I'm going to run ahead. Have you got that?'

Cliff squirmed under her fingers but nodded. 'Yeah, sure.' He was eight years old but to her, he seemed almost an adult.

'Straight back. Don't stop anywhere, you promise?'

'Yeah.'

She took one look at the five of them and understood they'd caught something of her fear. They wouldn't go anywhere. She turned and ran, barely stopping to draw breath.

Right up until the moment she lifted the receiver to dial 911 she thought Maryam might be found any minute now. It was fourteen minutes past one. Forty minutes since she'd woken up to find the children gone. There was a second's pause as the numbers went through, then the calm, professional voice of the operator came down the line. 'Emergency services. How may I direct your call?'

She opened her mouth but nothing came out. 'I . . . I . . .'

'How may I direct your call? Law enforcement, fire or ambulance services?'

'P-p-police. Law enforcement. There's a child missing,' she gasped. There was another pause as her call was re-routed. A man's voice came on the line and suddenly, the full weight of what was about to happen came down upon her.

457

It seemed to her as soon as she put down the phone that she'd been waiting for the call – or one like it – from the moment Maryam was born. When Tash had managed to choke out the words she'd been waiting nearly a year to hear, she put down the phone with hands that were surprisingly calm. Julian was sitting on the bed, his back to her, barking instructions into the mobile. Their suitcases were beside the door. His and hers. Black leather, Tumi badges, red trim. Details. Strange to think she had the capacity to notice.

'Ju-Julian.' She tried out the word on her tongue. He took no notice, still yelling into the phone, sorting out whatever it was that had to be sorted, back home. Home. Where was home? Where her children were, surely? 'Julian.' She said it louder this time. He half-turned towards her, impatience written in both his face and stance.

'What is it?' He held the mobile away from him.

'It's Tash.' She wasn't sure how she'd said it. 'Tash,' she repeated woodenly.

'What? What's the matter?'

'She . . .' She stopped, unable to say it out loud.

'*What?*'

'Maryam.' There. She'd said her name.

He was beside her in an instant. She heard his mobile drop as if from a very great distance. She began to make a noise she'd never heard before – a half-groan, half-grunt – and saw the alarm in his face, quickly replaced by the rising terror she was sure was mirrored in hers. 'Maryam,' she said again, her voice quivering, breaking.

'What's the matter? What's wrong with Maryam?' He put out one hand to hold onto her and with the other, grabbed the phone she'd just replaced. 'What is it, Rebecca?' She covered his hand with her own, holding onto it as though for dear life. She tried again and again to speak, to tell him what Tash had just blurted out. But he was already dialling.

ANNICK

In one of those surprising moments of clarity in which the future is suddenly revealed, Annick knew that she would remember for the rest of her life the relief that flowed through her when she heard it was Maryam who was missing and not Didier. She gave out a strangled cry, causing Yves to look up from his laptop in alarm.

'What is it?' He threw the computer to one side and scrambled out of bed.

'Th-thank you, yes . . . yes, we'll be right there. Does her mother know? No, not her godmother, her *mother*. Rebecca. Rebecca Harburg, she's—'

'What is it?' Yves was beside her. He took the phone from her. 'Hello? This is Yves Pas—Ameyaw. Who is this?' There was a few seconds' silence as the police officer she'd just spoken to relayed the same facts to Yves. A child was missing. No, not *their* child. Mr and Mrs Lovell's child, Maryam Lovell. Yes, a driver had been called. He'd be at the hotel in a few minutes, if they wouldn't mind returning to Martha's Vineyard? 'We'll be right there,' Yves said, reaching out to hold Annick's arm. 'Thank you. What was your name again? Detective Sergeant Vargas? Varga. Thank you, Detective Varga. We'll see you shortly.' He put down the phone and turned to her. 'Maryam's missing.' He said it slowly, as if he were dazed.

Annick swallowed. Shame welled in her throat like nausea. 'I know . . . she . . . I thought—'

'I know what you thought,' Yves said quickly. He pulled her towards him roughly, pressing her head against his neck. She began to sob – great heaving, dry sobs that shuddered through her. 'Don't,' Yves said quietly, stroking her hair. 'Don't think about it, *chérie*. Let's just get there first.'

'Th-they thought Tash was the mother; they got it wrong . . . I told her, Tash is her godmother, not her mother and—' She had to stop. Her teeth were chattering.

'We've got to go, Annick. Help me.' Yves gave her a gentle shake. 'Come on. We've got to pack up. The detective said they were sending a car over. Let's go.'

She followed him numbly. She couldn't think straight. What the hell had happened? Missing? What did *that* mean? As they emptied the suite, hurriedly gathering up their possessions, something else came to her . . . why wouldn't Yves look at her? He was avoiding her eyes, just as she was avoiding the shame of her own relief. Something wasn't right.

TASH

'Ma'am?' She looked up. It was a female police officer. She couldn't focus properly on the woman's badge. 'You need to come with me.'

'Wh-where? Wh-where are you taking me?'

The woman's voice was surprisingly gentle. 'Ma'am. You need to get dressed.'

Tash looked down at herself. She was still wearing the long linen shirt and the red bikini she'd been wearing that morning. Her eyes filled with tears. 'Y-yes,' she stammered. 'I'll . . . I'll just go upstairs . . . my bedroom . . .'

'Ma'am, I need to accompany you. Will you show me the way?'

In silence, with the woman's hand on her arm to guide her, Tash walked unsteadily out of the room.

The woman detective – Detective Sergeant Maria Varga of Troop D-4, Field Section of the Massachusetts State Police, Middleborough HQ – was still talking to her, her calm voice barely raising a notch as Tash fumbled her way into a pair of jeans and a long-sleeved T-shirt. It was nearly two thirty. Maryam had been missing for two hours. The house was now full of people. Within half an hour of making the call, police and officers from the various departments and agencies trained to deal with such emergencies had descended upon them. Rebecca and Julian were on their way; Annick and Yves would follow shortly. The scared and confused children had been taken upstairs. Maria Varga was asking her something. She frowned and tried to concentrate.

'Wh-what d'you mean?' she stammered, her hands refusing to do the work of buttoning a cardigan.

'Were you drinking, Miss Bryce-Brudenell?' Detective Sergeant Varga's voice was steady. 'We found an almost-empty bottle of gin on the kitchen counter. How many did you have before you went outside with them?'

460

Tash opened her mouth to explain. 'It's not like that. I'm not . . . I don't—'

'You don't need to explain anything to me. I just want the facts, Miss Bryce-Brudenell. How many drinks *did* you have?'

REBECCA

She remembered little of the terrifying dash from the hotel to the airport, a journey of no more than an hour; it seemed triple that. She was dimly aware of Julian's hand holding hers tight and hard throughout. A cold, terrible dread seeped through her every pore so that she could barely breathe. Her thoughts were confused and incoherent; Maryam, Tariq, Tash, Julian, the boys, her mother . . . round and round, forwards and backwards, this way and that, each possibility more terrifying than the next, until she thought she might actually be sick. The dreaded phone call that every parent reads about but deep, deep down, prays will never be one that *they* will receive, bobbed back to the surface of her consciousness, over and over again. 'Maryam's gone missing, Rebecca . . . we've searched everywhere . . .' Tash's voice. What had happened next? Did she drop the phone? Say something? Explode? She couldn't remember. Other things came back to her – Julian's back, the fine fabric of his light-blue shirt stretched across his muscles as he leaned forwards into his telephone call; the dark plum velvet of the curtains, herringbone weave of the carpet, the colours of the satin bedspread. But not her response, not that.

The same driver who'd picked them up barely a week earlier was waiting for them. There was another man with them: a tall, lean man with a craggy, weather-beaten face. Detective Carducci. She took in the name numbly. It was Julian who did the talking. Nearly a year old, dark hair, dark eyes . . . he pulled out his wallet and handed the photo over across the seats that divided them. Rebecca looked away. She had to hold her hands, one on top of the other, to stop herself reaching over and tearing it from his hands. Maryam's picture had no place being passed from father to detective in the back of a chauffeur-driven car. She swallowed and swallowed again. It seemed inconceivable that they were driving along the same route, rolling blue sea on one side, houses of unimaginable splendour on the other, a beautiful, early summer day just like the one they'd landed on . . . there was nothing in the landscape that even hinted at the terror lying within her, lying within them all. Julian still had hold of her; every now and then she felt a tremor pass through his fingers. She sat numbly beside him, speechless, as though paralysed. The car glided along smoothly, braking when necessary, picking up speed as they left the town behind, each of the four occupants lost in their own terrible, private fears.

TASH

The dread they brought with them blew into the house like one of those storms that came up off the ocean suddenly, mowing down everything in its path. She could feel it even before the car came to a juddering stop. Feet running across the pebbles, officers getting to their feet, the 'crack!' as the front door burst open and suddenly there they were. Rebecca and Julian.

Rebecca's face was twisted, made ugly with dread. 'Where *is* she? What have you done with my child?' The words exploded like gunshot. Tash jumped to her feet.

'No, no . . . it's not . . . I was watching her, Rebecca, I swear . . . I don't know what happened. They were all there, all of them. It was just for a moment, Rebecca, I swear. I just shut my eyes for a moment—' Her teeth were chattering; she couldn't get the words out fast enough. They were all looking at her with the same wild-eyed stare. A stare of accusation, of disbelief . . . of hate. She felt her stomach turn over.

'Mrs Lovell, please.' There were three law enforcement officers in the room – she'd forgotten their names already. The detective who'd accompanied the driver – Carducci? Carlucci? – quickly moved forwards, taking Rebecca by the arm. She shook it off angrily.

'Don't you *dare* try and squirm out of this one, Tash!' she screamed. 'This isn't something you can buy your way out of! Where's my *child?*'

Tash took a step backwards. Buy her way out of it? What was Rebecca saying? 'I—'

'Rebecca, darling, don't say that. It's probably just—' Annick stepped in, putting an arm round Rebecca, who was almost bent double. Julian was looking from side to side, as if he couldn't quite grasp what was

462

going on. Rebecca shook off Annick's arm in the same way she'd pushed aside the police officer.

'Don't you fucking tell me what to say! You're just relieved it's not your child! Go on, *admit it!* You're all just *standing* there! Why don't—'

'Mrs Lovell,' one of the female officers was more forceful. 'Don't. None of this is helpful. I need to ask you a few questions and—'

Tash stood by, open-mouthed with fear and shock. A sudden burst of static from a walkie-talkie shattered the air and then the officers all began to talk at once, that strange, surreal mixture of words and phrases familiar to her from American television shows – *AMBER alert; primary officers; securing the site; anything with her scent* – each bringing on a new wave of deeper, more terrifying fears. Everything seemed to happen at once. She watched one of the officers whisper to the other and then they both moved towards Rebecca, gripping her firmly by both arms. She struggled, of course, but they were not only stronger, they were professionals. Weeping uncontrollably, Rebecca was led out of the room. Outside she could hear more cars arriving and the sound of a hysterical Clea being questioned in the hallway. Betty Lowenstein was in the corner, her face as hard as stone. It was Betty who'd come upon her in the study and it was Betty who'd prized the glass of vodka out of her clenched hand. She'd said nothing; she didn't need to.

'It's not my fault,' Tash screamed suddenly, the pressure erupting in her chest. 'It's not my fault. Please, please believe me . . . it's not my fault!'

No one spoke. No one even looked at her.

119

TARIQ MALOUF
Martha's Vineyard

He looked at his watch. It was almost a quarter to three. Across from him, Maryam sat in a high chair that the friendly waitress had so kindly found for them. Father and daughter. His wife, he explained with a practised ease that astonished him, had taken the car with their other two children, leaving him alone with Maryam, their youngest. Her pushchair was in the boot; they'd forgotten to take it out.

'Oh, no problem,' she said, cheerfully empathetic in the way that only Americans can be. *No problem.* Two minutes later, she was back with the chair. 'What would she like?' she'd asked, gazing in open admiration at Maryam. 'She's a lot like you. Her mom must be really beautiful, too.'

He felt his throat constrict and it took him a few seconds to compose himself sufficiently to answer. 'Mashed bananas. With cream, if you've got any.' It was her older sister's favourite and had been since she was the same age. The older sister Maryam would never see, never know. 'And a black coffee for me.'

One look at her. That was what he'd promised himself. Just one glimpse. After that terrible day in Jerusalem where he'd forced himself to walk away – from Rebecca, Maryam, the affair, the Harburgs, *everything* – he'd tried to put her out of his mind and, for the most part, he'd succeeded. But then he'd seen an article about some society wedding or other in one of the magazines his wife devoured endlessly . . . and it all came flooding back. It took him a few seconds to recognise Rebecca in the photograph. She'd left dozens of messages, saying where they were going. It was a two-hour drive from his home in Connecticut. One glimpse, that was all. He wanted to be *sure*.

He found Tash Bryce-Brudenell's home easily enough. All the while he was driving along Interstate 95, he thought about the madness of it all. What would he say if Julian saw him? He was deluding himself if he thought Julian wouldn't recognise him. And then there was Rebecca to think about. What would she do? What would she say? What *could* she say? He shook his head as he drove, unable to find an answer that would satisfy anyone, least of all him. All he knew was the burning desperation to see this daughter of his once – just once. That was all.

He was parked halfway across the road, his car partially hidden by the man-made grassy knolls that stood in place of fences in this most upmarket of residential neighbourhoods. He saw the taxi bearing the two young girls pull out of the driveway, and the tall woman with the short blonde hair, whom he recognised as Tash Bryce-Brudenell, standing in the doorway, waving them off. His heart was hammering in his chest as he got out of the car and made his way down the lane that separated the two properties, hidden from each by the tall line of trees that were almost in full bloom. He could see the pool, its blue-green skin shimmering in the afternoon sun. He slipped behind the little white cabaña. It seemed a logical place to wait whilst he figured out what to do next.

And then events seemed to overtake him. He saw Tash come out to the pool with the children. Rebecca's twins first. He recognised them straight away. They took after the father. Then a small, dark child, trailing possessively behind Tash, who was carrying a baby. He felt a tightness in his chest as he watched her put the baby down, tucking her carefully into the seat, making sure the sun was out of her face. Maryam's face. He was too far away to see her clearly and it took almost all the self-control left to him not to simply walk out from around the small pool house, calmly introduce himself as the father of the child and walk off with her. He had no idea who else was in the house. One glimpse, that's all, he kept telling himself. He just wanted to be *sure*. He saw Tash come out with a drink in her hand and then heard the twins ask her when Mummy and Daddy would be back. 'On Monday, darling. Only another day to go.' So Rebecca and Julian weren't around? 'Your mummy and daddy, too, Didi. They're having a nice time together, just like we are, aren't we?' He saw the children shrug, completely unself-consciously, in the way only children can be. His heart lifted. Tash was clearly the only adult left in the house. He debated with himself for a moment whether to just go up and talk to her, but something held him back. He wanted to see Maryam first. Properly.

And then Tash fell asleep. She'd barely taken three or four sips of her drink before he saw the glass tilt dangerously towards the grass. She let go of it and it fell to the ground silently, spilling its contents immediately. He saw the boys look over at her uncertainly, then at Maryam, who seemed to be sleeping in her chair. They drew together for a few minutes; one, the slightly taller of the two, was clearly planning something. Exaggeratedly silent, they tiptoed away from the pool, heading for the house next door, leaving the sleeping adult and the sleeping child. He waited for a while – ten minutes, fifteen? He couldn't tell. And then it all happened so fast. Tash suddenly woke up, whether jolted out of sleep by a noise or the absence of it, he couldn't tell. She looked around her, focusing on the fact that the children were gone. She jumped up, grabbed her sarong and ran into the kitchen. A few seconds later, he saw her running wildly towards the beach. He didn't stop to think. He moved forward out of the bushes and walked up to her. When he saw her, and she opened her eyes to focus on his, all rational thought deserted him.

*

465

And now here he was, sitting in a Denny's somewhere in the middle of Edgartown with a baby, looking for all the world as if they belonged there, father and daughter, like all the others. Except they weren't. The child was of his begetting, but she wasn't his child.

It was time to take her back.

120

TASH/ANNICK/REBECCA

The door closed behind the detective sergeant and, for the first time since they'd arrived back at the house, Rebecca and Julian were alone. Rebecca was standing by the window watching the police fan out in a team, with their dogs straining at the lead. Their dark blue-and-white jackets with the letters MSP blazoned across the back could be seen all the way to the trees at the edge of the property. She couldn't think straight. Her teeth were chattering. Rage was building up inside her, more powerful and insistent than any emotion she'd ever felt. Julian must have sensed it; he came to stand beside her but said nothing. All the way from New York he'd held some part of her – a hand, a wrist, her arm – as if to keep her from falling but now nothing could hold her up. Why had she agreed to it? *Why?* Tash wasn't capable of looking after anyone, let alone four children. She was mad to have agreed to it! Everyone pretended they didn't know about the drinking and the lapses of control but they all knew! Everyone knew. So why hadn't anyone said anything? Was it the money? The fact that Tash had paid for every-thing, been so generous, wanting so badly to please? She'd practically shoved them out the door. 'Go, *go* . . . I promise you, nothing'll happen.'

Julian cleared his throat. He seemed about to say something when there was a tap at the door. They both spun round. Rebecca's heart leapt into her chest. 'Wh-who is it? Yes?'

The door opened slowly. It was Tash. For a long, dreadful moment they stared at each other. Tash's face was completely ashen; she'd never seen her so pale. Her hair was sticking up and there were dark circles underneath her eyes. She'd been crying, of course. 'Rebecca?' she said haltingly, taking a step forward. Someone was standing behind her. It

466

took Rebecca a second to work out that it was Annick. For reasons she didn't care to examine, the sight of the two of them – one with her child safe, the other the cause of her terror – forced the rage right out of her stomach, pushing it upwards through her chest and neck until it exploded, flooding her mouth like saliva, blinding her with its ferocious intensity.

'You . . . you *fucking bitch!*' The words were torn from her throat, winding her. She felt Julian's arm on hers, pulling her back but he could no more have stopped her than he could have stopped a storm. She saw Tash flinch, as though she'd been slapped. 'How could you? I left my child with you, you . . . *you fucking drunk*! My *child*! All you had to do was keep her safe! You've got a fucking *army* of servants here who'll do everything else . . . feed them, bathe them, all the things you can't be bothered to do. Just keep her safe, that's all!' She felt the world slipping away from her. Julian was trying to grab hold of her flailing arms but she shook him off with a strength that surprised him. She lifted her arm and with all the force she could muster, she slapped Tash, once, twice, and the scream that came from her throat was unlike any sound she'd ever heard. Everyone jumped. She heard footsteps coming up the stairs, the deep baritone of the police officer who'd been on hand to meet them; Adam and Annick were in the doorway, Annick's panicked face swinging wildly from her to Tash and back again. Yves and Adam both pushed past her, trying to reach Tash in the tangle of arms and palms. Tash was holding onto the doorjamb; her chest was rising and falling and there were two ugly red welts across her face. As hard as it was to believe, the sight only made Rebecca crazier with rage. She lifted her hand again but Adam caught it. At that moment, she was beyond herself. Blind fury had taken hold of her, shaking her in its fist like a leaf. 'You're just jealous, that's what it is,' she screamed.

'Rebecca!'

'Somebody get her out of here!'

'Take that woman downstairs!'

'Will someone . . . ?'

'You can't have children of your own *so you've taken mine!*' It was the beginning of a sentence that, once embarked on, would have no end. She knew that much. She saw Tash wince and the wide-eyed, faraway look in her eye was something Rebecca recognised; it was the look she'd always had, the look of an outsider, gazing in on something she longed to take part in, but couldn't. Another cry broke forth from her throat but Julian was holding her arms, pressing her to him. Adam had his arm round Tash and, together with the policewoman, they prised her fingers from the doorjamb and led her away.

In the confusion, no one heard the doorbell until Betty Lowenstein suddenly began to scream.

Epilogue

ANNICK
Martha's Vineyard, Cape Cod, USA

It was almost midnight. The house was finally quiet, struck by a silence that, after the emotions unleashed by the day, seemed almost eerie. Tash and Rebecca were upstairs, both utterly wrung out by events. Adam had gone with the police and Tariq Malouf, the man who'd simply walked up to the front door, a gurgling Maryam in his arms, and handed her over. To everyone's surprise, Adam had offered to go. 'He looks as though he could use some support,' he said in an aside to Annick and Yves. 'No one's going to press charges but . . . shit, I wouldn't want to be in his shoes. What a mess. What a fucking mess.' Annick watched him go, a new respect for Adam slowly surfacing in her. He'd phoned an hour or so ago to let them know that Tariq would be released without charge within the hour. Under the circumstances, the police thought, it would be better for Mr Malouf to spend the night somewhere in town and then drive back to his home in Connecticut the following morning.

Now the three of them, she, Yves and Julian were still sitting downstairs in the living room, not speaking, yet not disconnected either, reluctant to get up and put an end to the day that had been more dreadful than each could possibly have imagined.

'D'you want something?' she asked them both, finally getting to her feet. She pushed both hands into her hair, pulling it back from her face before letting it spring free again.

'Something?' Julian looked up. His eyes were bloodshot and his expression weary.

'A drink, maybe?' she offered. Despite everything, it seemed the only appropriate thing.

He glanced quickly, almost shyly, at Yves. 'A drink. Yeah, why not?'

'I'll get them. You stay.' Annick quickly left the room.

She came back a few minutes later with a tray, balancing the three large brandies carefully as she set it down. 'Rémy Martin. Good,' she said, half-apologetically. 'Trust Tash.'

Julian nodded slowly. 'Yeah,' he sighed. 'Trust Tash.'

Annick served both men, then sat down beside Yves. The day was over. She'd seen and heard more in it than she cared to think about. The hysteria that the day had unleashed would take days, weeks, months to subside.

'Listen,' Annick said suddenly. The other two looked up. 'I want to say something.' She held the brandy glass in both hands, warming it. The day was over, in the strict sense of time passing; it was after midnight and another was about to begin. But it wasn't over, not by a long shot. Tomorrow would be another word and another world and she wanted to forestall that. Someone ought to say *some*thing – what had been said couldn't be un-said – and she realised it was up to her. It didn't matter that Rebecca and Tash weren't there to hear her. She loved them; they loved each other, even if they'd lost sight of it. She saw Yves' look of disquiet and she shook her head. *It's all right*, she wanted to say. *I know what I'm doing.*

'This is what I want to say. Things don't always turn out the way you think they will. Things just . . . happen, somehow. Without you thinking about them, or planning them . . . it's what Americans always say. Shit happens. But nothing *happened* today. Oh, I know, it's easy for me to say,' she said, glancing at Julian. He was looking at her expectantly. She felt confident now she had their attention. 'It wasn't my child that went missing. But I *know* Rebecca and I *know* Tash and the way it was said, the way it came out, that's not how either of them meant it. I know that. We've been through so much together – too much – for this to be the end of it. They'll find their way back, I promise you.' She looked at Yves and Julian; their eyes were fixed intently on her.

'I suppose, for me, the most shocking thing about today isn't just what happened to Maryam or the fact that Tash drank too much and fell asleep. It could happen to anyone. No, what's worse is how far from the truth we've all strayed. Everyone has secrets; that goes without saying. And yes, some of us have more secrets than others.' She stopped for a moment, looking at each of them in turn. Then she looked at Yves. 'You once said to me that Rebecca and Tash were all I had, that without a family, my friends were everything. It's still true. Yes, I've got my own family now . . . you and Didi . . . but we're *all* each other's family. All of us. You, me, Didi, the twins, Julian. And Tash and Adam, of course.

Even Tariq. We're all bound together, whether we like it or not. And secrets and lies, even little white ones, don't belong in families.' She stopped and looked at her glass for a moment before bringing it to her lips. 'That's all,' she said. 'That's all I wanted to say.'

Neither Yves nor Julian said anything. The silence between the three of them was deep but strangely comfortable. After a moment, Annick got up and walked into the kitchen. She drained her glass, feeling the brandy burn its way down her throat, warming her belly. She walked over to the sink and turned on the tap, rinsing the glass carefully, setting it down on the drainer. Someone had left a bunch of flowers on the island counter – peonies, from the garden – in thanks, perhaps, for Maryam's safe return? She picked them up, pulled off the few already-dead leaves and looked around for a vase. There was one on the bottom shelf of one of the cupboards and she bent down to pick it up. When she straightened up, Julian was standing in the doorway.

She smiled at him, a little embarrassed by her long speech, and began arranging the stems. 'Would you like a cup of tea?' she asked after a moment. He said nothing but sat down patiently like a child at the kitchen table. She could hear Yves' slow tread on the stairs. It was just the two of them, alone now. She switched on the kettle and the silence between them was filled by its throbbing. She made them both a mug and sat down opposite him, sliding it across the warm grain of the wooden surface.

'What I've always liked about you, Annick,' he said after taking a sip, 'is the way you see everything. Every detail.'

She blushed deeply. She hadn't meant to show off. 'No, I—'

He shook his head, forestalling her. 'It's true. You see beyond the surface of things, to where things really matter. You're right.' He took a sip of his tea. 'Secrets and lies. It's time to stop. We've all got too many of them, myself included. Thank you,' he said in his oddly formal way.

They sat for a little while longer, neither speaking. The wind had picked up outside, stirring the trees. A night owl flitted past, emitting a long, soulful hoot. Something barked in response – a fox perhaps . . . the trees stirred again. Night ploughed on, and would continue ploughing until the sun came up, bringing with it all the bright, expectant promise of a brand new day.